W9-CBP-742

HELL'S GATE

Baen Books by David Weber

Honor Harrington:
On Basilisk Station
The Honor of the Queen
The Short Victorious War
Field of Dishonor
Flag in Exile
Honor Among Enemies
In Enemy Hands
Echoes of Honor
Ashes of Victory
War of Honor
At All Costs

Honorverse:
Crown of Slaves (with Eric Flint)
The Shadow of Saganami

edited by David Weber:
More than Honor
Worlds of Honor
Changer of Worlds
The Service of the Sword

Mutineers' Moon
The Armageddon Inheritance
Heirs of Empire
Empire from the Ashes

In Fury Born

The Apocalypse Troll

The Excalibur Alternative

Bolos!
Old Soldiers

Oath of Swords
The War God's Own
Wind Rider's Oath

with Steve White:
Crusade
In Death Ground
The Stars At War
The Shiva Option
Insurrection
The Stars At War II

with Eric Flint:
1633

with John Ringo:
March Upcountry
March to the Sea
March to the Stars
We Few

with Linda Evans:
Hell's Gate
Hell Hath No Fury (forthcoming)

Baen Books by Linda Evans

Sleipnir

Far Edge of Darkness

The Road to Damascus
(with John Ringo)

with Robert Asprin:
Time Scout
Wagers of Sin
Ripping Time
The House That Jack Built
For King and Country

HELL'S GATE

DAVID WEBER
& LINDA EVANS

HELL'S GATE

A Baen Books Original

Baen Publishing Enterprises
P.O. Box 1403
Riverdale, NY 10471
www.baen.com

ISBN 10: 1-4165-0939-9
ISBN 13: 978-1-4165-0939-4

Cover art by Kurt Miller

First printing, November 2006

Distributed by Simon & Schuster
1230 Avenue of the Americas
New York, NY 10020

Library of Congress Cataloging-in-Publication Data

Weber, David, 1952-
 Hell's gate / by David Weber & Linda Evans.
      p. cm.
   "A Baen Books original"—T.p. verso.
   ISBN 1-4165-0939-9
  1. Space warfare—Fiction. 2. Life on other planets—Fiction. I. Evans, Linda. II. Title.

   PS3573.E217H45 2006
   813'.54—dc22

                                        2006019700

10 9 8 7 6 5 4 3 2 1

Pages by Joy Freeman (www.pagesbyjoy.com)
Printed in the United States of America

For Sharon, always.
Because with her on my side,
I can face the multiverse head-on.

For David & Aubrey, who keep me smiling,
and for Bob, always, for his endless technical assistance.
I couldn't whiff or trace without him.

CHAPTER ONE

THE TALL NONCOM could have stepped straight out of a recruiting poster. His fair hair and height were a legacy from his North Shaloman ancestors, but he was far, far away—a universe away—from their steep cliffs and icy fjords. His jungle camo fatigues were starched and ironed to razor-sharp creases as he stood on the crude, muddy landing ground with his back to the looming hole of the portal. His immaculate uniform looked almost as bizarrely out of place against the backdrop of the hacked-out jungle clearing as the autumn-kissed red and gold of the forest giants beyond the portal, and he seemed impervious to the swamp-spawned insects zinging about his ears. He wore the shoulder patch of the Second Andaran Temporal Scouts, and the traces of gray at his temples went perfectly with the experience lines etched into his hard, bronzed face.

He gazed up into the painfully bright afternoon sky, blue-gray eyes slitted against the westering sun, with his helmet tucked into the crook of his left elbow and his right thumb hooked into the leather sling of the dragoon arbalest slung over his shoulder. He'd been standing there in the blistering heat for the better part of half an hour, yet he seemed unaware of it. In fact, he didn't even seem to be perspiring, although that had to be an illusion.

He also seemed prepared to stand there for the next week or so, if that was what it took. But then, finally, a black dot appeared against the cloudless blue, and his nostrils flared as he inhaled in satisfaction.

He watched the dot sweep steadily closer, losing altitude as it came, then lifted his helmet and settled it onto his head. He bent his neck, shielding his eyes with his left hand as the dragon back-winged in to a landing. Bits of debris flew on the sudden wind generated by the mighty beast's iridescent-scaled wings, and the noncom waited until

1

the last twigs had pattered back to the ground before he lowered his hand and straightened once more.

The dragon's arrival was a sign of just how inaccessible this forward post actually was. In fact, it was just over seven hundred and twenty miles from the coastal base, in what would have been the swamps of the Kingdom of Farshal in northeastern Hilmar back home. Those were some pretty inhospitable miles, and the mud here was just as gluey as the genuine Hilmaran article, so aerial transport was the only real practical way in at the moment. The noncom himself had arrived back at the post via the regular transport dragon flight less than forty-eight hours earlier, and as he'd surveyed the muck below, he'd been struck by just how miserable it would have been to slog through it on foot. How anyone was going to properly exploit a portal in the middle of this godforsaken swamp was more than he could say, but he didn't doubt that the Union Trans-Temporal Transit Authority would find a way. The UTTTA had the best engineers in the universe—in *several* universes, for that matter—and plenty of experience with portals in terrain even less prepossessing than this.

Probably less prepossessing, anyway.

The dragon went obediently to its knees at the urging of its pilot, and a single passenger swung down the boarding harness strapped about the beast's shoulders. The newcomer was dark-haired, dark-eyed, and even taller than the noncom, although much younger, and each point of his collar bore the single silver shield of a commander of one hundred. Like the noncom, he wore the shoulder flash of the 2nd ATS, and the name "Olderhan, Jasak" was stenciled above his breast pocket. He said something to the dragon's pilot, then strode quickly across the mucky ground towards the waiting one-man welcoming committee.

"Sir!" The noncom snapped to attention and saluted sharply. "Welcome back to this shithole, *Sir!*" he barked.

"Why, thank you, Chief Sword Threbuch," the officer said amiably, tossing off a far more casual salute in response. Then he extended his right hand and gripped the older man's hand firmly. "I trust the Powers That Be have a suitable reason for dragging me back here, Otwal," he said dryly, and the noncom smiled.

"I wish they hadn't—dragged you back, that is, Sir—but I think you may forgive them in the end," he said. "I'm sort of surprised they managed to catch you, though. I figured you'd be well on your way back to Garth Showma by now."

"So did I," Hundred Olderhan replied wryly. He shook his head. "Unfortunately, Hundred Thalmayr seems to've gotten himself delayed in transit somewhere along the way, and Magister Halathyn was quick enough off the mark to catch me before he got here. If the magister had only waited another couple of days for Thalmayr to get here to relieve me, I'd have been aboard ship and far enough out to sea to get away clean."

"Sorry about that, Sir." The chief sword grinned. "I hope you'll tell the Five Thousand I *tried* to get you home for your birthday."

"Oh, Father will forgive you, Otwal," Jasak assured him. "*Mother,* now . . ."

"Please, Sir!" The chief sword shivered dramatically. "I still remember what your lady mother had to say to me when I got the Five Thousand home late for their anniversary."

"According to Father, you did well to get him home at all," the hundred said, and the chief sword shrugged.

"The Five Thousand was too tough for any jaguar to eat, Sir. All I did was stop the bleeding."

"Most he could have expected out of you after he was stupid enough to step right on top of it." The chief sword gave the younger man a sharp look, and the hundred chuckled. "That's the way *Father* describes it, Otwal. I promise you I'm not being guilty of filial disrespect."

"As the Hundred says," the chief sword agreed.

"But since our lords and masters appear to have seen fit to make me miss my birthday, suppose you tell me exactly what we have here, Chief Sword." The hundred's voice was much crisper, his brown eyes intent, and the chief sword came back to a position midway between stand easy and parade rest.

"Sir, I'm afraid you'll need to ask Magister Halathyn for the details. All I know is that he says the potential tests on this portal's field strength indicate that there's at least one more in close proximity. A big one."

"How big?" Jasak asked, his eyes narrowing.

"I don't really know, Sir," Threbuch replied. "I don't think Magister Halathyn does yet, for that matter. But he was muttering something about a class eight."

Sir Jasak Olderhan's eyebrows rose, and he whistled silently. The largest trans-temporal portal so far charted was the Selkara Portal, and it was only a class seven. If Magister Halathyn had, indeed, detected a class *eight*, then this muddy, swampy hunk of jungle was about to become very valuable real estate.

"In that case, Chief Sword," he said mildly after a moment, "I suppose you'd better get me to Magister Halathyn."

* * *

Halathyn vos Dulainah was very erect, very dark-skinned, and very silver-haired, with a wiry build which was finally beginning to verge on frail. Jasak wasn't certain, but he strongly suspected that the old man was well past the age at which Authority regs mandated the retirement of the Gifted from active fieldwork. Not that anyone was likely to tell Magister Halathyn that. He'd been a law unto himself for decades and the UTTTA's crown jewel ever since he'd left the Mythal Falls Academy twenty years before, and he took an undisguised, almost childlike delight in telling his nominal superiors where they could stuff their regulations.

He hadn't told Jasak exactly why he was out here in the middle of this mud and bug-infested swamp, nor why Magister Gadrial Kel-bryan, his second-in-command at the Garth Showma Institute, had followed him out here. He'd insisted with a bland-faced innocence which could not have been bettered by a twelve-year-old caught with his hand actually in the cookie jar, that he was "on vacation." He certainly had the clout within the UTTTA to commandeer transpor-tation for his own amusement if that was what he really wanted, but Jasak suspected he was actually engaged in some sort of undisclosed research. Not that Magister Halathyn was going to admit it. He was too delighted by the opportunity to be mysterious to waste it.

He was also, as his complexion and the "vos" in front of his sur-name proclaimed, both a Mythalan and a member of the *shakira* caste. As a rule, Jasak Olderhan was less than fond of Mythalans . . . and considerably less fond than that of the *shakira*. But Magister Halathyn was the exception to that rule, as he was to so many others.

The magister looked up as Chief Sword Threbuch followed Jasak into his tent, the heels of their boots loud on its raised wooden flooring. He tapped his stylus on the crystal display in front of him, freezing his notes and the calculations he'd been performing, and smiled at the hundred over the glassy sphere.

"And how is my second-favorite crude barbarian?" he inquired in genial Andaran.

"As unlettered and impatient as ever, Sir," Jasak replied, in Mythalan, with an answering smile. The old magister chuckled appreciatively and extended his hand for a welcoming shake. Then he cocked his canvas camp chair back at a comfortable, teetering angle and waved for Jasak to seat himself in the matching chair on the far side of his worktable.

"Seriously, Jasak," he said as the younger man obeyed the unspoken command, "I apologize for yanking you back here. I know how hard it was for you to get leave for your birthday in the first place, and I know your parents must have been looking forward to seeing you. But I thought you'd want to be here for this one. And, frankly, with all due respect to Hundred Thalmayr, I'm not sorry he was delayed. All things being equal, I'd prefer to have *you* in charge just a little longer."

Jasak stopped his grimace before it ever reached his expression, but it wasn't the easiest thing he'd ever done. Although he genuinely had been looking forward to spending his birthday at home in Garth Showma for the first time in over six years, he *hadn't* been looking forward to handing "his" company over to Hadrign Thalmayr, even temporarily. Partly because of his jealously possessive pride in Charlie Company, but also because Thalmayr—who was senior to him—had only transferred into the Scouts seventeen months ago. From his record, he was a perfectly competent infantry officer, but Jasak hadn't been impressed with the older man's mental flexibility the few times they'd met before Jasak himself had been forward-deployed. And it was pretty clear his previous line infantry experience had left him firmly imbued with the sort of by-the-book mentality the Temporal Scouts worked very hard to eradicate.

Which wasn't something he could discuss with a civilian, even one he respected as deeply as he did Magister Halathyn.

"The Chief Sword said something about a class eight," he said instead, his tone making the statement a question, and Magister Halathyn nodded soberly.

"Unless Gadrial and I are badly mistaken," he said, waving a hand at the letters and esoteric formulae glittering in the water-clear heart of his crystal, "it's *at least* a class eight. Actually, I suspect it may be even larger."

Jasak sat back in his chair, regarding the old man's lined face intently. Had it been anyone else, he would have been inclined to dismiss the preposterous claim as pure, rampant speculation. But Magister Halathyn wasn't given to speculation.

"If you're right about that, Sir," the hundred said after a moment, "this entire transit chain may just have become a lot more important to the Authority."

"It may," Magister Halathyn agreed. "Then again, it may not." He grimaced. "Whatever size this portal may be—" he tapped the crystal containing his notes "—*that* portal—" he pointed out through the open fly of his tent at the peculiar hole in the universe which loomed enormously beyond the muddy clearing's western perimeter "—is only a class three. That's going to bottleneck anything coming through from our putative class eight. Not to mention the fact that we're at the end of a ridiculously inconvenient chain at the moment."

"I suppose that depends in part on how far your new portal is from the other side of this one," Jasak pointed out. "The terrain between here and the coast may suck, but it's only seven hundred miles."

"Seven hundred and nineteen-point-three miles," Magister Halathyn corrected with a crooked smile.

"All right, Sir." Jasak accepted the correction with a smile of his own. "That's still a ridiculously short haul compared to most of the portal connections I can think of. And if this new portal of yours is within relatively close proximity to our class three, we're talking about a twofer."

"That really is a remarkably uncouth way to describe a spatially congruent trans-temporal transfer zone," Halathyn said severely.

"I'm just a naturally uncouth sort of fellow, Sir," Jasak agreed cheerfully. "But however you slice it, it's still a two-for-one."

"Yes, it is," Halathyn acknowledged. "Assuming our calculations are sound, of course. In fact, if this new portal is as large as I think it is, and as closely associated with our portal here, I think it's entirely possible that we're looking at a cluster."

Despite all of the magister's many years of discipline, his eyes gleamed, and he couldn't quite keep the excitement out of his voice. Not that Jasak blamed him for that. A portal cluster . . . In the better part of two centuries of exploration, UTTTA's survey teams had located only one true cluster, the Zholhara Cluster. Doubletons were the rule—indeed, only sixteen triples had ever been found, which was a rate of less than one in ten. But a cluster like Zholhara was of literally incalculable value.

This far out—they were at the very end of the Lamia Chain, well over three months' travel from Arcana, even for someone who could claim transport dragon priority for the entire trip—even a cluster would take years to fully develop. Lamia, with over twenty portals, was already a huge prize. But if Magister Halathyn was correct, the entire transit chain was about to become even more valuable . . . and receive the highest development priority UTTTA could assign.

"Of course," Magister Halathyn continued in the tone of a man forcing himself to keep his enthusiasm in check, "we don't know where this supposed portal of mine connects. It could be the middle of the Great Ransaran Desert. Or an island in the middle of the Western Ocean, like Rycarh Outbound. Or the exact center of the polar ice cap."

"Or it could be a couple of thousand feet up in thin air, which would make for something of a nasty first step," Jasak agreed. "But I suppose we'd better go find it if we really want to know, shouldn't we?"

"My sentiments exactly," the magister agreed, and the hundred looked at the chief sword.

"How soon can we move out on the magister's heading, Chief Sword?"

"I'm afraid the Hundred would have to ask Fifty Garlath about that," Threbuch replied with absolutely no inflection, and this time Jasak did grimace. The tonelessness of the chief sword's voice shouted his opinion (among other things) of Commander of Fifty Shevan Garlath as an officer of the Union of Arcana. Unfortunately, Sir Jasak Olderhan's opinion exactly matched that of his company's senior noncommissioned officer.

"If the Hundred will recall," the chief sword continued even more tonelessly, "his last decision before his own departure was to authorize Third Platoon's R and R. That leaves Fifty Garlath as the SO here at the base camp."

Jasak winced internally as Threbuch tactfully (sort of) reminded him that leaving Garlath out here at the ass-end of nowhere had been his own idea. Which had seemed like a good one at the time, even if it had been a little petty of him. No, more than a little petty. Quite a bit more, if he wanted to be honest. Chief Sword Threbuch hadn't exactly protested at the time, but his expression had suggested his opinion of the decision. Not because he disagreed that Fifty Therman Ulthar and his men had earned their R&R, but because Shevan Garlath was arguably the most incompetent platoon commander in the entire brigade. Leaving him in charge of anything more complicated than a hot cider stand was not, in the chief sword's considered opinion, a Good Idea.

"We'd have to recall Fifty Ulthar's platoon from the coast, if you want to use him, Sir," the chief sword added, driving home the implied reprimand with exquisite tact.

Jasak was tempted to point out that Magister Halathyn had already dragged *him* back from the company's main CP at the coastal enclave, so there was really no reason *he* shouldn't recall Fifty Ulthar. Except, of course, that he couldn't. First, because doing so would require him to acknowledge to the man who'd been his father's first squad lance that he'd made a mistake. Both of them might *know* he had, but he was damned if he was going to *admit* it.

But second, and far more important, was the patronage system which permeated the Arcanan Army, because patronage was the only thing that kept Garlath in uniform. Not even that had been enough to get him promoted, but it was more than enough to ensure that his sponsors would ask pointed questions if Jasak went that far out of his way to invite another fifty to replace him on what promised to be quite possibly the most important portal exploration on record. If Magister Halathyn's estimates were remotely near correct, this was the sort of operation that got an officer noticed.

Which, in Jasak's opinion, was an even stronger argument in favor of handing it to a competent junior officer who didn't have any patrons . . . and whose probable promotion would actually have a beneficial effect on the Army. But—

"All right, Chief Sword," he sighed. "My respects to Fifty Garlath, and I want his platoon ready to move out at first light tomorrow."

*　　*　　*

The weather was much cooler on the other side of the base portal. Although it was only one hour earlier in the local day, it had been mid-afternoon—despite Jasak's best efforts—before Commander of Fifty Garlath's First Platoon had been ready to leave base camp and step through the immaterial interface between Hilmaran swamp and subarctic Andara in a single stride. The portal's outbound side was located smack on top of the Great Andaran Lakes, five thousand miles north of their departure portal, in what should have been the Kingdom of Lokan. In fact, it was on the narrow neck of land which separated Hammerfell Lake and White Mist Lake from Queen Kalthra's Lake. It might be only one hour east of the base camp, but the difference in latitude meant that single step had moved them from sweltering early summer heat into the crispness of autumn.

Jasak had been raised on his family's estates on New Arcana, less than eighty miles from the very spot at which they emerged, but New Arcana had been settled for the better part of two centuries. The bones of the Earth were the same, and the cool, leaf-painted air of a northern fall was a familiar and welcome relief from the base camp's smothering humidity, but the towering giants of the primordial forest verged on the overpowering even for him.

For Fifty Garlath, who had been raised on the endless grasslands of Yanko, the restricted sightlines and dense forest canopy were far worse than that. Hundred Olderhan, CO of Charlie Company, First Battalion, First Regiment, Second Andaran Temporal Scouts, couldn't very well take one of his platoon commanders to task in front of his subordinates for being an old woman, but Sir Jasak Olderhan felt an almost overpowering urge to kick Garlath in the ass.

He mastered the temptation sternly, but it wasn't easy, even for someone as disciplined as he was. Garlath was *supposed* to be a temporal scout, after all. That meant he was supposed to take the abrupt changes in climate trans-temporal travel imposed in stride.

It also meant he was supposed to be confident in the face of the unknown, well versed in movement under all sorts of conditions and in all sorts of terrain. He was *not* supposed to be so obviously intimidated by endless square miles of trees.

Jasak turned away from his troopers to distract himself (and his mounting frustration) while Garlath tried to get his command squared away. He stood with his back to the brisk, northern autumn and gazed back through the portal at the humid swamp they had left behind. It was the sort of sight with which anyone who spent as much time wandering about between universes as the Second Andarans did became intimately familiar, but no one ever learned to take it for granted.

Magister Halathyn's tone had been dismissive when he described the portal as "only a class three." But while the classification was accurate, and there were undeniably much larger portals, even a "mere" class three was the better part of four miles across. A four-mile disk sliced out of the universe . . . and pasted onto another one.

It was far more than merely uncanny, and unless someone had seen it for himself, it was almost impossible to describe properly.

Jasak himself had only the most rudimentary understanding of current portal theory, but he found the portals themselves endlessly fascinating. A portal appeared to have only two dimensions—height, and width. No one had yet succeeded in measuring one's depth. As far as anyone could tell, it *had* no depth; its threshold was simply a line, visible to the eye but impossible to measure, where one universe stopped . . . and another one began.

Even more fascinating, it was as if each of the universes it connected were *inside* the other one. Standing on the eastern side of a portal in Universe A and looking west, one saw a section of Universe B stretching away from one. One might or might not be looking west in that universe, since portals' orientation in one universe had no discernible effect on their orientation in the other universe to which they connected. If one stepped through the portal into Universe B and looked back in the direction from which one had come, one saw exactly what one would have expected to see—the spot from which one had left Universe A. But, if one returned to Universe A and walked *around* the portal to its western aspect and looked *east*, one saw Universe B stretching away in a direction exactly 180 degrees reversed from what he'd seen from the portal's eastern side in Universe A. And if one then stepped through into Universe B, one found the portal once again at one's back . . . but this time looking west, not east, into Universe A.

The theoreticians referred to the effect as "counterintuitive." Most temporal scouts, like Jasak, referred to it as the "can't get there" effect, since it was impossible to move from one side to the other of a portal in the same universe without circling all the way around it. And, since that held true for any portal in any universe, no one could simply step through a portal one direction, then step back through it to emerge on its far side in the same universe. In order to reach the far side of the portal at the other end of the link, one had to walk all the way around *it*, as well.

Frankly, every time someone tried to explain the theory of how it all worked to Jasak, his brain hurt, but the engineers responsible for designing portal infrastructure took advantage of that effect on a routine basis. It always took some getting used to when one first saw it, of course. For example, it wasn't at all uncommon to see two lines of slider cars charging into a portal on exactly opposite headings—one from the east and the other from the west—at the exact same moment on what appeared to be exactly the same track. No matter how carefully it had all been explained before a man saw it for the first time with his own eyes, he *knew* those two sliders had to be colliding in the universe on the other side of that portal. But, of course, they weren't. Viewed from the side in that other universe, both sliders were exploding out of the same space simultaneously . . . but headed in exactly opposite directions.

From a military perspective, the . . . idiosyncrasies of trans-temporal travel could be more than a little maddening, although the Union of Arcana hadn't fought a true war in over two centuries.

At the moment, Jasak stood roughly at the center of the portal through which he had just stepped, looking back across it at the forward base camp and the swamp they'd left behind. The sunlight on the far side fell from a noticeably different angle, creating shadows whose shape and direction clashed weirdly with those of the cool, northern forest in which he stood. Swamp insects bumbled busily towards the immaterial threshold between worlds, then veered away as they hit the chill breeze blowing back across it.

This particular portal was relatively young. The theorists were still arguing about exactly how and why portals formed in the first place, but it had been obvious for better than a hundred and eighty years that new ones were constantly, if not exactly frequently, being formed. This one had formed long enough ago that the scores of gigantic trees which had been sliced in half vertically by its creation had become dead, well-dried hulks, but almost a dozen of them still stood, like gaunt, maimed chimneys. It wouldn't be long before the bitter northern winters toppled them, as well, yet the fact that it hadn't already happened suggested that they'd been dead for no more than a few years.

Which, Jasak told himself acidly, was not so very much longer than it appeared to be taking Fifty Garlath to get his platoon sorted out.

Eventually, however, even Garlath had his troopers shaken down into movement formation. Sort of. His single point man was too far from the main body, and he'd spread his flank scouts far too wide, but Jasak clamped his teeth firmly against a blistering reprimand... for now. He'd already intended to have a few words with Garlath about the totally unacceptable delay in getting started, but he'd decided he'd wait until they bivouacked and he could "counsel" his subordinate in private. With Charlie Company detached from the battalion as the only organized force at this end of the transit chain, it was particularly important not to undermine the chain of command by giving the troops cause to think that he considered their platoon CO an idiot.

Especially when he did.

So instead of ripping Garlath a new one at the fresh proof of his incompetence, he limited himself to one speaking glance at Chief Sword Threbuch, then followed along behind Garlath with Threbuch and Magister Kelbryan.

Although Jasak had enjoyed the privilege of serving with Magister Halathyn twice before, this was the first time he'd actually met Kelbryan. She and Halathyn had worked together for at least twenty years—indeed, she was one of the main reasons the UTTTA had acquired the exclusive use of Halathyn's services in the first place—but she normally stayed home, holding down the fort at the institute at Garth Showma on New Arcana which Halathyn had created from the ground up for the Authority. Jasak had always assumed, in a casual sort of way, that that was because she preferred civilization to the frontier. Or, at least, that she would have been unsuited to hoofing it through rugged terrain with the Andaran Scouts.

He still didn't know her very well. In fact, he didn't know her at all. She'd only reached their base camp three weeks earlier, and she seemed to be a very private person in a lot of ways. But he'd already discovered that his assumptions had been badly off base. Kelbryan was a couple of years older than he was, and her Ransaran ancestry showed in her almond eyes, sandalwood complexion, and dark, brown-black hair. At five-eight, she was tall for a Ransaran... which meant she was only eight inches shorter than he was. But delicate as she seemed to him, she was obviously fit, and she'd taken the crudity of the facilities available at the sharp end of the Authority's exploration in stride, without turning a hair.

She was also very, very good at her job—as was only to be expected, given that Magister Halathyn must have had his choice of any second-in-command he wanted. Indeed, Jasak had come to realize that the true reasons she'd normally stayed home owed far less to any "delicacy" on her part than to the fact that she was probably the only person Magister Halathyn fully trusted to run "his" shop in his absence. Her academic and research credentials were impressive proof of her native brilliance, and despite the differences in their cultural heritages, she and her boss were clearly devoted to one another.

It had been obvious Magister Halathyn longed to accompany them this morning, but there were limits in all things. Jasak was prepared to go along with the fiction that vos Dulainah wasn't far past mandatory retirement age as long as the old man stayed safely in base camp; he was not about to risk someone that valuable, or of whom he was so fond, in an initial probe. Magister Kelbryan had supported him with firm tactfulness when the old man turned those longing, puppy-dog eyes in her direction, and Magister Halathyn had submitted to the inevitable with no more than the odd, heartfelt sigh of mournful regret when he was sure one of them was listening.

Now the hundred watched the team's junior magister moving through the deep drifts of leaves almost as silently as his own troopers. Despite—or possibly even because of—the fact that he'd never worked with Kelbryan before, he was impressed. And, he admitted, attracted.

She opened a leather equipment case on her belt and withdrew one of the esoteric devices of her profession. Jasak was technically Gifted himself, although his own trace of the talent was so minute that he was often astonished the testing process had been able to detect it at all. Now, as often, he felt a vague, indefinable stirring sensation as someone who was very powerfully Gifted indeed brought her Gift to bear. She gazed down into the crystal display, and her lips moved silently as she powered it up.

Jasak saw the display flicker to life and moved a little closer to look over her shoulder. She sensed his presence and looked up. For an instant, he thought she was going to be annoyed with him for crowding her, but then she smiled and tilted her wrist so that he could see the display more clearly.

In many ways, it looked a great deal like a standard Authority navigation unit. He quickly identified the latitude and longitude readouts, and the built-in clocks—one set to the base camp's time, and one which automatically adjusted to local time on this side of the portal—and the compass and directional indicator arrows. But there was another arrow in the glassy heart of the sphere of sarkolis crystal, and it was flanked by two waterfall displays which had never been part of any navigation unit he'd ever used.

"This one," she said quietly, tapping the green waterfall, "indicates the portal's approximate distance. And this one," she tapped the red waterfall, "indicates its measured field strength. And the arrow, of course," she grinned, "indicates the direction."

"I've never seen a unit quite like that one," Jasak admitted, and she snorted in amusement.

"That's because Magister Halathyn and I built it ourselves," she told him. "Actually, he did most of the design work—I was just the grunt technician who put it together."

"Oh, I'm sure," he said, shaking his head.

"No, it's true!" she insisted. "The beauty of it is in the theoretical conception. Once he'd done the intellectual heavy lifting, actually building the spells was relatively easy. Time consuming, but not difficult."

"Maybe not for *you*," Jasak said dryly, and she shrugged. "But the important thing," he continued, allowing her to drop the subject of her own competency, "is that I've never had a nav unit that pointed me directly at an unexplored portal before. It beats the hell, if you'll pardon the language, out of humping the standard detectors around the countryside on a blind search pattern. Especially someplace like this—" he waved a hand at the heavy tree cover "—where it's all but impossible to get a dragon, or even a gryphon, in for aerial sweeps."

"That's exactly why Magister Halathyn's been working on it for several years now," Kelbryan agreed. "In fact, the whole reason I let him come out here in the first place—" somehow, Jasak felt confident, her choice of the verb "let" was probably painfully accurate "—was to let him field test the spellware."

"And is that the reason *you're* out here, if I may ask?" Jasak inquired.

"Well, for that . . . and to keep an eye on Magister Halathyn," she admitted with a slight smile.

"Which suggests to my keen intelligence that you were, indeed, being overly modest about your contribution to the project," Jasak said. "Somehow I don't see the Institute letting both of its top magisters wander around three or four months' travel from home if they weren't both needed."

"I suppose there might be some truth to that," she conceded after a moment. "Although, to be completely honest, and without trying to undervalue my own contributions to the R&D, the real reason I insisted on coming was to keep *him* from wandering around out here to handle any field modifications the spellware might require. Besides—" she smiled infectiously "—it's the first 'vacation' I've taken in over five years!"

"But why all the secrecy?" Jasak asked. She looked at him, and he shrugged. "The UTTTA must be champing at the bit to get this deployed, so why was Magister Halathyn so busy insisting that he wasn't *really* up to anything?"

"It didn't have anything to do with UTTTA, or any other official part of the Union," she replied. It seemed evident from her tone and her expression that she really would have preferred to leave it at that, but after glancing at him consideringly for a second or two, she shrugged.

"You may have heard that magisters can be just a *little* . . . paranoid about their research." She smiled briefly, and Jasak managed to turn a laugh into a not particularly convincing cough. "A little paranoid," in this case, was rather like saying that White Mist Lake was "a little damp."

"Well, all right, maybe it goes a bit further than that," she said with a reluctant grin. But the grin faded quickly, and she shook her head. "In fact, it goes a lot further than that where Magister Halathyn is concerned. Especially for something like this. There's no way he was going to let even a whisper about this project out where the Mythalans might hear about it before he was ready to publish."

Jasak nodded in suddenly sober understanding of his own.

"While I'd never like to suggest that Magister Halathyn doesn't hold you in the highest respect, Hundred Olderhan," she continued, "the real reason we're out here? It's the farthest away from the Mythal Falls Academy he could get for his field test. And—"

She paused, looking at him with the sort of measuring, considering look he was unused to receiving. After a moment, she seemed to reach some inner decision and leaned closer to him, lowering her voice slightly.

"Actually," she said quietly, "we've done a bit of refining on his original theoretical work, as well. The sort which requires absolute validation before anyone publishes. I have to admit that I didn't really expect to be able to test all of the features in a single trip, but take a look at this."

She tapped the unit with her wand, and both waterfalls and the arrow disappeared instantly. A brief moment passed, and then they lit again . . . but this time, they were noticeably different.

She looked up at Jasak, one eyebrow crooked, and he frowned. Then, suddenly, his eyes widened and he gave her a very sharp glance indeed.

"Exactly," she said, even more quietly. "Magister Halathyn's original idea was to produce a unit which would detect the closest portal and home a survey team in on it. But once we got into the theory, we discovered that we could actually nest the spells."

"So that—" Jasak indicated the display, "—means there's a *second* gate out here?"

"If it's working properly. And—"

She tapped the display again. And again. And a *fourth* time. With each tap, the process repeated, producing new directional arrows and new distance and strength displays, and Jasak swallowed.

"Is *that* why Magister Halathyn's been talking in terms of a cluster?" he asked, and she nodded.

"Either the thing's completely screwed up—which is always possible, however little we might want to admit it—or else there is *at least* a total of five portals associated with this one." A jerk of her head indicated the swamp portal. "Or, more precisely, this one is one of at least five associated with *this* one," she amended, bringing up the original display on the strongest and nearest of the other portals.

"You said 'at least,'" Jasak observed intently, and she nodded again.

"We never expected to hit anything like this on our first field test, Sir Jasak, so there are only a total of six 'slots' in the spell-ware. In theory, we could nest as many as fifteen or twenty—it just never occurred to us to do it. I suppose that was partly because the Zholhara Cluster only has six portals, and it seemed unlikely anyone might find one even bigger."

"Gods," Jasak breathed. He stared at the unit for several seconds, then shook himself. "I'm beginning to see why you were keeping this whole thing so quiet!"

"I thought you might. Still," her eyes brightened, "as happy as I am with how well it seems to be performing, I think you may still be missing something about this cluster as compared to Zholhara."

"What?" He moved his gaze from the unit to her face.

"The Zholhara portals are as much as three thousand miles apart. The maximum range on our detector—assuming we got our sums right—is only about nine hundred miles. In fact, according to the readouts, the *farthest* one we've detected is less than six hundred miles from this portal right here."

Jasak sucked in a deep, hard breath. A *minimum* of five virgin portals, all within a radius of only *six hundred miles* of one another? Gods! They could have five entirely new transit chains radiating from this single spot! It took him several seconds to wrap his mind around the implications, and then he smiled crookedly.

"So that's why Magister Halathyn's like a gryphon in a hen-house!"

"Oh, that's *exactly* what he's like," she agreed with a grin. "And it'd take a special act of God to get him out of here before every one of these portals is nailed down. Assuming, of course, that they're really there. Don't forget that this is our first field trial. It's going to be mighty embarrassing if it has us out here chasing some sort of wild goose!"

"Not very likely with both of you involved in chasing the goose in question, Magister Kelbryan," he told her with an answering grin. She waved one hand in an almost uncomfortable gesture, and he gave a tiny nod of acknowledgment and shifted conversational gears.

"Well, I guess we'll know one way or the other pretty soon," he said. "How far away from the nearest are we now?"

"Assuming Magister Halathyn and I got it right when we built this thing, it's about thirty miles that way," she replied, pointing almost due north, directly away from White Mist Lake.

"About fifteen hours hard hike, in this terrain," Jasak said thoughtfully. "Twice that with rest breaks, a bivouac, and the need to find the best trails. And that assumes basically decent going the entire way."

He glanced at the local time display, then craned his neck, looking up through a break in the autumnal canopy at the sun, and grimaced. The local days were getting short at this time of year, and there was absolutely no way they were going to make it before dusk, he decided, and raised his voice.

"Fifty Garlath!"

"Sir?" Shevan Garlath was a lean, lanky, dark-haired man, almost ten years older than Jasak, despite his junior rank. Although he'd been born in Yanko, his family had migrated from one of the smaller Hilmaran kingdoms barely fifty years earlier, and it showed in his strong nose and very dark eyes as he turned towards the hundred.

"We need to swing a little farther east," Jasak said, chopping one hand in the direction indicated by Kelbryan's illuminated needle. "About another thirty miles. We'll move on for another three or four hours, then bivouac. Keep an eye out for a good site."

"Yes, Sir," Garlath responded crisply enough to fool a casual bystander into thinking he was actually a competent officer. Then he nodded to his platoon sword.

"You heard the Hundred, Sword Harnak," he said.

"Yes, Sir," the stocky, neatly bearded noncom acknowledged, and went trotting briskly ahead to overtake the platoon's point and redirect its course. Jasak watched him go and reflected on how fortunate Garlath was to have inherited a platoon sword good enough to make even him look almost capable.

*   *   *

Platoon-Captain Janaki chan Calirath jerked upright in his sleeping bag so suddenly the nearest sentry jumped in surprise. Under-Armsman chan Yaran whipped around at his platoon commander's abrupt movement, then flinched as a huge, dark-barred peregrine falcon launched itself from the perch beside the sleeping bag. The bird screamed in hard, angry challenge, hurling itself into the clear, cold night to circle overhead furiously . . . protectively.

Yaran stood for a moment, waiting for the platoon-captain to say something—anything. But the platoon-captain only sat there. He didn't even move.

"Sir?" chan Yaran said tentatively. There was no response, and the under-armsman stepped a little closer. "Platoon-Captain?"

Still no response, and chan Yaran began to sweat, despite the chill breeze blowing across the encampment. There was something . . . ominous about the officer's total immobility. That would have been true under any circumstances, but Janaki chan Calirath wasn't any old Imperial Marine officer. No one was supposed to take any official notice of that, but every member of the platoon-captain's command was a Ternathian (which, chan Yaran knew, wasn't exactly an accident), and that made *this* officer's petrified lack of response downright frightening.

Chan Yaran moved to the side until he could see his CO's face in the firelight. The platoon-captain's eyes were wide open, unblinking, glittering with reflected fire, and chan Yaran swallowed hard. What the *hell* was he supposed to do *now*?

He looked around, then leaned closer to the officer.

"Your Highness?" he said very, very quietly.

The wide, fixed eyes never even flickered around their core of firelight, and he muttered a soft, heartfelt curse. Then he drew a deep breath and crossed to another sleeping bag and touched its occupant's shoulder lightly.

Chief-Armsman Lorash chan Braikal twitched upright almost as abruptly as the platoon-captain had. Unlike the officer, however, Third Platoon's senior noncom was instantly and totally aware of his surroundings. Chan Braikal hadn't drawn his present slot by random chance, and his eyes tracked around to chan Yaran like twin pistol muzzles.

"What?"

The one-word question was quiet and remarkably clear of sleepiness for someone so abruptly awakened. It came out almost conversationally, but chan Yaran wasn't deceived. Chan Braikal wasn't the sort to jump down anyone's throat without thorough justification. Gods help you if you screwed up seriously enough to *give* him that justification, though.

"It's the platoon-captain, Chief," chan Yaran said, and chan Braikal's eyes snapped wider. "He just . . . sat up," the under-armsman said. "Now he's just staring straight ahead, right into the fire. He's not even *blinking*, Chief!"

"Vothan's chariot," chan Braikal muttered. He shoved himself upright and crossed to the Platoon-Captain's side. He knelt there, looking into the young officer's eyes, but taking extraordinary care not to touch him.

"Shouldn't we . . . well, *do* something, Chief?" chan Yaran asked. Chan Braikal only snorted harshly, never looking away from Third Platoon's commanding officer.

"There's fuck-all anyone *can* do," the chief-armsman growled. "Not till it runs its course, anyway."

"Is . . . is it a Glimpse?" Chan Yaran's voice was almost a whisper, and chan Braikal barked a laugh deep in his throat.

"You've seen just as many Glimpses as I have," he said. "But I'm damned if I can think of anything else that would hit him like this. Can you?"

Chan Yaran shook his head wordlessly.

"What I thought," chan Braikal grunted, and sat back on his heels. He gazed at the Crown Prince of Ternathia's profile for several seconds, then sighed.

"One thing we can do," he said, looking up at chan Yaran at last. "Break out that bottle of whiskey in my saddlebag. He may just need it in a little while."

Chan Yaran nodded again and hurried off. The chief-armsman scarcely even noticed his departure, although half his reason for sending chan Yaran off had been to give the other Marine something to do as a distraction. Now if someone could just distract *him*, as well.

The tough, experienced noncom snorted again, without a trace of humor. Third Platoon was still a week out from Fort Brithik on its way forward to reinforce Company-Captain Halifu. The mountains were far behind them, as they headed out across the broad stretch of plains to Brithik, but the autumn nights were cold under the brilliant stars. They were also indescribably lonely out here under the endless canopy of the prairie heavens. The ninety-seven men of Third Platoon—outfits this close to the frontier were always at least a little understrength, and Third Platoon was lucky to be only eleven men short of establishment—were a tiny band of humanity amid these ancient mountains which had never known the step of man.

Lorash chan Braikal had joined the Imperial Marines seventeen years before largely because he'd known Marines tended to get sent places just like this. Places on virgin worlds, where the emptiness stretched out forever, wild and free. Over his career, he'd seen thousands of them, and along the way he'd discovered that he'd made exactly the right choice when he enlisted.

But tonight, he felt the vast emptiness of a planet not yet home to man stretching out around him in all directions, sucking at his soul like a vacuum as he knelt here in this fragile bubble of firelight, watching the heir to the imperial crown in the grip of a precognitive Glimpse of terrifying power.

Gods, the chief-armsman thought. *Gods, I wish we'd never left Fort Raylthar!*

But they had, and there was nothing he could do but wait until Prince Janaki woke up and told them what vision had seized him by the throat.

Well, wait and pray.

*   *   *

The next morning dawned clear and considerably chillier. There was frost on their bedrolls, and Jasak found it difficult to radiate a sense of lighthearted adventure as he dragged himself out of his sleeping bag's seductive warmth. Magister Kelbryan, on the other hand, looked almost disgustingly cheerful. She'd taken being the only woman in the expedition in stride, but Jasak had unobtrusively seen to it that her sleeping bag was close to his. Not because he distrusted his men—the Second Andarans were an elite outfit, proud of their reputation—but because his father's maxim that it was always easier to prevent problems than to solve them had been programmed into him at an almost instinctual level.

And, he admitted cheerfully as he watched her rolling her bag as tightly as any of his troopers, because he enjoyed her company. It was even more enjoyable talking with her than looking at her, and that was saying quite a bit.

He chuckled, shaking his head in self-reproving amusement, but

then his humor faded a bit as he listened to Fifty Garlath issuing his morning orders.

His "discussion" with Garlath the evening before had been even more unpleasant than he'd anticipated. The fifty had always resented Jasak. Everyone in the Second Andarans—and in the entire Arcanan Army, for that matter—knew Sir Jasak Olderhan was the only son of Commander of Five Thousand Sir Thankhar Olderhan, Arcanan Army, retired. Who also happened to be His Grace Sir Thankhar Olderhan, Governor of High Hathak, Duke of Garth Showma, Earl of Yar Khom, and Baron Sarkhala . . . and more to the point, perhaps, the man who had commanded the Second Andaran Scout Brigade for over fourteen years before his medical retirement. The Second Andarans were, for all intents and purposes, an hereditary command of the Dukes of Garth Showma, and had been for almost a hundred and seventy years. In fact, they had originally been raised as "The Duke of Garth Showma's Own Rangers."

All of which meant that although Jasak might on paper be only one of the brigade's twelve company commanders, he was actually a little more equal than any of the others. Jasak himself had always known that, and the knowledge had driven him to demonstrate that he deserved the preferential treatment an accident of birth had bestowed upon him. Unfortunately, not everyone recognized that, and the Arcanan Army's tradition, particularly in its Andaran units, was for officers and noncoms to remain within their original brigade or division for their entire careers. It produced a powerful sense of unit identification and was an undoubted morale enhancer, but it could also enhance petty resentments and hostilities. Family quarrels, after all, are almost always nastier than quarrels between strangers.

Shevan Garlath remembered the day a skinny, gawky young Squire Olderhan, fresh out of the Academy, had reported for duty. Shevan Garlath had been a commander of fifty then . . . and he still was. Barring a miracle or the direct intervention of the gods themselves, and despite the fact that he was the younger cousin of a baron, he would still be a commander of fifty when he reached mandatory retirement age. Not even his aristocratic cousin possessed the pull to get someone of his demonstrated inability promoted any higher than that. But since he wasn't prepared to admit that it was because of his own feckless incompetence, it had to be because other people—people like then-Squire and now-Commander of One Hundred Olderhan—had stolen the promotions *he* deserved because their connections were even loftier then his own.

He'd listened to Jasak expressionlessly, without saying a word . . . and certainly without ever acknowledging that a single one of Jasak's tactful criticisms or suggestions was merited. Jasak had wanted to strangle him, but he'd been forced to admit that it was his own fault. He ought to have jerked Garlath up short six weeks ago, when the man was first transferred from Baker Company to Charlie Company as an emergency medical relief for Fifty Thaylar. But he'd told himself it was only a temporary arrangement, just until Thaylar returned from hospital and he could pack Garlath back off to Baker. So instead of sorting the idiot out—or getting rid of him—then, Jasak had let things slide. And now, as his father had always warned him, he was discovering just how much more difficult it was to correct a problem than it would have been to prevent it in the first place.

"I regret that the Hundred is dissatisfied with my efforts," Garlath had said in a cool voice when Jasak finished. "I believe, however, that my deployment of the men under my command has been both prudent and adequate."

Despite everything, Jasak had been flabbergasted.

"I don't believe you quite understand my point, Fifty Garlath," he'd said after several seconds, once he was confident he could control his own tone. "My point is that we were very slow getting started this morning and that I disagree with your assessment as to the adequacy of our formation once we did get moving. I want it changed."

"I believe, Sir, that—as my report will make clear—the reasons for any delay in our departure time were beyond my control. And my understanding of Regulations is that my chosen formation and interval fall within my own discretion, as this unit's commanding officer, so long as my deployment meets the standards laid down by Army doctrine and general field orders."

"This isn't about standards," Jasak had replied, trying to keep the anger out of his tone as he realized Garlath truly intended to defy him. "And it certainly isn't about regulations, Fifty. It's about getting the job done."

"I understand that, Sir. And I would point out that First Platoon, under my command, has successfully accomplished every task the Hundred has assigned to it."

"Whenever you finally got around to it." Jasak's response had come out a bit more icily even than he'd intended, but the defiance flickering in Garlath's eyes—the challenge, which was what it amounted to, to officially reprimand him, despite his patrons, when there was no overt failure in the field to point to—had infuriated him. As, he'd suddenly recognized, it had been intended to. Garlath, he'd realized, was actually attempting to provoke him into words or actions which the fifty would be able to claim proved the hundred's no doubt scathing endorsement of his efficiency report stemmed solely from the fact that Jasak nourished some sort of private vendetta against him.

It was the kind of cunning which proved the other man's fundamental stupidity, but that hadn't changed the parameters of Jasak's current problem, and he'd inhaled deeply.

"Listen to me, Fifty," he'd said then, "this isn't a debate, and this isn't some sort of Ransaran democracy. Tomorrow morning, you will place your point element the required two hundred yards ahead of your main body. You will place a man between your point element and your main body, in visual contact with each, and you will deploy scouts a maximum of one hundred yards out on either flank, where *they* can maintain adequate contact with the main body. Moreover, you *will* maintain one squad at immediate readiness, with its dragon locked and loaded. And when we return to base camp, you and I will . . . discuss our little differences of opinion about the adequacy of your command performance. Is all of that understood, Fifty Garlath?"

Garlath's already dark face had darkened further, yet he'd been left little room for maneuver. His jaw had clenched, and his eyes had blazed hotly, but he'd drawn himself up and saluted with a precision that was a wordless act of insubordination in its own right.

"Yes, Sir. Understood. And I assure the Hundred that his instructions will be obeyed to the letter. Is that all, Sir?"

"Yes, it is."

"By your leave, then, Sir," Garlath had said with frozen formality, pivoted on his heel, and stalked off to find Sword Harnak.

*　　*　　*

"I hope I'm not out of line, Sir Jasak, but you and Fifty Garlath don't exactly seem to like one another."

"Oh?" Jasak looked across at Magister Kelbryan, once more following along behind Garlath with him, and his mouth quirked in a humorless smile. "What makes you say that?"

"I could say it's because I'm Gifted, and that I was always good at social analysis spells. Which happens to be true, actually." Her smile had considerably more amusement in it than his had. "On the other hand, those spells have always been overrated in the popular press. They work quite well for mass analyses, like the polling organizations undertake, but they're pretty much useless on the microlevel." She shrugged. "So instead of falling back on the prestige and reputation of my Gift, I'll just say that he seems a trifle . . . sullen this morning."

The magister had a pronounced gift for understatement, Jasak reflected. In fact, Garlath's "sullenness" had communicated itself to his platoon. Sword Harnak had obviously done his best to defuse the worst of it, but Garlath had made his own air of martyred exasperation only too plain when he ordered his troopers to assume the formation Jasak had insisted upon. He'd been careful about the actual words he used, obviously determined to provide the hundred with no overt ammunition if it came to charges of insubordination. But tone and body language could be remarkably eloquent.

Jasak had considered making a point of just that. Punishable offenses under the articles of war included one defined as "silent insubordination," which could certainly be stretched to cover Garlath's attitude. He was tempted to trot it out—Garlath was busy creating the very situation Jasak had hoped to avoid by refraining from criticizing him in front of his men—but he resisted the temptation. Whatever else he might be doing, the fifty *was* complying, however ungraciously, with the specific instructions he'd been given.

Of course, he was sending out only a single point man, instead of the entire section Jasak himself would have assigned. The hundred recognized that as yet another petty defiance, but Garlath had obviously figured out that Jasak was reluctant to ream him out in front of his men. So the fifty was challenging him to demand that he change his orders, or to simply overrule him and "usurp" command of his platoon. And Jasak had been almost overwhelmingly tempted to do just that.

But the very strength of the temptation had warned him that it was born at least as much of anger as of professional judgment, and anger was not the best basis for making command decisions. Better to wait until he was certain his own temper wasn't driving him . . . and until he could bring the hammer down as Garlath deserved without doing any more damage to the platoon's internal discipline while they were in the field. If there'd been any prospect of running into some sort of opposition, or even any dangerous predator, it might have been different. But this was a virgin portal. There wouldn't be even the threat of the frontier brigands or claim jumpers the Army was occasionally called upon to suppress.

"I'm afraid the fifty and I don't exactly see eye to eye on the proper conduct of a first survey," he said after a moment, answering the magister with rather more frankness than he'd initially intended.

"And *I'm* afraid that that's because the fifty is a frigging idiot," Magister Kelbryan replied tartly.

Jasak blinked in surprise, and she giggled. It was an astonishingly bright, silvery sound, almost as unexpected as her earthy language had been.

"I'm sorry, Sir Jasak!" she said, her tone genuinely contrite despite the laughter still bubbling in the depths of her voice. "It's just that Magister Halathyn and I had to put up with him for almost six full days after your departure, and I've never met a man more invincibly convinced of his own infallibility. Despite, I might add, the over-whelming weight of the evidence to the contrary."

"I'm afraid it would be quite improper for me to denigrate the abilities of one of my officers, especially in front of a civilian," Jasak said after a moment.

"And the fact that you feel constrained to say that tells me every-thing I really need to know, doesn't it, Hundred?" she asked. He said nothing, only looked at her, smiling ever so faintly, and she giggled again. Then she eased the straps of her pack across her shoulders, inhaled hugely, and looked up at the crystal blue patches of autumn sky showing between the dark needles of evergreens and the paint brush glory of seasonal foliage.

"My, what a magnificent day!" she observed.

*   *   *

Trooper 2/c Osmuna swore under his breath as the rock shifted under his right heel. His left arm rose, flailing for balance as he teetered in the middle of the broad, shallow stream. The heavy infantry arbalest in his right hand threatened to pull him the rest of the way off center and down, and the prospect of tumbling into the crystal clear, icy water rushing over its stony bed wrung another, more heartfelt obscenity out of him.

He managed, somehow, not to fall. Which was a damned good thing. Sword Harnak would have had his guts for garters (assuming that Gaythar Harklan, Osmuna's squad shield didn't rip them out first) if he'd fucked up and given Fifty Garlath an excuse to pitch another damned tantrum. Garlath was a piss-poor substitute for Fifty Thaylar, and he was already in a crappy enough mood. Fifty Thaylar would only have laughed it off if his point man fell into a river; Garlath would probably rip everyone involved a new anal orifice just to relieve his own emotional constipation.

Personally, Osmuna reflected, as he continued on across the stream, stepping more cautiously from stone to stone, he thought the bee the Old Man had obviously gotten into his bonnet was probably a bit on the irrational side. Oh, sure, The Book insisted that point elements and flanking scouts be thrown out and that they maintain visual contact with one another at all times. But despite all of that, it wasn't like they were going to run into hordes of howling savages, and everyone knew it. No one ever had, in two centuries of steady exploration and expansion. Still, between the Old Man and Garlath, Osmuna knew which *he* preferred. Officers who let themselves get sloppy about one thing tended to get sloppy about other things . . . and officers who got sloppy, tended to get their troopers killed.

His thoughts had carried him to the far bank, and he started up a shallow slope. The line of the stream had opened a hole in the forest canopy, which permitted the growth of the sort of dense, tangled brush and undergrowth which had been choked out elsewhere in the virgin mature forest. As he began to force his way through it, a flicker of movement higher up the slope, on the edge of the trees, caught his attention. He looked at it, and froze.

*   *   *

Falsan chan Salgmun froze in disbelief, staring down at the river.

The man—and it was, indisputably, a *man*, however he'd gotten here—looked completely out of place. And not simply because this was a virgin world, which meant, by definition, that no one lived there.

It wasn't just his uniform, although that pattern of dense green, black, and white would have been far better suited to a tropical rain forest somewhere than to the mixed conifers and deciduous trees towering above him. Nor was it his coloring, which, after all, was nothing extraordinary. It was the totality of his appearance—the peculiar spiked helmet, covered in the same inappropriate camouflage fabric of which his uniform was made; the clubbed braid of bright, golden hair spilling over the back of his collar; the knee-high, tightly laced boots; the short sword at his left hip . . . and the peculiar looking *crossbow* carried in his right hand.

It was like some weird composite image, some insane juxtapositioning of modern textiles and manufactured goods with medieval weaponry, and it couldn't be here. Couldn't exist. In eighty years of exploration under the Portal Authority's auspices, no trace of any other human civilization had ever been discovered.

Until, chan Salgmun realized, today.

And what the fuck *do I do now?*

*   *   *

Trooper Osmuna stared at the impossible apparition. It wore brown trousers, short boots, and a green jacket, and its slouch hat looked like something a Tukorian cattle herder might have worn. It had a puny looking sheath knife at one hip, certainly not anything anyone might have called a proper *sword*, and something else—something with a handgrip, almost like one of the hand crossbows some hunters used for small game—in an abbreviated scabbard on the other hip. It was also holding something in both hands. Something like an arbalest, but with no bow stave.

It couldn't be here, he thought. Not after two hundred years! Despite all of his training, all of his experience, Osmuna discovered that he'd been totally unprepared for what had been laughingly dismissed as "the other guy contingency" literally for generations.

His heart seemed to have stopped out of sheer shock, but then he felt his pulse begin to race and adrenaline flooded his system. He didn't know exactly what the other man was holding, or how it worked, but he knew from the *way* he held it that it was a weapon of some sort.

And what the fuck *do I do now?* he wondered frantically.

*　　*　　*

Chan Salgmun shook himself. He was only a private employee of the Chalgyn Consortium these days, working for one of the private firms licensed by the Portal Authority to explore the links between the universes. But in his day, he'd served in the Ternathian Army, which considered itself the best on Sharona, with reason, and he recognized the other man's confusion. Confusion that could be dangerous, under the circumstances.

Here we both stand, armed, and scared as shit, he thought. *All we need is for one of us to fuck up. And that damned crossbow of his is cocked and ready to go. I know I* don't *intend to do anything stupid . . . but what about* him?

His thumb moved, very carefully disengaging the safety on his Model 9 rifle.

*　　*　　*

Osmuna saw the not-arbalest move slowly, stealthily, and the level of adrenaline flooding his system rocketed upward. Doctrine was clear on this point. In the inconceivable event that another human civilization was encountered, contact was to be made peacefully, if at all possible. But the overriding responsibility was to ensure that news of the encounter got home. Which meant the people who *had* that news had to be alive—and free—to deliver it.

And if Osmuna intended to stay alive and uncaptured, it probably wouldn't be a very good idea to let this stranger point an unknown weapon at him.

He moved his left hand to the forearm of his arbalest and tipped it upward slightly.

*　　*　　*

Craaaacccccckkkkk!

"What the he—?"

Jasak's head snapped up at the sharp, totally unexpected sound. He'd never heard anything like that flat, hard explosion. It was almost like a tiny sliver bitten off a roll of thunder. Or perhaps the sound a frozen branch made shattering under an intolerable weight of winter ice. But it was neither of those things, and whatever it *was*, it wasn't a natural sound, either. He didn't know how he could be so positive, yet he was, and his first instant flare of astonishment disappeared into a sudden, terrible suspicion.

CHAPTER TWO

SHAYLAR NARGRA-KOLMAYR DUCKED under the open flap of her tent, stepped out into the early chill, and sucked in a deep double lungful of morning. The crisp autumn air tasted like heaven, and she stretched, closing her eyes to sort out the delightful scents floating on the breeze. Cinnamon-dry leaves underfoot mingled with the soft, green fragrance of moss, and the deep, rich scent of wet earth from the forest floor. She grinned in sheer delight, then opened her eyes to watch the gold-tinted mist that hung in a thick, whisper-soft curtain along the stream they'd been following for three days. She could hear the broad creek—it nearly qualified as a river—gurgling and chuckling its way through the ravine it had cut through the forest.

Her husband, Jathmar Nargra, emerged from the tent behind her, and slanting sunlight turned his thinning sandy hair into copper fire. The ends curled slightly from the dampness, like the baby curls in the pictures Jathmar's mother had shown her after their marriage. Field equipment festooned his sturdy canvas web gear: metal canteen, waterproofed compass, field glasses, canvas rucksack. He had his rifle slung across one shoulder for greater ease in carrying, and a Halanch and Welnahr revolver rode his belt.

The lever action rifle and heavy single-action pistol were for protection against inimical wildlife—today, at least. There was literally no chance that they'd run into anything like claim jumpers or a gang of portal pirates in a virgin universe, but that wasn't always the case out here on the leading edge of the frontier. Shaylar was more than a little relieved that he wasn't going to need all that hardware today, but she had to admit he made a brave and dashing figure, standing there in the golden sunlight that filtered down like shafts of molten butter through the gorgeously colored leaves overhead.

28

Jathmar's sun-bronzed face broke into a broad grin as her delight sparkled to him through their marriage bond.

"It *is* a good morning, isn't it?" he observed. "Even with my unheroic figure squarely in the middle of it."

"Oh, absolutely!" Shaylar laughed.

"You wound me, woman." His long face took on a crestfallen tragedy that would have fooled anyone else. "You weren't supposed to *agree* with me!"

"My dear, you're armed and dangerous enough to take on any black bears, timber wolves, wild boars, or cougars native to this part of the world." She batted her eyelashes at him. "What more could any delicately reared maiden ask?"

"Hah! That's more like it!"

He waggled his eyebrows and swaggered over for his good-morning kiss. Rather, his *fifth* good-morning kiss since they'd rolled out of their sleeping bags, twenty minutes previously, she thought with an inner laugh as he enfolded her in his arms. Jathmar Nargra was nothing if not an opportunist. And since they'd spent the vast bulk of the past four years in the company of forty unmarried men—give or take the odd one or two security types who'd hired on, then decided to homestead, or gotten eaten by the odd crocodile—Jathmar made the most of whatever opportunities came his way.

So did Shaylar, for that matter. Since most of the universes explored to date did have cougars in this region, and since—so far as anyone had been able to tell after eighty years of constant exploration—every portal's universe was very nearly identical to every other, Shaylar didn't mind in the least Jathmar's tendency to run about armed like a proper brigand. His various bits and pieces of lethal hardware might get in the way at moments like this, but that was just fine with her.

When Jathmar finally decided their kiss had been adequate, for now, at least, he stepped back, and she grinned as she noticed the sketchbook peeking out of his rucksack.

"Planning to loaf today, are we?" she inquired sweetly, and his clear hazel eyes twinkled.

"Tease me all you like, faithless wench. One of these days, I'll have to beat the art buyers off with a club, and we'll find ourselves retired, rich, and happy."

"I'm happy now," she smiled. "And with all of this," she swept an expansive arm at the pristine wilderness surrounding them, "who needs to be rich?"

"Who, indeed?" he echoed, brushing a lock of raven-black hair from her brow. A few strands always escaped the practical braids she wore while in the field. "You really *are* happy," he said, smiling as he read her emotions through the special bond between married Talents. "I worried about it, you know. When we first started our crusade to place you on a field team."

"Yes, I know," she said softly. "And I know how hard you pushed the Board to pull it off."

"Halidar Kinshe turned the tide of opinion, not me," Jathmar demurred. "And you've known the parliamentary representative a lot longer than I have, dear heart. Still," he grinned, "if you want to lavish thanks on your husband's humble head, far be it from me to discourage you."

"You," she said severely, swatting him with her rolled up tube of charts, "are incorrigible!"

"Not at all. *En*couragable, now . . ."

She laughed as he waggled his eyebrows again. Then he tipped his head up to peer through the crimson and golden clouds of fall foliage high overhead.

"It is a grand morning for sketching, isn't it? Not to mention perfect weather for a survey. The mist ought to burn off early, I think."

"Not that you *need* a clear day," Shaylar chuckled. Jathmar's Talent was the ability to "see" terrain features in a five-mile circle around him, regardless of weather or ambient light—or the complete lack thereof. "But weather like this should make the hike more exhilarating. I'll give you that. In fact, I think I'm jealous about being stuck in camp while you go gadding about!"

"You're happy as a pearl in a bed of oysters," he told her, tweaking her nose gently. "Besides, after that last universe, you should be thrilled by any sunshine we can get."

"I'll say."

Shaylar's shudder of memory was only half-feigned. The universe they'd mapped prior to entering this one had connected via a portal in the middle of what had to be one of the rainiest spots in any known universe. Back home, it would have been northwest Rokhana, near the mouth of the Yirshan River where it spilled into the immense Western Ocean. They'd been incredibly lucky in that their arrival portal and the portal leading to *this* universe were less than three hundred miles apart, and they knew it. Portals in such close proximity to one another were almost unheard of, and correspondingly valuable.

Despite that, and despite the guidance Darcel Kinlafia, their Portal Hound, had been able to give them, it had taken them almost a month and a half to cover the two hundred and sixty-five dripping wet miles between them, and the last three weeks had been horrible. They hadn't seen the sun for twenty-three straight days, and most of their gear had sprouted mold that had required copious amounts of bleach once the rains finally stopped. After six weeks spent in perpetually soggy clothes, squelching through perpetually soggy wetlands, pushing through perpetually thick undergrowth with machetes, and sleeping under perpetual shrouds of mosquito netting and the smoke of smudge pots, this crisp, clear autumn air was heaven itself.

"I'm not complaining," she said cheerfully. "At least we could come through the portal and leave the rain behind. Poor Company-Captain Halifu had to build a *fort* in that mess. I don't think I've ever seen such an abundance of unenthusiastic soldiers in my life."

Grafin Halifu had favored Jathmar and Shaylar—carefully out of earshot of the men of his command—with a piquant rendition of his opinion of the multiverse's inconsiderate ill manners in placing a portal in that particular godsforsaken spot. And since Uromathians worshiped just about as many deities as there were individual Uromathians, a spot had to be nigh well lost at the back of forever before *all* the Uromathian gods decided to forsake it.

For some odd reason, the company-captain had seemed less than amused by Ghartoun chan Hagrahyl's decision to name that universe "New Uromath" in honor of Halifu's homeland.

"No, Grafin's troops weren't very happy, were they?" Jathmar chuckled. "Of course, I wouldn't have been very happy if Regs had required *me* to build on the already-mapped side of that particular portal, either. There they sit, sinking slowly into the mud, and right in front of them is all of *this*."

It was his turn to wave expansively at the towering forest giants all about them.

"At least Darcel wasn't bound by the PAAF's policy," Shaylar pointed out.

"I think some of Grafin's troopers were ready to commit mayhem when they realized he was bugging out for a better spot," Jathmar agreed.

"They couldn't possibly blame him," Shaylar replied primly, eyes laughing wickedly. "He's a telepath. And everyone knows that not even the best Voice can transmit *through* a portal."

"That's what all of you keep telling the rest of us, anyway," Jathmar said. "I'm not too sure Grafin's troopers were buying it this time around, though."

Shaylar chuckled. Like her, Darcel Kinlafia was a Voice, a Talented long-distance communications specialist. Voices, who were born with the gifts of perfect recall and the ability to connect, mind-to-mind, with other Voices, were essential in many aspects of Sharonian society.

Governments, the Portal Authority, and private industries ranging from manufacturing to news broadcasters used Voices to transmit complex messages that were word- and image-perfect. The military used Voices, as well, for its long-range communications. But as useful as Voices were throughout Sharona's multiple-universe civilization, they were utterly indispensable to the work of surveying *new* universes.

Every survey crew fielded a bare minimum of two Voices. One remained at the portal giving access to a new universe, serving as a link between the field team conducting the survey and the established settlements in the universes behind them. The more portals a field team surveyed, the more Voices it needed to cover the portals in their particular transit chain. And when their team reached the distance limit of Shaylar's transmission ability, they would need to move Darcel forward and replace him with a new Voice in a game of telepathic leapfrog.

This portal, in particular, was part of the reason they were so stretched for manpower. During the past ten months, Chalgyn Consortium's teams had found no less than three new portals, including New Uromathia and this one, which they hadn't named yet. That had forced them to split up, trying to claim and explore them all, and that was before they crossed into this universe and started to realize what they might have stumbled across. Their discoveries were going to be a massive windfall, and not just for them and their employer. In all of its eighty previous years of exploration, the Portal Authority had located and charted only forty-nine portals. The Chalgyn teams had already increased that total by over six percent, and if Darcel was right about *this* portal, the consequences for their entire civilization (not to mention their own bank accounts) would be stupendous.

All of that was wonderful, but it also left them incredibly shorthanded. Ghartoun chan Hagrahyl had split their team twice, already, claiming the other two portals and exploring the universes beyond them. As a result, they were down to only two Voices and a bare minimum of other crewmen, not to mention supplies, but nobody was complaining.

Fortunately, the Portal Authority was in charge of all portal transit traffic, which meant the units of the PAAF—the Portal Authority

Armed Forces, composed of multinational military units assigned
to Authority duty—built the portal forts and provided most of the
personnel to man them, including at least one Portal Authority Voice.
Or, that was the way it was supposed to work, at any rate. *This* portal
was so new, and there were so many other portals along what had
been designated the Karys Chain that needed forts, as well, that the
military hadn't been able to bring in a new Voice, yet.

All of which left Darcel Kinlafia holding down the listening post for
their team until a fort-based Voice could be moved in. Darcel would
pass their field reports along from one Voice to the next, creating a
chain of rapid communications. They could, if emergency required it,
get a message all the way back to humanity's birth world, Sharona,
in little more than a week. If not for the water gaps between some
of the portals, which had to be crossed by ship, since no one could
permanently post a relay Voice in the middle of an ocean, they could
have gotten a message home in a matter of hours.

Shaylar was grateful that she would never be the Voice stuck at the
portal, just waiting for someone else's messages. She wasn't merely the
Voice assigned to the survey team, she was married to—and inextri-
cably linked with—its primary Mapper. That made her not only an
integral part of the survey, but meant she was critical to the team's
primary mission: mapping a new universe. Jathmar could "See" the
terrain around him, but Shaylar was the team's actual cartographer.
It was her job to translate Jathmar's mental "pictures" of distant
terrain features into the maps which would guide later exploration
and settlements. Even if they stumbled across another portal, they
wouldn't—couldn't—leave Shaylar there to cover it. They would have
to send word back to field another survey crew to explore the new
universe, or else to take over the exploration of this one so that *they*
could concentrate on the new one.

Then again, they couldn't really leave Darcel, either. Not for long,
anyway. He might not be as essential to the everyday operations of
the field team as Shaylar and Jathmar were, but his secondary Talent was, in its own way, even more important to the Consortium's
long term operations.

She knew exactly how lucky she was. Not just to escape the tedium
of portal sitting, while others enjoyed all the fun of exploration, but
to be out here at all. On the whole, Sharonian women enjoyed equal
status with Sharonian men, although legal rights varied from one
kingdom or republic to the next. After all, there was no question
about female intelligence or inherent capabilities in a population where
one in five people possessed at least some degree of Talent. That sort

of discrimination had gone out with the dark ages, thousands upon thousands of years ago, during the first Ternathian Empire.

But mapping virgin universes was arduous, frequently dangerous work. The Portal Authority, whose governing members were drawn from each of Sharona's dozens of nations and city-states—not to mention the current Ternathian Empire—had decreed that women should not risk the dangers routinely braved by virgin-portal survey teams.

Shaylar was the Portal Authority's first exception to that ironclad rule, which had carried the weight of eighty years of precedent. She was very much aware that her performance was under scrutiny. She had the chance of a lifetime—the chance to blaze the way for other women who wanted to explore where no other human had ever set foot—but she was equally conscious of her responsibility to prove once and for all that it was time to set that long-standing rule permanently aside.

Shaylar had helped survey two other virgin universes before this expedition, not to mention putting in her time, along with Jathmar, pushing back the frontiers of other, already claimed universes. Each portal gave access to an entire planet, after all, and however physically similar all of those duplicate worlds might be, they still had to be explored and surveyed. And that wasn't the sort of chore which could be accomplished in the snap of your fingers. Besides, that sort of exploration was the final training period—the internship—the Authority required before it was prepared to turn a team loose on the far side of an unexplored portal.

It was just as rugged a life as everyone had warned her it would be. The frontier wasn't gentle, and it didn't make allowances for the "frailer sex." But despite the worries of the general public and the dire predictions of the naysayers—not to mention the very real harshness of conditions, and the ever-present dangers any pioneer faced in the wilderness—she was profoundly happy. Not to mention tremendously successful.

Having Jathmar at her side to share the experience only deepened the wonder of it all. Her eyes met his and the love that came rolling to her through their marriage bond was so strong and sweet tears prickled her eyelids. Jathmar leaned down the seven inches between their mismatched heights and placed a gentle kiss on her brow, a more tender expression of his feelings than a mere ardent lip-lock. Then he grinned and jerked his head towards the deep timber.

"Time's a-wasting," he said. "Let's see how much we can get mapped before lunch. And the sooner we talk to Ghartoun, the sooner we'll get started."

Their camp was nestled in a natural clearing where the stream looped its way through the timber. It had taken them three days to come this far, and they'd been here for nearly three more days, mapping the region. Shaylar knew she would miss the campsite when they moved on, but she was just as anxious as the others to see what lay ahead. Any survey was always slow work, of course, but it had taken five full days just to map the portal itself. Not surprisingly, since it was by far the largest any of them had ever seen, far less mapped.

In fact, at over thirty miles wide, it was actually larger than the Calirath Gate. That made it the largest portal ever discovered, and their first task on stepping through it had been to map the actual portal and lay out the grid coordinates of what would become this universe's primary base camp, one day's journey from Company-Captain Halifu's fort. This one would be a substantial affair—a fully manned fort and forward supply depot that would house Portal Authority administrators, medical teams, more soldiers, and enough equipment and supplies to serve as the staging area for other exploration teams, construction crews, miners, and the settlers who would inevitably follow.

Once they'd found a suitable site for that base of operations and sent its coordinates back for the Chalgyn Consortium to begin organizing the follow-on construction crews, they'd set out along a line to the south. As they pushed forward, they'd built small brush enclosures at the end of each full day's travel, designed to keep out unfriendly local wildlife. They'd remained in place at each camp long enough to thoroughly map the surrounding region—which meant hiking far enough to telepathically Map a twenty-mile grid-square—then pushed forward another full day's journey and built another camp to start the process all over again.

It was no accident that the Portal Authority had drawn upon the Ternathian Empire's method of expansion. Ternathia had been building empires for five thousand years, after all. That was an immense span of time in which to develop methods that *worked*, and the Portal Authority had borrowed heavily whenever and wherever appropriate, including the custom of building fortified camps along any line of exploratory advance through virgin territory. The fact that Ternathia provided over forty percent of the PA's multinational military contingent, and something like half of its total attached officers, might also have had a little something to do with it, Shaylar supposed.

With only twenty people on their currently understrength crew, she and her crewmates couldn't build the elaborate stockades which had comprised the Ternathian system of day-forts. But they could construct a perimeter of interwoven branches that served to keep out anything short of a herd of charging elephants. There were even tales from veteran crews of stampeding cattle and bison herds numbering in the tens of thousands, turning aside and flowing around the camp, rather than run directly into the jagged, sharp projecting branches of its brush wall. All in all, the system worked as well for the Portal Authority as it had for the Ternathians.

Ghartoun chan Hagrahyl was intimately familiar with that system, since he'd served with the Ternathian Army, as the honorific "chan" in his name proclaimed. He'd been an engineer, and after fulfilling his commitment to the Army, he'd returned to school. He had taken advantage of a major scholarship offer to pursue graduate studies in engineering and actually taught engineering at the branch of the Ternathian Imperial University in New Estafel on New Sharona, the first major colony established outside Sharona's home universe.

After a decade in the classroom, however, he'd succumbed to the lure of the portals. That had been almost twenty years ago, and for the last seven, he'd been with the Chalgyn Consortium.

She and Jathmar both found Ghartoun's experience comforting. Jathmar was especially conscious of it, since he himself had never served in any military force. The Republic of Faltharia, colonized long after the last real shooting war had rampaged across Sharona, had only two neighbors, neither of whom were interested in expanding their territories through conquest. Not when there was free land for the taking in unexplored universes, just waiting to be colonized. Jathmar had learned his woodcraft during his childhood, living near and honing his Talent in the trackless Kylie Forest, the greatest of Faltharia's protected state forests, which preserved the wilderness Faltharia's earliest settlers had found when they arrived from Farnalia nearly three hundred years ago.

Jathmar was grateful that Farnalians—and their Faltharian descendents—understood the multiple values that large tracts of wilderness bestowed on a nation. And for giving him a place to hone the skills which had helped earn him a slot on a survey crew.

And if he lacked formal military training, he'd been through the Portal Authority's own rigorous training program. Coupled with a lifetime as a hunter, he felt more than capable of holding up his end of anything that came his team's way. Not that he spent very much of his time in camp.

His Mapping duties were the main reason it had taken them three days to move this far south. They could have made the same trip much more quickly—they were little more than a single day from their entry portal for someone hiking at his best emergency speed—but you simply couldn't Map that quickly. While Darcel Kinlafia loafed around at the portal with a fishing pole and a stewpot full of whatever he could bring down with his rifle, Jathmar and Shaylar were hard at work, earning every cent of their fat paychecks.

They frequently toiled well past darkness to lay down their expanding grid. Jathmar didn't need daylight to "see" terrain features, and Shaylar could work by the light of the oil lamps they carried in their packs, with reflectors to give her plenty of light to fill in the charts and field reports she was responsible for creating. With any luck, their chosen direction would carry them straight toward some kind of valuable real estate that they could claim for the Chalgyn Consortium.

The consortium's main income, of course, would come from portal-usage fees. Once a survey crew discovered a new portal, the company which employed them earned the right to charge fees for every person and every load of goods that traveled through it. The Portal Authority actually ran the portals and set the fees, which were very low on an individual basis. But the cumulative totals added up to a staggering annual income for busy portals.

That was the driving force behind fielding survey crews. Any crew that found a new portal guaranteed a potentially massive income for its company. Mineral wealth and other natural resource rights simply added to the lucrative venture, and the team which found them shared in the money derived from them.

Now Jathmar offered his wife an arm, and Shaylar giggled as she laid her hand regally on his elbow. The gesture was curiously refined, in that subtle and mysterious way Harkalan women seemed to master in their cradles. For just an instant, the grubby, dirt stained dungarees and scuffed hiking boots wavered as his mind's eye showed him a vision of his wife in High Harkalan formal dress. She looked stunning in its multitude of embroidered layers, each one dyed a different, luminous color, setting her skin aglow with the colors of sun-struck emeralds and gold-flecked lapis and the rich, burgundy tones of Fratha wine.

Blue lapis remained to this day the most precious gemstone in *any* Harkalan culture, for reasons Jathmar still wasn't sure he entirely grasped. Harkalan mythology tended toward the complex, with layers of meaning Shaylar was still explaining after nearly ten years of wedded bliss. Of course, most of Shaylar's lessons ended prematurely, since virtually all of Harkalan mythology revolved around the pleasures of intimacy shared between willing participants. . . .

Shaylar caught the drift of his emotions and smiled gently, with a seductive promise that hit Jathmar like a blow to the gut. That smile made him grateful all over again for the victory they'd won, securing Shaylar's place in this survey crew. He couldn't have done field work without her. *Wouldn't* have, rather, for the simple reason that being separated from her for extended periods of time would have felt entirely too much like premature death.

"I love you, too," Shaylar murmured, drawing his head down for another kiss that was altogether too brief. He sighed regretfully and promised himself an early end to the evening, thankful that they'd pitched their tent just a little farther from the others, for privacy's sake. Shaylar picked up *that* emotion through their marriage bond, too, and her eyes smoldered as they met his. Then she schooled her features, patted his arm in a decorous, wifely fashion, and headed him toward the center of camp, where Ghartoun chan Hagrahyl's voice rang out clearly above the chatter of birds defending their chosen territories.

"Ghartoun sounds just like them, doesn't he?" Shaylar chuckled, nodding toward the deep timber and its glorious explosion of bird-song. "Defending what we've marked on our charts and figuring ways to outfox our competition when the rival survey teams arrive."

"I'd lay money that nobody else has ever suggested that Ghartoun chan Hagrahyl shares *anything* in common with birds," Jathmar laughed. The stocky Ternathian looked more like a Tathawirian bison than anything avian. The former soldier's black hair was cut short, military fashion, despite thirty years on the civilian economy, and his blue eyes were as crisp as the morning air.

He wasn't a brilliant man, but he knew his job, and a lively intelligence lived behind those intense blue eyes. At six-feet-one-inch, he was taller than Jathmar, and far more heavily built, brawny with muscle. At five-two, Shaylar looked like a child beside him. Her chin barely reached his chest, and she weighed a hundred and five pounds, soaking wet, but appearances were deceiving. She was an experienced outdoorswoman, capable of holding her own on any march they'd ever had to make—and that ghastly three weeks-slog through wetlands and riverine floods had taxed *all* of them to the limits of their endurance.

"You're ready?" chan Hagrahyl asked, glancing up from sharpening his camp ax at their approach. He tested the edge with a cautious thumb, then grunted in satisfaction. He'd dulled it thoroughly yesterday, cutting branches for the camp's brush fence.

"Do you have a preference for which direction we start this morning?" Jathmar asked.

"Not really. Just bear in mind that Falsan headed southwest about thirty minutes ago, following our creek downstream. He's after something he can bag for supper. I told Cookie that if he served up another slop-pot of trail-rats, I'd scalp him alive."

Jathmar laughed. He was delighted that their team leader was such an ardent believer in saving their dried and canned emergency rations for genuine emergencies. He enjoyed eating fresh meat from the game they brought down, along with whatever edible plants were in season where they'd camped. Still . . .

"Fair's fair, Ghartoun, and we're lucky to have him," he pointed out. "Naldar's the best cook on any team this side of Sharona. He can even make trail-rats edible."

"That's what *you* say," Shaylar muttered. "I'd almost as soon eat shoe leather."

"A woman after my own heart," chan Hagrahyl chuckled. "At any rate, I trust Falsan's judgment. He's not going to shoot at something he can't see, but there's no point taking chances. I'd just as soon you didn't jostle his elbow when he's trying to stalk whatever's out there, either. If you head straight south, you might cross his firing line, so I'd recommend going east."

"Agreed," Jathmar said dryly. Unlike Shaylar, Falsan was not a telepath, and without something like their own marriage bond, not even a Voice as strong as Shaylar could contact someone who *wasn't* telepathically Talented. Falsan chan Salgmun was as steady and reliable as they came, but accidents happened, and Jathmar didn't want to risk trailing a man with a loaded rifle in unknown territory. Not when the man didn't realize he was being trailed.

"All right, I'll hike a mile out along the eastern line and work around the perimeter toward the terminus of the southern transit. That'll let Shaylar build up a detailed record of everything within six miles of our camp in that grid quarter. My terrain scans are picking up a fork in the stream, about a mile east of here. The main creek runs almost straight east, and the other branch flows south, so I'll follow those as a rough guide. I'll use the compass for directional corrections when the streams twist out of true with the baselines."

"You always were a cautious fellow, Jathmar," chan Hagrahyl observed with another chuckle. "You've got the best directional sense of any terrain scanner I've worked with—and that's saying a lot, I might add. But you still carry a compass."

Jathmar shrugged off the compliment to his skill, although Shaylar's grin could have cracked solid oak and her delight fizzed in his awareness.

"A careful Mapper lives to map the next portal, my friend," he smiled. "Careless Mappers, on the other hand, can get themselves and their crews killed." He wrapped an arm around Shaylar's shoulders. "And just between you, me, and the fence we put up yesterday, I plan to survive long enough to see worlds we never dreamed were out here!"

Chan Hagrahyl grinned and clouted him across one shoulder.

"Well spoken, Jathmar. Well spoken, indeed." Then his manner settled back into professionalism. "Will you be able to complete the baseline grid today?"

Jathmar frowned thoughtfully up at the sky as he considered the question. Then he tossed his head in something which was almost a nod.

"Probably," he said, "although it should take us most of the day, at a minimum. At least this," he waved one hand at the towering trees of the mature climax forest about them, "means we don't have much underbrush to slash our way through, thank the gods. But I'll be following streambeds for a fair portion of the day, and there's enough understory along these banks to slow me down a good bit. Once I start the perimeter swing down toward the southern baseline, the terrain ought to be easier going."

Jathmar would essentially be walking along an L-shaped path that would fill in a square-shaped area of ground. Survey base grids were always square, given the nature of a terrain scanner's Talent. This morning's first square would begin the newest section of their base grid for this day-fort. Once that grid was completed, they would decide which direction to move to begin the next grid-square of exploration. Ideally, that would depend on where they were, and what valuable resources might be nearby.

"If we can get a good look at the stars tonight," Shaylar said hopefully, "we ought to be able to place our location a little more precisely."

"That'll make me feel better, I don't mind admitting," chan Hagrahyl agreed with a nod. "It's one thing to know approximately where you are, but I'll be happier when a star-fix pinpoints our location more accurately."

The clear autumn day was welcome for more than the simple absence of rain. The skies had remained overcast since their arrival, almost as though the rain clouds had followed them through the portal and dogged their heels before finally attenuating with distance. That was actually possible, Jathmar mused, given the size of that portal and the collision of air masses between the two universes.

Based on the vegetation and wildlife, Jathmar was betting they were somewhere in the northern portion of what would have been his own birth country, back on Sharona. The massive oak trees, sugar maples, tulip poplars, and sycamores, coupled with the cardinals and chipmunks, and the majestic white-tail deer they'd spotted, all suggested a spot within perhaps two or three hundred miles of the lakeshore city of Serikai in his native Faltharia.

If so, the five immense lakes of Faltharia—larger than many a Sharonian sea—should lie very close to their present position. Jathmar had made a private bet with himself that they would end up fixing their position within a few days' hike of this universe's analog of Emlin Falls. Emlin was one of the two most spectacular waterfalls on Sharona—and, of course, on any of its many duplicates which had already been discovered and at least partially explored. But Jathmar wasn't thinking solely about the scenery. If they were near Emlin Falls, they wouldn't be too terribly far from some valuable iron ore deposits. Still, he didn't want to raise anyone's hopes yet, so he said nothing about his suspicion to chan Hagrahyl.

"We'll get started, then," Jathmar told their expeditionary leader instead. "I'll plan to rendezvous back at camp around noon."

Chan Hagrahyl grunted his satisfaction and turned back to carefully finish sharpening his ax blade.

Jathmar and Shaylar headed for the eastern end of the camp, passing Rilthan's tent, where the gunsmith was busy making field repairs to one of the rifles which had started jamming yesterday. The tools of his trade were spread out around him, along with pieces of the partially disassembled weapon. It was one of the Model 9's. The Ternathian Army had disposed of thousands of the lever-action .48-caliber rifles on the civilian market over the last several years. They were powerful, reliable weapons, especially with the newly developed "smokeless" powders, even if their tubular magazines made it unsafe to use the equally new (and ballistically far superior) "Spitzer-pointed" rounds. They were certainly sufficient for any civilian need, at any rate, and the Army had just about completed reequipping its active-duty formations with the newer bolt-action Model 10.

Past Rilthan, the drovers were working on the pack saddles, examining their tack carefully while a dozen sturdy donkeys stood slack-footed and bored in the temporary pen. Pack animals were essential to a long expedition, and donkeys were sturdy enough to require very little veterinary care. They were also rugged enough to subsist on vegetation on which horses would have starved, although they couldn't match the speed and carrying capacity of the mules the military used as pack animals. The mingled scents of gun oil, dust, warm hide, and dung lent a pungent note to the early morning air.

Several of the little animals shook their heads and followed Jathmar and Shaylar with hopeful eyes, wanting fresh carrots or a handful of grain. Shaylar reached across the rope that served to pen the animals into one corner of the stockade and scratched one of them between its ears. It butted her hand, begging for more, and she laughed.

"Sorry, pet. That's all the scratching I have time for. And I'm fresh out of carrots."

Jathmar grinned as Shaylar followed him out through the rough gate in the stockade and trailed him a short distance into the trees. Her dark hair caught the early sunlight with a silky gloss, like a blackbird's wing. She looked . . . not out of place in this towering timberland, but still somehow alien. Like a visitor from another, very different world, not just another universe.

Perhaps it was just that Jathmar knew exactly what world she'd been born to, for he'd visited Shaylar's home before marrying her. The diminutive beauty who'd captured his heart was not Faltharian. Shaylar had been born in Shurkhal, a prosperous kingdom of ancient Harkala that sprawled across a hot and arid peninsula between the eastern coast of Ricathia and the great triangular jut of land that lay a thousand miles across the Harkalan Ocean.

Shaylar's features bore the unmistakable stamp of Harkalan ancestry, as well they might, since Shurkhal had once been the cultural center of the Harkalan Empire. Swallowed up by the massive Ternathian Empire, ancient Harkala had prospered, thanks to its placement along the trade routes running east and west. When Ternathia had finally dissolved most of its empire, retreating back to its core provinces, the Harkalan kingdoms had come into their own again as independent realms. Shaylar's family wasn't part of the wealthy traders' class, let alone the ruling families, but they had welcomed him—a genuine outsider—with open arms and that worlds-famous, genuine Shurkhali welcome that Ternathian bards once had written of so eloquently.

Shaylar's dark eyes lifted, meeting his as she caught the nuances of his emotions.

"Well, why wouldn't my family welcome you?" she asked softly. "You were quite a coup for a girl like me."

"A girl like you?" He chuckled. "Do you have any idea how many Mappers at the Portal Authority I had to knock over the head to get myself assigned to you?"

Shaylar laughed out loud.

"Jath, you never had a chance! Not after I'd made up my mind. Which I did about five minutes after meeting you in Halidar Kinshe's office."

He grinned, hazel eyes dancing impishly with the delight that could speed her pulse even after ten years of marriage. They'd met while interning at the Portal Authority during the early phases of their training. Halidar Kinshe was a royal parliamentary representative from Shaylar's kingdom, who also held a position on the Portal Authority's board of directors. No portal survey crewman—or crew*woman*—could accept employment from anyone, not even a private consortium like Chalgyn, without being bonded by the Portal Authority. And the Authority wouldn't bond anyone who hadn't completed its rigorous coursework successfully. Part of that included a political internship with a Board director, whose evaluation of an intern's performance literally made or destroyed that intern's hope of future employment.

Shaylar had sometimes despaired of surviving those grueling years of intensive classwork, combined with field expeditions and mandatory training in things like marksmanship and self-defense. They'd taxed her to the utter limits of her intelligence, Talent, and endurance. But she'd made it—one of only sixteen women who'd ever completed the full course, and the only one allowed to join an active survey team. While Halidar Kinshe had proven himself an unexpected ally and mentor, for which she would always be grateful, it was Jathmar who'd helped get her through the classwork and the agonizing fieldwork, which was designed to weed out as many applicants as possible. She'd fallen hard for Jath, as he'd been called then, long before their graduation from the Portal Authority Academy.

He'd done the same. He'd even adopted the customary "-ar" suffix married couples from Shurkhal added to their first names once they'd exchanged wedding vows. It wasn't a Faltharian custom, but he'd told her he wanted to follow it before she could work up the nerve to ask if he might consider it. His offer had melted her heart with joy, and not just because it had underscored how much he loved her. She'd also recognized what it would mean to her family, and she'd been more afraid than she'd been prepared to admit even to herself that her family wouldn't approve of her independent-minded Faltharian and his republican notions and dreams that her father, at least, would never fully understand.

Her father was, at heart, a simple agriculturalist, tending admittedly large flocks of russet-wool sheep, silk-hair goats, and the surly, hump-backed dune-treaders that Shurkhali merchants had used for centuries to cross the desert trade routes between their coast and the rich markets far to the east. He couldn't understand the dream that drove Jathmar . . . and he understood Shaylar's dreams even less well.

But he loved her, and he seemed to realize that her mother's dreams had been reborn and reshaped in her own heart. Shaylar's mother was a cetacean translator. A very good one, in fact, employed by one of the largest cetacean institutes on Sharona. Shalassar Kolmayr-Brintal had come to Shurkhal as a young woman, following her own dreams. She'd helped found the Cetacean Institute's Shurkhali Aquatic Realms Embassy, which was—as sheer happenstance would have it—located on land the Institute had purchased from Thamin Kolmayr. Their unexpected courtship was still Institute legend.

Shaylar had grown up with "playmates" whose playground was the long, narrow Finger Sea that lapped against Shurkhal's eastern shoreline, linking the Mbisi Sea—by way of the Grand Ternathian Canal—with the Rindor Ocean. Dolphins and whales from the Rindor Ocean swam to the embassy to pass messages and conduct treaty negotiations with the Cetacean Institute, by way of the embassy. The embassy passed those messages to the Cetacean Institute's headquarters in Tajvana, as well as passing the Institute's messages to the whales and dolphins.

Jathmar had been as delighted as an eager adolescent, not only meeting but swimming with dolphins who could hold actual conversations with Shaylar's mother. *Their* approval of Jathmar had gone a long way toward endearing him to her mother's heart. Like all cetacean translators, Shalassar had a high opinion of Sharona's ocean-dwelling citizens. An opinion that Shaylar—and now Jathmar—shared.

But there wasn't all that much wealth in dune-treaders and goats, no matter how you added up the small change. And while her mother was a respected and Talented professional, there wasn't a great deal of money in cetacean translation, either. Not even at the embassy level.

Of course, if that black liquid seeping up through the sand in her family's ancient holding proved to be as valuable as some of the Ternathian engineers thought it might, Clan Kolmayr might just find itself possessed of more wealth than their entire lineage—stretching back nearly two thousand years—had ever possessed. That was what everyone else seemed to think, at any rate, although Shaylar wasn't so sure there was enough of the "crude oil" beneath the family holdings to make it worth the developers' while. Investing the time and machinery necessary to drill wells and pump out whatever oil might be there would surely take a hefty chunk of money up front.

And once they'd pumped out whatever was there, what would they *use* it for? She couldn't help feeling skeptical about those newfangled engines that used the refined products made from oil. She couldn't imagine a world where the noisy, smelly, dirty things would ever be as widespread and useful as the more wide-eyed fanatics claimed they would. But the thought of her parents and cousins wearing silks and building fancy houses and gardens was enough to tickle her sense of humor. Those images flickered across the marriage bond into Jathmar's awareness, and his eyes twinkled.

"Of course they'll be rich as kings. Why do you think I married you, my little sand flower?"

Shaylar thumped him solidly on the shoulder with the best glower she could produce. It wasn't very convincing. Jathmar was the least money-oriented human being she'd ever known.

He laughed and kissed her lightly, then sighed.

"Time to get busy," he said. "Give me time to get into position before making contact. Call it at least half-an-hour, given that underbrush."

He was eying the thick growth along the stream's steep banks.

"Half-an-hour, then," Shaylar nodded, and he turned and headed east along the creek.

Shaylar watched him vanish around the bend, allowed a small sigh to escape her—mostly because she wanted to go with him this morning—then shook herself firmly and returned to camp. She set up her work table, which was a lap desk that unfolded to give her a smooth writing surface. The donkey assigned to them carried it, when they were on the move, since that level writing surface was a necessity. Mapping was ninety percent of the reason they were out here, after all.

She chose a spot on the eastern edge of camp, outside the stockade, since chan Hagrahyl had most of the survey crewmen taking their gear apart to check for damage. It was a ritual they performed each time they stopped. Frayed straps could lead to damaged equipment, which could put lives at risk, and chan Hagrahyl was too good a team leader to risk that kind of sloppiness.

While most of the crew busied themselves inside the stockade, Shaylar laid out her materials, sitting within visual range of the remaining three crewmen who were busy along the stream. Braiheri Futhai, the team's naturalist, was peering through the weeds, sketching something in his notebook. Elevu Gitel, the team's geologist, was dutifully absorbed in taking soil samples. Futhai had already laid out his collecting nets, waiting until the mist burned off and the dew dried from the grass before scooping butterflies and other insects out of the air. Both men were self-absorbed, scarcely aware of one another.

The third man caught Shaylar's eye, rolled his own at the scientists, and gave her an irreverent grin. Barris Kasell was a former soldier, an Arpathian who'd served his time in the infantry of his native kingdom, which made him something of an oddity. Most Arpathians were horsemen, renowned for their equestrian skill and ferocity, both of which they needed to guard their borders from the powerful Uromathian kingdoms and empires south and east of them.

Unlike chan Hagrahyl, Kasell had a wicked sense of humor. He usually drew guard duty, watching over the scientists—and her, as well—because he didn't mind the job and was extremely diligent. His almond-shaped eyes, legacy of the mixed blood in that region of Arpathia, twinkled at her.

Shaylar wore her own handgun at her hip, as did every other member of chan Hagrahyl's team. But she couldn't do her job *and* pay attention to her surroundings, so Kasell watched out for danger while she charted and the others did their collecting.

The heavily forested region around them teemed with birdlife and dozens of small mammal species, one of which had already sent Futhai into fits of ecstasy, since it was a completely unknown type.

"A black-and-white chipmunk! Gods and thunders, a black-and-white chipmunk! And look—there are *dozens* of them, so it's not an isolated deviant individual!" Over the course of their three-day march, that had become Futhai's favorite cry. "They're everywhere! It's not an isolated population! Black-and-white chipmunks! A true new subspecies!"

Braiheri Futhai was a man whose fastidious nature showed itself not so much in the way he carried himself, or engaged his surroundings—he was every bit as good a woodsman as any other member of the team—but in the way he thought, down deep at the core of his Ternathian soul. Futhai was *not* Braiheri chan Futhai, for he'd never served in Ternathia's military. Not because he was unpatriotic, but because soldiering was not a gentleman's occupation.

Futhai was a very good naturalist, with a veritable treasure trove of scientific information stored in memory. His knowledge ranged from geology to meteorology, from zoology and botany to physics, and the mathematical precision with which all worlds—including their beloved Sharona—whirled through the ether in their journeys around duplicates of Sharona's sun. He had a keen eye and a keen mind, and a gift for detailed observation that made him a valuable member of the survey team.

Unfortunately, those excellent qualities shared brain space with all too many notions about proper attitudes and behaviors for a certifiable (by birthright and exalted pedigree) gentleman of Sharona's most ancient, prestigious empire. Worse, he expected others to treat him with the deference he, himself, believed he merited, as the grandson of a Ternathian duke. And he treated everyone else in accordance with those same social rules, as carefully learned as his science. He wasn't demanding or petty, or even rude about it, which only made matters worse, as far as Shaylar was concerned. He was insufferably polite, in fact, particularly with her, treating her to an unending barrage of courtesies, looking after her every need . . . whether she wanted him to or not.

But the thing that drove Shaylar craziest was his unshakable conviction that his notions and customs were as unalterably and exclusively correct as the physical laws of the universe he so delighted in studying. It had simply never occurred to Braiheri Futhai that not everyone on Sharona thought the Ternathian way of doing things was the best way. He possessed just enough Talent for Shaylar to realize he truly believed, in his innermost heart, that someday every enlightened Sharonian would metamorphose himself or herself into a clone of a Ternathian gentleman or lady. He simply didn't grasp the basic truth that Shaylar *preferred* her Harkalan viewpoint and beliefs, just as Jathmar preferred his Faltharian ones, and Elevu Gitel preferred his Ricathian ones.

Not that there weren't profound similarities between most of Sharona's great societies. With psionic Talents running through at least a fifth of the world's population, there were bound to be some similarities. And given the enormous territory the Ternathian emperors had once ruled, and the colonies that had spread across vast oceans from Ternathian shores, at least half of Sharona's population could claim at least some Ternathian heritage, whether it was by blood relation or the holdovers of colonial civic administration. Personally, Shaylar preferred Ghartoun chan Hagrahyl's straightforward military mindset to Futhai's more civilized notions. It was probably rude of her, but she simply couldn't help it when Futhai went to such pains to make himself so utterly, unctuously disagreeable.

So she grinned back at Kasell, rolled her own eyes toward the self-absorbed naturalist, then sat down facing the stream and tuned out the distractions around her with the practiced ease of an experienced professional. She unrolled the chart they'd compiled to date, weighted it down so that it couldn't roll up again, and marked off the section due east of their campsite. Then she laid out her tools: compass with pencil fixed in place, steel ruler, protractor, a second pencil, and a template with precut map symbols to speed and simplify her work. She wouldn't ink the chart until she and Jathmar had gone over it tonight, double-checking her accuracy after supper.

She also laid out her field notebook, and one of the piston-fill pens she and countless other survey crew members—not to mention ordinary clerks and officials—blessed on a daily basis. She filled the pen from a metal flask of ink she'd carried with her through three virgin universes, made sure the flask's cap was screwed into place, and carried it back to her tent.

By the time she returned to her work table, Jathmar had hiked far enough to start picking up new terrain features. When Shaylar reached out to contact him—the nature of his Talent meant she had to contact him, since he could See but wasn't able to transmit to her or anyone else—the pictures in his mind started flowing into hers. The process was second nature to her, now, although she paused now and again to reflect on how dull life must be without any Talent at all to turn the multiple universes into a maze of fascinating playgrounds.

The glorious, crisp morning and the sunshine that glowed across her shoulders combined to keep her contented with life. She hummed under her breath, not even really aware that she did so, and concentrated on what Jathmar was seeing—and on what he was Seeing, since there was a distinct difference. When she'd first begun her training, Shaylar had found it difficult to sort out the images Jathmar saw with his two physical eyes from those he Saw with his "third eye." The screen in Jathmar's brain Saw a far wider slice of terrain than mere eyes could take in, and that screen was what Shaylar tapped when establishing her link with him.

Her husband was actually looking at a bend in the creek that already existed on their chart, since it was well within his five-mile radius from camp. Although that image was the stronger of the two, she ignored it with practiced ease and focused on the other, ghostlier image he was Seeing.

For Jathmar, the mechanics involved seemed to be a sort of looking "up" and then "out" along an invisible gridwork that registered as faint threads of light. He Saw terrain superimposed across that gridwork, like shadows glimpsed through mist. For Shaylar, the mechanics of her Talent took the form of a sudden gestalt, a totality of impressions that simply appeared, complete, in her own mind's eye. She Saw what he did as a whole, complete image—like a stage play containing nothing but scenery. Had Shaylar been in contact with another Voice, the images would have been far sharper, more like seeing it with her own eyes, rather than catching shadows that had the look of a watercolor painting left too long in strong sunlight.

She had to reach out consciously to pluck the images from Jathmar's mind, which took concentration. But he was close enough to camp that it wasn't particularly taxing. The farther apart she and Jathmar—or another telepath—were, the more concentration it took to make contact and maintain it. Shaylar's maximum range was just over eight hundred miles. That put her in the top ten percent of all Voices, although at that distance it took every ounce of concentration she could summon to hold contact.

Other Voices had even more limited ranges, which gave her team a distinct advantage. When she and Darcel had first been assigned to the same team, Darcel had been startled at the range she achieved. Startled and a little worried, since his own maximum range was barely two-thirds as great as hers. It was entirely possible for Shaylar to go far enough out of his range that he could pick up her transmissions, yet be too far away for him to transmit a reply back to her. They'd worked carefully together in a well-established colony world before heading for the wilderness, using the railroads in a very serious game of leapfrog to gauge effective distances at which they could both make contact. In the end, they'd found that he could Hear her at up to eight hundred miles, whereas she could Hear him at almost six hundred and fifty. Unfortunately, at anything over five hundred and eighty miles, he could Hear her only if he knew she would be trying to contact him and went into Voice trance to Listen for her, which limited their *effective* maximum range to that figure.

Once deployed, that maximum effective range dictated how far they could travel from any new portal before a relay team had to follow them out, to serve as a connection that would enable them to push deeper into the wilderness. It was an awkward arrangement, in some respects, but far better than the alternative would have been. If the survey crews hadn't been able to report without physically sending a member all the way back to the portal, it would have taken decades longer to reach as many portals and virgin universes as Sharonian teams had already mapped. As it was, the exploration of the intricately connected universes was moving forward at a steady pace. The one thing *everyone* wished for was a Talent that would lead them directly to new portals.

The best they could manage at the moment was to push outward with as many teams as they could reasonably field, with at least one member of each team sensitive to the still unexplained physics behind portal formation. Some—and only a few—Talented people, like Darcel, could actually sense the presence of other portals well enough to at least provide a compass direction to them, which was enormously better than nothing. Still, the task of actually locating no more than one or two portals anywhere within any given universe, when an entire planet identical to their own had to be searched, was far worse than hunting a needle in a haystack.

Shaylar shuddered every time she thought about the Haysam Portal, for example. The inbound portal from New Sharona was almost eight thousand miles from the outbound portal to Reyshar, and over six thousand of those miles were across the Western Ocean. Getting to *that* portal must have been an indescribable nightmare, she often thought. Indeed, she considered it remarkable that Sharonian exploration teams had managed to find as many portals as they had, even after eighty years of steady exploration.

Meanwhile, she and her husband were doing their part to further that exploration. The Portal Authority had already sent a full contingent of soldiers and supplies down the transit chain to build forts at each of the new portals they'd opened up. The Authority didn't conduct exploration, but it maintained absolute jurisdiction over every portal into a new universe. Private companies hired teams like Shaylar and Jathmar's to push forward into new universes, with the greatest incentive known to humanity: profit. The Portal Authority charged only "users' fees" on traffic through a portal, but it was the internationally appointed guardian of all of the other rights and commerce which passed through the portals. And the rights to land and minerals and other valuable natural resources belonged to whatever company or individual got there first and staked a claim to them.

That was one reason Shaylar's notebooks and charts were so valuable. The Chalgyn Consortium could lay claim to everything she and Jathmar—and the rest of the team, who made their presence here possible—could map. Other companies' teams could, and eventually would, follow them through the portal, but the first-comers held all the advantages.

As soon as a team could figure out exactly where it was, which took a combination of painstaking mapping and star-fixes, combined with strong backgrounds in the natural sciences—geology and biology in particular—all the team had to do was compare their location here with master charts of Sharona to figure out which areas to reach *first*. If, for instance, they had emerged near a spot where valuable iron deposits existed on Sharona, they would head straight there and claim them before any other company's teams got word that a new portal had opened at all, let alone where it led.

The team which made it through a portal first could make a great deal of money for the company which employed it. And since survey crews were paid, in part, on a system of shared stocks in the assets of the company, team members could get rich, as well, with just one or two lucky breaks. This was the third virgin universe Shaylar and Jathmar had "pushed" on behalf of Chalgyn. There wasn't much in the way of value anywhere near the swampy mess just behind them, but they'd mapped some valuable terrain in the one prior to that, which meant they would have quite a nest egg built up for their retirement years. As for what they might yet find in *this* universe . . .

They'd had to wait for the Portal Authority's garrison to arrive before stepping through into this universe, but they were the only team anywhere near this end of this particular transit chain. The other major consortiums were going to chew nails and spit tacks when word of this lovely little cluster of portals filtered back. Shaylar grinned at the very thought, having been on the other end of the stick all too often. She'd lost track of the number of times they'd jumped through portals somebody else had already opened up, crossing miles and miles of someone else's claim in the hopes of reaching a valuable area nobody else had claimed, or—best of all—finding a new portal of their own.

This time, she told herself happily, *we get first choice of what's out here.*

But for now, Jathmar's images were coming through steadily as he began a long, leisurely sweep from the eastern edge of his morning's hike, turning toward the south to begin the leg that led him down parallel to the end of the southern transit. By the time he finished the long day's hike, they would have filled in the blanks remaining in the southeastern transit zone. The portal lay behind them, almost due north of their present camp, clearly marked on Shaylar's chart. Once they'd filled in the entire region around their current day-fort, they would compare what they had to the master charts and see if they could come up with a correlation to Sharona. She doubted it, given the immense sweep of land that usually had to be charted before a terrain feature large enough or distinctive enough emerged to make that accurate a determination possible. But a few more days of charting ought to do the trick. Then all they had to do was decide which way to head to secure the best chunks of land for the Chalgyn Consortium.

Shaylar plotted out more terrain features as Jathmar sent new images, with new topographical features—gullies, a deep ravine, another stream that came trickling in from the east of Jathmar's current position. She jotted down a running commentary, as well, on the images flickering through her awareness. She and Jathmar would go over her notes tonight, while the information and both their impressions remained fresh. They would make whatever amendments were necessary before calling it a night, then begin again the next morning.

When Jathmar halted for a rest at midmorning, Shaylar sat back and was almost startled by the sound of voices behind her. They'd gone virtually subliminal during the previous two hours, no more noticeable than the murmuring sound of insects. The noise was startling, now that she'd come up for air, so to speak. From the sound of things, Futhai was trying to talk chan Hagrahyl into letting him hike farther along the stream than the team leader thought prudent.

"—if you would just authorize a guard, that wouldn't be a factor!"

"Not until Jathmar and Shaylar complete the basic grid around this camp," chan Hagrahyl rumbled in the tone that most of their team understood as "subject closed; don't bother to debate it." Futhai, however, was a zealous naturalist surrounded by new species—several of them, in fact. He'd also already established a most unusual co-mingling of species from different climatic regions. As far as he was concerned, that clearly confirmed Darcel's belief that they'd found an actual cluster. How else could so many species that didn't belong here have wandered into the area?

He obviously wanted to be out there collecting more specimens, and it appeared he wasn't prepared to take "no" for an answer. Not when his professional standing in the community of scientists was virtually guaranteed by the notes he was making in this camp alone. His enthusiasm for discovery was wreaking havoc with standard protocol, however, and chan Hagrahyl didn't sound amused.

If he hadn't been such an irritant, Shaylar might have felt a sneaking sympathy for Futhai. She knew only too well what it felt like to have something wonderful dangled in front of her, only to be told "no, you can't." Braiheri Futhai was only doing what she herself had done: fight to get what she wanted. Unfortunately for Futhai, chan Hagrahyl was a tougher customer than the combined weight of the Portal Authority's governing board and her own people's conservatism.

She grinned at that thought, then caught a glimpse of blackberry brambles all around Jathmar, along with a hint of deep satisfaction that the birds hadn't gotten all of the berries yet. Shaylar chuckled aloud, then relaxed back from the discipline of prolonged telepathic contact. She rose from her makeshift desk and shook the cramps out of her fingers and shoulders. Her work with Jathmar wasn't difficult, so much as intense. Her concentration needed a breather almost as much as Jathmar's legs—and taste buds—did.

She strolled west along the bank of the creek, casting a sharp woods-wise eye around the entire area, looking for any trace of hostile wildlife. She didn't expect any, given the amount of noise they'd made since setting up camp yesterday, but you could never be certain in a virgin universe. None of the animals in *this* Sharona had ever even seen a human being. They had no reason to be afraid of humans, which could be delightful, but could also be dangerous, since it meant their reaction to the presence of those humans was often difficult to predict. Personally, however charming she might find it to have wild deer willing to take food from her hand, Shaylar was in favor of having cougars or grizzly bears be wary enough of humans to leave her in peace.

She was also too experienced a field operative to take her safety for granted in the wilderness. All it would take to injure her, possibly fatally, would be a moment's carelessness, and the presence of several armed men in camp did nothing to absolve her of the responsibility for her own safety. This lovely forest doubtless had snakes in it, at the very least, and a rattle-tail's bite would be serious, indeed, even with Tymo Scleppis available. The telempathic Healer could speed the healing of deep cuts or broken bones, or help repair internal injuries, but pharmacological trouble like snake venom was another matter entirely, and their team was a long way from the nearest medical clinic. She scanned the terrain for potential trouble, aware almost peripherally of the weight of the handgun at her hip. She'd never needed it, but it was there, just in case of danger, and she knew how to use it. Very well, as a matter of fact.

Once she was sure of her environs, Shaylar descended the steep bank and crouched down to wash smudges of graphite off her hands. The water was shockingly cold, sending an ache up the bones of her hands to her wrists. Somewhere far upstream, several miles away, from the sound of it, a distant CRACK of rifle fire split the silence. Shaylar grinned, wondering what Falsan had bagged for the cookpot. He'd have plenty of time to clean the carcass, lug it back to camp, and butcher it properly before it was time to throw supper on the fire.

Given the distance, she doubted he'd brought down a deer, since he would've had to dress and haul the carcass all the way back alone. A wild turkey, maybe, she thought, straightening up and shaking excess water from her hands. Then she dried them on her heavy twill pants, and her grin turned into a fond smile as she recalled her father's reaction when he'd learned Shaylar would be wearing trousers all the time.

"But, my dear! That's—it's—"

"Practical, Papa," she'd said firmly. "That's the word you're looking for: practical. You don't object when Mama swims with her dolphin clients. She wears less in the water than *I'll* have on anytime I'm outside our sleeping tent."

"Yes, but your mother stays *in* the water. She doesn't traipse out and about on land dressed that way, and even when she comes *out* of the water, she's still on our property, after all."

"Oh, Papa, try to understand. The world is changing. Our little corner of Shurkhal isn't the whole multiverse, you know."

Her drollery had coaxed a wan chuckle from her father, which had, of course, been the beginning of the end to his resistance. It hadn't taken much more to convince him that she knew what she was doing, regardless of what her aunts and cousins would think about her running about the universes without a single skirt or tunic in sight.

Shaylar looked around the towering forest giants and shook her head, still bemused by her parents' notions of decorum and still a little mystified by her own determination to be so stubbornly independent. Most of her relatives halfway suspected she was a changeling of some sort, since no other member of Clan Kolmayr had ever evinced a desire to wander as far as Sethdona, the capital city of Shurkhal, let alone through even one portal, never mind the fifteen or twenty-odd between Sharona and this glorious forest.

She peered into one of the deep pools nearby and thought about trying a dip net on the truly immense trout she could see lurking in the dark water, back under the overhanging rocks that jutted out just a little farther along the bank. They would be mighty tasty eating, and she licked her lips as a hunger that matched Jathmar's made itself felt in her midsection. Maybe she could try netting the fish during lunch. Of course, they wouldn't need fish if Falsan brought back something substantial. Shaylar smiled a farewell at the fish, at least for now.

Another day, maybe.

She stood there for several more minutes, just looking at all the incredible beauty around her. The great forest was like a shrine, unlike anything Shaylar had known growing up in the arid Shurkhali peninsula. The motes of sunlight drifting down through the bright foliage danced and shifted on the dappled, dark water of the stream, which flashed an almost painful gold where light struck ripples and eddies in the swift moving current. The whispering laughter of the water was a hushed and beautiful sound.

This, she sighed, stretching luxuriously, *is the way to really live.*

Shaylar consulted her pocket watch, which hung from her neck on a sturdy silver chain—steel would rust under most field conditions—and realized her fifteen minutes of break time were up. She climbed the bank, resettled herself at her field desk, and contacted Jathmar. She caught a brief glimpse of the blackberry brambles—greatly denuded, now—then he shook the dust out of his trousers and got busy again.

The ghostly pictures began to flow once more as she and her husband settled back into the familiar routine.

CHAPTER THREE

THE SHARP CRACKING sound echoed and faded into a silence that was as unnatural as the sound which had produced it. Not a single bird was singing; even the squirrels ceased their barking chatter for a long, startled moment, and Gadrial Kelbryan looked at Sir Jasak Olderhan.

"What was that?" Her voice was hushed, as though she feared the answer.

"I intend to find out."

The hundred kept his voice to a whisper, too, prompted by an intuition he couldn't explain. But he meant every word of it, and one glance at Fifty Garlath had already told Jasak that he *was* going to have to be the one who did the finding out. Any officer worth his salt would already have ordered teams out to contact their drag and point men, their flanking screen. Garlath hadn't done that. He simply stood there, gazing thoughtfully at the same stretch of forest canopy he'd been contemplating before the sudden, sharp sound.

If Jasak hadn't been looking at the fifty at exactly the right moment, he might not have seen the way the older officer had jerked. The way his head had snapped around toward the mysterious sound. The flash of fear in those dark eyes before Garlath returned to that pose of studied nonchalance.

But Jasak had seen those things, all too clearly, and his jaw tightened. Unfortunately, he couldn't accuse the platoon leader of the cowardice his current indifference screened. Despite his own sudden, intuitive suspicion that something was wrong—terribly wrong—Jasak had no proof that it was. And a gut feeling wasn't grounds for making a charge as serious as "cowardice in the face of the enemy," despite the fact that both of them knew exactly why Garlath wasn't responding to the crackling danger that sound represented.

Or might *represent,* Jasak reminded himself. It wasn't easy, but he made himself step back just a little, determined to keep an open mind precisely because he recognized his own hairtrigger willingness to attribute the worst possible motives to Garlath's conduct as an officer of the Second Andaran Scouts.

All the fifty had really done, after all, was to ignore a sound that might be nothing more threatening than an old tree coming down somewhere. Jasak might be willing to bet his next five paychecks that the cause of that sound had been nothing so benign, but until he had more information—

Squad Shield Gaythar Harklan burst suddenly through a screen of brilliantly colored poplars, crushing a patch of toadstool mushrooms underfoot in his wild, headlong rush. He actually shot straight past Fifty Garlath and came to a gasping halt directly in front of Jasak.

"Sir!" His salute was a hasty affair, sketched with a hand that shook violently. "Sir, I beg leave to report a hostile contact—"

"*Hostile contact?*" Garlath snarled, abandoning his contemplation of the treetops to charge forward like an angry palm-horned bull moose. "Don't play the hundred for a fool! And how *dare* you desert your post without orders?"

"S-Sir—" Harklan stuttered, swinging irresolutely between Jasak and the irate Garlath. "It's just that Osmuna—he's *dead*, Sir!"

"Dead?" Jasak asked sharply, cutting off another vitriolic outburst from Garlath with a brusquely raised hand. "What killed him?"

He'd meant to ask "who," rather than "what," but he had a sudden feeling that his meager Gift must be functioning, because Harklan's answer should have shocked the living daylights out of him.

"That's just it, Sir. I don't *know* what killed him. None of us know. I-I think he missed the halt order for the rest break, Sir. I was just about to pass the word to our flankers that I was moving forward, trying to catch up with him, when that sound came." He gulped hard. "It was right on the line to Osmuna, whatever it was, but it took me a while to get through the brush and find him. He's dead, Sir. Just fucking *dead*, and the right-flank patrol caught up to me, and we can't any of us figure out why he's dead or even *how*—"

"That is quite enough!" Garlath's dark complexion had acquired a nearly wine-purple hue. "You're hysterical, soldier! Place yourself on report and—"

"Fifty Garlath."

The ice-cold voice cut Garlath off in mid-snarl.

"Sir?" The fifty's response was strangled.

"We have a dead soldier, Fifty. I might suggest making that our immediate priority. Discipline can wait."

Garlath's jaw muscles bunched visibly, and the enraged flush spread abruptly down his neck and under the line of his uniform's collar. His furious, frightened eyes snapped to Jasak's face, and for just a moment, it looked as if he might actually explode. But then his eyes fell.

"Of course, Sir," he grated.

If his jaw had been any stiffer, the bone would have shattered like ice, and the glare he turned on Harklan was deadly with a promise of vengeance. Jasak took note of that, too, and made himself a promise of his own where Shevan Garlath and the squad shield were concerned. Then the fifty wheeled away and began barking furious orders of his own.

Despite that, it took him nearly ten minutes to shake First Platoon into anything approaching proper threat-response posture.

Jasak watched the platoon commander with eyes of brown ice. At least half of Garlath's snarled orders only contributed to the confusion of the moment, and the fifty's collar was soaked with sweat, despite the morning air's persistent chill.

It was simple fear, Jasak realized. Or perhaps not so simple, given the dynamics at play. It didn't require a major Gift to detect the sources of Garlath's pronounced lack of courage: fear of whatever had killed Osmuna, fear of making a mistake grave enough to finally get him cashiered, fear that he'd already *made* that fatal mistake . . .

Well, a man can dream, *can't he?* Jasak thought sourly, wondering once again how Garlath had managed to outlast every other commander of one hundred assigned to ride herd on him.

"When we move out," he told Gadrial quietly without looking at her, his attention fully focused on the abruptly hostile shadows, "stay close to me."

He glanced at her, and she gave him a choppy nod. She looked tense, but not overtly frightened. Or, rather, on a second and longer look, she was scared spitless, but she wasn't letting the fear dominate her. Fifty Garlath ought to take lessons from this mere civilian—if anything about this particular civilian could be labeled "mere."

His brief glance lingered on her longer than he'd intended for it to. She didn't notice, because she was too busy sweeping the forest with an alert and piercing gaze that tracked any motion instantly. Her focused attention had a sort of dangerous elegance, almost a beauty, like a hunting falcon's, or a gryphon searching for a target to strike, and Jasak wondered quite abruptly if the slim magister had any self-defense warding spells tucked away as part of her extensive training in magical theory and applications. That might explain her composure. Then again, she struck Jasak as a thorough and competent professional, well aware of her skills—and weaknesses—and more than capable of weathering whatever unpleasant surprise the multiple universes might conspire to throw her way.

He reminded himself sternly of his own responsibilities and turned his attention away from her. It was surprisingly difficult. His attraction to the magister was deepening rapidly into profound respect as she resolutely refused to let death's unexpected arrival tumble her into panic.

It took nine and a half minutes too long, but Garlath did get his troopers moving within ten minutes, which was undoubtedly a personal record. He even managed to deploy them in the correct formation for responding to an unknown threat in close terrain. Privately, Jasak was willing to bet that it had taken Garlath those extra nine and a half minutes to *remember* the correct formation.

Once underway, it took almost twice as long as it should have to reach Osmuna's resting place. Mostly because Garlath was jumping at shadows . . . and a forest this size had a *lot* of shadows.

Jasak put Gadrial directly behind him as they moved through the trees.

"Stay right behind me," he told her.

With another civilian, he might have added a warning to keep quiet, but *this* civilian made considerably less noise than Garlath did as they moved cautiously forward through the brittle autumn leaf litter. The scent of the crisp leaves underfoot—a dry, incongruous cinnamon smell—reminded Jasak of holiday pastries. Unfortunately, that scent mingled with the stink of electric tension flashing from trooper to trooper as Garlath's insecurity filtered through the entire platoon. Jasak felt the fifty's fear corroding the confidence of the men under him and once again stamped on the overwhelming desire to take direct command of the platoon.

The temptation was the next best thing to overwhelming, but bad as things were, taking over from Garlath right in the middle of things would only have made them even worse. They didn't need anything confusing the chain of command at a time when half the platoon was out of visual contact with its CO and senior NCOs. He had no choice but to let the commander of fifty do his job, so he hugged his irritated impatience tightly to himself and took comfort in the fact that Gadrial remained a constant, exact two paces behind him.

Which, perversely, only made his frustration still worse. Garlath was supposed to be trained to do what Magister Kelbryan was actually *doing*.

Despite his concentration on Garlath and the men of First Platoon, a corner of the hundred's attention noted that Otwal Threbuch had stationed himself as his own silent shadow. Actually, it was a tossup as to whether the chief sword had taken that position more to protect Jasak or the petite woman behind him. It scarcely mattered, since Jasak had carefully placed her close enough to himself for the chief sword to do both, but he nursed a mild intellectual curiosity as to Threbuch's primary motivation.

Even odds he just doesn't want to explain to Mother if anything goes wrong on his watch, the hundred thought with a small, tight grin.

The men of Shevan Garlath's platoon finally reached the contact zone and deployed under Jasak's—and Threbuch's—silent scrutiny. Garlath, for once, actually followed the Book as he directed the platoon's squads to set up a perimeter defense to completely secure the area. He probably did it for the wrong (and entirely personal) reasons, but at least he'd done something right for a change.

As three of the platoon's four squads disappeared into the forest on divergent lines, the troopers communicated via the birdcall signals the Andaran Scouts had developed for covert movement. Somebody had even remembered to use the correct bird species for this part of this particular universe. Somehow, Jasak doubted that it was Fifty Garlath who'd drilled the platoon in proper communications procedure.

While they waited for the rest of the platoon to move into position, Jasak glanced at Gadrial and raised a finger to his lips, signaling for silence. The warning was pure reflex, and almost certainly superfluous. She was alert, motionless except for her eyes, which continued to study their surroundings with a strange blend of intense concentration and something that puzzled Jasak for a moment. He couldn't quite put a finger on it, until he realized that she hovered somewhere between fear and excitement.

She was certainly afraid—only an idiot, which she manifestly was not—wouldn't have been. But she wasn't *terrified*, which put her considerably ahead of Garlath, and she was deeply, intensely curious. Where the fifty looked like a man who wanted nothing so much as to run away and hide, *she* sensed the mystery as clearly as Jasak did, and she wanted to understand what was happening. No one needed to tell her that she—and they—could die at any moment, but the brain inside that lovely head was still working, still sifting clues, still looking for answers.

A sharp, trilling whistle finally sounded from the heavier brush just ahead to signal a successful perimeter deployment. Garlath twitched at the signal, but he didn't respond. Chief Sword Threbuch's nostrils flared, and he glanced at Jasak, who nodded slightly.

Threbuch whistled the approved countersignal Garlath had failed to give, and leaves parted as Jugthar Sendahli stepped from concealment. The dark-skinned soldier who'd fled Mythal and his menial status as a member of the non-Gifted *garthan* caste was one of Jasak's best troopers. He was also smart as they came, and he proceeded to prove it once again. He met the chief sword's gaze and glanced respectfully at Jasak, but wisely saluted Fifty Garlath, instead.

"Sir, beg leave to report the area is secure. The perimeter screen is in place. Arbalestiers are cocked and locked, and the dragons' accumulators are loaded and primed. Osmuna is this way, Sir."

Jasak frowned behind his eyes. Despite an obvious effort to keep his delivery cool and professional, Sendahli's voice was violin-string tight. What the devil had these men so spooked? They were seasoned veterans, who'd fought claim jumpers, border brigands, and commerce pirates. Death was hardly new to any of them, but the men of Fifty Garlath's platoon were shaken to their bones.

A trickle of sweat ran down Garlath's temple as he reacted to his command's mood, and Jasak glanced again at Gadrial. Her frown was narrow-eyed and speculative as she, too, took note of the fear in Sendahli's eyes.

The trooper turned to lead the way, and Jasak, Garlath, Threbuch, and Gadrial followed him, pushing cautiously through dense undergrowth towards the sound of running water.

They halted at the edge of a good-sized stream's embankment. The men who'd provided Osmuna's original flankers had sorted themselves out properly, forming an outward-facing picket line against any hostiles. They'd remained in position, even though the rest of the platoon had extended their own perimeter by several dozen yards. They hadn't slacked off despite the new arrivals, and Jasak reminded himself to say a few words of praise to Platoon Sword Harnak.

Osmuna's body lay in the stream itself. Garlath had already started down the slope, moving like a man who devoutly wished he were somewhere else. The hundred followed him wordlessly, wondering if Garlath even suspected how much *Jasak* wished the fifty were someplace far, far away. Chief Sword Threbuch followed Jasak, in turn, watching his back more closely than ever, but Gadrial stayed where she was, looking more than happy to obey Jasak's restraining hand signal.

Osmuna was dead, all right. His body lay half-submerged in the boulder-strewn creek. He'd struck one of the boulders on the way down, and flies were already busy about the huge smear of blood he'd left across the luxuriant green moss which covered it. He'd rolled off that boulder, and splashed into the stream, with his entire head immersed in a deep pool between the rocks. Had he drowned after being struck by whatever had produced that much blood?

Jasak frowned and stepped cautiously closer. The Scout had come to rest on his right side, so that his chest, back, and left shoulder were above water, and Jasak could see the hole in his chest. It was a very small hole, almost insignificant looking, and Jasak's frown deepened as he tried to imagine what the devil could have made a wound like that?

It wasn't the right size or shape for a crossbow quarrel. Nor was there any sign of a quarrel, or even an ordinary arrow. He'd seen what both of those missiles did when they entered flesh, and Osmuna's odd wound didn't look like that. Nor did it look like the sort of wound left behind when someone pulled a quarrel or arrow out again, either. The hole had drilled straight through Osmuna's camo uniform blouse as easily as a hot poker thrust through cheese. But the fibers hadn't been slashed through—not the way a knife would have cut them. They'd been stretched and ripped by the force of something which had driven bits of fabric into Osmuna's chest. A powerful enough arbalest might have produced that effect, but the wound would have been much larger. And it couldn't have come from a sharp-pointed blade, not even something like an ice pick, either, because a weapon like that wouldn't have stretched, ripped, and embedded those fibers into the wound.

Jasak balanced carefully on the rocks, moving around to look at Osmuna's back, and froze in sudden, ice-cold shock.

Graholis' bollocks! What the hell *caused that?*

Jasak abruptly understood the shaken look in the men's faces.

Osmuna's back had been blown open.

Literally.

The hole just to the right of Osmuna's left shoulder blade was almost the size of a human fist. In fact, Gadrial could probably have pushed *her* fist deep into that gaping wound without the slightest trouble. The flesh was mangled, looking as if someone had set off an explosive incendiary spell *inside* Osmuna's body.

Horror, sudden and total, crawled down Jasak's spine and lodged in the vicinity of his belt buckle. He'd never heard of any explosive spell that would penetrate human flesh like a crossbow quarrel, then blow up from the inside, and Sir Jasak Olderhan's education had been the finest any Andaran noble's son could have hoped to acquire. He'd studied the bloody history of Arcana, including its Wizard Wars—during which hair-raising atrocities had been unleashed on helpless, non-Gifted populations—but no one had ever come up with a battle spell that would do what Jasak was looking at right now.

Movement at his shoulder jerked his head around. Otwal Threbuch hissed between his teeth at his first sight of the victim's back, then lifted worried, deeply shocked eyes to Jasak's.

"Do you have any idea what did that, Sir?" he asked, clearly hoping Jasak's education might have the answer the chief sword needed to hear.

"No. I don't." Jasak shook his head, and Threbuch cursed foully under his breath.

"I was afraid you were going to say that," he muttered through clenched teeth. "What the *fuck* do we do now, Sir?"

Jasak looked pointedly at Shevan Garlath. The platoon commander was also staring at Osmuna's back, swallowing hard. Every few seconds he looked away, darting wild-eyed glances up the stream banks toward the ominous trees, but every time, that gaping wound dragged his unwilling eyes back to the corpse at his feet.

"Fifty Garlath?"

"Sir?" Garlath's voice sounded constricted, and his eyes were unsteady as they skated across to Jasak's.

"I would suggest you try to find the bastards who did this."

Garlath nodded, the motion choppy and strained. It took him three deep gulps of air to find enough of his voice—or courage—to begin issuing orders.

"Spread out. Look for any trace of the attackers. We're going to find the whoreson who did this."

Oh, yes, Jasak promised the slain man's ghost. *We most certainly are.*

*   *   *

Shaylar was busy filling in yet another new stream on her chart when a sudden sound broke her concentration. It was a hoarse, gasping cry, so faint it was almost inaudible in the background noise of the stream, and it came from very nearly under her feet.

"Shaylar!"

She jumped as though stung, her pencil skidding across the paper. Then she peered down the bank toward the creek and gave a sharp cry of her own. Someone was trying to crawl up the bank. Even as she realized who it was, the wiry scout slithered weakly back into the water with a mewling pain sound.

"Falsan!"

She cast one wild glance around the clearing, searching for Barris Kasell. He was a good fifteen yards further east along the bank, where Braiheri Futhai was poking into more bushes.

"*Barris!*" Her cry snapped him around in surprise. "Get Tymo!"

Then she flung herself down the bank, skidding through damp leaves and a slick spot of clay. Falsan was struggling doggedly to get his hands under himself, trying to stand back up. She reached him, braced him with one arm as she tried to help him up, and—

Pain struck with a brutal fist. It caught her right in the chest, robbing her of breath even as a ghastly sound broke through Falsan's lips. He collapsed again, sliding sideways, away from her, down the bank. He splashed into the stream and rolled almost prone in the icy water. He came to rest on his back—which let her see the dreadful red stain on his shirt. It had soaked the whole front, spreading outward from something that had penetrated cloth and flesh.

"*Ghartoun!*" she screamed in a voice edged with knife-sharp horror.

Falsan clutched at her blouse with one blood-smeared, shaking hand. He whispered through gray lips, his thready voice almost too weak to catch.

"Man . . . shot me . . . stayed in . . . water . . . no trail . . . can't foll—"

His breath wheezed away to nothing. His eyes didn't close. They remained open. Horribly, sightlessly open.

She felt him go. Felt the unseen force that was Falsan chan Salgmun vanish like smoke in her hands, even as she searched frantically for the wound. Her fingers touched metal. Stupid with shock, she stared down at it, found a thick steel shaft protruding nearly two inches from his flesh. Her hands were hot with his blood, but the rest of her was frozen. She sat half immersed in ice-cold water, shaking violently and trying to focus her spinning mind on the impossibility of what he'd just said.

A man had shot him.

A man . . .

Theirs was the only team anywhere in this universe. That meant—

Barris Kasell, Tymo Scleppis, and Ghartoun chan Hagrahyl plunged down the bank, literally on one another's heels. Chan Hagrahyl cursed horribly as he splashed into the water beside her. Their Healer slithered down next, took one look, and groaned.

"Too late," Shaylar heard him say. "He's gone."

She lifted her head. It took forever, that simple effort, like lifting a mountain with her bare hands. She met Ghartoun's stunned gaze.

"Somebody shot him." Her words came out like ax blows on solid ice. "He said a man shot him."

Chan Hagrahyl wrenched his gaze away from her face and stared at the ghastly metal shaft buried in Falsan's flesh.

"My gods," he whispered.

Suddenly the whole stream was looping and rolling in wild gyrations. Shaylar felt rough hands on her shoulders, heard somebody saying her name, and fought the roaring in her ears and the black tide trying to suck away her consciousness.

I will not *faint like a schoolgirl!* a small, hard voice grated somewhere deep inside her, and she shook off the hands trying to drag her up the bank. She went to her knees as they released her, but she forced her wildly spinning senses to steady.

She found herself kneeling in a tangle of tree roots, panting and trembling, but in control once more. She raised her head, and a worried pair of dark eyes swam into focus. Barris was crouched beside her, one hand bracing her so she didn't slide back down the bank.

"That's better," he said softly. "For a minute there, I thought you were going to collapse."

Her face tried to heat up. But she was still too shocky and pale to flush with humiliation, and his next words eased some of the shame which had wrapped around her like a blanket.

"You've had a nasty psychic shock, Shaylar, and you're not combat trained."

"Combat trained?" she parroted, appalled by the hoarse croak which had replaced her voice, and Barris nodded.

"When a Talented recruit joins the military, he's trained to handle something as brutal as combat death shock, especially at point-blank range. Nobody teaches that to civilian survey scouts."

The rough burr in Barris' voice seeped through the numb ice encasing her. Anger, she realized slowly. It was anger that she'd been exposed to something that ugly, that unexpected. And a deeper anger that one of their own had been murdered. Even shame that *he* hadn't seen Falsan struggling along the streambed.

When that realization sank in, some of her own shame eased. The abrupt loosening of her grip on her shuddering emotions was followed almost instantly by a flood of tears and violent tremors. She struggled grimly to hold them back, but without much success. Barris took her by one elbow and Tymo took the other. They helped her to climb to the top of the bank, and Tymo slipped an arm around her.

"Let them come, Shaylar. Let the shakes run their course. That's the way emotional shock will drain, as it should, not fester in your mind and poison your body."

That almost made sense. The fact that it didn't make complete sense, when it should have, rang faint alarm bells. But Tymo knew what he was talking about, if anyone did, so she sat there in the warm sunlight and waited for the tremors to ease up. When they did, she drew down a final, ragged gulp of air and looked up again.

"I heard his rifle," she said. "That must've been when . . ."

"Yes, I heard it, too." Barris nodded, his voice bitter with self-condemnation. "To think he'd been struggling all that time, trying to make it back, and we didn't do *anything*—"

"It's not your fault, Barris!" Ghartoun's voice interrupted sharply, and Kasell looked up at the team leader.

"I used to be a *soldier*, curse it!" he snarled almost defiantly. "I should've—"

"Done *what*?" Ghartoun chan Hagrahyl demanded, his own expression angry and shaken. "Snatched the truth out of thin air? You're not Talented. Neither was Falsan. Shaylar's a *Voice*—the best telepath in the five nearest universes—and *she* didn't feel a thing. There's not a Voice that's ever been born who could have picked up something like that from a nontelepath. So just stow the frigging guilt, right now!"

Kasell's jaw muscles clenched for a moment. Then he nodded and relaxed a fraction.

"Yes, Sir. You're right, of course. It's just—"

"I know. *Triad*, but I know. And I'd like to know where his rifle is, too. It's not with him."

Kasell swore one filthy, ugly word.

"Fanthi," Ghartoun called to a rugged hulk of a man who'd always given Shaylar the impression that every stretch of ground he walked across was a potential battlefield, "set sentries in a perimeter fifty yards out in all directions. We don't know where these bastards are, or how close they might be, let alone how many of them there are."

Fanthi chan Himidi, who'd served a double stint in the Ternathian infantry before signing on with Chalgyn Consortium, nodded sharply and organized the rest of the survey crew with swift, efficient dispatch. They had eight men with at least some military experience, who took charge of the others, sending their cook, their drovers, their smith—even Ghartoun's clerk—out to form a circular guard around their little camp. Shaylar felt better just watching the process chan Himidi had set in motion.

Ghartoun hesitated, looking unhappily into her eyes, then crouched down beside her.

"Shaylar," he said gently, "I have to ask. Did Falsan say any-thing?"

"He—" She drew an unsteady breath and made herself repeat those pitiful few words, then added, "I'm pretty sure he started to say 'They can't follow,' there at the last. But he didn't get the whole thing out before he—"

She stopped and swallowed hard.

"*They?*" Ghartoun asked, his voice sharp. "You're sure of that? Not 'he'?"

"No," she said slowly. "I'm not sure. He said 'can't follow,' but the impression I got was 'they.' I don't know if that means he saw several of them, Ghartoun, or if he was simply afraid there might be more of them nearby."

The expedition's leader exchanged grim glances with Barris Kasell. Then he looked back at Shaylar.

"Did you pick up anything else? Anything at all that could help us figure out what in the gods' names really happened out there?"

Shaylar drew another deep breath and shook her head to clear it, then held up one impatient hand when he misconstrued her meaning and started to speak. She closed her eyes and sorted through every impression she'd been able to catch during those fleeting seconds of contact. Falsan hadn't been Talented, but Shaylar had been touching him, which helped. She couldn't See anything that he'd seen, but the emotions behind those gasped-out words of warning had slammed their way into her awareness, along with the words themselves. If she could just get a solid grasp on them . . .

"I don't think there was more than one when he was actually shot, Ghartoun," she finally said. "I'm not picking up a sense of 'me versus them.' It's more a 'me versus *him*.' I think he was just afraid that there *would* be others who could follow a blood trail back to us."

"Which is why he stayed in the water," Ghartoun muttered.

"Where there's one, there are bound to be more," Kasell said with quiet intensity. "And did you get a good look at *what* killed him?"

"Oh, yes. A crossbow bolt."

"*Crossbow?*" Shaylar stared at the expedition's leader. "But that's—that's *medieval!*"

"So are clubs and rocks," Ghartoun snapped, his eyes crackling with suppressed fury. "And they'll still kill a man just as dead as a rifle will. Crossbows were weapons of war in our history for damned near a thousand years, come to that, until we finally figured out how to make gunpowder. These people don't have to be our technological equals to kill us."

"That's a fact," Kasell muttered in a voice of steel, and Ghartoun chan Hagrahyl glanced back at Shaylar.

"Can you pick *anything* else out of those impressions?"

She tried, but nothing else came.

"I'm sorry," she whispered miserably. "I only touched him for just a few seconds, and..." Her voice went unsteady. "I'm sorry. I just can't get anything more."

"I'm grateful you got as much as you did," chan Hagrahyl told her, squeezing her shoulder with surprising force, as though he'd forgotten she was barely the size of a half-grown Ternathian child.

"All right." He stood up, hands curling around the butt of his handgun and the hilt of his camp knife, both sheathed at his wide leather belt. "We don't know exactly who or what we're up against, but we do know they're nasty tempered and don't like company." He met Barris Kasell's gaze, his own hard and grimly determined. "We *may* have some time, especially if Shaylar's impression is right and there really was only one of the bastards. If Falsan hadn't nailed him with his first shot, we'd probably have heard at least two. And if Falsan got him, it may be a little while before his friends figure out he's not coming home. But we have to assume that there were others of them fairly close by, and that they'll at least be able to backtrack him to camp. And they *will*, too, after something like this. So we've got to get back to the portal before these bastards overrun us, and it's been a while since we heard that rifle shot."

Shaylar's breath caught. She hadn't thought about that, and the thick woods, so hushed and lovely, suddenly menaced their little party from every shadow, every movement of sun-dappled leaves in the breeze. In a single blink of her eyelashes, the entire forest seemed to be in sinister motion, tricking the eye and confusing the senses. And somewhere out there, well over two miles east of their camp, Jathmar was alone and unaware of what had just happened. She started to make contact when Elevu Gitel's voice jolted her out of her reverie.

"We've got to warn Company-Captain Halifu. Shaylar has to send a message. Immediately."

Shaylar looked up, and chan Hagrahyl nodded, meeting her gaze.

"Contact Darcel. Let him know what's happening. Have him take the message to Company-Captain Halifu, then come back to our side of the portal to listen for additional messages from you. Then try to contact Jathmar. I know you can't talk to him, but we've got to warn him to break off the survey and rendezvous with us."

"Rendezvous?" Braiheri Futhai's voice was incredulous. "Don't you mean return to camp?"

Chan Hagrahyl met the naturalist's astonished gaze.

"No, I do *not* mean return. We're abandoning this camp as fast as humanly possible. I want everyone to pack up the absolute essentials and be ready to march in ten minutes."

"We can't possibly be ready to leave in only ten minutes!" Futhai protested.

"If you can't pack it that fast, leave it," Ghartoun snapped. "And if you can't carry it at a dog-trot from now until we reach the portal, abandon it. Is that clear enough?"

"But—but what about Falsan?"

"Falsan's dead! And it's my job to make sure none of the rest of us join him!"

Futhai's eyes widened at the harshness in the expedition's leader's voice. But his jaw muscles clenched, and he gave chan Hagrahyl the obstinate glare Shaylar had come to associate with the naturalist at his absolute worst.

"We are *not* leaving this camp until that poor man is properly buried!"

"We don't have time." Chan Hagrahyl's voice was a glacier grinding up boulders.

"We are civilized people, Sir, and civilized people bury their dead," Futhai shot back, and Kasell's nostrils flared as he rounded on the naturalist.

"Not when the godsdamned natives are *shooting* at them!" he snarled in a voice of withering contempt.

"Nobody is shooting at *us.*" Futhai pointed out in maddeningly reasonable, patiently courteous, *patronizing* tones. "And since we're not in immediate danger, we can at least behave with respect for that poor man's death."

Barris Kasell's right hand clenched into a white-knuckled fist around the carrying sling of his rifle. From his expression, he would have vastly preferred to have the naturalist's neck in that fist's grasp, instead.

"If you're that nonchalant about the danger," he grated, "*you* stay behind to bury him. But don't, by all the gods, expect the *rest* of us to hang around here waiting for a pack of murdering bastards to follow Falsan's trail back to us!"

"He stayed in the water, so there isn't a trail to follow," Futhai pointed out almost pityingly. "You said as much yourself, and—"

"*Enough!*" Chan Hagrahyl's bellow silenced the entire clearing. "We don't have the luxury of time—not for funerals; not for arguments. Yes, Braiheri, he stayed in the stream on his way *back* to us, but there wasn't any reason for him to try to hide his tracks on the way *out*, was there? It may take them a little while to get organized, but they won't have any trouble finding us once they do!"

He glared at the naturalist for a moment, then turned back to Shaylar.

"Shaylar, send the message to Darcel immediately. Then pack your essential gear and abandon the rest. And don't leave behind *anything* that would let Falsan's murderers trace us beyond the portal. Carry all your maps, your notes—everything."

He shifted his gaze to include the others.

"Don't abandon any technology higher than knives and sticks, either. These people don't know a solitary thing about us, and I'd like to keep it that way. Braiheri, if it'll make you feel better, strip Falsan's gear and cover him with a cairn of rocks. Preferably in the stream, so they don't find his body and realize they've killed one of us. You can pack your notes, or bury him: your choice. And that's *all* you have time for."

He switched his attention back to Shaylar again.

"You understand why Jathmar will have to rendezvous with us *en route*? Or catch up with us as best he can? My duty's to get as many of us out as possible. I can't wait for anyone."

He held Shaylar's gaze, pleading with her to understand.

Her heart cried out with the need to protest, but he was right. She nodded, stiffly, instead, her muscles rigid with the knowledge that Jathmar was completely alone out there in a forest where someone had already committed murder.

Thank you, chan Hagrahyl's gaze seemed to say. Then he turned back to the others.

"Let's get busy, then. Take only enough trail rations to get us to the portal. We're marching light and fast."

Shaylar saw eyelids twitch as several of the men started to glance down at her. All of them—except Futhai—managed to abort the movement. But their thoughts were as clear as if each of them had been a full-blown Voice, and she swallowed hard as the import of those not-quite-glances sank in.

I'm going to slow us down. They know it; and I know it. And we can't afford it.

Something hard and alien stirred deep inside, giving her strength as she pushed herself to her feet. She surprised herself when she realized she'd already shoved aside the shock of Falsan's death. She had a job to do. It wasn't precisely the job she'd signed up for, since a shooting war with unknown people was the last thing anyone had expected to occur out here. But that didn't change the facts.

"I'll send the message to Darcel from my tent," she said in a hard voice she barely recognized. "While I'm packing. And I'll do my best to warn Jathmar."

Her voice actually held steady, and Ghartoun chan Hagrahyl looked into her eyes for a long moment, taking careful measure of what he saw reflected there. Then he nodded.

"Good. Let's rip this camp apart and hit the trail."

CHAPTER
FOUR

THEY FOUND THE footprints first, naturally.

"Whoever it was," Gaythar Harklan said, pointing toward the far bank, "they came down that into the water."

Jasak studied the steep slope opposite them, and his eyes narrowed speculatively. The other bank was steeper, rising a good ten or eleven feet above Osmuna's body. Had the killer entered the water before he attacked? Or to investigate the body after the killing was done? Or, the hundred's eyes hardened, to make *certain* his victim was dead?

Nothing offered any answers, just as nothing he saw could explain the sharp cracking sound which had split the morning apart.

"What's up there?" he asked Osmuna's squad shield.

"Nothing much, Sir. Looks like he'd been following the stream bank when he spotted Osmuna."

"Show me."

"Yes, Sir."

Harklan started back across the stream, with Jasak wading alongside. Threbuch followed the hundred, and Garlath tagged sullenly along behind.

"Here's where he slid down the bank, Sir," Harklan said. "See the gouges and footmarks?"

Jasak saw them clearly. Whoever had come down that bank had been clumsy as hell doing it. No Andaran Scout worth the uniform on his back would have left a trail like that to follow. In fact, Jasak couldn't think of anyone who would have.

He very carefully didn't glance at Fifty Garlath for *his* reaction. Instead, he stooped closer to the mud, peering intently.

"Send a couple of men both directions along this creek, Fifty Garlath. Tell them to look for a blood trail."

"Blood trail?" Chief Sword Threbuch muttered to himself. He peered more closely at the same marks, then grunted.

"By damn, Sir, you're right. Osmuna nailed the bastard. I didn't even think to check his arbalest to see if he'd fired it," the chief sword admitted in a chagrined tone.

"We're all a little rattled," Jasak answered, his voice dry as brittle weeds. "What I can't tell from this is how *badly* Osmuna nailed him."

There were only a few drops of blood splashed into the mud, but whoever had slithered down this bank had been wounded when he did it.

"Search this whole area," he told Garlath. "I want every inch of this ground run through a sieve, if necessary. Get me some gods-cursed *facts* to look at here!"

Garlath nodded sharply and turned to spit orders with a brisk efficiency that Jasak tried—hard—to give him credit for, since they were actually the *right* orders for a change. Search teams spread out, looking for a trail to follow and whatever else might be out there waiting to be discovered.

"Fifty Garlath!" someone called only moments later. "I've got something, Sir. I just don't know what it *is*."

Jasak followed Garlath to the top of the bank. Evarl Harnak, the platoon sword, was crouched down in a tangle of weeds almost directly above Osmuna's body.

"Look here, Sir," he said. "Here's a set of footprints. You can see where he must've been standing when Osmuna came along."

The noncom pointed to a distinct pair of footprints in the soft earth. Unlike the prints on the slope, these were undistorted and crisp, and Jasak studied them closely.

The feet which had made them had been wearing boots, he realized. Not soft-soled ones, either. They showed deeply ridged treads, the sort of treads found in the footgear of soldiers, or civilian outdoor enthusiasts. A design had been worked into the tread, he noticed uneasily. The kind of design an Arcanan bootmaker would use as a maker's mark, cut into the thick leather of the sole. If that footprint hadn't been left by a manufactured boot, Sir Jasak Olderhan would eat the ones on his own feet.

The realization chilled him even further. Osmuna's killer was no primitive half-wild savage. He was wealthy and sophisticated enough to wear manufactured boots and wield weapons of frightening, unknown power.

"You said you'd found something you couldn't understand?"

"Yes, Hundred." Harnak nodded and pointed into the clump of weeds. "The sunlight caught it as I was bending down to look at the footprints. It's metal, Sir. But I'm hanged if I can figure out what it is."

Jasak crouched for a closer look of his own.

It was a metal cylinder, closed on one end, open on the other. There was a small, distinct ridge or lip formed into the metal around the closed end, as if to form a base, and there were faint marks on the metal. Striations that were discolored. It smelled sharp, sulfurous, a deeply unsettling smell.

Jasak measured the distance between the footprint and cylinder with his eyes. Four and a half feet, give or take. It hadn't been dropped, he realized. It had been *thrown* into the weeds. Deliberately? Or had the man hurled it away accidentally, in reflex perhaps, when Osmuna's quarrel struck flesh? It didn't look like a weapon, or even a part of one. And it was certainly far too small to hold anything big enough to punch a hole that big through solid flesh. Unless—

Jasak frowned in fresh speculation. The hole in Osmuna's back was enormous, yes. But the hole in his *chest* was small. Very small. Just about the diameter of that cylinder, in fact.

"He used this to kill Osmuna."

"*How?*"

Jasak hadn't realized he'd spoken aloud until the chief sword's one-word question told him he had. Threbuch didn't sound incredulous—quite. But he did sound . . . perplexed, and Jasak scowled up at the grizzled noncom.

"Beats hell out of me, Otwal. But look." He fished the thing gingerly out of the weeds, picking it up by inserting a small twig into the open end. "It's the same diameter as the hole in Osmuna's chest."

"That couldn't possibly have gone through Osmuna." Fifty Garlath's tone was scathing enough to cross the line into open insolence. "There's no blood on it, and the angles are wrong, and it landed in the wrong place. If that thing had gone through Osmuna, it would've landed on the other side of the creek, not up *here*."

"I didn't say *this* had gone through the poor bastard," Jasak snapped, gripping his temper in both hands.

"Maybe whatever was *in* it went through him?" Chief Sword Threbuch mused, and Jasak tilted the cylinder so that sunlight fell into it as he peered inside.

"If there was anything in here, there's barely a trace of it left." He sniffed again. "Something smells . . . burnt?"

He reached into the open neck with one fingertip and felt some kind of residue inside. The chief sword twitched violently, as though he'd just suppressed a need to jerk Jasak's hand away, and the hundred managed to summon a wry smile.

"I think it's fairly safe to say Osmuna wasn't *poisoned*," he said.

"And you're sure of that because—?" Threbuch growled.

"Point taken. So I won't lick my finger, all right?"

"Sir!" Threbuch's eyes widened. "*Look* at your finger."

Jasak glanced down, startled, and discovered a black smudge on his fingertip.

"That's carbon," he said wonderingly. "It's like ordinary lampblack."

"But—" Garlath began, then clicked his teeth on whatever he'd been about to say.

"Go on, Fifty," Jasak said quietly.

"It doesn't make *sense*, Sir. Osmuna wasn't burned, any more than he was poisoned!"

"No," Jasak agreed thoughtfully. "No, he wasn't. But something was burned inside this thing, burned so completely that all that's left is a film of lampblack. And the end of this cylinder is the same size as Osmuna's wound. So there's a connection somewhere, even if we can't see it."

"An incendiary spell-thrower, Sir?" Gaythar Harklan asked nervously, and Jasak glanced at him.

"I'm not ruling anything out at this point, Shield," he said. "How close were you to Osmuna when he died?"

"About thirty yards away, Sir. Maybe forty." The trooper pointed to the other stream bank, where Gadrial sat on a boulder in the sun, waiting with commendable calm for a civilian plunged into the middle of a military emergency an entire universe away from the nearest help. "I was behind all that mess of underbrush. Shartahk's own work getting through it, too, Sir."

"And how loud was that cracking sound we all heard?"

"Damned loud, Sir. Hurt my ears, and that's no lie."

"It was loud enough where we were that I can well believe it," Jasak said, nodding absently.

He stood frowning at the enigma perched on the palm of his hand. Harklan was certainly right about how obstructive the underbrush was. The noncom's own nervousness—not to mention his military training's insistence on advancing cautiously in the face of the unknown—undoubtedly meant it had taken him even longer to get through it. Which, unfortunately, had given Osmuna's murderer a priceless gift of time in which to make his own escape.

He realized that his frown at the bland metal cylinder had become a glower, instead, and felt a burning frustration that he couldn't make any of the puzzle pieces fit together.

But whether he could do that or not, they still had a wounded killer to track.

"He went into the water," Jasak said. "*After* he threw this into the weeds. Was he just trying to rinse his wound, or was he trying to accomplish something else? Was anything of Osmuna's missing?"

He glanced at Evarl Harnak, who gave him a hangdog look of sudden guilt.

"I don't know, Sir," he admitted. "We, uh, didn't look."

"Then look *now*, curse you!" Garlath snapped so viciously Harnak paled.

"Yes, Sir!"

The platoon sword threw a sharp salute and scrambled down the bank, and Jasak bit back an acid comment. Harnak should have checked Osmuna's gear immediately; he and Garlath actually shared that opinion. But the men were already shaken, as it was. Snarling at them would only make them more nervous—and mistake-prone—than ever.

Garlath caught Jasak's tight-lipped disapproval and glared back defiantly, as though daring Jasak to reprimand him for ordering a trooper to repair his dereliction of duty. But the hundred couldn't do that, of course, however severely tempted he might be. If he reprimanded Garlath, even in private, it would only add weight to any charge of personal prejudice against Garlath the fifty might make.

In that moment, Jasak realized just how much he truly hated Shevan Garlath. Any man who abused shaken troops in the middle of a crisis—let alone a crisis bigger than anything the Union of Arcana had weathered since its founding—was a man who deserved to be cashiered. Preferably with his head stuffed up his nether parts.

Jasak wanted, more than he'd ever wanted anything in his life, to do that stuffing. The fact that he couldn't only fanned his cold fury, and his voice was an icy whiplash when he spoke.

"I want that killer's trail found and followed, Fifty. Send First Squad west, with one section on this side of the creek, and the other section on the far bank. Have them look for a place our man might've crawled out of the streambed. We know he's been hit, but we don't know how seriously, or which way he went. It'd be rough going for a wounded man to wade very far through all those boulders, though, so send them, say, half a mile.

"If we haven't found any trace of him by then, chances are he headed back east again. His footprints certainly appear to have come from that direction. So, in the meanwhile, send Third Squad east, looking for the same thing."

"And you, Sir?" Garlath bit out.

Jasak held the older man's eyes coolly, staring down the hostility in them. Hostility and a dark flare of pure hatred. Both of them knew precisely how badly Jasak wanted to be rid of Shevan Garlath, yet both of them also knew they were stuck with one another—at least for the duration of this crisis—and Jasak's reply would have frozen a lump of lava.

"Chief Sword Threbuch and I will backtrack the only solid evidence the bastard left behind. That trail." He pointed toward the faint line of footprints along the stream bank, prints that disappeared into the tangle of undergrowth. "Give me a couple of point men—preferably a fire team that's trained together."

He needed someone to watch out for Gadrial, and neither he nor Threbuch could devote the proper attention to that job. Not while tracking a murderer through *this* terrain. But they couldn't leave her behind, either. The multiple Mythalan hells would freeze solid before Jasak Olderhan entrusted Magister Gadrial Kelbryan's safety to the likes of Shevan Garlath.

"Yes, Sir!" Garlath made the snappy precision of his salute an insult in itself. Then he spun away and started snarling orders.

"Begging your pardon, Sir," Threbuch muttered, "but whoever this bastard is, he would have done us a grand favor if he'd killed that asshole instead of poor Osmuna."

Jasak didn't respond. The chief sword was way too far out of line for a noncom of his seniority, and he knew it. Worse, though, he obviously didn't care. And, worse still, Jasak couldn't blame him. So he simply ignored the remark entirely and gave the order no commanding officer liked to give.

"Chief Sword, please see to it that someone collects Osmuna's personal effects. We'll have to forward them to his widow. Then find Kurthal. He's the best draftsman we have. Have him render a sketch of those wounds, front and back, to proper scale."

Threbuch nodded, and Jasak drew a shallow breath.

"When he's done," he said, his voice flat as the ice on Monarch Lake, "prepare Osmuna's body for field rites. We can't just leave him, and we can't spare anyone to take him back to camp."

"Yes, Sir."

The older man's expression told Jasak he was about as happy with those orders as Jasak was. Nobody enjoyed that particular duty, least of all Threbuch, who'd conducted field rites over the years for more troopers than any man cared to recall. Jasak's father had very nearly been one of those troopers, and something in the chief sword's eyes said he was determined to make certain *Jasak* didn't become one, either.

While Threbuch went to deal with that unpleasant chore, Jasak glanced across the stream to where Gadrial sat, unobtrusively watched over by troopers who stood a yard or so above her with loaded arbalests, their gazes roaming ceaselessly for possible danger. She was watching Jasak. Even at this distance he could practically see her blazing curiosity over what they'd found. Not out of any ghoulishness, but because she was worried. More than worried, however splendidly she was concealing the fear he knew she must be feeling.

There was no point keeping her in suspense, and he motioned for her to join him.

*   *   *

Gadrial rose from her perch on the boulder, waded carefully across the swiftly moving stream, and climbed the far bank to join Jasak. She carefully kept her face calm, her manner composed, but she feared her eyes would betray her inner agitation. She wasn't afraid, precisely, but she was gripped by a strong emotion she couldn't readily identify. She was unsure whether to call it anxiety, worry, nervous jitters, or healthy caution, but whatever it was, she was determined to remain in control of it.

She dug her boots into the soft earth of the stream bank, resisting the temptation to rub her posterior, which hadn't enjoyed its stony resting place. It was a steep scramble, but she finally reached the top, where Sir Jasak Olderhan stood watching her through hooded eyes.

Military secrets, she thought, and sighed mentally. He would tell her only what he thought she needed to know. Which wouldn't be much. That was going to be frustrating enough, but the slight chill in his manner distressed her almost more, since she knew its probable source.

She hadn't looked at Osmuna as she waded the stream.

Sir Jasak didn't understand that, she was sure. Mired in his rigid Andaran codes of behavior, he probably thought she was being callous, possibly even coldhearted. He'd expected her to stare, perhaps blink on tears and bite her lip in an emotional display, because she wasn't Andaran, and therefore didn't share an Andaran woman's set of responses to such situations. He'd expected her to display curiosity, at the least, particularly since his men hadn't let her get close enough to see the wounds that had killed the poor man.

She had yet to meet any Andaran male who'd bothered to learn the attitudes held by other cultures' women on much of anything, let alone something as rigidly prescribed as the Andarans' views on death and the proper responses to it. Gadrial, on the other hand, wasn't particularly interested in learning the proper responses to death, because she held a profound respect for the sanctity of *life*, and murder violated that sanctity unforgivably.

Staring at a murdered person's remains was deeply disrespectful to the soul which had inhabited those remains. Worse, that soul was usually still there, confused by the sudden, brutal shift in its state and unwilling to move on until the shock had worn off. But more important even than that, her main concern—as always—was for the living, not the dead. There was nothing she could do to help Osmuna's brutalized soul, whereas there were a number of things she could do to help Sir Jasak Olderhan and his soldiers. If Hundred Olderhan *allowed* her to help. Being a stiffnecked Andaran noble, he was far more likely to order her wrapped up in cotton gauze and protected like a child.

She bit back a sigh and scrambled up the last two feet of the bank to level ground. She found herself more upset than she'd expected to be by Jasak's cool manner. It disturbed her that she wanted so deeply for *him* to understand, even if none of the others did. But there was nothing she could do about that, so she simply drew a deep breath and looked up a long way to meet his hooded eyes.

"Did you find anything?" she asked quietly.

"Nothing but more mysteries," he admitted. "That, and a trail to follow. More precisely, to backtrack. We're still looking for traces of where he went after he splashed into the stream."

"At least we've got something *to* follow," she said with a wan smile that lightened a little of the grim chill in his brown eyes. He studied her for a silent moment, then seemed to come to a decision.

"Ever see anything like this?"

He held a small metal cylinder on the palm of his hand. Gadrial peered closely without touching it, then frowned as she realized what she was seeing.

"Somebody burned something inside that," she said, and he nodded, one eyebrow flicking slightly upward.

"Yes, they did," he agreed.

"What?"

"I was hoping you might be able to tell me that."

The morning air felt suddenly colder. He didn't know what had killed Osmuna. He had no more idea than she did, and she stared at the object on his hand.

"It's so simple there's nothing you could use as a clue, trying to figure out what it *does*," she said. "Of course," she frowned, "someone who'd never seen a personal crystal might wonder what *it* was for, let alone how to retrieve any notes stored in it."

"Why do you say that?"

She looked up, a bit startled by the sharp edge in his voice and the sudden intensity of his eyes.

"What?"

"What in particular made you think about someone who'd never seen a PC before?" he amplified, and she pursed her lips.

"Well," she said, "the men under your command are scared. I mean, really scared. There's something wrong—terribly wrong—about Osmuna's death. None of you seem to know what caused the poor man to die, and now you're showing someone who isn't even a soldier an unknown device found near the dead man. That suggests to me that you have no idea who killed Osmuna, no idea how. And that means . . ."

Her voice trailed off as the full import of her own subconscious insight came sputtering up to the surface.

"That means somebody who isn't Arcanan did the killing," she said finally, slowly, and realized she was rubbing her arms in an effort to persuade the fine hairs to lie back down. She wanted desperately to stare into the woodline, and kept her gaze on Sir Jasak's face instead through sheer willpower.

"I'm right, aren't I? Otherwise, you wouldn't have asked me if I'd seen something like that."

He drew breath, visibly stepped back from whatever white lie he'd been about to utter, and nodded.

"Right on all counts," he said simply, and she shivered.

"You're sure it isn't a spell accumulator of some kind, Magister?" Chief Sword Threbuch asked. The question startled her, since she'd been concentrating too hard on what Sir Jasak was saying to realize the noncom had returned behind her.

And that's not the only *reason it "startled" you, either, is it?* she told herself tartly. There was something unnerving about having a grizzled combat veteran old enough to be her grandfather ask her such a question. Especially, in a voice filled with such flagging hope. She wished she didn't have to, but she shook her head.

"No, Chief Sword," she said almost gently, hating to kill even that tiny hope. "It isn't an accumulator. At least, it's nothing like any accumulator *I've* ever heard of, and I've had plenty of exposure to odd bits and pieces of experimental equipment. It doesn't seem to contain any sarkolis at all, so I don't see any way it could have been charged in the first place. And there isn't even the faintest whiff of magical energy clinging to it. Not even a faint residue. It's not connected to anything arcane."

When she glanced at Jasak again, she found a curious blend of relief and unhappiness in his eyes.

"Well," he muttered, "at least you didn't identify it as some sort of super weapon cooked up by a theoretical magician."

She couldn't stop the glance she cast at Osmuna, sprawled so obscenely below their vantage point.

"You're afraid it's a super weapon?"

"I don't know what the hells it is," he admitted with a frankness which astonished her.

"Then you really *don't* know what killed him?" she said, and Jasak's mouth went hard as marble.

"We know exactly what killed him." His voice was as hard and flat as his expression. "Something was driven through his body, straight through the heart."

"But you don't know what went through him?"

"No."

Gadrial peered at the innocuous metal cylinder again, then sighed.

"I'm sorry, Sir Jasak, but I haven't the faintest idea what that thing might be." She met his gaze once more. "And you have no idea how much I wish I could help you with this."

His response surprised her.

"If anything crops up that you *can* help with, be sure I'll call on you. We're a long way from home. A long way from the nearest help. Before this business is done, we may need the Gifts of every Gifted person we have. Meanwhile, stay close to the Chief Sword and me, but stay behind us."

She started to speak, but he held up one hand and surprised her again.

"That isn't Andaran chivalry," he added, his eyes glinting briefly with what might almost have been an odd little flash of humor. "It's my duty to see that any civilian is as safe as possible during a military emergency. That goes double for a magister with a Gift strong enough for Magister Halathyn to handpick her to head his theoretical research department."

His eyes dared her to protest that assessment, when both of them knew his standing orders contained no such official statement. Besides, Gadrial *wasn't* a civilian—not precisely, since she was officially on the payroll of the UTTTA and currently on sabbatical from her Academy position to serve as a research liaison to the Second Andaran Scouts.

But she wasn't about to take that particular gryphon bait, much less run with it. She was no adolescent, and the agony she'd endured at the Mythal Academy had taught her which battles were worth fighting, so she conceded the point.

"I appreciate your position, Hundred Olderhan."

The relief in his eyes told her he'd expected her to protest. She was, after all, Ransaran, with notions most Andarans regarded as rife with anarchy and social chaos. Gadrial didn't know whether to be irritated or amused. Then his eyes darkened, and she was suddenly gazing at another person, a grim stranger with skulls reflected in his suddenly frightening gaze.

"We're trying to find a wounded killer, Magister Kelbryan," he said softly, his near whisper far more chilling than another man's ranting. "This isn't going to be a simple hike through the woods. We're hunting the most dangerous quarry any human can hunt, and the only thing we have to track him by is the trail he left walking to this spot. I don't mean to give offense, but you're not an experienced tracker. You could damage a faint spoor without even realizing it."

"No offense taken. I'm a good outdoorswoman, but I'm no soldier, and I won't pretend to possess skills I don't."

"I appreciate your honesty. We're going to be moving fast. Very fast. You're not combat trained, Magister—"

"Gadrial," she interrupted, and one of his eyebrows quirked. The light in his eyes changed, the balefires flickering and dimming as surprise misted through the flame.

"I beg your pardon?"

"My name is Gadrial. If we're going to face death together, I'd just as soon do it on a first-name basis. Death is a little personal, don't you think? Much too intimate to face with a stiff formality between us. If I were a soldier, it would be one thing. But I'm not. Frankly, I'll feel better if you stop being so aristocratically formal and just *talk* to me."

He blinked. Actually blinked, started to speak, and paused. He blew out his breath, and then a tiny smile crooked one corner of his mouth.

"You have a point. Several points, all of them valid." The smile flickered larger for a moment. "In fact, you rather remind me of someone else. All right." He nodded. "Where was I?"

"You were telling me I'm not combat trained," she said in a dry voice which surprised another tiny smile from him. Then he regained his equilibrium.

"Yes. Well, the point I was going to make is that we'll be moving fast, trying to catch up. You may find it difficult to keep up the pace," he said, not formally, but certainly diplomatically, and she grinned.

"Is *that* all that's worrying you? My dossier must not have mentioned that I run competitively. Distance running. I may not match your speed," she added with a droll glance at all those muscles in a body that was certainly easy on the eyes, "but I've got endurance, and that's what we'll need most, isn't it?"

Jasak was beginning to think this delightful woman was just this side of perfection. But before he could decide how to respond, she continued.

"There's something else you need to know about me. You know I have a very strong primary Gift, but I have two or three minor *arcanas*, as well. One of those may be useful before this business is done."

"Oh?"

Gadrial tilted her head, studying him for a moment before answering. His tone sounded hopeful, rather than challenging or dismissive. Sir Jasak Olderhan might be a blue-blooded Andaran noble to his bootsoles—he was, after all, destined to become the next Duke of Garth Showma, Earl of Yar Khom, Baron Sarkala, and at least another half-dozen equally improbable titles—but that didn't seem to have atrophied any of his brain cells.

"I would be grateful for *anything* you can contribute," he said very quietly.

"Thank you. I'll be glad to help however I can. And among other things, I possess a minor Gift for healing. I'm no miracle worker, mind. Not even remotely in the same class as a school-trained magistron, or even an army surgeon with a fair dollop of Gift. But I can heal relatively minor wounds all day long, if necessary. And if a man's injured critically, I might be able to save his life. At the very least, I could probably stabilize him until a real healer can take over and do a proper job of tissue renewal."

"Magister Kelbryan—Gadrial," he said softly, "you have no idea how glad I am to hear that."

The glorious sunlight faded to a pale blur, and the sounds of birdcalls, wind in the treetops, and the bubbling wash of water below their feet all vanished from her awareness when the depth of worry behind those quiet words hit home. He was expecting trouble. Big trouble. Injuries worse than his platoon medics could handle. His surgeon was with Fifty Therman Ulthar, a universe away and seven hundred miles from the swamp portal. No one had expected to run into anything like this, and she glanced down at her hands, which could heal minor things. Sprains and contusions, broken toes or fingers. Those lay within her capabilities, and she hoped with sudden desperation that she wouldn't be called upon to handle more than that.

For the first time since their departure from the swamp portal, Gadrial Kelbryan was truly afraid.

CHAPTER
FIVE

JATHMAR FELT WONDROUSLY alive as he sent his mind quest-
ing across the surrounding folds and dips of land.

Mapping was as close to flying as he ever expected to come. Oh,
he'd gone ballooning, of course. That was part of every licensed survey
crewman's mandatory training. But ballooning was a slow-motion,
ponderous activity, and the balloon was merely pushed hither and
thither by whatever capricious winds happened to be blowing. He'd
heard rumors about balloons fitted with one of the newfangled
"internal combustion" engines some of the more wild-eyed lunatics
were tinkering with back on Sharona. He didn't expect much to come
of it, though. And even if it did, the earsplitting racket and stink
wasn't going to be very conducive to enjoying the experience.

But Mapping, now. Mapping felt more like what Jathmar imagined
birds must feel, soaring silently across the sky as forests and fields
flashed beneath one's wings. Jathmar had always envied birds, even
drab and commonplace little sparrows.

But, then again, sparrows can't Map.

Jathmar grinned at the thought, but Mapping was a Talent only
humanity possessed, and only a tiny fraction of the ten billion or
so human souls in existence could lay claim to that specific Talent.
Of course, that was still a pretty damned large absolute number.
Nearly a fifth of the population had been blessed with some kind of
psionic Talent. Given the best current estimate, that worked out to
around two billion Talented people, of whom only two percent had
inherited the ability to Map. That meant there were—theoretically,
at least—something like forty million Mappers, but there were several subtypes within the Talent, and they were clearly concentrated
in specific bloodlines. Not to mention the fact that at least half of

those technically Talented with the ability had Talents too weak to bother training for professional use. Both of Jathmar's parents had been Mappers, however, and so had three of his grandparents, which explained why his own Talent was so strong.

Unlike Shaylar, Jathmar's mother and grandmother hadn't been able to join survey crews. But they'd found ways to make use of their Talents on the home front, working for the Park Service: mapping virgin woodland without impinging on it, doing geological survey work, planning new highway routes, doing the occasional Search and Rescue work for lost hikers. Mappers can't find people. Even taking on odd jobs like inspecting dams and culverts for structural soundness.

Mapping was a Talent which was always in high demand in the commercial sectors. Considerably higher demand than his wife's usually was, actually. Voices were always valuable, but they were also among the most numerous of all the psionic Talents, the true telepaths of Sharonian society, with nearly as much variety in potential employment as there were individual variations between Voices. Shaylar was a very special case, however. Very few Voices could match her sheer strength and range, which would have been more than enough to make her extremely valuable to someone like the Chalgyn Consortium. But when the sheer strength of her Talent was combined with the precision with which she was able to use it *and* her marriage bond with Jathmar, it produced a team which could have written its own ticket with just about any survey concern.

Jathmar's professional assessment of his own Talent was tempered by a realistic view of his shortcomings, as well as his strengths. He knew he was a good Mapper—very good—and that Shaylar was a first-class Voice. But it was the combination of their Talents, the way they interlocked and complemented one another, which made them such a truly formidable team, especially in virgin wilderness.

The reasons for that were simple enough. Jathmar could See not only the topography of the ridgeline that lay two miles due south of him, and the abrupt turn this creek took a mile northeast, frothing through a white-water staircase of rapids, but he could also See what lay *under* the ground. Only a small percentage of Mappers had that degree of Talent, and that was what made Jathmar so valuable to a survey crew.

And Shaylar's ability to share that Sight with him was one of the reasons Halidar Kinshe, her government sponsor, had fought so hard to put them into the field together as a team.

Now, as he stretched his awareness to its furthest limits, Jathmar caught a glimpse of something vast and dense beneath the soil. It was large enough to cause a wavering, almost like heat-shimmer, in the faint but discernible—to a Mapper—magnetic field.

That magnetic field lay across his Sight of the world like a precisely cast fishnet of crosshatched lines. But the line just ahead of him was bent slightly out of true. That caught his immediate, full attention, for he'd come to know exactly what spawned that dark, massive magnetic anomaly. There was a major iron deposit in this region, big enough to warrant immediate investigation. If the deposit were large enough—and if the clues they'd gathered so far added up to what he suspected, it would be enormous—it would shortly be a magnet (Jathmar grinned at his own word choice) for development by the Chalgyn Consortium's Division of Mining and Mineral Extraction.

If DOMME developed the deposit into a profitable mining venture, every ton of ore extracted, smelted, and turned into tools would put finder's royalties into this survey crew's bank accounts. And if he really had stumbled across the same iron deposit as Sharona's fabulously valuable Darjiline Mines, the Consortium certainly would develop it.

It was one of the conundrums of trans-temporal exploration that in a society with access to multiple, duplicate worlds, with all the vast treasure troves of mineral resources, rich untouched farmland, and incalculable numbers of wild birds and animals that implied, there were actually a limited number of key resources and all too many companies in competition to grab them. With no fewer than fifteen major corporations and consortiums—not to mention nearly a hundred smaller independent outfits which operated survey crews on a shoestring budget—contending for the riches on the far side of any new portal, prizes like the Darjiline Mines were actually scarce.

Which was the whole reason survey crews worked so hard to figure out where they were when they crossed the eerie boundary of a new portal. News that the Portal Authority had sent troops to construct a new portal fort would race outward through the web of development companies literally at the speed of thought, despite all that a company's Voices could do to encrypt their transmitted reports.

No telepath was ever permitted to invade another's mind without permission. Prison sentences went with that kind of abuse, not to mention massive fines and the ever-present threat of closing down any company which knowingly used or tolerated such practices. But industrial espionage tiptoed around that particular law with increasingly sophisticated ways of deducing the truth. Once the

Portal Authority had taken the step of sending out a troop detachment to build the fort, rival teams would start sweeping into the area, looking for the fastest way to reach the most valuable tracts of land before anyone else.

Shipyards went up first, in many cases, built with surprising speed, since the only practical way of reaching many of those valuable tracts would be to sail there. The company that owned the forests and iron mines necessary to build those ships would make a ton of money selling them to rival outfits. Once they'd grabbed the best land for themselves first, of course.

It was usually a free-for-all along any portal border, which was why the Portal Authority insisted on building its forts. Portal Authority troops weren't there to fight a war, since there was nobody in any of the worlds they'd ever explored. They were there to prevent claim jumping and timber piracy and all the other uncivilized behaviors which went with the territory when multiple groups jockeyed for position along a vast, steadily expanding frontier. And, of course, to collect the Authority's portal transit fees.

It was, on the whole, a delightful and exhilarating time to be alive. He grinned and pulled out his field notebook and pencil, making careful notations that included compass headings, then set out again, eager to finish the routine work so they could get to the iron deposit.

*　　*　　*

Jathmar's Talent was strained to its utmost, feathered-out edge, feeling out the contours of the iron deposit he couldn't quite See from its distortions of the magnetic field, when it struck.

The psychic blow was so savage that he literally lost stride, stumbled, and went to one knee.

Shaylar!

He exploded back to his feet and whirled, blindly seeking the source of his wife's abrupt anguish, and his hand blurred toward his hip. Steel hissed with an angry-snake sound in the suddenly menacing silence as the H&W cleared leather. But there was nothing to shoot. He was miles from camp. Whatever was happening, he couldn't possibly get there in time to do anything about it. Fright chittered along his nerves while the rest of him stood frozen for long, soul-shaking moments.

Shaylar's terror and shock rolled across him in battering waves, but Jathmar wasn't a *telepath*. He didn't know what was happening. Couldn't glean the tiniest detail from the jagged emotions tearing through him. Every nerve in his body quivered with the need to run towards camp, but he bit down on the panic and remained where he was, forcing himself to breathe deeply.

You can't help anyone if you go crashing through the trees in a headlong charge.

The steel in that mental voice, put there by years of intense training and hardscrabble field experience, steadied him. It was hard to do—the hardest thing he'd ever done—but he managed to disassociate himself from the tidal wave of Shaylar's emotions. He stood silent for several more moments, just listening to the forest, but he couldn't detect anything out of the ordinary. The birds still chirruped and called through the trees. Squirrels and chipmunks still frolicked like happy children on a scavenger hunt. Wind rustled in the glorious crimson-golden foliage high overhead, and rattled through the thickets of blackberry brambles. The stream still bubbled its way across the rocks, splashing from one boulder to the next on its long journey to the sea.

In all that ordinary sound, Jathmar could detect not one single, solitary thing that might have threatened Shaylar. And, by extension, the entire camp, since Ghartoun chan Hagrahyl would never have permitted Shaylar to wander away from the base camp's protection. Nor was she foolish enough to do so. All of which meant one simple thing; if he wanted to find out what was wrong, he would have to return. Immediately.

Jathmar eased his slung rifle off his shoulder, holding the pistol one-handed while he clicked the safety off the long gun. There was no sign of danger in his immediate vicinity, but Jathmar wasn't taking any chances. He holstered the revolver and worked the lever on the rifle, chambering a round in one easy, fluid motion.

The metallic sound of the action was profoundly reassuring. The Sherthan Model 70 had been designed as a short, handy saddle gun, but it was still a powerful weapon. Chambered for a .48 caliber, three hundred-grain round based on the old Ternathian Army Model 9's. Its muzzle velocity was lower than the military weapon's, due to its shorter barrel, but with the new "smokeless powder," it still pushed the heavy, hollow-pointed round at over nineteen hundred feet per second, producing a muzzle energy of over two thousand foot-pounds. That gave the weapon a nasty kick, but it was also sufficient to blow a hole right through a man and lethal enough to deal with anything short of one of the huge grizzlies.

At the moment, Jathmar found that thought comforting. *Very* comforting.

Some survey crewmen routinely carried their rifles pre-chambered, so a bullet was available to fire instantly if a man needed to shoot in a hurry. Jathmar had more shooting experience than most scouts, however. He could load, lock, and fire a rifle or handgun in a fraction of a second, in total darkness or blinding rain, and under normal circumstances a round carried in the chamber was an accident waiting to happen.

This, however, was not a normal circumstance.

So he loaded the chamber, then moved forward cautiously, Model 70 in both hands (and trigger finger outside the trigger guard), senses alert for the slightest hint of danger. The emotional link with Shaylar had shifted. Horror had faded away into a sense of desperate urgency that threatened to swamp his hard-won calm. He literally could not imagine what was happening at their base camp, but he commanded himself once again not to panic and moved forward at a steady pace.

He forced himself to move more slowly than he would have preferred, repeating to himself the Authority *mantra* that coolheadedness was both a survey scout's first line of defense and his most effective weapon. Yet the urgency in the bond tugged at him, urged him forward as it grew stronger. It felt almost as though Shaylar was shouting "*Hurry!*"

Which, given the strength of her Talent and their marriage bond, might be exactly what she was doing.

Despite his determination to move with caution, Jathmar found himself speeding up. He couldn't help it. The forest was utterly normal, yet Shaylar's emotions were a goad, driving him faster with every passing minute.

He was never sure when he'd broken into a run, but he realized he was, in fact, running when he slid down a leaf-slick gully, thrashing through the underbrush, and found himself hurtling up the other side.

He paused at the top, panting, cursing his carelessness, and listened again. Still he heard nothing. Not a solitary, damned thing out of the ordinary. He checked his watch and tried to calculate how far he'd come. Half a mile, maybe. Jathmar grimaced, then set out again, opting for a compromise between the utter silence of caution and the pell-mell dash of panic.

Pushing through the dense underbrush along the stream was heavy work. The luxuriant growth's widespread, tangling limbs and brambles caught at his rugged clothing and slowed him down. He slogged through it, cursing its hindrance, then paused with another curse—this one directed at himself.

He was a *Mapper*, damn it. He was following the stream out of sheer habit, because it was the way he'd come on his way out. But the sense of direction which came with his Talent told him the precise bearing to the base camp, and he changed course, angling sharply away from the creek. The open forest floor away from the streambed's understory was vastly easier—and quicker—going, and his ability to See the terrain in front of him let him pick the best, fastest way through it.

I should've thought of this sooner, he told himself savagely. *Guess I'm not quite as calm as I'd like to think I am.*

There was no point in kicking himself over it, and he settled down to the steady lope the better going permitted.

*   *   *

It took Jathmar another thirty agonizing minutes to reach the campsite, where he found a rude surprise.

It was empty.

He stood in a screen of thick shrubs at the edge of the clearing, too uneasy to just step out into the open without taking a careful look first. The brushwork palisade stood silent in the glorious autumn sunlight, a circle of protection lacking only its gate. He could see the tents inside it, still pitched where they'd been this morning. The donkeys were still there, too, looking bewildered and lonely. But there wasn't a single *person* in sight, and not a single man-made sound anywhere in the clearing.

An icy fingertip touched Jathmar's heart. Deadly cold, unreasoning, it robbed him of breath for several shuddering, superstitious moments. Then his gaze, wandering in shock from one edge of the camp to the other, caught on something totally unexpected. His eyes jerked to a halt, fixed with sudden white-faced horror on something that shouldn't have been there.

It was a *cairn*.

Someone had piled rocks across something sickeningly man-sized and human-shaped. It lay at the top of the stream bank, in the shadow of the abandoned brush wall, and for a truly agonizing moment, Jathmar feared the worst. But then reason reasserted itself. He could still feel Shaylar through the marriage bond, closer than before. She was alive, not buried under that pile of cold stone. He shuddered and forced himself to push that terrifying image away, forced his mind to begin functioning once more.

He frowned. He'd heard a distant rifle shot, quite some time ago. Had someone accidentally shot one of their teammates? It was hard to credit. Every member of this crew, including Shaylar, knew weapons-handling inside and out. You didn't shoot at a target you couldn't see. You didn't point the muzzle at anything—like someone else on your team—that you didn't *want* a bullet to go through. You didn't carry your gun with a round chambered.

So who the hell was dead? And *how?* They hadn't even been felling timber, so there were no fallen trees to have crushed anyone.

He pondered for a moment longer, then moved cautiously into the open with the rifle butt snugged into the pocket of his shoulder, muzzle down, so no one could knock the barrel aside or rip it out of his hands. His finger was no longer outside the trigger guard. Instead, it rested on the trigger itself, ready to fire in an instant as Jathmar stepped through the unfinished gate.

Nothing stirred but the wind. The tent flaps, left open as though abandoned in a great rush, whiffled in the breeze that wandered in over the tops of the interwoven branches. Jathmar walked a quick perimeter recon inside the palisade, making sure no one was hiding out of sight in one of the tents. He felt like a fool, hunting for brigands who couldn't possibly be there. And he was right. No one *was* there. The camp was deserted.

He went back to chan Hagrahyl's tent. The expedition's leader had obviously raked hastily through his possessions, and Jathmar frowned again. What in the names of all the infinite number of Uromathian gods could have rattled chan Hagrahyl badly enough to simply abandon camp and run for the portal? That was an unheard of decision for any expeditionary leader. Teams only broke and ran from certifiable disasters: volcanic eruptions, earthquakes, forest fires. Even when facing brigands, running was inherently more risky than standing one's ground in a prepared camp. Their team was large enough, and well enough armed, to have dealt with any typical band of border brigands. But the ex-soldier had run for the portal. Run so fast he'd left Jathmar behind.

Jathmar was so rattled by the implications that he found himself wondering why he was so convinced his team was, in fact, running.

Because, idiot, his common sense muttered in some exasperation, *you're married to a Voice who's trying her damnedest to warn you to follow as fast as your big, flat feet will carry you.*

A swift check of his own tent confirmed his suspicions. Shaylar had packed in the same haste evident from chan Hagrahyl's tent. She'd abandoned clothing, food supplies, cooking utensils—everything but her camp ax, guns, and charts. Or that was what he thought, until he suddenly spotted his own backpack leaning against his sleeping bag.

She'd pinned a note inside the flap, written in obvious haste.

Someone's murdered Falsan. We don't know who or how many there are or where they came from. Ghartoun says we can't wait for you. Head for the portal—and be careful, beloved.

That was all . . . and it was more than enough.

The shock burst between his ears like an artillery shell. Falsan had been *murdered?* His shoulder blades twitched as a chill crawled its way down his spine. He'd felt foolish, looking for someone in the abandoned camp, but his instincts had been correct. There *was* someone out here besides themselves. Someone who'd already killed once. Someone unknown.

"Dear gods above . . ." he whispered.

An unknown *human* contact?

No wonder chan Hagrahyl had bolted for the portal. They were in over their heads, *way* over, and Jathmar didn't hesitate a second longer. He paused only to swiftly check the contents of his pack, nodding approval at Shaylar's selections—rations for two days, pistol and rifle ammunition, and his camp ax. Every one of their charts and notebooks was missing, undoubtedly in *her* pack.

Jathmar slung the pack onto his back, abandoning the rest of their meager possessions, then filled his canteen at the stream and headed out at a hard jog. Falsan's killers might well be mere minutes behind him—it had been a long time since he'd heard that rifle shot—which made speed more important than caution.

He made no particular effort to cover his tracks. Any experienced tracker would have no trouble following their trail, regardless of anything he might do. The footprints, broken branches, and bruised leaves left behind by eighteen people in a hurry would be as easy to follow as a Ternathian imperial highway. The more quickly he left the vicinity, the safer he'd be, and if it came to a fight, his two guns might make the difference between survival and something else.

He refused to think about a pitched battle between Falsan's killers and their survey crew, with Shaylar caught in the middle of it. The very thought robbed him of breath he needed for running, and Jathmar was grateful—profoundly so—that Falsan's route this morning had been nearly a hundred and twenty degrees off the bearing directly back to the portal. Whoever had killed him would have to locate their camp first, before following their tracks back to the portal. If they ran fast enough, there was a chance they could reach Company-Captain Halifu's fort and its contingent of soldiers in time.

He found himself cursing silently in time with his strides. *Eighty years!* Sharonian expeditions had spent *eighty years* exploring the multiverse, and not once had they found a trace of other humans. Why *now*? Why *them*?

He stamped on the anger. He knew it was merely a smokescreen, a way to divert his mind from his own terror, and he couldn't afford to let either emotion distract him. Nor was there any point in railing at the multiverse for putting Shaylar in danger. *He'd* done that, fighting to get her included on the field teams.

Well, he told himself grimly, *you got her into this, so you'll just have to get her out again.*

The whisper of her presence through their marriage bond seemed to chide him for blaming himself. They'd *both* fought to put her out here, not just him. Jathmar grimaced, knowing she was right, and tried to stop kicking himself. But he couldn't help it. So he tried to at least seethe at himself more quietly as he followed the trail the others had left. He scanned for pitfalls ahead, where he might twist or even break an ankle if he put his foot wrong, and listened intently for any hint of pursuit.

The one thing he couldn't do, and wished bitterly that he could—was to See what was behind him. Or, rather, *who*. Unfortunately, Jathmar could See only the land itself, not animals or people moving across it. It wasn't like looking with his eyes. He didn't See the land as a faithful image of reality. He Saw contours, shapes, protrusions and depressions, dense places and less dense ones, that he had learned to recognize as streambeds, mineral deposits, soil types, and all the other features which made up the bones of the world. He would have given a great deal to be able to scan the terrain behind him for the people who'd murdered Falsan, but what they needed for that was a Plotter, or a Distance Viewer.

What they *had* was one outclassed and nervous Mapper.

He ignored the crawling itch between his shoulder blades, told his spine to stop anticipating a blow from concealment, and concentrated on moving as rapidly as possible.

The trail—of course—led uphill all the way. Jathmar was in excellent physical condition—anyone who spent as much time hiking as a survey crewman had to be in good shape—but he hadn't pushed himself this hard in a long time. His thighs and calves were feeling the strain, and his breathing was heavier than he would have liked it to be. His Model 70 grew heavier with every stride, but he gritted his teeth and kept going. He'd been running for the better part of fifteen minutes when he heard a low voice from behind a screen of wild spirea bushes just ahead.

"Jathmar!"

He slid to an instant halt, breathing hard and turning his head to follow the sound.

"Ghartoun?" he panted, and the stocky ex-soldier rose from a cautious crouch.

"Any sign of pursuit?" he asked, his voice urgent but quiet, and relief jellied Jathmar's knees. He shook his head, stiffening both weary legs in grim resolution.

"Not yet. The camp hadn't been disturbed when I got there. And I haven't heard anything behind me."

"That's something, at least," chan Hagrahyl muttered. "You made good time catching up to us. Let's hope to hell Falsan's killer doesn't do the same. All right, we're moving out."

Jathmar pushed through the spirea behind chan Hagrahyl, and Shaylar flung herself into his arms, holding on tightly. She wasn't quite trembling, but he felt the distress tightening her muscles, and spikes of emotion ripped through their bond.

"I was so *scared*," she whispered against his chest. "Thank all the gods you made it back to us!"

"Shhh." He lifted her chin and kissed her gently, then frowned as he glanced at her bulging pack. "That's too heavy for you."

"Yes, but I didn't dare leave any of this behind, in case . . ."

She swallowed hard, and he brushed a fingertip across her lips.

"Never say it, love. It didn't happen. Here." He slid off his pack, opened hers, and redistributed the weight. "That ought to help."

She gave a sigh of relief when he helped her shrug the straps back across her shoulders.

"Oh, that's lovely. Thanks."

"Don't mention it, M'lady," he said with a courtly bow, and her smile wavered only slightly as she squeezed his hand.

She headed out behind the others, and Jathmar followed, carefully placing himself between her and whatever might be coming up behind them. They moved at a rapid pace, not quite jogging, but the difference was so tiny as to hardly matter. The trail wasn't a friendly one. It still drove inexorably uphill, and it was littered with underbrush, deadfalls, and deep gullies that hindered their progress. It hadn't seemed like such rough country coming through in the other direction, he thought bitterly, then gave himself another mental shake.

Be fair, he told himself. *It* isn't *that* rough—*you're just scared to death and trying to get through it five times as fast!*

Chan Hagrahyl kept them moving for two hours without stopping. Shaylar strode grimly forward, outwardly holding her own, but Jathmar could feel her aching weariness and the need for rest that she managed to keep hidden from the others. He'd never been so proud of her, nor so frightened *for* her, but he wasn't surprised when chan Hagrahyl finally called a halt and she cast pride to the winds and simply sank to the ground, panting.

The stocky Ternathian who'd once been an imperial officer cast uneasy glances at the forest behind. Probing glances that tried to see into the shadows behind far too much underbrush, far too many trees. Barris Kassel and the other ex-soldiers spread themselves into a defensive ring without a word, silently standing guard while everyone gulped a few swallows of water and caught their breath. Shaylar had her breathing under control again, but he could feel the aching weariness in her.

She can't keep going hour after hour at this pace, Jathmar thought despairingly. *Not all the way to the portal.*

He wasn't sure the *rest* of them could keep up this wicked pace, for that matter. Jathmar already felt the strain, and Braiheri Futhai was at least as badly winded as Shaylar. Jathmar tried to keep his worries quiet, tried to keep Shaylar from catching them, but he didn't succeed. When she lifted her head, meeting his gaze levelly, he tried to smile, and her answering smile's courage, and the strength of her love, nearly broke his heart.

Being here with you is worth it, worth the risk and the danger, her smile told him, and he smiled back, aware that he'd never loved her more.

Far too soon, chan Hagrahyl gave the soft-voiced order to move out again.

CHAPTER
SIX

"THAT'S NOT A campsite, Sir. It's the next best thing to a godsdamned *fortress*," Chief Sword Threbuch breathed in Sir Jasak
Olderhan's ear, and Jasak nodded grimly. It was an exaggeration . . .
but not much of one.

They'd found no trace of where their quarry had gone after
murdering Osmuna, which told Jasak that he'd turned back in the
direction from which he'd come, keeping to the stream to throw off
the scent. It also meant the only clue they had to follow was the
trail he'd left on his way to the site of the murder.

So they'd backtracked him. It hadn't been especially difficult; whoever he was, he hadn't bothered to cover his tracks when walking
towards his murderous rendezvous with Osmuna, so the trail itself
was easy to pick up. On the other hand, that trail had wound its
way through the underbrush along the stream like something a snake
with epilepsy might have left behind, and after what had happened
to Osmuna, Fifty Garlath's men moved with a certain understandable caution.

Jasak told himself the killer couldn't be very far in front of them
now. Not when he was wounded and struggling through the boulder-
strewn stream. Jasak had halfway expected to overtake the bastard
somewhere along the creek, but they'd found no trace of him. And
he had to admit that they'd taken at least two or three times longer
than they ought to have to get their pursuit organized in the first
place. He knew he could legitimately blame most of that delay on
Garlath's inefficiency, but innate honesty forced him to admit that
he'd been more than a little slow off the mark himself.

In fairness to himself—and Garlath—the sheer, stunning impossibility of what had already happened would have thrown *anyone*

off stride. And despite the importance of finding the killer and anyone else who might be with him, Jasak knew he'd been right to take the time to try to learn everything he could before setting out in pursuit.

However little "everything" turned out to be in the end, he thought glumly, lying belly-down beside Threbuch with his chin on his folded forearms while they studied the natural clearing on the far side of the stream.

The camp in the middle of that clearing made it painfully obvious that whoever he was, Osmuna's killer wasn't out here alone. One man could never have built the palisadelike wall they were studying from their vantage point across the streambed. Not by himself. That high brush barrier of interwoven branches and cut saplings surrounded an area at least thirty yards in diameter, and it was too high to see over from their present position.

There was too much timber down around the edge of the clearing, too, all of it showing the white scar of newly cut wood, for one man to have felled it all. If he'd cut down that many branches and small trees by himself, the oldest cuts would have started losing that raw, pale look of just-hacked-down timber.

"At least fifteen or twenty, you think?" he murmured to Threbuch.

"Couldn't be much less than that, Sir," the chief sword replied. "Not from all the work the bastards've put in over there."

Jasak nodded again and thought some more.

If that estimate was accurate, First Platoon had the mysterious strangers substantially outnumbered. In addition to the fifty-seven men of his four line squads, Garlath had an attached six-man engineer section, four quartermaster baggage handlers, and a hummer handler. Adding Jasak himself, and Chief Sword Threbuch, that came to seventy men, which ought to provide Jasak with a comfortable superiority.

But he couldn't be sure of that. Threbuch's estimate was based on the *minimum* number the construction of that palisade would have required, but it was large enough to house a considerably bigger number. A simple division of labor could easily have put fifteen or so to work building it while others hunted for food, prospected for minerals—there was a substantial iron deposit in the area, Jasak knew—or even pillaged some nearby village unfortunate enough to have been targeted by pirates. There simply wasn't any way to know from out here how many people really were occupying that camp. Which meant someone had to go inside to find out. Yet Jasak didn't feel like rushing forward and risking the lives of more of his men unnecessarily.

The palisade was strong enough to repel anyone who wanted to get inside, unless he had a convenient field-dragon to blast it down with explosive spells, which Jasak didn't. The thick wall of saplings—cut from the stream bank where there was enough open sunlight to allow heavy shrubs and saplings to grow—had been interwoven with tough brush, much of it thorn-covered, to create a high, virtually impenetrable barrier. His scouts' infantry-dragons, far lighter than the field-dragons the artillery used, would find it extremely difficult to blow gaps in it.

Despite the chief sword's comment, it wasn't quite a fortification. But it was more than stout enough to keep out any wild animals, and the number of people who could have been concealed in the area inside that high, thorny wall was dismayingly large . . . especially when those people were equipped with whatever unknown sort of weaponry they'd used against Osmuna.

Worse, the camp had been placed by someone with an excellent eye for terrain. The land rose towards it from the streambed, not steeply but steadily, and that location and its wall—higher than necessary to stop any native predator, but perfect for hiding its interior from an aggressor and preventing him from seeing the placement of men and weaponry on the other side—spoke of military planning. That much was unmistakable, but who had built it? And—more to the point—why?

In the face of so many unknowns, Jasak was unwilling to assume anything. What he needed was hard evidence, the answers to at least his most pressing questions, and he had nothing. For all he knew, this might not even be the killer's encampment. It might belong to someone else entirely—someone the killer had been scouting, prior to attacking.

Yet Jasak didn't believe that for a moment. Indeed, he was becoming more and more convinced that what he was looking at was a base camp for another multi-universal civilization. The very notion was absurd, but no more absurd than what had already happened. And they were close to what Magister Halathyn and Gadrial strongly believed was a class eight portal. If they were right, no one could possibly have lived in the vicinity without literally stumbling across the thing. A class eight wasn't the sort of thing that could escape notice for very long. The class three portal leading to their own swampy encampment was almost four miles across; a class eight would be closer to twenty-five or even thirty.

With something that size and the swamp portal only a couple of days travel apart by foot, Jasak couldn't believe any natives in the general vicinity would have failed to notice them. Which meant they should have built cities, or at least villages and transportation systems, to take advantage of them. Yet all the Andaran Scouts had found was this tiny, semi-fortified camp.

Which meant Osmuna's killer had probably been doing much the same thing they were: mapping and exploring.

Jasak conscientiously ordered himself not to wed himself to any sweeping conclusions without more evidence. They could be in the middle of some noble's huge game preserve, after all. Whoever had killed Osmuna might have thought he was eliminating a locally born trespasser or poacher. Or Jasak and his men might have unknowingly trespassed upon sanctified or unsanctified ground, in which case Osmuna might have been killed for blasphemy. But however firmly he reminded himself of those possibilities, he kept coming back to the totally alien nature of whatever had been used to kill his man.

This isn't getting me anywhere, he told himself. *And every minute I waste speculating is another minute for anyone inside that camp to make his ambush nastier, if he's planning one.*

The problem was what to do about it. Anyone who stepped out into that open clearing would undoubtedly find out if there was someone waiting inside that palisade with a terror weapon in his hands. Getting holes blown through more of his troopers didn't exactly strike Jasak as the best way of going about finding out, though. Oh, for one lowly reconnaissance gryphon to do an aerial sweep!

That gave him an idea.

He caught Fifty Garlath's eye, which wasn't all that difficult since the platoon commander was staring at Jasak with something close to panic in his eyes. The hundred pointed silently toward the nearest tree, then upwards into its widespreading branches. It stood along the bank of the creek where they lay prone, and Garlath nodded convulsively, with a look of relief that would have been comical under other circumstances but managed to look mostly pathetic under these.

The fifty signaled to Sword Harnak, then pointed at the same tree. Harnak, in turn, signaled to Jugthar Sendahli, who nodded, tapped one of his squad mates on the shoulder, and disappeared into the concealing brush.

It took the two troopers the better part of six sweat-filled minutes to work their way around to the back of the tree through the brush. Its trunk was more than broad enough to conceal them when they finally reached it, and Jasak heard the slightest of rustles as Sendahli's squad mate boosted the *garthan* high enough to reach the lowest of the widespreading limbs.

The dark-skinned scout went up the tree in slow motion, each movement silent with caution, each toehold tested gently before he used it to boost himself higher. He scarcely jostled a single leaf on his way up, and Jasak gave an internal nod of approval, pleased that Garlath's tenure hadn't ruined the *garthan* yet. Jasak had recommended Sendahli for promotion, and he hoped it went through.

The man was Mythalan, but hardly *shakira* or even *multhari*. The *garthan* caste was the lowest of the low in Mythalan society, comprised of the vast masses born without any Gift at all. In most parts of the Union of Arcana, those born without the ability to use magic were simply ordinary citizens. They might not be able to aspire to the magistery like Gadrial, but they could look forward to ordinary careers and the same basic opportunity to earn a good living as anyone else.

But not in Mythal.

Jasak's jaw muscles knotted as he watched Sendahli's slow, skillful execution of his orders and felt his Andaran sense of civilized behavior towards other human beings rising up in fresh indignation. A *garthan* wasn't legally property any longer. Chattel slavery had been outlawed two centuries ago, under the Union of Arcana's founding accords. But the accords had only limited power inside a country's national borders, which meant most local laws had remained the same. And in countries which had embraced the Mythalan culture and its rigid stratifications, those born without the ability to use magic faced lives little if any better than those of a Hilmaran serf from Andara's first age of conquest.

People born to the *garthan* caste lived painfully limited lives. Their employment choices were a matter of heredity—a butcher's son became a butcher, even if he was better suited to building wagon wheels—unless the whim of their *shakira* lords and masters willed otherwise. The magic-using castes and sub-castes, with the ruthless support of the traditional *multhari* military caste, still ruled Mythal and her allied colonies—including those in several new universes—with an iron hand. They jealously guarded their hereditary privileges and frothed at the mouth at the slightest suggestion of abolishing the caste system that relegated men like Sendahli to third-class citizenship and a grimly limited future.

Jasak had never learned the details of the debacle which had finally driven Magister Halathyn to sever all connection with the great

Mythal Falls Academy, *the* premier magic research and development academy in all of Arcana's many universes. Much as he personally detested the *shakira* caste, Jasak had to admit that, historically, the majority of the great breakthroughs in magical theory had originated with the Mythalans. Which, of course, only made them even more insufferably overbearing and arrogant.

It undoubtedly also helped to explain what had happened with Magister Halathyn. Jasak *did* know that Halathyn had infuriated many of his *shakira* peers by devoting so much of his time and talent to the needs of the UTTTA even before he left the academy. It wasn't so much that they'd objected to trans-temporal exploration, but the *shakira* as a caste harbored a fierce resentment for the fact that the military (which meant Jasak's native Andara) dominated trans-temporal exploration. The Mythalans had tried for years to secure control of the Union's exploration policies, only to be frustrated by Andara and Ransar. Whatever their own differences might be, the Andarans and Ransarans had formed a unified front against *shakira* arrogance literally for centuries, which had only made Mythal's resentment of the UTTTA's policies worse. Halathyn had never had much patience with that particular view, and he'd actually taken the time to find out how he could best aid in the exploration process.

And then had come Gadrial Kelbryan. She'd been only a lowly undergraduate, at the time—not yet seventeen, which had been an almost unheard of age for *anyone*, even a *shakira*, far less a Ransaran, to win admission to the academy—but every story agreed that she'd been at the heart of whatever had driven Halathyn vos Dulainah out of Mythal Falls forever in a white-hot rage. Given what Jasak had come to know of Halathyn, added to the obvious strength of Gadrial's Gift and the deep and abiding Ransaran faith in the individual, he rather suspected he could guess how it had happened. And he was absolutely certain that the *Mythalan* version—that Gadrial had been Halathyn's out-of-caste lover, trading sexual favors for better grades—was a total fabrication.

Ransaran and Mythalan societies, and the religious beliefs which underpinned them, could not have been more different. Mythalans believed in the reincarnation of the soul, and that lives of virtue were rewarded by successive incarnations in steadily higher castes on the path to a fully enlightened existence. Virtually all Ransaran religions, whatever else they might disagree about, were monotheistic and believed in a *single* mortal incarnation and a direct, personal relationship with God.

The Mythalan belief structure validated the superiority of the *shakira* and bolstered the monolithic stability of the structure which rested upon the *garthan*'s total subjugation. After all, how could someone become a member of the *shakira* in the first place, unless he had attained the right to it in his previous incarnations? But Ransaran theology engendered a passionate belief in the right and responsibility of the individual to take command of his own life, to make of himself all that his own God-given abilities and talent made possible. The Mythalan caste system was a loathsome perversion in their eyes, and the clash between the two cultures was long-standing and bitter.

The discovery that a *Ransaran* possessed such a powerful Gift would have been gall-bitter for most *shakira*, and it was widely believed that the Mythal Falls faculty had a habit of washing out "unsuitable" students any way it had to. Or, if the student in question was too academically strong for that, using the requisitely brutal form of harassment to drive him—or her—away.

Jasak had no way of knowing if that was what had happened in Gadrial's case, but the towering fury of Halathyn's vitriolic letter of resignation when he broke off completely with his fellow *shakira* and formally joined the faculty of the academy that served the Union of Arcana's military headquarters at Garth Showma was legendary. And Gadrial Kelbryan, then a lowly third-year undergrad, had accompanied him as his protégée and student.

Over the two decades since, Magister Halathyn had assembled the staff—including Gadrial—which had built the Garth Showma Institute into a true rival for Mythal Falls and improved the UTTTA's field capabilities by at least twenty-five percent. In the process, he'd carved out his own special niche in field operations . . . and continued his ruthless demolition of Mythalan stereotypes wherever he encountered them.

It had been one of the greatest pleasures of Jasak's military career to watch the aging magister convert the suspicious *garthan* soldier now swarming so carefully up the massive oak—a man who'd joined the Andaran Army as a way to escape Mythal and buy a better future and higher social status for his children—into an ally and friend.

There was only one Magister Halathyn, he thought. And the swamp portal where Halathyn was currently camped, in a flimsy tent with only a single squad to provide security, was far too close to whoever had come out of *this* fortified camp.

Jasak peered upward, trying to spot Sendahli, but he couldn't see a trace of the trooper. Good. If *he* couldn't see Sendahli, even knowing he was there, nobody inside the palisade ought to see him, either.

On the heels of that thought, a piercing trill came wafting down from the treetop.

All clear.

Jasak grimaced. So their mystery camp was empty, but was it merely unoccupied at the moment, or abandoned?

He glanced at Fifty Garlath, who was sweating profusely again. Garlath darted a nervous glance back at Jasak, then motioned to Gaythar Harklan. The squad shield lay prone at the edge of the creek, but he rose at the gesture and scrambled his way down the bank, across the swift-moving main current, and up the other side. He scuttled across the ground in a swift, crouching dash that carried him to the base of the palisade, then came fully upright. He kept his back as close as he could to the brush wall's outermost, sharply jutting branches, taking no chances Sendahli's all clear might have been mistaken, but at least no one was shooting at him with anything.

So far, so good, Jasak thought. *And now . . .*

Harklan edged sideways along the wall, then whipped through the opening in a rollover prone that took him into enemy territory literally at ground level. Silence gripped the waiting platoon. Flies whirred and buzzed past Jasak's ears, and still the silence held. Then Harklan reappeared.

"It's abandoned," he called across, "but they haven't been gone long. There are several fire pits in here, and the coals're still hot enough to cook over. And they've left their pack animals."

Jasak exchanged glances with Threbuch.

"Whoever they are, they're in a tearing hurry to be somewhere else, Sir," the chief sword observed quietly, and Jasak nodded, then glanced at Gadrial.

"They're headed for your class eight portal, is my guess," he said.

"It's not *my* class eight," she muttered. "If it's anyone's, I'd say it's *theirs.*" She waved at the abandoned camp. "They obviously got to it before we did. It's even possible the class eight leads into their home universe."

"You don't think they're from this one?" Jasak was curious to see if her logic paralleled his own.

"I don't see how they could be," she said, shaking her head. "I'm no soldier, but it seems to me that if there were more of them nearby, they'd have sent a messenger for help and holed up behind those spiky walls while they waited for it. But they didn't do that. They ran. That suggests they're feeling outnumbered, guilty, or maybe just scared to death. Whatever their motives, they're obviously determined to go someplace where they can get help. That camp may look formidable from out here, but it's actually pretty rudimentary. If there weren't very many of them, they could've built that just to keep out bears and panthers and what-have-you so they wouldn't have to post a sentry to watch for predators."

Jasak was impressed. She might be "no soldier," but her reasoning tallied closely with his own. And from the flicker of respect in the chief sword's expression, it tallied with Otwal Threbuch's, too.

"You'd have made an effective military analyst, Gadrial," the hundred said, and her eyes glinted.

"One of these days, you Andaran bully boys will be civilized enough to let us ladies join your ranks. The effect ought to be bracingly beneficial."

"Ladies in uniform?" The chief sword snorted. "Carrying arbalests and throwing war spells? Ransaran democratic madness."

"I'm qualified expert with a hand arbalest," she said tartly. "And I can throw spells that would singe your braided Shalomarian hair. Literally," she added sweetly.

The chief sword just grinned, unrepentant.

"I would suggest," Jasak interrupted, before Threbuch succeeded in digging himself in any deeper, "that we discover what we can about that."

He nodded toward the palisade, and Fifty Garlath took his cue from that and ordered the platoon forward. First and Second Squads split up and did a sweep of the treeline surrounding the clearing, looking for possible ambushes or snipers. Third Squad unlimbered its crew-served infantry-dragon, setting it up in a cover position on this side of the stream. Fourth Squad followed First and Second across the creek and bellied down under cover of the far bank, waiting.

Gadrial watched with quiet intensity from her vantage point in the scrub. She was perfectly aware that Jasak had no intention of walking out there until the security sweep was complete and the platoon's heavy weapons were in place to respond to any threat. Had she not been present, he would probably be out there already himself, but she was along for the ride, so he was left with the responsibility for her safety.

He obviously placed a high priority on keeping her in one piece, and she was scared enough to appreciate that, yet independent-minded enough to flush with embarrassment as she admitted to herself that she *wasn't* able to hold her own out here. She had no formal military training. She truly was a crack shot with a hand-sized arbalest, but she'd never fired a shoulder weapon in her life, and she couldn't even give the dragon gunners a hand. As strong as her various Gifts were, she'd never used artillery and had only the vaguest sense of how it operated.

Gadrial's main interest in the infantry-dragons, and the heavier field-dragons of the true artillery, was in the battle spells that powered them. She'd spoken to combat engineers and knew battle spells were complex. Building them demanded intense concentration frequently under conditions that were challenging, to say the least, and not all of them were directly related to the artillery. Infantry companies included not just the dragons and their gunners, but also an attached squad of combat spell engineers with multiple responsibilities.

Combat spell engineers were among the highest-skilled and highest-paid men in the Union of Arcana's armed forces. There were never enough of them to go around, though, and they were too valuable to put at the sharp end and get them shot at if it could be avoided, so units like Hundred Olderhan's routinely carried plenty of extra spell packs for emergency use.

Infantry platoons were built around squads, each twelve men strong. A squad was subdivided into two maneuver teams, each consisting of three arbalestiers commanded by a noncom, and supported by an infantry-dragon. It took both of a dragon gunner's assistant gunners and two of the squad's six arbalestiers to carry enough accumulator reloads to fight any sort of sustained engagement, but in the absence of someone who could recharge them, a team had only the ammunition it could carry.

Now Gadrial shivered, watching the heavy weapons deploy defensively. She was afraid a battle was exactly what was going to happen. The question was whether it would break loose here, or somewhere else.

When the final "all clear" whistled across the open space, Fourth Squad rose out of its cover, spread into a skirmish line, and headed into the abandoned camp. Jasak strode ahead, leaving Gadrial in the care of two men assigned as her bodyguards. She deliberately fell behind his rapid stride, making sure she didn't get in anyone's way. Still, she'd nearly reached the gap in the brush walls when she realized Jasak had stopped dead in his tracks.

He stopped so abruptly she almost collided with him, and when she stepped around him to see what he was staring at, she caught her breath. A cairn of rocks lay in the shadow of the brush wall, piled up between the interwoven branches and the edge of the stream, and she felt a tremor in her knees, and another in her chest, as she recognized its shape and depth.

The fact that someone had died here shouldn't have shocked her so brutally. She knew that. But as she stared down at the pile of rocks over what had been a human being, there was no doubt in Gadrial's mind that they'd found the man who'd killed Osmuna.

Dismay stabbed deep as the sickening import crashed home. There'd been only one man on the bank above the creek where Osmuna had died. Only one trail through the forest led back to this camp. Which meant that only two men knew what had happened out there in the wilderness.

And both of them were dead.

She recognized the same understanding in the grim look in Jasak Olderhan's eyes, the knotted muscles in his jaw and the tension in his shoulders. She wondered what he was thinking, then decided she didn't really want to know. Then Jasak raised his gaze, granite eyes tracking like a hunting gryphon after prey as they sought out his commander of fifty.

"Search this camp," he said flatly. "I want to know how many men were here. What they left behind. Anything that might give us an idea of where they're from, and why they're here."

"Yes, Sir!"

Garlath started spitting orders. They sounded industrious enough, but they lacked a certain clarity, and Jasak locked eyes with his chief sword. The grizzled noncom nodded crisply and moved immediately to organize the search Garlath was attempting to direct.

Once Chief Sword Threbuch waded in, the swift, methodical search went so smoothly it was like watching a choreographed dance, Gadrial thought. Except for the fact that there was no music but the jittery rattle of wind in dead leaves that scuttled across the rocky cairn where Osmuna's killer lay, that was. She supposed she ought to be glad—in a retributive, just-desserts fashion—that the man who'd murdered Osmuna was dead, and a portion of her did want to be glad, shocking as that seemed. But it was only a small part of her, and the rest was horrified by what had transpired out here.

The Union Accords, the cornerstone of the Union of Arcana, had put an end to the savagery of the Portal Wars two centuries previously. They had united the various warring kingdoms and republics into one cooperative entity, dedicated to exploring the multiple universes and giving everyone in the Union a better life. The opportunity to build something new and worthwhile in pristine universes, the chance to amass wealth in a civilization which was wealthy in a way pre-portal Arcanans couldn't possibly have imagined.

Those Accords had governed the use of portals and new uni-verses for two hundred years. And they also laid out the rules and contingency plans for contact with another human civilization in the clearest possible terms. Every soldier in the Union's military forces was put through training on how to conduct such a first contact, which aimed above all else to be peaceful. The last thing anyone had wanted was a shooting war with another human civilization.

Yet in all the years of the Union's existence, no such other civilization had ever been encountered. The rules were still there, the troops were still trained in them, but *only* as a contingency. No one had actually expected to ever require them. Not really. Surely if there'd been other human beings in existence, Arcana would have discovered them long ago.

But they hadn't . . . until today. Until two total strangers had met in a trackless wood. Met in fear and suspicion, and despite the strictures of the Accords, promptly slaughtered one another. Gadrial hadn't known Osmuna, but he'd seemed a bright enough fellow, dedicated to his duty in the Andaran Scouts. He'd seemed unhappy with Fifty Garlath, but proud to serve Hundred Olderhan, and Gadrial found it difficult to believe he would have thrown the Accords into the garbage can without extremely good cause.

Her gaze returned again and again to the silent grave while Jasak's men searched the camp for clues. Ten minutes elapsed in grim silence, punctuated by the sounds of angry men ransacking what had been an orderly camp, and their ugly mood frightened her. These men had blood in their eyes, looking for something—or some*one*—to rip apart in retaliation for a comrade's murder. She couldn't really blame them, but that made their anger no less frightening, and when she glanced at Jasak, she saw him frowning as he, too, watched the camp's destruction.

The facts they shook loose were few and far between.

"We're not looking at more than eighteen or nineteen people, at most," Chief Sword Threbuch reported to Jasak and Garlath. "There's damn near nothing here but spare clothes, sleeping rolls, and abandoned foodstuffs. We found more of those little metal things we recovered on the bank above Osmuna's body, though, and you're right, Sir. There is something inside."

He produced several shiny metal cylinders, each of which had a duller metal object stuffed into the top. They weren't all identical; some were larger, some smaller. Most of the metal caps were round-nosed, although some were flatter than others. All of those had hollows in their tips, but there were also three longer ones, each of which had a solid, sharply pointed tip.

"That looks like lead," Jasak frowned as he touched one of the round-nosed cylinders. "But this one—" he took one of the three pointy ones "—looks more like . . . copper?"

He glanced up at Threbuch, but the chief sword's expression was baffled. Jasak looked at Gadrial, who extended her hand. He laid the cylinder in her palm, and she turned it, examining it from all angles.

"It is copper," she agreed. "But look here." She tapped the end. "It's not *solid* copper. It's more like a jacket around something else. And I think you're right about that, too. The core is lead."

"I wonder . . ." Jasak murmured as he took the mysterious object back from her.

"Sir?" Threbuch asked.

"I wonder how much force it would take to propel this," Jasak tapped the cylinder's pointed cap with one fingernail, "across fifteen or twenty feet of space and drive it through a human body?"

Garlath lost color and made a strangled sound that drew Jasak's eyes to him.

"That—that's barbaric!" the fifty protested.

"But damned effective," Jasak pointed out.

"You can't be sure that's what happened," Garlath objected. "There's not enough of *anything* inside that little cylinder to do such a thing."

"Just because we can't imagine how to do it, Fifty Garlath, doesn't mean someone else couldn't *figure out* how to do it," Jasak observed.

Garlath flushed, the color looking even darker against his fearful pallor, and Jasak turned back to Threbuch.

"Go on, Chief Sword," he said, and Threbuch produced some other odd cylinders of metal. These were much larger, as broad as his palm, and six inches long.

"There's a whole stash of these, whatever they are, Sir. We found them in every tent. They don't seem to be weapons of any sort, but there something inside them. You can feel it slosh when you shake the thing."

"You shook one of them?" Jasak frowned, and Threbuch snorted.

"One of the men had already been shaking them, Sir. It didn't explode in *his* hand, so after I'd ripped him a new asshole—pardon, Magister." He glanced at Gadrial and colored slightly himself. "Anyway, I figured it was probably safe enough to handle them."

"See if someone can cut into one of them. But not here. Take it out to the woodline, just in case."

As the unhappy trooper who'd drawn that particular job headed out with the dense metal object and his short sword, Threbuch continued his situation report, such as it was.

"They haven't been here more than a couple of days, Sir. If I were to hazard a guess, I'd say this was a forward observation post, or a base camp of some kind. A relay station, maybe, for others to follow. They're no primitives, whoever they are and wherever they've come from. You've seen their metalwork. That matches ours, but it's just the beginning."

He motioned to another trooper, who brought over an armload of examples.

"Their cloth is high quality," he said, holding up a length of what looked like sturdy canvas. "If this wasn't machine-loomed, I'll—" he flicked another glance at Gadrial and amended the phrase on his tongue to "—eat my shirt."

The magister just grinned, which stained the hard-bitten noncom's cheeks pink once more. Then he jerked his gaze back to his commanding officer.

"The same pattern repeats everywhere you look, Sir," he said, doggedly ignoring the humor glinting in Hundred Olderhan's eyes, despite the tension of the moment. "We found high quality leather goods sewn on a machine. Metal mess kits, with eating utensils and plates tucked inside collapsible cookpots. Personal toiletry kits with combs and brushes that look like something manufactured for a mass market, not locally produced by some village shop."

"If they left dishes and combs behind, they left in a damned hurry," Garlath muttered.

"And they weren't too worried about replacing them, either," Threbuch replied. "That kind of gear's hard to replace when you're at the end of a long transit chain."

"They may not be at the end of a long chain," Jasak said quietly.

Utter silence reigned for a long moment, broken only by the wind and rustling leaves.

"They're running for the portal we came out here to find," he continued after a moment. "I'm certain of it. Not only did they abandon most of their gear so they could move faster, they abandoned the donkeys they used to carry it here, as well." He nodded toward the sturdy little beasts penned in one corner of the camp behind a fence made of rope. "I'm betting they have another fortified base on the other side. Not a little camp like this, either. A large base, with plenty of troops."

The chief sword swore colorfully. Then he stopped himself abruptly. He looked at Gadrial again, started to say something apologetic, then obviously decided he had more serious things to worry about than her possible reaction to a little rough language.

"We can't afford to let them reach that portal ahead of us, Sir," he said. "If you're right, and if they get to a bigger fort before we get to them, we'll be outnumbered. Given what they did to Osmuna, and how fast they did it, I don't like that scenario. Not one damned bit."

He glanced at Gadrial again as he spoke, but this time his expression was very different. The tough-as-dragons-scales chief sword looked terrified. And not, she realized abruptly, for himself. He was horrified by the thought that someone would kill *her* the same way they'd killed Osmuna. She had to blink hard, and she looked away, unwilling to embarrass him with her abruptly watery emotions.

"Hundred Olderhan," Fifty Garlath said before Jasak could respond to Threbuch, "given the chief sword's astute analysis, I respectfully recommend a course of extreme prudence. The enemy has an unknown troop strength and a head start. They're moving fast and light, whereas we're burdened with considerable equipment, including the dragons. Magister Kelbryan's calculations suggest that the portal's close enough they'll undoubtedly reach it well ahead of us. And with Fifty Ulthar's platoon at the coast, instead of the swamp portal, we're badly understrength."

"Your point?" Jasak tried hard to keep the acid out of his voice.

"In my considered opinion, Sir, pursuing at this time would be the height of folly. The only prudent response is to return immediately to our base camp in the swamp and send for reinforcements from the coast before attempting to run these people down."

Jasak stared at the older man, disbelief warring with rage as Garlath looked defiantly back. An ugly, triumphant glow lit the backs of his eyes, and Jasak felt his jaw muscles aching as he clenched his teeth in comprehension.

Garlath's spineless cowardice was equaled only by his incompetence as an officer and his hatred for any officer promoted past him. But he was clever in his own way. So damned clever it turned Jasak's stomach. Clever enough to wrap his desire to flee from anything that looked remotely like danger in the mantle of considered, prudent tactics.

Volcanic rage sizzled through Jasak Olderhan, but before it could boil over Gadrial Kelbryan shocked him by rounding on Garlath like a hissing basilisk. Her almond eyes flashed with lethal lightning as she advanced on Garlath, who actually backed away from her slender fury with an expression of almost comical astonishment.

"Don't you *dare* use *my* research as an excuse to cut and run!" she snarled.

"Magister Kelbryan, you mistake my meaning!" Garlath replied, speaking so quickly the words came out gabbled. "I didn't say we should *run away*. Not at all! That would be as foolish as rushing forward. All I'm recommending is a tactical retreat, just a temporary maneuver to concentrate our forces. If we stay scattered, we won't be able to withstand a united attack by an enemy of unknown strength using weapons we can't even understand. We can't afford to risk walking into some sort of ambush. We have to be sure we survive to carry word of this staggering discovery to our superiors. And then there's your own value as one of our finest magisters. If anything were to happen to *you*, or if you, gods forbid, fell into enemy hands, then—"

"Oh, stuff it someplace interesting, Garlath!" Gadrial snapped.

"Magister," Garlath said almost fawningly, "I only meant—"

"I know exactly what you meant! I've been trapped in your revolting company for *weeks*, Shevan Garlath. You are the most pathetic excuse for an officer I've ever seen. One of your own men has been murdered—*murdered*, damn you!—and the only thing *you* want to do about it is run away and hide someplace safe! And you have the unmitigated gall to use *me* as an excuse for your cowardice?"

Gadrial realized she was literally shaking with fury, and a corner of her mind wondered how much of that stemmed from her own fear and her own need to find something to lash out at. Not that it made her contempt for Garlath any less merited, even if it did.

"We have to find out what's going on out here," she continued in a marginally calmer, icy voice. "We have to find out *now*, before things get any further out of hand. If we can't do that—and do it before it all goes totally out of control—then I'm not going to be the only one at risk. And I warn you, *Fifty* Garlath. If *anything* happens to Magister Halathyn because of your fuck-ups, I will come after you for blood debt. And I'll keep coming, through as many godsdamned universes as it takes to track you down and feed your miserable excuse for a soul to the crows!"

Naked shock flared behind Garlath's eyes, and Jasak stepped in quickly.

"Magister Kelbryan, I fully appreciate your concern for Magister Halathyn's safety. Believe me, I want to protect him as much as you do. As for getting a message back to our superiors," he swung his gaze to Garlath, who flushed dark red under its withering contempt, "that's why we carry hummers. Chief Sword, see to it. Send a priority message to Javelin Kranark at the forward base, and another to Commander of Five Hundred Klian, at the coast. Given the urgency

of the situation, I want Fifty Ulthar and his platoon recalled immediately. And I'm sure Five Hundred Klian will also want to get a
message off to Five Hundred Grantyl at the Chalar base. Record and
release immediately with my chop on the header."

"Yes, Sir!" Threbuch saluted crisply and darted one disgusted
glance at Garlath before heading for Javelin Iggar Shulthan, Charlie
Company's senior hummer specialist. Jasak watched him go, then
turned back to the infuriated woman still glaring at Garlath.

"Magister Kelbryan," he said quietly and formally, breaking her
concentration and drawing her carefully away from the object of her
rage, "I would consider it a great personal favor if you would add
your own message. Your Gifts are far superior to mine, and I want
Five Hundred Klian to have as much information as possible."

"Of course," she said stiffly. "I would be delighted to help in any
way I can."

She flicked one final, fiery glance at Garlath, then strode vigorously
across the camp to join the chief sword and their hummer handler.
Jasak watched her for a moment, then took a firm grip on his own
temper and returned his attention to Fifty Garlath.

As much as he wanted to, he couldn't follow Gadrial's explosive
example and call the man a sniveling coward. She was dead-on accurate, but that didn't matter. Garlath had given too many plausible,
outwardly militarily sound reasons to retreat. He knew how to play
the game, all right. Jasak had to give him that. That skill—playing
the nasty little game of power politics which was the worst curse
of the patronage system within the Arcanan military—was the one
thing Shevan Garlath was actually good at.

A deep and abiding hatred crystallized in Jasak's blood, turning
him cold as ice, and Garlath backed up another involuntary step
before his expression.

"Your tactical concerns are noted, Fifty Garlath." Jasak's eye was
granite-hard as he bit his words out of solid ice and spat them at the
older man like hailstones. "Your assessment of the situation does not
tally with mine, however. It's imperative that we stop these people
before they reach the portal. I don't want a damned battle, Garlath. I
want *answers*. And I want to control the situation. Until we get those
answers, until we get to the bottom of what happened out here, we
don't *know* anything. But if these people are as confused as we are,
and if they get back to their superiors and tell them *we* started it,
it's going to change from a disaster to a godsdamned catastrophe.

"We won't get any answers if they reach the portal—and whatever base may lie beyond—before we've caught up. And we won't

be able to put the brakes on this, either. Shartahk seize it, we don't even have any idea how to *communicate* with them if we do catch up with them! So the only option *I* see is to find them, stop them, and try to make some sort of controlled contact with them, just like the first contact protocols require. And, failing that, we at least need to take them into custody and return them to base where someone else, with the kind of diplomatic experience none of us has, can try to figure out how to talk to them and, gods willing, straighten this fucking mess back out. Do you read me on this, Fifty Garlath?"

Garlath's jaw worked as he glared back at Jasak. The fusion of fear, resentment, and hatred bubbling away inside the man must be like basilisk venom, Jasak thought. He doubted that explaining his own analysis had done a bit of good, but he'd had to at least try to get through to this excuse for an Andaran officer.

"Do you *read* me?" he repeated very softly, and Garlath jerked his head in a spastic nod.

"Good," Jasak said, still softly. "Because we're facing a fast, hard march, and I expect you to pull your weight. Is that clear?"

"Yes, Sir." Garlath's tone was so brittle Jasak wondered why his tongue hadn't shattered.

"Then get the men ready to march within the next three minutes. May I assume you're capable of carrying out that order, Fifty?"

"Yes, Sir." Hatred seethed in Garlath's dark eyes. For a moment they met Jasak's. Then they skittered away, and the fifty jerked out a salute and turned on a bootheel, snarling orders at his men.

But they were, by the gods, ready to march in three minutes.

CHAPTER
SEVEN

JATHMAR FROWNED AS Ghartoun chan Hagrahyl and Barris Kasell exchanged grim looks for the fifth time in ten minutes. He glanced at Shaylar for a moment, then moved closer to them.

"Trouble?" he asked quietly, and chan Hagrahyl nodded choppily. "We're being followed."

Jathmar's stomach did a creative dip and dive. His eyes went instantly to Shaylar, then he wrenched them back to the other two.

"You're sure?" he asked, and Barris nodded.

"For the last two miles, at least. They're still behind us a good ways. Probably haven't spotted us yet. But it's only a matter of time."

"Then how can you be sure anyone's there?"

"Look," Ghartoun grunted, and jerked his head sideways.

Jathmar frowned again. Then his eyes followed the gesture, and it was his turn to grunt as if someone had just slugged him in the belly.

A rabbit bounded past, not loping from place to place but moving at a determined run. Moments later he saw another, then a third. Chipmunks, too, were running through the sparse undergrowth, and a quick glance at the trees revealed agitated squirrels bounding from branch to branch, streaking along in the same direction their survey crew was traveling.

His jaw clenched in instant understanding, mingled with chagrin. He'd grown up in these woods, damn it. He should have seen it for himself, even sooner than chan Hagrahyl and Kasell.

And you probably would have, if you weren't so worried about Shaylar, a little voice told him.

"Something's spooked them," he said, knowing it was unnecessary even as he spoke, and both the others nodded.

"My guess is," Barris said as they continued to move steadily forward themselves, "that they've hit our trail and fanned out into a line. They're trying to circle around and cut off any escape attempt. If I'm right, we're going to see animals cutting across our path from the sides any moment now."

Jathmar grimaced. He drew breath to ask what he could do . . . just as a good-sized rabbit shot past, running on a diagonal path that slashed from their right to their left. His eyes tracked it, and he swore with quiet, heartfelt passion.

"We're not going to make the portal, are we?" he said quietly.

"No." Barris Kasell was watching the trees, not the rabbit, but he answered anyway. "We aren't."

Jathmar worried his lower lip with his teeth.

"I'm no soldier, but there's got to be something we can do. Something *I* can do. What do you suggest?"

Chan Hagrahyl was also watching the forest. Now he looked back at Jathmar, his gaze like sharpened steel.

"There's not much we *can* do, except try to find a place to make a stand of some kind, and out here, that isn't likely. There's nothing here but forest. No high ground, no streambeds or gullies, not even a mountain pass to defend—just open trees. Gods know how many of them are out there, let alone what they intend to do once they overtake us."

"We've only got four real choices," Barris Kassell added in a low tone, flipping his eyes back to the trees. "We can keep going, even try to pick up the pace. We *might* outrun them over a short distance, especially since we have the advantage of already knowing where we're going. But we can't run all the way to the portal; we're a long, hard day's march away. Or, we could pick a spot to make a stand, but Ghartoun's right. There's not much out here that lends itself to digging in against a siege. We certainly can't hide, not from trained trackers, and given how quickly they've overtaken us, we're up against men who know their business."

"So we can run, make a stand, or hide. What's the fourth option?" Jathmar asked, not liking any of the others.

"We can turn and carry the fight to *them*," Kasell said. "I doubt they'd expect us to do that, which would give us the advantage of surprise, initially at least."

"I thought about that," chan Hagrahyl agreed, "but there are several major drawbacks. Among other things, we don't have any idea how badly outnumbered we might be, and we don't have all the ammunition in the world, either. Judging by the number of animals they've spooked into running, I'd say there's a fair sized group out there, so we'd probably need all the ammo we've got and then some."

"I could take Fanthi," Kasell said very quietly. "Maybe Rilthan and Elevu. Load up with all our spare ammo. This kind of terrain—" he jerked his head at the trees "—three or four experienced grunts could do a hell of a lot of damage to somebody armed with crossbows."

"But Ghartoun just said—" Jathmar began, only to be cut off by chan Hagrahyl.

"He's not talking about a stand, Jathmar. He's talking about slowing them down, forcing them to deploy and waste time. And he's right, the four of them could do a lot of damage. But," he moved his eyes from Jathmar to Kasell, "I don't think you could do enough. Not to buy us long enough to get all the way to the portal. Besides, I'm kind of fond of all four of you."

"Four of us against all these civilians," Kasell replied quietly, and Jathmar swallowed as he realized Barris was arguing in favor of a virtual suicide mission.

"I know."

For just a moment, Ghartoun chan Hagrahyl's face was simultaneously hard and haggard, but then he shook his head again.

"No," he said. "And not just to keep you from getting your stubborn Arpathian self killed, Barris. We still don't know what happened out there, and I'm beginning to wonder if *they* know for certain, either. Judging from how long it took these people to catch up with us, fast as its been. They certainly weren't hard on Falsan's heels. And Falsan couldn't have moved very quickly with that damned crossbow bolt in his chest before somebody who wasn't wounded could have caught up with him. I'm starting to think he really did run into just one of them, initially, at least. Maybe their man is wounded—maybe even dead—too. They may have been delayed giving him first aid. Hell, they may even have needed time just to *find* him after they heard the shot! That might just explain why it could have taken them so long to backtrack Falsan."

"You're saying this is all some kind of *misunderstanding*?" Kasell demanded incredulously.

"I'm saying it *might* be. And even if it isn't, so far we've only lost one man and, as far as we *know*, they haven't lost any of theirs. At the moment, it's still at least remotely possible we could settle this whole thing without anybody else getting killed. But to be effective at slowing them down, you'd have to open fire from ambush. That's definitely a hostile act—the kind that ups the stakes all around."

Kasell looked for a moment as if he were prepared to continue arguing. But then he grunted unhappily and nodded in acquiescence.

"So what *do* we do?" Jathmar asked.

"A variant of forting up." Chan Hagrahyl sounded like a man who'd made his mind up. "Can you See anything we might use for shelter, Jathmar? Anything at all?"

"I can't guarantee what I'll find, but I'll Look."

"That's all I ask."

Jathmar had already crossed this ground once, on their outbound leg, which helped. The dips and low undulating hills, masked from ordinary eyesight by the dense covering of the forest, stretched for long, unchanging miles. The land revealed to his inner eye was stark and easy to read. Unfortunately, there wasn't a single spot in any of that rolling terrain that would shelter them, or at least give them a fighting chance to defend themselves.

He blinked, returning his awareness fully to his body, and met chan Hagrahyl's worried eyes.

"Did you—" the expedition's leader began, only to break off as a magnificent ten-point buck came crashing through the trees at an oblique. Only this time, the animal crossed their path from left to right.

"Nothing, Ghartoun." Jathmar shook his head. "I'm sorry."

Ahead of them, Fanthi chan Himidi broke abruptly left, signaling for the others to remain where they were. He moved swiftly and silently, vanishing between the thick tree trunks like a ghost.

Jathmar halted, heart pounding, breathing heavily, and gripped Shaylar's hand. Her slim fingers trembled against his, but they both drew comfort from the contact. She peered worriedly up into his face, and he tried to summon a smile, but she could read his agitation too easily through the marriage bond.

A moment later, Fanthi returned, jogging straight up to chan Hagrahyl.

"There's a clearing we can use. Looks like a twister touched down at some point in the past year or so. Lots of trees down. Tangled brush, tree trunks the size of temple pillars. Good cover, as well as plenty of concealment. We won't find a better spot."

Even Jathmar knew the difference between "cover" and "concealment." The former was a physical barrier between you and enemy bullets, like a shield. The latter merely hid you from view. A screen of leaves concealed, but did nothing to stop incoming fire; a solid tree trunk did both.

Chan Hagrahyl looked at chan Himidi for a moment, then nodded.

"Take point." He raised his voice. "Listen up, people. We're following Fanthi. Move it!"

Chan Himidi had, indeed, found a good spot. Little more than an acre across, the clearing overflowed with raw distraction. A spinning funnel of wind from some long-ago storm had ripped trees out of the earth, snapped them like kindling, and twisted them apart, leaving jagged knife blades of wood stabbing the sky. Small splinters had been driven into other, still standing trees with such force that they were embedded like nails. Tree trunks had crashed to earth in a jumbled pile, digging broken branches into the ground.

"We know they're coming at us from three sides," chan Hagrahyl said quietly. "We'll take position there." He pointed to a confusion of tangled wood on the far side of the clearing. "I want clear firing lanes, and someone to watch our backs, in case the bastards succeed in circling all the way around us."

"I'll cover our rear until you're all in position," chan Himidi volunteered through clenched teeth.

"Good." Chan Hagrahyl nodded. "But listen to me, everyone! No one shoots unless *I* say so. Got that? *Nobody* shoots. I know we all want revenge for Falsan, but there are men out there with weapons. If we have to fight, we fight all out, but first we try and work things out so that nobody else gets killed. Is that understood?"

Heads nodded all around, one or two of them a bit unwillingly, and he grinned tightly at them all.

"Good," he said again. "In that case, let's get under cover and dig in."

They took their positions in utter silence, facing south, the direction from which the bulk of their pursuers would approach, and fanning out slightly. Jathmar stationed himself and Shaylar in a sheltered pocket where a massive black walnut trunk, nearly five feet in diameter, formed a solid barricade. It was the best protection he could find, and branches thicker than his own torso jutted up and out from the main trunk, forming angled braces he could use to steady the rifle if it came to that.

Tymo Scleppis took up a position to Jathmar's left, near the center of their all-too-ragged line. The Healer was opening his pack, trying to ready himself for casualties if it came to open fighting. Rilthan—their best marksman, by a wide margin—crawled in just to Shaylar's right. The gunsmith was the only member of their party armed with the new Ternathian Model 10 bolt-action rifle, with its twelve-round box magazine. He said nothing as he settled into position, but he flicked one glance briefly in Shaylar's direction before meeting Jathmar's gaze. It was only a fleeting look, but it told Jathmar that Rilthan had chosen his spot deliberately, and Jathmar's throat was tight as he nodded, acknowledging Rilthan's intention to protect her.

Beyond Rilthan was chan Hagrahyl's clerk, a dark-skinned Ricathian who'd joined straight out of high school. Not yet nineteen, Divis' color was closer to last week's ashes than its normal warm chocolate hue, and his hands shook as he tried to load his own rifle. The drovers formed their flank guards, such as they were, but they had barely five men on either side.

Jathmar crawled up onto one of the immense branches, using it as a firing step to get just high enough to shoot over the top of the trunk. It was too tall for him to shoot across standing on the ground, but thanks to other branches that had slammed into the earth, the fallen tree bole didn't quite reach the forest floor. There was a gap, about fourteen inches high, which allowed Shaylar to lie prone behind one of the big branches, protected from incoming fire, yet able to shoot through the gap if need be.

Everyone was checking weapons, including Shaylar, and Jathmar's hands felt clumsy as he pulled cartridge boxes out of his pack. He'd fired hundreds of rounds through the Model 70, and thousands of rounds through other rifles he'd owned, over the years. He'd hunted for food and for sport, and he'd run into bandits more than once, trading shots with desperate, lawless men. But he'd never seen real combat, and his hands refused to hold steady as the reality of what they faced hit home.

He slid his H&W out of its holster and curled his fingers around the reassuring solidity of its walnut grips. The big .44 caliber, seven-shot revolver was single-action. The hammer had to be pulled back for each shot, but the six-and-a-half-inch-barreled pistol was deadly accurate, and it had immense stopping power.

It was also too big and heavy for Shaylar to shoot accurately. She carried a Polshana—a much smaller and lighter .35 caliber weapon, with a four-inch barrel and smaller grip. Unlike the H&W, the Polshana was double-action, and Rilthan had worked long and hard to tune its action for her until it was glass-smooth. It held only six shots to the H&W's seven, but unlike Jathmar, Shaylar had four speedloaders, and he watched her tuck them into the right hand pocket of her jacket.

He swung out the H&W's cylinder and loaded the chamber he normally left empty for the hammer to rest on. Then he slipped it back into its holster and finished arranging his ammunition boxes

around him. At his feet, Shaylar was doing the same thing with
the ammo boxes from her pack. From his slightly elevated vantage
point, Jathmar could see others settling into equally favorable spots
amongst the fallen trees.

Fanthi chan Himidi had abandoned his post, watching for pursuers from the south, now that everyone else had gotten into position.
He settled into a new spot of his own, behind everyone else, facing
north into the forest behind them and scanning restlessly for any
sign of the men trying to circle around to close the trap. Jathmar
spotted chan Hagrahyl at the center of their little group, hunkered
down in an angle where two tree trunks had fallen against one
another as they crashed down.

Braiheri Futhai had crawled as far as possible from the expected
line of fire, hiding in visible terror and doing nothing to prepare for
self-defense. Elevu Gitel had hunkered down between Jathmar and
chan Hagrahyl. The geologist was loading his rifle in grim silence,
and glancing in the other direction, Jathmar found Barris Kasell less
than a yard beyond Rilthan.

Try as he might, he couldn't see the others, which he took as a
good sign. They settled in, uneasy, on edge—waiting in a classic
ambush position to see what their pursuers would do.

*   *   *

Shevan Garlath had never seen a likelier spot for an ambush.

He stared, mesmerized, at the jumble of timber a tornado must
have toppled in some relatively recent storm. The entire clearing was
a twisted mass of jagged, broken wood, tree trunks, and branches
that jutted out like the sharp stakes of a basilisk trap.

And he had to search it.

Had to go out there, into that deadly maze, and *search* it.

There was no question that their quarry had gone into it. The
trail was clear to see—even he could follow it without difficulty—and
the birdcall signals from the Scouts who'd worked their way around
to the other side indicated that they hadn't come back out again.
But the question was *why* they'd stopped here . . . and what they
intended to do next.

And of all the thousands of soldiers spread out through this
multi-universe, godsforsaken transit chain it had to be *him* that
drew the job of finding out. Finding out if the murdering whore-
sons who'd killed Osmuna—that lazy-assed, sleep-on-duty, *worthless*
piece of dragon-bait—planned on killing anybody else today. Garlath
cursed the dead man, wishing desperately that there was a way to
weasel out of this particular duty. If he'd dared, he would have sent

his point men in alone. Would have stayed back here in the trees, where it was safe.

But Hundred fucking Olderhan—the name and rank stuck in his craw like a fishbone—was watching him. Watching, waiting with bated breath for Garlath to screw up. Regs—and tradition—were clear: a commander of fifty went out with his platoon. He had to be right on top of the action, especially in close terrain like this, to coordinate his troopers' movements and respond instantly to any change in the situation.

Garlath cursed the Regs, cursed the officers who'd written them, cursed the "follow-me" junior officer tradition of the Andaran military, cursed the judge advocates who'd established the punishments for failing to follow Regs . . . and, with a passion and a fervor which surprised even him, cursed Sir Jasak Olderhan for ever having been born to make Garlath look so bad in comparison.

The Duke's Golden Brat could do no wrong, he thought viciously. Fine, then. Garlath would just have to do such an outstanding job on this operation that he'd make *Olderhan* look sorry-assed inadequate for a change.

He ground his teeth together, bitterly aware that it would take a miracle to do that, given Olderhan's infernally good luck—not to mention his fucking birthright. But there was nothing he could do about *that*, either, and so he forced himself to stand there and listen to the bastard's voice.

* * *

"Remember," Jasak said, making his voice as calm and matter-of-fact as he could. "We want this situation *contained*. We know they're in there somewhere, and we need to make certain we don't lose any of them. But I want this settled without shooting, if it's at all possible."

He looked at Garlath, trying to will him to comprehend.

"Understand me, Fifty. We're responsible for the lives of our own people, but our *overriding* responsibility is to the Union. To preventing this from getting any further out of hand. You and your men will *not* fire unless and until you are attacked."

Garlath stared at him, face sweaty and eyes wide. Jasak could almost literally feel the protest just barely locked behind the other man's teeth.

"I understand your concern for your men's safety," he said, his voice as soft and reasonable as he could make it even as both of them knew whose safety Garlath was truly concerned about, "and no officer likes giving an order like that. But it's a direct order, and it *will* be obeyed, Fifty Garlath. On the other hand, I'll understand if you feel unable to order your men to obey my instructions under these circumstances. If you do, I will relieve you without prejudice and assume command of your platoon and responsibility for any casualties it may suffer."

He felt Gadrial stiffen where she stood beside Chief Sword Threbuch, but he kept his own gaze on Garlath's, staring deep into the fifty's eyes, almost begging the man to accept his offer. Jasak didn't feel any more eager than the next man to wade out into that tangled, torn mass of timber, but he was completely willing to offer Garlath a way out of the duty which obviously terrified him.

*   *   *

Shevan Garlath managed—somehow—not to glare back at the officious, sanctimonious bastard in front of him. Relieve him "without prejudice"! Oh, yes. Garlath believed *that*, didn't he? If he declined the "honor" of walking out into that maze, his career would be over. Whatever he might say *now*, Olderhan's official report would slam him for "cowardice in the face of the enemy," and his own request for relief would "prove" the charge.

Which was a capital offense, if a court-martial convicted.

Besides, he told himself, searching frantically for something to bolster his own courage, *he knows perfectly well that whoever's actually in command when we finally make contact with these bastards—however it comes out—is going to be made for life. And if he has to relieve me for "cowardice" to take over command, it'll only make him look better!*

"No, Sir," he grated. "It's my platoon, my job. I'll do it."

*   *   *

Jasak swallowed a vicious, silent curse as Garlath spurned the offer. But there was nothing he could do about it. Whatever he might suspect, or even know, about Garlath's terror, he had no overt evidence of cowardice, and Garlath was right. It *was* his platoon, and under both Union military law and the Andaran code of honor, Jasak *had* to leave him in command unless he requested relief or openly violated regulations or the articles of war.

"Very well, Fifty Garlath," he said frostily. "You have your orders. Good luck."

*   *   *

Garlath clenched his jaw so tightly it hurt all the way down his neck as he nodded to Gaythar Harklan. The Second Squad shield nodded back, and started forward, slowly and gingerly, with the squad's arbalestiers deployed in a skirmish line.

Garlath followed behind them, hands wet with sweat as he gripped his loaded arbalest. The squad advanced slowly, painstakingly searching every twisted pile of branches that offered a hiding place, and the fifty felt his heart battering against his rib cage like a hammer.

Whoever these bastards were, wherever they'd come from, they were *not* going to get the drop on Shevan Garlath.

*   *   *

Shaylar watched the advancing men from her hiding place through a screen of barren branches, long since deprived of their leaves.

These men meant trouble. Big trouble. They were dressed in military style uniforms, practical and suited to an active life in rough country. Yet their appearance was so incongruous, so odd, that it took a concentrated effort to focus on them and what they were doing, rather than what they wore and the anachronisms they carried.

Their bizarre, medieval weapons made them look like play actors . . . until you got a good look at their faces. Even at a distance of fifty yards, it was clear the men behind those grim expressions were capable of carrying out any kind of violence to which they might set their hand. Shaylar hadn't grown up around soldiers, but she'd seen a lot of them since joining the survey crews, and the tough air of dangerous competence which surrounded these men left her trembling.

Not even a rabbit could have evaded their meticulous search. In fact, several didn't. Rabbits and chipmunks darted into the open several times, running in panic as men with swords—honest-to-goodness *swords*—poked them into hiding places into which no human being above the age of six months could possibly have shoehorned himself.

Each animal that exploded out of hiding tightened the thumbscrews on Shaylar's ragged nerves. From the reactions of the soldiers, particularly the man behind their advancing line, who seemed to be in charge, the strain was no less acute on their side. On an immature, emotional level Shaylar wanted to be glad these killers were afraid of them, but common sense and a chilling voice at the base of her skull told her how dangerous their fear could be.

Their advance narrowed the gap steadily, bringing them within thirty yards of her hiding place. They continued to search with methodical, terrifying thoroughness. It was only a matter of time before one of those grim-faced men thrust a sharp steel blade through a pile of branches and came sword-point-to-gun-muzzle with Shaylar or one of her companions. She didn't dare move her head even to look for Jathmar or Ghartoun chan Hagrahyl. She scarcely dared to breathe. Surely it *couldn't* be much longer now!

The same thought must have crossed chan Hagrahyl's mind. The nearest soldier was twenty yards out, and chan Hagrahyl stood up.

Without his rifle. Without even a handgun. He simply *stood up*, in the most stunning display of pure, cold courage Shaylar Nargra-Kolmayr had ever seen in her life.

"If you don't mind, that's far enough," he said in a voice that sounded like someone talking to his grandmother, not to a pack of armed strangers who'd already murdered a friend of his.

He held his hands out in the open, empty, nonthreatening, trying to show them he was no danger. The men in the clearing whirled at the sound of his voice, then froze where they stood, taking stock through wide eyes. They stared from chan Hagrahyl's empty hands to his tense but pleasant smile, and two or three of them turned uncertainly toward the trees behind them, rather than towards the man Shaylar had *thought* was in charge.

Then she realized that *that* man wasn't frozen in surprise.

*   *   *

The sound of a voice shouting alien gibberish sent terror scalding through Garlath even as his mind shrieked the word: *Enemy!* The jabbering stranger thrust himself violently out of hiding, ready to strike with some terrifying murder weapon, and the sorry-assed men of Second Squad weren't even *moving*.

Terror fluttered at the back of Garlath's throat, like a trapped basilisk, yet even as it strangled him, a sudden wild exultation swept through him, as well.

I've got him! He's mine! *Not Jasak Olderhan's, not anyone else's, but mine!*

Visions of glory, of promotions and the adoration of all of Arcana roared through him like dragonfire, spreading to his fingertips and toes, and his arm came up.

*   *   *

Jasak saw Garlath's arbalest twitch as the stranger stood up, calling out in a friendly voice. He saw the weapon start to swing up, start to track around towards the voice.

"Hold fire!" he shouted. "*Hold fire, Fifty Garlath!* Damn it, I said hold—"

Thwack!

*   *   *

The crossbow quarrel hit chan Hagrahyl directly in the throat.

Shaylar screamed under Jathmar's feet, echoing his own shock. Blood drenched the pile of wood, spraying hot and terrible over chan Hagrahyl's hands as he clawed at the shaft, choking on blood and steel. And then he was falling backwards, against the pile of wood.

Jathmar snarled and threw his rifle to his shoulder, but Barris Kasell beat him to the first shot. The ex-soldier's rifle cracked like doomsday, and the bastard with the crossbow staggered. Jathmar's shot slammed into him a sliver of a second later, and then the entire survey crew opened up.

*   *   *

Sir Jasak Olderhan stared in horror. Thunder shook the world. Crack after sharp, ear-splitting crack tore the air, and he couldn't even see the *weapons*, let alone the men using them. Puffs of smoke jetted from the toppled timber here and there, and blood fountained from his commander of fifty. The projectiles smashing into Garlath exploded out of his back, ripping it open, turning him into so much torn and shredded meat.

He went down, and before Jasak could react to the stunning, horrifying response, Shield Harklan's skirmish line returned fire. They brought their arbalests up, shooting at the puffs of smoke which were the only targets they could see, and then the entire clearing erupted.

CHAPTER
EIGHT

DARCEL KINLAFIA WAS worried.

The initial message from Shaylar—terse, shaken—had been too wild to believe, too threatening to grasp with anything but cold horror, and yet too vividly accurate to doubt. She'd sent him not only the message from chan Hagrahyl, but also the images of herself splashing down into the creek, watching Falsan die under her hands. Darcel had felt everything *she'd* felt, and he wanted to do murder. He wanted his hands around the throat of whoever had killed Falsan and put Shaylar through something so horrifying.

Worst of all, there was absolutely nothing Darcel could do to help. Even if Company-Captain Halifu emptied the entire half-built fort and set out *now*, Shaylar and Jathmar, Barris and Ghartoun—all of the people who'd become his family over the past several years were simply too far away.

And so he paced his solitary camp, not wanting even the company of Halifu's soldiers, since anyone's presence would rub him raw, like sand in a open wound.

My fault, he thought bitterly, even though he knew—in his saner moments—that it was a lie. He wasn't responsible for whatever was happening out there, but he was the one who'd sent them to meet it, because Darcel Kinlafia wasn't just a Voice; he was also a Portal Hound.

That wasn't the technical name for his secondary Talent, but it was the one everyone associated with the Portal Authority used. No one had yet found a way to actually detect and pinpoint the locations of portals, but a Hound had a special affinity to whatever disturbance in the fabric of creation brought them into existence. No Hound could reliably quantify what he sensed, he couldn't pluck distances and classifications out of thin air, and yet Darcel simply "knew" the compass bearing to the nearest portal. He had absolutely no way of knowing how far away it might be, but he knew which way to go to find the closest one.

Well, that wasn't entirely correct. A larger portal might *appear* to be closer than a smaller one which was actually much nearer to a Hound's physical location. But the Hounds, who were even rarer than Mappers of Jathmar's strength, were utterly invaluable to any exploration team.

It was Darcel who'd found the immense portal which had first admitted them to this universe. It was Darcel who'd realized that they'd stumbled upon yet another lobe of the cluster which had brought them here.

And it was Darcel Kinlafia who'd sent his dearest friends towards the nearest/strongest portal he'd been able to "scent" . . . and directly into the horror which had been awaiting Falsan.

Stop that! he snapped at himself. *Ghartoun's one of the most experienced people in the game. He knows how to handle himself and a crew. They'll be all right. Surely they'll be all right.*

Shalana's mercy, please *let them be all right.*

He'd already relayed Shaylar's message. Even now, it was rushing back along the transit chain, Voice to Voice, portal to portal, universe to universe, through dozens—hundreds—of telepathic Voices, all passing along the frantic message.

Warn the homeworld!

The Portal Authority wasn't designed to meet this kind of emergency. Oh, the notion had been bandied about, but not seriously. Not in the eighty years mankind had been exploring through the portals. There were—thank all the gods—forts at every portal, and larger military bases at central nodes, even this far out. But that was entirely to police the homeworld's own portal traffic and to provide security for settlers and survey crews threatened by bandits. The possibility of something like this had been only a *theoretical* one, and one which had become increasingly less likely seeming as exploration spread further and further outward with absolutely no sign of any other human civilization.

When Shaylar's warning had come in, he'd gone back through the portal to relay, then found Company-Captain Halifu and delivered the disturbing message to him in person. Grafin Halifu had dispatched Platoon-Captain Hulmok Arthag and half his cavalry platoon—the only one assigned to him—to find the civilian crew and escort them safely back, if they could only make rendezvous with one another in time.

Darcel had asked—almost begged—for permission to accompany that platoon, but Halifu had denied it. And rightfully so, Darcel admitted, however grudgingly. He was the only Voice Halifu had. If anything happened to him, Halifu would have no one to relay his own reports farther up the chain.

And so, Darcel could only stay here, pacing, worrying, wondering if Arthag and his men would reach Shaylar and the rest of his family in time. But that, he knew, was up to the unknown adversary, to the faceless person or persons who'd killed poor Falsan. Blood had already been shed, but surely it wouldn't come to open warfare? Only madmen would want to provoke that kind of—

We're under attack!

The scream was a knife, tearing into his brain.

Then the connection deepened, and the images thundered like a runaway freight train into his shocked senses. He staggered, actually went to his knees. Men in uniforms were shooting at him—shooting with *crossbows*. A quarrel thudded into thick wood two feet from his head. Gunfire cracked everywhere. Men screamed. A hail of bullets mowed down the uniformed soldiers standing out in the open. Only one of them survived long enough to drop and disappear in the tangled timber about him, and Darcel gasped as his gaze swung to another pile of shattered trees.

Ghartoun!

Dead, sprawled obscenely across a tangle of broken branches. Sightless eyes widened, shocked, face twisted in pain and terror.

"Reload!" Barris Kasell was shouting from somewhere just to his right. "There's more of them back in the trees, trying to work around! Rilthan, watch our flank!"

"Shaylar." It was Jathmar, his voice choked with fright. "Shaylar—are you all right?"

"Yes. Yes, I'm—*Here they come!*"

Three men appeared, carrying . . . something. A strange object, perhaps four feet long and two or three inches in diameter, made out of what looked like glass. No, not glass. Rock crystal? It didn't seem to be either, but it certainly wasn't metal, and—

Crossbow fire screamed out of the woodline to their right. Somebody shrieked in agony behind him. Darcel—or Shaylar, if there was a difference—jerked around and saw Braiheri Futhai writhing on the ground. A steel shaft protruding from his chest, high and to the right. Blood pooling, foaming on his lips, and—

Flame erupted from nowhere at all.

A huge, incandescent fireball ripped into the toppled trees. Smoke blinded him. Someone else was screaming.

"Shoot the gunners!"

It was Barris, shouting through the smoke and confusion, and Darcel's eyes whipped back to the men with the not-crystal tube. It was mounted on a tripod, now, pointed in their direction, like some sort of weird fieldgun.

"*Shoot the gunners!*" Barris bellowed again.

Darcel felt his hands move as Shaylar snatched up the rifle. It shook wildly.

Steady! he told the portion of his mind that was Shaylar. *Better... Yes, much better... Brace it... That's right. Sight picture—front sight—center it—NOW!*

The rifle kicked, the bullet cracked, and one of the enemy gunners jerked, screamed, and went to one knee.

Again!

Others were shooting, too, picking off the gunners steadily.

"They're coming in from the right!" Elevu Gitel shouted, and Jathmar spat curses above Darcel's head and twisted around, shooting at the fresh crossbowmen coming in along their vulnerable flank. Two men went down... three...

"How many of them *are* there?" the Mapper gasped. A quarrel thwacked wood two inches from his cheek, buried in the tree trunk he crouched behind. "Bastards!"

He fired at them again, cursed, and ducked down to reload, shoving the cartridges into the loading gate while all the universe roared and screamed madly about him.

Another fireball erupted from somewhere. Dried leaves and twigs burst into flame. Someone was screaming—high and mindless, on and on.

"Where's it *coming* from?" Jathmar demanded hoarsely.

There were two of the not-artillery things out there now, and the original one had acquired a new crew. The other was fifty yards from the first one, identical to it. And pointed almost dead at Darcel. It started to *glow*, like eldritch fire, or the northern lights at midwinter, and—

Flame was everywhere.

Darcel flung himself to the ground. Heat seared its way past, just above his back. He didn't dare breathe. He squeezed both eyes shut. Heard ghastly howls that belonged to human beings in mortal agony...

Blessed cool air rushed in. He gulped down, coughed on smoke and the acrid stench of burnt wood and what smelled sickeningly like roasting meat. The tree trunk above him was smoking, bark blasted off in places.

"*What the fuck* was *that?*" It was Jathmar's voice. Thick, terrified.

"*DOWN!*" Shaylar screamed.

Another fireball ripped across them. Someone was still shooting. Cursing monotonously and shooting, mindless with terrible rage. Darcel grabbed for the rifle he'd dropped, shouted at Shaylar's stunned mind.

They're coming in a mass! Shoot!

Infantry erupted across the smoldering wreckage of the clearing. Fifteen, maybe twenty of them. Shaylar snatched the rifle to her shoulder, pulled the trigger. Worked the lever, took another shot . . . worked the lever . . . took another shot.

They fired the rifle dry, and the bastards were still coming. No time to reload. Darcel went for Shaylar's Polshana, but it was Shaylar who acquired the first target. She brought the gun up two-handed, centered a charging soldier, squeezed the double-action trigger. The man staggered, clutched at his chest, and then his face exploded as their second hollow-nosed slug hit him squarely in the forehead and she shot him down like carrion.

Rilthan wreaked havoc on the center of the charging line. Each time his rifle cracked, a soldier screamed and sprawled in the debris, leaving a widening gap in the middle of their line. Shaylar tracked to the side, acquiring a target at the right hand end of the charge and firing, again and again, as she worked her way inward, and Darcel knew their revolver was almost empty.

The charge wavered. Halted. Broke apart. Shaken soldiers ran back into the cover of the trees, and someone was shouting orders from back there. More men were moving into position. Gods—how many of them *were* there?

Reload! Darcel shrieked at Shaylar through their connected minds. *Reload!*

Shaylar swung out the Polshana's cylinder, tipped it up, hit the ejection rod. Empty cases fell glittering to the leaves, and her left hand steadied the cylinder as her right snatched the speedloader from her pocket. The fresh rounds slid into the cylinder, perfectly aligned despite her choking terror, and she twisted the speedloader's release knob and dropped it, even as her left hand snapped the cylinder back into place. Then she reholstered the revolver and reached for the ammunition box ready at her elbow. Reloaded the rifle with hands which had steadied down to a mind-numbed, rote-smooth motion. Cartridge in, press it down, next cartridge in, press it down—

Darcel caught motion from the corner of his eye. He slewed around, and Shaylar brought the rifle with them, rising to a half-crouch and firing as a *third* artillery crew laid in their fire mission.

"Jathmar! *Down!*"

Two blasts erupted from the mouth of hell.

A fireball ripped through the fallen trees again—and writhing through the incandescent flames came a jagged streak of lightning. It slammed into Barris Kasell, who was still shouting orders. For one horrifying second, he twisted in midair, lit by blue actinic fire that burst from his very skin.

Thunder struck. Fire crackled everywhere. The entire world was ablaze. Then the cool air was back again, and they gasped, shuddering, fighting for breath.

Shaylar passed her rifle to Jathmar to give him a backup weapon and fumbled for her pack. She yanked it open and started dragging out her maps, her notebooks—the records of every universe they'd mapped, with the locations of every portal in the cluster they'd been exploring, and—far worse—every portal between here and Sharona itself.

She dragged them out, snatched a branch from a blazing pile of deadwood, touched flame to each and every map in her possession. Burned them to ash. Ripped out notebook pages and fed them to the flames, as well. Rifles cracked, men screamed horribly, and still she consigned pages to the flames, destroying her work in a desperate bid to keep the savage killers from overrunning every portal they could reach. And even as she burned them, Darcel heard fewer and fewer rifles still firing, knew his friends—his family—were dying around her under the fury of those impossible, horrifying balls of flame and bolts of lightning.

She set the final page aflame, then tossed the leather binder and map case themselves into the burning deadwood. Only a handful of rifles were still spitting defiance, and she snatched out her Polshana again, turned back towards her firing position.

And then it happened.

Jathmar had realized what she was doing, and how important it was. He'd stood over her, firing steadily, protecting her while she worked. But as she tossed the final load into the flames, he jumped down to pull her back to a safer spot . . . just as another fireball struck. It caught his back, flung him against a fallen, crosswise tree branch. His belly and chest struck hard, and he doubled up around the wood, pinned for horrible seconds with flames scorching his back.

His clothes ignited. Fire crisped hair and skin.

"JATHMAR!"

This scream tore her throat. Shaylar and Darcel were scrambling forward, trying to reach Jathmar as he slid off a branch and fell to the ground. Lightning branched and slammed inches away. The concussion of thunder hurled them sideways. Their head struck something incredibly hard with bone-crushing force—

Darcel exploded back into his own body.

The air was clear. No smoke. No screams. No dying men. The portal, silent as sunlight, stood thirty yards to his left as he lay sprawled across the ground. Psychic shock held him immobile for long, soul-shaking moments. He heard distant voices shouting and saw someone running toward him from the far side of the portal, where a slow but steady rain was falling. Darcel shoved himself into a sitting position, groped for a rifle that wasn't there. Then he realized who it was running toward him. Grafin Halifu, himself. Commander of the new fort that was only three hundred yards from where Darcel lay sprawled, stunned, in the sunlight.

"What's wrong?" Halifu demanded, his own rifle in his hand as he closed the last ten yards. "You started shouting something about soldiers in the woodline!"

Darcel lifted unsteady hands, scrubbed his face, tried to reorient himself.

"Attack," he managed to say in a wheezing groan. "Our crew's under attack. Infantry, artillery fire—"

"*What?*" Halifu's face washed white with shock.

"I was linked with Shaylar." Darcel shut his eyes. "Oh, gods— *Shaylar!*"

He tried to contact her, tried frantically to get through. But he found only deathly cold silence.

"She's not—" Halifu's horror-choked voice broke off, unwilling—or unable—to complete the question.

"I don't know." Darcel was shaking, unable to control the runaway tremors. "We were hit by an artillery blast of some kind. Thrown by the concussion. Hit our head on something."

He wrapped his arms about himself, gulped down air.

"Ghartoun's dead. So are Barris Kasell and Braiheri Futhai. Elevu Gitel. And if Jathmar's still alive—oh, gods, the burns were horrible—"

He realized he was rocking back and forth only when someone else's arm around his shoulders steadied him and Halifu pressed something metallic against his chattering teeth.

"Drink!"

Darcel gulped, choked, wheezed as the whiskey went down. His eyes smarted . . . but his whirling senses steadied.

"Thanks," he whispered as the world stopped looping around him.

More people were arriving from the fort, armed for battle and staring a little wildly at the trees around Darcel's camp. Company-Captain Halifu got a second deep gulp of whiskey into him, then waited until the worst of the shakes had eased up.

"Can you give me a report now?" he asked quietly.

Darcel couldn't look into the officer's worried eyes. He knew if he did, he wouldn't be able to speak at all. So he stared at the ground instead and started to talk.

He rambled, his voice unsteady and hoarse, trying to convey the horror, the terrifyingly alien attack, the inexplicable weapons that had sent death crashing across the terrified, outnumbered survey crew. Most of them were *civilians*, totally unprepared to deal with something as brutal as an all-out attack by trained troops.

Darcel realized he'd finished talking when Company-Captain Halifu ripped out a hideous oath. He clenched his jaws so tightly his teeth creaked, still sitting on the ground.

"Stinking *bastards*!" Halifu snarled. "I may be supposed to have a company here, but all I've got is two understrength platoons, less than a hundred and fifty men, and Platoon-Captain Arthag's cavalry detachment. And *he's* riding straight into a trap with half of his men right fucking now! I can't possibly meet an attack by weapons like that—not without reinforcements—and we're over five thousand miles from the nearest railhead! The column from Fort Salby's due any day, but how close it is yet is anyone's guess."

The fort's commander made himself stop, draw a deep breath. He stepped back from his rage and fear and shook his head.

"Armsman chan Therson!"

"Sir!"

Chief-Armsman Dunyar chan Therson, Bronze Company's senior noncom, snapped to attention.

"Get Bantha. Tell him we need to get a dispatch to Petty-Captain Arthag *at once*. He's to stop where he is and hold position."

"Yes, Sir!" Therson said.

"Then find Petty-Captain chan Shermayr. His infantry's going to have to assume full responsibility for our security here; I want the rest of Arthag's men in the saddle and moving up to reinforce him inside the next five minutes. See to it that Arthag knows they're coming and that he's not to move another yard until the rest of the rescue party catches up with him."

"*Rescue party?*" Darcel choked out. "What's the fucking point?"

Company-Captain Halifu went white again.

"Surely there must be *some* survivors," he said hoarsely.

Darcel never knew what showed on his face, but suddenly Halifu was crouched in front of him, gripping his shoulders with bruising force.

"Don't give up yet," the Uromathian said in a voice full of gravel and steel grit. "*I'm* sure as hell not giving up, not until we've seen *proof*. If I were the commander of that military force, I'd *want* survivors, someone I could question—"

Darcel flinched, and Halifu bit his lip.

"I'm sorry, Darcel. I know they're friends, almost family."

"Shaylar," Darcel groaned, closing his eyes in despair. He was half in love with her himself. He'd treated her like a kid sister, mostly to convince his heart it didn't actually feel what it stubbornly insisted it felt. Oh, yes, he'd loved Shaylar, just as he'd loved Jathmar for treating her like a queen, as well as a beloved spouse and professional partner.

Shaylar, he whispered into the dead silence of his broken telepathic link. *Wake up, please.* Please, *Shay!*

But her voice remained lost in a black nothingness at the center of his soul, and Darcel slowly lifted his head. He came to his feet, scrubbed at wet eyes while the others scuffed tufts of grass with their boots and dug divots out of the ground rather than embarrass him by noticing the tears.

"Company-Captain Halifu," he said in a voice of steel-sharp hatred. "I believe you said something about needing reinforcements?"

Halifu met his gaze levelly—met and held it. Then he nodded.

"Yes, I did. If you'd be so kind as to transmit a message for me, requesting them, we'll get started on that rescue mission."

"Compose your message, Sir," Darcel said very, very softly. "I'll be waiting when you're ready to send it."

He turned away then, without another word, and started breaking out the ammunition boxes in his gear.

CHAPTER
NINE

"CEASE FIRE! *CEASE fire!*"

Jasak plowed into the nearest infantry-dragon's crew. He caught the closer assistant gunner by the collar and heaved him bodily away from the weapon. The gunner didn't even seem to notice . . . until Jasak kicked him solidly in the chest.

"*Cease* fire, *godsdamn you!*"

The gunner toppled over with an absolutely astonished expression. For just an instant, he didn't quite seem to understand what happened. Then his expression changed from confusion to horrified understanding, and he shook himself visibly.

Two of First Platoon's four dragons were still firing, blasting round after round into the tangle of fallen timber. There hadn't been a single return shot in well over a minute, but the gunners didn't even seem to realize it. They were submerged in a battle frenzy, too enraged by the slaughter of their fellow troopers—and too terrified by the enemy's devastating weapons—to think about things like that.

"Graholis seize you, *cease fire!*" Jasak bellowed, charging into a second dragon's crew while Chief Sword Threbuch waded into the third.

The fourth dragon hadn't fired in some time; its entire crew, and six other troopers who'd taken their places, were sprawled around it, dead or wounded.

Threbuch tossed the last operable dragon's gunner into a tangle of blackberry bushes at the clearing's edge just as a final lightning bolt sizzled from the focus point and slammed into a fallen tree trunk. Bark flew, smoke billowed up with the concussive sound of thunder, and then the discharge fizzled out.

Silence, alien and strange, roared in Jasak's ears.

He stood panting for breath, his pulse kicking at the insides of his eardrums like a frantic drumbeat. He made himself stand there, fighting his shakes under control, then dragged his sleeve across his face to clear his eyes of sweat and grime. Only then did he make himself look, make himself count the bodies.

His men lay sprawled like gutted marionettes across ground that was splashed with far too much blood. There were bodies everywhere, too many of them motionless, not even moaning, and his stomach clenched in the agony only a commanding officer could know.

Graholis' balls. Half his entire platoon was down out there. *Half!*

"You're bleeding, Sir."

The quiet, steady voice punched through his numb horror. Shocked, he slewed around to find his chief sword tearing open a medical kit.

"What?"

"You're bleeding, Sir. Let's have a look."

"Fuck that!" Jasak snapped. "It can't be more than a scratch. We've got to search for the wounded—*all* the wounded. Theirs as well as ours."

"So order a search. But you're still bleeding, and I'm still going to do something about that."

"I'm not—"

"Do I have to knock you down and *sit* on you, Hundred?" Otwal Threbuch snarled so harshly Jasak stared at him in total shock.

"You're our only surviving officer, Sir," Threbuch's voice was like harsh iron, fresh from the furnace, "and you will *damned* well hold still until I find out why there's blood dripping off your scalp and pouring down your side!"

Jasak closed his mouth. He hadn't realized he was bleeding quite that badly, and he made himself sit quietly while the chief sword swabbed at the scalp cut he hadn't even felt. Worse was the furrow that *something* had plowed through the flesh along the edge of his ribs. Whatever it was, it had barely grazed him, but it had left a long, stinging wound in his side, ripped his uniform savagely, and left an impressive bloodstain that had poured down over his side. Another few inches inward, and it would have gone straight through a lung, or even his heart.

Jasak gritted his teeth, directing his surviving noncoms—there weren't many—to search for the wounded while Threbuch applied a field dressing. The instant the chief sword finished, Jasak strode out into the clearing, checking on his own wounded as he headed for his real objective: the enemy.

Some of his men had already reached them.

"We've got a survivor, Sir!" Evarl Harnak called out. "He's in bad shape."

Jasak hurried over to Garlath's platoon sword wondering what miracle had brought the sword through alive, since Harnak had led the charge the other side's weapons had torn apart. It was hard to believe that *any* of those troopers could have survived, Jasak thought bitterly. And that, too, was his fault—he'd been the one who'd thought the dragons had suppressed the enemy's fire.

He climbed through a tangle of fallen tree limbs and hunkered down beside Harnak. The sword was kneeling beside a man whose entire left side was badly burned. He'd taken a crossbow bolt through the belly, too, doing untold and probably lethal damage, even without the burns and the inevitable severe shock.

He was breathing, but just barely. It was a genuine mercy that he was unconscious, and Jasak was torn by conflicting emotions, conflicting duties and priorities. This whole disaster was *his* fault, which meant this man's brutal injuries were his fault. He reached for the wounded man's unburnt wrist and found the pulse. It was faint, thready, failing fast. Helpless to do anything else, he watched the stranger die.

"More survivors, Sir!" another shout rang across the smoke-filled clearing. "Oh, gods! One of them's a *woman!*"

Jasak ran, sickness twisting in his gut. He cursed the debris in his way, fighting to find a path through it, then flinging himself down, crawling under a fallen tree trunk to reach them. There were four survivors, fairly close together. Three had been burned badly; the fourth was scorched, but the infantry-dragon's breath had barely brushed her, thank Graholis.

She was unconscious. One slim hand was still wrapped around a weapon that was the most alien thing Jasak had ever seen. Drying blood caked the hair on the right side of her head, and a ghastly bruise was already swelling along that side of her face. A nasty lump ran from her temple to the back of her head.

"She must've been thrown against the tree trunk," he said, turning his head, eyes narrowed.

Yes, there was hair and blood caught in the rough bark, and it took all of Sir Jasak Olderhan's discipline not to slam his bare fist into the bark beside them. His only medic was dead—had been shot down, trying to reach wounded dragon gunners—and at least three of these people were so badly hurt they probably wouldn't have survived even with a medic.

"I need Magister Kelbryan," he barked over his shoulder, turning back to the savagely wounded survivors. "*Now*, damn it!"

Somebody ran, shouting for Gadrial, and Jasak bent over the unknown woman. Her pulse was slow under his fingers, but it was steady, strong, thank the gods. She was tiny, even smaller than Gadrial, with a beautiful, delicate face. She looked like a fragile glass doll lying crumpled in the ruins, and Jasak's heart twisted as he raged at Garlath and even at this woman's companions for coming here, for killing Osmuna and starting this whole disaster. And worst of all, for bringing this lovely girl into the middle of the killing his men—and hers—had unleashed in this clearing.

He'd kept Gadrial back at the very edge of their own formation, flat in a shallow ravine where she—and the men he'd assigned specifically to guard her—were out of the line of fire. Why the *hell* hadn't these men done the same?

Because, the stubborn back of his mind whispered in self-loathing and disgust, *you left them no choice, circling around them to cut off their escape* . . .

Someone came crashing toward him through the underbrush, and he lifted his gaze to see Gadrial running recklessly through the tangled wood, past dead soldiers and smoking rubble.

"Where?" she gasped, and Jasak reached out and lifted her across the five-foot fallen trunk as if she'd been a child. He set her down beside the wounded, and her breath choked on a sound of horror.

All three of the male survivors were burned. Two had been caught facing the fireball when the dragon's breath detonated amongst them, and their crisped skin and the stench of their burnt flesh twisted Jasak's stomach all over again. The third man had been facing away, or at least partially away, leaving him burned across the back. His shirt was a tattered wreck of blackened cloth. He'd been slammed into a jutting limb and fallen sideways, landing on one shoulder before sprawling across the ground, and broken ribs were visible through the tattered shirt.

"Rahil," Gadrial whispered. Jasak looked at her, saw her eyes, and flinched inwardly.

"Can you save them?" he asked, his voice hoarse. "Can you save *any* of them?"

She swallowed hard and nerved herself to test the pulse of the nearest burn victim. He was semi-conscious, and a hideous, gurgling scream ripped loose as his arm shifted. Gadrial whimpered, but she didn't let go.

"Rahil's mercy," she breathed, then forced herself to inhale deeply. "The others?"

Jasak led her to them. She tested their pulses in turn, her eyes closed, whispering under her breath. Power stirred about her, gripping hard enough to twist Jasak with a sharper nausea.

"It's bad—Heavenly Lady, it's bad. I can't save them all. I'm sorry. I might—I can probably keep one of them alive. Maybe..."

She stood, staring down at them, and Jasak felt her inner, helpless horror as she realized the hideous choice which lay before her. He started to open his mouth, to *tell* her which to try to save, to take the burden of that choice from her. It was both his responsibility and all he could offer her, but before he could speak, her shoulders twitched suddenly.

"Look!" She pointed at the woman's wrist, and Jasak frowned! The tiny, unconscious stranger wore a bracelet—a cuff of flexible metal that looked like woven gold. He'd already noticed that, but Gadrial was pointing at one of the wounded men, as well. He wore a matching cuff.

"That one," the magister said. "I'll—"

Her voice broke as she turned away from the others, the two who would die. The two she must *let* die.

She knelt beside the man with the wrist cuff. He was broken, as well as burned. The savagery of his wounds bled back through her hands, carried by her minor healing Gift, and she moaned involuntarily in the face of so much pain, so much damage...

She closed her eyes, rested her hands carefully on his chest, and summoned the power of her Gift. Whispered words poured from her lips, helping her shape and direct the energy she plucked from the air about her. That energy was everywhere, a vast, unseen, seething sea that rolled and thundered like a storm-swept tide. It poured out of the emptiness between mortal thoughts and the power of God and scorched down her arms, out through her hands into the injured man. It was enormous, that sea of energy, an unimaginable, infinite boil of power flying loose and wild for anyone with the Gift strong enough to touch and take it.

But Gadrial's healing Gift was only a minor arcana. She could take only a little, only a sliver of the power someone with a major healing Gift could have taken, and even that small an amount had a price.

"He's...stabilized..." she managed to whisper, and the smoke-filled clearing looped and whirled around her.

Someone caught her shoulders, steadied her, and she leaned against a shoulder that took her weight effortlessly.

She needed that support—badly—as voices swam in and out of focus. The universe seemed to dip and swerve, curtsying like a ship in a heavy sea, and the start of a brutal headache throbbed somewhere behind her eyes.

Gift shock, her trained mind told her through the chaos. The strain of someone pushing a Gift far beyond its safe limits. It had been a long time since she'd felt it, and she wandered through seconds and minutes which stretched and contracted weirdly as she tried to find her way through the chaos of the backlash.

It took what seemed a very long time, but then her senses finally cleared, and she realized she was sitting propped against Sir Jasak Olderhan himself. His arm was about her, holding her there, while he issued a steady stream of orders.

"—and when that's done, Chief Sword, I want you to take one man and confirm that class eight portal. I want to finish that, at least, whatever else we do. I hate to give you up, but I want my best man in charge out there. Just be *damned* careful. We didn't— I didn't—mean to massacre these people, and I don't want *anyone* shooting at anyone else. Is that clear?"

"Very clear, Sir."

"Good. Just tiptoe in and tiptoe out, do whatever it takes to avoid further contact. Any questions?"

"No, Sir."

"Move out, then. The sooner you go, the likelier you are to get there and back before anyone realizes these people aren't coming home."

Jasak's voice went bleak and grim on the final few words. He could only hope the other side hadn't sent a runner ahead with a message. If they had . . .

"Keep your eyes open, Chief Sword, but don't dawdle. If they've dispatched a runner, I want him—alive and unharmed."

"Yes, Sir."

Threbuch saluted and turned away. Jasak watched him go, then noticed that Gadrial was watching him.

"Feeling better?" he asked quietly, moving the arm which had held her upright, and she nodded and sat up.

"Yes. Thanks." Her voice was hoarse, but it didn't quiver. "What we do now?"

Jasak glanced at the still-unconscious woman and the man Gadrial had pulled back from the brink.

"We have to get them back to the swamp portal before we can airlift them out. We can't get a dragon here in time. The nearest is at the coast, seven hundred miles from our entry portal. First it'd have to get there, then fly cross-country to meet us, and once it touched down out here—" he pointed at the clearing "—it wouldn't be able to take off again. Not enough wing room to get airborne fast enough to clear the trees. A battle dragon might be different—they're smaller, faster. They can dive, strike, and lift off again in a much smaller space. But transport dragons need a lot of wing room."

He sounded so calm, so controlled, Gadrial thought. Except for the fact that that calm controlled voice of his was telling her things he knew perfectly well she already knew.

"What about clearing a landing zone?" she asked. "Could you burn down some of the trees with the infantry-dragons?"

Jasak shook his head and gestured at the scorched trunks the enemy had found shelter among. They were smoldering, badly scorched, but mostly intact.

"Look for yourself. A dragon is designed to burn people," he said bitterly, "not to knock down trees. We do have some incendiary charges that could bring down even a tree that size," he nodded towards a towering giant, six feet thick at the base, "but not enough to clear a landing field long enough for a dragon to take off again. We'd need ten times as many as we've got to do that.

"We're Scouts, Magister Kelbryan, not heavy-combat engineers. No. The only hope is to get the wounded back to the swamp portal, or at least to someplace with enough open space for a transport dragon to take off, as well as land." Jasak glanced at the man Gadrial had saved. "*Can* he be moved? Without jeopardizing his life?"

"I don't know." She ran a weary hand through her hair while she struggled to focus her thoughts. "Probably. I'll know more when I touch him again. He shouldn't be moved right away, though. We'll have to get them out of this, I know." She motioned at the smoldering wreckage surrounding them. "But not far—not yet. Even the little I've done so far will have exhausted him."

Jasak nodded somberly. He'd seen what saving the man had done to Gadrial, and the healing Gift drew deeply upon the reserves of the injured person, as well.

"We can do that," he said. "And he'll have at least a little while to stabilize before we can pull out. We have a few things to do that will take some time."

He looked out across the open ground where so many of his men—good men, among the best in the Andaran Scouts—had died because of one man's colossal stupidity. And because of another man's even greater stupidity in not relieving a dangerous, incompetent fool of command, whatever regulations and the articles of war said.

Gadrial turned her head, following his gaze, and her eyes were dark.

"What will you do with them?" she asked softly.

"The same thing the Chief Sword did for Osmuna." Jasak had to clamp his jaw tighter for a moment.

"Field rites," he said then, and looked down at her. She looked back, her expression puzzled, and his lips tightened. "I take it you've never seen them?" he said almost harshly.

Gadrial shook her head. The only thing she knew about "field rites" was that military commanders were sometimes forced by necessity to abandon their dead. Procedures had been developed for just that sort of emergency, but that was all she knew about it. She thought he might explain, but he didn't. Instead, he turned to Platoon Sword Harnak, his senior noncom now that he'd sent Otwal Threbuch away, and indicated the other two wounded men with a gentle, curiously vulnerable wave of his hand.

"Have someone stay with these men until . . . until they're not needed, Sword. No man should die alone."

Harnak nodded grimly, and Jasak inhaled and nodded at the girl and the man Gadrial had saved.

"I want *these* two moved out of this hellish pile of timber. But for pity's own sake, take care with him. He's *got* to survive, Harnak."

Gadrial realized there was more to Jasak's almost desperate insistence than any mere intelligence value living prisoners might represent. Jasak Olderhan was a soldier, but no murderer, Gadrial realized, and even she recognized that these people hadn't stood a chance once his support weapons opened fire on them. Now she felt his granite determination to snatch at least some of them back from the jaws of death . . . whatever it took.

"Yes, Sir." Harnak's acknowledging salute, like his voice, was subdued. Exhausted.

Gadrial knew how the sword felt. She watched Jasak smooth a tendril of long, dark hair away from the unconscious woman's face. His fingertips were so gentle, so tender, Gadrial felt tears prickle at the corners of her eyes.

"I'm sorry," she thought she heard him whisper, but it might have been only the wind. Then he pulled himself together and got busy organizing his surviving troopers for the farewell they would soon bid to far too many brave men.

And to one arrant coward, a small voice whispered deep inside Gadrial Kelbryan. She looked at the wounded, the dying, the dead, and knew it would be hard not to spit on Garlath's grave.

*   *   *

Shaylar didn't want to wake up. She wanted to be dead. For long moments, she couldn't remember why—she was just certain that whatever ghastly thing waited for her was too terrible to bear living through. She whimpered, wanting her mother. Wanting someone who could hold her close and whisper that everything was all right. That everything would be as it should, and not as it was, torn with screams and flame, the sight of her beloved—

She jerked back from the memory, but not in time. Pain—hot and terrible—gripped her heart with savage, shredding claws.

Jathmar!

She tried to touch him through the bond, but there was something wrong, dreadfully wrong, inside her head. Pain throbbed relentlessly, leaving her dizzy and sick. And, far worse, Voiceless. She couldn't Hear Jathmar, and even though she tried, she couldn't Hear Darcel, either. There was nothing but pain. Nothing else in the universe...

Someone touched her.

She flinched violently, whimpering again as fresh pain exploded through her. But the touch returned, gentle, soothing her, drawing her back from the crumbling edge of sanity. Reluctantly, she opened her eyes and blinked in the dappled light streaming down through golden treetops.

A woman knelt beside her. Not a uniformed soldier—a woman, dressed much the way Shaylar was, in sturdy and practical clothes. She was lovely, in the delicate, porcelain way of Uromathian women, but Shaylar knew this woman didn't come from Uromathia. Nor from anywhere else Sharonians had ever set foot.

The stranger's dark eyes were shadowed with grief and the lingering shock of having witnessed something too horrible to face. There was strength in those eyes, the strength of gentle compassion and something else Shaylar couldn't quite define.

The not-Uromathian woman moved slowly and carefully, as if she understood without words that a rapid movement would send Shaylar skittering in terror. She held up a canteen—despite its unfamiliar shape, it couldn't be anything else—and poured carefully into a small metal cup. A hand eased under Shaylar's head, lifted a little—

—and pain exploded through her. A cry choked loose, and her hands dug into the ground in spastic response. But she felt the other woman touch the side of her head. She murmured something, so softly Shaylar wasn't even sure she'd heard words at all, and then the pain in her head eased a little. Shaylar opened her eyes and stared, wondering what had just happened. She knew from experience what the touch of a telempathic Healer felt like, and this was *nothing* like that.

Fear stirred uneasily once more, despite the dampening down of the pain and nausea. Whoever—and whatever—she was, the woman held the cup to Shaylar's lips, and Shaylar drank deeply. The water felt glorious to a throat made raw by screams and smoke.

Memory struck her down again. Smoke. Flame. Jathmar *burning* in the center of the fireball. She began to cry, helplessly, and the woman held her, rocked her gently.

Shaylar's Talent roared wide open. She couldn't hear thoughts; her wounded head throbbed without mercy, and the language would have been wrong, in any case. But the other woman's emotions spilled into her, hot as peppered Ricathian whiskey, yet gentle and filled with sorrow and compassion.

They didn't mean for this to happen.

She didn't know how she knew it, but Shaylar *knew*. As certainly as if the woman had told her, mind to mind, she knew . . . and knew it was the truth. They hadn't meant for the fighting, the death, to happen at all. Deep currents of someone else's emotions washed over her: bitter regret, a sorrow so deep it ached, a sense of helpless grief, smoldering anger at someone—a specific person, somehow to blame for all the agony and destruction. Shaylar felt it all, and with it came a bleak, terrible desolation all her own.

Deep, wrenching sobs shook her, and then the other woman was urging her to turn around. Was speaking softly but urgently, pointing at something nearby. Shaylar turned reluctantly, resisting the pressure, unwilling to face whatever it was, but the not-Uromathian was gently, implacably insistent, and Shaylar was too weak to resist.

And then her breath caught. He lay beside her. His hair was singed; his shirt—what little remained of it—was scorched; and her breath faltered at the sight of the raw, oozing burns along his back. But his ribs were lifting and falling, slowly, steadily.

"*Jathmar!*"

The shriek came from her soul, and she tried to fling herself at him. But the other woman caught her back, speaking urgently again. Her fear gradually seeped through Shaylar's wild need to throw her arms about her husband and protect him from further harm. The other woman had captured Shaylar's face between her hands, was speaking in a frantic tone, trying to make Shaylar understand something vitally important.

And then she did. Jathmar was badly, desperately injured. He might yet die, and Shaylar stopped struggling to reach him. The relief in the other woman was so strong it caused the slender not-Uromathian to sag and gulp in air. Then she released Shaylar, and watched as Shaylar ruffled Jathmar's flame-damaged hair, brushed a fingertip across his cheek.

Shaylar's eyes were wet. When she looked up, so were the other woman's. They sat beside Jathmar, both of them weeping, and somehow the worst of the horror faded away. Whoever these people were, whatever ghastly "mistake" had ended in such carnage, there were decent and caring people among them.

Other sounds gradually penetrated Shaylar's awareness. Voices—men's voices, close by, sounding well organized, busy, and deeply grim. She looked around, trying to find other survivors, and saw no one else she knew. They were no longer in the clearing at all. Someone had carried them under the trees, away from the toppled timber and the scene of the massacre.

But some of that massacre's slaughter had come with them. She, Jathmar, and the woman trying to help them were surrounded by other men, men in torn and bloody uniforms. Many of them were swathed in bandages. Some lay motionless, faces waxen, hardly breathing. Others moaned in pain, and Shaylar felt a sudden, shockingly vicious stab of satisfaction as she saw the proof that her friends—her family—had not gone easily into death.

There were two other people in sight. Two more men in uniform, but these weren't wounded. They stood less than two yards away, although they weren't watching Shaylar, which both surprised and relieved her. She felt far too fragile to be stared at by men who had, just minutes previously, tried their best to murder her.

Instead, they were staring into the trees, their gazes sharp and alert. Sentries, Shaylar realized abruptly, and bitterness choked her. They might as well have saved themselves the effort standing guard. They'd already slaughtered the only Sharonians in this universe, except Darcel Kinlafia, and he was probably on his way back to the previous portal, taking with him the horrifying last minutes they'd spent in linked communication.

He probably thought she was dead—that all of them were dead. There would be no rescue attempt, unless she somehow found a way around the pain and the fracture in her Talent that had left her Voiceless. Without that, Darcel would have to believe they were dead, and Company-Captain Halifu had too few men to risk confronting these people's terrible firepower just to recover a dozen dead bodies.

Her fragile self-control wavered, threatened to break apart. She

was alone, cut off from anyone who could help her, awaiting only
the gods knew what fate. . . . Then she thought of Jathmar and his
terrible injuries. He would need her even more desperately than
she would need him, she told herself fiercely, and felt fear and the
beginnings of hysteria recede. They were alive and together, and
Jathmar needed her. That was all that mattered.

She looked up dully as someone walked across and stopped in
front of her. He was tall and ruggedly handsome, but his eyes were
burnt holes, filled with the afterimage of what he'd witnessed. There
was a huge, invisible weight on his shoulders, one she'd seen a handful of times in her life. Most recently, it had rested on Ghartoun
chan Hagrahyl's shoulders. It had been there when he decided they
couldn't wait for Jathmar. And again, when he stood up and faced
armed men without so much as a pocket knife in his hands.

He's their commander, she realized with a shock like icewater. He
was simply standing there, looking at her, and his eyes held hers the
way Ghartoun's had, pleading with her to understand. To somehow
refrain from hating him.

∗   ∗   ∗

Jasak watched the play of emotions across the tiny woman's face.
They were as transparent as glass, and his heart ached. He'd never
felt so helpless in his entire life, but there was literally nothing he
could do to erase the agony that lived behind her eyes. He didn't
even dare to step closer; he didn't want to see her flinch away from
him.

He looked at Gadrial. She'd been crying, but she wiped her face
dry, waiting for him to say what he'd come to tell her.

"We're ready to begin the field rites," he said quietly. "If you'd
rather not watch . . ."

"I knew some of those men well enough to grieve for them," she
said, her own voice low but steady as she stood.

"Field rites aren't for the faint of heart."

"Not everyone has an Andaran view of death." Her voice was as
level as before, but it had suddenly turned much cooler.

"No, not everyone does," he said, holding her eyes steadily. "But
there's been too much burning of flesh already for anyone to relish
witnessing more. That's what field rites do, Gadrial. Cremation."

He'd heard the harsh burr in his own voice, and her face changed.
The cool aloofness vanished, replaced by something almost like
contrition.

"I'm sorry," she said. "I was thoughtless and rude. They were
your men. . . ."

She looked away, but not before he saw fresh tears glittering on her eyelashes. That nearly proved his undoing, but she pulled herself back together and her eyes met his once more.

"Thank you for letting me know it was time," she said softly, and glanced down at the woman Jasak had carried here. Then she looked back at him.

"If I were her, I'd want to know," she said, even more softly.

Jasak's soul flinched, but he nodded, and Gadrial crouched beside the other woman, speaking very softly. She urged the tiny, injured woman to her feet and steadied her as her balance wavered. She was probably suffering from a concussion, at the very least, Jasak thought bitterly, hoping fervently that the blow hadn't fractured her skull.

Don't be stupid, he told himself sharply. *Gadrial wouldn't have let her stand up if there were broken bones anywhere in her body.*

*   *   *

Shaylar had to lean heavily on the other woman, but she managed to take the few tottering steps back to the open clearing. The smoke had dissipated, but the smell lingered, and Shaylar swallowed nausea, certain she would carry this stench to her grave. Then they reached the edge of the trees, and her footsteps faltered. She would have fallen, if the other woman hadn't been holding her so tightly.

She couldn't count the bodies. There were too many of them, and the world was spinning again, trying to drag her down into darkness. She fought off the vertigo and the tremors, fought to regain control of her swimming senses. Why had they brought her out here? Why did they want her to see the pitiful remains of the people she loved—and the foul remains of the men who'd killed them? She wanted to scream at them for making her come out here and face this again.

What finally caught her attention was the way the surviving soldiers were standing. They were silent, helmets in hand, and then the tall man began to speak. His voice was very quiet, and Shaylar finally realized what he was doing. It was a eulogy—sacred rites for the dead.

And not just his own, she noticed, forcing herself to look again. She saw the bodies of her own companions, laid out with the same care they'd taken with their own dead. Limbs had been straightened, hands crossed over breasts, crossbow quarrels removed . . .

Her crippled, frustratingly erratic Talent was still functioning well enough to catch the emotions of the woman she leaned against, and she winced as they flooded through her. These people were nearly as devastated as she was, with guilt added to the grief. They were trying to show proper respect, according her people the same honors and rites as their own. Someone was moving among the bodies, now, laying a small object on each man's chest. Whatever the objects were, they were placed with reverence and care. Rectangular and dense, they caught the sunlight with the same odd, crystalline sheen as the terrifying weapons which had hurled fire and lightning at them.

The last one was placed, and the man who'd placed them returned to the edge of the clearing and rejoined his companions. Their commander said something further, then turned once again and looked at Shaylar, with something terrifying and almost pleading in his eyes. He took something from the pocket of his uniform blouse, looked at his men, and spoke again.

His voice was harsh with command, and every one of his men snapped to attention. Their right hands struck their left shoulders in what was obviously a salute, and they held it as the commander drew a quick breath, as if for courage, and touched something on the object he taken from his pocket.

Light flared, so bright Shaylar had to look away, her eyes clenching shut in reflex. When she got them open again, her entire body stiffened. The bodies laid so carefully on the ground were *burning*.

She choked, tried to whirl away, and lost her precarious balance. She was falling, dragging the other woman with her. Someone was screaming mindlessly, and a corner of her mind realized it was her. Strong hands caught her, kept her from sprawling across the ground, and she fought like a wildcat, striking out with her fists and nails, frantic to escape this newest horror. She might as well have tried hitting a mountain. The hands were strong, terrifyingly strong, yet strangely gentle, and their owner was saying something in a voice filled with raw pain.

And then her Talent betrayed her once again.

His emotions battered her bleeding senses with someone else's regret, so sharp it was like a knife in her own heart. And that wasn't all. She felt his aching desire to erase her suffering, and a bitter acknowledgment that his attempt to show respect to her people had backfired hideously. He would have done *anything* in that moment to ease her pain, and she knew it. Knew it with the absolute certainty possible only to a telepath.

It was the cruelest thing he could have done to her. She needed an enemy to hate, and he gave her *this*—his bleeding heart and the agony of a man whose every instinct was to protect and who *knew*, with a certainty which matched her own, that he'd destroyed her very life, instead.

Shaylar opened her eyes and stared up into his, and then shuddered violently and went limp, undone by that last realization.

*   *   *

Jasak stared helplessly at the tiny, wounded figure slumped in his arms. He'd tried to show her companions the same honor he'd paid his own fallen men. He'd hoped—prayed—she could understand that there were too many dead, too few living to carry them home again. Too many for them to bury in earthen graves if they had any hope of getting the wounded back to safety in time for it to do any good.

He couldn't—wouldn't—leave any of them for the buzzards and the carrion crows. Her companions had been as human as his own men, and he was already beginning to suspect that they hadn't been soldiers at all. They'd been *civilians*, but they'd fought trained soldiers with a courage—and a ferocity—any man of honor must respect. If anyone had ever deserved proper treatment from their enemies, these men had.

But he should have realized what those fiery bursts of light and flame would do to someone who'd just seen all of her companions slaughtered in deadly explosions of fire. Especially when there was no way for any of them to *explain* to her what they were doing.

Jasak didn't know what to do. No training manual, no officers' course, covered something like *this*, and he glanced up at Gadrial, hoping for enlightenment, or even a simple suggestion. But he found her biting her lip, her own face twisted with guilt and a sense of helplessness which matched his own.

But then the slender woman he held lifted her head. Her eyes were wet and wounded, reddened from too many tears, but they studied him for a brief, dreadful eternity. He was unaware he'd been holding his breath until she turned that deadly gaze away, releasing him from the paralysis which had gripped him, and looked out at the still fiercely blazing funeral pyres.

She wrenched away from him and stood watching the flames, her body swaying for balance, her face ashen. When she started to speak, Jasak's pulse jumped in shock. Her voice was a thin, fragile sound against the roar of magic-induced flames. He couldn't know if she was invoking a deity, or speaking a eulogy, or simply saying their names, but a chill ran across his skin as he watched her face the flames and all they meant.

Everyone else was staring at her, as well, and several of his men shivered. Jasak wondered how many of his men she'd killed. She'd still had a weapon in her hand when they found her. Who was she?

They didn't even know her name, much less what she was, or why she was here, and the totality of his ignorance appalled him.

She finished speaking at last and closed her eyes. She stood silently for long moments, tears sliding down her cheeks. Her face was bruised and swollen, blood had dried in her hair, and the poignancy of her grief tore at his heart like pincers. She nearly crumpled when Gadrial wrapped an arm around her shoulders, and Jasak started forward to catch her. But she caught herself, stiffened her knees, and stayed on her feet.

"Jathmar," she whispered brokenly, and Jasak watched Gadrial guide her back into the trees and help her sit down beside the man who wore the cuff that matched hers.

Jasak watched for a moment longer, then dragged his attention away and focused on the next task at hand. Somehow, he had to transport his own wounded, a woman with an obvious concussion, and a man so badly injured he literally hovered at death's door, through almost twenty miles of rough wilderness. And somehow, he had to figure out what had happened here, and how a handful of people had slaughtered Fifty Garlath's command in such a tiny handful of minutes. First Platoon had gone into the fight with fifty-six arbalestiers and dragon gunners. Twenty-seven of them were dead, and another nineteen were wounded, some of them critically.

With Threbuch and one other trooper dispatched to find the other side's portal, he had fewer uninjured men than he had wounded, even counting his six engineers and the baggage handlers.

He didn't look forward to the rest of the day.

* * *

Haliyar Narmayla struggled to hold back tears as the carriage clattered through the cobbled streets of New Ramath. The cavalry escort riding in front of her cleared the way, giving her carriage absolute priority, and the port master had already been alerted to expect her arrival. The dispatch boat was undoubtedly raising steam even as the well-sprung, rubber-tired carriage swayed and vibrated over the cobbles.

It was impossible to see much, or would have been, if she'd had the heart to look out the window in the first place. New Ramath was a respectable small city—or very large town, depending on one's standards—but it was no huge metropolis. It was also out towards the end of the explored multiverse. In fact, its only reason for existence was to serve Fort Tharkoma, perched in its mountainous aerie almost four hundred miles inland, where it covered both the exit portal from the universe of Salym and also the railhead from

Sharona itself. Additional track was being laid beyond Tharkoma, of course. In fact, the *actual* railhead was currently no more than a few hundred miles short of Fort Salby in the universe of Traisum.

But New Ramath was a critical link in the chain which bound the ever expanding frontier to the home universe. The entry portal for Salym was guarded by Fort Losaltha, almost fourteen hundred miles from Fort Tharkoma. The rail line could have been extended from Losaltha directly to Tharkoma, but Losaltha was located at the Salym equivalent of Barkesh in Teramandor, where the fist of the Narhathan Peninsula and the Fist of Bolakin closed off the eastern end of the Mbisi Sea. A rail line would have had to skirt the northern coast of the Mbisi and penetrate some of the most rugged mountains to be found in any universe. With its long experience, the Portal Authority and the shareholders of the Trans-Temporal Express had opted to avoid the huge construction costs and delay that would have entailed and utilize the water route, instead.

The city of Losaltha, built on the splendid harbor which had served Barkesh for so many thousands of years back in Sharona, was in the process of becoming a major industrial city. For now, however, the Express and Portal Authority were still shipping steamships through to Salym by rail. They arrived as premanufactured modules, which were assembled at Losaltha and then put into service, closing the water gap between Losaltha and New Ramath. In fact, it had amazed Haliyar when she realized just how big the modules the Trans-Temporal Express's specialized freight cars could transport really were. Of course, most of the shipping here in Salym was still of local manufacture—small, wooden-hulled, and mostly powered by sail. That was the norm in the out-universes, after all.

But given the fact that New Ramath's sole reason for being was to handle the bigger, faster TTE freighters and passenger vessels plying back and forth between Losaltha and the Tharkoma Portal, its dockyards and wharves were several times the size one might have expected, with not a few luxury hotels under construction. But it remained a provincial city, for the most part, with few of the amenities those closer to the heart of civilization took for granted. Which had struck Haliyar as particularly amusing when she was first assigned here, since Tharkoma was little more than two hundred miles from Larakesh, the Ylani Sea seaport serving the very first portal ever discovered, and little more than three hundred miles from Tajvana itself. Or, rather, from the locations Larakesh and Tajvana occupied in Sharona.

And why are you letting your mind run on like a crazed tour guide at a moment like this?

Her mouth tightened as the question drove through her brain, but she knew the answer. It was to keep from thinking about the message locked in the agonized depths of that self-same mind.

If only Josam hadn't taken ill, she thought bitterly.

But he had. Josam chan Rakail was the Voice assigned to Fort Tharkoma, and he had the range to reach Chenrys Hordan, in the small town of Hurkaym. Hurkaym was actually little more than a village, built on the island which would have been Jerekhas off the toe of the boot of the Osmarian Peninsula to serve as a link in the Voice chain between Fort Tharkoma and Fort Losaltha. Josam could reach Hurkaym easily, but Haliyar's range was far more limited. That was why she'd been assigned to serve as the New Ramath Voice and link the city to the portal fortress. But Josam had come down with what sounded like pneumonia, and his assistant Voice at Tharkoma had even less maximum range than Haliyar did. Which meant all he'd been able to do was to relay the message to her for her to pass on to Chenrys.

And since I don't have the range to do it from here, either, I'm going to have to get into *range in the first place*, she thought.

She finally glanced out the window. It was the middle of the night in New Ramath, and without gas streetlamps, the city was wrapped in slumbering darkness, sleeping peacefully. She wondered how that would change when its inhabitants discovered the news she was about to pass on.

Her fingertips traced the hard, round outline of the pocket watch in the breast pocket of her warm jacket. It was hard to believe, even for a Voice, that less than half an hour had passed since the vicious attack on the Chalgyn Consortium's survey crew, five universes, two continents, and an ocean away from New Ramath. Haliyar bit her lip, fighting back a fresh burst of tears.

She'd met Shaylar Nargra-Kolmayr and her husband on their way through Salym. As a Voice herself, although never one in Shaylar's league, she'd been unable to avoid feeling the echoes of their mutual devotion. Their marriage bond was so strong that no telepath—whether of Voice caliber, or not—could spend five minutes in their company *without* feeling it, whether she wanted to or not. And that made the agony of Seeing Jathmar's horrible death before Shaylar's very eyes, and then Seeing—and feeling—the even more terrible moment when Shaylar's Voice went abruptly silent, even worse. The experience had been like an ax blow, and now it was *her* job to pass that dreadful, soul-searing experience on to Chenrys in all its horrifying detail.

She wouldn't have had to do this if Josam hadn't fallen ill. She might have managed to avoid the unbearable immediacy of knowing *exactly* what had happened to two people she had both liked and admired deeply . . . and envied more deeply still.

The carriage slowed, and she drew a deep breath, preparing to climb down when the door opened. The dispatch boat—an incredibly fast little vessel, powered by the new steam turbines and capable of sustained speeds of thirty knots or more—lay waiting for her, smoke pluming from its two strongly raked funnels. It wouldn't have to take her all the way to Hurkaym. Haliyar's range was almost three hundred miles; getting her as far as the west coast of Osmaria would allow her to reach Chenrys, and that would take the dispatch boat less than four hours. Then the message—and all its grim, horrible imagery—would go flashing further along the transit chain literally at the speed of thought.

There were still water gaps which couldn't be closed by convenient relay stations like Hurkaym, Haliyar thought as the carriage came fully to a halt. Those were going to impose delays much greater than just four hours. Still, the message would reach Tajvana and the Portal Authority's headquarters there in less than a week.

And what happens then, she thought as the coachman's assistant opened the door for her, *scarcely bears thinking on*.

She stood for a moment, gazing at the dispatch boat under the bright, gas-powered lights of the TTE wharf, and tried not to shiver.

CHAPTER
TEN

JASAK HAD TO send another message. However little he might relish the thought, he had no choice, and he strode over to Iggar Shulthan.

"Iggy, I need two more hummers."

"Yes, Sir. I thought you would, Sir."

The hummer handler opened a small wire cage, made of heavy gauge mesh rather than the sort of wires and crosspieces wealthy ladies used to house chirping canaries or rainbow-winged near-sprites.

He moved carefully and gently, whispering the whole time, as he retrieved one of the ten remaining hummers from the dozen he carried everywhere First Platoon—or whichever of Charlie Company's subunits he was attached to at the moment—went.

Hummers were so aggressive they required not simply soothing handling, but also carefully controlled incantations that turned off their natural attack instinct. The bird Shulthan had retrieved was a beautiful creature, with iridescent green feathers and a ruby throat. And it was also five times the size of any wild hummingbird, with a stiletto beak that was even larger in proportion.

The Andaran Scouts, like all other trans-universal military organizations, bred magically augmented hummers by the hundreds of thousands. Incredibly fast in the air—a hummer could top a hundred and fifty miles per hour—male hummers were aggressive enough to ward off attacks by any airborne creature smaller than a gryphon. They formed the backbone of the Union of Arcana's long-distance communication network, routinely flying distances of well over a thousand miles.

The most remarkable thing about hummers, to Jasak's thinking, was how they transported messages. Rather than strap a message to the outside of a large, slow bird vulnerable to gryphon attacks, the inventor of the hummer system—an Andaran Scout, Jasak thought, with a touch of familiar smugness even now—had found a way to embed a message inside a smaller, faster bird. Every hummer in service was surgically implanted with a message crystal, wafer thin yet capable of storing complex and surprisingly long messages.

Just as Gadrial and Halathyn used spells to store their notes in personal-crystal displays, hummer handlers used spells to store urgent messages which could be retrieved by the receiving hummer handler. Dragons always gave Jasak's spirits a lift, but hummers were sheer artistry.

"Ready to record your messages, Sir," Shulthan said. "Destination?"

"First bird to the coast," Jasak said. "The second to Javelin Krankark at the portal."

Shulthan nodded and spoke the proper spell to implant the first destination's coordinates, then looked back up at Jasak.

"Begin message, Sir."

"Hundred Olderhan, second Andaran Scouts to Five Hundred Klian, Commander, Fort Rycharn. Urgent. First Platoon of my company has sustained heavy combat casualties. The platoon's combat strength has been reduced to eight—I repeat, eight—effectives after an encounter with what I believe to have been a survey party from another transtemporal civilization." Even as he said the words, they still sounded impossible, even to him. "Several of my casualties have serious internal injuries," he continued. "They are in critical condition and urgently require a healer's services. I am transporting them to our base camp as quickly as possible, but I estimate that it will require twenty-plus hours from the time chop on this message to return."

Jasak paused, considering what he'd said, wondering if he should say still more. But what *could* he say until he got back to report in person and answer all of the no doubt incredulous questions Five Hundred Klian was certain to have?

He grimaced and tossed his head.

"Hundred Olderhan reporting," he said. "End of message."

Shulthan spoke again, locking the message properly into the crystal. Then he stroked the hummer gently, whispered to it, and tossed it into the air. It sped away so rapidly Jasak couldn't follow the motion with his eyes even though he'd been waiting for it.

He drew a deep breath, trying to visualize the consternation that hummer was going to create when it reached Fort Rycharn. Then he turned back to Shulthan.

"Second hummer, please," he said.

At least he could include one piece of good news with the message to Krankark. He could reassure Magister Halathyn vos Dulainah that Gadrial had taken no harm, despite the fact that Halathyn had trusted her safety to Sir Jasak Olderhan.

He recorded the message and tried to watch the second bird streak away through the forest. He failed again, as always, and steeled himself to turn back to the remnants of his shattered platoon. He'd done all he could; it remained to be seen whether that—and Gadrial's minor Gift for healing—would keep the wounded alive.

He hoped twenty-five hours of travel time wouldn't turn out to have been an overly optimistic estimate.

*   *   *

Andrin Calirath felt twitchy.

It was an uncomfortable sensation, like feeling swarms of honeybees buzzing just under her skin. It plucked at her nerve endings with a constant, jarring twang, until it threatened to drive her mad. It had plagued her most of the afternoon, too vague to consider a true Glimpse, yet far too insistent to ignore.

The weather hadn't helped. The last week had been fair and fine, like a holdover of summer, but today had set out to remind everyone that autumn was upon them. Like the sensations under her skin, the weather was maddeningly neither one thing nor another, for today had been one of those perpetually drizzling days, too wet to call a mist, too halfhearted to call rain. Below the vast expanse of glass that served the Rose Room as a window, the gardens were all but obscured by the combination of misting rain and approaching evening, and her mood matched the garden—cold, foul, and unsociable. The cheerful chatter of her younger sisters was almost enough to drive her from the room, ripping out handfuls of hair as she went.

Andrin bit down on the impulse—hard. A grand princess of the Ternathian Empire did not display public fits of temper, no matter what the provocation. That stricture—not to mention responsibility—weighed heavy on shoulders that had seen only seventeen changings of the seasons, but she didn't really mind the pressure of her birth rank. Not much, anyway. She enjoyed her many opportunities to help people, to make a difference in their lives. She was grateful for what she had, and for what she could do, but she never forgot who—and what—she *was*. She was a Calirath, born to a tradition of service to her people, her family, and to herself. Everything else, including any private dreams she might nourish, was secondary.

A coal fire burned steadily behind her in a fireplace built when coal had been little more than a funny sort of black rock and trees and peat had been the only fuel on the island. The vast fire pit could have held half a mature oak tree; instead, it held five separate coal fires, spaced evenly along the length of the fireplace. The scent of coal dust, sharp and thick at the back of her throat, was just one more irritant to be weathered. Winter in Ternathia was nothing like the snow-laden ordeal of Farnalia, and it was still only early October, but the wet, raw day had brought an early chill to the palace. It was more than enough to make her grateful for the fire's heat, and she'd draped a woolen shawl around her shoulders, as well. Its soft, warm touch was like a soothing caress, offering at least a little comfort against the angry honeybees.

The little clock on the mantle chimed the hour with a sprinkling of liquid crystal notes, and the silver-sweet bells were a reminder that yet another hour of her life had been devoured by someone else's schedule. The honeybees snarled louder at the thought, whittling away another few notches of her temper, and she sighed. She loved her mother and her sisters, but on days like this, with the Talent riding hard with sharpened spurs, Andrin desperately needed time alone. Time to focus inward, to ask—demand—of this inner agitation what message lay beneath it.

Another clock chimed, farther down the mantle, setting her teeth on edge. Her mother loved fussy little bric-a-brac, like clocks that chimed with the sound of real birdcalls. The Rose Room, Empress Varena's private domain, was filled with her collection of delicate breakables. Andrin had been terrified to move in this room for the first ten years of her life, for graceful deportment had not come naturally to her. Unlike her younger sisters, she'd been forced—grimly—to learn it in the same way a fractious schoolboy might be forced to learn his arithmetic.

I want out *of here!* her soul cried out. *Out of this room, this palace, this awful sensation of doom . . .*

Andrin's Talent never made itself felt for joyous things. That blistering injustice was the reason she was so agitated—*no, be honest, afraid,* she thought harshly—standing here beside the window, staring hard at the garden she could barely see through the mist and the misery. On days like this, she would have given a piece of her soul to be an ordinary milkmaid or shop clerk somewhere, untroubled by anything more serious than helping some wealthy fribble choose which color of ribbon looked best with a card of lace. Shop clerks didn't have inscrutable portents buzzing like angry bees under their skin.

Precognition was a curse of royalty.

At least Janaki is the heir, she consoled herself.

The stiff set of her face eased a little at that thought. Her older brother was in the Imperial Ternathian Marines, assigned to border patrol in a newly colonized world at the edge of Sharonian exploration. She envied him enormously. The open sky, the freedom to gallop one's horse for the sheer mad delight of it, the ability to actually step through portals, not just read about them from the confines of stone walls and garden hedges. She would have been happy just to ride her palfrey through the streets of Estafel today, despite the drizzling rain that had—by now—turned the capital city's cobbled streets into slick and dangerous ribbons of stone.

She started to sigh again, but checked the impulse before it could become audible. She didn't want to inflict her sour mood on her mother or sisters.

The door clicked open.

Andrin turned, grateful for any diversion, yet so anxious about what might be happening somewhere in the many universes Sharonians now called home that her heart stuttered until she saw that the sound was merely her father's arrival for dinner.

She tried to summon a smile, grateful that bad news hadn't actually arrived on their doorstep . . . yet, at least. Her father was a large man, as were most Ternathians. Not stocky, and certainly not fleshy, but he was built like a bull, with the massive shoulders and thick neck that were the hallmark of the Calirath Dynasty. To her private dismay, and the despair of her dressmaker, Andrin looked altogether too much like her father, and not a bit like her mother. The Empress Varena might stand nearly five feet eleven inches in her stockings, but she looked delicate, almost petite, standing beside His Imperial Majesty, Zindel XXIV, Duke of Ternath, Grand Duke of Farnalia, Warlord of the West, Protector of the Peace, and by the gods' Grace, Emperor of Ternathia.

The emperor who, at that moment, wore a look which so nearly matched Andrin's own mood that she felt herself trying not to gape openmouthed.

*   *   *

Zindel chan Calirath caught the grim set of his daughter's jaw, the stiffness of her shoulders, and knew, without a word spoken, that Andrin felt it, too. He halted in the doorway, halfway in and halfway out, and nearly had the door rapped into his heels. The doorkeeper had been opening and closing the Rose Room door every day at six p.m. sharp for the last twenty years, and not once in all that time had the emperor stopped dead in the middle of the doorway.

But Zindel couldn't help it. The warning that vibrated through him when his gaze locked with his eldest daughter's was as brutal as it was unexpected. He sucked in a harsh breath, totally oblivious to the doorkeeper's frantic, last-minute grab at the door handle. He never even realized how close the door had come to slamming into him as his entire body vibrated with the Glimpse.

Something was going to smash her life to pieces. Soon.

Dear gods, no, not Andrin, a voice whispered inside his head, and his eyes clenched shut for just an instant. Clenched shut on a bewildering dazzle of half-guessed images, so fleeting, so jumbled, they were impossible to capture. Explosions of flame. Weeping faces. A powerful locomotive thundering along a desert rail line, with the Royal Shurakhalian coat of arms displayed on either side of its cab. A great whale rising from the sea in an explosion of foam. Gunfire stabbing through darkness and rain. A city he'd never seen yet *almost* recognized, a ship flaming upon the sea, a magnificent ballroom, and his tall young daughter weeping like a broken child . . .

His nostrils flared under the dreadful cascade of almost-knowledge which had been the greatest gift and most bitter curse of his line for twice a thousand years and more. He was no Voice, yet he could taste the same splinters of vision ripping through Andrin, as if the proximity of their Talents had somehow sharpened the fragmented Glimpse for both of them, and he bit his lip as he felt her anguish.

But then he fought his eyes open again and saw Andrin biting down on her own distress. He understood the tension singing just beneath her skin, the shadows in her eyes. They were echoes of his own fear, his own gnawing worry, and his eyes held hers as the cheerful greetings from his wife and younger daughters splashed unheard against him, drowned out by the terrible prescience. Andrin's eyes were dark with its heavy weight, all the more terrible because they could give it neither shape nor name, and when she smiled anyway, it broke his heart.

She'd grown so tall, these last two years, too tall for mere courtly beauty. She was strong beneath the silks and velvets of an imperial princess. She wasn't a beautiful girl, his Andrin, not in the conventional sense. Her chin was too strong, her nose too proud, her face too triangular, for that, but strength lived in those unquiet eyes and the firm set of her mouth. Her long sweep of raven hair, shot through with the golden strands which were borne only by those of Talented Calirathian blood, lent her an almost otherworldly grace she was entirely unaware she possessed, and her eyes were as clear and gray as the Ternathian Sea.

"Hello, Papa," she said, holding out one hand.

He crossed the Rose Room swiftly and took her into a careful embrace, denying himself the need to crush her close, to protect her. He was careful, as well, to hug each of his younger daughters in turn—and his wife—in exactly the same manner, for exactly the same amount of time. He didn't want Varena to guess his Talent was riding him with cruel spurs. Not yet. Not until he'd Glimpsed more of whatever terrifying thing he might yet See.

"Now, then." He smiled at Razial, who'd just turned fifteen, and Anbessa, whose eleventh birthday had been celebrated two months previously. "How did your lessons go today?"

He let their youthful voices wash across him, finding comfort and even mild humor in little Anbessa's complaint that she saw no need to learn what Ternathia's imperial borders had been eight hundred years previously, since the Empire's current borders were far smaller. Then there was Razial. His middle daughter's bubbling enthusiasm over her latest art lesson was, Zindel knew, motivated more by the physical attractiveness of her art tutor than it was by any real love of watercolor painting. But he also knew the tutor's proclivities did not include nubile young grand princesses. And since Janaki was not only old enough to hold his own in affairs of the bedroom, but out of the palace and several universes removed, Zindel had no real worry about the safety of his offspring under the roving eye of a handsome young art instructor. Razial's current infatuation was merely entertaining, in a gentle and soothing way that dispelled some of the gloom after a day like today. He gave Razial another six months, at most, before some other gloriously handsome devil caught her eye and the tension of her raging hormones. He'd worry about *that* devil when the day came.

Meanwhile . . .

Zindel sat beside his wife, drawing comfort from Varena's warmth at his side, while they waited for the servants to arrive with their supper. Varena's needlework—a new cover for their kneeling bench at Temple—was a work of art in its own right. Varena's designs were copied eagerly throughout the Empire, viewed as instantaneous must-haves for anyone on the Society list, or anyone with the aspiration to be on it, and not simply because of who she was.

*　　*　　*

Her Imperial Majesty Varena smiled as her husband sat beside her, but her skilled hands never paused in their work. She drew no small pleasure from the work she created with nimble fingers, needle, and thread . . . and if her hands were busy making something beautiful, no one would see them twist into the knots of fear which came all too often for an imperial wife.

She was Talented, of course; it was legally required for any Calirath bride. But hers wasn't a very *strong* Talent, just a middling dollop of precognition. It was nothing like the Glimpses her husband and her older children experienced, yet it was enough to set up tremors in her abdomen which threatened to upset the balanced poise of her busy fingers. Something was wrong. She could feel it in her own limited way, and she knew the signs to look for in her husband and her daughter, but she let them think they were succeeding at hiding their inner agitation, because it was kinder to give them that illusion.

Neither of them wanted to add stress to her life, so she carefully hid her own disquiet, aware that whatever was wrong would come in its own good time. She saw no sense in rushing to meet trouble before it arrived, unless one had a clear enough Glimpse and sufficient time to alter what *might* be coming.

Which happened all too seldom.

"Well," Zindel said to Razial at last, "while I'm delighted to hear your art studies are coming so well, I'm not at all sure Master Malthayr is quite prepared to pose nude for you." He glanced down at Varena with a tender, droll humor which was heartbreaking against the background tension she felt quivering through him. "What do *you* think, love?" he asked her.

"*I* think," she said calmly, setting her needlework aside as the doors opened quietly and supper began to arrive, "that your sense of humor requires a sound whacking, Your Imperial Majesty."

"No!" He laid one hand on his heart, gazing at her soulfully. "How could you possibly say such a thing?" he demanded while Anbessa giggled and Razial looked martyred.

"I believe it has something to do with having been married to you for over twenty years," she said with a smile.

He chuckled and took her hand as she stood. But the darkness still lingered behind his eyes, and she squeezed his strong fingers tightly for just a moment. Awareness flickered through his expression at the silent admission that she was only too well aware of the frightening black cloud of tension wrapped around him and Andrin. Then she smiled again.

"And now, it's time to eat," she said calmly.

*   *   *

After the gut-wrenching cremation of the dead, Shaylar's captors stayed where they were for over an hour, camped mercifully upwind of the remains in the toppled timber. Despite the insight her Talent had given her into these people and their intentions, Shaylar felt an inescapable measure of grim satisfaction as she contemplated the heavy price they'd paid for slaughtering her friends. They didn't have enough unhurt men to carry all of their wounded, she thought fiercely, and she also felt a slight, fragile stir of hope as she thought about what that might mean.

Darcel probably thought she was dead, but he couldn't be positive, and as far as he could know, some of the others might have survived, even if she hadn't. Under the circumstances, Company-Captain Halifu would almost certainly have to be sending out a party to rescue any possible survivors, and if these people couldn't retreat because of their own injured men . . .

The woman who'd been trying so hard to comfort her was moving among the wounded who lay sprawled in the trees. She paused at each man, touching him lightly and whispering something. She also consulted frequently with their commander, but she obviously wasn't a soldier. Shaylar was virtually certain of that. She'd already noticed the other woman's lack of a uniform, but Shaylar wondered if she might be a civilian healer assigned to this military unit. Certainly what she'd done for Shaylar's throbbing head and her current attentiveness to the wounded suggested that might be the case, which surprised Shaylar on two separate levels.

Healers assigned to the Sharonian military were full-fledged members of that military, part of the Healers' Corps. They were also all men. Women didn't serve in the Sharonian military. Even in Ternathia, which was deplorably "progressive" by the standards of other Sharonian cultures, only a tiny handful had ever been accepted for military service, and then, inevitably, only in staff positions or as nurses well to the rear. Officers and even enlisted men could marry, of course, and their wives and children could travel with them to their assigned duty posts. But those wives and children remained in military-built and financed housing in the civilian towns which sprang up around the portal forts. They didn't accompany their men on missions, whether in the wilderness or to put down the occasional outbreak of banditry in more settled country, and not even Ternathian female nurses were ever assigned to the Healer Corps which served units in the field.

Whoever this woman was, she finished tending the wounded and returned to Shaylar's side. She sat beside her, looked into Shaylar's eyes, and pointed to herself as she spoke slowly and clearly.

"Gadrial," she said. It was an odd name, but a name was clearly what it was.

"Jathmar?" she continued, pointing at Jathmar and confirming Shaylar's guess.

"Yes." Shaylar nodded, wincing at the movement of her aching head. "Jathmar."

Gadrial nodded back, then cocked her head, waiting expectantly, and Shaylar touched her own breastbone.

"Shaylar," she said, and a lovely smile flickered like sunlight across Gadrial's face.

"Shaylar," she repeated, then said something else. Shaylar tried desperately to make contact with Gadrial's mind, hoping that this woman might be some sort of telepath, but she could touch nothing. The place inside her own mind where such connections were made was a throbbing mask of blackness and pain. She was still Voiceless, and panic nibbled at the edge of her awareness. If the damage proved permanent . . .

Don't borrow trouble.

Her mother's voice echoed through her memory, and grief and the fear that she would never see her mother again were nearly Shaylar's undoing. She felt her mouth quiver, felt fresh tears brimming in her swollen eyes, but then Gadrial took her hand gently and pulled her back from that brink.

"Shaylar," she said again, then something else. She pointed to Jathmar and the others, then to the south. Shaylar frowned, and Gadrial pantomimed walking with two fingers on the ground, then pointed again.

Shaylar felt herself tensing internally once more. They were leaving, walking toward something in the south . . . which was the direction Darcel had sent them to locate the nearest portal to another universe.

She looked at all of the other wounded, then back at Gadrial, cursing the whirling unsteadiness of her own senses and thoughts. She couldn't imagine how the remaining fit soldiers could possibly transport all of their wounded fellows, and her heart sank as she realized Gadrial might be referring only to her and Jathmar. If their own portal to this universe was as close at hand as Darcel had thought, they might want to get their prisoners safely away for future interrogation, and that thought was terrifying.

But if they want prisoners to interrogate, they'll have to keep us alive until they can start asking questions, a little voice said somewhere deep inside her. *And that means they'll have to get Jathmar proper healing as quickly as possible.*

Her jaw clenched as the exquisite anguish of her plight gripped her like pincers. Every step, every inch, toward the south would take them farther and farther from any possibility of rescue. But those same steps might very well take Jathmar towards healing and survival.

Shaylar had known the risks when she signed up for this job, but she'd never dreamed how devastating it would be to face a moment like this, knowing her beloved needed medical care only their enemies could provide. Yet in the end, that was the only chance fate was likely to put into her trembling hands, and so she nodded, and felt as if she were somehow sealing their doom.

And either way, it's not as if I have very much choice, she thought grimly.

*   *   *

"I know you're frightened," Gadrial said gently to the other woman—Shaylar—and touched her arm. "But I swear Sir Jasak will do everything he can to save Jathmar for you."

Shaylar's mouth trembled again briefly at the sound of her companion's name. She reached down, touching Jathmar's forehead with heartbreaking gentleness, and Gadrial's own heart twisted as she recognized the grief and despair in the gesture.

Then she heard the sound of approaching footsteps, and she and Shaylar both looked up as Jasak went to one knee beside them. Weariness showed in the commander of one hundred's face and the set of his shoulders. It was obvious from the way he moved that the wound along his ribs, especially, was causing considerable pain, but the shadows in his eyes as he looked down at Jathmar and Shaylar had nothing to do with *his* wounds.

"How's it going?" he asked.

"I've got their names," Gadrial said. "And I think I just got her to understand and agree to walk with us to the swamp portal."

"Gods, I hope so." His voice was full of smoke and gravel. "She's suffered enough without us having to drag her every step of the way."

"They're your prisoners."

Gadrial tried to keep from speaking between clenched teeth, but it was hard. She wasn't at all happy in her own mind about taking Shaylar and Jathmar back as military prisoners. Surely they'd already done these people enough hurt! The thought of what Shaylar and Jathmar might face at the hands of government and military interrogators, on top of all they'd already suffered, was enough to stiffen her with rage.

It must have showed, despite her effort to control her voice, because Jasak gave her a quick, very sharp look. Then he nodded.

"Yes, they are," he said flatly. "And my responsibility."

Ah, yes—responsibility, Gadrial thought. That most Andaran of all traits. *Noblesse oblige.* The duty to codes of honor instilled into Andaran children—girls, as well as boys—from the cradle itself. She wanted to ask if that responsibility would protect these battered people from the military hierarchy that would want to peel their minds like apples. She had no idea what kind of magic might be brought to bear on the mind of a prisoner of war, and, frankly, she didn't want to find out. But if the Union of Arcana and its military decided that extracting information from Shaylar and Jathmar was vital to the security of the Union, there wouldn't be a single damned thing Gadrial could do about it.

So she did the only thing she *could* do. She introduced Sir Jasak Olderhan, son of the Duke of Garth Showma, to his prisoners.

* * *

Jasak saw the worry and anger in Gadrial as clearly as he saw the terror and exhaustion in Shaylar. The slender girl repeated his given name with a bruised weariness he recognized as post-battle trauma. He hated seeing it in Shaylar's eyes as much as he hated seeing the suspicion in Gadrial's, but he couldn't expect the magister to understand that. She was Ransaran, raised in a culture where the formality of military duty, of knowing one's obligations to a stratified social order, wasn't an ingrained part of everyone's basic childhood training. She didn't understand what Jasak's responsibility entailed. Not yet. But she would, he promised himself, and hoped that the worry and anger would fade from Gadrial's eyes as quickly as he hoped the terror and shock would fade from Shaylar's.

Yet neither of those things was going to happen quickly enough, and Gadrial's worry—and Shaylar's exhaustion—were probably both going to get worse before they got better. And that, too, would result from his responsibilities, including his responsibility to push everyone, including this poor, brutalized young woman, ruthlessly, even brutally, in a relentless effort to get Jathmar the healing he so desperately needed.

He doubted either of the women would understand why that was so important to him. Important to Jasak Olderhan, not to Commander of One Hundred Olderhan. And there was no way in this universe, or any other, that he could hope to explain it to them in the time he had.

So he did what he could do to try to reassure both of them. He lifted Shaylar's hand and stroked it the way he would have stroked a frightened kitten.

"Don't be afraid," he said gently. "No one will hurt you again. *No one.* I know you don't understand, yet, but I swear that on my honor, Shaylar. And I'll do everything I can to help you understand it."

Her hand was limp, broken feeling, in his grip, and her dark eyes were glazed. He sighed and turned back to Gadrial.

"We'll strike camp as soon as you determine it's safe to move him." He nodded at Jathmar. "My baggage handlers survived, so at least we'll be able to lift the most critically wounded. But even so, it's not going to be a picnic stroll through the park getting them safely back to the portal and transport."

He glanced again at Jathmar, wondering if the wounded man's unconsciousness was a mercy or a bad sign.

"We'll rig a field litter for him," he said. "And one for her, as well, if she needs it."

"Get it ready, then," Gadrial said. "The sooner we move him, the faster we'll get back. As long as his litter doesn't jostle him too much, he should be all right. I'll do what I can for him as well as your men."

"I appreciate that. Immensely." He smiled, the expression tight with worry and fatigue, yet genuine. "I'll get right on it, then."

It took only minutes to break out the collapsible field stretchers that were part of the baggage his platoons carried in the field. Jasak couldn't imagine what battle must have been like before the development of Gifts made it possible to move heavy loads with spells, rather than muscle power.

All four of his baggage handlers had survived, along with their equipment. The most critically wounded were placed on proper field litters, canvas slings mounted between poles to which the handlers attached standard spell storage boxes. They didn't have enough of the standard litters for the less critically hurt, but Sword Harnak threw together field expedient substitutes, using uniform tunics for slings and hastily cut branches for poles. They looked like hell, but they ought to do the job, and Jasak watched the baggage handlers attaching the sarkolis crystal storage boxes.

The storage devices were all pretty much the same size and shape. Only the markings varied, with a color coding that told the soldier at a glance whether it contained spells that powered infantry-dragons, spells that lifted baggage, or spells that illuminated a landing area to guide living dragons during night airlifts. As an added precaution, those which carried weapon-grade spells featured carefully contoured shapes which would fit only into the weapons they were intended to power, but that wasn't immediately apparent at first glance.

Jasak supervised preparations closely, speaking to wounded men in a low, reassuring voice. Gripping shoulders where a bracing moment of support was required to stiffen a man's weary spine. Making sure every bit of captured equipment was secured for analysis back home. He still didn't understand how the long, hollow tubes they'd found beside the dead—or the smaller versions several had carried, as well—had managed to wreak such havoc, but he intended to find out.

When it was time to shift the unconscious Jathmar onto one of the litters, Jasak abandoned the captured equipment to the handlers he'd detailed to haul it out and personally accompanied Lance Erdar Wilthy. Wilthy was the senior, most experienced of First Platoon's baggage handlers, and Jasak had assigned him specific responsibility for transporting Jathmar. The lance had been doing his job for years, but Jasak found himself hovering, unable to restrain himself from taking personal charge of the delicate operation of getting Jathmar onto the litter despite the fact that he knew Wilthy had far more experience than he.

Shaylar sat beside her husband, one hand resting gently on his scorched brown hair, when Jasak and Wilthy approached. Her unguarded expression was full of anguish, and Jasak crouched down beside her.

"Shaylar," he said gently. She looked up, and he pointed to the canvas sling Wilthy was unrolling on the ground beside Jathmar.

"We're going to put Jathmar on this stretcher," he continued, pantomiming the act of picking something up and setting it down again. "We won't hurt him. I promise."

Shaylar looked at him, and then at the litter. Since they would have to transport Jathmar face down, the litter had to be rigid, or the sling would bend his spine painfully in the wrong direction, not to mention the tension it would put on the burned skin of his back. Harnak's improvised stretchers would never have worked, Jasak thought, watching Wilthy slide crosswise slats into place, turning the canvas sling into a rigid platform.

When it was ready, Jasak pantomimed their intentions to Shaylar again, and she nodded.

"Easy, now," Jasak cautioned Wilthy. "I'll take his shoulders, Erdar. You take his feet. Gadrial, support his waist. We only need to lift him a couple of inches off the ground. On the count of three. One, two, three—"

They lifted him two inches and slid him smoothly onto the canvas. Shaylar hovered, holding Jathmar's head, biting her lips when he stirred with a sound of pain. Gadrial whispered over him, and he subsided again, lying quietly on the litter.

So far, so good, Jasak thought.

"All right, attach the accumulator and let's lift him, Erdar."

"Yes, Sir," Wilthy said, and pulled out the box and attached it to the receptacle on the litter.

Shaylar had been looking down at Jathmar's face, but she looked up again, attracted by the lance's movement. For just a moment, she showed no reaction, but then her eyes flew wide and she came to her feet with a bloodcurdling scream.

Jasak flinched in astonishment as she leapt past him, snatched the box off the litter, and hurled it violently away. Then she spun to face him—to face *all* of them, every surviving member of First Platoon. She was a single, tiny woman, smaller than Jasak's own twelve-year-old sister, but he could literally feel the savagery of her fury as her fingers curled into defensive claws. She was prepared to attack them all, he realized. To rip out the throat of any man who approached Jathmar with her bare teeth, and he recoiled from her desperate defiance, trying frantically to understand its cause.

"Oh, dear God!" Gadrial cried. "She thinks we're going to cremate him alive! They all look alike to her—the accumulator boxes!"

Comprehension exploded through Jasak, and he swore with vicious self-loathing.

"Get that box, Wilthy!" he snapped. "Fasten it to something else—*anything* else. Show her what it does."

The white-faced trooper, his expression as shaken and horrified as Jasak's own, scrambled to retrieve the accumulator. He scrabbled it up out of the leaves where Shaylar had thrown it and fastened it to the nearest object he could find—a section of decaying log about three feet long and eighteen inches in diameter. The box was equipped with twenty small chambers, each with its own control button, and he pressed one of them, releasing the spell inside.

The log lifted from its leafy bed. It floated silently into the air and hovered there, effortlessly.

Shaylar watched, her eyes wide. Then she sagged to her knees, gasping as she panted for breath, and Gadrial knelt beside her.

"It's all right, Shaylar," she said gently, reassuringly. "It's all right. We're not going to hurt him. It'll just pick him up. See, it lifts the log."

She pointed, pantomiming moving the accumulator back to Jathmar's litter, then lifting Jathmar the same way. Shaylar trembled violently in the circle of Gadrial's left arm, and the magister glanced over her shoulder at Jasak.

"For the love of God, lift the other wounded men. She's half crazed with terror!"

"Get them airborne!" Jasak barked to the other handlers, who were watching with open mouths. "Damn it, get them airborne *now!*"

Wilthy's subordinates obeyed quickly, lifting all of the critically wounded. Shaylar watched them, her body taut, her eyes wide. But the wildness was fading from them, and she began to relax again, ever so slowly.

"It's all right," Gadrial told her again and again. "Let us help him, Shaylar. Let us help Jathmar. Please."

Jasak watched as Shaylar's obvious terror began to ease. The furious fear for Jathmar which had given her strength seemed to flow out of her. Her mouth went unsteady, and her eyes overflowed. Then she crumpled, and Gadrial caught her, held her close, rocked her like a frightened child, stroking her hair and soothing her.

A badly shaken Jasak turned back to Wilthy.

"Lift Jathmar's stretcher, Erdar. But move carefully, whatever you do. She's not strong enough to take many more shocks like that one."

"Yes, Sir. I'll be gentle as a butterfly, Sir."

Gadrial urged Shaylar to her feet as Wilthy slowly and carefully, pausing between each movement to let Shaylar see every step of the process, lifted Jathmar's litter until it floated just above waist level.

Shaylar watched, still panting, and Gadrial wiped the other woman's cheeks dry with the corner of her own shirt. Then the magister gave her a smile and squeezed her hand for just a moment, before moving it to rest on Jathmar's. Wilthy had tucked the injured man's arms down at his sides, which was an awkward placement, but better than leaving them hanging over the edges of the litter.

Shaylar curled her slender fingers carefully, delicately, around his. Then she drew a deep breath. Her chin came up, and she met Jasak's gaze once again.

"All right, People." Jasak gave the order. "Move out."

CHAPTER ELEVEN

"*WHAT?*" COMPANY-CAPTAIN BALKAR chan Tesh stared at Petty-Captain Rokam Traygan in total disbelief. "You can't be serious!"

"I wish to all the Uromathian hells I wasn't, Sir," Traygan said harshly. The Ricathian Voice's face was the color of old ashes, and his hands shook visibly. He looked away from chan Tesh and swallowed hard.

"I—" He swallowed again. "I threw up twice receiving the message, Sir," he admitted. "It was . . . ugly."

Chan Tesh stared at the petty-captain, then shook himself. He didn't know Traygan as well as he might have wished, hadn't even met the man before the Voice caught up with his column in Thermyn. But they'd traveled over a thousand miles together on horseback since then, from the rolling grasslands of what would have been central New Ternathia and across the continent's deserts and rocky western spine. The heavyset, powerfully muscled Voice hadn't struck chan Tesh as a weakling, yet he was obviously shaken—badly shaken—and chan Tesh was suddenly glad that *he* wasn't a Voice.

"Tell me," he said quietly, almost gently, and Traygan turned back to face him.

"Company-Captain Halifu didn't know exactly where we were," the Voice said, "and I've never worked with the Chalgyn Voice, Kinlafia. So instead of trying to contact us directly, he had Kinlafia pass the report straight up the chain with a request that Fort Mosanik relay to us. I got Kinlafia's entire transmission."

He swallowed again and shook his head.

"I never imagined anything like it, Sir," he said, his voice a bit hoarse around the edges. "It was—It was like Hell come to life. Fireballs, explosions, *lightning bolts*, for the gods' sake! And Shaylar Nargra-Kolmayr and her husband caught right in the middle of it."

Chan Tesh felt his own face turn pale. He was Ternathian, himself, not Harkalan, but Nargra-Kolmayr was virtually a Sharona-wide icon. The first woman to win the battle for a place on a temporal survey crew; one of the most powerful Voices Sharona had ever produced; daughter of one of Sharona's most renowned cetacean ambassadors; half of one of Sharona's storybook, larger than life romantic sagas. The fact that she was beautiful enough to be cast to play herself in any of the (inevitable) dramatizations of her own life had simply been icing on the cake.

"Was she hurt?" he asked urgently.

"Yes," Traygan half-groaned. "She was linked with Kinlafia, and somehow she held the link to the end. Held it even while whoever the bastards were slaughtered her crew—even her *husband*!—all around her. And then—"

His face twisted with what chan Tesh realized was the actual physical memory of the last moments of Nargra-Kolmayr's transmission.

"She's *dead*?" chan Tesh almost whispered.

"We don't know. We think she hit her head, so she might just be unconscious." Traygan sounded like a man whose emotions clung desperately to what his intellect knew was false hope, chan Tesh thought grimly.

"All right, Rokam," he said. "Tell me exactly what you know. Take your time. Make sure you tell me everything."

*   *   *

It was the news a transport pilot least wanted to hear.

Squire Muthok Salmeer's quarters, such as they were, were almost adjacent to the hummer tower. The handler on watch had handed the message straight to Salmeer, and Salmeer had run all the way from his quarters to the CO's office to deliver the ghastly news.

"*Combat* casualties? Combat with *what*?" Commander of Five Hundred Sarr Klian demanded incredulously as he scanned the message transcript the duty communications tech had pulled off the incoming hummer's crystal. It was, Salmeer recognized, what was known as a rhetorical question, and the pilot waited tensely for the five hundred to finish reading.

By the time he was done, Klian was swearing blisters into Fort Rycharn's roughly finished wooden walls. He glared at the authorizing sigil at the foot of the message, then shook his head, looked up, and glared at Salmeer.

"He met someone from another universe and *attacked?* Has Hundred Olderhan lost his blue-blooded *mind?*"

"Sir," Salmeer said, leaning forward and jabbing a finger at the two words in the entire message which had meant the most to him, "I don't know who attacked who, but he says he's got *heavy casualties,* Sir. Whatever his reasons, whatever's going on out there, he needs a med team. We've got to scramble one *now,* Five Hundred. My dragon's got seven hundred *miles* to fly just to reach the portal."

The pilot was almost dancing in impatience. Sarr Klian swore once more, explosively. Then, as Salmeer opened his mouth to protest the delay, Fort Rycharn's commander shook his head savagely.

"Yes, yes, of course! Throw a medical team into the saddle and *go,*" he said sharply.

Salmeer paused just long enough to throw an abbreviated salute. The five hundred returned it with equal brevity, and Salmeer whipped around. He was already back up to a run by the time he hit the door, but even so, he heard Klian muttering behind him before the door closed.

"He *attacked* them? What the *fuck* is Olderhan *doing* out there?"

Twenty minutes later, Fort Rycharn's sole permanently assigned transport dragon was lumbering out to the flightline, loaded with an emergency medical transport platform, several canvas bags of medical supplies, two surgeons, four herbalists, and Sword Naf Morikan, Charlie Company's journeyman Gifted healer, whose R&R had just been cut brutally short.

"Sir Jasak *attacked?*" Morikan demanded as he fumbled his way into the saddle on the already-moving dragon. "Attacked *what,* in the gods' names? There's nothing *out* there!"

Salmeer bit his tongue to keep himself from pointing out that there obviously *was* something out there, since Sir Jasak Olderhan had gotten into a blood-and-guts fight with whatever it was. The pilot found it impossible to believe it really had been representatives of another trans-universal civilization. That was simply too preposterous for him to wrap his mind around without a *lot* more evidence. But he didn't have any better explanation for what it might have been than anyone else at Fort Rycharn did, and he reminded himself that Morikan was Olderhan's company healer. He knew every one of the men of Fifty Garlath's platoon personally. Of course the noncom was worried half out of his mind.

"I have no idea, Sword," he said instead. "Be sure your safety straps are buckled tight."

"Yes, Sir," Morikan replied. "Ready when you are, Squire," he added after a moment, and Salmeer gave Windclaw the signal.

The dragon launched quickly, as if he'd caught his pilot's urgency, and he probably had. Windclaw was a fine old beast, a century old last month, and as smart as a transport ever got. Of course, that wasn't much compared to a battle dragon, but Windclaw was no mental midget, and his experience made him doubly valuable in the field, particularly in an emergency. A canny old beast like Windclaw knew every trick in the book for coaxing extra speed during an emergency flight.

Salmeer wished bitterly that they'd had even one more dragon available to send with Windclaw, but this universe was at the ass-end of nowhere, almost ninety thousand miles from Old Arcana. Worse, it was over twenty-six thousand miles back to the nearest sliderhead at the Green Haven portal, and almost ten thousand of those miles were over-water. A transport dragon like Windclaw could cover prodigious distances—up to a thousand miles, or possibly a bit more in a single day's flight—but then he *had* to rest. That meant landing on something, and the water gaps between Fort Rycharn and Green Haven were all wider than a dragon could manage in a single leg.

That made getting *anything* all the way to the fort an unmitigated pain in the ass. But Salmeer was used to that, just as he was used to the fact that Transport Command promotion was slow to the point of nonexistence. Muthok Salmeer himself had almost thirty years in, but he was never going to be a combat pilot, and he still hadn't been promoted as high as a fifty. Taken for granted, overworked, underappreciated, and underpaid: that was a Transport Command pilot's lot in life, and most of them took the same sort of perverse pride in it that Salmeer did.

None of which made his current problem any more palatable.

The Arcanan military—and the UTTTA civilian infrastructure, for that matter—were notoriously casual about extending the slide rails out into the boondocks. It was hard to fault their sense of priorities, Salmeer supposed in his more charitable moments. After all, even Green Haven boasted a total population of considerably less than eight hundred thousand. That wasn't a lot of people, spread over the surface of an entire virgin planet the size of Arcana itself, and it wasn't as if other portals, much closer to Arcana, couldn't supply anything the home world really needed. Exploration and expansion were worthwhile in their own right, of course, and there were always homesteaders, eager to stake claims to places of their own. But simple economic realities meant the inner portals were far more heavily developed and populated and invariably received a far greater proportion of the Transit Authority's maintenance resources as a result.

And it's the poor bloody transport pilots who make it all possible, Salmeer thought bitterly. *Not that anyone ever notices.*

He supposed it was inevitable, but every bureaucrat, whether uniformed or civilian, seemed to assume there would always be a transport dragon around when he needed one. The sheer range a dragon made possible was addictive, despite the fact that even a big, powerful, fully mature beast like Windclaw could carry only a fraction of the load a slider car could manage. Most of the freight that needed moving on the frontiers was relatively light, after all. But the demands placed upon the Air Force's Transport Command were still brutal. The Command was always short of suitable dragons, and Cloudsail, Windclaw's partner in the two-dragon teams which were supposed to be deployed, had torn three of the sails in his right wing colliding with a treetop. They'd had to ship him back to the main portal for treatment, and, *of course,* there'd been no replacement in the pipeline.

All of which explained why Windclaw was the only dragon currently assigned to Fort Rycharn when Salmeer was desperately afraid that Sir Jasak Olderhan might well need far more than a single beast.

He glanced back, craning around in the saddle which ran securely around the base of Windclaw's neck, to be sure his passengers were still with him. Straps passed behind the dragon's forelegs, as well, to keep the saddle from slipping sideways. It put Salmeer in the best position to see where Windclaw was going and to communicate his orders to the dragon. Behind the saddle, Windclaw's back supported the emergency medical lift platform—a low-slung, aerodynamically streamlined lozenge made of canvas, leather, and steel tubing.

The platform was broad enough to accommodate two people lying flat beside one another, and deep enough to allow for a bottom shelf and top shelf for the storage of reasonably small items of cargo. It also ran most of the way down Windclaw's spine, which made it long enough to permit the transport of up to twenty critically injured people on stretchers laid end-to-end. A turtle-backed windbreak of taut canvas was stretched over the front two thirds of the framework to keep the slipstream off the medical casualties during transport.

Passengers who weren't incapacitated could ride in one of three saddles strapped in front of the lozenge, and both surgeons and the Gifted healer had opted to do so. All three wore helmets with full-length visors to keep the wind—and insects—out of their faces during flight. The herbalists, the most junior members of the medical team, rode inside the transport lozenge itself.

The terrain below them was a morass of mud, standing water, low-growing swamp forest, and vast stretches of reed-filled marsh. Waterbirds by the hundreds of thousands—probably by the millions, if he'd been able to count them—were visible below, some winging their way above the swamps, some dotting the marshes like a variegated carpet in shades of gray, white, brown, and pink. Still others rested among the trees, in what Salmeer suspected were vast rookeries, given the season in this part of this particular universe.

It was a breathtaking sight, even for a man accustomed to piloting transport dragons through empty universes. He loved the vast sweep of nature at its pristine best, and vistas like this one still raised his spirits. A wry grin formed behind the wind shield fastened to his leather-padded steel riding helmet. Despite all of his complaining about overwork and lack of respect, there was a reason he'd signed up for the Air Force, after all! He always felt sorry for the soldiers who had to slog across most universes on foot, like the Andaran Scouts did.

*   *   *

Shaylar walked in a daze, stumbling forward at Jathmar's side. He lay so still she would have been afraid he was dead if not for the faintest of flutters under her fingertips, where his pulse beat against the skin. It was the only way she could tell he wasn't, because she couldn't sense him through the marriage bond at all. Black acid lay at the core of her brain, preventing anything—even Jathmar—from connecting.

It was terrifying, that silence. And yet, given the agony he was in, or would be when he awoke, it might be a mercy, as well.

Her world had shrunk to a tightly constricted sphere around herself and Jathmar's hand. Everything beyond was lost in a haze, out of focus and rumbling with a strange, muted roar, like freight trains whispering in the distance. The strongest reality was the unrelenting, raw agony inside her own head—an ache with spiked heels, doing a raucous Arpathian blade dance behind her temples and eyelids.

She had no idea how much time had passed since the attack, no idea how far she would be forced to struggle through this endless wilderness. Her awareness faded in and out, unpredictably, with an occasional louder noise close by. An explosive crack as a dried branch broke under someone's foot; a murmur of voices speaking alien gibberish. The sounds whirled around her like a slow cyclone, leaving her lost and dizzy in the middle of nothing at all. . . .

She awoke brutally, with her face against something rough and uneven. Ground, she thought distantly. The roughness was the ground, covered with drifts of leaves. Confusion shook her like a terrier with a wounded rat, and voices rose in alarm on all sides. For long, terrifying moments she had no idea where she was, or why. Then memory slammed her down, and she bit back the scream building in her throat. She wanted to fall back into the delicious nothingness, couldn't find the strength to face what had happened or was yet to happen.

Someone was sobbing uncontrollably, and she realized slowly that it was her.

Then a voice came to her. It was a gentle voice, the voice of a woman whose name she knew but couldn't find in her broken memory. An equally gentle hand touched her hair, and the whirling confusion steadied. The voice came again, more sharply focused this time, and someone's arms were around her. They lifted her gently, laid her on a soft surface.

Cloth, she realized. Cloth cradling her from head to toe. She collapsed against it, sinking into its supporting embrace, boneless with gratitude for the chance to simply lie still and rest.

*   *   *

"Is she asleep?"

Gadrial glanced up. Sir Jasak Olderhan was bent over her shoulder, peering worriedly at Shaylar, his eyes dark.

"Very nearly," she said. "Let's get her litter up to transport height."

She let Wilthy adjust the levitation spell in the accumulator. Once Shaylar was floating between waist and hip height, Wilthy passed guidance control to a strapping soldier with a bandage on one thigh and livid bruises across the right side of his face. The trooper's expression as he gazed down at the slender girl was a curious blend of wonder and apprehension, as though he expected her to mutate into a basilisk at any moment. Given the damage Shaylar had helped inflict on the soldier's unit, Gadrial supposed the analogy might be apt, at that.

She watched the litter float away, then drew a deep breath and looked up at the afternoon sky visible through occasional breaks in the leaf canopy. It was later than she liked, for their progress had been agonizingly slow, with twelve litters to guide through primeval wilderness and far too few able-bodied soldiers to do the piloting. They should have been no more than twelve hours' hike from the portal when they began their homeward trek, but she was beginning to fear that Jasak's twenty-five-hour estimate had been too optimistic.

"You're worried," Jasak said quietly.

"Terrified!" she snapped, then bit her lip. "I'm sorry. But Shaylar isn't strong. I think there's some internal injury, something inside her skull. I'm trying to keep it stabilized, but it takes constant attention, and I think she's slipping away from me slowly, anyway. And Jathmar—"

She lifted both hands helplessly in admission of a deep, unfamiliar sense of total inadequacy, and saw Jasak's face tighten.

"If we could only get a transport dragon in here," he murmured. His voice trailed off, but then, suddenly, his eyes snapped to life. He, too, glanced skyward for a moment, obviously thinking hard, then nodded sharply.

"It might just be possible," he muttered to himself, then refocused on Gadrial. "Excuse me," he said, almost abruptly, and wheeled away, walking straight to Javelin Shulthan.

"Send another hummer back to camp, Iggy," he said. "Tell Krankark to send the medical evacuation team through the portal the instant it reaches camp. Have them meet us at the stream where Osmuna was mur—"

He paused, glancing at the litters where Jathmar and Shaylar lay crumpled and broken, and the verb he'd been about to use died in his throat.

"At the stream where Osmuna died," he said instead, looking back at Shulthan. "A transport dragon should have the wing room to take off if he flies down the streambed. Tell Krankark to send a reply hummer, homed in on these coordinates, to confirm receipt of our message. Stay here until it returns, then catch up to us at the stream. It's less than ten minutes from here to the portal for a hummer, so you shouldn't have to wait too long."

"Yes, Sir!"

The hummer shot away through the trees less than two minutes later, like a feathered crossbow bolt. Jasak watched it disappear into the towering forest, willing it to even greater speed, then turned to find Sword Harnak with his eyes.

"Let's get them moving again, Sword," he said briskly. "We're heading for the stream where Osmuna died."

Jasak was grateful that he'd entered the exact coordinates for the spot of Osmuna's death into his personal navigation unit. He'd done it for the purposes of making sure his report was complete and accurate, of course, but now it was going to serve a second, even more important purpose. With that for guidance, they could follow a cross-country course directly to the same place, and they set back out, moving steadily . . . and unbearably slowly. Someone's litter hung up on *something* every few moments, which made walking a straight line—difficult in this kind of terrain, under any circumstances—outright impossible. Only the coordinates in Jasak's nav unit made it possible to follow a reliable bearing towards their destination at all, and the terrain was actually rougher on their new heading.

Jasak winced inside every time one of his wounded men stumbled, or cursed under his breath, or blanched, flinching as an unexpected, leaf-hidden foot-trap jarred his ripped and torn flesh. As a first combat experience, it—and he—had been a dismal failure, he thought. Too many good men were wounded or dead, and he still had no answers. He hadn't prayed—really prayed, and meant it—in years, but he did now. He prayed no one else would die out here; that no one else would pay for his errors in judgment. And while he prayed, he moved among his men as they struggled forward, pausing to murmur an encouragement here, to jolly someone into a painful smile there, anything to keep them on their feet and moving forward.

He wasn't sure he'd made the right decision now, either. But he'd made it, for good or ill, and the sound of the stream, musical and lovely in the silence, was a blessed sound as it guided them across the last, weary stumbling yards to its banks several hours later.

The sun was barely a hand's width above the treetops when they finally caught sight of the rushing, sparkle-bright water. Jasak longed to fling himself down, surrender at least briefly to his fatigue and the pain of his own wounded side, give himself just a few moments of rest as a reward for getting his survivors this far. But this late in the season, and this far north, full darkness would be upon them quickly. The rescue party couldn't possibly reach them before nightfall, and probably not before dawn, and the night promised to be clear and cold. Some of his wounded would die before sunrise without a hot fire . . . and Jathmar would be among them.

So Jasak didn't fling himself down. Instead, he ordered his exhausted men to pitch camp. He put those still capable of heavy manual labor to work cutting enough firewood to keep half a dozen bonfires going all night, asked Gadrial to check on his own wounded as soon as she'd tended to Jathmar and Shaylar, and then got a work party of walking wounded organized to assemble the tiny two-man tents they used only during the worst rainstorms into a single tarpaulin large enough to shelter all of the critically injured.

Lance Inkar Jaboth got busy cobbling together a hot meal from trail rations, local wild plants, and what Jasak had always suspected was a dollop of magic. *Something* made the concoctions Jaboth whipped up for special occasions—and emergencies—not just edible, but actually *palatable*. Whatever it was, it would be a gift from the gods themselves, under conditions like these. Jasak wished it had been possible to detach someone to hunt game for the pot, but he'd needed every able-bodied man he still had just to transport the wounded. Besides, if there were soldiers close enough to that other portal, out there, Jasak might find himself facing counterattack tonight. Under the circumstances, he had no arbalest bolts to waste.

He set perimeter guards and established a sentry rotation that would take them through the night. He put his best, most reliable troopers on the graveyard watch, the long, cold hours between midnight and first dawn. The men were spooked enough, as it was; he didn't want some overwrought trooper with a bad case of vengeance on his mind firing an infantry-dragon at shadows. Or worse, at Otwal Threbuch, returning from the portal they'd come here to find.

By the time darkness fell, half a dozen small bonfires crackled, driving back the pitch-black shadows under the trees and warming the crisp night air. Jasak worried about providing a homing beacon for a possible enemy scouting force or counterattack, but they had to have the warmth. So he did his best by moving his sentries as far out as he dared, then saw to his people, pausing at each fire to speak with exhausted soldiers, praising their courage under fire and seeing that their wounds were properly dressed.

Those wounds horrified him.

The sheer amount of trauma made him wonder just how much force was behind those tiny lead lumps. None of the bland metal cylinders they'd found looked dangerous enough to cause this kind of damage. Some of the wounds they'd inflicted, like the one in his own stiffening, throbbing side, were long, shallow trenches gouged out of skin and muscle at the surface. Others were more serious. Korval, one of his assistant dragon gunners, would never have the use of his left hand again. Not, at least, without some very serious Gifted healing. Korval had just unwrapped the bloodied bandages, waiting white-faced while the water heated over the fires so the wound could be properly washed, as Jasak crouched down to look. The bones had shattered, and the muscles and tendons looked as if they had literally exploded from within.

Korval looked up, met his shocked gaze, and managed a wan smile.

"Could've been worse, Sir. Might've been through m'balls, eh?"

"Watch your language, Soldier," Jasak growled. "There are ladies present." But he gave Korval's shoulder a hard squeeze and said, "You did a damned fine job today, keeping that dragon crewed under heavy fire. I've never seen anyone operate an infantry-dragon one-handed. Frankly, I don't know how you did it. I'll send Ambor to dress that properly; there should be some herbs in his kit to help with pain, at least," he added.

"That'd be just fine with me, Sir," Korval said, and Jasak smiled and gave the wounded man's shoulder another squeeze.

Then he moved on, still smiling, while behind his expression he cursed his own decision to send his company surgeon back to the coast with Fifty Ulthar's platoon for R&R. Layrak Ambor was rated surgeon's assistant, but he was only an herbalist, with neither the trained skill of a field surgeon, nor a Gift. But he was doing his dead level best, and he was far better than nothing. However limited his skills might be, Jasak was thankful they had at least that much medical help to add to Gadrial's healing Gift.

The men who'd been shot through the body, rather than an extremity, were in serious condition. Most were still shock-pale, and the low moans of grievously wounded men, floating above the steady, musical tones of rushing water, left Jasak Olderhan feeling helpless and useless. Anything he could do for them was hopelessly inadequate, and while cursing Garlath relieved some of his own emotional pressure, it did nothing to ease their suffering.

He paused briefly at the makeshift tent where Ambor worked frantically to keep their worst casualties alive. When Jasak hunkered down beside him, the herbalist was nearly wild-eyed, overwhelmed by the sheer number of ghastly wounds he had to treat, and by the appalling number of lives held in his trembling hands.

"You're doing a fine job, Ambor," Jasak said quietly. "Under conditions like these, no one could do better. Where can Magister Kelbryan help the most?"

A little of the wild panic left Ambor's eyes. He swallowed, then looked around his charges, obviously thinking hard.

"Ask her to look after Nilbor and Urkins, if you would, Sir. They're in bad shape. Gut wounds, the both of them, Sir. Unconscious and in shock, despite everything I've tried, and they're getting weaker. Without the Magister—"

He shrugged helplessly, and Jasak nodded.

"I'll send her in immediately."

"Thank you, Sir."

Ambor looked and sounded steadier, and the heat of the fire just outside the casualty tent was beginning to take hold, radiating at least a fragile comfort over the semi-conscious wounded. Jasak paused for just a moment, looking back at the herbalist over his shoulder, then strode quickly back out into the darkness.

He found Gadrial kneeling beside his injured prisoners. The tender look on her face as she stroked Jathmar's scorched hair with gentle fingertips, sounding his pulse with her other hand, touched something deep inside Jasak. He, too, was worried about the unconscious man. Jathmar hadn't roused even once, although that might have been as much Gadrial's doing as the result of his injuries.

Gadrial looked up as Jasak approached Jathmar's litter, which someone had adjusted to float ten inches above the ground.

"You need me for someone else?" she asked, and he nodded, his expression unhappy at the demands he was placing upon her.

"How are you holding up?" he asked quietly, and her eyes widened, as though his question had surprised her. Then a smile touched her lips.

"I'm tired, Sir Jasak, but I'll manage. Where do you need me?"

"In the tent. We've got two men Ambor's losing—belly wounds, both of them. They've slipped into a coma."

She paled and bit her lower lip, then simply nodded and rose in one graceful, fluid motion he couldn't possibly have duplicated. He escorted her into the tent, then stepped back outside, giving her privacy to work.

He looked around the bivouac one last time, then inhaled deeply. He'd done everything he could to settle everyone safely, however little it felt like to him, and curiosity was riding him with spurs of fire. Since there wasn't much else he could do about any of their other problems, he decided he could at least scratch that itch, and pulled out some of the strange equipment they'd recovered, both from the stockade and from the massive toppled timber.

He took great care with the long, tubular weapons every man—and woman—had carried. There seemed to be several different types or varieties of them, and he rapidly discovered that they were intricate mechanical marvels, far more complex than any war staff his own people had built. Of course, war staffs—including the infantry and field-dragons which had been developed from them—were actually quite simple, mechanically speaking. They merely provided a place to store battle spells, and a sarkolis-crystal guide tube, down which the destructive spells were channeled on their way to the target.

Jasak had no idea what mysterious properties these tubular weapons operated upon. Nor could he figure out what many of the parts *did*, but he recognized precision engineering when he saw it.

A dragoon arbalest, like the one Otwal Threbuch favored, used a ten-round magazine and a spell-enhanced cocking lever. The augmented lever required a force of no more than twenty pounds to operate, and an arbalestier could fire all ten rounds as quickly as he could work the lever. It had almost as much punch—albeit over a shorter range—as the standard, single-shot infantry weapon, and a vastly higher rate of fire, but no man ever born was strong enough to throw the cocking lever once the enhancing spell was exhausted. Infantry weapons were much heavier, as well as bigger, and used a carefully designed *mechanical* advantage. They might be difficult to span without enhancement, but it could be done—which could be a decided advantage when the magic ran out—and they were considerably longer ranged.

The workmanship which went into a dragoon arbalest had always impressed Jasak, but the workmanship of whoever had built these weapons matched it, at the very least. Still, he would have liked to know what all of that craftsmanship *did*. Even the parts whose basic function he suspected he could guess raised far more questions than they answered.

For example, the weapon he was examining at the moment was about forty-two inches long, over all. The tube through which those small, deadly projectiles passed was shorter—only about twenty-four inches long—and it carried what he recognized as at least a distant cousin of the ring-and-post battle sights mounted on an arbalest. But the rear sight on *this* weapon was set in an odd metal block mounted on a sturdy, rectangular steel frame about one inch across. The sides of the rectangle were no more than a thirty-second of an inch across, as nearly as his pocket rule could measure, and its frame could either lie flat or be flipped up into a vertical position.

When it was flipped into the upright position, a *second* rear sight, set into the same metal block as the first, but at right angles, rotated up for the shooter's use. But the supporting steel rectangle was notched, and etched with tiny lines with some sort of symbols which (he suspected) were probably numbers, and the sight could be slid up and down the frame, locked into place at any one of those tiny, engraved lines by a spring-loaded catch that engaged in the side's notches.

Jasak had spent enough time on the arbalest range to know all about elevating his point of aim to allow for the drop in the bolt's trajectory at longer ranges. Unless he missed his guess, that was the function of *this* weapon's peculiar rear sight, as well. If so, it was an ingenious device, which was simultaneously simple in concept and very sophisticated in execution. But what frightened him about it was how high the rear sight could be set and the degree of elevation that would impose. Without a better idea of the projectiles' velocity and trajectory, he couldn't be certain, of course, but judging from the damage they'd inflicted, this weapon's projectiles must move at truly terrifying velocities. Which, in turn, suggested they would have a much flatter trajectory.

Which, assuming the sophisticated, intelligent people who'd designed and built it hadn't been in the habit of providing sights to shoot beyond the weapon's effective range, suggested that it must be capable of accurate shooting at ranges *far* in excess of any arbalest he'd ever seen.

There was a long metal oval underneath the weapon. It was obviously made to go up and down, and he suspected that it had to be something like the cocking lever on Threbuch's dragoon arbalest. In any case, he had absolutely no intention of fiddling with it until they were in more secure territory, away from potential enemy contact. And when he let the very tip of his finger touch the curved metal spur jutting down into the guarded space created by a curve in the metal oval, his fingertips jerked back of their own volition. That startled him, although only for a moment. Obviously, that curved spur was the weapon's trigger—it even looked like the trigger on one of his own men's arbalests—and his meager Gift was warning him that it was more dangerous than the cocking lever (if that is what it was).

The metal tube itself was made from high-grade steel, and when he peered—very cautiously—into it, adjusting it to get a little firelight into the hollow bore, he saw what looked like spiraling grooves cut into the metal. Interesting. The Arcanan Army understood the principle of spinning a crossbow bolt in flight to give it greater stability and accuracy. He couldn't quite imagine how it might work, but was it possible that those spiraling grooves could do the same thing to the deadly little leaden projectiles *this* thing threw?

He put that question aside and turned his attention to the snug wooden sleeve into which the tube had been fitted. It was held in place with three wide bands of metal that weren't steel. They looked like bronze, perhaps. The wood itself continued behind the tube to form a buttplate—again, not unlike an arbalest's—so a full third of the weapon's length was solid wood.

The long, tapering section of wood, narrowest near the tube, widest at the weapon's base, had been beautifully checkered by some intricate cutting process. It was the only decoration on the weapon, and it was obviously as much a practical design feature as pure decoration. As Jasak handled it, he realized that the checkering would serve exactly the same function as the fishscale pattern cut into the forestocks of arbalests, making them easier to grip in wet weather.

Other items ranged from the obvious—camp shovels, hatchets, backpacks—to the completely mysterious, and he gradually realized that what *wasn't* there was as interesting as what *was*. Although Jasak searched diligently, he found no trace of maps or charts anywhere in their gear. He found notebooks, with detailed botanical drawings and startlingly accurate sketches of wildlife, but no trace of a single chart.

The implication was clear; they'd realized—or, feared, at least—that their position was hopeless, so they'd destroyed the evidence of where they'd been. If they were, indeed, a civilian version of Jasak's Scouts, working to survey new universes and map new portals, they would have carried detailed charts that showed the route back to their home universe. From a military standpoint, losing those maps was a major disaster for Arcana. From a political standpoint . . .

Jasak thought about the reaction news of this battle was bound to trigger—particularly in places like rabidly xenophobic Mythal, whose politicians trusted no one, not even themselves. *Especially* not themselves. As he thought about them and their probable response, Jasak Olderhan was abruptly glad these people had destroyed their maps, even as the Andaran officer in him recoiled from such blatant heresy.

He told the Andaran officer to shut up, and that shocked him, too. Yet he couldn't help it, for a shiver had caught him squarely between the shoulder blades, an odd prescience quivering through him like a warning of bloodshed and disaster.

Than a log snapped in the fire, jolting him out of his eerie reverie, and the uncanny shiver passed, leaving him merely chilled in the night air. He rubbed the prickled hairs on the back of his neck, trying to smooth them down again, and his glance was caught by a small, flat circular object lying wedged into the box of jumbled gear at his feet. He picked it up, and was surprised by its weight. The object was made of metal, rolled or cast to form a strong metal casing. After fiddling with it for a couple of moments, he determined that the top section was a lid that unscrewed. He removed it . . . and stared.

Inside were two . . . machines, he decided, not knowing what else to call them. In the lid section, there was a glass cover that sealed off a thin metallic needle, flat and dark against a white background. Tiny hatchmarks were spaced evenly around the circular "face" with neat, almost military precision. More alien symbols—letters or numbers, he was certain—marked off eight points around the perimeter.

Someone moved beside the casualty tent, and Jasak glanced up, automatically checking to see if it had been Gadrial. It hadn't, and when he turned back to the device in his hand, his gaze snapped back to the needle. He'd moved the case with the rest of his body, but the needle—which appeared to be floating on a post, able to spin freely—hadn't moved with the rest of the case. Or, rather, it *had* moved, swinging stubbornly around to point in the same direction as before despite the case's movement.

The discovery startled him, so he experimented, and found that no matter how he turned the case around, the needle swung doggedly to point in the exact same direction: north.

Understanding dawned like a thunderclap. It was a *navigation* device. But this was no spell-powered personal crystal that oriented its owner to the cardinal directions, as every Arcanan compass ever built did. It was nothing but a flat needle on a post, an incredibly simple mechanical device, powered by nothing he could see. How the devil did it work?

The bottom section of the metal case was much heavier than the lid, providing most of the heft he'd noticed when he first picked it up. Clearly, it housed something dense, and this object, too, had a flat glass face, under which lay another dial with hatchmarks, and another series of letters or numbers of some kind, beside each of the twelve longest hatch lines. There were *three* needles on this device: a short one which scarcely seemed to move at all; a long one which moved slowly; and a very thin one that moved continuously, sweeping around the dial in endless circles.

Its purpose, too, came in a flash of understanding as the slow, audible click-click of the long needle reminded him of the changing numbers in his personal crystal's digital time display. Yet this was no spell-powered device, either. Or, he didn't think so, at any rate. He discovered a small knob at one side which could be pulled out slightly to change the positions of the needles, or simply turned in place. Turning it without pulling it out resulted in a slight clicking sound inside the device, and a gradually stiffening resistance which increased the pressure needed to turn the knob. He stopped before it got too stiff to turn at all, lest he damage it by trying to force it.

He laid the two halves of the case in his lap, gazing down at them in the firelight, and frowned in unhappy contemplation. He was no magister, but his touch of Gift should have been enough to at least recognize the presence of any sort of spellware. Yet he hadn't detected even the slightest twitch of magic. He would have liked to believe that that meant the weapons he'd examined had exhausted whatever powered them, but he knew that wasn't the case.

Instead, what he had was a weapon which had amply proved its deadly efficiency; a navigation device which, for all its simplicity, looked damnably effective; and another device which obviously kept very precise track of time, indeed.

And none of them—not *one* of them—depended on spellware or a Gift. Which meant they would work for anyone, anytime, anywhere.

The night wind blew suddenly chill, indeed.

CHAPTER
TWELVE

THE SUN HAD disappeared into darkness when Windclaw
reached the swamp portal camp after almost seven arduous
hours of high-speed flight. There were few landmarks to navigate by,
but the camp's scattered lights stood out sharply against the unre-
lieved blackness of a world mankind had discovered considerably
less than a year earlier.

Windclaw backwinged neatly to a landing between the base camp's
tents and the portal itself. An icy breeze blew across the camp from
the portal, rustling the dead trees that speared into the sky on the
other side, rattling the reeds on this one. The vast sweep of black-
velvet heaven visible above the trees revealed brilliant stars, in an
unnerving northern constellation pattern, vastly different from the
southern skies it was pasted across.

It didn't seem to matter how many portals Salmeer saw or stepped
through; the spine-tingling awe never changed, and he'd been flying
portal hops for the better part of thirty years.

Windclaw had barely furled his wings when a soldier ran across
the muddy ground, holding what proved to be the transcript of
another hummer message. He climbed up the foreleg Windclaw had
been trained to offer, and Salmeer recognized him. He didn't know
Javelin Krankark especially well, but he'd always impressed Salmeer
as a competent trooper, utterly dedicated not only to the Second
Andaran Scouts, but also to Hundred Olderhan.

"Thank the gods you're here, Squire!" Krankark panted as he
handed Salmeer the transcript. "The hundred's halted at these grid
coordinates. He didn't dare keep moving his wounded after dark. He
needs you to bring the dragon through for an emergency evacuation
of the worst wounded."

Salmeer stared at Krankark in disbelief. He hadn't taken Windclaw through the portal, but he'd made enough deliveries to the base camp when it was daylight on the far side to have a pretty fair grasp of the sort of terrain—and tree cover—waiting on the other side.

"Is he out of his mind?" the pilot demanded harshly. "He wants me to try to set a *dragon* down out in the middle of those fucking *woods*?"

"You can't do it?" The javelin's expression was barely visible in the darkness, but the horror in his voice was clear, and Salmeer winced. The critically wounded men out there were this man's brothers in arms, the closest thing he had to a family out here.

"I've seen that canopy out there, and it's murder," the pilot said in a marginally gentler voice, waving one hand at the looming portal. "I haven't actually flown over it, not in *that* universe, anyway. But I've seen plenty of forests like it. That's a solid sea of trees, Krankark, stretching for hundreds of miles. A transport dragon can't slide sideways between branches that are damned near interwoven!"

"Is that all?" Krankark replied, hope glittering in his voice once more. "The hundred said he's camped along an open stream. He says there's plenty of wing room for a skilled dragon to get in and take off again."

"'*Skilled dragon*,' huh?" Salmeer muttered, interpreting that phrase to mean there was just enough clear space for it to be dangerous as hell, but doable . . . if your set was big enough, and your brain *small* enough, to try it.

In, of course, the opinion of a man who wasn't—and never had been—a qualified dragon pilot himself.

There are old pilots, and there are bold pilots, but there are no old, bold pilots. The flight school training mantra ran through the back of his mind, and he hovered on the brink of refusing. After all, Windclaw was an incredibly valuable asset out here. If Salmeer flew him into a treetop, then the possibility of evacuating *any* of the wounded to Fort Rycharn went straight out the window.

"Just how many casualties are there?" he asked, temporizing while common sense fought against his own sense of urgency.

Krankark's muscles seemed to congeal. The javelin went absolutely motionless, and his voice went wooden and hollow.

"There were twenty-one. There are only twenty now. Hundred Olderhan took a full platoon through the portal—sixty-seven men, counting the supports. Twenty-five of them are dead now."

"Mother Jambakol's eyelashes!" The filthy curse broke loose before he could stop it, and he made a furtive sign to ward off "Mother Jambakol's" evil glance.

"Please, Sir." Krankark gripped his arm. "Please, at least *try*," he begged. "All the hundred's got out there is an herbalist. We've got men unconscious, and the hundred says Ambor can't bring them out of the coma. . . ."

Krankark's voice shook, and Sword Morikan leaned forward behind Salmeer's shoulder.

"Their situation's desperate, Sir. You've got to get me to those men. I can't heal that many with magic alone, but I can save the most critically wounded, and we've got trained surgeons for the others. Except that unless I get there soon—and from the sound of it, we're talking about minutes, not hours—the death count's going to get worse. Feel that wind blowing through the portal? Badly wounded men won't last the night in that, even with a good hot campfire."

Salmeer swore again.

"All right. All right, I'll get you there, Sword. I won't take Windclaw in unless *I* decide there's enough room to get airborne again, but I'll lower you through the trees on a frigging *rope*, if I have to."

Morikan nodded sharply, and Salmeer looked past the healer at the two surgeons and the herbalists.

"I need to lighten the payload, especially if I've got wounded to haul out," he said. "You two dismount and wait for us here."

One of the surgeons looked a question at Morikan, who nodded again, as sharply as before.

"Go ahead, Traith," he said. "I'll take Vormak and two of the herbalists with me; you and the other two can set up here and be ready to work by the time the Squire and I get back. Don't worry," he smiled grimly, "it sounds like we're all going to have plenty to keep us occupied."

Salmeer snorted in bitter amusement and agreement, then turned back to Krankark as two of the herbalists and the surgeon Morikan had addressed began unstrapping and climbing down with their equipment.

"Okay, Javelin. You've convinced me," he said. "Jump down so I can get this boy airborne." The pilot smiled thinly. "Hell, he may just be crazy enough to actually try landing if I ask him to!"

He took the printout the javelin thrust into his hand, with the all-important coordinates of Hundred Olderhan's camp. Then, the moment Krankark and the others were clear, Salmeer patted Windclaw's neck and urged the dragon back aloft.

Windclaw took a running start, snapped his great wings wide, and lifted slowly, rumbling into the air across the open campsite. Windclaw needed nearly a hundred yards just to reach treetop height, because he was big, even for a transport dragon. That gave him lots of lifting power, but he was simply too large and too slow to lift off on his tail, the way some of the smaller fighting dragons could. The fighters—especially the ones bred to go after enemy gryphons—had to be fast and agile, since gryphons were small, swift, and brutally difficult to catch in midair.

Salmeer didn't usually mind Windclaw's lack of agility. Tonight, though, it might pose a major problem. But it might not, too, he reminded himself loyally, for he was proud of his dragon. He and Windclaw didn't share any sort of special bond, like the ones bred into some of the more spectacularly expensive pets wealthy Arcanans sometimes commissioned. No pilot or dragon did. But he'd come to know his beast's moods and temperament. They'd come to . . . respect one another, and Windclaw was fond enough of him—in a dragonish sort of way—to make their working relationship satisfying on both sides, and tonight, Windclaw's decades of experience might just make up for his lack of nimbleness.

Now Salmeer whistled sharply, and the dragon made a wide circle, building speed as he flew. Starlight and moonlight burnished his wings with a metallic shimmer, glittering as they touched the elaborate wing patterns that represented Windclaw's pedigree, as well as his current unit assignment. They swept around toward the opening between universes, gaining speed and more altitude with every wing stroke. By the time he actually reached the portal, Windclaw was moving at very nearly his top velocity and climbing steeply to clear the trees on its far side.

They flashed through the portal, with the inevitable pop of equalizing air pressure in one's inner ear; then they were climbing through clear, cold night air. Windclaw straightened the angle of his climb and leveled out, cruising through a crystalline night sky ablaze with stars and a wondrous moon which wasn't the same one they'd left behind.

Salmeer tapped his personal crystal with the spell-powered stylus that allowed him to plug in Hundred Olderhan's grid coordinates, even though Salmeer himself had no Gift at all, and the crystal obediently displayed a standard navigational grid, with the familiar compass points in a sphere around the circle that represented Windclaw. A blinking green arrow pointed the direction to fly, giving Salmeer a beautifully clear, easy-to-read three-dimensional display to follow. When they reached the target zone, a steady red circle would appear, directly at the grid coordinates Hundred Olderhan had sent.

But before that red circle appeared, they had a good, swift bit of flying to do . . . not to mention the minor matter of figuring out how to thread the needle and land a dragon Windclaw's size, in the middle of the night, along the banks of a frigging *stream*, of all godsdamned things!

Squire Muthok Salmeer shook his head, not quite able to believe even now that he'd agreed to this. Then he set himself to ignore the biting chill and concentrated instead on the warmth of the extra layer of clothes under his flying jacket and a truly spectacular sky awash with brilliant stars.

*   *   *

Shaylar awoke to darkness, confusion, and the scent of woodsmoke. For long moments, she lay completely still, trying to figure out where she was. She remembered the attack, the frightful cremation of the dead, the strange device they'd used to lift Jathmar and their other wounded on floating stretchers. She even remembered walking beside Jathmar, holding his hand as they evacuated the contact area. But she couldn't figure out where she was now, which suggested a prolonged period of unconsciousness. That made sense, although very little else did. Her head still throbbed with a fierce rhythm, and she still couldn't hear Jathmar, but she felt more rested, which was a mercy.

Unfortunately, she was also beginning to feel the bruises and contusions where that last fireball had blasted her into the fallen tree. Her face was painfully scraped along one cheek and jaw, and the deep abrasions stung like fire. Bruises left that whole side of her face swollen, and they were probably a lurid shade of purple-black by now. She reached up to touch the damage, only to abort the movement when her entire shoulder locked up. A white-hot lance of fire shot straight up the side of her neck, and she hissed aloud in pain.

Someone spoke practically into her ear, and she gasped in surprise, skittered sideways—

—and promptly rolled off the edge of whatever she'd been lying on. She bit off a scream, but the fall to the ground was only about ten inches. Which was still more than enough to knock the wind out of her and jar her painfully, especially with her previous injuries.

Whoever had spoken leaned over her almost before she landed, making worried sounds that quickly turned soothing. Gentle hands straightened her bent limbs and tested her pulse, and Shaylar whimpered, cursing the pain that exploded through her with every movement.

Her eyes opened, and she looked up.

She couldn't remember his name, but she knew his face: the enemy commander. He was speaking softly to her, his gaze worried and intense. She hissed aloud and flinched back when he touched the bruises along her jaw with a gentle finger, and his face drained white at the pain sound. What was obviously a stuttering apology broke from him, and she wanted to reassure him. But the unending pain and fear and the silence in her mind left her weak, and far too susceptible to new shocks. She was horrified to discover that all she could do was lie on the cold ground and weep large, silent tears that stung her eyes and clogged her nose.

He bit his lip, then very carefully lifted her. Even through her misery, she was astonished by his strength. She knew she wasn't a large woman, but he lifted her as easily as if she'd been a child, and he held her as if she'd been one, too. A part of her was bitterly ashamed of her weakness, but as he held her close, she rested the undamaged side of her face against his broad shoulder.

He'd been wounded himself, her muzzy memory told her, yet there was no evidence of any discomfort on his part as he held her. He didn't rock her, didn't croon any lullabies, didn't even speak. He simply held her, and despite everything, despite even the fact that he was the commander of the men who'd massacred her entire survey team, there was something immensely comforting about the way he did it.

Perhaps, a small, lucid corner of her brain thought, her Talent was still working, at least a little. That was the only explanation she could think of for why she should feel so safe, so . . . protected in the arms of these murderers' commanding officer.

She was never clear afterward on how long he held her, but, finally, her tears slowed, then stopped. He held her a moment longer, then very carefully placed her back onto one of the eerie, floating stretchers. When she began to shiver, he produced something like a sleeping bag, which he tucked around her. Then he moved her entire stretcher with a single touch, guiding it closer to a bonfire that warmed her deliciously within moments.

The shivers eased away, leaving her limp and exhausted, but she didn't go back to sleep. Her mind was strangely alert, yet wrapped in fog. It was a disquieting sensation, but she found it easier to cope if she just relaxed and let herself drift, rather than struggling to make everything come clear. Thinking clearly was obviously important, perhaps even critical, in her current predicament, but she couldn't see any sense in struggling to do something physically impossible at the moment.

So she lay still on her strange, floating bed, and wondered in a distant, abstracted sort of way, how these people made their stretchers float. There was no logical explanation for it, any more than there were logical explanations for the other mysteries she'd already witnessed: glassy tubes that threw fireballs with no visible source of flame. Seemingly identical tubes that hurled lightning, instead of fire. The odd little cubes that had somehow packed enough explosive force to immolate an entire human body—yet did so without any actual explosion, just a sudden and inexplicable burst of flame.

Sorcery, the back of her wounded brain whispered, and Shaylar was so befuddled, so lost in this unending bad dream, that she didn't even quibble with her own choice of words. Whatever these people used for technology, it looked, sounded, and even smelled like magic. At least, it did to her admittedly addled senses.

As she drifted there in the darkness, she gradually became aware of something else. The scent of food tickled her nostrils, and despite the pounding in her head and the lingering bite of nausea in her throat, sudden, ravening hunger surged to life. The last food she'd eaten had been a hastily bolted lunch, just before Falsan staggered into camp and died in her arms. She had no idea how long ago that had been, or what time it was now, but the stars were brilliant overhead, and the moon was high, nearly straight overhead. It had obviously been up for hours.

It was the middle of the night, then, which left her puzzled by the smell of something cooking over a fire. Most people tramping about in the wilderness did their cooking early in the evening, at or shortly after sundown. But then the commander returned to her, with a bowl and spoon. He smiled and said something that sounded reassuring, and helped her sit up. Her stretcher continued to float, rock steady despite the fact that it was only canvas and ought to have shifted as she moved. Its motionlessness was yet another strangeness she couldn't understand . . . and didn't want to think about yet.

She would much rather think about the contents of the bowl. When he handed it to her, after making sure she was able to grip it, she discovered a surprisingly thick stew, with what looked and smelled like wild carrots—thin and pale golden in the firelight—chunks of what might have been rabbit, and other things she couldn't readily identify. She took a tentative taste, unsure how her uneasy stomach would react to food, and was instantly transported to a state of near-ecstasy.

She actually moaned aloud, wondering how any camp cook could create something this magnificent under such primitive conditions.

Then she forgot everything else in this or any other universe and simply *ate*. Flavors rich and savory with spices she couldn't identify exploded across her tongue, and the hot food warmed her from the inside out. Some of the pounding in her head eased as her body responded to its first nourishment in hours, and she didn't even mind the savage ache in her bruised jaw when she chewed.

By the time she'd ravened her way through the entire bowl, she felt almost human again. A battered and bedamned one, but human, nonetheless. When she lifted her head, she found the enemy commander watching her, his expression wavering between intense curiosity, pleasure at how much she'd obviously enjoyed the food, deep concern, and lingering guilt. She looked back at him for several seconds, and his name finally floated to the surface of her memory.

"Jasak?" she asked tentatively, and his eyes lit with pleasure.

"Jasak," he agreed, nodding. He touched his chest and added, "Olderhan. Jasak Olderhan."

He waited expectantly, and Shaylar considered the intricacies of Shurkhali married names. Better to opt for simplicity, she decided.

"Shaylar Nargra," she said, and he repeated her name carefully, then glanced at Jathmar. His stretcher floated less than a yard from hers, close enough to the fire to keep him warm, and someone had laid a lightweight cover over him, so that the blistered skin and scorched clothing wasn't visible. He was still unconscious though, which terrified her, and her eyes burned.

"Jathmar Nargra," she said through a suddenly constricted throat, and an expression of profound contrition washed across Jasak Olderhan's face.

He said something, then gestured helplessly, unable to convey what he obviously wanted to tell her. His frustration with the insurmountable language barrier was obvious, and he took her hand, trying to reassure her.

Shaylar stiffened in shock. She remained Voiceless, yet his emotions were so powerful, so strong and uncontrolled, that they rolled through her like thunder anyway. It was all she could do not to jerk her hand away from that sudden, roiling tide, but she didn't dare antagonize him, and she could learn more—much more—when he touched her. If he became aware he was transmitting information, he would almost certainly stop doing it, and she couldn't risk that. The understanding she might glean was the tiniest of weapons, but it was also the only one she had.

He was speaking in low, earnest tones, and she fought the blackness and pain in her head, soaking in as much information as she could.

He was trying to help them. There was a sense of waiting for something or someone, with a feeling of great importance and urgency behind the need to wait. Someone was coming, she realized with a sense of shock. Someone who could help.

It shouldn't have surprised her, she realized a moment later. This universe didn't strike her as the home of these people. Contact with Jasak Olderhan reinforced that impression, but if they were as much strangers to this universe as Shaylar's survey crew had been, who was coming? More soldiers, undoubtedly—Jasak must have sent a message to another group of his people. But how *many* more soldiers? And from where?

Shaylar had no idea how his message had gone out. Did these people have a Voice with them? Or had Olderhan been forced to send a messenger on foot? In either case, they needed medical help urgently, given the seriousness of Jathmar's injuries and how many wounded Olderhan had. Yet he was waiting here, rather than pushing on. The help he expected must be close, then, however he'd summoned it. She didn't know whether to feel relieved that help for Jathmar might arrive soon, or alarmed by the threat another, probably larger, military force posed to Darcel Kinlafia and to Company-Captain Halifu's understrength force.

Once more, she tried desperately to contact Darcel, but her Voice remained nothing but a black whirlpool of pain and disorienting vertigo. The effort to establish contact turned the whirlpool into a thundering maelstrom so intense, so jagged with anguish, she actually cried out.

She jerked back, breaking contact with Olderhan to clutch at her temples and bend forward on the stretcher, hunched over with the torment in her head. And then she felt large, capable hands cradle her face. Fingers rubbed gently above her pounding temples, then moved down to her neck, where her muscles had knotted painfully. They massaged with surprising gentleness and skill, and she could sense Olderhan's genuine horror at the sudden onslaught of her pain, as well as his anxiousness to alleviate it.

That helped, as well, but her strength abruptly faded away to nothing. One moment, she was sitting up with Olderhan's fingers rubbing her neck; the next, she lay draped bonelessly against a broad chest once more, cheek pillowed against his shoulder yet again. She hated her own weakness. Hated the injuries that left her reeling in confusion, helpless to do *anything*.

She felt a tentative touch on her hair. The effort to use her Voice had scrambled her ability to sample his emotions once more, but he spoke to her, the words low and soothing, and it felt as if he were making vows of some sort. Promises to protect, or perhaps to defend; she couldn't grasp the nuances with no words or shared concepts, and with her Talent so crippled. Still, it was sufficiently reassuring to leave her limp against his shoulder, at least for the moment.

She'd rested against him for quite some time. She was actually drifting back towards sleep once more, when they were abruptly interrupted. A strange sound penetrated her awareness—a rhythmic flapping, like someone shaking out the largest carpet ever woven. Then someone shouted, and Olderhan responded with what sounded and felt like intense relief. He eased her back down onto the stretcher and hurried to the edge of the broad stream their camp had been pitched beside.

He stood there, peering out into the stream. But, no, she realized, that wasn't quite right. He was peering *above* the stream, with his head tipped back. He stared up at the stars, and the sound of shaken cloth was louder, much louder. Within moments, it had changed from rhythmic flapping to equally rhythmic thunder. A huge, black shadow swooped suddenly between Olderhan and the stars, then an overpressure of air blasted across the camp. The bonfires flared wildly as sparks, ash, and scattered autumn leaves flew before the whirlwind, and she jerked her gaze upward.

Scales, like a crocodile's armored hide in glowing, iridescent colors like shoaling fish. Immense wings, so thin the firelight glowed through them. Bats' wings the size of the sails on a ninety-foot twin-masted schooner. Claws, a foot long and razor-sharp, glittering bronze as they reached down to grasp boulders in the stream when it landed. A long, sinuous neck, like a serpent twenty feet long, still as thick as her own torso where it met the triangular, adder-shaped head. Spikes, immense spikes, jutting out over eyes of crimson flame, and an eagle's beak of metallic bronze, sparkling in the wildly flaring firelight.

Its mouth opened, revealing rows of sickle-bladed teeth, and it was looking directly at *her*. Shaylar's wounded mind shrieked at her to run, even as she sensed an alien, inhuman presence behind those fiery eyes, malevolent and barely under control.

The nightmare apparition hissed. The sound was an angry steam-engine shriek, and Shaylar flinched back, drew breath to scream—

—and the man strapped to its neck spoke sharply. He emphasized his words with a jab from an implement that looked part-cattle prod and part-harpoon. It would have to be sharp, she realized through waves of unreasoning terror, to make itself—and its owner's displeasure—felt through hide that tough.

Wings rattled angrily, like agitated snakes, and the prod came down again, sharper and harder than before. The beast reared skyward and let out a shriek of rage that battered Shaylar's bleeding senses. She did scream, this time, and cowered down with both arms over her head—not to keep the creature's teeth off her neck, but to keep its fury out of her mind.

She heard men's voices raised in angry shouts and what sounded like bafflement. Someone touched her shoulder, and she flinched, then realized it was Gadrial. The other woman seemed as baffled as the men—baffled, surprised, still half-asleep. But she also seemed determined to interpose her own body between Shaylar and the enraged beast in the streambed if that was what it took to protect her.

*   *   *

Gadrial cradled Shaylar in a protective embrace, blinking in still-sleepy confusion and utterly perplexed. She'd never personally seen an angry dragon, but that was the only way to describe this one, and it was glaring unnervingly straight at her. Or, rather, she amended, at *Shaylar*. The injured young woman was trembling, and Gadrial spoke quietly, soothingly, stroking her hair while she felt the tremors rippling through that slender body. Fear had stiffened Shaylar's muscles so tightly the tremors were like an earthquake shaking solid stone.

She's been through too much in too little time, Gadrial thought grimly. *No wonder she's all but hysterical!*

Despite the distance to the streambed's edge, Gadrial could hear Sir Jasak speaking with the dragon's pilot. They could probably hear him back at the base camp, she thought, and the pilot didn't look too happy at being on the receiving end of the . . . discussion. But then Jasak paused, hands on hips, head cocked, and the pilot shook his head.

*   *   *

"I've never seen Windclaw react like that, Sir," Muthok Salmeer said. "Never! He's an old fellow, smart as a transport dragon gets, with plenty of lessons in good manners. He's no war dragon, to be hissing at everyone but his pilot. He's spent his entire life in Transport and Search and Rescue work. It beats hell out of me, Hundred, and that's no lie. It's like he took one look at the girl there, and went berserk."

The squire's tone sounded as confused and upset as Jasak felt. It was obvious Salmeer was completely and totally perplexed, but the pilot had reacted quickly and decisively to his dragon's impossible-to-predict rage. That fact, coupled with his obvious concern, disarmed much of Jasak's initial fury.

The hundred made himself step back mentally and draw a deep breath. He glanced back at his prisoner, who sat huddled against Gadrial. Shaylar looked up, her face ashen as she risked a glance at Windclaw, then instantly pressed her face back against the magister, and he frowned as he got past his immediate reaction and started considering the implications of the dragon's behavior.

"That's . . . interesting, Muthok," he said after a moment, turning back to the pilot. "Damned interesting."

"You don't have any idea who they are, Sir?" Salmeer asked. "You could've knocked me down with a puff of air when that hummer message arrived, and that's a fact."

"No, we don't know who they are. But I intend to find out, and we won't do that if we lose them. The girl's hurt—I don't know how badly—but the man's critical. He won't last the night if we don't get him to a true healer, and some of my own men are almost as bad."

"Then it's a good thing I brought you one, Sir," Salmeer said with a smile. He gestured to the passengers still strapped to the saddles on Windclaw's back, and Jasak's eyes followed the gesture. The dragon's reaction to Shaylar had kept him from paying much attention to Windclaw's other riders, but now his face lit with delight as he recognized Sword Morikan.

"Naf!"

"Good to see you on your feet, Sir," the healer replied. "And Muthok brought more than just me. I've got Vormak and two good herbalists riding the evacuation deck, and Traith and two more herbalists are waiting back at the base camp. Muthok needed to lighten Windclaw, and I figured it would be better to avoid doing any surgery we don't absolutely have to do out here. It's a hell of a lot warmer on that side of the portal, and we'll have tents to work in, as well."

"Good man!" Jasak said, nodding hard. "Good work, both of you."

"Least we could do, Sir," Salmeer said. "On the other hand, this isn't exactly what I'd call a proper landing ground you've got out here, if you'll pardon my saying so. We can probably take out most of your critically wounded now, but getting airborne before we run into the trees is going to be tricky, and Windclaw's already flown a long way today. He's going to need at least several hours' rest after we get back to camp, so we'll have to come back for the others tomorrow." His eyes glinted. "Next time you decide to fight a battle, Sir, try to pick a spot easier to get dragons into, eh?"

"I'll bear that in mind," Jasak replied, with a smile he hoped didn't look forced. Then he smiled more naturally. "And I'm more grateful than you'll ever know to you for reaching us this quickly."

Jasak angled his head up to watch as Morikan, the surgeon, and the herbalists started to dismount. They hauled their gear down Windclaw's shoulder, then stepped across from his foreleg to the stream bank, where several of First Platoon's troopers waited to help them with their baggage.

Firelight caught the dragon's iridescent scales and set him aglow when he rustled his wing pinions or took a breath. He still looked agitated, and the sound of his breathing, the deep rush of air through cavernous lungs which no one could ever forget, once he'd heard it, was faster than usual. It was also higher pitched, almost whistling.

It's the sound a fighting dragon makes just before battle, Jasak realized with a sudden, shocking flash of insight. Humanity hadn't pitted dragons against one another in almost two centuries, and no one living had ever heard that pre-battle steam-kettle sound. Not in earnest, at any rate. But it had been too frequently described in the history books and the aerial training volumes—even in those silly romances his younger sister mooned over—for him to mistake what he was hearing now.

Which didn't make any more sense than all the other impossible things which had already happened this day.

Jasak stared up at the furious transport beast towering over him, and wondered a little wildly what had set off Windclaw's battle stress. Salmeer had been right about one thing, though; he was sure of that. Shaylar Nargra was the source of the dragon's anger. Yet what in all the myriad universes about that terrified, injured girl could cause a dragon to react so violently to her mere presence?

The question simmered in the back of his brain. Intuition and logic alike argued that it was an important one, but he had more immediately urgent problems at the moment.

"Can you keep him under control well enough to put her on his back?" he asked Salmeer, twitching his head at Shaylar. "Her and the others?"

The pilot had been gazing at Shaylar, as well, obviously asking himself the same questions which had occurred to Jasak. Now he refocused his attention on the hundred, and his jaw muscles bunched.

"Oh, yeah, Sir. I'll keep him in line, all right. He might get around some greenhorn handler, but he won't try any tricks with me. If I might make a suggestion, though, Hundred?"

"Suggest away," Jasak said with a sharp nod. "You know your beast—and your job—better than I ever will."

Salmeer's eyes narrowed, as if Jasak's tone had surprised him. Then he twitched his own head in Shaylar's direction.

"Put her up last," he said. "He won't try anything that would endanger his passengers once he's got wounded aboard. He's a smart old beast, Windclaw is, Sir, and he knows his duty. He's responsible for the safe transport of wounded men, and he knows it. Not like a man would, you understand, but he's smarter than any dog you'll ever own, and dogs are smart enough to look out for those under their care."

"Yes, they are. It's a good suggestion, Muthok, and one I appreciate. Deeply."

Salmeer ducked his head in an abbreviated nod of acknowledgment, then gave Jasak a grim little smile.

"I've answered the call of more than a few commanders of one hundred, Sir, and I'll tell you plain—you're the first who's ever given a good godsdamn about the opinions of a transport pilot."

Jasak frowned, his gaze locking with Salmeer's, and his nostrils flared.

"I can't say that fact makes me very happy, Muthok. But thank you for the information. It won't be wasted."

Salmeer blinked. Then his eyes narrowed as he remembered whose son he was speaking to. Jasak saw the memory in the pilot's eye and felt a flicker of harsh inner amusement.

No, Muthok, he thought. *It* won't *be wasted, I assure you.*

The Duke of Garth Showma, who also happened to be Commander of Five Thousand Thankhar Olderhan (retired), would light quite a few fires under certain officers when *that* piece of intelligence hit his desk. Officers too haughty—or stupid—to consider the insights of specialists with experience far superior to their own were officers who got their men killed when things went to hell.

Rather like I *managed to do this afternoon*, he thought, and felt his face tighten for an instant.

Salmeer met Jasak's gaze for a moment longer, almost as if he could hear the younger man's thoughts, then gave him a sharp salute.

"You take care of the wounded then, Sir. I'll start prepping the platform cocoons."

Jasak nodded, then turned as Naf Morikan finished passing his own equipment over to Sword Harnak and waded ashore.

Morikan was a North Shalomarian—one of the towering variety. A big, rawboned man, nearly six-foot-seven in his bare feet, he still managed to move so quietly, almost noiselessly, that Jasak had sometimes wondered if it was a part of his Gift. The healer had huge shoulders, enormous physical strength, and a Gift for healing which made the hulking giant one of the gentlest souls Jasak had ever known. He'd never pursued the research necessary to earn the formal title of magistron, the healer's equivalent of Gadrial's magister's rank, so he was technically only a journeyman, which also explained why he wasn't a commissioned officer in the Healer's Corps, himself. But Jasak wasn't about to complain about that today. Not when it meant having a healer as powerfully Gifted as Morikan out at the sharp end when the remnants of First Platoon needed one so desperately.

"It's good to see you, Naf," he said quietly, clasping the sword's hand. "I've got four men in comas, and one of them's the only male survivor from the people we ran into out here. That girl there," he pointed at Shaylar, "was with him."

Morikan's eyes glinted. Jasak could almost physically feel the questions simmering under the big noncom's skin, but the healer visibly suppressed them.

"Five Hundred Klian wants a full briefing, Sir. I'm dying of curiosity myself, for that matter. But that can wait, and the wounded can't. Which one is most critical?"

Jasak led him straight to Jathmar. Morikan knelt beside the injured man's litter, then hissed aloud when he touched him.

"Gods, Sir! I'm a *healer*, not a miracle worker! He's holding on by a thread! And it's so frayed, it's about to snap!"

"You think I don't know that?" Jasak snapped back. "Magister Gadrial is the only reason he's still alive at all!"

The big healer looked up, then whistled softly.

"Magister *Gadrial* kept him alive? With nothing but a minor arcana for healing?" He glanced at Gadrial, who'd given him a demonstration of her minor Gift when she'd first arrived in-universe. "Magister, you have my deep respect, ma'am. I wouldn't have believed this was possible."

He gestured at Jathmar, and Gadrial nodded to him across Shaylar's shoulder.

"Thank you," she said quietly. "And for Rahil's sake, do whatever it takes to save him. I'm convinced he's this girl's husband." She tightened her embrace around Shaylar, who was watching them, her hazy eyes wide and frightened. "She's hurt, herself, and she's in a fragile state. If she loses him—"

The magister broke off, her mouth tight, and Morikan nodded in comprehension.

"Their last names are the same," Jasak added. "I found that out when she woke up. They're either married or brother and sister, and I'm inclined to agree with Magister Gadrial's theory that they're married."

The big healer looked into Shaylar's eyes, took in the ghastly bruises that had turned half her face into a swollen, black mass of pain, and his jaw turned to granite.

"Start getting your less critically wounded onto the dragon, Sir Jasak," he said briskly. "I'll tend to them once we get back to the base camp, but I don't dare wait that long with this one."

Jasak nodded tightly and turned away to begin giving orders, and Naf Morikan crouched down over Jathmar's still form. He drew a deep breath, closed his eyes, and reached out, summoning the healing trance that gave him the power to work the occasional miracle.

*   *   *

Shaylar had no clear idea what the giant leaning over her husband was doing, but it was obvious he was the person Jasak Olderhan had been waiting for so anxiously. The newcomer was so huge he reminded her painfully of Fanthi chan Himidi, but the difference in his personality and chan Himidi's was blindingly evident, even to her presently crippled Talent. Chan Himidi had been one of Shaylar's dearest friends, yet she'd always been aware of his capacity for violence. Trained and disciplined, it had always been firmly under control, yet it had always been there, as well.

This man might wear the uniform of a soldier, and his personality was certainly just as strong as chan Himidi's had ever been, but *his* battles weren't the sort one fought with weapons.

The newcomer had lifted the blanket off Jathmar's burnt back and hissed aloud at the damage he'd found. But he didn't appear to be *doing* anything else at all. He was just kneeling there, hands extended over Jathmar's stretcher, eyes unfocused, staring at nothing. . . .

And then, suddenly, Jathmar began to *glow*.

Shaylar gasped. Light poured from the big man's hands, enveloping Jathmar's entire body. Then, despite the whirling black pain in her head, the marriage bond roared wide. Shaylar flinched violently in Gadrial's arms as Jathmar's pain blasted through her. She sensed Gadrial's sudden twitch of hurt as her fingers sank deep into the other woman's upper arms, but she couldn't help it. Her back was a mass of fire, her chest a broken heap of agony wrapped around ribs shattered like china someone had dropped to the floor, and her insides were bleeding.

Then she felt an odd presence, like a tide of warm syrup flowing over her—*into* her—and there was intelligence in the syrup. There were thoughts and emotions, a sense of awe that she was alive at all, and a determination to *keep* her among the living.

A soothing wave of light and energy she could sense but couldn't see sank down into her blistered back. The sensations were soul-shaking. She could literally feel her skin growing as blisters popped, drained, vanished. The damage ran deep . . . and so did whatever was sinking into her, repairing the deep layers of skin and tissue damaged in the hellish vortex of the enemy's fire.

It sank deeper still, down into her bleeding abdomen. She felt half-glued wounds knitting themselves together as new tissue closed the gaps and fissures in blood vessels, intestinal walls, muscles and organs. Pain flashed through her, bright and terrible, as ribs shifted, moving on their own, grating back into proper alignment. She writhed, whimpering, and the pain in her chest burst free in an agonized cry.

*   *   *

Shaylar's sudden scream yanked Naf Morikan straight out of the healing trance. His head whipped around, and he stared, shaken and confused, as Shaylar writhed in Gadrial's arms. Motion under his hands jerked his attention back to Jathmar, and his eyes went wider still as he realized Jathmar was moving in exactly the same way.

"What the living hell is going on?" the healer breathed in shock.

"I don't know," Gadrial Kelbryan gasped, her own face wrung with pain from the crushing grip of Shaylar's daggered fingers as they sank into her biceps. "I don't know, but for pity's sake, man, *finish the job!* They're both in agony!"

The magister was right, and Morikan returned to the trance. He was shaken, intrigued, and utterly mystified, but he forced all of that aside, out of the forefront of his attention, and reached out to that healing flood of power once more.

Now that Jathmar was semi-conscious, the healer took care to stimulate the centers of the brain and spinal cord that produced natural pain killers. The patient's body flooded with his own internally produced pain-fighting serum in moments, which quickly put an end to his semi-aware thrashing about, and Morikan was dimly aware that his wife's cries had faded as well.

By the time the job was done, Morikan felt as if he'd spent the day slogging through a jungle under a hundred-pound pack. But Jathmar's grievous wounds were healed, and the healer let his hands drop into his lap.

"He's sleeping naturally." He sighed, sitting up from his hunched position over the stretcher. "He'll sleep for several hours, while his body replenishes its energy, mending itself. We'll need to wake him briefly to take some nourishment, but I'd rather wait until we've got him back to our side of the portal before doing that."

Jasak Olderhan had returned from overseeing the loading of his other wounded, and he arrived in time to overhear the healer's last sentence.

"Thank you, Naf. Thank you." He clasped the sword's hand in a firm grip. "Now let's get you back into the saddle. And let's get Shaylar onto the dragon, too. Magister Gadrial, I'd like you to go with us. Shaylar trusts you more than anyone else, and she'll need you to keep her steady."

"I'll just get my pack," Gadrial agreed, and bent her head, murmuring into Shaylar's ear.

*   *   *

Shaylar roused from deep confusion and the oddest dreams of her life and realized Gadrial was urging her to get up. She managed to obey, still supported by the other woman's arms, and realized Jathmar's stretcher had moved. She looked around, quick alarm cutting through her confusion, then relaxed—slightly—as she discovered that several men were maneuvering Jathmar and his stretcher upwards, toward a long platform strapped to the back of the immense animal still crouched in the stream.

At least the beast that couldn't possibly exist—the *dragon*, her mind insisted, because that fairytale label was the only one she could think of—wasn't still staring at *her*. That was a massive relief.

It had swiveled its head to watch the men climbing up its side with an almost absurdly attentive air, instead. The way its head was cocked, the intentness with which it watched what was going on, reminded her of the freight master on one of the famous Trans-Temporal Express's endless trains.

Cinches like the belly bands of an ordinary saddle, but far larger, were drawn up tight every four feet and buckled securely, securing the platform on its back. Sidewalls around the top of the platform, a foot and a half high, bore plenty of cleats for ropes or straps, and the purpose became clear as Jathmar's stretcher was hoisted up and roped into place so that his "bed" couldn't shift. They fastened straps to Jathmar, as well, so that he wouldn't roll off the stretcher.

It's a mobile hospital, Shaylar marveled. Or, rather, an aerial ambulance for evacuating wounded to the nearest real hospital.

They didn't load all the wounded soldiers onto it, however; only those with wounds serious enough to prevent them from walking out on their own. There were quite a lot of them, and she was glad of that. So fiercely glad it frightened her, that Sharonian lives hadn't been sold cheaply. She only wished there were more *dead* soldiers, because however kindly Gadrial might treat her, however gentle and patient Jasak might be, she could not forget the slaughter they'd perpetrated. She would *never* forget it. Whether or not she could ever *forgive* it was a question for the future, and she was too battered to think even a few minutes ahead, far less weeks or months.

Then it was her turn.

Any faint hope Shaylar had nourished that they might release her, at least, died when Jasak himself escorted her toward the waiting dragon. She didn't want to go near that beast. Didn't want to come within striking distance of those lethal bronze claws, or those dagger-sized teeth. She was three or four yards away when it angled its head back around to glare at her. It started to hiss—

The dragon's handler spoke in a sharp, angry voice and swatted the beast smartly between its ears with his long, metal-tipped pole. At least, it looked like the blow had landed between its ears; they might have been mere armored spikes with hollow cores, but they were in the right *place* for ears. A cavernous, disgruntled grumble thunder-muttered from its sharp-toothed jaws, but it offered no further protest.

Men in uniform, balanced on the dragon's foreleg and shoulder, reached out to steady her across, then hauled her unceremoniously up to the low-walled platform. She trembled violently on the way up and would have fallen without the grip of strong hands on her wrists and hips.

At the top, she found herself seated beside Jathmar. A cushioned pallet, several inches thick, had been laid across the wood to form a softer surface for the wounded men, or their stretchers, to lie on, but Shaylar scarcely even noticed. She was too busy staring at her husband in disbelieving wonder.

The healthy, pink skin visible beneath his scorched shirt was a soul-deep shock. She'd *felt* it healing, but the very idea of such an uncanny miracle had been so alien that she'd more than half-feared it was no more than an illusion brought about by her own head injury. Something she'd wanted so badly, so desperately, that she had imagined it entirely.

But she hadn't. His hair was still a singed mess, but the terrible burns were gone, and her eyes stung as she leaned down to press a kiss across his cheek. She wished she could fling her arms around him and cradle him close, but the webbing around his body made that impossible. Straps stretched taut to either side, fastened securely to cleats that looked strong enough to hold a full-sized plow horse in place. The other injured men had been webbed down, as well, and lay head-to-foot along the narrow platform, filling it for almost its entire length. The man who'd healed Jathmar was kneeling beside another unconscious man, whose body glowed with that same eerie light.

Then Gadrial climbed up beside her and helped Shaylar with the unfamiliar webbing. Unlike the wounded men, Shaylar and Gadrial sat up, able to see over the low side walls, and the straps around her waist gave Shaylar a sense of security, despite their height above the ground. A few moments later, Jasak Olderhan scrambled up and helped the dragon's handler rig a windbreak around the front of the platform. It was made of sailcloth, and she was surprised—and grateful—that it didn't extend above her, Gadrial, and Jasak, as well. Instead, the dragon's handler gave each of them a set of goggles made of wood and round panes of glass that fit snugly around the head. Then he climbed into the oddest saddle Shaylar had ever seen.

The pommel and cantle rose high before and behind the rider's body, creating a snug cradle that hugged his waist. Straps from front to back held him firmly in place, adding to his security. Iron stirrups secured his booted feet, and a wide leather saddle skirt protected his legs from the dragon's tough neck scales, some of which were spiked in the center. The saddle skirt was soft, supple leather, and while it was well worn, showing signs of extensive use, it was also ornately tooled and bore flashes of silver where studs and roundels had been fastened to it. Intricate patterns in a totally alien design teased Shaylar's somewhat fuzzy eyesight.

Beneath the broad leather skirt was a thick pad of what looked like fleece from a purple sheep. She stared, unsure of her own senses in the uncertain, flickering light from the bonfires, but the fleece certainly *looked* purple. She wondered a little wildly if it had been dyed, or if people who raised genuine dragons also produced jewel-toned sheep.

Beneath the fleece pad, in turn, lay a saddle blanket woven in geometric patterns, and she blinked in surprise when she realized that the pattern in the saddle blanket was repeated in the dragon's scaly hide. Despite the straps and the bulky platform which hid so much of the beast, and despite the dimness of the firelight, she could see the same intricate, ornate swirls and chevrons in the iridescent scales along the dragon's side. She wondered whether the blanket had been woven to match a naturally occurring pattern, or if the beast had been decorated somehow to match the blanket. She was still trying to see more of the beast's hide when the man in the saddle called out a command.

The dragon crouched low, muscles bunching in a smooth ripple. Then they catapulted forward as the dragon's huge feet gripped tight on the stream's boulders and its powerful legs hurled them almost straight upward. The force of the sudden movement clacked her teeth together with bone-jarring force, but before she could even groan, the wide wings snapped open. The sheer breadth of the dragon's wingspan came as a distinct shock, despite its size, for they were even larger than she'd initially thought. They beat strongly, far more rapidly than she would have believed possible, and she felt the creature climbing in elevatorlike bursts with each downstroke.

They flew parallel to the stream, barely clearing the water and the brush-filled banks to either side at first, for more than a hundred yards. Then the creek turned south, forcing the dragon to follow the curve of its bed. Another hundred-yard straight stretch gave it the room it apparently needed to get fully airborne.

Each massive sweep of its wings, loud as thunder cracks in her ears, lifted them steadily higher. By the time they reached the end of the second straightaway, the immense dragon had finally cleared the treetops. They flashed past a rustling canopy of leaves, argent and ebony in the moonlight, then sailed into clear air above the forest.

Shaylar discovered that she'd been holding her breath and her fingers had dug into the straps holding her securely in place. She glanced back and saw a brilliant spot of light in the darkness, where the bonfires in the camp they'd left burned like jewels against velvet. Moonlight poured across the treetops with an unearthly beauty, creating a billowing silver leaf-sea which stretched for miles in all directions. Wind set the silver sea in motion, with a constant ripple and swirl that was dizzying, exhilarating, like nothing Shaylar had ever experienced before. The windbreak shielded her from about mid-torso down, but the skin of her face was cold, except where the goggles shielded it, in the icy wind buffeting past its upper edge.

We're flying, she breathed silently. *Actually flying!*

For a time, the sheer delight of the experience pushed everything else out of the front of her brain. But as the novelty of it began to wear off in the cold wind, the implications of a military force which possessed aerial transport—and the far more frightening capacity for aerial combat—made itself abruptly known. Given the dragon's tough armor, not to mention its sheer size, Shaylar wondered if a rifle shot could be effective against it. There were hunters who took big game, of course, especially in sparsely settled universes where elephants, rhinos, immense—and aggressive—cape buffalo, thirty-foot crocodiles, and even vast herds of bison were a serious danger to colonists. There were some pretty heavy guns and cartridges for that kind of shooting, but Shaylar wondered if even those weapons could be effective at much greater ranges than point-blank into a dragon's belly or throat.

And what kind of weapons might something like a dragon bring to combat? Would it do what the legends of her home world said dragons could do? Breathe fire? Eat maidens for breakfast? She recalled the beast's fury at her, its rage battering her senses, the firelight glinting on claws and teeth as it reared up, and could imagine only too clearly what it would be like to have something like that actually attack her with lethal intent.

I have to warn our people! she thought desperately.

She closed her eyes behind the goggles, fought the black pain in the center of her head, and reached frantically through the spinning vortex to contact Darcel Kinlafia. The headache exploded behind her clenched eyelids, but she faced its anguish, refused to surrender to it.

Darcel! she cried into the black silence. *Darcel, can you hear me? Please, Darcel!*

She tried to send an image of the beast she now rode, tried to project the memory of it rearing above her in hissing fury, but her head spun. The whole world revolved in dizzy swoops and plunges, a drunken ship at sea in a typhoon . . .

Gadrial's voice reached her, repeating her name with some urgency. Shaylar felt the touch of gentle hands on her temples, felt Gadrial trying to ease the pain. But she flinched back, clinging to the effort—and the pain—as she fought to reach Darcel, whatever the cost to herself, and—

A massive, metal-bending screech tore the air.

The dragon slewed sideways in midair. It actually *bucked*, and Shaylar's eyes flew open as her teeth jolted together and the whole platform creaked against the violent motion of the beast under it. Her head jerked, and she felt herself bounced backward against her safety straps as a raging red fury lashed at her mind.

The dragon bellowed again, whipped its own head violently around, and snapped at her with huge teeth. Shaylar screamed, then clutched her head, her senses bleeding. Someone was shouting, a voice white-hot with fury, and the dragon's violent gyrations ceased as abruptly as they'd begun. The rage in her mind was still there, still hot as lava, but the beast was no longer trying to throw her off or bite her in half, and she collapsed against Gadrial, shuddering.

"Help me," she pleaded brokenly, fingers clutching at the other woman's clothing. "Get it out of my mind!" she moaned. "*Please. Oh, please . . .*"

Gadrial had both arms around her, and, gradually, the pain receded and the nausea dropped away. Shaylar's throat loosened around the terror she'd been fighting, and a delicious lassitude stole along her nerves. It eased her down into a comforting darkness, a lovely darkness, one that shut out the pain and the mortal fear of the beast in her mind.

She barely felt the cushioned pad as her back touched it.

*   *   *

Gadrial eased the tiny woman gently down, rearranging the safety straps so that Shaylar could lie flat beside her. Once she'd secured the straps in their new configuration, she brushed dark hair back from Shaylar's bruised face and stared down at her.

Who are you, really? she wondered. *How far did you journey to reach us? And why should a transport dragon* hate *you the way this one obviously does?*

"Is she all right?" Jasak demanded, half-shouting above the wind.

"Yes. I've helped her go to sleep."

"Thank the gods! What in *hell* just happened?"

"I don't know! Is the dragon under control?" she counter-demanded, and he nodded.

"He is now, but it was damned touch-and-go for a second, there." He'd twisted around to stare at the unconscious girl beside Gadrial. "She's the source. Whatever's going on, *she's* the source." Gadrial could see the intense frustration in his expression even in the uncertain moonlight and despite his flight goggles. "Did you see or hear anything? Anything from her that could have triggered it?"

"No." Gadrial shook her head. "One minute she was fine. The next she was screaming, and Windclaw was trying to throw us off his back!" Then she frowned. "But there was something strange, right before she lost consciousness. She was saying something, and it felt—I don't know. It felt like she was begging for help. Not protection, *help*. Something to do with the dragon and her mind . . ."

She trailed off, wondering abruptly how she knew that. Because she *did* know it; knew it as certainly as if Shaylar had spoken aloud.

"What is it?" Jasak asked, and she shook her head to clear it.

"I'm not sure. It's just . . ." She stumbled, trying to put it into words.

"She was trying to tell me something, and I think I understood her. Not the words; they made no sense at all. But I *understood* her, Jasak. It's eerie." She swallowed. "Scary as hell, in fact. She was asking me to help her."

"Help her with the pain?"

"No." Gadrial shook her head again, trying to put her bizarre, elusive certainty into words. "No. She wanted me to help her ... get the dragon out of her mind?" It came out as a question, because she knew it made no logical sense. "I don't have the faintest idea why I know that, but I *know* it, Jasak. She was clutching at me, babbling, and that's what came into my head."

Sir Jasak Olderhan, commander of one hundred, stared at Gadrial as though she'd suddenly sprouted wings herself. For a moment or two, she suspected that he thought she'd gone off the deep end, but then he gave a sudden, choppy nod.

"That's damned interesting," he said abruptly. "Has anything like that happened before?"

She shook her head again.

"I don't think so."

"Well, pay close attention to every impression you receive when you're talking to her, or she's trying to communicate with you, Gadrial. *Something* about her caused Windclaw to react violently, and more than once. We don't understand anything about these people! Except that they use weapons and equipment that are the most alien things I've ever seen. We can't assume they're like us in *any* respect, which means the door's wide open for totally inexplicable technologies, or whatever it is she was using or doing to set off the dragon."

Gadrial nodded, feeling far colder than the frigid night wind could account for, and wondered what terrifying discoveries lay ahead. Shaylar looked so ... normal lying unconscious beside her. Normal, lost, and frightened out of her wits.

Gadrial stroked the night-black, windblown hair back from Shaylar's brow once more, and glanced at Jathmar, wondering what matching discoveries lay behind his face.

It was obvious the two of them came from racial stock as different from each other as Jasak's pale Andaran skin and round eyes differed from her own sandalwood complexion and dark, oval eyes. And although she'd had little time to study Shaylar and Jathmar's dead companions before their cremation, even that brief examination had told her the entire survey party had been as racially diverse as anything on Arcana. These people obviously came from a large, mixed-heritage society, whether it occupied only one universe or several, and she wondered abruptly how that society's members might differ from one another.

Did they have Gifts of their own? Different, perhaps, from any Gadrial had ever heard of, but equally powerful? Did different groups of them have *different* Gifts? How might *their* Gifts compare to those of Arcana? And what about their society's internal structure and dynamics? Had they evolved some sort of monolithic cultural template, or were they composed of elements as internally diverse—even hostile—as her own Ransarans and most Mythalans?

*　　*　　*

Jasak glanced back at Gadrial and noted her thoughtful frown. She was obviously thinking hard, sorting back through all of her impressions, and he nodded mentally in satisfaction. The brain inside that lovely head of hers was frighteningly acute. He had no doubt at all that if there were any clues buried among those impressions, Gadrial Kelbryan would pounce upon them as surely as any falcon taking a hare.

Satisfied that the bloodhound was on the trail, Jasak turned around again in his own saddle. He gazed straight ahead, but his attention wasn't focused on Salmeer's back, nor on Windclaw's shimmering wings as they beat powerfully in the moonlight. Not even on the glorious silver sea of leaves speeding past below them, with the dragon's moon-shadow racing from one bright treetop to the next in a flowing blur.

No. What *he* saw was Osmuna lying dead in a creek. A stockade filled with abandoned tents, foot-weary donkeys, and strange equipment. And a terrifying montage of battle images that flashed through his memory in bright bursts, like exploding incendiary spells.

And behind them was the frightening thought of what would happen if, by some unimaginable means, these people *had* successfully gotten a message back through the portal to their nearest base.

He couldn't imagine how they might have done it. A careful sweep around the battle site had found no tracks leading away from all that toppled timber, and there'd been no sign of messenger birds, like the hummers his own platoons carried. But these people had all manner of strange, inexplicable abilities and devices. If they had a sufficient command of magical technology—or, he thought with a shudder, some *other* sort of technology—to send messages across long distances without any physical messenger, Arcana could be in serious trouble already.

That thought was more than simply worrisome. It was downright terrifying. So far, he'd found nothing—nothing at all—in their captured gear which resembled arcane technology. An Arcanan crew that size would have been carrying all manner of spell-powered devices, but he hadn't seen a trace of anything made of sarkolis, hadn't sensed even a quiver of spellware. He couldn't even begin to visualize how anyone could possibly build an advanced civilization without arcane technology, but all he'd seen were fiendishly intricate, clever, totally *non*-arcane machines.

Was it really possible that one of those machines—possibly one he hadn't even found yet, one they might have *destroyed* to prevent him from finding it, as they'd destroyed their maps and charts—might have allowed them to send a message without a runner or a hummer?

The more he thought about how little he knew about Shaylar and her people, the more he wanted to avoid contact with any of them until Arcana had managed to fill in at least a few corners of the puzzle, punch at least a few holes through the fog of total ignorance which was all he could offer his superiors at the moment. And as he considered it, it occurred to him that if there was, in fact, something odd about Shaylar Nargra's mind, something which upset dragons, it was equally clear from *her* reaction that Shaylar had never seen anything remotely like Windclaw.

They don't have dragons, he realized. *And if they don't have dragons, is it possible that they don't have* anything *that flies?*

His frown intensified as that possibility hovered before him. He might simply be grasping at straws, but one thing he knew: dragons—unlike donkeys, soldiers, or civilian surveyors—left no footprints. If Shaylar and her companions *had* gotten a message back to their people, picking up his own route from the swamp base camp to the site of the battle and backtracking it wouldn't be particularly difficult for even semi-competent woodsmen. But simply finding the base camp wouldn't help them very much.

It was over *seven hundred miles* from the swamp to Fort Rycharn, with no roads, no trails, between the fort and the swamp portal. Everything at the portal base camp had been airlifted in from Fort Rycharn, and even Fort Rycharn was only a forward base. The actual portal into this universe was over three thousand miles away—across equally trackless ocean—on the island which would have been Chalar back on Arcana.

He nodded, mouth firming with decision. He couldn't undo what had already happened, but he could at least buy some time, and he intended to do just that. Pulling everyone back from the swamp portal to Fort Rycharn wouldn't be easy with only a single transport dragon available, but it would be one way to dig a hole and fill it in behind them.

If Shaylar's party had summoned a rescue party, it would find only the abandoned camp. Let it hunt through seven hundred miles of virgin, trackless swamp if it wanted to. By the time it could find Fort Rycharn, even *that* wouldn't do it any good, if Jasak had his way. Not if he could convince Five Hundred Klian to pull all the way back to the Chalar arrival portal and put twenty-six hundred more miles of water between any search party and the route to Arcana.

Time, he thought. *That's what we need—time. Time to get word back up the transit chain. Time for someone who knows what the* hell *he's doing to get back here and handle the* next contact with these people. *Time to figure out a way to somehow get a handle on this situation before it spins totally out of control.*

And the way to get that time was to make sure that anyone from the other side couldn't find a trace of Arcana.

Not until Arcana was good and ready to be found.

CHAPTER
THIRTEEN

JATHMAR FLOATED IN the darkness of the still, warm depths,
drifting slowly and steadily toward a sunlit surface far above
him. The light grew stronger, reaching down towards him, and
something stirred in sleepy protest. He reached out to the darkness,
wrapping it about himself, like a child burrowing deep into a goose
down comforter. He didn't want to wake up, didn't want to leave the
safe, still quiet. He didn't remember *why* he didn't want to wake, but
his drowsy mind knew that something waited for him. Something
he didn't want to face.

His eyelids flickered, and he reached out, as automatically as
breathing, for Shaylar's familiar touch.

Panic struck like a spiked hammer.

She wasn't there. Where Shaylar should have been, he found only
a roaring, pain-filled blackness. The shockwave of loss jolted him
into full consciousness with a sharp gasp of anguished terror, and
his eyes snapped open.

Sunlight burned down over him, hot and humid. There was no
trace of the glorious autumn woods he remembered; all he could see
was a vast stretch of muddy water and rank vegetation, heavy with
the smell of rot and mold and fecundity. The trees growing at the
water's edge, some growing in the water itself, were tropical varieties, heavy with vines, with no trace of the colors of a northern fall.
The voices of birds—some raucous, some musical, some like those
he'd never heard before—sounded through the hot, dense stillness,
huge butterflies drifted over and among the swamp grasses, like
living jewels, and the whine of insects hung heavy on the thick,
steamy air.

He lay on something simultaneously firm and yet soft-textured, like a folding canvas camp cot, and his thoughts fluttered and twisted, trapped between confusion and the strobing panic radiating from the *absence* where Shaylar ought to have been. He hung transfixed between seriously broken thoughts. Then voices registered, and movement, as well, close by. He sat up and—

He yelled and scrambled wildly backwards on the seat of his trousers. The "camp cot" under him never even wiggled, but he shot over its edge, sprawling onto muddy ground a full two feet lower than whatever had been supporting him. He panted, groping instinctively for his rifle, for his revolver, even for his *belt knife*, and his scrabbling hands found nothing but more mud.

The ... *thing* ... turned its horror of a head to peer down, down, down at him just as his frantically searching hand closed on a dead branch. The improvised club would be useless against a thing like that, but it was better than blunt fingernails, and he came to his knees, swinging the branch wildly up between himself and it.

The sudden flurry of shouts behind him barely registered. He ignored them, all of his attention fixed on the scaled monstrosity, until a uniformed man with a crossbow stepped in front of him. The soldier shouted and pointed his impossible weapon, but not at the horror looming over them. He aimed it at *Jathmar*. Then another man appeared, wearing the same uniform and snarling orders—or spitting curses—in a voice of white-hot fury. The first man lowered his crossbow and sent the second a hangdog look with something that sounded like an unhappy apology. The second man—the officer, Jathmar realized—said something else, his tone considerably less sharp but still reprimanding, and the crossbowman came to what had to be a position of attention and saluted oddly, touching his left shoulder with his right fist.

The officer nodded dismissal, watched a moment while the crossbowman marched off to wherever he'd come from, then turned his own attention to Jathmar.

Jathmar clutched his stupid stick, panting and sweating in the supercharged swampy air, and the officer met his gaze squarely. He held it, never taking his eyes from Jathmar's, and issued what was clearly another order.

Another man appeared and shouted at the beast, and Jathmar's eyes snapped back to the towering horror. It looked down at the man who'd shouted, rustled enormous demon's wings, and hissed, but it also moved away. The soft ground sucked at its immense, clawed feet as it slunk off, if anything that size could be said to slink ...

"Jathmar."

The sound of his own name whipped him back around to the officer. Aside from a long knife or short sword at his left hip, the other man wore no obvious weapon, but Jathmar had no doubt that he faced the commander of all the other armed men surrounding him and dared make no move at all. Then he frowned.

"How do you know my name?" he demanded.

The other man clearly didn't understand his question. He held up both hands in a trans-universal sign for "I don't have the least idea what you just said." Despite his own panic, despite the terror pulsing through him at the marriage bond's continued silence, Jathmar's lips quirked in bitter amusement. But then the officer in front of him said another word.

"Shaylar."

"*Where is she?*" Jathmar snarled, any temptation towards amusement disappearing into the suddenly refocused vortex of a panic far more terrible than he could ever have felt for himself. The club came up again, hovered menacingly between him and his enemy, and his lips drew back from his teeth in an animal snarl.

And then memory struck with such brutality he actually staggered, crying out in remembered agony. He was on fire, caught in the withering heat of an incandescent fireball, flesh blazing even as he fought to reach Shaylar, but he *couldn't*, and—

Someone moved toward him urgently, and the club came back up. A guttural sound clogged his throat, hot and hungry with primeval rage and a berserker's fury. He heard the officer saying something else, something sharp and urgent, and he didn't care. The club came back, poised to strike, and then it froze as his eyes focused on its target.

It wasn't another soldier; it was a girl. A slender, lovely Uromathian girl, taller than his Shaylar, but still small, delicate. She was saying his name, then Shaylar's name, pointing urgently to one side.

It's a trick! his mind shrieked, but he looked anyway.

The tents registered first. There was an entire encampment of them, in orderly rows, and more incongruously armed soldiers swam into view, their crossbows pointed carefully at the muddy ground. Then he saw the glassy tubes, and sweat and terror crawled down his back as he remembered the fireballs.

Then he saw the wounded. The brutal carnage of gunshot wounds registered in a kaleidoscope of torn flesh, shattered limbs, blood splashes on bandages, clothing, and skin. Someone cried out, the sound knife-sharp and piteous, as a wound was re-bandaged. The sights and sounds shocked him, horrified him ... gratified him. And while those conflicting emotions hammered each other in his chest, he saw her.

She was literally so close he'd overlooked her, caught by the deeply shocking sights further afield. He fell to his knees beside her, barely aware of his own anguished moan, completely oblivious for the moment to the way her strange "cot" hovered unsupported above the ground.

She was alive, breathing slowly, steadily. But her face . . . His breath caught. One whole side of her face was a swollen, purple mass of damage. Bruises had nearly obliterated her left eye, and it looked as if her nose might well be broken. Cuts and scrapes along her swollen cheek and brow told their own story, and memory struck again.

The fireball exploded all around them once more, as if it had just happened. He could literally *feel* himself flying into the tangle of deadwood while his skin and hair crisped in unbearable agony. He groped for his own face, the back of his neck, shocked all over again by a complete and impossible absence of pain. He found no charred skin, no blisters, no burns at all, and that was impossible. His rational mind gibbered—he'd been burned, horribly. He *knew* it, and his flesh shuddered and flinched from the memory of it. Yet he wasn't burned *now*, and that simply couldn't be true.

He knelt in the mud beside his wife and literally trembled in the face of far too many things he couldn't comprehend. Then her eyelashes shivered, a soft sound—half-sigh, half-whimper—ghosted from her lips, and he dropped everything. Dropped the club he still held, his vast confusion, even his attention for the enemy, and swept her up in his arms. He folded her close, held her like fragile glass, rocking on his knees, and buried his face in her singed and scorched hair.

"Shaylar," he gasped raggedly. "*Shaylar*, gods. You're still *with* me, love!"

The silence in her mind terrified him. He could feel her slender weight in his arms, feel the steady beat of her heart, hear her breathing, but when he reached with his mind, she simply wasn't there. Fresh horror rolled through him as the savagery of her bruised and battered face coupled with the silence of her mind in nightmare dread. What if—

Her eyes opened. They were hazy, at first. Blank with confusion . . . until she saw him.

"*Jathmar!*"

Her arms were suddenly around him. Jathmar was no giant. Falthar-ians tended to be tallish, and he was, yet he was also whipcord thin, built more for speed and endurance than brawn. Shaylar, on the other hand, was tiny, even for a Shurkhali. She was a most satisfactory size for hugging, in his opinion, but she'd always said she felt like a kitten trying to hug a mastiff when she returned the favor. They'd laughed over it for years, but today she clutched him so tightly he knew her fingers were leaving fresh bruises on the miraculously undamaged skin of his back, and it felt good. So good.

She buried her face against his chest, weeping with shocking strength, and he brushed back her hair, smoothed the scorched tresses and tangles which would take shears to put right. When he could finally bear to let go of her long enough to sit back and peer into her eyes, she touched his face, wonderingly.

"Oh, Jath," she whispered, huge eyes still brimming with tears. "You're a miracle, love."

"I—" He swallowed. "I was burned. Wasn't I?"

"Yes." The single word was barely audible, and she nodded. "Their Healer came. He—" It was her turn to swallow hard. "You were dying, Jath. I knew you were. But he gave you back to me. He touched you, just *touched* you, and the burns healed. Like the gods themselves had reached down to make you whole again."

The swamp and even her face wavered in his awareness. No Talent could do something like that. Even the most Talented Healers were limited mostly to healing minds which had been shattered, or encouraging the body to heal itself more effectively. They could work wonders enough, but none that came close to *this*.

The shiver began in his bones, and he turned his head almost involuntarily to stare at the man who stood watching them. Just watching. Not threatening, not intruding. Their officer looked like an ordinary man, *they* looked ordinary, and yet . . .

"I don't understand." He brought his gaze back to Shaylar. "If they could do this for me, why haven't they healed you? Or," he added, his voice turning harsh and bitter, "the men we shot to pieces?"

"I don't know." She shook her head. "None of it makes sense. But these people, Jath, they're not like us. Not at all. I think their Healers are more . . . more energy-limited than ours are." It was obvious to him that she was searching for words, trying to explain something which had puzzled her just as much as it did him. "I don't think they encourage the body to heal; I think they *make* it heal. When their Healer was working on you, you *glowed*, and there was this tremendous sense of energy, of power, coming from *somewhere*. I think they can do things our Healers could never even imagine, but they can only do so much of it before they . . . exhaust themselves.

And they only have one real Healer, so I think they must be ration-
ing the healing he can do, using it for the most critical cases."

"Or the ones with valuable information," he said bitterly before
he could stop himself.

"That's probably part of it," she said unflinchingly, "but I don't
think that's all of it. They put you first in line because you were
the worst hurt of all."

Doubt flickered in his eyes, and she shook her head.

"I mean it, Jath. The woman with them, Gadrial, she's some kind
of Healer, too, but not a very strong one. Or not by *these* people's
standards, anyway. She wasn't strong enough to heal either of us,
but . . ." Shaylar bit her lip. "Without her, you would have died before
their real Healer ever got to you."

Her voice had dropped to a terrible whisper, and his blood ran
cold. Yes, his memories were brutal enough to believe that. He didn't
need the inexplicably broken marriage bond to sense her deep anguish,
the horror of her belief that he was already dead still burning in
her memory, and his mind flinched like a frightened animal from
the vision of her all alone among their enemies.

"It's all right," he whispered raggedly, pulling her close again. "It's
all right, I'm still with you."

But even as he cradled his shaken wife, his gaze sought and found
the girl—Gadrial—who stood a few feet from the officer. She wasn't
Uromathian, no matter what she looked like. It took a real effort to
dismiss his preconceived notions, to remind himself that she wouldn't
think like a Uromathian or hold the same opinions, attitudes, biases,
or customs. And he owed her his life. For a Faltharian, life-debt was
a serious business, entailing obligations, formal courtesies, reciprocal
bonds of protection, none of which she would understand.

And none of which he particularly relished.

He would owe the other, stronger Healer, as well, he realized,
wherever he or she might be. That didn't make him any happier, he
admitted. And meanwhile, Gadrial was watching *him*, her expression
uncertain. When he met her gaze, she gave him a tentative smile.
Very sweet, very human. Very . . . normal.

Another shiver touched his impossibly healed back, which, he
realized for the first time, was bare. Startled, he glanced down and
discovered that his entire shirt was missing. Momentary disorientation
swept over him as he found himself kneeling on the ground beside
his wife, shirtless, just beginning to realize that he had absolutely
no idea where he was, or how far he and Shaylar were from the site
of that hideous battle, or how much time had passed. The totality

of his ignorance appalled him, and he looked back into Shaylar's worried eyes and frowned as something important nibbled at the edges of his scattered thoughts. Then he had it.

"Shaylar? Where are the others?"

Her composure crumbled. She began to cry again—helplessly, this time, softly and hopelessly, shaking her head in mute grief—and horror sent ice crystals through Jathmar's blood.

"No one?" he whispered. "Nobody else? Just us?"

She nodded, still unable to speak. Her struggle to hold herself together, to stop herself from falling to pieces, broke Jathmar's heart again. He drew her close, held her while she trembled, and he realized their bond wasn't gone, so much as wounded. Too badly wounded to function properly, but not so badly he couldn't feel her grief, her sorrow and despair.

"I'm sorry," he groaned. "I'm sorry I dragged you out here, into this—"

"No!" She looked up swiftly and shook her head with startling violence. "Don't say that! It isn't true!"

She was right, but at the moment, that was a frail defense against his own crushing sense of responsibility and guilt. His awareness of his complete inability to protect her.

It was painfully evident they were prisoners, but how did their captors treat prisoners of war? They must have some sort of procedures to deal with captured enemy personnel, and a further thought chilled him. Would these people think he and Shaylar were *soldiers*? Even he knew soldiers and civilians received different treatment from the military during armed conflicts. It had been a long time since any major Sharonian nation had gone to war, but even on Sharona there was the occasional border dispute, the "incident" when a patrol from one side wandered across the other side's frontier, the "brushfire" conflict between ancient and implacable enemies. And there'd been more than enough violent conflict in Sharona's pre-portal history to make such procedures necessary.

But how in the multiverse could he convince these people he and his wife were only civilians, when they'd killed so many genuine soldiers and wounded so many others? If Company-Captain Halifu sent real troops after them, these people would get a taste of what Sharonian *soldiers* could do, but would that help him and Shaylar? If the crossbows he'd seen were the best individual weapons their soldiers had, if they'd never before even seen what rifles and pistols could do, would they believe that ordinary civilians carried such weapons, even in the wilderness?

The memory of that frantic, dreadful fight replayed itself once more in jagged, terrifying flashes, but one thing was clear to him. It was only their artillery—that terrifying, unexplainable artillery—which had turned the tide against Ghartoun chan Hagrahyl's survey crew. As severely outnumbered as they'd been, they'd still been more than holding their own until the fireballs erupted among them.

No wonder those crossbowmen were so twitchy.

He'd already seen evidence that the regular troopers were poised on a hair-trigger where he was concerned, but how would their commanding officer behave toward him and Shaylar? If anyone hurt Shaylar, he'd . . .

Jathmar bit his lip. He couldn't do that. Couldn't even defend his own wife. If he tried, he'd wind up dead, and Shaylar would be at the mercy of his killers. His pain and self-blame doubled—tripled—but wallowing in misery accomplished nothing, so he dragged his attention back to the present.

"Where are we? Do you know how far we've come?"

"No. I was asleep when we came through that."

Shaylar pointed to something behind him, and he turned, then blinked. A *portal*. Gods, he really was a scattered, distracted mess to have missed seeing or even sensing a portal literally right behind him. It led into the forest their survey crew had discovered just days ago, but it clearly wasn't the one they'd used to enter that forest. This pestilential swamp was nowhere near the cool, rainy universe on the far side of their portal, and this portal was tiny compared to theirs.

"They took us out in the middle of the night," Shaylar murmured. "On a . . . dragon."

She hesitated over the word, but Jathmar glanced at the hideous creature and grunted in agreement. If there was a better word for that monstrous beast, *he* couldn't think of it.

"They put all the most critically wounded on its back," Shaylar continued. "They rigged up a special platform, like an ambulance, or a hospital car. Only this hospital car can fly. I tried to contact Darcel, but something's wrong inside my head. I can't hear anyone—not even you. There's a roaring blackness where my Voice should be, and I have a terrible headache. It never stops."

"That's what I sensed when I tried to touch the bond," he muttered. "When I first woke up, it was all I could hear. I . . . I thought it meant you were gone."

He met her gaze, saw the pain burning behind her brave eyes, saw it in the furrows that never quite smoothed out between her brows and the tension in her neck and face, where the bruises and swelling so cruelly disfigured her.

"Why the hell haven't they healed *you*?" he demanded again, much more harshly this time.

"I told you," she said, her tone clearly an explanation, not an excuse for their captors. "Their Healer has his hands full, Jathmar. And as decent as Gadrial and their commander have been, I'm *glad* their hands are full. I wish they were *fuller.*"

The bitterness in her normally gentle voice shocked Jathmar. He'd never seen such cold hatred in his wife. He wouldn't have believed she was capable of it, and the discovery that she was appalled him.

"I'm sorry." Her voice was sharp as steel. "But what they did to us . . . I may never be able to forgive them for that. I'm trying, but I just can't."

"Who the hell wants you to?"

"I do," she whispered. "My soul hurts, feeling this way."

His heart twisted, and the look he turned on the enemy commander who'd ordered their massacre could have frozen the marrow of a star.

There's not enough blood in your veins to make up for what you've done to her, his icy eyes told the other man.

The officer looked back, meeting that hate-filled glare squarely. Whatever else he might be, this wasn't a weak man, Jathmar realized. His regret for what had happened appeared to be genuine, but he met Jathmar's steely hatred unflinchingly. They shared no words, couldn't speak one another's language, but they didn't need to in that moment. They looked deep into one another's enemy eyes, and Jathmar could actually taste the other man's determination to do his duty.

Whatever that duty was; wherever it led. Whatever the consequences for Jathmar . . . and Shaylar.

There was no hatred behind that determination, no viciousness. Jathmar was sure of that. But there was also no hesitation, and so Jathmar bit down on his own hatred. He held it in his teeth, knowing he dared not loose it, dared not let it tempt him into even trying to strike back.

He knew it, but as he stared at that enemy's face, he realized that the other man recognized the depth of his own hatred.

*　　*　　*

Jasak Olderhan looked back at the kneeling prisoner with the eyes of icy fire. He understood the causes of that lethal glare only too well, although he doubted Jathmar would have been prepared to accept how *well* Jasak understood . . . and how deeply he sympathized.

But understanding and sympathy might not be enough. Unconscious, barely clinging to life, Shaylar's husband had been an obligation, a responsibility. Jasak's duty—both as an officer of the Union and as a member of the Andaran military caste—had been to keep him alive, at all costs. Everything else had been secondary.

But Shaylar's husband, awake and conscious, was another kettle of fish entirely. And from the look of things, a dangerous one.

"Is he a soldier?" Gadrial's question broke into his own brooding chain of thought, and he glanced at the slim magister. She, too, was looking at Jathmar, and her eyes were worried.

"Why do you ask?"

"He doesn't seem to be afraid. Not the way I'd expect a civilian to be, anyway. That look of his . . . that's not the kind of look I'd expect from someone who's frightened."

"No," Jasak said slowly. "It's not. But that's because he *isn't* 'frightened.' He's terrified."

"He's *what?*" Her gaze jerked away from Jathmar, snapping up to meet his.

"Terrified," Jasak repeated. "And in his place, that's exactly what I'd be, too. I don't know, at this stage, whether he's a soldier or not. I'm strongly inclined to think he isn't, but he knows *we* are, and he knows we've slaughtered his friends. That gives him a very clear notion of our highest priority."

"That being?" she asked uncertainly.

"Getting them safely back to Arcana so we can learn everything we possibly can about their people. I won't abuse them, but he can't know that. He'd probably face the possibility of his own abuse with courage, even defiance. But he's not alone. If I'd ever doubted that you were right about their relationship, I wouldn't now. That's his *wife*, Gadrial. You can see it in the way he's holding her, the way he looks at her, touches her. The idea of someone abusing her, possibly even torturing her for information, terrifies him. He already hates us for what we did to the rest of his friends. That's bad enough. But he also hates us for what we might do *next*. He knows he couldn't stop us if we tried to hurt her, but if it comes down to it, he'll *damned* well die trying, and that's something we can't afford to forget. Ever."

Gadrial frowned, then looked back at Jathmar and Shaylar and realized just how accurately Jasak had read the other man.

"So how can we convince him that we *won't* hurt them?" she asked, and Jasak sighed in frustration.

"Honestly? We can't. Not until we've learned their language, or they've learned ours. And not until enough time's passed for us to *demonstrate* our good intentions. Until then—"

His eyes narrowed, and he glanced at Gadrial again.

"Until then, that's one damned dangerous man," he said. "I hate to put you in the dragon's mouth, so to speak, but I really need your help."

"Of course. What can I do?"

"I want you to be our official go-between. If any of us," a tiny flick of the fingers indicated himself and the men of his command, "try to talk with them, his defenses will snap into place so strongly we couldn't possibly actually communicate. He'll be too busy worrying about an assault on his wife, and we'll be too busy worrying about an attempt to grab a weapon, or a hostage, or something else desperate."

"Whereas I wouldn't threaten him as much?"

"Exactly," he said, and she looked him straight in the eye.

"He might try to use *me* as a hostage," she pointed out, and he nodded slowly.

"It's a possibility, yes. I won't pretend it isn't. But if he's smart enough to realize how hopelessly outnumbered he is, and that he has no idea how far he is from their portal, with a wounded wife and no supplies, he won't try it."

"*If*," she repeated dryly, then snorted and gave him a wry smile. "Somehow, I can't imagine Shaylar marrying anybody that stupid. Not marrying him voluntarily, anyway," she added, realizing they knew nothing of the marriage customs among Shaylar's people.

"And I can't imagine that lady marrying anyone *in*voluntarily," Jasak said even more dryly. "Besides, it's obvious how devoted to one another they are. So even if her people are as 'enlightened' as, say, Mythal, these two seem to have adjusted to each other quite nicely, wouldn't you say?"

Gadrial's eyes glinted with amusement at his choice of examples, and her lips quirked in a brief smile.

"Let's just agree that we shouldn't make any assumptions about their marriage customs," she nodded toward Jathmar and Shaylar, "when our own are so varied. But if you want my opinion, theirs certainly isn't an arranged marriage. I can't imagine Shaylar doing this kind of work, out in the wilderness, if she were simply following her husband in the pursuit of *his* career, either. That doesn't make sense, just from a practical standpoint. Everybody's got to pull their weight and perform an important function on a team like theirs, so there's no room for the luxury of someone's spouse tagging along for the ride."

"I agree." Jasak nodded.

"So. What do you suggest I do now? We can't just stand here, staring at each other."

"No," he smiled faintly, "we can't. Do you think you could get through to Shaylar, somehow? She trusts you, at least a little."

"I'll try. But what, exactly, do I try to communicate? I don't know your plans, you know," she said, her tone tart enough to put a slightly sheepish smile into his eyes.

"Sorry about that." His cheeks actually turned a bit pink, she observed. "I've been so focused on getting them here alive that it hadn't occurred to me to share my plans with you. Despite the fact that you're fairly central to them."

Gadrial grinned. Sir Jasak Olderhan was adorable when he was embarrassed, she decided. And if she really wanted to complete his demolition, all she had to do was *tell* him so.

"So tell me now," she said, womanfully resisting the temptation. He looked decidedly grateful and rubbed the back of his neck, clearly gathering his thoughts.

"I intend to abandon this camp," he said. "Withdraw completely from this portal and evacuate everyone to the coast. There's no way anyone can track us if we evac by air, and that's critical, because the armed confrontation has to stop here. None of us are trained diplomats, and that's what we need. If we get a diplomatic mission out here, there's at least a chance we can keep anyone else from getting killed. At this point, it doesn't matter whether Osmuna shot their man first, or whether he shot Osmuna first. What's going to matter to *them* is that we slaughtered their entire crew; what's going to matter to *us* are the casualties we took, and the weapons capability they revealed inflicting them. We didn't mean for any of this to happen, but they're going to have trouble buying that, and there's going to be a lot of pressure on our side for a panic reaction when people higher up the military and political food chains hear about what's happened. Especially if the other side sends in some sort of rescue mission that leads to additional shooting."

"Which is why we need a diplomatic mission to help convince them it was all an accident." Gadrial nodded. "And civilian diplomats won't be as . . . incendiary as a camp full of soldiers. There'd be less chance of another confrontation ending in shots fired."

"Right on all counts," he said, and Gadrial gave him an intent look.

"At the risk of airing my own prejudices, Sir Jasak, I have to admit that that's the last thing I expected to hear from a professional officer.

I also happen to think it's the best idea I've heard since Garlath got his stupid self killed."

Jasak's eyes flickered, and she snorted.

"Never mind," she said. "I know you can't agree. Proper military discipline, stiff Andaran upper lip, all of that." She smiled sweetly at his expression. "Since, however, you've elected to proceed with such wisdom, how soon can we leave? And exactly what do you want me to try to convey to them about it?"

She nodded toward Shaylar and her husband once more.

"I intend to put them—and you—on the first flight I send out of here, along with the most seriously wounded Sword Morikan hasn't been able to heal yet."

Gadrial nodded. A Gifted healer, even a fully trained one like Naf Morikan, could stretch his Gift only so far before depleting his own energy. Gifts dealing directly with living things—like healers and the other magistrons and journeymen involved in things like the dragon breeding and improvement programs, the hummer breeding program, and even the agronomists who were constantly seeking to improve food crops and sources of textiles—were quite different from Gadrial's own major arcanas. Those Gifted in such areas required special training, and no one had yet succeeded in figuring out how to store a major healing spell, although Gadrial was confident that the coveted vos Lipkin Prize waited for whoever finally did.

Actually getting the spellware loaded into the sarkolis didn't seem to be the problem. It wasn't one to which Gadrial had devoted a great deal of her own attention—her major Gifts lay in other areas—but she suspected that the difficulty lay in the inherent differences between each illness or injury. The sort of blanket spells involved in most preloaded spellware were frequently a brute force kind of approach. That was acceptable for inanimate objects, but even small glitches could have major—even fatal—consequences for living things. So each healer was forced to deal with an unending series of unique problems, each demanding its own unique solution.

She and Magister Halathyn had discussed the theoretical ramifications fairly often over the years, although neither of them had enough of the healing Gift to make it a profitable avenue of research for them. They'd come to the conclusion that the difference between a magister, trained in the "hard sorcery" dealing with inanimate forces and objects, and a *magistron*, trained in the "life sorcery" someone like Naf Morikan practiced, was the difference between a symphonic composer and a brilliant sight-reading improvisationist. Neither was really qualified to do the other's job, or even to adequately explain the inherent differences between their specializations to each other.

"I've still got a camp full of wounded men who are going to need Naf's attention," Jasak continued, "but Five Hundred Klian has his entire battalion medical staff at Fort Rycharn. I need to get the more critical cases off of Naf's back, and I'm worried about what you've had to say about Shaylar. She doesn't seem to be in a life-threatening situation, so I can't justify pulling Naf off of the men who really *need* him, but I want her to get proper attention as soon as possible."

"All right. I understand—and, for what it's worth, I agree. I'll try to get your message across to Shaylar. Wish me luck."

"Oh, I do."

"Thanks."

Gadrial dried damp palms on her trousers, drew a quick breath, and started across the open ground, dredging up the best smile she could muster.

*   *   *

Jathmar had never previously considered what it could mean to be a prisoner, let alone a prisoner of war. But as he and Shaylar sat together under their captors' gazes, trying to eat, he was altogether too well aware of the hostility directed at them. The soldiers who'd so brutally slaughtered the rest of their crew obviously hated them, regardless of what their commander felt.

You killed our friends, those hostile looks said, *and you tried to kill* us. *Give us an excuse to finish what we started. Please.*

He tried to tell himself he was reading too much hatred into their stares. That he might be projecting his own emotions onto them, whether they deserved it or not. That it was probably as much fear of the unknown he and Shaylar—and their firearms—represented as it was actual hatred.

Some of that might even have been true. But he couldn't *know* that. He didn't have Shaylar's ability to read the emotions of other people, which left him unable to trust even Gadrial the way Shaylar seemed able to do. Nor could he relax under the cold, unwavering stares coming their way.

He couldn't get away from them, either. He needed even a short respite, needed to go someplace private, where he and his wife wouldn't be the focus of such intense hatred, or fear, or uncertainty, or whatever the hells it was. And he couldn't. He couldn't even stand up and walk away from camp to relieve himself! If he tried, someone would put a crossbow quarrel through him.

It was intolerable. He and Shaylar had come out here, exploring new universes, because they treasured freedom. The freedom to move from one uninhabited place to another, to savor the silence, the exhilaration of no boundaries, no strict rules governing their every move, no limits on where they went, or what they did.

Now they'd lost all of that, and he had no idea when—or if—they would ever regain it. The long vista of captivity that stretched bleakly ahead of them, denied everything they valued in life, weighed like a mountain on his shoulders. And unendurable as it might be for him, watching *Shaylar* endure it would be still worse. Every time he looked at her battered face, the anger tightened down afresh. Watching her struggle to chew, struggle to put her own terror aside and try to smile at him—and at their captors—was a pain he could hardly bear.

The sound of alien voices washed across him like acid, leaving him on edge. He couldn't even ask these people what their intentions were, or read their emotions from their body language, because he had no reference points. Not everyone used the same gestures to mean the same things even on Sharona, and these people were from an entirely different *universe*. He had no knowledge of their language, or their customs, or even how they gestured to indicate nonverbal meaning.

"We have to learn their language," Shaylar said. "Quickly."

He glanced up. Their eyes met, and he smiled slightly, despite the snakes of anger and fear coiling inside him, as he realized how well she truly knew him. Despite their damaged marriage bond, she'd followed his own train of thought perfectly.

"They certainly won't bother to learn ours," he agreed. "Unless it's to interrogate us more effectively."

She shivered, and he kicked himself mentally. He couldn't unsay it, though, so he took her hand carefully and rubbed her fingers.

"Sorry," he said. "And I'm probably looking on the dark side. You say their commander's a decent sort, and you've seen a lot more of him than I have. Besides, I can't imagine they'd want to risk . . . damaging us with barbaric questioning methods. We're their only information source, and they need us, not just alive, but healthy and cooperative."

He knew he was grasping at straws, trying to reassure her, and the look in her eyes said she was perfectly aware of it. People capable of murdering an entire civilian survey crew were capable of *anything*, and torture could be undeniably effective. No Sharonian nation had used it—openly, at least; there were persistent grim rumors about the current Uromathian emperor and his secret police—in centuries.

But in Sharona's dim, grim past, torture had been an approved and often frighteningly effective method of extracting detailed information from captives.

"If I could just get past this *headache*," Shaylar muttered, "I could concentrate on learning their language. It wouldn't be easy without another telepath to help with translations, but I could pass anything I learned on to you. Verbally, if the bond's been permanently damaged."

Her voice went thin and frightened on the last two words, and Jathmar gave her hand a reassuring squeeze.

"Let's stay focused on what we can do, not what we can't, let alone what we *might* not be able to do. Agreed?"

"Agreed," she said in a much firmer voice. Then her gaze sharpened. "Who's this?"

A tall, aged man with the ebony skin of a Ricathian had emerged from one of the tents and was approaching them. His face was open and unguarded, almost childlike in his obvious curiosity about them. Curiosity and—

Jathmar blinked, startled, when he registered the other emotion in the older man's face: delight. He and Shaylar exchanged startled glances, then both of them looked back at the dark-skinned man again.

He gave them a curiously formal bow, then folded his long, lean body down to sit beside them. His voice was strangely gentle as he said something, then indicated himself and said slowly and carefully, "Halathyn. Halathyn vos Dulainah."

Shaylar glanced at Jathmar, then touched her own chest.

"Shaylar," she said, then indicated her husband. "Jathmar."

Halathyn's face blossomed in a beatific smile. He moved his hands in an intricate fashion, murmuring almost under his breath, and the air began to shimmer. Shaylar gasped, and Jathmar stiffened in shock as a flower of pure light formed in the air between the silver-haired man's palms. It was a *rose*, scintillating with all the dancing colors of the rainbow.

Halathyn moved his hand, and the rose of light drifted toward Shaylar. The older man took her hand, lifted her palm, and the impossible rose drifted down to rest against her fingertips. It shimmered there, ghostlike and lovely, for several seconds, then sparkled once and faded away.

Shaylar sat entranced for several heartbeats, staring at her empty palm, then turned to stare at the aged man beside them. Halathyn was grinning like a schoolboy, and she felt herself smiling back, unable to resist. Despite the pain in her head, she could feel the clean, gentle radiance of the black-skinned man's soul, and it washed over her like a comforting caress.

Then Gadrial said something in gently chiding tones. She'd been speaking with Jasak just moments previously, and she'd stopped at another campfire to pick up mugs of steaming liquid and carry them over. Now she stood gazing down at Halathyn, head cocked to one side, smiling for all the world like a tutor—or possibly even a nanny—at her favorite charge.

When she spoke, Halathyn merely waved one hand in a grandly dismissive gesture that left her laughing.

"What was that?" Shaylar breathed in Jathmar's ear while Halathyn and Gadrial were focused on each other.

"If there's a better word than magic, I don't know what it is," Jathmar murmured back in awe.

"Dragons, magical roses . . . Do you suppose what they used against us really was . . . magic? Honest to goodness *magic*?"

Jathmar raised one palm in a helpless "who knows" gesture.

"That doesn't make any logical sense," he said, "but neither does that rose." He shook his head. "There *is* no 'logical explanation' for that! Not any more than there's a logical explanation for what they hit us with in that clearing, or how they healed my burns. Until we know more, we'll just have to reserve judgment."

Halathyn, meanwhile, had produced a large crystal. It was clear as water, one of the most perfect specimens of quartz Jathmar had ever seen. The old man was fiddling with it, using a stylus to draw odd squiggles and shapes across its surface, which struck Jathmar as a fairly ludicrous thing to do. Ink wouldn't stick to a smooth crystal. Besides, Halathyn wasn't even *using* ink, just a dry stylus.

But then Halathyn angled the crystal so that they could see, and Jathmar leaned forward abruptly. The crystal was *glowing*. Or, rather, the strange *symbols* he'd drawn were glowing, squiggles and shapes that burned steadily down in the heart of the crystal. And there was something else strange about it, too. The crystal, large as it was, was no bigger than Jathmar's closed fist. Logically, anything contained inside it had to be quite small, yet those glowing symbols were clearly visible. He couldn't *read* them, because he had no idea at all what they might stand for, but when he focused his attention on them, they grew to whatever size they had to be for him to make them out in every detail.

"What *is* it?" he wondered aloud.

Shaylar leaned closer and "casually" rested one hand on the older man's arm as she peered over his shoulder. A familiar abstracted look appeared on her face, then she smiled wonderingly.

"It's a tool of some kind. Something to . . . store things in?"

She sounded hesitant, and Jathmar frowned.

"Store things in?" he echoed. "That looks like writing of some kind, but how could anyone store writing inside a *rock*?"

"Or light, for that matter," she said. "And that's what it looks like—*light*."

"I'm the wrong person to ask." Jathmar shook his head, baffled. "I can't begin to imagine how something like that works."

Whatever Halathyn was doing with the stylus, the squiggles of light shifted rapidly inside the crystal. It certainly looked like writing of some sort, and it did, indeed, look as if Halathyn were storing the words inside that water-clear rock. He glanced up, eyes twinkling, then he whispered something else, and the light faded.

He handed it to Shaylar, who took it with a deeply dubious expression. Then he spoke one word and tapped the crystal with his stylus, and the glowing text sprang back to life. It glowed deep inside, scrolling past at what would probably have been a comfortable reading speed, if they could have read it at all.

Shaylar stared, openmouthed, then looked up to meet Jathmar's amazed gaze, and Halathyn chuckled. He looked inordinately pleased with himself as he retrieved his crystal, and the look he gave Gadrial was just short of impish. She responded by rolling her eyes, and handed over the mugs she carried.

They contained a beverage that smelled like tea. Jathmar took a hesitant sip and let out a deep sigh. It was *tea*, spiced with something wonderful. He blew across the surface, sipping with pleasure while Gadrial cradled her own cup in both hands and drank deeply. The Uromathian-looking woman glanced at Halathyn, then turned to Shaylar and spoke again. She pointed to Shaylar and Jathmar in turn, then to herself and to the dragon.

"Looks to me," Jathmar muttered, "like we're about to be taken out of here."

"Yes," Shaylar agreed. "And look at Jasak. He's paying awfully close attention to this conversation."

Jathmar glanced up and decided that Shaylar's comment was a distinct case of understatement.

"I'd say our friend in uniform sent Gadrial over as his errand-boy," he said. Then he glanced at Gadrial's figure, whose shapeliness was quite evident, despite her bulky hiking clothes, and smiled crookedly. "Well, maybe not errand-*boy*, exactly," he amended. "I find it mighty interesting that he sent *her* over, rather than telling us himself, though."

Shaylar gave him an unusually hard look.

"He doesn't want to push you into starting something that one of his soldiers might decide to finish," she said sharply, and he nodded.

"You think I don't realize that? With you in harm's way," he added gruffly, "I won't be starting *anything* I'm not likely to win. But I'll admit it. If not for his trigger-happy soldiers, I might be tempted."

Her breath caught, and terror exploded behind her eyes. She took one hand from her mug of tea, reaching out to grip his forearm with painful force.

"Please, Jath," she whispered, "don't even *think* of trying that. I couldn't bear to lose you again."

That shook him, and he looked deep into her eyes, suddenly seeing that hideous fight from her perspective. When *he* remembered that ghastly fireball engulfing him, he remembered agony and terror, but they were *his* agony, his terror. When *she* remembered it, she remembered seeing him die.

Deep as that instant of consummate terror and pain had been as the fire took him, the memory which had followed his return to consciousness in this camp, before finding Shaylar alive beside him, had been far worse. For those few, ghastly moments, when he'd believed *she* was dead, the world had been an unbearable place, darker, deeper, and far bleaker than the far side of the moon. Yet even that, hideous as it had been, had been far less horrifying than it would have been to see *her* wrapped in the furnace heat of a fireball, burning to death before his very eyes.

"No," he choked out, pulling her close, burying his face in her hair. "Never. I'll never risk *anything* that would leave you here alone."

Her breath shuddered unsteadily against the side of his neck, but she held herself together, and when she finally sat up again, her courageous smile sent an ache of proud pain through his heart. He dried her face with gentle hands, careful on her bruises, but before he could speak again, they were distracted by a sudden shout.

Both of them slewed around in time to see another dragon come winging in from the east. Translucent leathery wings vaned and twisted, altering its flightpath and slowing its airspeed. There seemed to be something indefinably *wrong* about the way it braked, how quickly it lost velocity, but Jathmar reminded himself that he was scarcely in mental condition to make reliable hard and fast judgments about mythological beasts who couldn't possibly exist anyway.

Jasak Olderhan had turned with everyone else at the dragon's approach. Now he strode rapidly to meet it, his face set in grim lines, and Gadrial spoke to the dark-skinned man sitting beside them. She sounded worried, and Halathyn shrugged, peering with obvious curiosity of his own as the dragon backwinged with a thunderclap of its immense wings and settled with surprising delicacy at the edge of camp.

Jathmar frowned at the newcomer, and even more at the reactions he saw around him.

"Trouble?" he wondered aloud.

"Could be," Shaylar replied. "It's obvious that Jasak isn't rolling out the welcome mat for whoever's on that thing, anyway."

CHAPTER
FOURTEEN

JASAK OLDERHAN REMINDED himself not to curse out loud as he shaded his eyes with one hand, peering up at the approaching dragon.

Muthok Salmeer had made the condition of Cloudsail, Windclaw's assigned wing dragon, abundantly clear. It would be weeks, at least, before Cloudsail could return to service, which hadn't exactly filled Jasak with happiness when he found out. The distance between the base camp and Fort Rycharn was just long enough to prevent a single dragon from flying a complete round-trip without pausing for rest. With only Windclaw, that was going to limit him to at most one and a half round-trips per day, which was going to put a decided kink into his plan to pull back to the coastal enclave by air.

Under the circumstances, the sight of a second operable dragon should have delighted him. Unfortunately, since it couldn't be the injured Cloudsail, it had to be one of the additional dragons they'd been promised for months. Given the water gap between Fort Rycharn and Fort Wyvern, at the entry portal into this universe, it could only have arrived by ship. Which meant the next regularly scheduled transport from Fort Wyvern had also arrived.

Which almost certainly meant . . .

The dragon landed, and Jasak's mouth tightened as a stocky man in the uniform of the Second Andaran Scouts with the same silver-shield collar insignia Jasak wore climbed down from the second saddle. The newcomer turned, surveying the camp and the rows of wounded troopers with a hard, grim frown, and Jasak snarled a mental obscenity.

He *had* been looking forward to his replacement's arrival, or, at least, to going home himself for a well-earned bit of R&R. But that had changed the moment Shevan Garlath sent the situation crashing out of control by killing an unarmed man. His men were shattered and demoralized, and the thought of turning his command over *now* was thoroughly unpalatable.

"Hundred Thalmayr." Jasak saluted the newcomer.

"Hundred Olderhan." Hadrign Thalmayr returned Jasak's salute with a flip of the hand which turned the ostensible courtesy into something one thin inch short of a derisive insult. Then he reached into his tunic pocket and extracted an official message crystal. "As per the orders of Commander of Two Thousand mul Gurthak, I relieve you."

Jasak's jaw muscles knotted as he saw the contempt in Thalmayr's dark eyes. The man knew nothing about what had happened out here, but it was obvious he'd already made up his mind about it. Jasak's temper snarled against its leash, but he couldn't afford to release it. Not yet.

"Very well, Hundred Thalmayr," he said formally, instead, accepting the crystal. "I stand relieved."

"Good," Thalmayr said. "In that case, pack your prisoners onto your transport, Hundred Olderhan. There's nothing to delay your immediate departure."

"On the contrary," Jasak said, more sharply than he'd intended to do. "I have men in the field, on a reconnaissance mission. They haven't returned yet, and we can't possibly evacuate until they do."

"Evacuate?" Thalmayr repeated incredulously. He stared at Jasak for an instant, then curled his lip contemptuously. "You can't possibly be serious!"

"I'm deadly serious," Jasak snapped. "These people have devastating weapons we can't even comprehend, Thalmayr. Less than twenty of them—apparently *civilians*—killed or wounded two thirds of a crack Scout unit. That's over *eighty-five percent* casualties to First Platoon's combat element. Until we know more about them, the last thing we can afford is another armed confrontation. We need to make that impossible—pull back to the coast and establish a buffer zone they can't track us across until we get a team of trained diplomats in here."

"We wouldn't need diplomats," Thalmayr said icily, "if you hadn't totally botched the first contact! I may not have been an Andaran Scout—" a not-so-faint edge of contempt burred in the last two words "—as long as *you* have, but even a straight infantry puke knows standing orders are clear, Olderhan. In the event of discovery of any non-Arcanan people, every precaution must be taken to insure *peaceful* contact." He swept an angry gesture across the wounded waiting for medical treatment. "Obviously, *your* idea of 'peaceful' isn't exactly the same as mine, is it?"

Muscles jumped along Jasak Olderhan's jaw. He could hardly tell this pompous oaf that Fifty Garlath had been ordered to stand down. It would have sounded like a lame excuse, and the last thing he was prepared to do was sound as if he were making excuses to Hadrign Thalmayr. Eventually, there would be a board of inquiry. The odds were at least even that the board's conclusions would send his career into the nearest toilet, whatever else happened, but at the moment—

"That doesn't change the current tactical situation," he said instead. He made his voice come out levelly, as nonconfrontationally as possible, but Thalmayr's eyes blazed.

"Yes," he bit out, "it does. *You* may want to cut and run, but your actions have made it imperative—*imperative!*—that we remain firmly in control of this portal. First, because the Union Army will never yield an *inch* of Arcanan soil. Second, because it's the smallest bottleneck in three universes, which makes it the best possible spot to hold our ground if we have to. And third, because your own initial report to Five Hundred Klian makes it clear that the universe on the other side of *that* portal—" he jabbed an angry gesture at the swamp portal "—is a fucking *cluster*. Only the second true cluster ever discovered! We are *not* going to give up access to a cluster the size of this one. Especially not when somebody's already been stupid enough to start a fucking war with the people we'd be giving it up to!"

Jasak knew his face had gone white, and Thalmayr sneered at him.

"We'll get your 'diplomats' in here, all right, Olderhan. They'll shovel the shit and clean up your mess for you. But in the meantime, if the bastards who did this—" the same angry hand jabbed at the rows of wounded "—want to pick a fight, they'll get no further than that slice of dirt." The finger jabbed again, this time at the portal. "If they want Arcanan soil, we'll give them just enough of it to bury them in."

Jasak stared at him, too aghast even to feel his own white-hot rage.

"*Are you out of your mind?*" he demanded. "If you invoke Andaran 'blood and honor' now, you'll have a first-class disaster on your hands! And you'll get more of my men killed, you—"

"*My* men!" Thalmayr snarled back. "Or have you forgotten the orders in that crystal?"

Jasak started a fiery retort, then made himself stop. He sucked in an enormous breath, promising himself the day would come when Hadrign Thalmayr would face him—briefly—across a field of honor. But not today. Not here.

"Yours or mine, Hundred Thalmayr," he said as calmly as he could, "it's unconscionable to put these men back into the path of combat again when there's no need, and when another violent confrontation would be the worst political disaster we could come up with. Sitting here rattling our sabers and daring the enemy to cross our line in the mud isn't the way to resolve this situation without further bloodshed."

"Contact's already been botched." Thalmayr's eyes were volcanic. "Thanks to that—thanks to *you*—these people now represent a clear and present danger to the Union of Arcana. My job is to safeguard Arcanan territory—"

"Your *job* is to defend Arcanan *citizens* from further danger," Jasak hissed, "not to haggle over the ownership of a patch of mud!"

"—and I'll rattle as many sabers as it fucking well takes to defend it!" Thalmayr snarled, as if Jasak hadn't spoken at all. "*Your* job—assuming you can *do* it—is to transport your passengers back for interrogation. I suggest you get started. It's a long, long way to Army HQ on New Arcana."

Before Jasak could open his mouth again, Thalmayr shoved past him and strode directly toward the campfire, where Jathmar and Shaylar had risen to their feet and stood watching the heated exchange tautly. Jasak stalked after the idiot, shoulders set for another confrontation. He got it when Thalmayr reached the campfire and turned with another snarl.

"They aren't restrained!"

"No," Jasak said icily. "They aren't. And they won't be."

"You're out of line, Soldier! Those *criminals*—" the finger he was so fond of jabbing with jerked at Jathmar and his wife "—have slaughtered Arcanan soldiers—"

"*Who butchered their* civilian *companions!*" Jasak discovered that he suddenly didn't much care how Thalmayr responded to the flaming contempt in his own voice. The man might be technically senior to him, but he was also a complete and total idiot. A part of Jasak actually hoped he could goad Thalmayr into taking a swing at him. His own career was already so far into the crapper that the charge of striking a superior—especially if the superior had struck the first blow—could hardly do a lot more damage. And the resultant chaos would probably force Five Hundred Klian to put someone—*anyone*—else in command of Charlie Company while he sorted it out.

"Soldiers who slaughtered their *civilian* friends in a battle Shevan Garlath started against direct orders!" he continued, glaring murderously at the other officer. "*We're* in the wrong, Hundred—not them! All they did was defend themselves with courage and honor. That girl—" it was his turn to point at Shaylar "—that *civilian* girl—is braver than any soldier I've ever commanded! Her husband was so badly burned by our dragons he was barely alive, she was badly injured herself, and she was all alone in the face of the men who'd killed all of her friends, but she faced us with courage. With *courage*, damn your eyes! She even managed to hold herself together during field rites for every friend she had in that universe. Don't you *dare* call these people criminals!"

Hundred Thalmayr paled. Field rites were enough to give even hardened soldiers nightmares. But then the color flooded back into his face, which went brick-red with fury.

"I'll call these bastards whatever I fucking well want, *Hundred*," he said in a voice of ice and fire. "And I am in command here now, not you! You, Sword!" he barked to Sword Harnak. "I want field manacles on these . . . people. *Now*, Sword!"

"Stand fast, Sword Harnak!" Jasak snapped. Thalmayr whipped back around to him with an utterly incredulous expression. Jasak matched him glare for glare, and the other hundred leaned towards him.

"I don't give a good godsdamn *whose* son you are, Olderhan," Thalmayr hissed. "You give another order to one of *my* men, and I'll send you back to Fort Rycharn in chains to face charges for mutiny in the face of the enemy!"

"Try it," Jasak said very, very quietly. "'These people,' as you put it, are *my* prisoners, not yours."

"They—" Thalmayr began.

"Shut your brainless mouth," Jasak said coldly. "I was in command of the unit which took them prisoner. The unit which *disobeyed* my orders and opened fire on a *civilian* survey party whose leader was standing there without a weapon in his hands trying his best to make *peaceful* contact despite the previous death of one of his people at our hands. We . . . were . . . in . . . the . . . wrong," he spaced the words out with deadly precision, "and I was in command, and they surrendered themselves to me honorably." He locked his gaze with Thalmayr's, his expression harder than steel. "'These people' are *shardonai*, Hundred Thalmayr. *My shardonai*."

Thalmayr had opened his mouth once again. Now he closed it,

glaring back at Jasak. The term "*shardon*" came from Old Andaran. Literally, it meant "shieldling," and it indicated an individual under the personal protection of an Andaran warrior and his house. It was a concept which stemmed from almost two thousand years of Andaran history. There could be many reasons for the relationship, but one of the oldest—and most sacred, under the Andaran honor code—was the acknowledgment of responsibility for dishonorable or illegal actions by troops under a warrior's command.

"I don't care what else they may be," Thalmayr said after a moment. A corner of his mind knew he ought to drop it, but he was too furious. "They're also enemies of the Union who have killed Army personnel, and as long as they're on a post *I* command, they will be properly manacled and restrained!"

"Try it," Jasak repeated, and this time it came out almost in a croon. "*Please* try it. Violate my *shardon* obligation, and you'll be dead on the ground before you finish the order."

Thalmayr blanched, his face suddenly bone-white as he saw the absolute sincerity in Jasak's blazing eyes. Like Jasak, Thalmayr carried his short sword at his hip, but the restraining strap was firmly buttoned across the quillons, and he very carefully kept his hand well away from it as he backed up two involuntary steps.

Silence hovered between them, colder than ice and just as brittle. Then, finally, Thalmayr straightened his spine and scowled.

"You may be certain, *Hundred* Olderhan, that I'll be filing charges for insubordination and threatening a superior officer."

"File and be damned," Jasak said, still in that soft, deadly tone.

"*And*," Thalmayr continued, trying to ignore Jasak's response, "I'll also be lodging a formal protest over your handling of these people. *Shardonai* or not, enemy prisoners should be restrained to prevent escape attempts."

Jason looked at him disbelievingly, then barked a harsh laugh.

"*Escape?*" he repeated. "And just where would they go, Hundred? They're in the middle of a heavily guarded camp seven hundred miles from the nearest coastline. Unless I miss my guess, Shaylar's suffering from a concussion, they have no idea how far they are from the portal they came through, and the gods alone know how many miles beyond *that* portal they'd have to go to find help! With Shaylar too badly injured to travel far, no weapons, and no supplies, they can't run. Not together—and Jathmar won't abandon her."

"You sound awfully godsdamned sure of yourself for someone who's fucked up every single command decision for the past two days by the numbers!" Thalmayr snarled.

"Because he's right," another voice said, and Thalmayr's head snapped around as Gadrial Kelbryan stepped unexpectedly into the fray. He stared at her for a moment, and she looked back with an expression which reminded Jasak of a gryphon defending her chicks. Thalmayr started to glare back, then turned an even darker shade of red as he suddenly realized what sort of language he'd been using in her presence.

"Magister Kelbryan," Jasak said formally, "May I present Commander of One Hundred Hadrign Thalmayr. Hundred Thalmayr, Magister Gadrial Kelbryan, Director of Theoretical Research for the Garth Showma Institute, and special assistant to Magister Halathyn vos Dulainah."

"Hundred." Gadrial nodded, her voice cool, and Thalmayr actually clicked his boot heels as he swept her an elaborate bow. As his head dipped low, Gadrial looked across him at Jasak and rolled her eyes, then wiped the look away, replacing it with a cool, composed gaze as Thalmayr came back upright.

"I apologize for my language, Magister," Thalmayr said almost obsequiously. Obviously, he knew exactly who Gadrial was . . . and recognized just how fatal to his career it would be to make a mortal enemy out of the second ranking member of the Garth Showma Institute's faculty. Although she wasn't officially in the military, Gadrial carried the equivalent grade of a commander of ten thousand in the UTTTA's civil service.

"I've heard soldiers talking to each other before, Hundred," she said, after a moment, and his shoulders seemed to relax just a bit. "If seldom quite so . . . freely," she added in that same cool voice with perfect timing, and his shoulders tightened back up instantly.

"Ah, yes," he replied, then stood there for a moment, as if trying to think of something else to say. "Ah, you were saying, Magister?" he continued finally.

"I was saying that *Sir* Jasak," she said, eyes glittering as she stressed Jasak's title ever so slightly, "is quite right in his assessment of our unexpected guests. And of our obligations to them."

Thalmayr's eyebrows climbed, and Jasak wondered just how much Gadrial actually knew about the *shardon* relationship. He was willing to bet she didn't begin to understand all of the deep-seated obligations of personal and familial honor bound up in it—she was simply too Ransaran to grasp the implications of Andara's feudal past. Obviously Thalmayr was thinking exactly the same thing, but whatever Jasak's opinion of the other man's basic intelligence—or lack thereof—he was at least smart enough not to pursue that particular basilisk.

"How so, Magister?" he asked courteously, instead.

"I've spent a great deal of time with Shaylar and Jathmar since their capture," Gadrial replied. "He's utterly devoted to her, as she is to him. Think for a moment, Hundred, how *you'd* feel if you were hundreds of miles from help and—"

"They may not be that far from their portal. It's my understanding that the cluster of portals you and Magister Halathyn have detected are in very close proximity. That means—"

"How dare *you interrupt a Guild magister?"*

Gadrial's voice cracked like a whip. She bristled so furiously her very hair seemed to crackle and Thalmayr blanched and backed up—first one step, then another—as she advanced on him.

"Are you truly the unschooled, illiterate, brainless, unwashed *barbarian* you appear to be?" Her voice was like a sword. "Or does the Andaran military academy include courses on discourtesy as part of its standard curriculum? Because if it does, you obviously excelled in at least *one* subject!"

"Magister, I—"

"Enough!" The air sizzled around her—literally *sizzled* as static charges cracked and popped like the aura of a Mythalan firebird. "I'm tired of musclebound idiots insulting my intelligence, my professional competence, and my rank! Shevan Garlath was a disgrace to the uniform he died in, and so far, Hundred Thalmayr, I'm not any more favorably impressed by *you*!"

Hadrign Thalmayr swallowed hard. For a moment, Jasak almost felt sorry for the other man, despite his own blinding rage. The wrath of any full magister was something few mortals cared to incur; the wrath of *this* magister could destroy the career of a man with far better political and patronage connections than Thalmayr possessed.

"Magister Kelbryan, a thousand pardons! I beg your forgiveness for my deplorable discourtesy."

She tilted her head back, staring down her nose at him despite the fact that he stood two full hands taller than she did. She let him sweat for another long moment, then gave a minute, frost-rimmed nod.

"Apology accepted," she said coldly. Then added, "As for your objection, *we* know how relatively close we are to their portal; they don't."

Thalmayr started to protest again, then clamped his lips together and kept whatever it was carefully behind his teeth.

"Much better, Hundred Thalmayr." Gadrial's eyes glinted. "They don't know for the simple reason that they were both unconscious for most of the flight here. They have no way of knowing how far we brought them by dragon."

"Oh. Oh, I see." Thalmayr cleared his throat. "Well, yes. That does change the picture a bit, doesn't it?"

Jasak carefully refrained from snorting aloud.

"It certainly does," Gadrial agreed coldly. "Not only do they have no idea how far they'd have to go, but Shaylar can't bolt, and Sir Jasak is right—Jathmar won't, not without her. Look at them, Hundred Thalmayr. I mean that literally. *Look at them.*"

Thalmayr's head turned like a marionette's. Jathmar had placed himself squarely between the hundred and Shaylar. His eyes were slitted, his posture tense. He stood with his knees slightly bent, his hands half-fisted at his sides, coiled like a serpent ready to strike.

"He's already close to the breakpoint," Gadrial said in a quieter, softer voice. "Do you really want to push him over the edge and set off a violent confrontation that might well end in another death, Hundred? And do you think your superiors will thank you for managing to kill off one of the only two sources of information we currently possess just to restrain a man who isn't going to run away anyway?"

Hundred Thalmayr cleared his throat again.

"You . . . may just have a point, Magister."

"How *magnanimous* of you to agree, Hundred."

He flushed under the ice-cold irony of her voice. For just an instant Jasak thought he might actually take up her verbal gage, but apparently even he wasn't *that* stupid.

"Very well," he muttered instead, his voice brittle. "I'll concede the point."

"Thank you. My job is hard enough as it is, without fighting the Army every step of the way."

"Your *job*, Magister?"

"Yes, my job. Isn't it obvious?" she asked, deliberately needling him. But he only blinked, clearly not seeing where she was headed.

"I'm the only obvious civilian in this camp," she said in a deliberately patient voice, "since even Magister Halathyn looks more 'official and military' than I do, in their eyes. I'm the only person they're likely to even halfway trust. I've also seen virtually everything that happened out here. What I know, what I've already seen and done, make my inclusion in whatever happens to them imperative."

"That's the official position of the Guild?" he asked, knowing full well that the Guild didn't know anything about this situation as yet. Gadrial knew it, too, but she looked him squarely in the eye.

"It is," she said flatly, and it *would* be, as soon as the news broke. She'd see to that personally, if she had to. Meanwhile, the closer she stayed to them, the less likely it was that anyone in the Army—or in the halls of political power, for that matter—would be able to spirit them off under a veil of secrecy and do whatever they deemed "necessary" to extract information. Not even politicians and commanders of legions wanted to take on the Guild of Sorcerers, and the Guild would certainly back her. Especially with Magister Halathyn's guaranteed support.

Gadrial wasn't foolish enough to think that anyone, even Magister Halathyn himself, could—or even should—shield them from *any* prying. But there were right and wrong ways of obtaining information from them, and Gadrial was determined that the right way would prevail.

Hundred Thalmayr obviously wasn't made of sufficiently stern stuff to stand against her.

"Very well, Magister Kelbryan," he said in a conciliatory tone. Then he glanced at Jasak again. "The prisoners are yours, Hundred. See to it," he added, his voice heavy with warning as he turned back to Gadrial once more, "that you at least remember whose side you're on."

Gadrial bristled again, but he'd already turned on his heel and walked off, spitting orders as he went. She met Jasak's gaze and found a curious blend of respect, regret, and dark worry in his eyes.

"You'd best pack your things," was all he said. "Salmeer's going to be wanting to leave shortly."

"You think Thalmayr's wrong to stay?" she asked quietly.

"Think?" He snorted. "No, I don't *think* he's wrong. I know it."

"I agree with you about the need to prevent another violent confrontation, but he's right about the size of the portal," she pointed out unwillingly, hating to sound as if she were siding with Thalmayr about *anything*. "All of the upstream portals from here are larger. If it *does* come to more shooting, isn't this the best place to try and hold them?"

"Hundred Thalmayr doesn't have a clue what he's up against," Jasak said softly, his tone flat. "He hasn't seen these people's weapons in action, and he doesn't know one damned thing more than *I* do about how many of them are out there, how close they are, how quickly they can follow us back to this portal. He *won't* know, either, until Chief Sword Threbuch gets back here. But instead of pulling people out, he's going to be moving more of them *in*." He shook his head. "One of my—*his*—platoons is all the way back in Erthos, over four thousand miles from here. First Platoon's been effectively destroyed, and Five Hundred Klian's battalion's scattered around holding posts across at least three universes. That leaves Thalmayr with only two platoons—barely a hundred and twenty more men, even with supports, since they're both understrength. That's not going to be enough to hold against any sort of attack in strength, but it *will* be big enough to make it impossible for him to disengage and pull out quickly if something too big to handle comes at him."

"And he's not remotely prepared to listen to you," Gadrial worried.

"He's convinced I screwed up, probably because I panicked. He thinks I behaved dishonorably, and that my intention to retreat was an act of cowardice."

"*Cowardice!* Is he insane? And you did *not* act dishonorably! Why, that pompous, *stupid—*!"

"Peace, Magister." He held up one hand, and she subsided, still fuming. "This isn't your fight," he said gently. "And rest assured that that accusation will be raised again."

"Any jackass who makes *that* accusation will hear the truth from me," she said, eyes slitted, "even if I have to knock them down and stand on their chests while I shout at them!"

"My Lady," Jasak said with a slight smile, "that's a sight I'd relish seeing. But be that as it may, I still have to get them safely back to New Arcana. Pack for the journey, please. I have to speak with Magister Halathyn. Immediately."

"*Halathyn,*" she breathed, her face suddenly pale. "He has to go with us."

"Yes, he has to," Jasak agreed. "And he's a cantankerous, dragon-headed, opinionated old curmudgeon, far too accustomed to getting his own way, who shouldn't be allowed outside the precincts of the Academy without an armed keeper and a leash."

He half-expected her to be insulted, but instead, her lips quirked in a slightly strained smile.

"My goodness, you *do* know him rather well, don't you?"

"That I do, and he's not going to want to get any farther away from this damned portal cluster than he absolutely has to. So, if you'll excuse me?"

He turned away, and it was clear to Gadrial as he stalked toward Halathyn, beckoning urgently to the aging magister and pointing toward Halathyn's tent, that he cared for that cantankerous, dragon-headed, opinionated old curmudgeon almost as much as she did. And, she thought, biting her lip, he was absolutely right about how hard it was going to be to convince Halathyn to "abandon his post" on the cusp of uncovering the greatest single trans-temporal discovery of all time: not simply a portal cluster, but another entire trans-universal civilization! Could Jasak—or she—possibly come up with an argument potent enough to pull that off?

Fear, cold as a Ransaran winter wind, blew through her heart. She stood for a moment longer, watching Jasak and Halathyn bend to duck under the fly of Halathyn's tent. Then she trudged off toward her own tent, and started to pack.

*　　*　　*

"There's more trouble brewing," Jathmar said tersely, and Shaylar nodded.

Judging by the raised voices coming from the tent where Jasak and the elderly, dark-skinned Halathyn had retreated to speak in private, they weren't exactly in perfect agreement about something. Halathyn sounded reasonable and confident, if a trifle irritated, while Jasak sounded angry and frustrated. The newcomer—the man Jasak and Gadrial had called "Thalmayr"—strode toward the tent, and Jathmar tensed. His maddening inability to understand what anyone said hadn't prevented him from recognizing the fact that Thalmayr represented a serious threat to him and Shaylar . . . or the fury with which Jasak had confronted the other man over it.

But Thalmayr paused, just outside the tent flap, obviously eavesdropping. At least he didn't intrude and make whatever was going on still worse, but Jathmar would almost have preferred that to the man's nasty grin before he moved on.

Whatever Jasak and Halathyn were arguing about, Jathmar decided he'd better worry about it, if Thalmayr was glad it was taking place. Thalmayr scared him straight down to his socks, and he didn't mind admitting it. Not, at any rate, as much as he hated admitting that he and Shaylar *needed* Jasak and Gadrial as protection against the other man.

"Gadrial's packing her belongings, too," Shaylar said abruptly. "Look there."

She nodded toward the tent beside Halathyn's, where the slim, not-Uromathian woman was visible through the open flap. She was, indeed, packing, but nobody else was.

"Whatever's going on, they're not evacuating the whole camp," Jathmar muttered. "They must intend to stand their ground at this portal."

"Will Grafin order out a search party?" Shaylar wondered.

"I don't know. That's a military question, which means it's also a political one. On the other hand, Darcel won't rest until he locates us—or our bodies. And Darcel can be mighty persuasive."

He smiled crookedly at Shaylar, but his smile disappeared as she shook her head.

"He won't find any bodies, Jath," she said, her voice hollow, and Jathmar felt something prickle along his scalp at her expression.

"What do you mean? Surely they buried the dead!"

"No." She shook her head. "No, they burned them. Cremation, I guess I should call it. All of them. Theirs and ours with—" She swallowed convulsively. "I don't know what it was. It burned fast, and hot. It consumed . . . everything."

"Those sick, sadistic—" Jathmar began savagely, but she shook her head again, harder.

"No, it wasn't like that!" Her distress was obvious, but she felt carefully for the right words. "They treated our people just like theirs, Jathmar. It was . . . it was like some kind of funeral rite. They couldn't carry the bodies out. And there weren't enough of them left to bury all the dead. So they did the best they could, and they gave our people just as much respect as their own."

Jathmar stared at her, and she managed a tremulous smile. But then her eyes closed once more, and she leaned her forehead against him.

"I know that's what they were doing, what they intended. I read it off Jasak. But *seeing* it . . ."

She began to weep yet again, and he held her tight, whispering to her, begging her not to cry.

"No. I need to," she said through her tears. "Barris told me that, after Falsan died in my arms. He told me to go ahead and cry. It was the psychic death shock, he said, and he was right. And then I watched *him*. Just watched him burn to ashes . . ."

"Oh, love," he whispered into her hair, rocking her gently, eyes burning.

He started to say something more, then stopped himself and closed his eyes. He hadn't been there when Falsan died, but he knew Barris had given Shaylar the right advice. Now, hard as it was, Jathmar had to let her do the same thing when all he really wanted to do was comfort her until she stopped weeping.

He concentrated on just hugging her, and deliberately sought something else to distract him from his desperate worry over her and his fury at the people who had driven her to this.

He opened his eyes once more and looked up at Gadrial once again. The other woman was almost finished packing, it seemed, and he found himself wondering just who Gadrial was. It was obvious that it was her intervention which had brought the incandescent confrontation between Jasak and Thalmayr to a screeching halt. And, ended it in Jasak's favor, unless Jathmar was very mistaken. The tall, menacing Thalmayr had backed down from her like a rabbit suddenly confronted by a cougar. And she and Halathyn appeared to be the only civilians in the entire camp. So just who *were* they? And how important *was* Gadrial?

The confrontation continued to rage in Halathyn's tent. Gadrial stood beside a packed duffel bag, her head cocked to one side, her body language tense and unhappy as she listened to it. Then she obviously came to a decision.

"Oh, my," Shaylar murmured in his ear. She'd almost stopped crying, and she managed a damp smile as she and Jathmar watched Gadrial march toward Halathyn's tent. The other woman's mouth was set in a thin, hard line, and her almond-shaped eyes flashed.

"I don't think I'd like that lady mad at *me*," Shaylar added, and Jathmar produced a smile of his own.

"I always knew you were a smart woman, love," he replied

Gadrial disappeared into the tent. A moment later her voice joined the fray, pleading at first, then increasingly sharp with anger. It went on for quite a while until, finally, she let out an inarticulate howl and stormed back out again.

A part of Jathmar wanted to be glad. Surely any discord in the enemy's camp had to be a good thing from Sharona's perspective! But then he saw Gadrial's face. Her lovely, honey-toned skin was ashy white, her lips trembled, and tears sparkled on her eyelashes.

Shaylar saw it, too, and rose swiftly, taking Jathmar by surprise.

"Gadrial?" Shaylar lifted a hand toward her, part in question, part in sympathy, and Gadrial's face crumpled. She looked back at Shaylar for a moment, then shook her head and turned away, retreating back into her own tent and letting the flap fall. Shaylar bit her lower lip, then sank back down beside Jathmar.

"I hate that," she whispered wretchedly. "I can't stand seeing her that distressed, especially after the way she's tried to comfort *me*."

"It's not our affair," Jathmar said gently. Anger sparked in her eyes, but he laid a fingertip across her lips and shook his head.

"It isn't," he said again, gently but firmly. "There's nothing we can do, because there's nothing they'll *let* us do."

"You're right." A sigh shuddered its way loose from her. "That doesn't make it any easier, though."

"Not for you," he acknowledged. "Me, now, I'm just a bit less forgiving than you are. I think I could stand quite a bit of distress on these people's part!"

"But not on Gadrial's," Shaylar replied.

"Well, no," he admitted, not entirely willingly. "Not on Gadrial's."

She smiled and touched the side of his face, then both of them looked up as Halathyn's tent flap opened again and Jasak emerged. Actually, "emerge" was too pale a way to describe his explosive eruption, or the eloquent gesture he made at the sky. Then he stalked away, heading toward another tent on the opposite side of the encampment.

Halathyn's tent flap stirred again, and the long, frail black man appeared. He called out something, and lifted one hand in a conciliatory gesture, but Jasak refused to listen or even glance back, and the storm in his eyes as he raged past their campfire frightened Jathmar.

Protector or not, Jasak Olderhan obviously wasn't a man any sane individual wanted pissed off at him, Jathmar thought. But he'd already concluded that, watching Jasak and Thalmayr. It wasn't fear of Jasak's temper that tightened Jathmar's arm around Shaylar; it was the iron discipline which held that temper in check. Angry men were dangerous—men who could control and *use* their anger, instead of being used *by* it, were deadly.

Jasak was one of the the latter, Jathmar decided, and filed that information carefully away. There were precious few weapons available to them, but knowledge was one, and nothing he learned about these people was a waste of effort. So he watched Jasak stalk into his own tent. Watched Halathyn lower his hand, sigh, and shake his head regretfully. Watched the old man reenter his tent without trying to heal the breach again. And Jathmar watched as Jasak, too, began to throw things into a heavy canvas duffel bag.

So both of their . . . champions would be going with them, wherever they were going. That was interesting, and at least a little reassuring. As for those who stayed behind . . .

Jathmar's eyes narrowed once more, filled with bitter emotion. He could only hope that Company-Captain Halifu and Darcel Kinlafia avenged them—with interest. That shocked him, in a way, even now, but it was true.

Jathmar Nargra had never expected to be brought face-to-face with the sort of carnage which had destroyed his survey team. Yet he had, and he'd discovered that he wanted his dead avenged. He wanted the people who'd killed them repaid in full and ample measure. Part of him was shocked by that, but all the shock in the multiverse couldn't change that fact.

Deep inside, another wounded part of him—a part which might one day heal, however impossible that seemed at the moment—mourned the passing of the man he'd been. The man who would have been horrified by the prospect of yet more slaughter, whoever it was visited upon. But for now, hatred was stronger than horror in his heart, and that was precisely how he wanted it.

CHAPTER
FIFTEEN

ACTING PLATOON-CAPTAIN HULMOK Arthag mistrusted the shadows in this thick, towering forest. Then again, Hulmok Arthag mistrusted most things in life, including people. Not without reason; Arpathians learned the meaning of prejudice the instant they set foot outside Arpathia.

The other races of Sharona made Arpathians the butt of jokes and viewed them—some tolerantly, some nastily—as barbarians. But no one made jokes about Hulmok Arthag, and if *he* was considered an unlettered barbarian, no one said so within his earshot.

He'd also learned, growing up on the endless Arpathian plains, that no sane man put his faith in the vagaries of wind, weather, fire, or even grass. Wind could bring death by tornado, weather by the freezing howl of blizzards that quick-froze everything caught in them, or the slower death of drought. Fire could blaze out of control, driven by wind to consume everything in its path. Grass could wither and fail, leaving no fodder for the herds, and when the herds failed, eventually there would be no one left to bury or burn the dead.

What Arthag *did* trust were his own strong hands, his own determination, and the hearts of those under his command. Not their minds, for no man's—or woman's—mind could be guaranteed, let alone trusted. But a heart could be measured, if one looked into its depths with the sort of Talent that laid its innermost secrets bare, and Hulmok Arthag had that Talent. He didn't misuse it, as some might have, but when it came to assessing the men under his command, he used it ruthlessly, indeed, and he'd come up with many ways to get rid of any man who failed to meet his own rigorous standards.

"Platoon-Captain."

Arthag looked up. It was Mikal Grigthir, the trooper he'd sent forward as an advance scout. Grigthir trotted his horse up to the small campfire where Arthgag sat, waiting with the rest of the halted column for his report, reined in, and saluted sharply.

"Good to see you in one piece," Arthag growled, returning the salute.

"Thank you, Sir." Grigthir had been with Arthag for less than six months, only since the Arpathian had been brevetted to his present acting rank and given command of Second Platoon, Argent Company, of the Ninety-Second Independent Cavalry Battalion. But he was an experienced man, an old hand out here on the frontier, and Arthag had complete faith in his judgment.

"What did you find?" the petty-captain continued.

"I found their final camp, Sir. It's been pillaged. Most of their gear was abandoned, but there's not a weapon left in the whole stockade. Not even a single cartridge case."

"They took the donkeys, then?" Arthag asked with a frown.

"No, Sir. I found them wandering loose around the camp. But the attack didn't take place anywhere near the stockade. Voice Kinlafia was right—our people got out in time and started hiking back toward the portal. They got further than we'd thought, too. I found plenty of sign to mark their trail, both their own and their pursuers'. I'd estimate that they were followed by at least fifty men on foot."

"Fifty." Arthag swore, although it wasn't really that much of a surprise. "You say you found their back trail," he continued after a moment. "Did you find where they were attacked, too?"

"Yes, Sir." Grigthir swallowed. "I did."

"And?" Arthag asked sharply, noticing the tough, experienced cavalry trooper's expression.

"It's . . . unnatural, Sir."

Grigthir was pale, visibly shaken, and Arthag drew a deep breath. He looked around at the thirty-odd men of his cavalry platoon, then nodded sharply to himself.

"All right, Mikal," he said. "Show me."

* * *

The forest was eerie as the platoon moved out once more in column, following Grigthir. The woods were too silent and far too deep for Arthag's liking. He'd grown accustomed to soldiering in any terrain, but he was a son of the plains, born to a line of plainsmen that reached back into dimmest antiquity. His ancient forebears had halted the eastward Ternathian advance in its tracks. Able to live off the land, fade into the velvet night, and strike supply trains and columns on the march at will, the Arpathian Septs had destroyed so many Ternathian armies that the emperor had finally stopped sending them.

But the Septs had learned from the violent conflict, as well, and where Ternathian armies had failed, merchants and diplomats had succeeded. The Septs had ceased raiding their unwanted neighbors, learning to trade with them, instead. That had led to greater prosperity than they had ever before known, yet no septman or septwoman had ever adopted Ternathian ways. Sons and daughters of the plains felt smothered and suffocated by walls and ceilings of wood or stone.

And *this* son of the plains felt closed in and vulnerable in a place like this forest, where he could see no farther than a few dozen yards but hidden enemy eyes could watch his men, waiting to strike from ambush whenever and wherever they chose. Grigthir had estimated fifty men in the force which had pursued and attacked the Chalgyn Consortium survey party, but where there were fifty, there might be a hundred, or five hundred, or more. Not a comforting thought for a man with fewer than forty troopers under his command.

As he rode along, he couldn't help wondering if Sharona's first contact with other humans would have ended in violence if both sides had glimpsed one another at a distance on a windswept plain, rather than stumbling unexpectedly across one another's paths in this unholy tangle of trees?

He snorted under his breath. Questions like that were a waste of time. However it had happened, Sharona had met its first inter-universal neighbors in blood under these trees, and that was all that mattered. It was his job to find any possible survivors—and take prisoners of his own for questioning, if he could—not to ponder the imponderables of life.

So Arthag guided his horse with knees and feet alone, leaving his hands free for weapons. He carried his rifle with the safety off, the barrel laid carefully along his horse's neck to avoid tangling the muzzle in vegetation, while he watched his mount's ears carefully.

The Portal Authority had adopted the Ternathian Model 10 rifle for its cavalry, as well as its infantry. Arthag wasn't positive he agreed with the idea, but he had to admit that if they were going to issue a compromise weapon to cavalry and infantry alike, the Model 10 was about as good as it was going to get. The Ternathian Bureau of Weapons had designed the Model 10 for use by infantry, Marines, and cavalry from the outset. It was a bolt-action, chambered in .40 caliber, with a twelve-round box magazine. Its semi-bullpup design gave it a twenty-six-inch barrel, but with an overall length that was short enough to be convenient in close quarters—like in small boats, or on horseback.

It was a precision instrument in trained hands, and Arthag's hands were definitely trained.

So was his horse. Bright Wind was no army nag. His exalted pedigree was as long and as fine as any Ternathian prince's, and his schooling in the art of war had begun the day he'd begun nursing at his dam's teats.

Hulmok Arthag's people were nomads, and Arthag was the son of a Sept chieftain—a younger son, true, with no hope of inheriting his father's Sept Staff, but that had never been his dream, anyway. There were always some men—and women—who felt the call to wander more strongly than their brothers and sisters, and Arthag had always been one of them. In times past, men like him had led the Septs to new lands, new pastures and trade routes. In the shrunken, modern world, hemmed in by others' borders, those who felt the ancient call did what Arthag had chosen to do and sought new pastures beyond the portals. And when Arthag had left the Sept, he'd asked only one gift of his father: Bright Wind.

Under the Portal Authority's accords, any trooper had the right to bring his own horse with him, if he chose, and if the horse in question met the Authority's minimum standards. Less than a third of them took advantage of that offer, but Arthag had never met an Arpathian who hadn't, and his own mount was the envy of many a general officer. All of which explained why Arthag watched the stallion's reactions so carefully. Bright Wind could be taken by surprise, of course, but his senses were far keener than Arthag's, and both horse and rider had learned to trust them implicitly.

They were perhaps an hour or an hour and a half's ride from the abandoned stockade when Bright Wind suddenly laid back his ears and halted. Arthag felt the shudder that caught the stallion's muscles a single heartbeat before they turned to iron. And then a slight shift in the wind brought the scent to him, as well. Smoke: a complex, unnatural stink that mingled foully with the ordinary scent of wood smoke and less ordinary smell of burnt flesh. Bright Wind's golden flanks had darkened with sweat, but the stallion wasn't afraid. Nostrils distended, ears pinned flat, he was ready for battle.

"What in Harmana's holy name is that stench?" Junior-Armsman Soral Hilovar muttered softly. The Ricathian Tracer wore an expression of horror, and something inside Arthag quivered. He didn't share Hilovar's Talent, but he didn't need to—not with that stench blowing on the wind.

"Let's go find out," he said quietly. He turned in the saddle, waving hand signals to the column which had halted instantly behind him. Scouts peeled off from the flanks, spreading out. The precaution was almost certainly unnecessary, but Hulmok Arthag didn't care.

Once his skirmishers were in position, he touched Bright Wind with his heels. The stallion stepped forward, dainty yet tense, and Petty-Captain Arthag rode out from under the trees into a scene of nightmare.

It was even worse than any of them had been expecting, particularly for Darcel Kinlafia. The Voice really should have been left behind with Company-Captain Halifu, but he'd flatly refused, and he hadn't been at all shy about it. He might be legally under Halifu's authority, despite his own civilian status, but he hadn't really seemed to care about that.

Arthag's platoon had only been attached to Halifu's command for a couple of months. The Chalgyn Consortium team's rapid-fire chain of discoveries had the Portal Authority scrambling for troops to forward to the new frontier. Arthag's men had been among the units swept up by the Authority broom and whisked off to an entirely new universe—and attached to an equally new CO—with less than a week's warning. A man got used to that in the Authority's service.

But although Arthag scarcely knew Halifu well, he didn't think Kinlafia would have been able to browbeat the company-captain into acquiescence if it hadn't been for the fact that he was the Voice who'd received Shaylar Nargra-Kolmayr's final message. Unlike Arthag or any of his troopers, Kinlafia had already seen the battlefield through Shaylar's eyes. That meant he might be able to give Hilovar or Nolis Parcanthi, the Tracer and Whiffer Halifu had attached to Arthag for the rescue mission, some critical bits of information or explanation which would let them figure out what had really happened here.

But whatever Kinlafia had seen through Shaylar's eyes, it obviously hadn't been enough to prepare him for what he saw through his own. He let out a low, ghastly sound as his gaze swept across the killing field where so many of his friends had died. It was pitifully clear that he saw something Arthag didn't—and couldn't—and Parcanthi reached across to grip Kinlafia's shoulder in wordless sympathy and support.

"Standard perimeter overwatch. Chief-Armsman chan Hathas," Arthag said briskly, pretending he hadn't noticed the Voice's distress. "First Squad has the perimeter. Third has the reserve. Second Squad will dismount and prepare to assist Parcanthi and Hilovar on request, but keep them out from underfoot until they're called for."

"Yes, Sir!" Rayl chan Hathas, Second Platoon's senior noncom, saluted sharply and turned to deal with Arthag's instructions. For a moment, Arthag envied him intensely. He would far rather have buried himself in the comfort of a familiar routine rather than face the sort of discoveries he was afraid they were going to make.

"Soral, Nolis," he continued, turning to the two specialists. "Do what you can to tell us what happened here. The rest of the column will remain outside the clearing until you're finished."

Hilovar and Parcanthi nodded, dismounted—awkwardly, in Parcanthi's case—and tied their reins to fallen branches. Arthag allowed no trace of amusement to cross his expressionless nomad's face—the Septs had their reputation to maintain, after all—but neither the Whiffer nor Tracer were cavalry troopers. They were technically infantry, and Parcanthi looked like a lumpy bag of potatoes in the saddle. Hilovar wasn't a lot better, and Arthag found the two of them about as unmilitary as anyone he'd ever seen in uniform. Hilovar was a tall, solidly built Ricathian who'd been a Tracer for a major civilian police department before the fascination of the frontier drew him into the Authority's service. Parcanthi, a bit shorter than Hilovar but even broader, was a Farnalian with flaming red hair and a complexion which Arthag suspected started peeling about a half-hour before sunrise. On a rainy day.

Both of them, despite their relatively junior noncommissioned ranks, were the sort of critically important specialists the Authority was always eager to get its hands on. And as critically needed specialists often did, they had a tendency to write their own tickets—often without actually realizing they'd even done it. Which, when it came right down to it, was just fine with Hulmok Arthag. He suspected that both of them would be just about useless in a firefight, but they knew that as well as he did. If it came to it, both of them were smart enough to stay out of the line of fire (if they could), and that, too, suited Arthag just fine, because they were also far too valuable to *risk* in a firefight. As it happened, and despite their lack of horsemanship or military polish, he liked what he'd seen of both of them—a lot. And if they could tell him anything about what had happened here, he would forgive them any military *faux pas* they might ever commit.

He waited until he was confident chan Hathas had the perimeter organized, then dismounted himself with a murmured command to Bright Wind, whose ears flicked in acknowledgment. Until and unless he told the golden stallion it was time to move, Bright Wind would stay exactly where he was. Arthag patted the horse's shoulder gently, then stepped up to the edge of the clearing, rifle ready, and settled in to wait.

There'd been no rain and little wind, which was a godsend for Parcanthi. Even so, the residual energy had already begun to dissipate. A sense of horror and pain would doubtless linger for years, but raw emotion wasn't what Parcanthi—and the rest of Sharona—sought.

The Whiffer stepped out into the center of the toppled timber, closed his eyes, and reached out with quivering senses to taste the surviving residual patterns, and images flashed through him. Whiffs of what had been. Smoke. The crash and roar of rifle fire. Screams of agony.

He turned, eyes still closed, to face the trees where the Chalgyn Consortium's crew had sought cover. He caught a flash of Ghartoun chan Hagrahyl standing up, hands empty. Caught another flash of a uniformed man spinning around, raising a crossbow, firing. Yet another flash of chan Hagrahyl staggering back, throat pierced with steel.

Other flashes cannoned through him. Barris Kasell dying monstrously inside a massive lightning bolt. Men in strange uniforms falling to the broken ground, as bullets hammered through them. Other Sharonians back in the trees, caught by fireballs and crossbow fire.

He turned toward the standing trees where the enemy had formed his line, and more flashes came. Shouts in an alien tongue. Men rustling cautiously through the trees, circling around to get at the defenders' flanks. Strange, glassy tubes that belched flame and lightning, just as Kinlafia had described. And bodies. Everywhere he turned, Whiffing the air, Parcanthi saw bodies. Caught in tangled tree limbs, sprawled across toppled tree trunks . . . lying in neat rows.

He jerked his attention back to that flash and tried to recapture it, to wring more detail from it. He saw the dead laid out in careful rows, limbs arranged as if they were only sleeping. Other men moved among them, placing something small on each corpse. He could see Sharonian dead, as well as those of the enemy. They'd grouped the survey crew together, it looked like, but the images were so tenuous he couldn't tell for sure how many Sharonians there were. He was still trying to count when an unholy flash of light blinded him. The bodies began to burn with unnatural brilliance—

Parcanthi let out a yell and staggered back, gasping.

"What is it?" someone demanded, practically in his ear. "What did you Whiff?"

Parcanthi jerked around and found Hulmok Arthag standing at his shoulder.

"W-what?" he gulped, still more than a little disoriented.

"What did you Whiff?" Petty-Captain Arthag asked again, and Parcanthi swallowed hard.

"They cremated the dead," he answered, his voice hoarse. "With something . . . unnatural."

"I'm starting to dislike that adjective," the Arpathian officer growled. He glowered at the clearing for a moment, jaw working as if he wanted to spit. Then he shook himself and looked back at the Whiffer. "What else did you get?"

Parcanthi gave himself a shake, regathering his composure.

"Part of the battle Kinlafia described, Sir. Just faint glimpses. The details are already fading, dissipating. They cremated our dead, as well as their own, but the images are so tenuous, it's hard to tell how many of our people were burnt."

"Keep trying," Arthag said in clipped tones. "We need to know if there were *survivors*."

"Yes, Sir. I know. I'll do my best."

"Good man." Arthag put a hand briefly on his shoulder, then nodded. "Carry on, then."

As Parcanthi got back to work, Arthag turned toward Soral Hilovar, who was searching through the fallen trees where the Chalgyn crew had taken shelter.

"Anything?" he asked, and the Tracer looked up with a bitter expression.

"Whoever these bastards are, they left damned little behind. If I could get my hands on something of theirs, I could tell you a fair bit, but they were fiendishly thorough scavengers. I haven't found anything *they* left behind, and not a single piece of Sharonian equipment, either, for that matter. I've found spot after spot where our people set down packs, or what were probably ammunition boxes, but they're gone. All I've got so far is this."

He held up a handful of spent cartridge cases, and Arthag gazed at them through narrow eyes.

"They mean to learn all they can from our gear," he said flatly, then inhaled and grimaced at the Tracer. "Nolis says they cremated the dead. I know it won't be pleasant, but try reading the ash piles."

He nodded toward the most open portion of the clearing, where Parcanthi stood in the midst of fire scars the length and shape of human bodies. Hilovar's jaw muscles bunched, but he nodded with the choppiness of barely suppressed anger. Not at Arthag, the petty-captain knew, but at what he was going to find out there.

"Yes, Sir," he bit out. "I'll do whatever it takes, Sir."

The normally cheerful Ricathian stalked toward the fire scars. At least he wasn't a novice when it came to crime scene work. His ten-year stint as a homicide Tracer in Lubnasi, the city-state of his birth, had inured him to mere human cruelty and suffering. He understood that people did violence to one another, even in a world of telepaths. But this ...

The ash pits, while macabre, were less horrifying to a former homicide Tracer than they would have been to a civilian. Not that they didn't bother Hilovar anyway, of course. But that was because he could already tell they were tainted with something not quite right, something profoundly disturbing. Whatever it was, he'd already encountered it when he Traced the survey crew's actual death sites.

He put that memory out of his mind, focusing on the immediate task as he knelt beside the first human-sized scorch mark. There wasn't much left, not even bone. A few twisted, melted bits of metal glinted dully in the ashes, but there wasn't even much of that. Not enough to tell if the bits had been buttons, or buckles, or something else entirely. Just a few droplets, where something had melted and dripped away until it coalesced into ugly, formless flakes and bits too small even to call pebbles.

Simply touching the ashes and splashes of metal sent vile prickles up his arms. Everything he touched gave off the same feeling as the death sites had, only worse. More concentrated. The vibrations of the energy he would normally have sensed in a place where humans had been incinerated—a house fire, say—had been warped by something uncanny in these ash pits. The residues crawled along his skin uncomfortably, like being jabbed with thousands of microscopic pins.

When he double-checked with Parcanthi on the location of cremation sites that were almost certainly Sharonian, then cross-referenced with sites which had definitely contained the enemy's dead, he found exactly the same residues on both, which led to an inescapable conclusion. Whatever they'd used to cremate their own dead had been used to burn the Sharonian dead, as well, so the odd residue wasn't a signature given off by the enemy's *bodies*. And whatever it was, they'd used something similar to kill the Chalgyn Consortium's people in the first place, because that weapon had left behind the same unsettling energy residue, all over the death sites. It was exactly the same residue as whatever they'd used to ignite the funeral pyres, and he couldn't make any sense out of it at all.

"*How* were they burned?" he muttered to himself without even realizing he'd spoken aloud. "Whatever it was, it was damned odd."

It certainly hadn't been any fuel Hilovar had ever encountered.

There was no wood ash, so it couldn't have been a traditional, archaic funeral pyre. It hadn't been kerosene, either, or some kind of flammable vegetable oil, or anything else he could think of. Besides, each of these fire scars was exactly the size of a single body . . . and they'd been burned out of the surrounding leaf mold without touching off a general conflagration. He saw the proof of that right in front of him, but the very idea was still ridiculous. He'd never heard of *any* fire intense enough to totally consume a human body . . . not to mention one that burned a neat hole out of drifts of dry leaves without spreading at all!

He furrowed his brow, trying to identify the elusive, disturbing sensation. It was more like the energy patterns near portals than anything else he could think of, but it wasn't the same as that, either. It was . . . *different*.

He growled in frustration and stood, looking around until he spotted Acting Platoon-Captain Arthag and Parcanthi. They were standing together to one side, and he strode briskly over to them. When he tried to explain his confusing impressions, the cavalry officer looked baffled, but the Whiffer blinked. He frowned for a few seconds, then nodded vigorously.

"I think you're onto something, Soral," he said. "I kept getting a Whiff of something really odd in this clearing. It was pretty strong where our people died, but it was even stronger over there." He pointed into the standing trees opposite the clearing where the crew had made its fatal last stand. "I got the strongest sense of it where I caught the flashes of those weird, shiny tubes Kinlafia described."

"That's interesting." Arthag rubbed his chin thoughtfully, looking from one spot to the other. "You sensed it at the point of impact, and at the point of origin. But not between? Shouldn't there be a parabola of residue between them, along the trajectory?"

"You'd think so, Sir," Parcanthi agreed with a frown. "Let me Whiff this again."

He moved slowly and carefully across the open ground between the two spots, again and again. He quartered the area meticulously, but when he came back, he shook his head.

"There's not a damned thing between them, Platoon-Captain. Nothing."

He looked perplexed, and Arthag's frown deepened.

"That's impossible!" the officer protested. Then grimaced. "Isn't it? I mean, how can something *shoot* without following a trajectory?"

"I don't have the least damned idea, Sir, but that's what it looks like they did. There was some kind of powerful energy discharge at the enemy's gun emplacement." He pointed. "There was another one where the weapon's discharge *struck*." He pointed again. "But I'm telling you, Sir, that there's *nothing* between those two spots. Not even the ghost of a signature. And this energy feels so damned *weird* it would be impossible to mistake its signature if it was there in the first place."

The three men exchanged grim glances.

"Just what in hell are we dealing with?" Hilovar asked for all of them in an uneasy tone, and Arthag scowled.

"I intend to find that out." He glanced at Parcanthi. "Can I send the men in to search the site yet, or do you need to take more readings first?"

"Keep them away from our people's death sites, if you don't mind, Sir. I do want to take more readings there, see if I can pin down more information about who died and who might not have. And stay clear of that area for now." He pointed to a spot under the standing trees. "That's where they tended their wounded before evacuating. I want to take a close scan of that, as well. You can turn them loose anywhere else, though."

Arthag nodded and strode across the clearing to Chief-Armsman chan Hathas.

"Spread them out, Chief-Armsman. I want every inch of this ground searched, from there—" he pointed "—to there." He indicated the two off-limit sites Parcanthi needed to scan again.

"Yes, Sir. Any special instructions on what we ought to be looking for?" chan Hathas asked.

"Anything the Tracer can handle, Chief. We're looking for anything he can get a better reading off of. As it stands, we don't have enough surviving debris to give Hilovar a decent set of readings. Find something better for him."

"Yes, Sir." Chan Hathas looked out across the clearing, his jaw clenched, and nodded sharply. "If it's out there, we'll find it, Sir," he promised grimly.

"Good," Arthag said, and then turned to face the sole survivor of Chalgyn's slaughtered crew.

"Darcel." His gruff voice gentled as he called the man's name.

"Sir?" The civilian's question was hoarse, his expression stricken and distracted.

"Pair up with Nolis, please," Arthag said quietly. "Compare what you saw through Shaylar's eyes with what he's picking up. I know that's going to be hard on you, but we've *got* to know precisely how many of our people were killed."

"Yes, Sir." The words should have been crisp, but they came out as a shadow of sound, barely audible, and distress burned in Darcel's eyes. He turned without another word and headed out across the broken, fire-scorched ground, stumbling over the rough footing.

It wasn't just the debris that was responsible for his unsteady gait. Just being in this clearing was agony, but he also had trouble distinguishing between what his own eyes saw and what he'd Seen through Shaylar's eyes. The memories kept superimposing themselves over what he was seeing here and now. He kept trying to step over branches that weren't there, and stumbled over ones that didn't exist in the view Shaylar had transmitted. He blinked furiously, trying to clear his distorted vision, and cursed himself when he couldn't. He needed to be clearheaded, not muddled between past and present. He *had* to be if he was going to help spot something that would provide clues for Parcanthi and Hilovar.

He stopped, turning in place, looking for the exact spot where Shaylar had crouched, where the agonizing memories in his mind had been born of fire and thunder. There. It was somewhere in that direction, he decided, and started forward once more, moving with grim determination through the confusion of reality and remembrance. If he could find the spot, he and the others might dredge up something they could use. Darcel had little hope that anyone had survived, but he needed to *know*. One way or the other, he had to know, because anything would be better than this dreadful uncertainty. This doubt.

He cursed the men who'd done this, not only for the killing, but for burning the dead and stealing everything they'd been carrying. They hadn't even marked the ash piles in any way! What kind of barbarians didn't even mark a grave? If they'd simply marked the sites, just indicated which piles of ashes had held Sharonians, and which their own accursed dead, there wouldn't have been this horrible doubt. The column would have known how many people needed to be rescued.

And how many needed to be avenged.

Darcel couldn't even lay remembrance wreaths at the graves of his dearest friends because he didn't know whose ashes were whose! It was intolerable, and there wasn't a damned thing he could do about it, other than help the Whiffer and Tracer wring every scrap of information they could from this place and from his own memory, with its perfect recall.

Shaylar's entire transmission was still in his memory. He simply had to calm down enough to retrieve it, and he had to remain

detached enough to analyze every fleeting second of those harrow-
ing minutes. If Shaylar had known where everyone was, and if she'd
been aware of everyone's deaths as they occurred, then theoretically,
he knew that, too. Those were distressingly large "ifs," but he had
to start somewhere.

So did Platoon-Captain Arthag. The officer had to know if they
were on a rescue mission, or a punitive strike. So Darcel tramped
through the fallen trees, comparing views and angles with what he
saw in memory.

It took a long time, but he found it in the end. When he finally
located the spot, he stood peering down at it for a long silent moment.
Had she died here? Or "merely" been wounded badly enough to
knock her unconscious?

Most of the branches and tree trunks in a four-foot swath around
her place of concealment had been scorched during the battle. Dead
leaves had burst into flame and burnt to white ash, some of which
had fallen onto branches below, and some of which—protected
from the wind—still clung to branches and twigs, paper-thin ghosts,
holding their shape eerily . . . until the slightest touch of his breath
caused them to crumble to nothing.

He was tempted to crouch down to match the views precisely, but
he stayed carefully to one side. He didn't want to contaminate the
site with his own energy residues, but even so, his boot brushed a
thick clump of char that wasn't wood.

What the devil? Darcel frowned and bent over it. Someone from
the other side had clearly looked at it after the fight and dumped
it again, leaving it as useless. That was the only way it could have
gotten to where it was, because it wasn't where Shaylar had been
crouching, and the ground directly under it wasn't scorched. Most
of the ground wasn't, actually, he realized with another frown. It
looked like the fireballs had passed horizontally through the broken
trees several inches above the ground.

But there was *one* burnt spot down there, he realized. One directly
under where Shaylar's feet had been.

This is where she burned the maps, he realized.

An icy centipede prickled down his spine as he recognized it.
He'd found the remains of her map satchel, and the binder which
had held her meticulous records. Both of them had been made of
oiled leather, to resist rain, and the binder had been wrapped in a
waterproof rubber case, as well. None of them had burned completely, despite her frantic efforts. She'd ripped out individual pages
from the binder to burn her notes, just as she'd burned the maps

one by one, to ensure their destruction. Then she'd tried to burn the satchel and binder, as well.

He didn't even poke at the charred lump with a stick. He left it for the Tracer to examine, instead. Since both Shaylar and one of her killers had handled it, they might get something valuable from it, so Darcel marked its exact location and kept looking.

A moment later, his throat constricted as he discovered why she'd lost consciousness so abruptly. A thick branch behind the spot where she'd burned her maps and notes was marked by dried blood and several strands of long, dark hair. Darcel's fingers went unsteady as he reached towards the strands, but then he made himself stop. Parcanthi and Hilovar needed to examine everything here before he contaminated it.

Darcel looked for the branch where Jathmar had been flung when the fireball caught him and spotted a few shreds of scorched cloth on the ground directly beneath it. The branch itself, thick as Darcel's forearm, had been seared black . . . except for a spot exactly the width of Jathmar's body.

The Voice moved cautiously around, staying outside the actual spot while his eyes searched carefully. The unburnt bark of the limb into which Jathmar had been thrown was scraped and cut where gear and buttons had dug into it, and he peered at the ground to see if anything of Jathmar's had fallen into the leaf litter.

If anything had, their attackers had found it first and carried it off. Unwilling to risk stirring things up with a closer search, Darcel called the Whiffer and Tracer over to join him and explained what he'd found.

"You'd better go first, Nolis," Hilovar said, glancing at Parcanthi. "You need uncontaminated patterns. I'll touch the evidence once you've gleaned what you can."

Parcanthi nodded and started with Jathmar's spot first. He closed his eyes and went very still, and even though Darcel couldn't sense the energy patterns Parcanthi was carefully examining, he knew enough theory to recognize what he was doing.

Every living creature generated its own energy field, created by that mysterious, poorly understood force that animated a physical body. Inanimate objects had their own strange energies, as well, and all objects vibrated at a specific rhythm. A person sensitive to those rhythms could detect them, focus on them, separate them from one another and wrest information from them. Could discern what forces had worked upon them, could draw visions—the famous "flashes" of the Whiffer—of past events out of the energy flowing about them.

Someone like Soral Hilovar, on the other hand, could touch an object and trace the major events in its history. If a living creature handled or came into contact with an object, some of that creature's life energy remained behind. The residue was like a static charge, except that it never entirely dissipated. Details would fade eventually, yet for the most part, the energy patterns left behind endured for a long time. But where a Whiffer might use those patterns to determine *what* had happened, a Tracer, like Hilovar, was sensitive to the connection *between* the object and whoever had touched it. Unlike a Whiffer, a Tracer couldn't see the general vicinity of those events, couldn't pick up flashes of what *else* had happened in its vicinity. But in many ways, what a Tracer *did* see was considerably more detailed. He could frequently tell whether or not the person involved in an event was dead or still alive. And, somewhat like Darcel's own sensitivity to portals, a Tracer could determine a directional bearing to the person in question.

The residue Whiffers and Tracers worked with was even stronger when a complex living creature—like a person—took a specific action. A violent action, or one steeped in powerful emotion—terror, rage, passion—left the strongest residue of all. If someone picked up a rock and bashed somebody else with it, a ghostly imprint remained behind, creating a shadow copy of the action . . . and its results. The shadow copy didn't even need to be tied to a specific object, if the original action had been sufficiently intense. The stronger the emotions, the stronger the copy. Sometimes, the shadow could last for years, particularly indoors—

Parcanthi hissed aloud and flinched. Sweat beaded up on his brow and a cliff, trickled down his temples.

"Oh, sweet Marnilay," he whispered, his voice shaking. "They burned him *alive* . . ."

Darcel's mouth tightened into a thin, harsh line. He knew exactly what the Whiffer was Seeing. He'd already Seen it himself.

"He collapsed there," Parcanthi said in a low voice, eyes still closed, pointing to the ground. "He was still alive when they found him. Their emotions were strong. Excitement. Relief?"

The last words sounded puzzled, but a flare of hope shot through Darcel, sharp and painful. *Alive.* Jathmar had been alive!

But Parcanthi was still talking, and Darcel's heart clenched at the Whiffer's next words.

"He was burned something ghastly. His back was burnt black, the shirt was just *gone*—burned away. He was barely breathing. Someone's crouched over him, trying to help. Gods! I can See *bone* down inside the burns!"

Parcanthi shuddered, his face twisting.

"It's too faint, curse it," he whispered, "and there were too many people crowded into the spot. The energy patterns are all jumbled up, imprinted on top of one another. I can't sort them out."

His intense frustration was obvious, and he opened his eyes and shook himself.

"That's it," he said grimly. "I'm not going to get anything much clearer than that from here." His jaw muscles bunched for a moment, and his nostrils flared as he inhaled. "Let me try Shaylar. Where?"

"There."

Darcel pointed, and the red-haired Whiffer nodded. His lean, craggy face was pale, covered with cold sweat, but he walked across and crouched down, as Shaylar had, surrounding and centering himself in the residue. Bleak eyes closed again, and he gave another shudder . . .

"She's burning everything. Maps, notes. She's shaking, linked to Darcel. Jathmar's starting to climb down from there—" he pointed to a spot above them, without opening his eyes. Then his entire body flinched.

"*Fire!* There's fire everywhere!"

He was slapping at his own clothes, clawing at his hair, shaking. Then the fireball Darcel had seen through Shaylar's eyes passed, and the Whiffer sagged in relief. He turned, eyes still closed, toward the branch that had knocked Shaylar unconscious.

"She crashed into that." He pointed to the blood-crusted branch. "She's lying still. Her face is swelling up, turning purple and black. There are cuts and scrapes."

Darcel's breath faltered. This time, his hope was so terrible it actually hurt his lungs, his entire body. If her face was swelling and bruising, she was *alive*. Corpses didn't bruise—did they? He realized that he wasn't sure, and the uncertainty was intolerable.

"They found her, too," Parcanthi said. "They're shocked, horrified, that they attacked a woman."

Darcel's fists clenched at his sides. He didn't want to think of these bastards as people who could be shocked and horrified by what they'd done to an innocent, lovely girl.

"They can't wake her up," Parcanthi said abruptly. "There's something wrong, desperately wrong. Inside her head. They're trying. They're *frantic*, but they can't wake her up, and she's badly injured . . ."

His voice shook, frayed. Then he groaned.

"It's fading out! The whole godsdamned thing's wavering and fading away. They carried her out of here, but I can't See anything beyond that. It just fades into nothing. Or, rather, it blurs into that same mess Jathmar's did, with all the imprints jumbled up together. I can't see anything more than that."

"You have to!" Darcel cried, unable to stop himself. "We *have* to know what happened to her! Is she still *alive*?"

"I can't *tell*!" Parcanthi's eyes opened, filled with anguish. "Too many people died right here." He waved at the toppled trees around them. "And too damned many people came through here—trying to rescue survivors, trying to find every last piece of equipment. It all bleeds and blurs and fades like ink in the water." He furrowed his brow, rubbed his eyes. "Maybe if we can figure out where they took her and Jathmar, I can tell more from there."

Darcel choked down more frantic demands. Parcanthi couldn't do the impossible, and he knew it. So he turned to Hilovar instead, and the Tracer glanced at Parcanthi.

"Go on." The Whiffer nodded. "I've got everything I'm going to get out of this spot. I'll head over to the trees, where the enemy's lines were, try to find the spot where they tended the wounded. Maybe I can tell more there."

Parcanthi extricated himself from the spot where Shaylar and Jathmar had fallen. As he did so, Hilovar met Darcel's gaze squarely.

"You have to realize," the ebony-skinned Ricathian said in a low, cautionary tone, "that I may not be able to tell, either. I can tell you what happened to an object and the person or people most closely associated with it, but I may not be able to Trace anything beyond the event itself."

"But Tracers can find missing persons from hundreds of miles away!" Darcel protested. "I know they can. You've done it yourself!"

"Sometimes I can," Hilovar agreed. "That was useful in police work when I was still working homicide. But you have to understand, Darcel. The more traces there are at a crime scene, the harder it is to filter out just one. I worked a case once where an entire extended family had been killed by portal pirates. These bastards had a nasty habit of raiding isolated mining camps, taking off with years' worth of profits, and killing all the witnesses.

"There were so many members of the gang, so many victims, and so much violence done in such a small space, that I couldn't get an accurate Trace on anything. It took us over a *year*—and three more slaughtered mining camps—to run the bastards down. If there'd been only one or two victims, or fewer pirates, I could probably have nailed them in a matter of weeks. Maybe even days."

Hilovar's eyes were dark with remembered pain and frustration, and he sighed.

"We've got the same trouble here. There was so much violence the event residues have contaminated the objects caught in the middle of them. Everything I've touched so far has so many echoes clinging to it that I can't get accurate readings. If we had more objects to Trace from, the odds would be better. But with so little evidence, and so many strong residues, it's going to be tough. I'll do my dead level best, I promise you that. And if we can find the place where they took the wounded, if we can isolate something there that she and Jathmar touched, the odds will go up. But even then, it's going to be dicey. And if there's another portal nearby—"

He spread his hands, indicating helplessness.

"I don't understand," Darcel said, with a frown.

"Portals always screw up a Trace." Hilovar seemed surprised by Darcel's response. "You're a Voice—and a Portal Hound, too. Can you transmit a message through a portal?"

"Of course not. No one can trans—"

Darcel stopped abruptly, and Hilovar nodded with a compassionate expression.

"The energy around a portal is always weird stuff, damned weird. That's another reason it took us so long to trace those damned pirates. You can't Trace anyone *through* a portal any more than a Voice can send a message through one, or a Mapper can Map through one of them . . . and you can't just follow someone through and pick him up again on the other side. Stepping through a portal . . . scrambles the residue. Those pirates would slip through a portal, and every trace of them would literally vanish. It was like the gods had stepped down, erased their very existence. This—" he waved at the virgin forest surrounding them "—isn't anyone's home universe, which means the other side came through a portal, too. If they've taken any survivors back through it with them, the odds of Tracing them on the other side— Well, I'd be lying if I told you they even existed, Darcel."

Darcel cursed, then gritted his teeth and nodded. At least Hilovar was too honest to offer false comfort, he told himself.

"All right," he said. "I understand. Do what you can."

The Tracer took a deep breath, turned away, and grasped the branch Jathmar had struck. His knuckles locked, and a ghastly sound broke from his throat. His eyes shot wide, and his pupils dilated in shock, then shrank to pinpoints. He shuddered, then jerked his hands loose and shook them violently, as though flinging off drops of acid.

"Sorry," he muttered, scrubbing sweat from his face with one forearm. "I'll . . . try again."

He gripped the branch longer, this time, but his entire body began to shake. The muscles of his face quivered, veins stood out in his temples, and his voice, when he finally spoke, was thick with pain and shock.

"*Hurlbane's balls . . . !* Bones broken . . . bleeding inside, deep inside . . . burns from scalp to knees . . ."

Blood vessels popped up in terrifying relief along the backs of Hilovar's dark hands, hands like gray marble, carved from stone.

"He can't . . . he can't possibly have lived. Not with those injuries. Not more than a few minutes . . ."

Flashes of memory—that accursed, *perfect* memory of a Voice—showed Darcel Jathmar's easy laughter. His boundless enthusiasm, his sheer joy in the adventure that was life itself. There were hundreds of those memories, *thousands*, and Darcel Kinlafia closed his eyes as he felt his heart turn to cold steel.

Then he opened them again. Hilovar had let go of the branch. He stood flapping his hands, as though they, too, had been burned.

"And Shaylar?" Darcel asked after a moment. "What about Shaylar?"

The Tracer drew a shallow breath, as though it hurt to expand his chest more deeply. Then he cleared his throat.

"Is there something specific here I can Trace?" he asked, and Darcel pointed to the charred map satchel. And to the bloody branch with the dark hair caught in its bark. Hilovar looked at them both, then nodded.

"Only one way to find out," he muttered, and Darcel literally held his breath as Hilovar's strong fingers closed gently around the strands of hair and the blood-crusted branch. Dark eyes closed once more as Hilovar gave himself to the Traces.

"She was alive when they took her away," he said after a moment in a strong voice, and Darcel's hope leapt. But then Hilovar frowned. "Alive, but unconscious." He bit his lower lip, and his voice faded to a terrible whisper. "Blood pooling under the skull. Putting pressure on something critical. Swelling . . ."

His hands began to shake, and he shook his head hard, then released the branch and opened his eyes.

"I can't see anything beyond that, Darcel. She *was* alive, but . . ."

The pain was even worse because of that brief, thunderous stab of hope. But hemorrhaging in the brain sounded at least as serious as Jathmar's more overt injuries, and might well have been worse. Darcel looked away, blinking burning eyes, as the anguish stabbed through him.

"Could—" He stopped, cleared his throat. "Could she have survived something like that?"

"I don't know." The Tracer's voice was hollow, full of bleak uncertainty and exhaustion. "I'm no surgeon, Darcel. I can't even tell what *part* of her brain was injured, only that it felt . . . critical. If the injury wasn't in a life-threatening area, if they had a skilled surgeon close enough . . ."

Hilovar didn't have to finish. There were probably no more than a dozen surgeons in all of Sharona's far-flung universes who would have been capable of repairing the sort of damage Hilovar was sensing. What were the odds that a pack of crossbow-armed barbarians would have a surgeon with those skills with them out here in the middle of these godsforsaken woods?

Hope died, messily, and what grew in its place was colder than the frozen Arpathian hells. It cut through him, cruel as any razor, and it hungered.

Darcel Kinlafia looked into Soral Hilovar's eyes and caressed the butt of his revolver almost gently.

CHAPTER
SIXTEEN

JATHMAR REMEMBERED HIS own wistful thoughts about the joy of flight on the morning of the nightmare attack—was it really only two days ago?—and how he'd envied even a common sparrow's ability to wheel and dart and soar.

Now, as he peered down at the distant ground through the glass face shield and cold wind whipped over him in an icy hurricane, he discovered that anything he'd ever imagined fell far short of the truth. The sheer exhilaration of actually streaking through the sky was so great, so overwhelming, that it actually pushed his dread of the future awaiting him and Shaylar out of the front of his thoughts. That wasn't something he would have believed was possible, and a corner of his brain wondered if he was concentrating on his delight so hard in part to avoid thinking about that selfsame future.

Maybe he was, but that didn't change anything. The creature beneath the platform upon which he and Shaylar were seated, carefully strapped in for safety, was unquestionably the most powerful animal he had ever seen. The sheer strength in every downstroke of those seemingly fragile wings beggared every other notion of animal power he'd ever held, and now that he'd gotten over his initial shock, he could appreciate the creature's—the *dragon's*—metallic, glittering beauty. The flashes of bronze and copper-colored sunlight, reflected from its scales, were almost blinding, and the ornate pattern on its wings and hide gleamed. Shaylar had to be right, he told himself. That marvelous geometric design *had* to be artificial, although he couldn't imagine how such intricate patterns had been applied to a living animal's skin.

In fact, there was a *lot* about these people that he couldn't imagine, and whatever else befell them, he couldn't suppress his delighted grin as they raced the wind itself. He'd come out here in search of adventure, hadn't he? Well, when it came to unusual, unlikely experiences, riding the back of a dragon which dwarfed any elephant and soared as effortlessly as any eagle had to rank high on the list.

The sheer speed of the flight was enough to leave him gasping in amazement. Not even a train barreling down a miles-long straight track could have matched it. He couldn't begin to fathom how a creature so massive could fly so fast. It simply wasn't *natural.*

He snorted at the thought. He and Shaylar had already seen a dozen other impossible things, and no doubt they'd see still more. Things nobody on Sharona would even have believed possible. Beneath the anger, the hatred, the fear, the portion of Jathmar Nargra which had drawn him into the survey crews in the first place struggled to reassert itself. His genuine love of new sights, odd adventures, and places no Sharonian had ever set foot pressed tentatively against the deep traumas of the last ninety-six hours.

He felt it stirring and wondered what was wrong with him. How could he possibly feel anything except fear, anxiety, hatred for the people who'd murdered his friends, crippled his wife's Talent, almost killed him? How could there be *room* for anything else?

He didn't know. The fact that he couldn't banish his silly grin made him feel guilty, as if he were betraying his dead friends' memories, yet there it was, and he couldn't convince himself Ghartoun, or Barris, or Falsan would have begrudged him the feeling. It wasn't enough to set those darker, harsher emotions aside. Even if it had been, he wasn't prepared to do that yet, for many complex reasons. It would be a long time before he was prepared to even consider truly relinquishing that darkness. Yet there was a deep, almost soothing comfort in discovering that an important part of him, one he valued deeply, hadn't died with his friends among the toppled trees.

He recalled Shaylar's attempt to comfort Gadrial's distress and wondered if she struggled with some of the same feelings. Maybe she was simply braver than he was. Maybe it was just that she'd already recognized the truth in that ancient, banal cliché about life going on. Certainly there was an undeniable edge of bad melodrama in refusing to recognize that they had to make the best of whatever came their way. If they wanted to do more than merely survive, wanted to continue to be the people they'd always been before, then they had to discover things which could still bring them joy, people they could still care about. Perhaps Shaylar simply understood that better than he did. Or perhaps she simply had the courage to go ahead and admit it and reach out, risking fresh hurt because she refused to surrender to despair.

He reached down to cover Shaylar's hands with his own, where she'd wrapped them around his waist, and gave her fingers a gentle squeeze. He couldn't tell her why, not with the wind snatching sound away, but she tightened her arms around him in a brief return gesture, then leaned more of her weight against his back and the sturdy, borrowed shirt he wore.

It felt strange, that shirt. It was a uniform shirt, made of heavy cotton twill, comfortable, and certainly rugged enough for the purpose of exploring virgin universes, but with a cut unlike anything Jathmar had ever seen. Sharonian shirts were simply two panels of cloth which met in front and buttoned down the center, but this shirt had a complicated bib-like construction, with two rows of buttons where the left panel and right panel overlapped a third, which lay beneath the other two.

Jasak Olderhan had shown him how to fasten it up. It wasn't one of Olderhan's own shirts, since Jathmar would have been lost in the taller, broader man's garments. He suspected it had belonged to one of the men killed in the fighting, which gave him a distinctly odd feeling. Still, he'd needed a shirt, and clothing wasn't among the things Olderhan's men had taken away from the survey crew's abandoned camp.

Not that they hadn't taken plenty of other things. Several heavy cases—obviously purpose-designed canisters specifically intended to be transported by dragons—were strapped to the platform behind the wounded. Those cases contained all the guns and every piece of equipment they'd been carrying in the battle. From the looks of it, they also contained a fair percentage of the equipment they'd abandoned in camp, as well. Olderhan's men had even carried out the spare ammunition boxes.

At some point, Jathmar knew, Olderhan was going to "ask" them to demonstrate all of that equipment's use. Including the guns. He wasn't looking forward to that, but for the moment, streaking through the sky on a creature out of mythology, suspended between what had happened and what was yet to happen, he was able to set those worries aside and simply enjoy the breathtaking experience of riding the wind.

Below them, as far as he could see, lay miles and miles of trackless swamp. He'd discovered that his Mapping Talent worked just fine from up here—or would have, if not for the fact that he'd never in his life moved this quickly. Trying to sort out everything his Talent let him See was all but impossible simply because of the speed with which it came at him. He was sure he could have learned to compensate with practice, but for now he couldn't make a great deal of sense out of what he was Seeing. Which was particularly frustrating, since he rather doubted that his captors realized they'd given him the opportunity to chart a perfect escape route . . . if only he'd been up to the challenge.

But if he couldn't See all he would have liked to, there was more than enough he could see. Brilliant sunlight scattered diamonds across the open patches of water among the reeds, swampy hillocks, and patches of trees. Vast clouds of birds rose in alarm as the dragon flashed overhead: graceful waterbirds with snowy white wings and dove gray wings and wings of darker hues that were doubtless herons and cranes.

They were too high to see any of the other animals which inhabited that vast swamp, but Jathmar had little doubt that there'd be plenty of crocodiles or alligators of some sort down there, along with fish, water-loving mammals, and millions upon millions of crustaceans. He wished he could figure out where they were, though, and he couldn't. The shape of land masses never varied from one universe to the next, but one stretch of swamp was very like any other, and he had absolutely no reference points to try and figure out where *this* one lay. If he could look at the stars tonight, he would at least be able to tell whether they were in the northern hemisphere, or the southern, but he was unhappily certain that the information wouldn't do him a great deal of good.

Although I suppose I'll at least draw a certain amount of mental satisfaction out of putting my astronomy lessons to good use.

*   *   *

They'd flown several hundred miles, at least, when the dragon finally began to descend just as Jathmar spotted a clearing near the beach. A fort had been built along the edge of a sheltered bay, where a stream emptied from the swamp into the sea in a startling plume of dark water that stained the turquoise seawater for a surprising distance. Despite a lifetime spent Mapping, Jathmar had never consciously thought about dark, nutrient-rich water creating such a visible stain in much clearer seawater, let alone how it would look from the air. It was almost like a painting—swirls of color like the strokes of a brush across canvas, unexpected and beautiful.

Then they were circling over the fort itself, and he turned his attention to their destination. It was a fairly large structure, but scarcely huge, and he nodded inside. Everything he'd seen so far suggested that their captors were operating at the end of an extensive line of relatively unimproved universes, much as the Chalgyn Consortium crew had been doing when they blundered into one another. He'd seen scores of Sharonian forts very much like the one below him. Form followed function, so it was probably a multiversal pattern: an outer stockade, made of thick logs hewn from the clumps of forest dotting the vast swamp, wrapped around a fairly large open courtyard which held several buildings.

A sturdy, if roughly built, pier ran out into the bay from the seaward face of the fort. That, too, was something he'd seen many times before. What he *hadn't* ever seen was a ship like the one lying alongside that pier, and his eyes narrowed behind the protective glass shield as he studied it.

It wasn't especially huge—not more than three hundred feet, he estimated, though it could have been a bit more than that—and its sleek lines were unlike those of any ship he'd ever seen before. It was slim, obviously designed for high speed, with sharply flared clipper bows and a graceful sheer. The superstructure seemed enormously top-heavy to Jathmar, far bigger and blockier than any Sharonian ship he'd ever seen, but that might have been partly because there was so little other top hamper. It had only a single mast, whose sole function was clearly to support the lookout pod at its top, and there was no trace of the tall funnels a Sharonian steamer would have boasted. In fact, that was the strangest thing of all, he realized. The ship below him had neither sails nor funnels, so what in the names of all the Uromathian devils made it *go?*

He had little time to ponder the question before the dragon back-winged abruptly and touched down with almost terrifying suddenness. His mind shrieked that they were coming in much too quickly for safety, but the wide wings braked their forward movement at the last possible instant. Indeed, they slowed far more quickly than should have been possible with several tons of dragon in motion, then settled in a swirl of beach sand, flying debris from the tide line, and a solid *whump.* There was no doubt about the moment they touched the ground, but the actual landing was far less jarring than he'd feared from their approach speed. The beast's rear legs touched first, then it settled onto its forelegs, trotted briskly forward for a few dozen yards, and simply stopped.

Jathmar glanced back into his wife's wide, alarmed eyes, and made himself smile.

"We made it!" He chuckled, although his breath was a little unsteady. "And we got down in one piece, too! I had my doubts, right there at the end."

"That was . . . amazing." Shaylar sounded a bit breathless herself as she uncurled her fingers from their death grip on his waist. "Really . . . wow!" she added.

Gadrial appeared from behind them, smiling at their obvious reaction to the flight and landing. She showed them how to unbuckle the complex straps, then signaled for them to wait while the seriously wounded were offloaded first. The men who'd come out to meet the dragon—there were substantially fewer of them than a fort this size should have boasted, Jathmar thought—had sorted themselves out into two—no, three—types.

The first group guided stretchers that floated by themselves. Stretchers, Jathmar realized abruptly, like the "cot" upon which he'd awakened in the swamp base camp. *So that's how they transported so many wounded men out*, he thought as the stretchers floated straight up the dragon's side, where the wounded were carefully shifted onto them.

The second sort were either an honor guard or, more likely, a security detail charged with making sure he and his wife didn't attempt something rash. The third, Jathmar pegged as command-and-control types, given the deference the others accorded them. The crossbowmen of the security detail stood rigidly at attention and snapped out crisp salutes as the apparent officers strode past them towards the dragon.

Then it was the unwounded passengers' turn to descend. The ground abruptly looked much farther away, and Jathmar exchanged a single apprehensive glance with Shaylar, who still seemed distinctly unsteady on her feet.

"Why don't I climb down first, so I can brace you if you lose your grip?" he suggested.

She nodded, and he drew a quick breath, gave her a bright smile, and climbed over the edge, hooking his feet into the crosswise strands of the weblike ladder.

The beast's hide was surprisingly warm. He'd expected something so reptilian to be more, well . . . *reptilian*. But it was warmer than he was, even through the tough, spiky armored scales. One of the spikes caught at the leg of Jathmar's trousers, and he decided—a little queasily—that he really didn't want to know what was big enough and nasty enough for a beast this size to grow spiked armor to avoid being eaten by it.

He made it safely to the ground, then reached up to assist Shaylar down the last several inches to the sand. She swayed as her feet touched the ground, forehead creased with a furrow of pain Jathmar didn't like a bit. The distracting excitement of flying was wearing off quickly, he thought, and slipped his arm around her to help support her drooping weight, then turned uncertainly to look for Jasak Olderhan, who'd climbed down ahead of them.

Olderhan was waiting with grave patience, and when Jathmar turned, he gestured both of them forward with a reassuring smile. They approached him obediently, and he hesitated a moment, then offered Shaylar an arm. It was a gallant gesture, as well as a pragmatic one, given her unsteadiness. And it might just be Jasak's way of sending an important message to the people waiting across the beach, Jathmar thought. He looked down at Shaylar, nodded reluctantly, and watched her lean against the officer's forearm. She looked up at her towering captor and actually produced a smile, despite the bruises and swelling that turned it into a pathetic, lopsided expression that clearly caused her pain.

Jathmar saw a few widened eyes, and more than one look of sudden uncertainty that bordered on . . . guilt as Shaylar's tiny size and brutally battered appearance registered. He blinked in surprise when he identified that particular emotion. Then his eyes narrowed as he realized Jasak Olderhan clearly knew what he was doing . . . and that he appeared to be swaying at least a few opinions. Moving slowly, every step attentive to the bruised and battered woman he escorted, Jasak supported Shaylar across the wide beach while Jathmar walked at her other elbow, ready to catch her if she lost her footing in the loose sand.

They came to a halt before a cluster of three officers. All of them were older than Jasak—two of them by quite a number of years—and Jasak stopped before the eldest of them all. The older officer was a solid, rectangular plug of a man, six inches shorter than Jasak, but still the most imposing man on the beach. Jathmar recognized power when he saw it, and this man, with his iron-gray hair, bull-like neck, and arms that could have snapped Jathmar's spine almost absentmindedly, literally exuded power. His eyes, as gray as his hair, weren't cold so much as wary and observant. He swept his gaze across Jathmar from top to toe, but his granite expression gave away nothing of his thoughts. His gaze lingered considerably longer on Shaylar, and a vertical line drove between his brows as he studied her injured face—and everything else about her—in minute detail.

Last of all, that cool, appraising gaze centered itself squarely on Sir Jasak Olderhan. Jasak greeted his superior with that curious clenched-fist salute, and the older officer returned it—crisply enough, but with a good deal less formality. Jasak spoke briefly, and his superior asked a question. Jasak answered, and the older man nodded. Then, catching Jathmar by surprise, the man who obviously commanded this military outpost stepped back and gestured them past him and his official entourage.

Jasak saluted again, then solicitously escorted Shaylar—and, by extension, Jathmar—into the enemy fortress.

Jathmar's first impression from the air, that this fort wasn't so very different from Sharonian ones—just as the lives of the men stationed in it couldn't be so very different from Sharonian soldiers' lives—had been accurate enough. He readily identified barracks, officers quarters, and a central block which undoubtedly held the fort's command center. There was what looked like a mess hall to one side, and a particularly stoutly constructed building, which was probably the armory or the brig, or might well be both.

All of that was expected enough, but other things he saw had no Sharonian equivalents.

For one thing, there were cages along the far side of the open courtyard. There weren't many of them, but they were big enough to hold a really massive wolf or a small pony, and they obviously contained *something* which was violently alive. The cages were too far away to determine what kind of creature was penned inside, but he could see—and hear—enough to know they were unlike anything which had ever walked Sharonian soil or flapped through Sharonian skies.

They gave off metallic glints, for starters, rather like the dragons did. They also produced a noise like a steam whistle in a crowded railway station, and the breeze carried the smell of them across the courtyard to Jathmar. He wriggled his nose, trying to come up with something—anything—familiar he could compare it to. Nothing came to mind, though.

Other cages and pens were reassuringly normal looking. He could see chickens in coops and a pigpen with a number of live swine lolling in the mud, and he could hear the distinctive bleating of goats. What he *didn't* see was any trace of horses, or any similar draft animals.

Given the dragons' size, they certainly had to be housed outside the fort, but he hadn't seen any sign of external corrals for more mundane transport animals as they overflew the fort, which struck him as a little odd. All Sharonian portal forts stocked horses and mules. They were necessary for rapid deployment in the field against border bandits, portal pirates, or other serious threats to civilian lives in a frontier settlement. They were equally essential for the pursuit of armed desperadoes, the transport of supplies and equipment, rescue work in the face of natural disaster, or hauling supply wagons or the field artillery held at most of the larger portal forts.

Jathmar supposed it was possible that Jasak Olderhan's army hadn't brought horses to this particular fort because of the unsuitable terrain. Swamps and horses didn't get on well with one another, for multiple good reasons, and the thought of trying to drag *wagons* through that muck would have been enough to send any Sharonian quartermaster into gibbering fits. Then, too, with dragons to haul supplies, they probably didn't really need horses as pack animals, although Jathmar could envision all sorts of terrain where dragons would be useless. The dense forest in which he and his friends had first encountered these people came forcibly to mind.

Whatever they used for pack animals, though, one thing was clear: this fort was as well stocked and well organized as any Portal Authority fort Jathmar had ever seen at the end of a long transit chain, and he frowned as an earlier thought recurred to him. He couldn't tell how many men were housed here, but he had the distinct impression that the fort had been designed to hold a much larger garrison.

That was interesting . . . and worrisome. From what he could see, Grafin Halifu probably had almost as many men as these people did, despite the fact that his company was understrength. But even if that were true, it was clear this fort was intended as the base for a force much larger than Halifu's. So, was that larger garrison simply out in the field on exercises? That was certainly possible, and if true, it meant the enemy had sufficient reinforcements in close proximity to easily handle anything Halifu might throw at them.

On the other hand, if Jathmar was right that this was an end-of-the-line installation, built primarily to service the swamp portal, then it might very well still be awaiting the rest of its garrison. Gods knew that was common enough for the Portal Authority's forts! And if that were the case *here*, then that gray-eyed man on the beach might just find himself very hard pressed to hold off a prompt Sharonian strike.

Unless, of course, Jathmar reminded himself, *the reinforcements he's waiting for are almost here already. This fort's obviously been here for at least several months; that probably means the rest of its assigned personnel are somewhere in the pipeline on their way here. Grafin's first reinforcement column certainly wasn't all that far out when we headed through the portal.*

They reached their evident destination, and Jathmar found himself helping Shaylar into a roughhewn building whose wooden walls and floorboards had been roughcut from large logs. The first room was obviously an office of some kind, where a uniformed young man saluted Jasak and personally escorted their entire party into another, much larger room. Jathmar had halfway expected to find jail cells; instead, they entered an airy, breeze-filled room that was obviously an infirmary, where rows of cots had been laid out in readiness for the incoming wounded.

Several of the floating stretchers were maneuvered past them, with the more seriously hurt taking precedence over the walking wounded, including Shaylar. Men who were obviously physicians and orderlies handled the incoming casualties with brisk efficiency, although most of the medical personnel seemed to lose a bit of their professional detachment at their first sight of gunshot trauma.

A man with graying hair, slightly stooped shoulders, and gentle eyes the color of the North Vandor Ocean in winter gave Shaylar a kindly smile and gestured her over to a real bed, not one of the emergency cots.

She held onto Jathmar's hand as she sat down on the edge of the bed. The gray-haired man spoke at length with Jasak Olderhan and Gadrial. Jathmar didn't need to speak the language to recognize a physician at work, and he watched the—doctor? healer?—nodding slowly and jotting what were obviously notes into a small crystal the size of his palm. Like Halathyn's, this man's crystal held squiggles of text that glowed faintly. But he tucked that crystal away in a capacious pocket and pulled out a much slimmer one, long and thin, with a bluntly tapering point at one terminus. The new crystal's other end was rounded, shaped to fit into his palm, and he held it out and murmured something.

A beam of light streamed from the end. Shaylar twitched away in astonishment, but he only smiled reassuringly and allowed the light to play across the back of his other hand, demonstrating its harmlessness. She looked at him just a bit timidly, then smiled back and sat straight and still as he peeled back her eyelids, peered carefully into her pupils, and shined the beam of light right into her eyes to see how the pupils reacted.

He frowned and asked Gadrial a brief question.

Gadrial's answer was also brief, and the man shined the light into Shaylar's ears, paying particular attention to the one on the bruised, swollen side of her face. Then he murmured something else in an absent tone, extinguishing the crystal's light, and put the peculiar little device away. He stood for a moment, then laid very gentle hands on Shaylar's battered face. He closed his eyes, and his fingers moved slowly across her injuries, lighter than butterfly wings as he traced the extent of the damage. They moved around to the side of her head, then to the back, all while his eyes remained closed.

When they opened again, he stepped back and gave Shaylar a very reassuring smile. But Jathmar saw the worry in his eyes, and he spoke with Gadrial again. The questions were longer and more detailed, this time, and he listened very carefully to her answers. Jasak asked a question of his own, and the gray-haired man answered gravely, evidently trying to explain his findings. Jathmar had seen plenty of Sharonian Healers conducting examinations by touch and Talent, but that didn't seem to be what was happening here, although he couldn't have said precisely why it felt different.

At length, the man urged Shaylar to lie down. Gadrial touched Jathmar's arm, then pointed from the healer to Shaylar, folded her hands, and laid her head against them, pantomiming sleep. Jathmar nodded slowly. He didn't much like the idea of some strange healer putting his wife to sleep in order to do unimaginable things to the inside of her head, but she needed medical care badly, and this man seemed to be the best that was available.

Dozens of questions he couldn't possibly get across through pantomime streamed through his head, but even if he'd been able to ask them, he probably wouldn't have understood the answers. So he simply nodded and pointed to a chair, trying to ask if he could sit beside his wife. The healer hesitated. His expression was easy enough to decipher, Jathmar thought mordantly. Jathmar was an enemy who'd killed an unknown number of their people. The healer was afraid that he would react—badly—if anything went wrong during his wife's treatment.

Jathmar wished the other man was wrong, but he wasn't positive he was. The thought of letting this man go poking around through Shaylar's brain with whatever strange methods he used terrified Jathmar, and he could feel his self-control wavering under the pressure of that terror. But as with so much else, he had no real choice. Something was badly wrong with Shaylar's Voice. That suggested deep damage from the concussion, and whatever this man had sensed from his examination, it had him worried. It had Jathmar worried, too. Head injuries were the darkest fear of most of the Talented, whether they were willing to admit it or not. So little was known about the human brain, even now, and without the services of a Healer specifically trained in treating those with major Talents, the odds of Shaylar's ever recovering her Voice were probably much less than even.

But there was almost certainly no one in this entire universe with that sort of training. This man Jathmar couldn't even communicate with was the best available.

"We have to risk it," Shaylar said softly, correctly interpreting his stricken expression.

"I know," he said, his voice low. He started to say something else, trying to reassure her. Then he stopped himself and simply shook his head. "I'll be right here beside you the entire time."

"I know," she replied, and smiled. "Whatever happens, Jathmar, I love you."

He started to speak, but his throat tightened savagely. He had to clear it, hard, before he could get the husky words out.

"You're my life, Shaylar." He stroked her hair gently, smiling at her, willing his lips not to tremble. "I'll be right here when you wake up."

He pulled the chair over, his eyes silently daring anyone to countermand him.

After a brief moment of locked gazes, the healer simply sighed and nodded.

Jathmar sat down and held Shaylar's hand in his. The healer glanced at him once, then placed his own hands carefully on her temples and began whispering. *Something* was happening between his hands—an indefinable something that shivered around Shaylar's head. It wasn't quite a *glow*, so much as an odd thickening of the light, and as it strengthened, her eyes closed.

There wasn't anything to see, really. Jathmar was peripherally aware of activity behind him as more wounded men were brought in, groaning and trying not to cry out as they were transferred to beds, where other healers got to work. The man bending over Shaylar worked with his eyes closed and kept up a constant subvocal whispering the whole time he did whatever it was he was doing. Shaylar lay pale and still beneath his hands, looking broken, lost, and childlike in a bed whose frame was designed to accommodate one of the strapping soldiers assigned to this fortress.

Then the bruises began to fade.

Jathmar's eyes widened. Dark, ugly bruises—purple and black and crimson—paled to the yellows and browns of old trauma . . . then faded completely away. The swelling receded, as well, as some fantastic process he could only gape at sent the pooled liquids under her skin—blood serum and excess water—seeping back into the tissues and blood vessels from which they had come. The man spoke quietly, and Gadrial dampened a cloth and used it to gently cleanse the crusted cuts and abrasions. As she rinsed away the dried blood,

Jathmar saw that the skin beneath it had completely healed. All that remained of the ugly cuts and deep abrasions were the faintest traces of fine white scar along her temple, cheekbone and eyebrow. Her face, so fragile against the white hospital sheet pillowcase, bore no further traces of the desperate injuries she had sustained.

At last the healer sat back. His quiet whisper faded away, and the odd, thickened light around her face faded with it. The healer spoke to Gadrial again, very carefully, and she nodded.

He's giving her instructions of some kind, Jathmar realized. Then the implications of that sank in. *He's telling her what to do because they don't expect us to stay here very long.*

The man finished speaking to Gadrial and rested a hand on Jathmar's shoulder. That surprised him. The gesture was firm, reassuring, even friendly. None of the hatred Jathmar had seen in the eyes of Jasak's men shadowed this man's eyes, and he felt his own tension recede a notch.

"Thank you," he said slowly, carefully.

The healer gave him a brief smile, patted his shoulder once, and turned briskly to the wounded men still awaiting badly needed treatment. Shaylar was still asleep, and Jathmar wondered how long she would remain unconscious. Then, as if she'd heard his mental question, her eyelids twitched. They fluttered slowly open, and even before she was awake, the marriage bond roared wide open. He felt her confusion and wondering surprise that the pain in her head was gone. Then her eyes focused on Jathmar, and the rush of love and relief and gratitude that overflowed his heart poured into her senses.

She reached up and touched his face with gentle fingers that trembled ever so slightly.

"It's back," she whispered. "The bond . . . I can hear you again. . . ."

"And I can hear you," he whispered back, cupping the side of her face which was no longer bruised and swollen, fingertips tracing the faint white lines that remained. "The bruises are gone, the swelling—everything. If *that* wasn't magic, I don't know what else it could have been."

Her tremulous smile was radiant. She was so beautiful his throat ached, but when she tried to sit up, Gadrial reached down swiftly and stopped her, saying a single word which obviously meant "No."

Shaylar looked surprised. Then she touched her own brow, which had furrowed.

"My head feels really strange," she murmured, terrifying Jathmar for a moment. "Not in a bad way," she reassured him hastily.

"Just . . . odd. When I tried to sit up, it started buzzing like a swarm of bees. And there's an odd sort of tingling, down deep. I hadn't noticed that before I tried to sit up, either."

"Well, whatever he did, I think Gadrial's right. Lying still for a while is a very good idea," Jathmar told her.

"I don't feel like arguing the point." Her smile was more of a grin. "Besides, it's *heaven* to be lying in a real bed again."

He laughed softly and smoothed her hair again. It still needed the attention of a pair of shears and a good stylist to repair the damage, and he found himself wondering if these people's *beauticians* used magic, as well.

Behind him, Jasak Olderhan spoke briefly to Gadrial. She didn't look especially happy about whatever he'd said, but she nodded. Then Jasak touched Jathmar's shoulder and gestured to him. His meaning was plain enough; he wanted Jathmar to go somewhere with him.

Jathmar's stomach muscles clenched. So did his teeth, but he made himself give Shaylar's hand a gentle squeeze.

"Get some rest, love," he told her. "You need your beauty sleep."

His light tone didn't fool her. Their marriage bond was working at peak efficiency once more, and she knew exactly how scared he was. But she gave him a brave smile and touched her hair herself.

"If I can explain to Gadrial, maybe she can even find a comb and mirror somewhere so I can primp a bit before you get back."

He wanted to hold her close forever, so that nothing could ever harm her again. Instead, he gave her fingers one last squeeze, then stood up, squared his shoulders, and faced Jasak Olderhan.

"Lead the way," he said.

* * *

Jasak discovered a deep respect for Jathmar's courage as the other man faced him. Jathmar had already been hit with a variety of experiences which must have been utterly bewildering. Clearly, they'd shaken him to the core. Over the course of the day, his face had clearly revealed that he'd never seen anything like dragons, personal crystals, or Gifted healers. Yet he stood quietly, facing Jasak—and whatever Jasak had in store for him next—and if his eyes were understandably apprehensive, and if tension sang through his muscles, he met his captor's gaze unflinchingly.

Jasak wished there were some way he could tell Jathmar how much he respected him. But there wasn't, and so he simply bowed slightly and gestured for the other man to accompany him.

Jathmar followed him quietly, and their boots clattered hollowly across the rough boards of the hospital floor. Then they were out in the hot sunshine, with the breeze wandering in through Fort Rycharn's open gates. The tang of saltwater stung the nose, and the murky, thick scent of the swamp clogged the back of the throat, as they crossed the busy compound. Jasak headed for the commandant's office and wished he felt as brave as Jathmar looked. He wasn't looking forward to the coming interview. He'd sat through many a debriefing after firing shots in some brush with frontier bandits, but he'd never given a genuine *combat* debrief.

He discovered that the prospect became steadily more daunting as the moment approached. What had seemed the most reasonable course at the time seemed more and more questionable as he went over each step of the disastrous mission, trying to organize his thoughts. Doubts plagued him. Things he should've done, things he shouldn't, things he ought to have seen . . . but hadn't.

Then there was no further time to worry about it, because they were at the headquarters building.

"The Five Hundred is waiting for you, Hundred Olderhan," the adjutant at the outer desk said with a crisp salute, although he eyed Jathmar with open curiosity. Commander of Five Hundred Klian looked a bit taken aback, as well, when Jasak entered his office with Jathmar in tow.

"It's hardly standard procedure to bring a captured prisoner to an official debriefing, Hundred Olderhan. I trust you have a good reason?" he said after returning Jasak's salute.

"As a matter of fact, Sir, I have several reasons. Jathmar doesn't understand our language, so there's no risk of a security breach. And there's nothing in this office, Sir that could be even remotely considered classified. But my primary concern is for Jathmar's safety."

"His safety?" Klian echoed.

"My men are badly shaken, Five Hundred. Fifty Garlath's platoon outnumbered Jathmar's survey crew three-to-one, but we took massive casualties. Their weapons are devastatingly effective, and their rate of fire is considerably higher than even a dragoon arbalest's. Quite frankly, some of my survivors fear and hate him. They wouldn't try anything against his wife—they were properly horrified when they found out we'd nearly killed a woman—but I wouldn't care to leave Jathmar in the same room with any of them. Not without an armed guard to see that no one tried anything."

"I see. And you don't trust *my* men to do their jobs, either?" Klian's tone was biting.

"That's not at all an issue, Sir. My concern where *your* men are concerned rests entirely on Jathmar's state of mind, not theirs. He's been hammered by multiple shocks in a very short time. The slightest manifestation of sorcery shakes him to the core, and his wife is also our prisoner. That terrifies him, and I can't say I blame him for it. If our roles were reversed, I'd be *damned* worried about the interrogation methods my captors might intend to use."

Five Hundred Klian frowned, but it was a thoughtful frown, not an angry one.

"Go on," he said.

"I won't go so far as to say he trusts me, but I'm at least a somewhat known quantity, and I stood between them and Hundred Thalmayr when the hundred expressed . . . dissatisfaction over my decision not to chain them."

Klian's frown deepened, but he said nothing, and Jasak wondered whether Fort Rycharn's CO's displeasure was directed at Thalmayr or at Jasak's decision.

"In a fort filled with soldiers," Jasak continued, "I'm the *only* known quantity from his viewpoint. In my considered opinion, leaving him alone under the guard of men he has excellent reason to fear, would constitute a serious risk. He's desperately shaken and afraid. I don't want to take even the slightest chance of someone inadvertently pushing him across an edge we don't want him to cross. There's been more than enough violence already, and we need him—what he knows, what we can learn from him that we couldn't learn from his wife. I don't want to see us lose all of that because someone he doesn't know accidentally pushes too hard."

Klian's expression relaxed a couple of degrees, and he tipped back slightly in his desk chair.

"Very well, Hundred. Your solution may be a bit unorthodox, but your reasons seem sound enough, both militarily and politically. I would have expected no less of an Olderhan. Now, though, would you be so good as to explain exactly *how* this cluster-fuck occurred?"

Jasak drew a deep breath, looked Sarr Klian straight in the eye, and explained it. *All* of it. When he described Fifty Garlath's last action, the five hundred swore so sharply Jasak paused. Klian clamped his jaws, cutting himself off in mid-oath, and motioned for him to continue, and he did, right through the thunderous disagreement between himself and Hundred Thalmayr over the evacuation of the forward camp at the portal.

When he'd finally finished, Five Hundred Klian sat back, steepled his fingers, interlaced his fingers across his hard-muscled abdomen, and exhaled a long, slow breath.

"I appreciate your candor, Hundred. And your thorough analysis.

I'll be frank with you—in my opinion, you were handed one hell of a mess when we handed you Shevan Garlath. It wasn't my idea to transfer him into your company. From what I saw of him, you showed remarkable restraint in dealing with his . . . inadequacies. I wish I could say I'm surprised he shot an unarmed man who was clearly calling for a parley of some sort, but I can't. I'm *appalled*, not surprised." He shook his head. "In my crystal, Garlath's clearly at fault. But . . ."

Yes. Jasak gave a mental sigh. *But . . .*

"You realize, Olderhan, that your career may end over this?" Klian said almost gently, and Jasak met his eyes steadily.

"I do, Sir."

"Yes, I'm sure you do. Not all officers would."

Frustration colored Klian's last words. He hated to see a good officer caught in the jaws of a dragon this nasty, and he had a sinking feeling that Arcana was going to need good officers badly in the not-too-distant future. If *he'd* been sitting at a fort commandant's desk on the other side, and news like this had hit his desk, there'd have been hell to pay, with interest due.

"It isn't fair to you, son," he said quietly, "but it looks to me like we're staring a potentially ugly war right in the face, and politicians like to *blame* somebody for their wars. Military tribunals are supposed to be above that, but the men who sit on them are fully aware of political repercussions. Half the officers sitting on them have their own political ambitions, too. And Garlath's dead; you're not. They're going to want somebody they can point at, somebody they can look in the eye and say 'It's *your* fault, Mister!' Once they've got him, they can tell the politicians 'See? We found the guilty party, and we punished the guilty party.' It's ugly, it's brutal . . ."

He paused and looked into Jasak's eyes.

"And you knew all of that before you ever walked into this office, didn't you?"

"Yes, Sir." Jasak's lips twisted in what some people might have called a smile. "I did indeed."

"I'm sorry, son." Klian leaned forward. "I'll send my own sealed report back with you, along with some other official dispatches. It might do some good."

"Thank you, Sir."

"A lot will depend on the officers available for the tribunal when it's called. If you get a good board, it could still come right."

"Yes, Sir," Jasak agreed, but his voice was dry and not particularly hopeful. Then he sat forward. "If I might ask, Sir, what are your intentions regarding the portal camp?"

Klian sighed and sat back again, pinching the bridge of his nose.

"Could they have gotten a message out?" he said finally, glancing at Jathmar.

The prisoner sat very quietly, hazel eyes intent as he listened to the conversation he couldn't understand and tried to glean anything he could from their faces, their voices, their eyes. Olderhan was right, Klian thought. This was a deeply frightened man, and a dangerous one. One Sarr Klian wouldn't have cared to push too far without a truly urgent reason.

The five hundred met Jathmar's eyes, then turned back to Jasak, very carefully keeping his own expression impassive. The younger officer was pulling absently at his lip, frowning ever so slightly.

"I don't *know* if they got a message out, Sir," he said finally. "I don't think they could have, but we know as little about them and about their capabilities as they know about ours."

"So you're not sure?"

"No, Sir. We searched for any sign that someone might have headed back independently of the rest of their party, or the possibility that someone might have made a break for their portal during the fighting. My people know their jobs, and I had Chief Sword Threbuch available to help make sure they did them. I'm fairly confident no one carried a message physically back, and we didn't find anything remotely like hummers in their gear, either. Logically, every indication says they didn't, but there's no possible way to guarantee that."

Klian drummed lightly on his desktop, which was basically a rough plank supported by two on-end wooden chests that served as storage bins for data crystals, maps, and all the miscellany of command at a fort this size.

"One would assume they took the most direct route from their fortified camp to their portal," the five hundred said, thinking aloud. "But we can't assume they were traveling at their top speed. Which means a messenger could have gone on ahead of them, possibly even bypassed the fallen timber completely. For that matter, they could have sent someone by a completely different indirect route. I'm sure your people did search diligently, but suppose they thought about that possibility ahead of time? I'm not sure *I'd* have been smart enough to think of it in the middle of something like this, but the *smart* thing for them to do would have been to send someone further up the streambed, where he wouldn't have left any trail. Let him get another four or five miles from camp, then head cross-country by a completely different route, and you'd have needed a special miracle to cut his trail."

"It's certainly a possibility, Sir," Jasak conceded. "From the look of their camp, I'm inclined to think it didn't occur to them. I think they were thinking almost exclusively in terms of clearing out and avoiding additional contact with us completely. Which," he added a bit bitterly, "I certainly managed to prevent them from doing."

"Yes, you did. Which was exactly what you were supposed to do," Klian said. He frowned some more. "You say their ages varied?"

"Yes, Sir. Considerably. The youngest was probably in his early twenties; the oldest was in his fifties, at least."

"Were they soldiers?"

Klian looked at Jasak intently, and the younger officer paused before he answered.

"I'm almost certain they weren't, Sir," he said. "A survey crew, obviously, but a civilian one. They weren't in uniform, didn't even all have the same sorts of boots or trousers. They had the kind of gear you'd expect portal surveyors to have, but none of it was stamped or painted or embroidered with unit insignia, or any sort of military identification marks. And they had an awfully broad assortment of weapons, too. Most of them carried the same sort of hand weapon, but their shoulder arms differed a lot. I don't think any military unit would have accepted something as unstandardized as that. Spare parts and ammunition differences would play hell with the Quartermaster Corps, if nothing else." He shrugged most unhappily. "When you mix all of that together, I can only come up with one answer, Sir. Yes, they *were* civilians."

And we blew them to hell, Klian thought darkly. *May your worthless soul burn in hell forever, Garlath.*

"I see," he said aloud. "And I'm tempted to agree with you. Especially given the presence of that girl. Granted, you had Magister Kelbryan with *you*, but their young lady's situation would appear to be very different from the magister's, if she's married to one of the crewmen." He gave Jasak another keen glance. "You're sure they're married?"

"Yes, Sir. Magister Kelbryan concurs. In fact, she suggested it first, and everything I've seen only strengthens that assessment."

Klian nodded again, sitting back with pursed lips as he went over everything Jasak had said.

"It's possible they got a message out," the five hundred said finally, slowly. "On the whole, though, I think I agree with you that it's not likely. Magister Kelbryan's equipment put the portal you went out to find at no more than, what—thirty miles?"

"About that, Sir. I sent Chief Sword Threbuch ahead to confirm that," Jasak reminded him.

"Yes. The thing is, I'm trying to weigh risks. We don't know their protocol for handling portals. A civilian team in an uncharted universe suggests a radically different approach from ours, though, which leads me to wonder whether there's likely to be *any* military presence of theirs out this way."

"Is that a risk we can afford to assume, Sir?" Jasak asked quietly.

Klian met the younger officer's eyes. There was no challenge, no criticism, in his expression or tone. Just quiet worry. *Deep* worry. Gods and thunders, what had it taken to put that look in Jasak Olderhan's eyes? Jasak's expression brought home to the five hundred the fact that even having heard the description of the battle, even adding up the admittedly shocking number of casualties, he couldn't imagine what it had been like standing under those trees while some totally unknown form of weaponry cut down men all around him.

"You tell me, Hundred," he said abruptly. "You were the one who faced them out there."

Jasak sucked in air, then straightened in his chair.

"Sir, I've already said that remaining at that portal is a grave risk, in my opinion. Not only are my men badly shaken, but there's no military reason to remain, and a great many political reasons to pull out. Eventually, *someone* from their side's going to come looking for that crew. If they find an empty portal, with seven hundred miles of swamp between them and Fort Rycharn, they can't possibly reciprocate with a return assault. And unless something's changed in the last four days, I'm afraid we're too short of available manpower to reinforce Thalmayr."

He looked a question at Klian, who shook his head with a grimace.

"I'm *supposed* to have a full battalion out here already," the five hundred said sourly. "Did you happen to notice a thousand men or so out there on the parade ground, Hundred? No? Well, I haven't seen them either."

"So, basically, all Hundred Thalmayr will have is Charlie Company's second and third platoons, and what's left of First Platoon." Jasak shook his head. "With all due respect, Sir, that's not very many men to hold a portal three and a half miles across."

"No, it isn't. But at least the terrain would favor him. It's mostly flat as my mother-in-law's bread out there. He'd have the best sight-lines we're going to get for his infantry-dragons, and I've got half a dozen field-dragons I could send forward to him by air. That's a lot of firepower, Hundred."

"Yes, Sir, it is." Jasak's tone was deeply respectful. Which, Klian noted, wasn't exactly the same thing as agreement.

"There's another point to consider," the five hundred said, even as a part of him wondered why he was explaining himself this fully to so junior an officer. "As you say, your company is really all that's been sent forward to my command area right now. Oh, I've got the *supports* for an entire battalion, but under normal circumstances I'd be surprised if I saw more than another company or so any time in the next couple of months. Under *these* circumstances, I'm sure my dispatches are going to have sort of the same effect a well-placed kick has on an ant hill, of course. Give Two Thousand mul Gurthak a few days to react, and he's going to be reaching for every warm body he can find and shoving them in here. But that's going to take *time*, and until it happens, that swamp portal is the *only* place I can hope to hold with the combat power I've already got. I hate to say it, but Thalmayr's right about that."

"I know he is, Sir," Jasak agreed. "I guess I'm mostly concerned by two points. First, if their *personal* weapons could slaughter eighty percent of First Platoon, then gods only know what their artillery and *heavy* weapons are capable of."

Klian's mouth tightened in acknowledgment of the point, and Jasak continued.

"Second, and maybe even more important, I'm afraid that if *any* additional shots are fired, they'll cinch the certainty of open warfare. I'm talking politics, not military protocol, Sir. We need a team of trained ambassadors, and it's going to take time to bring them down the chain. Our next meeting with these people has to be peaceful, Sir, or we *will* be looking at war. A long, potentially disastrous, *nasty* war."

Five Hundred Klian winced at the image that conjured. Still . . .

"Everything you've said is true, Hundred," he said, fingertips drumming once more on the rough wood planking of his desk. "The question is one of timing. You say you saw nothing among their effects that might have paralleled our hummer communications system, which *ought* to mean the only way they could get a message back to their nearest support would be by runner. There's at least a chance they did exactly that, but even so, it's got to take them at least a few days to react.

"If we could be sure they had a military presence *at the portal you were looking for*, I'd evacuate our swamp portal in a flash. Or, at least as much of it as I could with only two dragons to pull everyone out. But even if they do have the equivalent of Fort Rycharn sitting out there somewhere, it's probably not all that close to their entry portal. We're only seven hundred miles from *our* entry portal to that universe, and you know as well as I do how short a hop that is compared to most distances involved. They'd have to have either a very heavy garrison deployed very far forward, or else a ridiculously short distance between portals, in order to put a powerful strike force into the field quickly."

Jasak nodded almost unwillingly, and Klian shrugged.

"Artillery can't fire *through* a portal, Hundred. If Hundred Thalmayr digs in properly, he can dominate everything on our side of the portal by fire. They'll *need* a substantial troop strength to break through that sort of defense, and presumably they'll know it, which should discourage adventurism on their side."

"Assuming they see things the same way we do, Sir."

"Always assuming that," Klian agreed. "Still, I'm inclined to leave Thalmayr where he is." He saw the alarm in Jasak's eyes, despite the younger man's best efforts to conceal it, and shrugged.

"I'll give him direct orders to dig in on *our* side of the swamp portal and stay there," he said. "The only way there could be another serious shooting incident would be for the other side to try to force a crossing. I don't really like it, but I think it's the best compromise I can come up with, at least until mul Gurthak gets more troops in here."

"I hope you're right, Sir," Jasak said. His voice was harsh, but that didn't bother Five Hundred Klian. The youngster was grim as hell, unhappy about the decision, but he recognized that the decision had been *made*. He might not like it—*Klian* didn't like it one damned bit, himself—but this was an officer who recognized that an order was an order.

"I hope I am, too," he sighed, then shook himself.

"I know you'll feel better, son, if you wait to hear Chief Sword Threbuch's report before you head for home with Magister Kelbryan and the prisoners. I'll arrange quarters for all four of you, apart from the rest of the men."

"Thank you, Sir. I appreciate that." Jasak met Klian's eyes levelly once more. "In fact, for the record, Sir, I'd like to officially inform you that Shaylar and Jathmar are my *shardonai*."

Klian stiffened—not in anger or outrage, but in dismay.

"Are you sure about that, Hundred?" he asked very quietly.

"Yes, Sir. I am," Jasak replied firmly, and Klian closed his mouth on what he'd been about to say.

The last thing this boy needed, duke's son or no, was to throw himself into the sort of catfight this was going to be. Klian didn't like to think about what was going to happen to Shaylar and Jathmar once higher authority got its hands on them. The military was going to be bad enough; the politicians and the internal security forces were going to be a nightmare. Given what was already hanging over Jasak's head, not to mention the inevitable tribunal, throwing himself between his prisoners and the entire Arcanan military and political establishment would be suicidal for his career. The five hundred couldn't conceive of any other possible consequence for his actions.

But when he looked into Jasak Olderhan's eyes, he knew the hundred didn't need *him* to explain that.

"Very well, Hundred Olderhan," he said instead, his tone formal. "I accept your declaration of *shardon*, and I will so attest, both in my dispatches and in your travel orders."

"Thank you, Sir," Jasak said, very sincerely. Klian wasn't obligated to do that, and by choosing to do so, anyway, the five hundred was putting himself in a position to be thoroughly splashed when the shit inevitably hit the fan. But his attestation, especially as part of Jasak's travel orders, which would go wherever Jasak went, would constitute a formal tripwire against . . . overzealous superiors.

"It's the least I can do for a young fellow who seems intent on pissing *everybody* off," the five hundred replied with a crooked smile. "And in the meantime, I'll post an armed guard outside your quarters, just to be *sure* no one gets any ideas about retaliating against Jathmar or his wife."

The prisoner's eyes glinted with sharp interest at hearing his name yet again. Klian looked at the man, recognizing his intelligence as well as the discipline which kept his inevitable anxiety in check. Knowing there was a sharp, active brain behind those eyes made his inability to communicate with the other man even more frustrating.

"Jathmar?" the five hundred said, and the prisoner gave him a jerky nod.

"Sarr," Klian said, touching his uniform blouse. "Sarr Klian." He waved his hand, indicating the room, the compound beyond the window. "I command this fort."

He pointed to the palisade walls visible through the window, then pointed at himself again. Jathmar studied him through narrowed eyes for a moment, then gave a slow nod. Clearly he'd already guessed as much.

"You," Klian said, pointing to Jathmar, "will go with Jasak Olderhan."

He pointed to Jasak again and pantomimed walking. Jathmar regarded him suspiciously for a moment, then nodded again. A fraction of the tension gripping him relaxed, but his eyes remained deeply wary. Klian would've given a great deal for the information behind those eyes. As he'd told Jasak, he wasn't at all happy about the decision he'd made; he just didn't see any other decision he liked better. But if more fighting *did* break out, Sarr Klian was going to be the one in the hot seat, and he was desperately short of information.

"Very well, Hundred." He switched his attention back to Jasak. "I'll make arrangements for those quarters immediately. Take him back to the infirmary for now. Let him sit with his wife until your accommodations are ready."

"Yes, Sir."

"And, Hundred Olderhan," Klian continued, standing and offering the younger officer his hand, "good luck. You deserve it . . . and you're going to need it."

"Yes, Sir. Thank you."

Jasak shook the proffered hand firmly, and Klian watched him leave with his prisoner. Then the five hundred sat back down behind his roughhewn desk and discovered he'd developed a raging headache.

Now there's *a surprise*, he thought with harsh humor, and then he got grimly to work.

CHAPTER
SEVENTEEN

DARCEL KINLAFIA STOOD moodily in the chill, rapidly falling evening under the mighty trees and tried not to look sullen.

It wasn't easy, not even when he knew all the reasons for the delay. Not even when his intellect *approved* of most of the reasons. For that matter, not even—or, perhaps, *especially*—when the delay was at least partly his own fault for insisting upon accompanying Acting Platoon-Captain Arthag's expedition in the first place.

Patience, he told the hunger coiling within him. *Patience, they're here now.*

And it was a damned good thing they were, too, he reflected, watching the head of the column.

The horsemen and their mounts looked exhausted, as well they might, given how hard they'd pushed themselves over the past five days. Kinlafia grimaced and walked across as Platoon-Captain Arthag looked up from his mess kit, then stood.

The column halted, and the man riding at its head beside the standard-bearer with the dove-tailed company guidon, embroidered with the three copper-colored cavalry sabers which denoted its place within its parent battalion, looked around. Kinlafia had never actually met him, but he recognized Company-Captain chan Tesh without any trouble, and the dark-skinned petty-captain beside him had to be Rokam Traygan. The fact that Darcel had seen chan Tesh's face through Traygan's eyes without ever seeing Traygan's was one of those oddities Voices quickly became accustomed to.

Chan Tesh's searching eyes found Arthag, and the Arpathian officer waited until the company-captain had dismounted before he saluted.

"Acting Platoon-Captain Arthag," he said crisply.

"Company-Captain chan Tesh," chan Tesh replied. The newly arrived cavalry officer looked almost Shurkhali, but he was a Ternathian, with an accent which sounded so much like Ghartoun chan Hagrahyl that Darcel winced. Chan Tesh's voice even had the same timbre.

"I'm glad to see you, Company-Captain," Arthag said.

Chan Tesh studied his face for a moment in the rapidly failing light. Kinlafia wondered if he was looking for any indication that Arthag actually resented his arrival. After all, chan Tesh's superior rank gave him command, which also meant *his* name was undoubtedly the one going into the history books. And his impending arrival had effectively nailed Arthag's feet to the forest floor, preventing the Arpathian from acting until chan Tesh got there. But if the Ternathian had anticipated any resentment from Arthag, what he saw in the other officer's expression clearly reassured him, because he smiled wearily.

"We're glad to *be* here, Platoon-Captain," he said. "Not least because our arses need the rest!"

*   *   *

"I think we can provide more than just a rest, Company-Captain," Hulmok Arthag said. "My people have a hot meal waiting for you."

"Now that, Platoon-Captain, is really good news," chan Tesh said. "I think my backbone's about ready to start gnawing on my belt buckle from the back!"

It was a humorous exaggeration, but not that much of one, chan Tesh reflected. He and his column had been just over twenty miles from the entry portal to New Uromath when the stunning news reached them. Chan Tesh was willing to admit privately that he hadn't been pushing the pace at that point, since he'd expected to relieve Company-Captain Halifu on routine garrison duty and hadn't really been looking forward to taking over Halifu's rain-soaked portal fort. The Uromathian company-captain's reports had made it abundantly clear just how soggy chan Tesh's new duty post was likely to be.

But word of the mysterious strangers who'd slaughtered the Chalgyn Consortium survey crew had changed all of that. Chan Tesh had quickly reorganized the transport column, leaving the infantry and the majority of the support troops, including his half-dozen field guns, with his executive officer while chan Tesh himself took a hard core of mounted troops ahead as quickly as he could. Over the last five days, he and his relief force had covered almost three hundred miles, most of it through dense, rainy forest. If it hadn't been the worst five-day ride of Balkan chan Tesh's life, it had to come close.

But we're here now, he thought grimly. *And if Arthag's report's as accurate as his reports've always been in the past, the bastards on the other side of that swamp portal aren't going to be a bit happy about that!*

He looked over his shoulder as the rest of the column came in. He was proud of those men. Tired as they were, weary as their mounts were, there'd been no straggling. These were mostly veterans, who didn't worry about parade-ground precision, but the column was well ordered and well closed up.

Chan Tesh's own cavalry company—Copper Company, First Battalion, Ninth Regiment, Portal Authority Armed Forces—led the column. He'd left one of his three platoons with his XO, and Copper Company had been a bit understrength to begin with, but he still had eighty-five experienced, hardened troopers. Then there were the two platoons of Imperial Ternathian Marines.

Most nations' marines were straight leg-infantry—not surprisingly, since marines were supposed to spend most of their time in shipboard service. *Ternathian* Marines were a rather special case, however. They prided themselves on their ability to go anywhere and do anything their orders required, and they'd been a mainstay of the Portal Authority's multinational forces for over half a century. There were those in the Ternathian Army who were firmly convinced that what had really happened was that the Marines had hijacked a lion's share of the Ternathian commitment to the Portal Authority purely as a means of preventing the Imperial Marine Corps' demise, and chan Tesh rather suspected that those critics had at least a semi-valid point. Certainly there'd been an ongoing struggle for the military budget between the Imperial Marines and Imperial Army for as long as anyone could remember. The *Navy,* of course, had always stood by and watched the squabble with a sort of amused tolerance. *No one* was going to suggest funding land troops at the expense of the Imperial Navy, after all.

But whatever the Marines' motives might have been, they'd succeeded in carving out a special niche in trans-universal operations. They did more of it than anyone else, and as they were wont to point out, they also, quite simply, did it *better* than anyone else. Despite his own Army career, chan Tesh couldn't argue about that. They still couldn't match the staying power and sheer, concentrated offensive punch of the Ternathian Army—they were *light* infantry, after all—but they had developed an almost incredible flexibility and took a deep (and well-deserved) pride in their adaptability. Which was why chan Tesh had left his Army infantry behind and brought his Marines along; they were just as competent in the saddle as they were on foot.

Unlike the cavalry troopers of chan Tesh's own company, or Arthag's, the Marines wore their normal Ternathian-issue battle dress. It was a comfortable uniform, with lots of baggy, conveniently placed cargo pockets. It was also dyed a low-visibility khaki color. Marines might be willing to ride to work, but they were still infantry—dragoons, at least—and they preferred to fight on foot. Whereas a cavalryman usually found it a bit difficult to conceal his horse, Marines were adept at using terrain and concealment.

And it's damned comforting to have them along, chan Tesh thought frankly. Again, they were a bit under establishment. Their nominal troop strength should have been two hundred and sixteen men, including officers and supports. Their actual strength was only a hundred and fifty-seven, but they more than made up for any lost firepower with the machine-gun squad attached to each platoon.

"I hope you'll pardon my saying so, Sir, but it looks like you came loaded for bear."

Chan Tesh turned back to Acting Platoon-Captain Arthag as the other man spoke.

"It seemed like the thing to do," the company-captain said, with a mildness which fooled neither of them.

"Can't argue with that, Sir," Arthag said grimly, and chan Tesh studied the man thoughtfully again for a moment or two.

Hulmok Arthag had a high reputation among the Portal Authority's military personnel, despite his relatively junior rank. Chan Tesh suspected that the Arpathian would have been promoted long since if his positive genius for small-unit operations along the frontier hadn't made him too valuable where he was to spare. Arpathians as a group tended to be good at that sort of thing, but Arthag was a special case, with an absolutely fiendish ability to get inside the thinking of portal brigands and claim-jumpers. In many ways, the promotion he so amply merited, and which was coming his way at last, was almost a pity. The Portal Authority was eventually going to get a highly competent regiment-captain or brigade captain out of it, but it was going to give up a truly brilliant platoon-captain to get him.

"I was relieved when they told me you were the man at the sharp end of this stick, Platoon-Captain," chan Tesh said. Arthag's Arpathian expressionlessness didn't even waver, of course. "I've heard good things about you. In fact, I've wanted the chance to work with you for a while now. I'm just sorry it had to come after something like this."

"I am, too, Sir," Arthag replied. He looked into the falling darkness, and chan Tesh felt a slight shiver as he followed the Arpathian's eyes and saw the tangled, seared timber where the survey crew had been massacred.

"To be honest, Sir," Arthag continued, turning back to his superior, "it's been...lonely out here. I was relieved when Company-Captain Halifu's dispatch reached me with the news you were on your way."

"I only wish we'd been able to let you know sooner," chan Tesh said, and Arthag's eyes narrowed very slightly.

"Voice Kinlafia's been extremely helpful to my Whiffer and Tracer, Sir," he said, very carefully not so much as glancing in Kinlafia's direction. "His special insight into what happened here's been invaluable in pointing them—and, for that matter, my scouts—in the right direction."

"I wasn't criticizing Voice Kinlafia," chan Tesh said mildly. "If I'd been in Company-Captain Halifu's position, I'd probably have made exactly the same decision. It's just unfortunate that Halifu didn't have another Voice to take up the slack. We had to get within forty miles of his fort before my Flicker could reach him."

Arthag nodded with what might have been the slightest possible trace of reassurance, and chan Tesh hid a grimly amused smile. He didn't doubt for a moment that at least some of the rear-area wonders were going to criticize Halifu for allowing his precious Voice to accompany the rescue force to the wrong side of this universe's entry portal. But, as he'd just said, chan Tesh felt the Uromathian officer had made exactly the right decision. And at least Halifu had two good Flickers of his own. They might not be Voices, but they were capable of teleporting—or "Flicking"—relatively small objects, like dispatch cases, for distances of up to thirty or forty miles. Some Flickers had managed as much as fifty miles, and they were prized by Sharonian military organizations. They might not have the reach or the flexibility of Voices, but they were a damned good substitute over their effective ranges, and there were often decided advantages to transmitting *physical* messages.

Junior-Armsman Tairsal chan Synarch, chan Tesh's senior Flicker, had managed to get word to Halifu less than twenty-four hours ago, and Petty-Armsman Bantha, Halifu's senior Flicker, had relayed that information to Arthag, in turn. Since chan Tesh and his column had crossed over into this universe, Traygan and Kinlafia had been in close communication, homing chan Tesh unerringly in on Arthag's position and bringing the company-captain fully up to date on everything Arthag's scouts had discovered.

"I'm sorry it took us as long to get here as it did, Platoon-Captain," chan Tesh said after a moment. "The last twenty-five miles to your entry portal were a copperplated bitch. Much worse than I'd anticipated, to be honest."

"I know. I've come to the conclusion that the sun simply isn't allowed to shine in that universe," Arthag replied, and chan Tesh snorted. Whether the Arpathian was right about that, or not, there was no getting around the fact that what appeared to be every creek, stream, rivulet, river, and puddle in New Uromath was well over its banks, which hadn't done a thing for his column's progress.

"At least I had plenty of time to scout the enemy position," Arthag continued. Once again, it could have been a complaint, since the peremptory order for Arthag to stand fast until chan Tesh arrived with his reinforcements had precluded any immediate action on Arthag's part. But it was apparent to chan Tesh that Arthag was sincerely relieved to see the column. The Arpathian's comment about the opportunity to scout the enemy was also well taken, and chan Tesh nodded in forceful agreement.

"Yes. I'm looking forward to seeing your sketches myself."

"Of course, Sir."

Arthag made a signal to one of his troopers, and chan Tesh watched the man in question—a tallish, but not huge, Farnalian with the two red pips of a petty-armsman—respond. It was a pity Arthag hadn't had a Flicker of his own. He'd been able to receive dispatches from Halifu, but he hadn't been able to send his own notes back. Now the petty-armsman marched over, saluted, and produced a leather dispatch case.

"Petty-Armsman Loumas, Sir," Arthag said. "He's my Plotter."

"Ah." Chan Tesh nodded in understanding. Plotters were highly valued in the military. Unlike Mappers, they could provide only limited information on terrain, or what lay under the surface of the ground, but—also unlike Mappers—they were sensitive to the presence and location of living creatures. Like Mappers, they were range-limited, and usually to much shorter ranges than a Mapper. Indeed, it was the rare Plotter who could reach beyond four or five miles. But they were still extremely useful as scouts, since it was impossible for any sentry or picket within their range to conceal himself from them.

"Loumas took our scouts right up to the portal," Arthag continued, opening the dispatch case and removing a carefully executed sketch map. "Chief-Armsman chan Hathas sketched the actual maps. He's out with the advance picket, keeping an eye on them, at the moment."

He handed the map across to chan Tesh, who unfolded it quickly.
Darkness had finished falling while he and Arthag were talking, and
there was insufficient light to make out details. He started to walk
across to one of the campfires, but Loumas produced a bull's-eye
lantern and opened the slide, letting its light fall across the map.

"Thank you, Petty-Armsman," chan Tesh said courteously, then
bent his full attention to the sketch.

"You didn't pick up *any* sentries on our side of the portal, Petty-
Armsman?" the company-captain continued as he studied the map.

"No, Sir," Loumas replied. "Picked up quite a few deer, and even
a couple of bears, but couldn't find hide nor hair of anyone else.
Proper idiots they are, if you don't mind my saying so."

"I don't mind at all, Petty-Armsman," chan Tesh said, glancing up
from the sketch map. "As long as we all remember that these people
can obviously do things we can't. It's possible they have some way
of keeping an eye on things that we've never heard of. Maybe they
didn't *need* sentries."

"Yes, Sir," Loumas said just a tiny bit stiffly. Then he grimaced.
"Sorry, Company-Captain. It's just seeing what these bastards did,
knowing where they are—"

He broke off with a shake of his head, and chan Tesh nodded.
Not necessarily in agreement, but in understanding. He'd already
seen exactly the same reaction in the men of his own column. The
news that a civilian survey crew had been cut down like animals
would have been bad enough under any circumstances. The fact that
Shaylar Nargra-Kolmayr had been caught in the middle of it, and that
Darcel Kinlafia hadn't been able to pick up even a whisper of her
Voice since, made it much, much worse. His men wanted payback,
and, to be completely honest, so did chan Tesh.

The company-captain returned his attention to the sketch and
shook his head mentally as he absorbed the details.

Maybe I was just a bit hasty there, he thought as he studied the
drawing. *If this sketch is as accurate as I think it is, then Loumas
damned well has a point about what these people use for brains!*

"You say your chief-armsman made the sketch?" he asked Arthag,
never looking up from the map.

"Yes, Sir." Something about Arthag's voice made chan Tesh look
up. The Arpathian acting platoon-captain was actually grinning, and
chan Tesh raised one eyebrow.

"Chief-Armsman chan Hathas is a much better sketcher than I am,
Sir. When Loumas and his scouting party got back and described
what they'd seen, I decided I needed to take a look for myself. I did,

but I didn't feel my own artistic abilities could do justice to it, so I got the chief-armsman to do the job. As nearly as I can tell you from my own observation, he got the details just about perfect."

"Vothan," chan Tesh muttered. "Maybe they really *are* all idiots."

Whoever was in command on the other side clearly wasn't very well versed in portal tactics. To be fair, portals—even relatively small ones like the one on the map in chan Tesh's hands—were always difficult to defend. The bizarre physics involved made that inevitable. On the other hand, there were intelligent ways to go about defending one, and then there was . . . this.

The chief-armsman had sketched the portal from both aspects, which the combination of the portal's relatively small size and the other side's failure to picket this side had made much simpler for him to do. And from the sketch, it appeared that the opposing commander was either terminally overconfident or else incredibly stupid.

Unless, chan Tesh conscientiously reminded himself, *he really does have some kind of god weapon over there.*

Which, given the fireballs and lightning bolts he'd already used on the Chalgyn Consortium crew, certainly wasn't impossible. But still . . .

The enemy had thrown up fieldworks—palisades, with what were obviously firing loopholes, protected with shallow earthen berms—to cover both aspects of his side of the portal. Because the portal itself separated them, he'd been forced to dig in two totally separate forces which were hopelessly out of visual contact and support range of one another, despite the fact that they were less than a hundred yards "apart." That much chan Tesh could readily understand, since every portal defender faced the same problem.

But the earthworks themselves puzzled him. They looked like something left over from the days of muzzleloading muskets and smoothbore cannon, he thought, except that they seemed a bit flimsy even for that. He didn't see a single bunker, and it was obvious from chan Hathas' sketch that there were no dugouts, either. In fact, chan Tesh didn't see *any* overhead cover.

"These ramparts of theirs don't look very . . . substantial," he commented. "You got a good enough look to confirm the berms are really that shallow?"

"Yes, Sir." Arthag shrugged. "I'm not sure, but I think Voice Kinlafia may have come up with an explanation for why everything over there looks so insubstantial."

"Indeed?" Chan Tesh looked up from the sketch once more, turning his attention to the one man in civilian clothing.

He hadn't ignored Kinlafia up to this point out of discourtesy, but rather because the Voice looked so bad. His face was tightly clenched around a mixture of anguish, fury, and gnawing impatience which chan Tesh needed no Talent to recognize. Kinlafia's eyes were like burnt holes in his face, and chan Tesh wondered if the man's jaw muscles had truly relaxed even once since the rest of his crew was butchered. Chan Tesh had no desire to intrude upon the man's obvious pain, but if Kinlafia had a theory to help explain what chan Tesh was seeing in this sketch, he wanted to hear it.

"You have a theory, Voice Kinlafia?" he asked courteously, and Kinlafia nodded. It was a jerky, almost convulsive nod, and his expression was taut as he waved back towards the fallen timber chan Tesh hadn't actually seen yet.

"I'm not sure what they use for 'artillery,' Company-Captain," he said, "but whatever it is, it isn't anything like ours. I know Voice Traygan has relayed Whiffer Parcanthi's and Tracer Hilovar's reports about the odd residues they've picked up to you. We still don't have any sort of explanation for what could have created them, but during the time Voice Nargra-Kolmayr—" his voice went flat and dead for a moment as he used Shaylar Nargra-Kolmayr's formal title, chan Tesh noted "—and I were linked, I Saw their heavy weapons in action. They have a lot of blast effect, and the . . . 'lightning bolts,' for want of a better word, they throw seem to affect targets in a remarkably deep zone. But neither of them seems to have very much in the way of penetrative effect."

"No?" Chan Tesh cocked his head, one eyebrow raised, and Kinlafia shrugged.

"They seem to rely entirely on the direct effect of the heat or lightning they generate. The 'fireballs,' in particular have a pronounced blast effect, but I think it's actually secondary. And they seem to . . . detonate the instant they encounter any sort of target or resistance, even if it's only a tree limb or a screen of brush."

"Obviously, none of us—" Arthag's micrometric nod indicated the troopers of his platoon "—actually saw the battle, Company-Captain. But after examining the damage patterns out there, I'd have to say I think Voice Kinlafia's on to something. There's no sign anywhere of the sort of punch-through effect you'd get from our own artillery. And no shell splinters or shrapnel, either. Their artillery seems to be spectacular as hell, and it's certainly devastating to anyone actually caught in what Voice Kinlafia calls its 'zone of effect,' but that zone is smaller than we originally thought, and I don't believe their 'guns' are going to be able to punch through very much in the way of serious cover."

"So you and the Voice think the reason their fortifications seem so . . . spindly is that their own weapons wouldn't be able to penetrate them and they've assumed that since theirs wouldn't, ours can't?"

"Something along those lines, Sir," Kinlafia said, and surprised chan Tesh with a tight smile. "I've noticed that people—whether they're military or civilians—tend to think in terms of the things they 'know' are true. It's called relying on experience, and in general, it's a pretty good idea, I suppose. But in this case, no one *has* any experience. Not really."

"A very good—and valid—point, Voice Kinlafia," chan Tesh said, impressed by the other man's ability to think when he was so obviously on fire with grief and fury. The company-captain nodded respectfully to the Voice, then turned back to Arthag.

"These here," he said, tapping the sketch with his forefinger. "These are those tube things—the artillery—Voice Kinlafia's just been describing?"

"Yes, Sir," Arthag agreed, and chan Tesh nodded.

There were, he conceded, a dismayingly large number of the odd artillery pieces. Some of them were also clearly larger than others, which to chan Tesh's mind suggested that they were probably more powerful and longer ranged. From the way they were positioned, he suspected they'd been emplaced to sweep the relatively flat ground on the far side of the portal with fire. Given their demonstrated potency, even without the secondary fragmentation effect of Sharonian artillery, that probably made sense. But why in the gods' names had they put them right on top of the portal that way? And with no better cover than they had?

"I think they're going to have a little problem here, Platoon-Captain Arthag," chan Tesh said after a few seconds. He looked up with a thin smile. "I've brought along a mortar company."

Arthag's eyes narrowed. Kinlafia's, on the other hand, began to glitter with fierce satisfaction, and chan Tesh nodded.

"There's a spot right here, Sir," Arthag said, indicating a point on the sketch map. "There's a nice little ravine on our side of the portal, deep enough to give cover to a standing man. It doesn't have a direct line of sight to the portal, but I think it would do just fine for mortars."

"Good." Chan Tesh gave the map another look, then folded it up.

"I believe you said something about supper, Platoon-Captain," he observed. "We're going to need to rest the horses for at least several hours, and I don't mind admitting that I could use a little sleep myself. Let's go find that food, and while I eat, I'd like to talk with your Whiffer and Tracer and Voice Kinlafia."

"Of course, Sir. Right this way."

*   *   *

Once the animals had been picketed for the night, chan Tesh's weary men devoured the supper Arthag's troopers had held ready for them, then fell into their sleeping bags, dead to the world within minutes. Chan Tesh would desperately have liked to join them, but he had other duties to discharge first. So he sat propped against a tree at Arthag's campfire, finishing his second bowl of stew, and listened quietly to the reports from Arthag, Kinlafia, Parcanthi, and Hilovar.

It wasn't a pretty story. Chan Tesh had already heard Kinlafia's report of the initial attack, relayed by Rokam Traygan, but it was different hearing it directly from Kinlafia himself. As the Chalgyn Consortium Voice made himself recount every detail of the horrendous attack, chan Tesh could literally taste the man's anguish and hatred. He wanted to reassure Kinlafia that they would do everything in their power to track down any survivors, but the chances of there *being* any survivors didn't sound good. None of these men—himself included, he admitted—really hoped to find anyone alive, but they were determined to try.

And failing that, Balkar chan Tesh reflected grimly, *I want the opportunity to exact some serious vengeance.*

The company-captain was Ternathian by birth and rearing, but his family hadn't always been. In fact, his father had immigrated to Ternathia with his own parents as a youth. Emigrated, in fact, from Shurkhal. Chan Tesh didn't normally think of himself as Shurkhali, but he'd just discovered, over the last five days, that the blood of his father's people still ran in his veins. If Shaylar Nargra-Kolmayr *had* died in that blood-stained clearing over there, there wasn't a hell deep enough for the enemy to hide in.

Watch yourself, Balkar! he chastised himself dutifully. *You're not really some Shurkhali nomad out stalking another clan for vengeance. You're also an imperial Army officer, with a responsibility not just to the Authority, but to His Imperial Majesty, as well. Neither of them need a hotheaded, out-of-control junior officer at the other end of the multiverse committing them to all-out war with another transuniversal civilization!*

All of which was true enough, but didn't change a thing about the way he felt. Or about his determination to seek punishment for the individual responsible for this debacle. He was honest enough to admit that he would prefer to squeeze the life out of the bastard himself, with his own bare hands, but he'd settle for having the butcher's own rulers, whoever the hell they were, hang him for the murderer he was. And Balkar chan Tesh was grimly certain that punishment exactly like that would be one of Sharona's demands whenever diplomatic relations were finally established.

"The one thing that really worries me," he said at length, having absorbed everything as well as his weary mind was able to, "is how close they may be to reinforcements of their own. We have no idea how far this fortified swamp portal of theirs is from their own next entry portal. Or of how long a transit chain they may be dangling from."

"You don't think they could be native to that universe?" Kinlafia asked, twitching his head in the general direction of the swamp portal.

"I suppose it's remotely possible," chan Tesh replied. "I think it's extremely unlikely, though. That's an exploration camp over there, Voice Kinlafia. They—"

"Please, Company-Captain," Kinlafia interrupted with another of those pain-filled but genuine smiles, "I'm not really all that fond of formal titles, and I'm a civilian. I don't have any formal standing in your chain of command, and I fully realize how out of my depth I am when it comes to any sort of military operations. So it seems a little silly to be going all formal when you talk to me. My name's Darcel."

"Of course . . . Darcel," chan Tesh said. "And mine's Balkar."

He smiled back at the Voice for a moment, then continued.

"As I was saying, Darcel, that's a small, very crude camp on the other side of that portal. They're still sleeping in tents, and that indicates they've only recently arrived at the portal site. If that were their home world on the other side, surely they'd already have known about the portal and explored it long since. I realize from Platoon-Captain Arthag's scouts' reports that this isn't a very *old* portal, but it didn't just come into existence last week, either, so—"

He shrugged, and Kinlafia nodded slowly.

"That's pretty much what I've been thinking," he admitted.

"Which brings me back to my original point," chan Tesh said. "How close are they to the next node in *their* transit chain? For that matter, how quickly did they get *their* report of what happened back to higher authority? Do they have a relief force on its way already, the same way we're responding to Voice Nargra-Kolmayr's cry for help?"

"I suppose that depends on whether or not they had a Voice of their own with them," Kinlafia said, but chan Tesh shook his head.

"It depends on a more fundamental question than that, Darcel." Kinlafia looked at him, and the company-captain shrugged. "It depends on whether or not they have Voices *at all*."

"Surely they do—they must!" Kinlafia said, but chan Tesh only shook his head again.

"You're the one who just pointed out to me—quite rightly—that people tend to operate on the basis of what experience tells them is true," he said. "Well, *our* experience tells us that there have to be Voices on the other side. But *do* there?"

"I—" Kinlafia paused, then grimaced. "All right, I see your point. I can't conceive of how they couldn't have Talents, but I suppose it's possible. On the other hand, can we risk assuming they don't?"

"Oh, no." Chan Tesh shook his head vigorously. "I intend to assume they *do*—I'll be a hell of a lot happier to find out I was wrong about that than I would be to find out I was wrong about assuming they *didn't*! But how quickly they can respond is the question that worries me the most. Well, that and the fact that they don't know any more about us than we know about them."

Kinlafia looked puzzled, and chan Tesh snorted. It was too harsh to be called a laugh.

"The only thing we know about these people is that they've encountered another party scouting an obviously virgin universe and killed or captured them all." Kinlafia winced, but chan Tesh continued calmly. "And that's all they know about us, too. I'll bet you my last pair of boots that they're wondering whether or not *our* people got a message out, and for a lot of the same reasons. But we're both only groping in the dark out here, and that makes me nervous as hell. People who don't *know* what's going on have a tendency to make worst-case assumptions . . . and then act on them."

"I agree, Sir." Hulmok Arthag nodded. "They're going to be nervous, too, if not downright spooked. Our people hit these bastards hard. It's obvious from their trail that they had a *lot* of wounded to transport. You should see all the bandages at the bivouac site we found earlier today! They've got to be wondering what's going to come after them next—and how much worse it's going to be. The fact that they've dug in shows they're at least taking precautions. They're probably ready to shoot first and ask questions later. Just like they did last time," he added bitterly.

"Exactly," chan Tesh agreed. "And let's be honest here—so are we." He looked around the faces in the firelight. "None of us is going to be inclined to take any chances. And, frankly, I'm not going to be exactly brokenhearted if these bastards give us an excuse to blow them straight to hell. Not after what they did to our people. And *that* worries me, too."

Kinlafia didn't say anything, but the sudden tightening of his face made his reaction to chan Tesh's last few sentences abundantly clear. The company-captain looked at him for a moment, then leaned forward.

"I know you want revenge, Darcel," he said quietly. "Well, so do I. And, as I say, I'm not going to be taking any chances. But if we just charge in there shooting, we're going to make any possibility of establishing real contact with these people even more difficult. And—" he raised his voice slightly as rebellion flickered in Kinlafia's eyes "—if there are any of our people still alive over there, charging in shooting is probably the best way to get them killed after all."

Kinlafia sat back abruptly, and chan Tesh looked at Arthag.

"Our first responsibility is to get any survivors back alive and unharmed. Or, at least, without their suffering any additional harm. If there *aren't* any survivors," he continued unflinchingly, "then our primary responsibility becomes establishing contact—hopefully without still more violence—and demanding that whoever ordered the attack on our people be held accountable and punished for it. I'm not going to risk any of our people if I can help it, but I'd far rather see the son of a bitch responsible for this arrested and hanged than see this turn into some sort of general war."

Kinlafia looked at him for a long, silent moment, then shook his head.

"I understand what you're saying. Intellectually, I even agree with you. But my heart?" He shook his head again. "Whatever my head says, my heart hopes to hell that these bastards do something— *anything*—else to give us the excuse to shoot every godsdamned one of them."

He rose, and stood looking down at chan Tesh and Arthag. His expression wasn't really challenging, but it was definitely unyielding, and chan Tesh couldn't blame him a bit for that.

"I'm going to try to get some sleep," the civilian said after a moment. "Good night."

It was said courteously, even pleasantly, but behind the courtesy, Balkar chan Tesh sensed the iron portcullis of the Voice's hatred. The company-captain watched Kinlafia walk away, and wished he didn't understand the Voice's feelings quite as well as he did.

*   *   *

"Sir!"

Chan Tesh reined up as one of Arthag's troopers came cantering back towards the column. The cavalryman reported to his own platoon commander, not chan Tesh, exactly as he should have.

"Yes, Wirtha?" Arthag said as the trooper saluted.

"Sir, we've found another bit they dropped," Wirtha said, and Arthag's eyes narrowed. Then he looked at Parcanthi and Hilovar.

"You two had better go check it out," he said, without checking with chan Tesh. Which, chan Tesh reflected as the Whiffer and Tracer trotted off in Wirtha's wake, was precisely what a good subordinate was supposed to do.

The two officers, accompanied by Darcel Kinlafia, followed the Talents at a bit more leisurely pace. Chan Tesh rather wished that Kinlafia hadn't been present. He'd done his dead level best, tactfully, to suggest that Kinlafia should return to Company-Captain Halifu's fort, since it was essential that they have a Voice available to relay further up the transit chain if something unfortunate—something *else* unfortunate—happened out here.

Kinlafia, unhappily, hadn't been interested. And, unlike Rokam Traygan, the civilian Voice wasn't under chan Tesh's direct authority. It was obvious that the only way the company-captain could have sent Kinlafia to the rear would have been under armed guard, and he hadn't been able to bring himself to do that in the face of the civilian's obvious pain. So Traygan had been sent back, instead, and Kinlafia was still here. Here waiting for the next, crushing blow if they confirmed Shaylar Nargra-Kolmayr's death, and here where his brooding grief and the white-hot smolder of his thinly banked fury hung like a storm cloud in the back of every mind.

But there wasn't much chan Tesh could do about that. Even if he'd been inclined to change his own mind about ordering Kinlafia to the rear, it was too late. Traygan was already more than halfway back to Halifu's fort, which left Kinlafia as the only Voice available at the sharp end.

Since there wasn't anything he could do about that, the company-captain put it out of his disciplined mind and concentrated on Wirtha's discovery. He wasn't very surprised that the scouts had found another bit of debris jettisoned by the people whose trail they were following back to the portal. If these people did have Talents, they appeared to be remarkably unconcerned about anything a good Whiffer or Tracer might be able to discern from their castoffs. Although, to be fair, given the number of wounded the other side was carrying with them, at least some bits and pieces were bound to get away from them.

It was a sign of how good Arthag's people were, though, that they were searching just as diligently this time around as they'd searched the first time they scouted the enemy's trail back to his entry portal.

The three of them caught up just as Hilovar and Parcanthi dismounted and walked across to the object the scout had found. As usual, Hilovar stopped short, allowing Parcanthi first crack at the energy residues, and the Whiffer crouched over whatever it was.

"A soldier dropped this," he said at length. "Not an officer, I don't think, but that's harder to be sure of. He's wounded, staggering. I can See more wounded all around him. Limping—cursing, it sounds like. They're carrying a fair number of men on those strange stretchers of theirs." He grimaced. "I still can't See how they get the damned things to *float* that way," he complained almost petulantly, then opened his eyes.

"Same as usual, Sir," he said, standing and turning to look up at Arthag. "They were moving slowly, but steadily. It was nearly dark when whoever dropped this dropped it." He indicated the item with his foot, without actually touching it, and glanced at his partner.

"Your turn, Soral."

Hilovar nodded and crouched down in Parcanthi's place. He stared down at what had been dropped, and his brow furrowed.

"What the hell *is* that?" he muttered under his breath.

It was a small, square object, made of something that looked almost like glass which had been deliberately opaqued. There were markings on it, but what the alien symbols signified was anyone's guess. Hilovar considered it for a moment, then shrugged and picked it up—

—only to let out a startled yelp and drop it back into the leaves on the forest floor.

"What's wrong?" chan Tesh asked sharply, watching the Tracer shake his hand as if he'd just burned it.

"Sorry, Sir." Hilovar looked a bit embarrassed. "It just took me by surprise. It's . . . unnatural."

"*That* fucking word again," Arthag growled.

"Sorry, Sir," Hilovar said again, glancing back at the scowling Arpathian. "But this thing—it's got the same feel as those accursed ash piles, only stronger. Much stronger. Concentrated as acid, in fact. It prickled my hand so hard it was like being swatted by wasps."

Chan Tesh winced at the image, then sighed.

"Do what you can, Junior-Armsman. We need anything you can dredge out of that thing—whatever it is."

Hilovar nodded, gritted his teeth, and picked it up again. It was obvious that just holding the thing caused him considerable pain, but he endured grimly.

"He's shot through the shoulder," the Tracer said, after a heartbeat or two, in a grating, savagely satisfied tone. "Bleeding into his bandages and hurting like a son of a bitch. Stumbling a good bit. Wishing he could ride on one of the stretchers, it feels like. He keeps looking at them, up ahead."

Then, suddenly, Hilovar shot upright.

"Great gods! There's a *woman* with 'em!"

"*Shaylar?*" The name tore from Darcel Kinlafia like a cry of pain, jerking Hilovar out of his concentration, and the Tracer turned to meet his tortured gaze.

"No," the junior-armsman said gently, watching the Voice's face crumple again. "I'm sorry, Darcel. She looked Uromathian—a little thing, pretty as a peach. She was walking beside one of the stretchers. I caught just a tiny glimpse of her. I think the man who dropped this," he held up the surprisingly dense object on his palm, "wanted her to help him."

"A Healer, then?" Arthag mused.

"Sounds like it," chan Tesh agreed, and cocked an eyebrow at Hilovar. "Can you get anything else off of it?"

"No, Sir. Not really," the Tracer said, obviously unhappily. "It's just more of the same. He's just moving slowly—very slowly. And hurting like hell."

"*Good!*" Kinlafia snarled, and Arthag leaned over in the saddle and gripped his shoulder wordlessly.

"Is there anything else on the ground here?" chan Tesh asked, and Wirtha shook his head.

"No, Sir. We looked around pretty carefully before I reported it to the platoon-captain."

"In that case, may I see it, Soral?"

Hilovar stepped over between chan Tesh's mount and Arthag's magnificent stallion. He held his hand up, allowing the officers to study the object on his palm. Neither of them offered to touch it lest they contaminate it for further Whiffing or Tracing.

"Doesn't look like much, does it?" Arthag murmured, and chan Tesh frowned.

"It looks like glass. But it isn't, is it?"

"It's made from the same thing as those godsdamned 'artillery pieces' of theirs," Darcel said harshly even as Hilovar shook his head.

"Now that's interesting," chan Tesh mused. He glanced at Kinlafia, then back at the Tracer. "It's heavy, isn't it?"

"Yes, Sir. Very dense," Hilovar added. "Surprisingly so, for its size."

"Are those buttons along the side?"

"That's what they look like, Sir," Hilovar agreed.

"Well, I'm damned if I'll try pushing one of them!" chan Tesh snorted.

"If you don't mind, Sir, I'd like to put it into an evidence bag. This thing *hurts* to hold. I don't know what it's made of, or what's inside it, but it's got that same foul, nasty—*unnatural*—" he added, meeting Arthag's gaze grimly "—feel. I'm not real anxious to push those buttons, either, Sir, and that's no lie. This thing is damned *weird.*"

"Very well." Chan Tesh nodded. "Put it away. Carefully."

Hilovar pulled a small canvas evidence bag out of his saddlebags and slid the dense little cube into it, then slid both of them into a larger canvas bag slung from his saddle horn, where he'd stored the other bits and pieces they'd found scattered along the trail.

"All right," chan Tesh said then. "We're getting close to that overnight bivouac of theirs, aren't we?"

"Yes, Sir," Wirtha agreed. "About another ten, fifteen minutes. There's quite a bit of stuff scattered around where their fires were. Most of it's little bits and pieces of personal gear, torn uniforms, that kind of thing. And lots of soiled bandages," he added with grim satisfaction.

"Let's move along, then," chan Tesh said.

*   *   *

"Here it is, Sir," Wirtha told chan Tesh shortly afterward, and the company-captain drew rein once more. The area before him, a clearer space along the bank of the same stream which had flowed beside the slaughtered survey crew's day-fort, showed the rings of half a dozen big bonfires and a handful of smaller ones. Even from here, he could see that there was a lot of debris strewn around, including a stained snowdrift of gore-crusted bandages.

"Has anyone been out there yet?" he asked.

"No, Sir," Wirtha replied. "We bypassed it on the way through."

Chan Tesh glanced at Arthag, and the acting platoon-captain shrugged very slightly.

"Nolis and Soral had their hands full with the debris we'd already found at the fallen timbers and at the Chalgyn crew's day-fort, Sir. I'd left them behind to deal with that while I went ahead. By the time we actually found the campsite, we also knew we were hot on their trail, so I took the point and pressed on in hopes we might overtake them. But they got to their own entry portal at least several hours before we did. By the time Nolis and Soral were ready to follow us up, we'd received the order to hold in position and wait for your arrival. It took a while to get a runner forward to my position to recall me to meet you, and Nolis and Soral stayed put in the meantime, as per their orders from Company-Captain Halifu. By the time I got back to camp and could have ordered them forward to the bivouac area here, you were only a couple of hours out."

"I see." Chan Tesh smiled thinly. "So that old saying about order, counter-order, *dis*order came into play."

"More or less, I'm afraid," Arthag agreed.

"Well, it's no one's fault." Chan Tesh sighed, and looked at Parcanthi and Hilovar. "Go ahead," he said.

The two noncoms saluted, dismounted, and headed forward. Hilovar, as usual, waited while Parcanthi moved into the bivouac area, sweeping from one cold ash pit to another, following the energy residues. It took him the better part of twenty minutes, but when he returned to the waiting officers, his eyes glowed.

"I got some good, solid Whiffs, Company-Captain!" he told chan Tesh. "There's a place a bit further down the creek over there," he pointed, "where *something* came in during the night."

"Something?" chan Tesh repeated. "What *sort* of 'something'?"

"Gods alone know," Parcanthi said frankly. "It was big. Dark. I could see firelight on what looked like . . . hide, maybe. If it *was* hide, the creature under it was big, Sir. *Really* big, like nothing I've ever seen. But it was too damned dark to get a good look at it. They were loading stretchers onto it, whatever it was."

"Some kind of transport," Arthag muttered. "So, that's what they did." Chan Tesh glanced at him, and the acting platoon-captain grimaced. "We knew they were traveling a little faster when they moved on from here. Didn't notice any particular decrease in the number of their walking wounded, but they were definitely moving more quickly."

"Did they load all the stretchers onto it, whatever it was, Parcanthi?" chan Tesh asked the Whiffer.

"No, Sir. It looked to me like they might've been loading up a dozen or so, like they were taking the most critically wounded out. Whatever it was, and however big it was, I don't think it had enough carrying capacity to take all of them. All I could see was something big and dark that moved off down the creek bed. Then I lost the Whiff."

"Down the creek," Arthag murmured with a frown which drew chan Tesh's attention back to him.

"Something's bothering you," the company commander observed. "What is it?"

"Just that something the size Nolis is describing damned well ought to have left a trail. Once you get to the other side of the creek, the terrain's just like it is on this side. And the underbrush along the stream banks is awfully dense. Anything much bigger than a house cat should've left *some* sign of its passage when it pushed through it, and we didn't see a thing. Or, rather, we didn't see the tracks of anything but the men on foot we'd been following all along."

"Could it have headed along the streambed to avoid leaving a trail?" chan Tesh asked.

"I suppose it's possible, Sir. I just don't see any reason why it should have. If the party on foot is still headed steadily south, then their destination must lie in that direction. Why should their transport have headed in some *other* direction?"

"I agree it doesn't make a lot of sense," chan Tesh said. "By the same token, it has to've gone *somewhere*. Parcanthi Saw it, so we know it was here. Unless you want to suggest that it just flew away, it had to leave tracks somewhere, too, and I know your men's reputation. They wouldn't have missed the sign something that size had to leave behind."

"I don't—" Arthag began, but Parcanthi interrupted, his voice a bit edged.

"I'm sorry, Sir. And I apologize for interrupting, but I hadn't finished my report."

Arthag and chan Tesh both turned back to him, and he waved back in the direction he'd already pointed.

"It was dark, like I said, but I might—I just *might*—have Seen one of our people among them." Both officers—and Kinlafia—jerked upright in the saddle, eyes narrowing, as he continued. "I could see someone's back, climbing up onto whatever it was. I couldn't see the face, or even get a good look at the hair, because whoever it was, they were wearing some kind of leather hat, or helmet. And they were out beyond the range of the firelight. But I'm positive that they weren't in uniform."

Darcel Kinlafia sucked down air in the sudden silence.

"Could it have been the woman you Saw, Soral?" Arthag asked quietly. "The one you said looked Uromathian. Was *she* in uniform when you Saw her?"

"She wasn't," Parcanthi said, before Hilovar could speak. "In uniform, I mean. But this wasn't her. I could See her clearly, standing on the bank. She couldn't have been anyone else, not from Soral's description earlier. It looked like she was waiting her own turn to climb up onto whatever it was."

"How . . . how big a person did you See?" Kinlafia whispered harshly.

"Small. Very small. Maybe this high," Parcanthi said, measuring with his hand.

"*Oh, gods!*" Kinlafia's voice was barely audible, and his throat worked convulsively. The others stared at him as he bowed his head over his saddle bow, eyes tight shut.

"Darcel?" Arthag said, very quietly, after a moment, and the Arpathian's eyes widened as he saw the Voice's face.

"*It's her*—Shaylar!" Kinlafia said hoarsely. "It's *got* to be her! Nobody else in the crew was remotely close to that small!"

"I didn't get a very good look at whoever it was," Parcanthi cautioned. "It was dark as sin out there in the brush, and they were climbing up whatever that thing was, which means I couldn't get a good contrast reading. All I could really see were dark shapes against the dark, black wall of hide, or whatever it was. It was a small person, slightly built, in civilian clothing. That much I could See. But I don't know that it was *Sharonian* clothing. And," he added in the tone of someone desperately trying not to step on the flaming hope in Kinlafia's eyes, "we already know they had at least one other woman—in civilian clothing—with them. If they had one, they might have had two."

All eyes turned to Hilovar, and the Tracer cleared his throat.

"If we can find anything Shaylar was holding, I'll know," he said. "But that's a big if, Darcel. A *damned* big if."

"I know." Kinlafia's voice was full of grit and gravel. "But I've got reason to *hope*, now. That's more than I've had ever since I lost contact with her."

"I agree," chan Tesh said, but his own voice was heavy. "If it was Shaylar, though, and she was conscious, up and moving, why didn't she contact you, Darcel? She had to know you'd be waiting, that you were well within her range. For that matter, I happen to know *you've* been trying to contact *her* every hour on the hour since you crossed to this side of our own portal."

Kinlafia looked at him, then cleared his own throat.

"She struck her head on something, remember? Hit hard enough to knock her unconscious, at least. And Soral's already said there was damage inside her head, serious damage. She could have been injured badly enough to be rendered Voiceless."

"But if she's hurt that badly, would she have been on her feet and climbing up whatever it was Parcanthi glimpsed out there?" chan Tesh asked.

"I don't know." It came out practically in a groan, and Kinlafia ground his teeth. "Mother Marthea, these monsters are capable of anything! If they're willing to force an injured girl to walk, to climb up this thing, when we *know* she's suffered a critical head injury, then what in the gods' names *else* are they willing to do? They could—"

"Stop it!" Chan Tesh's voice rapped out harshly, jerking Kinlafia back around to face him.

"There's no point to this," the company-captain growled, albeit more gently. "You're torturing yourself with visions we have no way to prove or disprove. The people who did this may be a complete unknown, Voice Kinlafia, but one thing we *do* know; if they have got surviving Sharonians, they're going to want them as healthy as possible."

"You're right," Kinlafia whispered. He sounded unsteady, but he drew another deep breath and slowly nodded. "You're right," he repeated. "I'm sorry. I'm just about out of my mind, worrying and wondering and feeling so gods-cursed *helpless....*"

"I understand," chan Tesh told him. "But none of us can afford to let anger swamp our thinking."

"Yes, Sir," Kinlafia said quietly. "I'll bear that in mind. The last thing in this universe—or any other—I want to do is something rash that jeopardizes *any* Sharonian lives. Ours—" he nodded to the column of mounted men "—or that of anyone they've taken with them."

"That's good," chan Tesh said quietly, and smacked him lightly on the shoulder before turning back to his two Talented specialists. "Soral, I think it's your turn in the barrel. See what you can find out."

*   *   *

A half-hour later, the Whiffer and Tracer had completed their reports. They'd managed to pick up quite a lot of additional detail about the individuals who had bivouacked here; very little of it did much good, unfortunately.

"So what do we really know?" chan Tesh asked, looking around the circle of faces around him. He and Arthag had been joined by the Marine officers in command of the two platoons he'd brought along. Hilovar and Parcanthi were both there, too, despite their noncommissioned ranks, available for consultation at need. And, of course, there was also Darcel Kinlafia.

"We know their wounded were hurt even more badly than we thought, Sir," Arthag said. "We know they sent at least ten or twelve of their people out aboard whatever the hells it was Nolis Saw down by the creek, and we know it was godsdamned big."

He grimaced. Guided by the Whiffer, some of his scouts had finally found a few footprints, in among the rocks, gravel, and water-washed sand. Whatever the enemy's transport animal had been, it had been *huge*. And its feet had been unlike anything Hulmok Arthag had ever seen—or imagined—in his life. It must have been actually standing in the stream itself, which explained the dearth of footprints, but the partial ones they'd found in the end had been frightening to behold. Long-toed, with huge claws, and damned near as long as Arthag was tall. Most maddening of all, they couldn't find a single track heading toward the bivouac . . . or heading *away* from it, for that matter! It was as if the creature had simply materialized where it was, stood around for a while, and then *de*materialized!

"I think Nolis is right that they were getting their most seriously wounded out of here," chan Tesh observed. "Makes sense. But they also sent out the one woman we know was with them, and at least one more civilian, at the same time, and both of them were at least mobile enough to climb up by themselves. So I'd say they were pulling out the people they thought were most valuable, as well as those who were worst hurt. That obviously would have included any of our people who were still alive."

"So what we've really got is just more puzzles," Kinlafia said a bit harshly.

"Any information is always valuable, Voice Kinlafia." An edge of formality frosted chan Tesh's measured reply. Kinlafia looked at him, and the company-captain looked back levelly.

"We know where their encampment is, Darcel," he continued, "and we have it under observation until we can get there and deal with it. In the meantime, any evidence we can get, any information we can cull, may be the one critical piece we need to tell us what to do when we *do* get there."

Kinlafia looked rebellious for a moment. Then his nostrils flared, and he nodded in unhappy agreement. But it *was* agreement, chan Tesh noted.

"All right," he said decisively. "I'm going to assume they do have at least one Sharonian prisoner. I may be wrong about that, but they were obviously pulling out *someone* besides their own wounded. We also know where their entry portal is, and we've got a good notion of how they've dug in on their side of it. I think it's time we took this the rest of the way to them."

Hunger sparkled in Kinlafia's eyes, and chan Tesh felt more than a small flicker of it deep within himself, as well. But he continued in that same, decisive voice.

"Given the size of the only other civilian Parcanthi Saw, I'm also going to operate on the assumption that Voice Nargra-Kolmayr *may* still be alive. If that's true, then getting her back is our number one priority. Our number two priority, however, is to try to put some sort of lid on this situation before it gets even worse. Much as I'd prefer otherwise, this isn't a punitive expedition. These aren't portal pirates, they aren't claim-jumpers—they aren't anything we've ever encountered before. But they are, clearly, representatives of another trans-universal civilization. So unless they start it, or unless we have convincing evidence that they're holding our people and won't give them up without a fight, I don't want any shooting."

The company-captain could literally taste Kinlafia's disappointment. Arthag and both of the Marine officers seemed just as unhappy, although they were too disciplined to let it show, and chan Tesh allowed himself a small, thin smile.

"I don't want any shooting from our side," he reiterated. "But if it should happen that *they* start the shooting—for a second time—I intend to be very certain that *we* end it. Is all of that clearly understood?"

Heads nodded all around, and he nodded back.

"In that case, gentlemen, let's get moving again. I want to be in position to . . . speak to these people before sundown."

CHAPTER
EIGHTEEN

CHIEF SWORD OTWAL Threbuch hated the taste of defeat.

He couldn't begin to count of the number of missions he'd carried out successfully over the course of his career. He'd cheated death ten ways from hell, dragged back commanding officers held together by little more than bandages and stitches, and somehow—some way—always gotten the job done.

But as he lay stretched out flat on his belly along the tree limb, staring at the tantalizingly close disk of the swamp portal, he tasted the most bitter failure of his life. His worst nightmare was right under his nose, and there was literally no way for him to warn Hundred Olderhan it was coming.

He'd done exactly what the hundred had instructed him to do. Neither he nor Emiyet Borkaz, the First Platoon trooper with him, had found any sign of a messenger as they left the site of the fight at the toppled timber behind and headed for what they hoped was the other side's entry portal.

That entry portal had turned out to be a monster when they finally found it. Threbuch had never seen—never imagined—one that size. It had to be at least thirty miles across, and as he'd gazed through it at the rain-soaked forest on the far side, he'd mentally apologized to Magister Halathyn and Magister Kelbryan for every doubt he'd cherished about their newfangled portal-finding gadget. If this wasn't a class eight portal, it could only be because it was a class *nine*.

Its size had been part of the problem. Threbuch had never before been assigned to scout anything that size with only two men. Finding the fort from which the survey party must have come had taken far longer than he'd liked, but the fall of night had prevented them from following the back trail all the way that first day. They'd been forced to bivouac overnight, and a cold and cheerless night it had been without so much as a palm-sized campfire.

The next day, they'd come within a hair's breadth of being snapped up themselves by a party of what were obviously mounted scouts. Threbuch and Borkaz had been crossing an open space left by some long-ago fire, and they'd been *damned* lucky to realize what was happening in time to disappear into a handy thicket of brambles. Threbuch had taken the opportunity to study the horsemen carefully, and he hadn't liked what he'd seen one bit.

Their horses weren't much to talk about, at least. They didn't look as if they'd been enhanced at all, although they appeared well cared for and were clearly well trained. The men on their backs had been another matter entirely. *These* men were obviously soldiers. They wore distinctive uniforms, with dark gray tunics and green breeches tucked into high cavalry boots, which blended into the forest surprisingly well ... and made it totally clear that the people the Andaran Scouts had fought and defeated—*slaughtered*, he'd thought, forcing himself to face the truth—had, indeed, been civilians.

He'd made himself put that thought aside, concentrating on the job in hand, and his jaw had set hard. There were three men, clearly the point of a larger column, moving with an alert, competent professionalism Threbuch had never seen bettered. He hadn't been able to see their faces, but the set of their shoulders and their overall body language had shouted both their focus and their fury, which had pretty much answered the question about whether or not they knew something had happened to the survey party. He still didn't have a clue how they'd found out, but if that wasn't a rescue party with blood in its eye, he'd never seen one.

They'd carried shoulder weapons like those of the civilians the Scouts had already encountered, although these were sheathed in saddle scabbards. They also carried more of the smaller, belt-sized version, and the first swords Threbuch had seen from the other side. Cavalry sabers, of course, but the swords—like the shoulder weapons—were saddle-carried. And unlike the shoulder weapons, it didn't look as if they were intended to be gotten at quickly. Small wonder. If *he'd* had ranged weapons as good as theirs, he'd have sold his own sword for beer money!

The chief sword had lain beside Borkaz, watching as the sweep men rode past. The horsemen rode with alert eyes, obviously taking little for granted, but it was apparent that they were far more focused on where they were going than upon where they were. They moved steadily on, without ever approaching the thicket in which Threbuch and Borkaz hid.

Threbuch had stayed exactly where he was, despite the impatience he had sensed from Borkaz, after the trio had disappeared along the same trail he'd been following in the other direction. Borkaz was too disciplined to actually complain, but he'd obviously hovered on the point of doing so when, several minutes later, the *rest* of the column had come into view.

Forty men, Threbuch had estimated, *all* of them with those same deadly shoulder weapons. They'd outnumbered Hundred Olderhan's remaining combat effectives by four-to-one, and they'd been accompanied by pack mules. Threbuch had no idea what had been on those mules. Rations, undoubtedly, some of it, but was that all? Or did they have yet more of their demonic weapons—weapons a mere civilian survey crew couldn't have matched—hidden away in those innocent looking packs?

There'd been no way to know, just as there'd been no possible way Threbuch and Borkaz could have beaten those mounted men back to Hundred Olderhan. The thought had been gall-bitter, but Sir Jasak was as coolheaded—and smart—as any junior officer Threbuch had ever served. He'd already be pushing to get back to their base camp at the swamp portal as quickly as possible. The only thing Threbuch could do was hope he made it before the pursuing cavalry force came right up his backside.

Well, that and continue with the mission the hundred had given him in the first place.

Once the patrol had passed, he and Borkaz had eased back from the immediate trail and continued far more cautiously to the north. They'd become aware of the huge portal shortly after dawn on the second day, although it had been mid-morning by the time they'd finally spotted the fort on the portal's far side.

That had been an unpleasant discovery, too.

The fort was little more than a rough, three-quarters-finished wooden palisade around a central courtyard. Threbuch must have seen hundreds of similar forts in his career. But *this* fort was a hornet's nest of activity, despite the rain falling steadily across it. There weren't as many men as he might have expected in the uniformed fatigue parties laboring on its construction, but peering through the unfinished, open gate from the dry side of the portal, Threbuch had seen additional buildings—barracks, obviously—going up. No doubt the prospect of getting watertight roofs over their own heads could have explained the workers' industry, but there'd been far too few troops in sight for the amount of bunk space Otwal saw going up.

"Graholis, Chief Sword!" Borkaz had muttered beside him. "Are they expecting a godsdamned *regiment*?"

"It's not *that* bad," Threbuch had replied. "It looks bigger to us because we're both scared shitless at the moment. Actually, it's probably not much bigger than one of our battalion forts."

"Whatever you say, Chief," Borkaz had said doubtfully.

They'd spent a while studying the fort. The bad news was all that barracks space; the good news was that, at the moment, they didn't seem to have the troops to put *into* those barracks. The more they'd looked at it, the more Threbuch had come to the conclusion that the column which had almost snapped up him and Borkaz must have represented virtually all the combat strength immediately available to the other side. If that were true, and if the hundred did beat that cavalry column through the portal, he should be in pretty good shape.

"All right," he'd said finally to Borkaz, turning his back—not without difficulty—on the fort and its work parties. "We've found their fort, and we already know their cavalry is past us. Not much we can do about that. So the next priority is figuring out just how godsdamned big this thing—" he'd waved an arm at the rainy half-disk of another universe looming over them "—really is. And if it comes to it, we're going to need a better idea of the terrain on both sides."

Borkaz had nodded, although he hadn't looked particularly happy. Threbuch hadn't blamed him, either. Neither of them had really anticipated a portal this size. Doing even a cursory tactical sweep was going to take the two of them at least a couple of days, and probably longer.

"I don't like it," Threbuch had continued, "but I think we're going to have to split up. We'll each take half the rations, then you'll sweep that way—" he'd pointed southeast; this portal's axis was aligned in a generally southeast-northwest direction "—and I'll go the other. How's the charge on your RC?"

Borkaz had reached into his pack and pulled out his reconnaissance crystal, which looked pretty much like any other PC, except for the bracket designed to allow him to affix it to the front of his helmet. He'd pressed a button on the side of the glassy cube and studied the readout for a moment.

"I've got ninety-six hours, Chief," he'd reported.

"Good. It looks like this fort's about right square in the center, so even if this thing's as big as it looks from the sky arc, it can't be much more than fifteen miles from here to the far edge in either direction. It shouldn't take more than a day or so for one man to travel that far, so you'll be able to leave it on record the whole way."

"I could do it in less than—" Borkaz had begun, but Threbuch had cut him off.

"Maybe you could, but you're going to be operating solo, with nobody to watch your back, and we have to get this one right. We *don't* fuck up this time, understood? So you take your time, and you hole up somewhere at night, and you don't cross over to the other side until you're at least five miles from their fort. Is that understood?"

"Yes, Chief Sword," Borkaz had said, rather more formally than usual.

"Good. Then get moving. I'll meet you here tomorrow afternoon. If you don't turn up in three days—or if *I* don't—then we both head back to camp on our own. And for gods' sake, be careful!"

*　　*　　*

That had been three days ago, and Otwal Threbuch had cursed himself long, soundly, inventively, and viciously for that delay when he and Borkaz had discovered what else had come through that portal while they'd been elsewhere.

The sweep of the portal itself had gone well. Once they'd been away from the immediate vicinity of the other side's fort, they'd both crossed over into the rain-soaked forest on the far side. Neither of them had enjoyed their drenching, although they'd at least been able to withdraw back to the dry side for occasional rests, but the recon crystals attached to their helmets had faithfully recorded everything either of them had seen after they'd been activated. In fact, the crystals had undoubtedly seen things neither Threbuch nor Borkaz had realized they were looking at. The Intelligence pukes would be able to generate detailed topological maps of the area in the portal's immediate vicinity and for as much as a mile or two on either side of it, once they got their hands on those RCs.

Threbuch had very carefully backed up each crystal into the unused memory of the other. If something happened to him, Borkaz would have the complete record, and vice versa. Personally, the chief sword intended to see to it that no one needed his backup, but a man never knew.

That thought had come back to haunt him as he realized that the people for whom the fort's barracks had been intended had obviously been closer than he'd allowed himself to hope. The trail he and Borkaz had followed to reach the portal was beginning to look like a godsdamned highway from all the traffic passing over it. He hadn't been able to make any sort of hard estimate from the hoof-churned leaves and mud, but it had looked to him as if at least another couple of hundred horsemen must have followed the original column. They couldn't have been more than a few hours—a day, at the outside—ahead of the chief sword and his companion, but that had still put them between Threbuch and Hundred Olderhan.

And left Threbuch no possible way to warn the hundred what was coming.

So he and Borkaz had done the only thing they *could* do. They'd headed back through the forest in the ground-covering lope of the Andaran Scouts, despite their fatigue and the fact that neither of them had eaten very well over the past several days. Threbuch was no spring chicken these days, and that fact had been mercilessly ground home by the pain in his legs and the fire in his lungs. Yet he'd actually managed to set the pace for the much younger Borkaz, and—thanks to their personal navigation crystals—they'd been able to cut directly across country through the woods, avoiding the considerably longer trail everyone else was following.

It had been a nightmare run, but they'd almost won the race.

Almost, unfortunately, wasn't good enough, Threbuch thought.

He growled yet another mental curse, and only a lifetime of discipline prevented him from slamming his fist into the branch on which he lay with bone-breaking force. There had, indeed, been close to two hundred men—maybe more—in that second column . . . and every damned one of them was between him and Borkaz and the portal.

What the fuck is the Hundred thinking *about?* he demanded of himself. *Where are the godsdamned* sentries? *Where are the* pickets?

It didn't make any sense at all. The bastards out there in the woods between Threbuch and the portal were good, no question. The chief sword had almost walked right into one of them without even seeing him. Only the gods' own luck had saved him, when the fellow—whose uniform was as different from that of the cavalry troopers Threbuch had seen as the chief sword's own—turned his head and whistled a birdcall as good as any Threbuch might have produced himself. Any temptation the chief sword might have felt about picking the sentry off and slipping through the gap it would create had vanished when replies had come back from three different positions, all within easy sight range of the first.

But good as they might have been, they should never have been able to get this close to the portal, with their infantry deployed in what was obviously a well laid out skirmish line, without being spotted. They certainly weren't any *better* in the woods than the Andaran Scouts, and Threbuch couldn't imagine what sort of idiocy could have prevented Hundred Olderhan from posting pickets to prevent them from doing exactly that.

Yet something obviously had kept the hundred from taking that elementary precaution, and getting himself or Borkaz captured or killed wouldn't do any good at all. The sound of one of the enemy's weapons *might* alert the troopers on the other side of the portal. It might not, too, and there was no guarantee these people would be stupid enough to use their thunder weapons. If there were enough of them—and gods knew there were—they could take him and Borkaz without firing a shot.

Besides, in the cold, hard calculus of military reality, the information he and Borkaz were bringing back was worth more than Hundred Olderhan's entire company. That monster portal had to be reported, and the detailed terrain scans he and Borkaz had carried out would be literally priceless if it came to operations against the portal's defenders.

And so there was nothing he could do but lie here, less than a thousand yards from the portal, and pray that the earthworks he could see on the other side might actually give the Andaran Scouts enough of an edge to survive.

*   *   *

Hulmok Arthag stood with Balkar chan Tesh in the ravine he'd told the company-captain about while two sections of the mortar company set up their heavy weapons behind them.

There were four of the ugly, deadly weapons in the ravine, and Platoon-Captain Morek chan Talmarha, the company's commanding officer, was personally overseeing their emplacement. He'd sent the two tubes of the company's third section to set up farther to the east, under Senior-Armsman Quelovak chan Sairath, his senior noncom. The terrain was less suitable there, but the weapons had a range of over six thousand yards, and chan Talmarha had managed to find a suitable spot to emplace chan Sairath's weapons out of sight of anyone on the other side. Chan Tesh would have preferred not to split them up, but he couldn't cover both aspects of the portal from a single firing position.

Arthag had been surprised when he saw the mortars attached to chan Tesh's column. The acting platoon-captain had expected the three-inch weapons which were the norm for mobile units of the PAAF; what chan Tesh had actually brought along was the heavy four-and-a-half-inch version. The three-inch weighed only a tad over eighty pounds in firing position; the four-and-a-half-inch weighed almost three hundred, and it was a pain to pack into position on mule back. Pack animals couldn't carry as many of the far heavier rounds, either, so the bigger weapon was more likely to be used from a fortified position, or when it was possible to move using wheeled transport. In fact, that was the role intended for them when they'd been sent along with chan Tesh in the first place.

There was no question which was the more effective weapon in action, though. Mortar rounds were thinner-walled than conventional artillery shells, which meant a higher percentage of their total weight could be given up to explosive filler. The three-inch mortar's round weighed less than seven pounds, with an explosive filler of only one and a half pounds; the four-and-a-half-inch round weighed twenty-seven pounds, with five and a half pounds of filler. Both were designed to fly apart along prefragmented lines when they exploded, but whereas the three-inch had a lethal radius of about twenty-five feet, the four-and-a-half-inch's lethal radius was forty feet.

Under the circumstances, and given the horrific effect of the other side's inexplicable weapons, Arthag didn't blame chan Tesh a bit for his choice of support weapons.

The mortar crews were busy leveling the base plates, using the spirit levels built into the weapons' bipods, while the Marines chan Tesh had detailed to support them unloaded the mule-packed, finned, base-fused rounds and stacked them neatly in place. Arthag watched them, then looked up as Petty-Armsman Loumas slithered down the side of the ravine and saluted.

"You wanted me, Sir?" he said to chan Tesh.

"Yes." Chan Tesh nodded. "What can you tell me?"

"Not much, I'm afraid, Sir," Loumas replied. "This close, the portal energies are playing hell with my Talent." He grimaced. "I could probably actually give you a better Plot from a half-mile back or so. I don't *think* there's anyone out there, but what I'm Seeing is way too 'foggy' for me to guarantee it. And," he admitted, "I may be feeling that way because there wasn't anyone the *last* time I Looked."

"I'm inclined to think you're probably right," chan Tesh said, making a mental note of the Plotter's awareness of the danger preconception posed. It wasn't every man, Talented or not, who could keep that in mind. And in chan Tesh's experience, it was even less common for a man to admit that it might be happening to *him*.

"If they'd been going to put sentries out at all, they'd have already done it," chan Tesh continued, thinking aloud.

"They did send those work parties across this morning, Sir," Arthag pointed out, and chan Tesh nodded in acknowledgment.

"There's not exactly very much firewood on their side," he pointed out. "I'd be sending out wood-cutting parties, too, in their place. But Chief-Armsman chan Hathas kept a close eye on them, and according to his count, all of them are back in camp. They didn't leave any of them behind on our side."

"True enough, Sir," Arthag conceded. "All the same, I wish they hadn't done it. I'd give half a month's pay if chan Hathas had been able to get a better look at whatever the hells that thing was!"

"Me, too," chan Tesh admitted.

The timing on the enemy's wood-cutting expedition couldn't have been worse. With only a handful of men to keep an eye on things, Chief-Armsman chan Hathas had been forced to spread them out if he wanted to keep both sets of fortifications under observation. The virtually simultaneous emergence of work parties from each aspect of the portal had forced him to pull back in obedience to his orders to avoid contact until chan Tesh could bring up the main body. Chan Hathas had managed the maneuver flawlessly, as was only to be expected out of a noncom of his experience, but he'd had to give up his initial, carefully chosen vantage points. Which meant he'd had only the most frustrating glimpses of some huge, metallic-colored creature which had apparently both arrived and departed in the course of no more than an hour or two. His angle of vision through the portal had been too acute for him to see more, but it was fairly obvious from his report that it must have been whatever they'd already used to evacuate their more critically wounded.

There'd been no sign of it at all since shortly after midday, and that had been enough to tighten Darcel Kinlafia's mouth into a hard, grim line. Chan Tesh understood that, but the truth was that if the other side had decided to send any prisoners somewhere else, they would probably have done it long before this.

Of course, they may not have decided to move them elsewhere at all, the company-captain mused.

Platoon-Captain Parai chan Dersal, the senior of his two Marine platoon commanders, came trotting down the ravine and saluted.

"We're in position on both sides, Sir," he said.

"Good." Chan Tesh smiled slightly. "May I take it from the lack of gunfire, shouts, and screams that you managed your deployment without anyone on the other side noticing?"

"I believe you can take that, Sir, yes," chan Dersal replied, absolutely deadpan, and chan Tesh heard Arthag chuckle slightly, despite the tension hovering in the ravine.

"There is one thing, though, Sir," chan Dersal said. "I was talking to Chief-Armsman chan Hathas. I wanted his advice on the best positions for my sharpshooters. In the course of the conversation, he mentioned that one of his men had reported seeing a civilian in the camp."

Darcel Kinlafia stirred slightly behind chan Tesh, but the Marine officer went on before the Voice could say anything.

"He said it was a man, definitely not a woman, and that he seemed to be moving about freely, which a prisoner wouldn't have been."

"That's right," Arthag said. "He didn't get a very good look at the fellow, but whoever he was, he definitely wasn't in uniform."

"Well, I think I got a better look at him when I was moving my people into position," chan Dersal said, touching the field glasses cased at his side. "He's a civilian, all right. Looks like a Ricathian. Unlike anyone else I saw in there, he's not armed, either, and he's old, Sir. Quite old, I'd say."

The Marine gazed at chan Tesh expressionlessly, but the company-captain knew what the man was really saying. They were both Imperial Ternathian officers, trained in the same tradition, after all.

"I take your point, Platoon-Captain," chan Tesh said, speaking a bit more formally. "And if you saw one obvious civilian in there, there may be more we haven't seen. I take that point, as well." He turned so that he could look at both Arthag and chan Dersal. "Pass the word to all of our people that there are probable civilians in that camp. No one is to take any unnecessary chances, but we're also not out here to butcher noncombatants."

"*They* did," Kinlafia muttered in a barely audible voice, and chan Tesh looked at him sternly.

"Perhaps they did. But *we* aren't them, and neither the PAAF nor the Ternathian Empire massacres civilians." Kinlafia still looked rebellious, and chan Tesh frowned. "I understand your point, Darcel," he said firmly, "but I also have to point out that your people most definitely were not *unarmed*. Civilians, yes, but not unarmed, and all the evidence is that they gave at least as good as they got until the artillery opened up. We're not going to do anyone any good if we kill people who are neither armed nor shooting back just for the sake of vengeance. More than that, I'm not going to let my people turn into the very thing I'm out here hunting down. Is that clear?"

Kinlafia glowered, and chan Tesh cocked his head to one side.

"I asked if that was clear, Darcel. I want your word on it. If you can't give it, I'll have you disarmed and held at the horse lines."

"It's clear," Kinlafia said, after a moment. "And you have my word." He grimaced. "Probably a good thing you do, really. I'd like to still like myself a few months from now."

"I'd like for you to, too," chan Tesh said with a little smile, but then his smile faded and he turned his attention back to Arthag.

"You're sure you want to be the one who does this, Hulmok?" he asked quietly.

"Sir, you're the one who said we have to give them a chance to deal fairly with us." The Arpathian shrugged. "I happen to agree with you, for several reasons. But if we're going to try for a peaceful contact, it ought to be an officer, and Bright Wind and I are the best team for it, anyway. With all due modesty, I'm the best rider you've got, and Bright Wind is the best horse you've got."

"All right." Chan Tesh sighed. He wasn't happy about picking *any-one* to take on this particular duty, but as he'd told Arthag, it had to be done. What had happened to the Chalgyn Consortium team could have been an accident. That sort of thing wasn't supposed to happen with properly trained and disciplined troops, but chan Tesh had seen enough monumental fuck-ups in Ternathian and PAAF service to know it could happen anyway, even to the best outfit in the multiverse. So it was time to see what happened under more controlled conditions, when panic couldn't be blamed for the other side's reactions. Which, unfortunately, meant sending someone in harm's way, and Arthag was right about the logical choice.

The company-captain looked at Arthag and chan Dersal, then up at the sky. The sun was settling steadily towards the western horizon, but there were at least a couple of hours of daylight left. There was time enough, he judged, and he couldn't count on these people to stay fat, happy, and stupid forever.

He gave his mortar sections one last glance. Chan Talmarha gave him a pumped fist sign, indicating readiness, and he nodded to himself.

"All right, Parai," he said. "Get back to your platoon. Hulmok, you come with me. I think we'll send you in from the west. At least that way they'll have the sun in their eyes if they decide to do something outstandingly stupid."

CHAPTER
NINETEEN

"YOU BE CAREFUL out there, Hulmok," Darcel Kinlafia said
quietly as Acting Platoon-Captain Arthag swung gracefully
back into the saddle.

"Oh, I will be," Arthag said with a smile. Then he clicked gently,
and Bright Wind stepped daintily forward.

"*Look* at him!" Kinlafia muttered to chan Tesh, watching the
Arpathian officer's ramrod-straight spine. "I'd be scared to death; *he*
looks like he doesn't have a care in the world!"

"He doesn't," chan Tesh said simply. The Voice turned to stare
at him, but chan Tesh, too, was looking after the single horseman
riding straight towards their dug-in enemies.

"Hulmok Arthag," the Ternathian officer continued softly. "Fifth
son of Sept Chieftain Krithvon Arthag." He glanced at Kinlafia finally.
"I've never served with him before, but I know his reputation. And
after ten months under Regiment-Captain Velvelig, I've learned a
bit about Arpathians, too. They've got so many hells full of demons
to worry about, if they've been stupid enough to live the way they
shouldn't have, that there's not a thing any mere mortal can do to
scare them. And if they *have* lived the way they ought to, why,
there's nothing here that can tempt them to stay on earth, given
the rewards waiting for the courageous in the afterworld. Hulmok's
less fatalistic about it than a lot of septmen, but it's still in there.
Which doesn't mean it takes an ounce less of guts to do what he's
about to do."

* * *

Hulmok Arthag asked Bright Wind for an easy trot as he moved
forward through the trees. The breeze of their passage was just
enough to spread the traditional green banner of parley he carried,

and he glanced up at it with a wry snort. He didn't expect the enemy to know what a Sharonian parley banner looked like, but it seemed likely that a lone horseman showing up with *any* banner in his hand was less likely to draw instant fire than a lone horseman without one.

Besides, as Company-Captain chan Tesh had pointed out, if he went out under a parley banner and they shot at him, anyway, there would be absolutely no question about the legal justification for unlimbering everything chan Tesh was prepared to throw at the people on the other side of that portal. When it came to starting a war—or trying to avoid one—such details mattered, and Arthag admired the way chan Tesh's mind operated.

He thought about the careful preparations the company-captain had made, and his lips twitched in an evil grin. He didn't really want a war any more than anyone else did, but that didn't mean he'd be particularly upset if the bastards gave chan Tesh's people an excuse.

He approached the portal and brought Bright Wind down to a dancing walk as he rode through the positions of the carefully hidden Marines. The stallion worried at the bit. The horse was aware of Arthag's battle-ready tension and ready for a fight himself, fretting against the restrained pace to which Arthag held him and so primed for instant combat that sweat darkened his neck.

Arthag saw two sentries on the far side of the portal. They should have seen *him* already, he thought, but they weren't looking in his direction at the moment. He walked Bright Wind steadily forward, waiting for them to notice him, and grimaced in exasperation as he got within eighty yards of the portal. Admittedly, the thick forest stretched right up to the portal, and chan Tesh's decision to send him in from the west meant the sentries had the blinding light of the afternoon sun shining straight into their eyes, but still...!

Close enough, he thought as the range fell to barely fifty yards, and let out a shrill whistle.

Their heads jerked up as if he'd poked them with a heated poker, and both of them whipped around towards him. They saw him, sitting his horse, just outside the treeline on his side of the portal, and one of them gave a startled shout and started to bring up his crossbow.

"Halt!" Arthag called out sharply, even as Bright Wind screamed in warning and lifted his front hooves off the ground. But the second sentry shouted something urgent at his companion, and the man with the weapon aborted the movement and stood frozen in place.

Then others began stirring behind the sentries. Arthag couldn't make out details, since the earthworks which had been thrown up blocked his view, but he had the distinct impression of purposeful movement. Well, that was to be expected, although the thought that the other side was busy manning its inexplicable—*unnatural,* he thought, smiling to himself as he used Soral Hilovar's favorite word—artillery didn't exactly fill him with joy.

After several tense moments, someone else turned up. A tall man, whose uniform was subtly different from that of the sentries. The newcomer was an officer, Arthag decided. The uniforms these people wore were too unfamiliar for him to explain why he was sure of that, but he was. And as he watched the other man, he suspected he was looking at the portal camp's commanding officer.

Even from fifty yards away, Arthag could clearly see the surprise—amounting to shock—on the officer's face. The man looked as if he couldn't believe his own eyes, although Arthag couldn't imagine what he found so difficult to accept.

*   *   *

Commander of One Hundred Hadrign Thalmayr stared in disbelief at the single horseman.

He was positive Commander of Two Thousand mul Gurthak would be funneling forward every reinforcement he could find, and every day Thalmayr remained in possession of the portal was one more day for those reinforcements to reach him. And after almost six days, Thalmayr had concluded that the enemy's total inactivity indicated that the murderous scum who'd massacred so many good Arcanan soldiers hadn't gotten a message out before that blunderer Olderhan managed to kill or capture all of them after all.

He'd never had much use for those over imaginative sorts who fretted themselves into panics over events no one could control. Indeed, he'd always prided himself on his own levelheadedness. Yet he suddenly realized that he'd been allowing himself to become if not complacent, at least . . . increasingly optimistic. If the other side didn't know what had happened, it might be weeks—even months—before they got around to coming looking, and he'd been settling more and more into the belief that that was what was happening.

The appearance of the man on that golden horse was like taking a bucket of cold water in the face. Not only had "someone" turned up, but one look at the someone in question told Thalmayr it wasn't another civilian.

The hundred swept the trees behind the mounted man through narrow eyes, shading them with his raised hand and cursing the blinding sunlight. The stranger was more than a bit difficult to make out, in his dark tunic and breeches, and Thalmayr was uneasily aware that he couldn't see very much through the light glare. Still, if there'd been more of these people around, surely his people would have seen them! The wood-cutting parties he'd sent out that morning hadn't seen any sign of them, so they couldn't have been here very long . . . however many of them there might be.

In fact, he thought slowly, it was possible this fellow was all alone. Thalmayr had already decided Olderhan was right about at least one thing; the people he'd encountered had been just as surprised as Olderhan had been. They hadn't expected to run into another trans-universal civilization, either, so there was no reason for their superiors to think that was what had happened to them. But they hadn't been far from their entry portal, either, so even if they hadn't gotten a message back—*and there's no fucking way they could have*, he told himself—it was possible whoever had sent *them* out had finally missed them and sent out search parties. And in a virgin universe, those search parties would have been thinking in terms of some sort of accident or natural disaster, not hostile action, so it would have made sense for them to split up their available manpower to cover as much area as possible.

A corner of Thalmayr's mind warned him against grasping at straws, but standing here on top of his parapet dithering wasn't going to accomplish anything, and he started forward.

*   *   *

Arthag watched the enemy officer, wondering what was running through the other man's brain. Whatever else the fellow might be, he didn't seem to be an extraordinarily quick thinker, the Arpathian decided with biting amusement.

But then, finally, the other man started forward, as if he intended to climb down from his earthwork. Arthag didn't want that. He wanted all of these bastards right where he could see them until he was confident they hadn't planned some sort of ambush his own scouts simply hadn't been able to spot.

"Stop!" he called out in a voice trained to carry above the din of battle, lifting his hand in a universal "halt" sign. "Stand right there!"

*   *   *

Thalmayr stopped as the horseman raised his hand. The other man's voice was authoritative, the words harsh and alien-sounding, and the hundred felt his face darken with anger. He didn't much care for the notion of having a single stranger giving *him* orders in front of his men! Besides, who the devil did this godsdamned fellow think he was, giving *orders* to an Arcanan officer!

"What do you want?" he barked back, hands on hips. "This portal is Arcanan territory!"

*   *   *

Arthag watched the enemy officer stop where he was. Then the other man shouted something that sounded belligerent. That might simply have been the difference in languages, he reminded himself conscientiously, but there was still something about the other man's body language that rubbed Arthag the wrong way.

"You've attacked my people!" Arthag shouted back, sweeping one arm around to point toward the distant battlefield. "And you've taken prisoners." That was still a shot in the dark, of course, but the other man wouldn't understand a word he was saying anyway. "I want to see Shaylar! Shaylar Nargra-Kolmayr!"

*   *   *

Thalmayr twitched. Most of the words the horseman had spouted were only so much more arrogant-sounding gibberish, but not all of them. He shouldn't really have been surprised—if this was a member of a search party, presumably he would have known who he was searching for, after all—but it still took him off guard. Perhaps the name had taken him by surprise simply because it was the only part of the other man's unintelligible speech he'd been able to recognize.

His mind flashed back to the confrontation with Olderhan, the tiny, beautiful woman with the brutally bruised face standing behind the other hundred, and remembered fury whipped through him. It stiffened his shoulders, and his eyes flashed angrily as his head came up.

*   *   *

Arthag's breath hissed as the name struck the other man with visible force.

That bastard knows Shaylar's name! He recognized *it!*

There was only one possible way for the enemy officer to have recognized Shaylar's name. She'd survived. Survived at least long enough to tell her captors who she was. Whether or not she still lived, though . . .

*   *   *

Despite the remembered flare of anger, Thalmayr made himself think. The woman—Shaylar—had been the *only* woman in the other party. No doubt the search parties would be especially concerned about her, so it made sense for this fellow to mention her name. But the fact that he was sitting out here talking strongly suggested he had no notion there'd already been shooting. He seemed far too calm, too unconcerned over his own safety. So if he didn't know—or even strongly suspect—that this Shaylar had been captured, the thing to do was to bluff, play for time. Besides, Thalmayr couldn't have produced the woman even if that was what the other man had demanded.

The hundred composed his expression into one of confusion, then shook his head and raised his hands, shoulder-high and palms uppermost in a pantomime of helpless incomprehension.

"I'm afraid I don't understand a single word you're saying, you stupid bastard!" he called back.

*   *   *

"Wrong answer," Arthag growled under his breath as the other officer shouted back something unintelligible. Then he raised his own voice, louder than before.

"Shaylar! Bring me Shaylar right now!"

*   *   *

Thalmayr's jaw clenched. He still couldn't understand what the other man was saying, but the repeated use of Shaylar's name in what certainly sounded like an increasingly angry tone, worried him. The mounted man wasn't asking general questions, wasn't following the sort of "take me to your leader" approach one might have expected from a first-contact situation. Whatever he was saying, he was being specific—*very* specific. And he kept using the woman's name.

"I can't understand you!" Thalmayr shouted back. "I don't have any idea what you're talking about!"

*   *   *

Arthag listened not to the words—which wouldn't have meant anything to him, anyway—but to the tone, and his eyes were narrower than ever as he studied the other man's body language.

Whatever this bastard's saying, he's lying out his ass, the Arpathian decided. He was fully aware that he knew nothing at all about the other's cultural template, the gestures his people routinely used among themselves. But Arthag's Talent was at work. Like any Talent, it couldn't penetrate the interface of a portal, but after so many years, so much experience of *knowing* what was behind a gesture, a shift in expression, a change in tone, he was prepared to back his own ability to read the hearts of others across any imaginable cultural divide.

"You're lying!" he shouted. "You know perfectly well who I'm asking for! You bring me *Shaylar*—Shaylar Nargra-Kolmayr—now! I want to see her here—right here!" His left hand pointed at the ground in front of Bright Wind. "*Shaylar*, now! Or we come in there, kick your cowardly, murdering ass, and pull her out ourselves!"

*   *   *

He knows, Hadrign Thalmayr realized abruptly. *He* knows *what happened!*

The other man's anger was painfully obvious, and the jabbing of that accusatory index finger could not be mistaken. He wasn't asking if they'd *seen* the little bitch; he was demanding that they *produce* her.

The hundred still couldn't imagine how anyone could have gotten word back, but they obviously had. Yet whatever they'd gotten back must've been garbled, or partial, he thought, his mind whizzing along at dizzying speed.

They know something *happened*, he told himself, fighting to stay calm, *but if they really knew what, they'd've come loaded for dragon, and they wouldn't have started out asking questions. And this bastard's here all by himself ... probably.*

Thalmayr's brain hurt as all the possibilities and ramifications spun through it. He didn't know that this single cavalryman really *was* here on his own. It seemed possible, although it was obviously far from certain. But even if he'd brought friends along, they were all still on the far side of the portal. Those shoulder weapons of theirs might be able to punch through the interface, just as arbalest bolts from Thalmayr's own men could, but artillery would be useless, and not even artillery could knock down his fortifications. So unless there were *hundreds* of the bastards out there in the woods, Thalmayr's positional advantage was still overwhelming.

I need more information, he told himself. *And I need to keep the other side guessing as long as possible. And these people's weapons are supposed to be noisy as hell, whereas our arbalests aren't, and he's well within my people's range. So if they* have *split up their search parties to cover more ground ...*

The decision made itself. Perhaps, if he hadn't been trying to juggle so many unknowns, so many imponderables, simultaneously, he would have thought it through a bit more clearly, realized just how many optimistic assumptions he was still allowing himself.

But perhaps not, either.

*   *   *

Arthag watched angrily as the other man shook his head again, forcefully. Then the lying bastard made a mistake.

He snarled something low ... and the sentries both whipped up their crossbows.

*   *   *

"All right!" Thalmayr shouted at the other man. "That's enough of this silly shit! You're my prisoner, godsdamn it!"

It was his turn to point at the ground with one hand while the other made a peremptory "get your ass over here!" gesture.

"Get over here *now*! Or, by all the gods, I'll nail you to that fucking saddle!"

*   *   *

"You must be as crazy as you are stupid," Hulmok Arthag said conversationally, although there was no way in any of the hells the other man could have heard him. Then he raised his voice.

"I don't think so!" he shouted back, his voice firm but calm, and shook his head.

*   *   *

"Fine!" Thalmayr snarled.

The horseman had obviously understood the surrender demand, but he didn't even seem to care. He only sat calmly in the saddle, exactly the way he had been, ignoring the arbalests aimed at him, and Hundred Thalmayr's simmering anger—and uncertainty—turned into pure, distilled fury at his failure to impose his will on the situation. And at that single, arrogant prick sitting out there as if he didn't have a care in the world. As if Hadrign Thalmayr were a threat too insignificant for him even to deign to notice.

"Have it your own way!" he shouted at the other man.

*   *   *

"They've fired on Platoon-Captain Arthag!" Balkar chan Tesh snapped.

He'd been peering through his field glasses from his own position on a tree branch fifteen feet off the ground. Now he raised his head and turned to look at the wiry noncom sitting on the branch above his and hugging the trunk for dear life.

"Instruct Platoon-Captain chan Talmarha and Senior-Armsman chan Sairath to open fire!"

"Yes, Sir!" Junior-Armsman chan Synarch replied, grateful for anything to distract him from his fear of heights. He closed his eyes for a brief instant, and one of the small metal dispatch cases he wore at his waist, on what looked for all the world like an outsized cartridge belt, disappeared from its loop. An instant later, a second dispatch case vanished as he Flicked it to Senior-Armsman Quelovak chan Sairath covering the eastern aspect of the portal.

The dispatch cases reappeared almost instantly. Chan Talmarha and chan Sairath snatched them up, opened them, and found the written orders chan Tesh had prepared for this very contingency before ever sending Arthag out. Chan Talmarha glanced at the order, then turned to his gunners.

"Time to open the ball, boys!" he barked.

*   *   *

Hadrign Thalmayr cursed as the golden horse twisted on its tail and lunged *sideways.* He'd never imagined an unenhanced animal could move that quickly. Had he been wrong in his original assessment of it?

The question flickered behind his eyes even as both arbalest bolts hissed past its flashing hind quarters. They missed by scant inches as the rider dropped like a stone and vanished behind the horse's side. He simply *vanished . . .* but he hadn't hit the ground. He was hanging off the side of his saddle, completely hidden by his mount, as the horse took off like a fiend. It whipped back into the trees, and Thalmayr swore again, viciously, as he saw the rider twist himself back up into the saddle.

Godsdamn it! That's torn it wide open! When that son of a bitch gets home he'll—

The hundred looked up suddenly as he heard a brief, abbreviated fluttering sound.

*   *   *

Balkar chan Tesh had his field glasses back to his eyes. He'd breathed a huge sigh of relief as Arthag thundered safely back into cover, but his attention was on the murderous bastard who'd just tried to have the Arpathian murdered.

That pretty well answers the question of whether or not the first *massacre was an accident, doesn't it?* chan Tesh thought viciously.

The idiot was still standing there, fully exposed, staring after Arthag, and chan Tesh bared his teeth in contempt.

You're not up against civilians this *time you miserable bastard!*

*   *   *

The fluttering sound ended in an abrupt, thunderous explosion behind Thalmayr, and the furious hundred's heart seemed to stop.

He'd never heard an explosion quite like it. It wasn't the sizzling, hissing crack of an infantry-dragon's lightning bolt, or even the thunderclap of a fireball. This explosion was . . . different, somehow. Deeper-throated, more hollow and yet louder. He heard screams of pain, shock, and terror as it erupted well behind the earthworks, and terror smoked through him.

They can shoot through *a portal!*

Disbelief warred with his terror as he whipped around, staring at the fountain of fire and dirt and the sudden crater at its foot. Even *that* was wrong! It was as if the explosion had erupted *underground*, and that was flatly impossible for any artillery spell!

That was his first thought. But then he realized something else, something almost as terrifying as the fact that *these* people's artillery spells did work across a portal interface.

That explosion had been *behind* his parapet. Somehow, they'd projected it *through* the parapet before it exploded!

* * *

"A little long, Sir!" a noncom reported to Platoon-Captain chan Talmarha as he opened the dispatch case which had suddenly appeared and pulled out the hastily scrawled note. "Not much—about thirty yards."

"Down thirty!" chan Talmarha barked, pointing at his number two mortar crew. An instant later, the big weapon gave its distinctive throaty cough and the second ranging shot went whistling off.

* * *

Hundred Thalmayr cringed as a second explosion roared. The first had erupted well behind his fortifications, among the neatly arrayed lines of tents. The second exploded right in the heart of his artillery positions, and this time the shrieks were shrill and sharp with agony. Something whined past him, and one of the sentries, still standing beside him, as stunned as he was, went down with a bubbling scream.

Thalmayr turned towards him and realized yet another horror. The impossible artillery explosions clearly weren't as powerful as a field-dragon could have produced, although they were far more powerful than the ones his infantry-dragons could generate. But unlike any infantry or field-dragon Thalmayr had ever heard of, *this* artillery hurled out some sort of secondary weapon, something that slashed outward from the heart of the explosion to claw down men as much as fifteen or twenty yards away!

* * *

"That's got it, Sir!" the noncom reading the incoming dispatches announced jubilantly, and chan Talmarha showed his gunners his teeth.

"Pour it on, boys!" he shouted. "Ten rounds rapid, fire for effect!"

* * *

"Take that bastard down!" Platoon-Captain chan Dersal barked as the mortar bombs began to land. He and his men were within less than two hundred yards of the portal. Woodland like this gave all the concealment a skirmish line of Imperial Marines needed, and his people had crept carefully, patiently, into position, waiting for the order.

Now it came, and two hundred yards was no challenge at all to men trained by the Imperial Marines' Pairhys Island firearms instructors.

*   *   *

Something smashed into Hadrign Thalmayr's hips. It slammed him savagely to the ground, with a scream of agony, an instant before the remaining sentry went down without a sound. Even through his anguish, the hundred heard sharp, vicious whip cracks of sound coming from the woods, heard the spiteful hiss of something tiny and invisible sizzling through the air.

He managed to heave himself up onto his elbows, but his body was totally nonresponsive from the hips down, and any movement was agony. He started to shout an order. Even he had no idea what it was going to be, but it didn't matter. Before he had his mouth fully open, the overture of the first two explosions was replaced by a horrendous crescendo.

*   *   *

Balkar chan Tesh's lips skinned back from his teeth as the heavy mortar bombs exploded. There was nothing to protect the men behind those earthworks from the full fury of chan Talmarha's fire. No bunkers, no overhead cover, not even any slit trenches! The splinter-spewing explosions marched across the enemy position in hobnailed boots of flame and turned the fortifications which had been supposed to protect their occupants into an abattoir.

*   *   *

Thalmayr's eyes bulged with horror as he watched the massacre of Charlie Company, Second Andaran Scouts. The "protected" area behind the parapet had become a killing ground, and his men couldn't even *see* the artillery slaughtering them. It couldn't simply shoot through a portal, or project its effect through solid objects, it was *invisible*, as well!

But, unfortunately for Charlie Company, its men refused to go down without a fight.

*   *   *

Chan Tesh's eyes widened in astonishment as the enemy's infantry swarmed up and over the parapet. They'd already taken hideous casualties—he *knew* they had—but they came on anyway. Armed only with crossbows, most of them, they charged straight into the face of concealed riflemen. Here and there he saw one of them carrying one of those strange, glittering weapons which spat fireballs, but his Marines had been briefed on those, and deadly accurate rifle fire brought them down.

Then the machine guns opened up.

The Faraika I was a crank-operated, twin-barreled weapon, firing the same basic .40-caliber round as the Model 10 rifle. The barrels were mounted side-by-side, each with its own breach mechanism. Effectively they were two complete individual rifles, and rotating the crank chambered and fired each of them in rapid alternation.

Firing belted ammunition, the Faraika I had a sustained rate of fire of almost two hundred rounds per minute. It couldn't keep it up indefinitely, of course, without overheating, but there were five of them covering each aspect of the portal.

*   *   *

"*No!*" Hadrign Thalmayr screamed as an inconceivable avalanche of fire swept over the Scouts. Blood flew in grisly sprays, and his charging men went down as heads and chests exploded under the impossible sledgehammer blows of the enemy's thunder weapons.

It was too terrible to call a massacre.

*   *   *

"Cease-fire! *Cease fire!*" chan Tesh shouted. "Tairsal, order the mortars to stand down—*now!*"

The Flicker sent the order as quickly as he could, but the big four-and-a-half-inch projectiles continued to smash down for another several seconds.

The moment they stopped falling, Hulmok Arthag's cavalry, as previously planned, led chan Tesh's own company in a thundering charge through the portal to secure the objective before the enemy could recover.

*   *   *

Hundred Thalmayr watched sickly as at least a hundred mounted men erupted from the forest. They rode straight over his own men, but even in his agony and despair, the hundred realized they were more intent on getting through the portal and into his camp then they were in massacring his troopers. They completely ignored his wounded, and they seemed almost equally willing to ignore the *unwounded*, as long as no one offered resistance to their passage.

Here and there, one of the Andaran Scouts, carried away by battle rage, or hatred—or duty—*did* offer resistance. But every one of those charging cavalrymen had one of their deadly hand thunder weapons in his fist, and Thalmayr groaned as still more of his men went down.

The golden stallion which had first ridden out of the woods led all the rest. Its rider put it across the parapet in an effortless, soaring leap, and the rest of the horsemen followed on his heels.

There were still a few dragon gunners on their feet, standing amid the mangled bodies of their fellows. Thalmayr saw one of them swinging his weapon around, saw him actually get a shot off. The fireball enveloped three of the charging cavalry troopers, and he heard someone screaming. But then a crackle of hand-weapon thunder cut down the gunner and his assistant, alike.

Half the cavalry spread out, sweeping along the parapet's inner face. The rest thundered straight ahead, heading for the tents.

Many of the riders flung themselves off their horses, storming into the tents, hand weapons ready, and Thalmayr felt horror grip him by the throat. He still had wounded men in those tents, less-critically injured and yet to be evacuated to the coast. Men unable to defend themselves. What if—?

Then a fresh blur of motion caught his eye. Magister Halathyn crashed backwards through the opening of his tent. He staggered, clutching at one visibly wounded arm, then went heavily to his knees on the muddy ground. An enemy trooper exploded out of the tent on his heels, shouting at him, holding one of those ghastly hand weapons and pointing it directly at the aged magister.

Magister Halathyn was gasping out something, pointing frantically towards the east, then jabbing the same hand at the tents full of wounded. The dismounted cavalryman glared at him for an endless instant, still pointing his weapon at the magister's head. Then he lowered it, holding it by his side, and reached out his free hand to help the wounded Halathyn to his feet.

Thalmayr gasped in relief—only to scream in useless denial a heartbeat later as a lightning bolt lashed out from his own parapet. It caught two more of the enemy horsemen . . . and slammed through them to catch Magister Halathyn and the man helping him to his feet, as well.

They went down, writhing in the actinic glare. Lightning lifted and twisted their bodies, then slammed them down into the mud. They lay hideously still.

"*Magister Halathyn!* Oh, *gods . . .*"

It took Hadrign Thalmayr a moment to realize the voice was his own. And then, finally, the merciful darkness pulled him under.

CHAPTER TWENTY

JASAK OLDERHAN WAS torn between impatience to get under-way, frustration, fury, and fear.

Otwal Threbuch was overdue. A soldier of his ability and experience should've made the hike to the class eight portal and back to the base camp by now. But his walking wounded had reported back two days ago, according to Hundred Thalmayr's hummer report to Five Hundred Klian, and still there was no sign of Threbuch or Emiyet Borkaz.

That was worrisome. Had Threbuch run into more of Shaylar's people? Even if he had, that didn't necessarily mean anything dire had happened. For one thing, it simply took longer to move without being seen or heard by an enemy than it did to hike through unoccupied territory. And, Jasak reminded himself, he really had no idea how big the portal he'd sent the chief sword to recon might be. If Gadrial and Magister Halathyn were right about it, its sheer size might well have delayed Threbuch—especially given the chief sword's idea of what constituted an adequate reconnaissance. For that matter, Gadrial herself had said her new portal-sniffer was experimental. It could have given a false reading on the portal's size, or on the distance to it.

In short, there were any number of nondisastrous reasons the chief sword might have been delayed. Unfortunately, given what had already happened, Jasak found it difficult to feel optimistic.

The fact that Therman Ulthar and his Third Platoon had been ferried forward by dragon to support Thalmayr's asinine forward defense of Arcana's "sacred soil" only added to Jasak's worry . . . and anger. The more Jasak considered Thalmayr's stance, the less sense it made even from a tactical perspective. He suspected he wasn't completely alone in that opinion, either. Five Hundred Klian might have decided to support Thalmayr's decision, but unless Jasak was badly mistaken, the five hundred nursed more reservations about it than he was prepared to admit.

At least Klian had sent a request back to Fort Wyvern for reconnaissance gryphons. In a more perfect world, they would already have been moved forward to Fort Rycharn, given the fact that Rycharn was the staging point for the exploration of this universe's only known portal. But, like everything else this far out along the frontier, recon gryphons were in short supply, and Commander of Five Hundred Waysal Grantyl, Fort Wyvern's CO, had only four of them. He'd decided—for reasons best known to himself—that it was more important to retain them under his own direct control, and he was senior to Klian. It was true enough that the heavy forest on the far side of the swamp portal was exactly the worst sort of terrain for gryphon reconnaissance, which undoubtedly figured in Grantyl's decision, but Jasak prayed nightly that he would relent in the face of Klian's request. Suitable terrain or not, Jasak had men in harm's way.

Of course, he reminded himself bitterly, even if Grantyl did change his mind, it would take over a week for Klian's request to reach Fort Wyvern and the gryphons to reach Fort Rycharn. And, he reminded himself even more bitterly, they weren't "his" men anymore. Not officially, anyway. That pompous, stiff-necked idiot Thalmayr had made that clear enough. But that didn't mean it was true; it simply meant there was no longer anything Jasak could do to protect them.

He'd had a brief conversation with Fifty Ulthar before the transport dragons moved Third Platoon back to the swamp portal. Military protocol had made it impossible for Jasak to discuss his reservations about Ulthar's new company commander frankly, but he and the fifty had known one another a long time. He was confident Ulthar had read between the lines of what propriety did allow him to say, and the fifty was the late, unlamented Shevan Garlath's antithesis. Jasak was confident Ulthar would do the best anyone in his position could. The problem, of course, was that there wasn't really all that much a platoon commander *could* do when his company commander had decided to insert his head into his anal orifice.

Jasak stood glowering eastward out the window of his assigned quarters across the beautiful tropical sea as the sun slid toward the western horizon. It should have been a soothing panorama, but at the moment, the softening shadows and the water's turquoise serenity only irritated him further. He hauled out his PC and checked the time, then snorted in mingled amusement and frustration. It would be dinnertime in another half-hour, which would kill at least another hour and a half or so. After which he could probably put his head back into Fort Rycharn's communications center, before he turned in, to see whether or not there'd been any word from Threbuch without seeming *too* anxiety ridden.

Not that he was fooling anyone, he knew.

He turned from the window, left his quarters, and headed across to the ones which had been assigned to Gadrial and their prisoners. The shortcut he followed took him past a rear corner of the armory, and his brisk stride paused suddenly—in surprise, more than anything else—as he heard a low, harsh voice hissing something vicious in Mythalan.

As the Duke of Garth Showma's son and heir, Jasak had been tutored in at least the basics of every major Arcanan language . . . including Mythalan. He'd made considerably less use of Mythalan than most of the others, over the years, but he'd enjoyed the opportunity to practice his language skills with Magister Halathyn. The magister had been gently amused at Jasak's atrocious accent, but at least their conversations had scoured much of the rust of disuse from Jasak's comprehension of Mythalan.

Now the hundred's eyes narrowed and his face darkened at what he was hearing.

"—fucking *garthan*! Are you *really* stupid enough to think that just because you've escaped your proper station in Mythal, you can put on grand airs out here and act like *my* equal?"

It took Jasak a second or two to recognize the voice. Then he placed it. It belonged to Lance Bok vos Hoven, a Gifted combat engineer who'd transferred into First Platoon along with Shevan Garlath when Garlath had arrived as Fifty Thaylar's temporary replacement. Vos Hoven's job had been to recharge the storage units for the platoon's infantry-dragons, and Jasak had been a bit surprised to see his obviously Mythalan name on First Platoon's roster. *Shakira* were rare—very rare—among the Arcanan army's noncommissioned ranks, aside from a relatively small number who were also *multhari*, and who were then properly known as "vos and mul," not simply "vos." The fact that vos Hoven wasn't *multhari* had piqued Jasak's curiosity mildly, but the man had kept largely to himself, and Garlath, his platoon commander, had seemed satisfied with him. Indeed, Garlath had specifically requested vos Hoven's transfer from his original platoon when he himself was assigned to take over First Platoon.

Which, Jasak thought grimly now, *should have been warning enough, right there!*

Vos Hoven had been wounded in the fighting, despite his position at the rear (which he'd shown absolutely no inclination to leave). He'd been hit through one shoulder by an obviously wild shot from one of those horrendous thunder weapons, which had done massive damage to his shoulder joint and explained his emergency evacuation. But from the strength of his voice, it was obvious the fort's medical staff had healed him quite nicely.

Unfortunately.

"Please, vos Hoven," another voice said, and Jasak's already simmering rage boiled up volcanically as he recognized Jugthar Sendahli's terrified, pleading tone. Sendahli had also been badly wounded—in his case, after crawling forward into the teeth of the enemy's fire to man one of the infantry-dragons whose original crew had lain in slaughtered heaps about him while he fired. "I meant no disrespect, Mighty Lord! I just—"

"You just *what*?" vos Hoven snarled. "You just thought you'd keep the money for yourself, did you?"

"It's my pay, Mighty Lord!" the *garthan* trooper who'd distinguished himself so thoroughly cried in a low, anguished voice. "It's all my wife and son have to live on, and—"

Sendahli's voice broke off in the sound of a fist striking flesh, and Sir Jasak Olderhan erupted around the armory corner like a charging rhino.

"*What the* hells *d'you think you're doing, vos Hoven?*"

The *shakira* whirled with a guilty start, eyes wide, right fist still cocked for another blow. Then he jumped back, releasing his left-handed grip on the front of Sendahli's uniform. The *garthan* staggered, and Jasak's fury redoubled as he saw the blood flowing from Sendahli's nose and mouth, the bruises, and the split eyebrow. The blow Jasak had heard land obviously hadn't been the first one, and fear flickered across vos Hoven's face as he saw Jasak's expression. But then something else flashed through his eyes, and a sneer replaced the instant of fear.

"Administering discipline to the troops, *Sir*," he said.

The combination of his sneer and the scathing emphasis on the "Sir" told Jasak exactly what was going through vos Hoven's arrogant Mythalan mind. He obviously expected Jasak to be cashiered, and in the society from which vos Hoven sprang, that sort of disgrace would automatically discredit any accusations Jasak might make—especially against someone legally entitled to put that accursed "vos" into his name. But they weren't in Mythal. The *shakira* might well be right about Jasak's career prospects, but until and unless he *was* cashiered, Jasak was an officer of the Union of Arcana. And whatever might happen to his career, he was also the son of Thankhar and Sathmin Olderhan.

"Bullshit!" he snapped. "You just landed your lying ass in the brig, *soldier!* Report yourself under arrest to the fort master-at-arms right damned now!"

"*What?*" Vos Hoven's jaw dropped. Then rage exploded behind his eyes. "How *dare* you? Do you have any idea who my family is?"

"What makes you think I give a flying *fuck* who your godsdamned family is?" Jasak didn't think he'd ever been so furious in his entire life—not even with Shevan Garlath, and that took some doing. "You just go right on running your mouth, soldier! There's plenty of room on the charge sheet!"

"*What* charge sheet?" Vos Hoven barked a contemptuous laugh. "Are you actually stupid enough to think *my* family would—"

Jasak took one long, furious stride that brought him chest-to-chest with the shorter, more slightly built *shakira*. Vos Hoven's eyes widened. He stepped hastily back for several feet, until the armory wall stopped him, and a flare of fear stabbed abruptly through the contempt and fury of his expression.

"I don't *care* who your family is, you arrogant Mythalan prick," Jasak told him in a voice which had gone quiet, almost calm, as his white-lipped fury moved from the realm of fire into one of ice. "Not even a caste lord can protect you from the Articles of War."

"Articles of War?" vos Hoven repeated, as if they were words from a language he'd never heard. Then he shook himself. "On what charges?" he demanded.

"We'll start with physical assault of a fellow soldier," Jasak said coldly. "Then we'll add extortion and coercion for financial gain, and conduct prejudicial to good discipline. And we'll finish up—unless you want to go right on running your mouth and dig it still deeper—with insubordination and the defiance of an order from a commissioned officer. And under the circumstances, the court will probably tack 'in time of war' onto the list."

Vos Hoven inhaled hard. Potentially, that last charge could put him in the dragon's mouth—that ancient euphemism for the execution of a soldier. At the very least, conviction would result in stockade time, dishonorable discharge . . . and the sort of disgrace no *shakira* caste lord would tolerate in a member of his clan. He stared at Jasak for a heartbeat or two, then straightened and shook himself.

"Sir, you misunderstand the situation completely," he said in a suddenly reasonable voice, all trace of defiance vanishing from his expression. "I realize how this situation could be misinterpreted, but with all due respect, I must protest the severity of your accusations. This trooper began by assaulting *me*. I may have overreacted in defending myself, but I never attempted to extort *money* from him!"

Jasak's lip curled with contempt, and he wondered if vos Hoven actually believed he could deceive the lie-detection spells which were part of any court-martial proceeding. The *shakira* looked at him for a moment, then shrugged and stepped away from the armory wall, moving to his left.

"I apologize for my initial tone," he continued, "but once I've explained, I'm sure—"

The combat knife seemed to materialize in his right hand even as he lunged forward.

Jasak's eyes snapped wide in disbelief, but his left arm swept out, striking the inside of vos Hoven's forearm to sweep the blade to one side. He twisted his torso simultaneously out of the original line of the thrust, and his right hand reached for the *shakira*. But vos Hoven fell away from him, evading his grip and circled quickly to his own right. Jasak's hand swept down to his own right hip, but it found nothing. He'd left his short sword in his quarters, since he was only headed for the dining hall, and he swore with silent, bitter venom at the memory. The *shakira* recognized his expression, and his lips drew back in a snarl, baring his teeth as he balanced himself for a second attack. He started forward again, but before he could move, the *garthan* he'd beaten lashed out.

It was the last thing vos Hoven had expected. His attention was totally focused on Jasak when Sendahli's right hand closed on his knife hand's wrist. The *garthan* stepped into him, his hand rising and circling to the left, pulling the *shakira*'s wrist up and around the fulcrum of his own forearm. Vos Hoven cried out in pain as the knife was forced up so sharply it almost punctured his own cheek, and then his fingers opened, and he dropped the weapon with another, harsher cry of pain, as Sendahli twisted harder, driving him to his knees. He crouched there, leaning to the left, left hand flat on the ground, as he tried desperately to relieve the white-hot pain in his right arm and shoulder.

Jasak straightened, glaring down at the immobilized *shakira*.

"I said there was still room on the charge sheet," he said flatly, "so we'll just add attempted murder of a superior officer."

The sound vos Hoven made was trapped between a snarl of fury and a whimper of anguish, and Jasak turned his attention to the *garthan* with the bleeding, bruised face.

"Thanks, Sendahli."

The trooper nodded silently, and his battered face was tight. Tight with fear, Jasak realized, and a fresh spasm of fury shot through him as he took in the other man's bruises, the eye that was already swelling shut. What he'd just done to vos Hoven was graphic proof that he'd *allowed* himself to be beaten.

"Stand him up," Jasak said, and reached into one of his cargo pockets as Sendahli hauled vos Hoven back to his feet. Jasak pulled out a small spell accumulator, then stepped close behind the *shakira* and yanked both the other man's hands behind him. He pressed vos Hoven's wrists together, then put the small block of sarkolis against them and pressed one of the several color-coded buttons on it.

Vos Hoven grunted, shoulders twitching in fresh discomfort, which didn't bother Jasak a bit. The spells stored in the standard army-issue utility crystal were designed to cover a broad spectrum of possible needs, from fire-starting to signaling a reconnaissance flight as it passed overhead. The spell he'd selected to secure vos Hoven was intended as a general binding spell for things like bundles of gear or firewood, without any particular concern for how tightly it might bite. It wouldn't do vos Hoven any permanent damage—not for the brief time it would be needed—but it probably hurt like hell, Jasak reflected with grim satisfaction.

He spun vos Hoven back around to face him, then shoved the *shakira*'s back against the armory wall once more.

"You just stand there," he said in a voice of ice. "You so much as *move* before I tell you to, and I'll see you *buried* under this fort."

Vos Hoven stared back at him, mouth working, expression stunned. Jasak glared at him for a moment, then turned his attention back to Sendahli. The *garthan* winced as Jasak tilted his head gently back with a finger under his chin to examine his injuries, and the hundred shook his own head.

"I'm going to need your testimony in a minute, Sendahli," he said quietly. "The moment you've given it, though, I want you to report back to the infirmary. And before the healers fix you up again, tell them I want record-crystal images and a detailed written—and witnessed—report on the damages."

"Yes, Sir." Sendahli's reply came out in a near-whisper, and Jasak's mouth tightened as he tasted the *garthan*'s shame. He knew, Jasak realized. Knew his company commander knew he'd let vos Hoven beat him.

"Jugthar." Jasak let the hand under Sendahli's chin move to grip the trooper's shoulder. "After we've taken your deposition and you've seen the healer, Five Hundred Klian will be presenting you with a commendation."

"Sir?" the Scout's dark eyes were confused and a little dazed.

"It's for bravery under fire," Jasak said. "What? You thought I hadn't noticed how you handled yourself out there? I'd already recommended you for promotion before we stumbled into combat. The way you performed after it all hit the fan only confirms my judgment, so you keep your head up, soldier. Despite what assholes like *this* may think—" he jerked his head sideways at vos Hoven "—you have *nothing* to be ashamed of, and a lot to be proud of. Do you hear me?"

The trooper who had escaped literal bondage in Mythal blinked rapidly and swallowed hard. Then he nodded and met Jasak's eyes levelly.

"Yes, Sir," he said. "Thank you, Sir." Then he inhaled deeply. "It's been an honor serving under you, Sir. I'll never forget it."

Jasak squeezed his shoulder again, touched by the *garthan's* sincerity, then turned his icy stare back to vos Hoven.

"And now, Lance vos Hoven, let's go to discuss your conduct with Five Hundred Klian."

Murder flared in the *shakira's* eyes, but he turned and marched towards the commandant's office without offering further resistance. Jasak retrieved his knife from the dirt and followed him in icy silence, with Sendahli a pace behind him.

Jasak was bitterly certain that this, too, was his own fault. He'd known Garlath had brought vos Hoven with him. That should have been enough to make him look very carefully at the *shakira*—closely enough, at any rate, to recognize what the man was doing to Sendahli. On the other hand, he thought after a moment, it was entirely possible, even probable, that vos Hoven had waited to put the *garthan* "back in his place" until Jasak's departure on the furlough which had been cut short by Magister Halathyn's detection of the class seven portal.

Mythalans! Jasak snarled silently, his eyes hot on vos Hoven's back. The *shakira* caste was enough to give all the rest of Arcana's Gifted a bad name, but this one, at least, would never terrorize another *garthan*. No wonder Halathyn vos Dulainah had left Mythal in disgust!

Jasak had often wondered how Magister Halathyn had escaped the *shakira*'s ingrained and cherished belief in their own superiority. He doubted anyone would ever know, and it didn't really matter, in the long run. However it had happened, the rest of Arcana had benefitted hugely from it, he reflected as he shoved vos Hoven through the office block's door. And, he admitted more grudgingly, as his mother had insisted for years, it served as graphic proof that not *everyone* born into the *shakira* caste deserved his contempt. Not that the Duchess of Garth Showma's own contempt for the *shakira* as a whole was one whit less blistering than her son's.

Five Hundred Klian's clerk's eyes widened when he saw the bound *shakira* and battered *garthan* . . . and the combat knife in Jasak's hand. The astonishment in his expression blanked abruptly at Jasak's terse explanation and request to see the commandant.

"Of course, Hundred," he said. "Just a moment, please."

He rose, knocked on the five hundred's office door, and disappeared through it for a few moments. Then he reemerged, holding the door open.

"The Five Hundred will see you right now, Sir," he said.

Jasak thanked him, then marched his prisoner into Klian's office.

"What's this all about, Hundred Olderhan?" the five hundred asked in a cold voice. Then he glanced at the battered trooper whose commendation he'd just signed, and his eyes went bleak.

"I'm sorry to disturb you, Sir," Jasak said as he laid vos Hoven's ten-inch combat knife on the commandant's desk, "but I believe we have a small problem here."

"What sort of problem?" Klian asked, and Jasak explained precisely what the nephew of a caste lord—one of the hundred or so most powerful men in Mythal—had just attempted to do with that knife. And what he'd been doing when Jasak interrupted him.

Five Hundred Klian's expression went from bleak to thunderous as the story came out. When Jasak reached the end of his own account, Klian directed half a dozen questions to Sendahli. The *garthan*'s responses were subdued, obviously more than a little frightened, but clear, and by rights Klian's glare should have incinerated vos Hoven where he stood by the time Sendahli finished.

"I see," he said coldly, and looked back at Jasak. "I presume you wish to formally charge your prisoner, Hundred Olderhan?"

"I do, Sir." Jasak repeated the charges he'd already listed for vos Hoven.

"I'll certainly endorse them," Klian said grimly, and Jasak watched from the corner of one eye as the *shakira* finally began to wilt. It was incredible, he thought. Vos Hoven had obviously thought, right up to the last moment, that Klian would quash the charges against him simply because of who he was.

"Since attempted murder is a capital charge, however," the five hundred continued coldly, "it must be heard before a formal court. I have neither the authority to convene such a court, nor sufficient qualified officers to form one. What I can—and will—do is endorse your charges, have this man brigged here at Fort Rycharn, and see to it that he is returned with you, under confinement, to Arcana to stand trial there."

Jasak was a bit surprised by Klian's last statement, and the commandant smiled bleakly.

"Nothing would give me greater pleasure than to hang him right here and now, Hundred," he said coldly. "And given what you and Trooper Sendahli have just told me, I have no doubt the charges against him will ultimately be sustained. However, the situation is complicated by what happened to First Platoon while this man was attached to it. Intelligence is going to want to talk to all of the survivors, I'm afraid."

A slight flicker of warning touched his icy eyes as they met Jasak's, and Jasak abruptly understood. Vos Hoven had been present at the botched contact and massacre. Jasak was confident that Klian believed his own account of what had happened, but both he and the five hundred knew there was going to be a court of inquiry. There had to be one. And if it looked as if Jasak had used a court-martial to silence a potentially damaging witness . . .

Jasak's jaw clenched. That thought had never occurred to him, and it ought to have. He'd realized all along that vos Hoven would never recognize that he merited punishment. Nor would the *shakira's* powerful family—their minds simply didn't work that way. He didn't doubt for a moment that they would use every bit of influence they possessed, every trick, every distortion, that occurred to them to avert the disgrace vos Hoven's conviction would spill across them. And Sir Jasak Olderhan, as the agent of vos Hoven's destruction, would find himself with implacably bitter—and extraordinarily powerful—enemies. Exactly the sort of enemies an officer already facing a court of inquiry didn't need.

"I understand, Sir," he replied steadily, and Klian nodded with a tight, approving smile.

"Yes, I believe you do, Hundred," he said. Then he looked past Jasak to his clerk. "Summon the Master-at-Arms, Verayk," he said.

"Yes, Sir." The clerk disappeared, and Jasak glanced at Jugthar Sendahli. The *garthan*'s eyes told him that Sendahli, too, knew what sort of enemies this affair was going to make Jasak, and that he was desperately sorry for adding to Jasak's troubles.

Can't be helped, Jasak thought, as philosophically as he could. It went with the territory, if a man was going to be worthy of the uniform he wore. Besides, Jasak's own connections were nothing to sneeze at. He'd deal with *shakira* caste lords when the time came; at the moment, he had another job to do.

He watched with grim satisfaction as Bok vos Hoven was marched out of Klian's office to the brig, and then personally escorted Sendahli to the infirmary. By the time they got there, the *garthan* trooper's shoulders had straightened and he was once again carrying himself like what he was, not what vos Hoven had tried to make him.

Jasak handed him over to the healers with a profound sense of satisfaction. If he'd accomplished nothing else in uniform, at least he'd salvaged the career of one damned fine soldier. Perhaps it wouldn't be the most noted epitaph a career could have, but given the circumstances, he was afraid they were going to *need* good soldiers badly.

He watched the healer examining Sendahli for a moment, then turned away, praying he was wrong as he headed back toward Gadrial's quarters to escort her to dinner, wondering—again—why Otwal Threbuch was late.

CHAPTER
TWENTY-ONE

ANTICIPATION CRACKLED THROUGH the Board room as Orem Limana, First Director of Sharona's Portal Authority, let his gaze run across the assembled directors. They obviously knew Something Was Up, and well they should. Whispers and speculation had been flying for weeks as coded Voice messages came flowing in to the Authority communications center from the frontier. Messages in code generally meant one thing: a new portal.

Each exploration company used its own internal, private codes, known only to its Voices and the Authority, to register its claim to any new portal. The Authority kept copies of each company's master codes, and any Authority code-clerk who broke the rigid rules governing access to them found himself—or herself—in jail faster than thought could fly. The Portal Authority was serious about protecting the rights of the companies and people who invested money, sweat, and blood in the hazardous work of exploration.

Limana had spent twenty years in the Portal Authority Director's chair, making sure everyone lived by those rules, because he believed in them. He was both respected and feared, and because he believed in the rules, he kept track of which players were dirty, and which played fair. Which ones took care of their people, and which ones found ways to cheat, denying benefits or manufacturing excuses to fire an employee unlucky enough to be disabled on company time. Orem Limana had shut down two exploration companies during his tenure—shut them down lock, stock, and barrel—for shady dealings and egregious violations of employee protection compacts filed with the Authority.

Knowing what he did about each and every company in the business, Orem was utterly delighted by the incredible good fortune

354

which had come to the Chalgyn Consortium over these last few months. Everyone in the Authority knew, of course, that portal discoveries must be on the rise in the Hayth Sector. The amounts of coded traffic coming in from the Voices along the Hayth Chain made that painfully obvious, as did the redeployment of the PAAF to send additional troops down the chain. But very few people had an accurate grasp of the situation, and Orem could hardly wait to tell them.

He caught the eye of Halidar Kinshe, one of the few people on Sharona who already knew, since quite a few of those coded messages had been directed to his personal attention. The twinkle in Kinshe's eyes told Limana his longtime friend and frequent co-conspirator was enjoying the moment as much as he was, and the First Director conscientiously suppressed his own smile as he picked up his mallet of office. He tapped the silver bell beside his chair, sending a ripple of notes shimmering across the room, and the buzz of conversation died instantly as thirty heads swiveled toward him.

"Ladies and gentlemen, it was good of you to come on such short notice. I know several of you have been traveling close to three weeks by steamship and rail." He nodded a welcome in particular to Lady Jagtha of New Farnal's Kingdom of Limathia, since she'd made the longest journey of any of the board members. "I asked you to come specifically to discuss the situation that's been developing in the Hayth Transit Chain."

He'd had their attention before. The mention of Hayth had turned it into *rapt* attention, and he smiled as he pulled down a rollup map at the front of the room, showing the beads-on-strings tracery of the forty-odd universes Sharona had explored. Most of those beads were threaded onto only a single string, indicating only a single entry and exit portal. Others, like Hayth, had three portals, although only one—Reyshar—had four. Wherever a triplet occurred, it gave its name to the new transit chain splitting off from its second exit portal, and Hayth—four portals, and almost fifteen thousand miles, from Sharona—was shown as the head of an eight-universe chain. The Hayth Chain split again at Traisum, with the primary chain continuing through Kelsayr and Lashai while a new secondary chain split off to Karys.

"As I'm sure you're all aware, with the exception of the Sharona Chain itself, this is the longest single transit chain we've explored so far. What none of you are aware of, since the newest developments have occurred since our last Board meeting, is just how much longer it's about to become."

He turned from the map to watch their faces.

"Over the past several months, survey teams fielded by the Chalgyn Consortium have discovered and claimed five new portals at the end of what we are now designating the Karys Chain."

Mouths dropped open, and Irthan Palben knocked over a water glass. He swore in sudden dismay as it soaked his notes and suit, and Orem grinned.

"Chathee, could you find a towel to mop up that spill?"

Chathee Haimas, his perpetually efficient assistant, was already halfway across the room, having apparently conjured a towel out of thin air. Sympathetic chuckles broke the silence as she handed it solemnly to Palben.

"That's a suit you owe me, Orem," Director Palben muttered, smiling despite the irritation in his voice. The massive blond Farnalian ordered his suits custom-dyed as well as custom-tailored, and silk wasn't known as a forgiving fabric when doused with water.

"Put it on your expense account, Irthan. I'm sure we can persuade someone to glance the other way just this once, since I did drop that on you with a certain, ah, relish, shall we say?"

That produced more laughter, and Limana allowed himself a smile of his own. But he wasn't quite done, and the laughter gradually ebbed as the men and women assembled in that Board room realized he wasn't.

"I probably will put it on my account," Palben said. "But before I do, suppose you drop the other half of your little bombshell, whatever it is. Just in case the damage gets worse."

"I doubt it could get *much* worse," Limana replied, examining his colleague's sodden state. "However, you're right. There is one other *small* discovery involved."

Every eye was fixed upon him, and the temporary relaxation of their laughter was a thing of the past.

"In addition to the five portals Chalgyn has fully explored, proven, and claimed," he said quietly, "their crews have also discovered what appears to be the first true cluster in the history of our exploration efforts. At present, it would appear that the cluster in question consists of a minimum of *seven* portals, including their entry portal, all within a very, very short distance of one another."

Stunned silence greeted the announcement, and Orem Limana hid a huge mental smile behind his own solemn expression. Chalgyn Consortium was going to make perfectly *obscene* amounts of money in the very near future, and that delighted him more than he could say.

It was his job to see that everyone had a fair and equal right to use the portals which had already been discovered, but it was also his job to protect the financial interests of any group which discovered a *new* portal. That was true for every exploration company, but it gave him considerably more pleasure and personal satisfaction in some cases than in others, and this was definitely one of the former. Chalgyn worked hard, on a shoestring budget, and it said something important that the best and brightest field crews had been flocking to Chalgyn's banner over the past several years anyway.

Including, he thought smugly, the brightest rising stars of all: Jathmar Nargra and his lovely wife. Limana had had his doubts, at first, but Halidar Kinshe's belief in Shaylar had been more than justified, and the risk of putting her into the field had paid off. Not only were she and her husband performing top-notch work, but she'd become a multiverse-wide celebrity. And it didn't hurt a thing that she was one of the loveliest young women he'd ever met, the First Director thought even more smugly.

No institution as powerful as the Portal Authority could be uniformly beloved, however rigidly honest and scrupulously fair its management might be. And while the Authority was supposedly above politics, no one with the intelligence of a rock believed that. Given the realities of human ambition, greed, and the hunger for power, it had no choice but to pick its course through waters frequently troubled by political tempests, and that required a constant—if subtle—battle for public opinion and support. Its First Director had to have the honesty of a saint, the fortitude of an Arpathian warrior-priest, the showmanship of a patent-medicine salesman, and the political instincts of a rattlesnake. Orem Limana had all four of those, and he and his public relations people had jumped on the chance Shaylar offered with both feet.

Shaylar Nargra-Kolmayr had become, in many ways, the human face of the Authority, and not just for the Kingdom of Shurkhal, either. Hers was one of the half-dozen or so most widely recognized faces in the entire multiverse (thanks in no small part to the efforts of one Orem Limana's PR flacks), and even Sharona's colony worlds adored her. Shaylar Nargra-Kolmayr was the best thing which had happened to the Portal Authority since the very first portal had popped into existence eighty years ago. She was shaking things up, in exactly the way they needed to be shaken, and he was delighted with her.

Then Director Ordras Breasal surged to his feet. Breasal was a thin, hatchet-faced man, habitually found near the back of any room in which he sat. His chin was shaped like the sharpened point of a bearded ax and jutted outwards, perpetually daring the world to break its fist against that thick, pointed bone. Now he thrust that chin right at Limana and pitched his voice in a tone designed to etch steel.

"First Director! I demand an explanation!"

"Breasal's arse would demand an explanation for having to let out the contents of his bowels," someone muttered behind Limana.

Orem Limana's cold stare had been known to make even Arpathian septmen break into a cold sweat. Now he turned it on the whisperer, Djoser Anzeti, who—as it happened—*was* an Arpathian septman. Anzeti didn't break into a sweat, but he did have the grace to flush red, although it was a pity to censure him, since Limana was in complete agreement with his sentiment. Director Breasal was the largest pain in Orem Limana's professional life . . . and that took some doing.

He gazed at Anzeti for a heartbeat or two, then turned his attention back to Breasal, who represented Isseth, one of the independent kingdoms sandwiched between the jagged mountains northwest of Harkala and south of Arpathia's wide and arid western plains.

"What, precisely, did you wish explained, Director Breasal?" he asked through teeth which were carefully not clenched, and Breasal drew himself up, basking in the attention he so seldom received—and even less frequently deserved—from his fellow board members.

"How is it that this Portal Authority has spent eighty years exploring new universes, finding new ones at the steady rate of one every two years or so, yet this upstart, brash little fly-by-night Chalgyn Consortium is about to lay claim to twelve—*twelve*, curse them!—in less than six months? Chalgyn's gotten away with its dirty work long enough, slipping teams into universes claimed by other companies and cheating honest organizations, like Isseth-Liada, out of their hard-earned profits! I demand an explanation! I demand an audit of their corporate records! I demand an investigation for collusion and conspiracy and fraud, and—"

Director Anzeti slammed to his feet and brought both hands down so hard the heavy conference table jumped.

"How *dare* you? If *anyone* deserves to be audited for collusion, conspiracy, and fraud, it's *Isseth-Liada!* The Septentrion's exploration teams have filed complaint after complaint about terror tactics, intimidation, wrecked equipment, *threats*—"

"Enough!" Limana roared.

Silence fell like broken shards of ice against a stone flagging.

Breasal curled his lip, his eyes cold and contemptuous, while Anzeti glared murderously.

"Director Breasal," Limana bit out, "if you wish to make formal charges, you're free to do so. But I will not tolerate vindictive slander from any director on the Portal Authority's governing board. Lay your proof on the table, Director, if you intend to make charges that serious. Prove it, or I swear by all the gods of heaven and hell, you will *never* serve as a director of this Portal Authority again. Do I make myself clear?"

Breasal's expression changed abruptly, and his eyes flared wide in shock. He opened his mouth, but nothing came out—not even a squeak—and Limana leaned forward, his own hands braced on the table.

"*Do I make myself* clear, *Sir?*"

Breasal nodded, suddenly pale.

"Good. I expect a memo on my desk, before the close of business today, Breasal, either laying out enough proof to warrant an investigation, or formally apologizing to this Board and to the Chalgyn Consortium for slander. The choice of which memo you write is entirely up to you, but you *will* write it. And you will also *sign* it, before witnesses, and it will remain on permanent file in my office as a legally binding document. Is that clear, as well?"

Breasal managed another jerky nod, and Limana switched his attention back to Anzeti.

"I expect to see a written summary of all complaints from the Septentrion's field crews on my desk no later than eight o'clock tomorrow morning. Or an apology to this Board and Isseth-Liada Corporation, whichever you prefer. Is that understood?"

"Oh, yes. Thoroughly understood, Sir."

Anzeti's eyes blazed, and Limana had little doubt that the Arpathian's memo would be extremely enlightening. He'd heard enough grapevine rumbles to have him itching to open a formal investigation of Isseth-Liada's practices, but no one to date had found the courage to make a formal complaint. He also knew why the Septentrion had remained silent. Of all Sharona's cultures, the Septs were—by choice—the least technologically sophisticated, which made them the brunt of unpleasant jokes, on one hand, and victims of outright prejudice, on the other.

Unfortunately, all too many septmen had learned that justice sometimes went to the party with the most money and political clout. Limana found that situation intolerable, which was why he'd insisted—forcefully—that a new directorship be established to represent the Septentrion. He wished a bit bitterly that Anzeti had trusted him enough to come forward before this, but at least the man had spoken up at last, which meant Limana could finally *act*.

Isseth-Liada's corporate officials weren't going to thank Breasal for the outburst of spleen which had provoked Anzeti, and that was another source of considerable pleasure for Orem Limana. Of course, he knew very well that those same corporate officials did nothing without the express permission of Isseth's rulers. That made the whole ball of nails *political*, as well, and he expected the looming conflict to be a nasty one. But he had, by all the gods, had enough. He was more than ready to tackle Isseth-Liada *and* its political masters.

"Very well," he said in a more normal tone. "If we're quite finished with that subject, I'll be happy to explain precisely how the Chalgyn Consortium has located so many portals in such a short span of time."

Across the room, Halidar Kinshe sat back with a smile. He, too, had been itching to take Breasal down a peg, if not three or four, and now he watched with great satisfaction as Limana produced charts and maps showing transit routes to the portals Chalgyn had stumbled across. The First Director also produced projected schedules to move the enormous amounts of materials and manpower necessary to build portal forts to properly cover that many portals. Fortunately, the Trans-Temporal Express's rail lines and shipping lanes had already been fully established as far as Salym. In fact, the railhead was most of the way to Fort Salby, in Traisum, by now. That was going to be a huge help with the logistics, but the sheer scale of the project was still daunting. It was going to be the biggest single surge of expansion in the Authority's entire history, and the scramble to pay for it was going to be . . . challenging.

Chalgyn's stockholders didn't know it yet, he thought cheerfully, but they were poised to become fabulously wealthy over the next few years from portal transit fees alone. *Everybody* was going to want a piece of that cluster. After so many years of picking up other teams' scattered crumbs, Chalgyn had hit the most spectacular paydirt anyone had struck since the very first portal.

Kinshe wasn't financially involved in the consortium, but Chalgyn was a Shurkhali company, which left a warm glow in his heart as he contemplated its achievements. It was like watching the child of his heart and spirit finally prove his worth. Chalgyn had just shot to the very pinnacle of a business dominated by Ternathians and Uromathians from the outset, and the consortium had outmaneuvered companies with far more capital and experience to do it. After centuries in Ternathia's shadow, Shurkhal was finally shining in her own light again, and it was a glorious feeling.

Limana was just getting to the estimated support costs to finance this unexpected surge in construction and staffing needs—expenses that would be repaid through portal use fees until the loans were retired in full—when the boardroom's door opened and Limana's junior assistant beckoned urgently to Chathee Haimas. The junior assistant's face was ashen as she whispered a message, and Haimas turned white. She asked a single question, and the younger woman shook her head, clearly hanging on the ragged edge of bursting into tears.

Haimas closed her eyes for just an instant. Then she turned and crossed directly to Orem Limana.

"First Director, I beg your pardon," she said calmly. "There's an urgent message for you. It's come in from the Voice network." She glanced directly at Kinshe and added, "I believe Director Kinshe should be present when you take the message, Sir."

Kinshe's worry turned to ice; Limana merely nodded.

"I'll ask the Board to be patient for a few minutes," he said smoothly. "Perhaps the directors could begin drawing up preliminary plans to meet our projected staffing needs for the new forts. Director Kinshe, if you'll join me in my office?"

"Certainly."

They had no sooner reached the corridor and seen the board-room door closed behind them than Limana's junior assistant *did* burst into tears.

"I'm sorry, Sir," she choked out. "I wouldn't let the Head Voice interrupt the Board meeting until he told me why, and it's—it's just dreadful. Hurry, please. He's waiting."

Limana's office wasn't very far from the boardroom, so Kinshe didn't have to worry in ignorance for long. The Head Voice was waiting for them, and Kinshe went cold to the bone after one glance at Yaf Umani's face. Umani had been the Portal Authority's senior Voice for just short of forty years, and he was a tough, no-nonsense executive, with one of the strongest telepathic Talents on Sharona. His range had been phenomenal when he was still in the field, and his personnel decisions were legendary, displaying a second Talent, for he invariably chose exactly the right person to fill each job, from the Portal Author-ity public relations office to field Voices. He tolerated no excuses, he backed down from no one, and he'd been known to terrify sovereign heads of state whose opinions differed from his regarding the proper operation of the inter-universal Voice network.

Which made the fact that Yaf Umani was trembling one of the most frightening things Halidar Kinshe had ever seen.

"What in Kefkin's unholy name has happened?" Limana asked, dashing a liberal amount of whiskey into a tumbler and thrusting it into Umani's unsteady hands.

The Head Voice gulped the liquor in two swallows. His eyes were shocked, haunted by something so dreadful Kinshe *knew* he didn't want to hear it.

"I'm sorry, Sir," Umani said in a voice that was thready and hoarse. "It's—oh, gods..." Tears hovered just behind his eyes, and his lips quivered. "I can't—I don't even know how to—"

He stopped, closed his eyes, took several deep breaths. Then he met Limana's gaze almost steadily.

"First Director, I beg leave to report that we're at war, Sir."

For just an instant, the office was totally silent. Then—

"*What?*" Limana actually seized Umani by the shoulders, while Kinshe sucked down a hissing breath. The First Director stared at the Head Voice, shock warring with disbelief, until he abruptly realized he was gripping the older man tightly enough to bruise. He closed his own eyes for a moment, then let go, stepped back, and drew a deep breath as he visibly struggled for control.

"One of our survey crews has been attacked." Umani's words wavered about the edges. "By foreigners. People, I mean, but not like us. Soldiers. Not Sharonian. What they did to our crew—"

His voice choked off, and Kinshe, focused on that last incomplete phrase, found himself speaking through clenched teeth.

"Which crew?"

The Head Voice flinched, and it was Kinshe's turn to seize his shoulder.

"*Which crew?*"

"Hers." The one-word answer was a whisper.

"How—" Kinshe's voice stumbled on the word, full of rust. Then he forced out the rest of the question. "How badly were they hit? Is Shaylar still alive?"

Umani, already ashen, went so deathly gray that Limana steered him hastily into the nearest chair. When the Head Voice could speak again, he did so flat-voiced, with his eyes closed, as though trying to shut out something too terrible to look at again even as he relayed what he had Seen through Shaylar's eyes.

"They ran for the portal. They didn't make it—not even close. The soldiers—" He stumbled over the word, drew a ragged breath. "The attackers were back in the trees. Hard to see. Our people took shelter. Ghartoun chan Hagrahyl tried..." Umani swallowed. "He tried to talk to them. Stood up without a weapon in his hands—and they *shot* him. Murdered him in cold blood."

Umani's flattened voice was brittle as glass.

"Our team shot back in self-defense, and they—" He shuddered. "They opened fire with artillery, or something like it. Flame throwers. Huge balls of flame, three or four yards wide and hotter than any Arpathian hell. Crisped—incinerated—everything they touched. Mother Marthea, *everything*. And something else—something that hurled *lightning*. Jathmar Nargra—" Umani's voice broke again. "He was burned, horribly burned, right in front of her eyes. He can't have survived. Then something hit *Shaylar*. I don't know what. I don't know if it just knocked her unconscious, or if it killed her, but we can't get through. We *can't*. Darcel's tried and tried..."

Tears trickled unheeded down gullies in the man's cheeks which hadn't been there when Kinshe had seen him in the corridor this morning, less than half an hour ago. Kinshe had never seen any Voice so shaken, not even in the midst of the most violent natural disasters.

"She stayed linked," Umani was whispering. "Right to the end. I can't even *imagine* how she did it. How she stayed linked with Darcel Kinlafia when her entire crew—her own *husband*—was being blown apart, burned alive, around her. She even burned all her maps, the portal charts leading back to Sharona. That poor, brave child, determined to get the warning out, to protect *us* at all costs..."

"I'll have to tell her parents." Kinshe heard his own voice, distantly shocked that it seemed to be speaking without his conscious control, and Limana and Umani turned to stare at him.

"Don't you understand?" he groaned. "We can't let a total stranger tell them. It's my fault she was out there. I'm the one who pushed for it, and—"

"I approved it, Hal," Limana said, cutting him off brusquely. "Don't take the blame for this on yourself. I'm the one who had the final say-so, and it's on my head, if it's on anyone's."

The First Director shook his head, then inhaled sharply.

"We'll come back to Shaylar's parents in a moment, Hal—I promise," he said. "But painful as it is to set that aside, there's far more urgent business in front of us."

Kinshe looked up into Limana's worried gaze, feeling dazed and shaken, and the First Director gripped his shoulder.

"I don't know how bad this is going to turn out to be, Hal. First reports are always the most terrifying ones, but this—" Limana shook his head. "I don't see how this one is going to get any better, especially if—forgive me—especially if it turns out Shaylar *is* dead."

Kinshe jerked as if he'd been struck, but Limana continued unflinchingly.

"We have to hope it was all some hideous mistake. Gods know there've been enough catastrophic border incidents no one wanted in *Sharona's* history! If this *was* a mistake, then maybe—just maybe—we can keep it from spinning completely out of control. But it's happening almost a full *week's* Voice range from here. We don't have any idea what's happened in the meantime, what local military commanders—on both sides—may have done by now. For all we know, it's *already* spun out of control, and that means we have to take a worst-case approach."

He held Kinshe's shoulder a moment longer, gazing into his old friend's eyes until the Shurkhali director nodded. Then Limana gave one last, gentle squeeze, folded his hands behind him, and began to pace.

"If Yaf is right—if we *are* at war—it's a job the Authority isn't designed to handle. We've got portal forts out there, thank all the gods, but they're designed for peacekeeping, not to resist attackers with heavy weapons. Not even attackers with *Sharonian* heavy weapons, much less whatever *these* people may have! And the only thing we know about the other side right this minute is that they apparently showed no mercy to our survey crew. Our *civilian* survey crew."

He looked up from his pacing long enough to see Kinshe nod again, then turned back to the Head Voice.

"I assume the Voices in the transmission chain have put a security lock on this, Yaf?" Umani nodded in confirmation, and Limana grunted. "Good! We can't afford to go public with it, not yet. Not until the families have been told, at least. We . . . might have to make a general announcement, because something this big will get leaked if we don't act fast. We could do the 'Names will be withheld until next of kin have been notified,' standard disaster spiel, but we can't do even *that* until we've notified the heads of state."

He stopped pacing to lean on his desk, hands splayed flat, spine rigid. Then he nodded in sharp, crisp decision.

"We have to call a Conclave. Now. This afternoon."

"Conclave?" Kinshe's head spun. "*The* Conclave? No one's called for a Conclave since the Authority was formed!"

"Do you have a better idea?" Limana demanded, raking a hand through his hair, and Kinshe thought about it. He thought hard, then swore under his breath.

"Now that you mention it, no."

"I thought you wouldn't." Limana actually managed a taut parody of a smile. Then his nostrils flared. "We won't have time to assemble the heads of state from every sovereign nation for a face-to-face meeting. It'll have to be over the Emergency Voice Network."

"That's going to leak, First Director," Haimas warned him. "You can't activate the EVN without popping warning flags all over the news media."

"Can't be helped," Limana said, and turned his attention back to Umani. "Head Voice, I'm formally invoking a Conclave. Please activate the EVN to inform all heads of state. Use government-bonded Voices only. First meeting to take place via the Voicenet in—"

He thought rapidly, making mental calculations about time zones, reactions to the message, and the slow grinding of bureaucratic wheels. Then he gave a mental shrug.

"The first meeting will take place in four hours," he said crisply. The other people in the office looked at him, and he snorted. "Yes, I said four hours—three-thirty, our time. Let 'em piss and scream all they want; it'll get their attention, and that's what I want. Their full, undivided attention."

Yaf Umani drew a deep breath.

"Very well. I'll see to it immediately, Sir."

Limana watched him go, then looked up and met Kinshe's gaze.

"That's begun, at least," he said softly. "In the meantime, we need to take some immediate steps of our own. We'll have to put all our portal forts on maximum alert and move PAAF troops toward the contact zone, and we have to get it done as quickly as possible. I can order all of that on my authority as First Director, then let the Conclave worry about what to do next."

Kinshe nodded, and Limana inhaled deeply.

"We won't be able to sit on this for long, Halidar. It's going to go public—quickly. But you can reach Shaylar's family by nightfall if you use the ETS. I'll authorize the transfer."

"Yes." Kinshe nodded, still fighting the feeling of stunned disbelief, compounded now by the shock of being given access to the ETS. "Yes, of course that's the fastest solution. I should have thought of it." He managed a wan smile. "It never even occurred to me. Probably because I've never been high enough on anyone's priority list to get clearance to use it."

The Emergency Transportation System was normally reserved for the use of heads of state and diplomats on time-critical missions. The ETS consisted of an interlocked matrix of teleportation platforms, located in the capitals of most of Sharona's nation states. The platforms themselves were restricted to a size of not more than eight square feet, and a maximum load no more than six or seven hundred pounds, and the telekinetic Talent required to power the system was rare. It could also lead to potentially fatal health consequences for those who possessed it, if it was overstrained, so the system was used only very sparingly.

And I was never important enough to use it . . . until now, Kinshe thought grimly, wishing with all his heart that the opportunity to experience it had never come his way. He dragged both hands through his hair, just trying to face it. Mother Marthea, how did a man tell loving parents something like *this* about their child?

"I'll red-flag your priority," Limana continued, and glanced at Haimas. "Chathee, I need you to take charge of this. As soon as Yaf's alerted the EVN, have him contact King Fyysel's personal Voice directly. Tell him Halidar's going to need a special locomotive and car. And tell him why—Fyysel may want to send someone with him."

Knowing his king, Kinshe could guarantee that there would be someone accompanying him. Several someones. King Fyysel was given to flamboyance, even when the occasion was trivial, which this one certainly wasn't. At least the railway lines ran all the way from the capital to the Cetacean Institute. They wouldn't have to drive overland by carriage—or worse, by dune-treader.

"Also tell King Fyysel's Voice I strongly recommend that he order the lines cleared the whole damned way from the capital to the Institute," Limana continued to his assistant. "I can keep a lid on this only so long, and the clock's already ticking. And ask Yaf to choose a senior Voice to go with Halidar, so he can join the Conclave en route."

"Yes, Sir." Haimas stepped out of the private office and began giving crisp, clear instructions to Limana's staff. While she did that, the First Director turned back to Kinshe.

"However this plays out, I'm counting on your support. Yours is very nearly the only moderate voice Fyysel will listen to, my friend. Given Shaylar's nationality, Shurkhal's going to be overrun with reporters asking questions about Shurkhali honor and blood vendetta. The last thing we can afford is to have the King of Shurkhal throw that burning black oil of yours on the kind of fire this will ignite."

Kinshe grimaced, able to picture his monarch doing that only too clearly.

"I'll do my best, Orem, within the confines of my own honor. But it may not be enough. It's worse than just our normal sense of honor, you realize? The Shurkhali people, from King Fyysel down to the lowest stable boy, have invested tremendous national pride in Shaylar. Even those who don't approve of her doing a man's job have taken pride in the fact that a *Shurkhali* woman was first. The king isn't the only Shurkhali male we'll have swearing vendetta. Trust me on that."

"You give me such cause for hope," Orem muttered.

"It won't be pretty." Kinshe's eyes narrowed as another thought occurred to him. "Not anywhere. You realize Uromath will cause trouble? And what happens when the Arpathian Septenates get word—" He shook his head. "It'll take some fast talking to keep *them* from sending every warrior above the age of fourteen through the portals for the chance to ride in the battle against the godless heathen."

"You think I don't know that?" Limana growled. "Gods and demons, this is going to be an unholy mess!" He blew out a deep breath and added, "From where I'm standing, Ternathia looks to be our best bet. And you know how *that* will play in certain quarters."

"Only too well," Kinshe said with a wince. "I'm not even sure you'll be able to convince *Ternathia*," he added, but Limana snorted harshly.

"Zindel chan Calirath's no fool," he said grimly. "He won't want it, but he's Ternathian. That'll tell, if nothing else will, and I think he's smart enough to know what our other options will be."

"You've got our whole future mapped out," Kinshe observed with a tight smile, "and the Conclave hasn't even been called yet."

"Care to place a friendly wager on the ultimate outcome?" Limana responded.

"Not on your life. You're too seldom wrong to throw my money away," Kinshe growled, and the corner of Limana's lips twitched.

"Hah! At last you admit it!" The flash of humor faded quickly, though. "We'll just have to do the best we can. If you think up any bright ideas on how to contain the rage—or at least channel it into something that won't worsen the situation—I'm all ears."

"If I do, you'll be the first to know."

"Good." Limana drew a deep breath. "Don't bother going back to the Board meeting. Go home and pack. I'll send a carriage to pick you up an hour from now, drive you to the ETS station. A senior Voice will meet you there. If that train isn't ready by the time you hit Sethdona, I'll have some railway official's guts for zither strings."

"I have every confidence," Kinshe said, his voice as dry as the sands of his homeland. "I'll take my leave, then." He gripped Limana's hand. "Don't let them do anything stupid while I'm gone."

"If it looks bad, I'll have my Voice flash yours to take your proxy vote. May the gods speed your journey, my friend."

Kinshe strode through the Portal Authority' imposing stone headquarters, his heels clicking against the marble, his attention tightly focused on what would have to be done to meet the crisis each step of the way between here and a distant Shurkhal. One thing he already knew, though, without any doubt whatever. It would take an act of the gods themselves to persuade King Fyysel not to send several thousand riflemen and an artillery division out to commit blood-vengeance genocide.

CHAPTER
TWENTY-TWO

"DEAR, YOU'VE HARDLY touched your breakfast."

Andrin Calirath looked up at the sound of her mother's gentle voice. Empress Varena wasn't the sort of parent who nagged, and she wasn't nagging now, really. That didn't keep Andrin from feeling as if she were, but the look in her mother's eyes stopped any protest well short of her vocal cords.

"I'm sorry, Mother," she said instead, and managed a wan smile. "I'm afraid I'm just not very hungry."

The empress started to say something else, then stopped, pressed her lips together, and gave her head a tiny shake. Her brain had already told her there was no point trying to get Andrin to eat. That the attempt would only make things worse, by pointing out that she'd noticed something her daughter was desperately trying to pretend wasn't happening. But what her mind recognized and her heart could accept were two different things.

She looked at her husband, sitting at the head of the table, and he looked back with a sad smile and eyes full of the same shadows which haunted Andrin. The smile belonged to her husband, her daughter's father; the shadows belonged to the Emperor of Ternathia, and not for the first time in her life, Varena Calirath cursed the crushing load the Calirath Dynasty had borne for so many weary centuries.

Andrin peeked up through her eyelashes, acutely aware of her parents' exchanged looks. She wished desperately that she could comfort her mother, but how could she, when she couldn't even explain her terrifying Glimpses to *herself*? Her father would have understood, but she didn't need to explain to him. It was painfully evident that he was experiencing the same Glimpses, and she refused to lay the

369

additional weight of her own fears, the terror curdling her bone marrow, on top of the other weights he must already bear.

Unlike her, he had to deal with all the crushing day-to-day burden of governing Sharona's largest, oldest, wealthiest, and most prestigious empire despite his own Glimpses. He didn't need a whining daughter on top of that!

She used her fork to push food around on her plate, trying to convince herself to try at least one more bite. There was nothing wrong with the food itself. Breakfast had been as delicious as it always was; it was simply that a stomach clenched into a permanent knot of tension couldn't appreciate it.

Almost a week, she thought. A *week* with the bumblebees crawling through her bones, the nightmares which woke her and skipped away into the shadows before she could quite grasp them. A week with visions of chaos and destruction, the outriders of heartrending grief to come, of loss and anguish. No wonder she couldn't eat! She knew she was losing weight, and she'd seen the shadows under her eyes in her morning mirror, and that didn't surprise her one bit, either.

She'd had other Glimpses in her life, some of them terrible beyond belief. The Talent of the Caliraths was . . . different. Unique. Precognition wasn't actually that uncommon. It wasn't one of the more common Talents, but it wasn't as rare as, say, the full telempathic Healing Talent.

But precognition was limited primarily to physical events and processes. A weather Precog could predict sunshine and rain for a given locale with virtually one hundred percent accuracy for a period of perhaps two weeks. Longer-range forecasts of up to two months could also be extremely accurate, although reliability tended to begin falling off after the first month or so, and the level of accuracy degraded rapidly thereafter. Other Precogs worked for forestry services, predicting fires. And along the so-called "crown of fire" around the Great Western Ocean, they watched for volcanic eruptions and tsunamis. They'd saved countless lives over the centuries with their warnings, like the one they'd issued before the island of Juhali in the Hinorean Empire—and its analog in every explored universe, for that matter—had blown up so devastatingly thirty-seven years ago.

Yet those events were all the results of *physical* processes. Of the movement of unthinking masses of air and water, the random strike of lightning bolts, the seething movement of magma and the bones of the earth. The Glimpses of the House of Calirath dealt with *people*.

Quite often, they also dealt with natural disaster, because people were trapped in them. But those disasters would have happened whether there'd been anyone there to witness them, or not. What Andrin and her father and their endless ancestors before them had seen in those cases was the human cost of the disaster. The impact on the lives of those trapped in its path.

There had been times when a Calirath Glimpse had been enough to divert or at least ameliorate the consequences of cataclysm. Andrin was grateful for that. She herself had saved possibly thousands of lives with her Glimpse of the Kilrayen National Forest fire in Reyshar before high winds had sent it sweeping over the town of Halthoma like a tidal bore of flame. She'd *Seen* the flames leaping the firebreaks, cutting the roads, consuming the town, burning women and children to death. It had been that human element—the terror and pain and despair of the *people* involved—which had generated her Glimpse . . . and her father's frantic EVN message had warned the Reyshar government in time to evacuate and thwart that very Glimpse. She treasured that memory, despite the nightmares of the disaster only she had Seen, which still came back to her some nights. And she was only too well aware from her history lessons of how often in Ternathia's past it had been a Glimpse, the Talent of the imperial house, which had plucked victory from defeat, or turned mere survival into triumph.

But there were times—like today—when all those accomplishments seemed less than a pittance against the cost of her Talent.

If only she could make it come clear! If only she could take it by the throat, choke it into submission. But it didn't work that way. Glimpses could be of events from next week, or next month, or next year. Some had actually been of events which had not occurred until the person who had Glimpsed them was long dead. Sometimes, they never came to pass at all, but usually they turned out to have been terrifyingly accurate . . . once they were actually upon you. And one thing the Caliraths had learned over the millennia was that the closer the event came, the stronger the Glimpse grew.

Which was the reason her stomach was a clenched fist and there were shadows under her eyes. This was already the strongest Glimpse she had ever endured, far stronger than the Halthoma Glimpse, and it was *still* growing stronger. The images themselves were growing sharper, even though she still lacked the context to place them, and she felt as if she were a violin string, tuned far too tightly and ready to snap.

"Andrin," her father said calmly, "I've been thinking that this afternoon, perhaps you and I might drop by the stables, and—"

He stopped speaking abruptly, and his and Andrin's heads turned as one, their eyes snapping to the breakfast parlor's door an instant before the latch turned. Andrin felt herself go white to her lips, and her father's hand tightened into a fist around his napkin, as the door opened and Shamir Taje stepped through it.

"Your Imperial Majesties," the First Councilor of the Ternathian Empire said, bowing first to Zindel and then to Varena and the rest of the imperial family, "I apologize for intruding on you."

Varena Calirath held her breath as she saw Zindel's face. His entire body had gone deathly still, and she bit her lip as she realized that whatever he—and Andrin—had awaited appeared to be upon them.

"I'm sure you had an excellent reason, Shamir." Her father's voice was amazingly calm, Andrin thought, when he had to feel the same jagged lightning bolts dancing along his nerves.

"It's an urgent message, Your Majesty," Taje said formally, and Zindel nodded.

"Very well." He glanced down into Varena's eyes. "I beg your pardon, my dear. Children," he added with an apologetic smile, then glanced at Taje again. "Will I be back shortly, Shamir?"

"I . . . doubt it, Your Majesty."

"I see." Zindel kissed each of his daughters in turn, beginning with little Anbessa and leaving Andrin until last. He gripped her hands for a moment, meeting the worry in her eyes with a steady gaze as she stood to kiss him back, and she actually managed to summon a smile for him.

"I'll let you know what I can," he said quietly, and she nodded.

"If you can't, I'll understand."

"Yes." He brushed a lock of hair from his tall, straight daughter's brow. "I know."

He gave her another smile, then turned briskly and stepped back through the door with Shamir Taje, and she discovered her knees were trembling. She all but fell back into her chair, not even bothering with proper deportment, but her mother didn't scold. She just bit her lip and tried to smile in a brave effort that didn't fool Andrin.

A moment later, the door opened again, and Andrin's head whipped back around. Her father stood there, pale as death, staring straight at her.

"Zindel?" the empress' voice sounded breathless, frightened.

"I'm sorry, dear. I didn't mean to alarm you." His eyes met hers, held for an instant, then moved back to his eldest daughter. "Andrin, I'm afraid you have to come with me. It's essential that you join the Privy Council's deliberations."

Andrin heard someone gasp and wasn't sure if the sound had come from her mother, or from her. She tried to rise, then paused to take a deeper breath, and made it to her feet on the second attempt.

"What is it, Father? What's happened?"

"It's just a precaution, Andrin, but it's necessary. I'll brief you with the rest of the Council."

Andrin saw the flicker in his eyes, the tiniest of speaking glances at her baby sisters, and swallowed down a throat gone dry.

"Of course, Father." She bent to press a kiss on her mother's suddenly cold cheek. "I'm sorry, Mama. Will you convey my apologies to Aunt Reza for missing my lesson this morning?"

"Of course, dearest."

Andrin followed her father into the passage, suddenly wishing her fears could remain nameless, vague, however terrifying. This morning, all she'd wanted was their resolution; now she harbored a terrible suspicion that the truth would be far worse than anything she'd yet imagined.

The walk to the Council Chamber seemed endless, yet it was also far too short, and Andrin drew a deep breath and straightened her spine as the doors finally opened before them. She'd never actually been inside the Privy Council Chamber, which wasn't as surprising as someone else might have thought, since Hawkwing Palace, the imperial Ternathian residence in Estafel, was the largest structure on the entire island of Ternath. The ancient palace in Tajvana had been substantially larger, and more opulent, just as the ancient empire had been larger and, for its day, even richer. But Andrin had difficulty imagining a building more immense than her birthplace, since the palace was a small city in its own right.

Nearly five thousand people lived and worked in Hawkwing Palace, which ambled across twenty acres of land, including the stables, kennels, and formal gardens. If one added the vegetable gardens and greenhouses, the palace and its grounds ate up nearly thirty acres in the heart of Ternathia's capital city, which boasted the most expensive real estate on the island. Or, for that matter, in the entire sprawling Empire as a whole. She'd never seen all of it, and probably never would. Those who governed—or were related to those who did—had no need to visit the vast kitchens, or the hothouses where vegetables were grown in winter and fruit trees were coaxed to produce fruit year round.

She'd been to the Throne Room, of course, but the chambers where her father consulted, planned, worried, and governed were alien territory, and she discovered that the Privy Council Chamber made a distinct contrast to the vast and ornate Throne Room. The Throne Room's function was to remind visitors of the power, magnificence, and ancient lineage of the Empire; this chamber, by comparison, was an almost cozy room, more than large enough to hold the entire Privy Council, yet small enough to feel almost intimate. Walls of the same gray stone used to build the entire palace had been left bare, rather than faced with marble, but ancient, beautifully polished woodwork lent the stone a softening accent, and colorful banners decorated two walls, representing the various nations and peoples who comprised the Empire.

A third wall was devoted almost entirely to a hearth, where a cheerful coal fire drove away the autumn chill when she stood close. The mantle was simple, compared with other fireplaces in the palace, and served mostly as a place to put clocks. At first, she thought it was an echo of her mother's love for bric-a-brac. But then she tipped her head to examine them more closely, and discovered one clock for each of the time zones within the Empire.

Andrin forgot the tension of the moment as she stared in delight at the simple but effective way to determine at a glance what time it was in any given city of the Empire. Each clock was labeled with the names of the major cities within its zone, and she even found clocks at the far end of the mantle that showed time zones in the rest of Sharona.

That discovery led her eyes to the map hanging across the far end of the room, where she could trace the familiar coastlines and pair them up with the mantle clocks.

The island of Ternath, itself, shown by the mapmakers as a vibrant green jewel, was the westernmost land bordering the rolling expanse of the North Vandor Ocean. Just to the east of Ternath lay Bernith Island, which stretched farther north and south than Ternath and was wider, as well. Beyond Bernith, with its landmark white-chalk cliffs, past the chilly waters of the Bernith Channel, lay the great continent of Chairifon, where most of Ternathia's empire sprawled across Sharona's northern hemisphere, two thousand and more miles from east to west, and fifteen hundred from north to south.

Her gaze traveled from the Bernith Channel south, to the Narhathan Penninsula, the enormous fist of land that bordered the Strait of Bolakin from the north. The strait itself was dominated by the Fist of Bolakin, jutting down from Narhath, and the Hook of Ricathia, reaching up from the south. The Fist took its name from the huge, steep-sided rock which was its most prominent feature, and from the Ricathian city-state of Bolakin, which had controlled the strait—and the Fist—for centuries. Ternathia had struck a deal with the Bolakini for possession of the Fist in a lucrative treaty, sealed with intermarriages and trade agreements, which included levies on all non-Ternathian shipping that passed the Fist.

From Bolakin, she traced the coastline that skirted the tideless Mbisi Sea, known to traders as the Sea of Commerce or Sea of Money, depending on how one translated the original Bolakini. Either translation was apt, considering the money made from the commerce crossing the Mbisi on any given day, especially since the emergence of the Larakesh Gate and the completion of the Grand Ternathian Canal. The long, fairly straight southern shore of the Mbisi was controlled by various wealthy Ricathian city-states, while the Ternathian coastline sprawled along the Mbisi's far longer and more winding northern shore.

The only land north of the Mbisi Sea that Ternathia *didn't* govern was the far northern strip that bordered the icy Polar Ocean, surrounding the north pole. The fjord-riddled coastline of the huge, vaguely spoon-shaped promontory of Farnalia formed the western boundary of the Farnalian Empire. That empire stretched from the North Vandor Ocean, lapping and slapping its way into those deep fjords, right across the top of the vast Chairifonian supra-continent that stretched clear to the Scurlis Sea, five thousand miles to the east. The Farnalian Empire was very narrow, viewed north to south, but so long it wrapped a quarter of the way around the world. And though it was sparsely inhabited, thanks for the most part to its climate, the people who lived there were as impressive as their land.

Farnalians were even taller than Ternathians, tending towards big, robust men with blond and red hair, and statuesque women who were as comfortable in the saddle or behind the plow as their menfolk—and just as capable of wielding a sword (or, these days, a rifle) in defense of their own homes. Once upon a time, the sea rovers of Farnalia had been noted for their fondness for axes, other people's possessions, and their own boisterous, brawling independence. That, Andrin supposed, might have been one reason her ancestors had established treaties with Farnalia, rather than attempting a more . . . energetic approach.

At one time, Ternathia had controlled almost all of Chairifon south of Farnalia and west of Uromath, but that had been long ago. Sometimes the sheer depth of history behind something as simple as that map took Andrin's breath away. It was difficult to comprehend the vast gulf of time which had passed since Ternathia had signed its first treaties of alliance with Farnalia, more than four thousand years previously. Trade between the two empires had been brisk and lucrative throughout that immense stretch of time, and the Farnalians themselves joked about how Ternathian influence had finally civilized their ancestors. Of course, that was partly because so many of those ancestors had been Ternathians themselves. Along the borders of the western half of Farnalia, intermarriage with Ternathians was so common that it had long ago become impossible to distinguish a person's nationality on the basis of physical appearance.

There were those—particularly in Uromathia—who muttered occasionally about "mongrels," but absorption had been the true key to Ternathia's successful expansion of its borders. Those borders had been extended primarily because of the Empire's need to protect its trade routes from the brigandage and unrest which always seemed to be simmering away just on the other side. Yet as each troubled region was acquired and pacified, the traders—and their rulers—found themselves facing yet another new area of unrest, where ship-based pirates and land-based brigands harassed Ternathian merchants from the other side of the *new* border. Which, inevitably, provided fresh impetus to expand still further.

And so, the Empire had grown ever larger. There had never really been a conscious plan to forge an empire in the first place. At every stage, it had been primarily a pragmatic matter of seeking border security, not fresh lands to rule, yet the result had been the same. Ternathia had become a spreading, irresistable tide, bringing Ternathian arts and technology to the cultures it had engulfed, learning from those cultures, in turn, and—always—intermarrying with them. The Calirath Dynasty had been wise enough to bind its subject peoples to it by making them full members in the Empire which had overrun them, and marriage had been one of the promises and guarantors of that equality. So had respect for local religions. The process of absorption had worked both ways, gradually and almost always successfully, over centuries, and one reason it had was the fact that the Ternathian traders had brought with them something far more valuable than gold or spices or precious stones.

Ternathians had been the first to harness the Talents of the mind. Legend had it that Erthain the Great, the semi-mythical founder of the House of Calirath, had been the very first Talent. Andrin took that with a hefty lump of skeptical salt, but there was no question that Ternath was, indeed, the birthplace of the Talents. The telepathy of the Voices, Precognition, Mapping, the prescient Glimpses which were the heritage and curse of Ternathian royalty, Telekinesis, Distance Viewing—all of them had been developed and nurtured in Ternath, and then bequeathed to the children of Ternathia.

Intermarriage had carried those Talents throughout the sprawling Empire. Eventually, they had spread far beyond Ternathia's borders, through other intermarriages, and today their possession wove throughout all Sharona, like a gleaming net of precious gold.

Yet the world had turned and changed, until, eventually, the vast territory under direct Ternathian rule could no longer be administered at an affordable cost. Ultimately, a Ternathian emperor had made the decision to set free those provinces the Empire could no longer afford to govern. Andrin had always been glad Ternathia's borders had shrunk not from the fire of rebellion, or the crumbling of internal decay, but because her ancestors had been wise enough to return control of its far-flung provinces to the people who lived there.

That was the reason the wealthy Kingdom of Shurkhal and the many smaller kingdoms which shared its cultural heritage were once again Shurkhal and her sister states, just as the Harkalan states were once again sovereign, with legal bonds to no one but themselves. It was better that way. Andrin knew that. Not only because her tutors—including her father and mother—had taught her so, but because she could see it for herself.

It was worse than folly to grip something one could no longer afford to keep, simply for the perverse joy of possession. It was cruel to do so, and cruel to hold people in bondage. Had they wanted to remain Ternathian, she thought, they would doubtless have found a way to make it profitable for Ternathia to keep them. But only a few kingdoms or republics or principalities had refused their freedom when it was offered.

Ternathia's empire had shrunk steadily, and for the most part gracefully, and those who ruled the Ternathian Empire had retained their humanity in the process. Andrin Calirath was proud to be part of that lineage, proud to be the daughter of Ternathia's current emperor, who still ruled five hundred and seventeen million souls, give or take a few hundred thousand. And she was proud that even as they had taken back their freedom, Ternathia's one-time provinces had retained much of what Ternath had brought them. Proud of their independence and individuality, yes, but also mindful of thousands of years of shared history and the common heritage which continued to bind them together, as well.

After Ternathia and Farnalia, the next largest "empires," if the term could be used, were the Arpathians of the Septentrion, famous for furs, amber, vast herds of horses, and nomadic warriors, and Uromathia.

In reality, there was no such thing as an "Arpathian Empire"—the Septs were far too fiercely independent for anything that centralized—

but the Septentrion formed a recognizable union of cultures, religion, and political interests. It gave all the Septs representation, enforced the peace between them, and dominated the immense sweep of land from the Ibral Sea to the Scurlis Sea, four thousand miles to the east. Even more importantly, it gave the Septs a unified voice in trade protecting the Septs from outside unscrupulous trade practices.

South of Arpathia lay the tangled kingdoms of the Uromathian culture. Those kingdoms included Eniath, whose fierce deserts had given rise to a people with a love of horses and hawks that rivaled Andrin's own, as well as to genuine empires and several smaller independent states. The larger of the two empires was the Uromathian Empire itself, which had given the entire culture its name and rivaled modern Ternathia in size.

The smaller Hinorean Empire was no welterweight, but it couldn't match its larger neighbor, Uromathia, in size or wealth. Uromathians tended to produce enormous population densities, far greater than Ternathia's or, indeed, than the rest of Sharona in general. There were so many Uromathians, in fact, that large numbers of them had migrated to the new universes discovered beyond the portals.

Andrin had never met any Uromathians in person, although she'd seen a handful of envoys who'd come to Hawkwing Palace on official business. They were an exotic people, but far smaller than most Ternathians. Andrin had been taller than any of the male Uromathians she'd seen, which doubtless would have made them uncomfortable had they actually met her face-to-face.

Sweeping her gaze back toward the west, she skipped over the triangular jut of land that was Harkala and its sister states, once part of Ternathia but long since independent once more. The long Ricathian coastline led her eyes up past Shurkhal—another former Ternathian province, famous for its vast stretches of uninhabitable desert—and the Grand Ternathian Canal, linking the Mbisi and the Finger Sea.

Then her gaze reached the portion of the map north of Shurkhal, along the Mbisi's eastern shore, where the nation of Othmaliz lay between the peoples of the west and the peoples of the east. Like Shurkhal and Harkala, Othmaliz had once been part of Ternathia's empire. Also like Shurkhal and Harkala, Othmaliz had returned to native rule when Ternathia withdrew from the eastern half of its empire.

Andrin's gaze stopped there, for in Othmaliz, lay Tajvana.

Her skin tingled with the strange fire of her still-undefined Glimpse as she moved her eyes past the long, narrow, knifelike promontory known as Ibral's Blade, which ran parallel to the incredibly long and narrow Ibral Straits. That narrow passage of water opened up into the Sea of Ibral, which lapped against the city's ancient shoreline, and her heart burned with a strange passion she stared at the name on the map.

Tajvana.

The very name was magical, imbued with a history so deep it could hardly be grasped. Capital city of Ternathia for twenty-three centuries. Beauty beyond imagining. Ancient power, unrivaled in the history of mankind. Wealth almost beyond calculation, because it had been wealthy for so many millennia. Tajvana, which could be reached from the west only through the Ibral Straits, straddled the even narrower Ylani Straits, beyond which lay the dark and chilly waters of the Ylani Sea.

The Ylani was totally landlocked, save for that one tiny outlet, through Tajvana. Historically, whoever controlled the Ylani Straits had controlled the rich trade routes between Ricathia and Ternathia in the west, and Arpathia and Uromathia in the east. The importance of that trade had begun to fade as colonization had spread from Chairifon across the globe of Sharona, opening new markets, new sources of raw materials and goods, but only until the Larakesh Portal had suddenly appeared in the mountains just west of the sleepy little Ylani Sea seaport of the same name some eighty years ago. The only way for shipping to reach Larakesh from the rest of the world was through the Ibral and Ylani Straits, which meant—once again—through Tajvana. The ancient city had become, if possible, even wealthier than before, and the Portal Authority's decision to locate its headquarters there had restored it to the very first rank of important cities. Yet it was still the sheer history of the city which resonated so deeply with Andrin's very blood and sinew. Tajvana was unique, the one city on the face of Sharona which had known both financial and political power, virtually without interruption, for at least five thousand years. The city was as old as Ternathia itself, a jewel the Ternathian emperors had voluntarily given up.

Despite Andrin's understanding of the economic and political reasons behind Ternathia's abandonment of Tajvana, she'd always felt that the city's loss had diminished not merely the borders of the Empire, but its prestige and culture, as well. To Andrin's way of thinking, at least, it was a matter of national pride—or, more precisely, national shame—that her ancestors had abandoned the richest and most culturally diverse city in the world. She'd often wondered if the people of Tajvana missed the Ternathians and the power and prestige the Empire had brought to their city, or if they'd been glad to see the people who'd conquered them so long ago finally return home.

Andrin had wanted to see Tajvana for as long as she could remember, which was unusual for her. She didn't normally chase after ghosts, or yearn for lost glory. But Tajvana was different. It felt . . . wrong, somehow, to live in this chill stone palace in cool, rainy Ternath, when whispers of memory ran through her blood, echoes of warm wind in her hair, the warmth of sun-heated marble beneath her hands as she leaned against a carved balustrade, drinking down the glorious light that washed across the city like a tide, along with the scent of exotic flowers, or the rattle of palm fronds against a star-brushed night sky—

Andrin blinked and focused on the Privy Council Chamber once more. Such clear memories of a place she'd never seen would have been disturbing, had she not been Calirath. But the blood in her veins was the same blood which had flowed through the veins of Tajvana's rulers for centuries, and her family's Talent often manifested odd little secondary Talents no one could quite explain. She had visited Tajvana in her dreams, walked its narrow streets through the memories carried in her blood and, quite possibly, her Talent, and she longed to actually go to Tajvana, just to see how accurate those whispers of memory really were.

She sighed, aware that it was highly unlikely she would ever travel there, and yet burningly conscious of the need. Somehow, despite the unlikeliness, she'd always secretly believed that one day she *would* see Tajvana. Yet she was an emperor's daughter. Her safety and her duties took precedence over any urge she might have had to make the long journey. And once she married—in what would doubtlessly be a politically advantageous marriage, whether the suitor was a Ternathian noble or a prince of some other land—her duty would be to remain at home and raise somebody's heirs. She regretted that more than any other part of her life, yet duty came first when one was born Calirath. And at least she could be intensely glad that Janaki would be the one to rule Ternathia after their father.

She felt a familiar stir of relief at that thought, but the relief was matched by a stronger prickle of her discomfiting Talent, which brought her back to the worrisome question of why her father had insisted on her presence at the Privy Council meeting.

Most of the councilors had arrived, but there were still a few holes in the ranks. First Councilor Taje was deep in conversation with her father, their voices too low for her to hear, when Alazon Yanamar, Zindel's Privy Voice, entered the chamber and made her way straight to the emperor. Yanamar was not a standing member of the Privy Council, although she frequently attended its meetings, for obvious reasons. But today, she carried a strange, disquieting aura with her, and as Andrin watched them—her father, Taje, and Yanamar—she tried not to shiver.

It got harder as Zindel and the Privy Voice stepped into the farthest corner of the room, standing alone while Yanamar delivered whatever message had pulled them away from breakfast.

The emperor's face drained of color, and Andrin's palms went cold and damp against her velvet skirt. Yanamar's trained face gave no indication of what the message had contained, but Zindel's eyes had gone dark and frighteningly shuttered, with a look Andrin had never seen in them.

The Privy Voice glanced once toward Andrin, not unkindly, but without a hint of the thoughts behind *her* shuttered gray eyes. Not sure what else to do, Andrin nodded politely back to Yanamar from where she'd seated herself in one of the chairs along the wall, rather than one of those at the council table. Her father glanced up, as if the movement of her head had drawn his attention, and gave a slight frown. But he didn't speak, so she remained where she was, on the sidelines, where she belonged. She was here to observe and learn, not participate. At least, she didn't *think* she was expected to participate. She was usually adept at reading her father's nonverbal signals, but today she was unsure of anything except the fear that buzzed beneath her skin, sharper now than ever.

So she watched and listened as the remaining privy councilors hurried into the room, summoned from whatever tasks had been interrupted by the command to assemble. The First Councilor was by far the most composed of the lot; Andrin couldn't remember ever having seen Shamir Taje lose his composure. He was like a five-masted barque, she mused—ponderous and steady, solid and dependable, whatever the weather between him and his destination. As a child, she'd thought him duller than the endless Ternathian rain; as a nearly grown woman, with a better appreciation for the requirements of statesmanship, she recognized him for what he truly was: an utterly indispensable advisor, whose solid judgment and unflappable resolve were precisely what the Ternathian Empire required.

She wondered if he even suspected how well she understood that, and decided the likelihood was vanishingly small. That thought caused her to smile to herself, which arrested the attention of several privy councilors, who paused in the middle of speculative conversations to wonder what their emperor's daughter knew that they didn't. They also wondered why she was in the chamber at all.

Most decided they would really rather not know, since the only reasons they could drum up to explain her presence were uniformly bad ones. Some bordered on catastrophic, so the councilors eyed one another and kept conversation light in an attempt to steady jangled nerves until everyone had arrived.

It took what seemed to Andrin to be an agonizingly long time before the last councilor hurried into the room, out of breath from having run most of the way, and her father stepped to his place at the head of the long table. The table's ornate inlay gleamed in the lamplight, which was necessary, because the Privy Council Chamber had no windows. The thick oak tabletop's warm honey-gold was inlaid with darker wood, ivory, silver, and even mother of pearl in beautiful patterns. The ancient eight-rayed sunburst imperial crest of Ternathia took up the entire center of the vast table, glittering with precious metals and gemstones, and faithful representations of trees, flowers, and fruits from all across the vast sweep of Ancient Ternathia swept around its periphery.

The councilors moved quickly to claim their own assigned chairs, but remained standing while the tall, reed-thin chaplain intoned the brief benediction which preceded all official imperial functions. His voice was surprisingly deep, coming from such a frail-looking chest, as he requested guidance from the double Triad which had watched over the Empire for five millennia. The emperor stood quietly, respectfully attentive, as he prayed, but the moment the ritual was completed, Zindel seated himself in the chair that had stood at the head of this table for three centuries, which allowed the councilors to sit down, as well.

*   *   *

Zindel XXIV's massive oak chair was as intricately decorated as the table, with matching inlays, including the glittering imperial crest which shone above and behind his head and the carved image of the famous Winged Crown of Ternathia which formed the top of its solid back. One thing Zindel chan Calirath's ancestors had understood very well was the power of symbolism. He was no less aware of it himself, and knew he would have to call on all of that power to shepherd his people through the coming crisis. He settled into the cushioned comfort of the chair, lingering briefly on the realization that this chair was a good deal more comfortable than many of his duties, then spoke in a brisk tone.

"Ladies, gentlemen, thank you for arriving so promptly. We've received an urgent message from the Portal Authority. First Director Orem Limana has invoked a worldwide Conclave, scheduled for this afternoon at one-thirty, Ternathian time."

"*Conclave,* Your Majesty?" Ekthar Shilvass, Treasury Councilor, repeated sharply.

"That's right, Ekthar. I've called this session to discuss the reason for it. We don't have much time to prepare, and I need advice, my friends—advice and information. Unless I'm very seriously mistaken, Sharona is at war."

A shocked babble exploded around the table. Zindel had expected it, and he used the momentary confusion to glance at his daughter. Andrin had jerked bolt upright in her chair, her face white, as the import of his words hit home . . . along with the reason for her own presence. Then Shamir Taje rapped his knuckles sharply against the table in a brusque signal for silence.

"Your Imperial Majesty," he said, using the deliberate formality to remind the other councilors of proper protocol during an imperial crisis, "the Privy Voice gave me only part of the message from Director Limana when she asked me to bring you here. Perhaps you would clarify my most urgent question."

Zindel inclined his head, positive he already knew what the question would be.

"With whom are we at war, Your Majesty?" Taje asked, and the emperor met his old friend's gaze levelly.

"That, unfortunately, is the question of the hour. No one knows."

"But—" Captain of the Army Thalyar chan Gristhane, the Ternathian Army's uniformed commander, blurted out, "how can that be? If we don't know *who* we're fighting, how do we know we're at war *with* them?"

"We don't know who *yet,*" Zindel said grimly, "but unless the gods themselves intervene, we are most definitely at war, ladies and gentlemen. At war with someone who's slaughtered one of our survey crews, apparently to the last man." He paused, then added harshly, "And woman."

Stunned silence held the room for three full heartbeats. A swift glance at his daughter caught the sudden knife-sharp grief in her eyes as his last two words registered, and she began to weep, silently, biting her lip to keep the sound from distracting the council. He was fiercely proud of her—and more frightened *for* her than she would ever know.

Then he turned his attention back to his councilors and explained—briefly but fully—what had happened. The Privy Voice answered question after question, as best she could, but there was a limit to what she could tell them. There were no answers to most of the questions, and Zindel finally interrupted the fruitless queries.

"Rather than use precious time speculating in the dark about people about whom we know nothing, I would suggest turning our attention to Ternathia's role in this afternoon's Conclave. The leaders of every nation on Sharona and those of our largest colony worlds will meet via the EVN, and, at that meeting, we'll have to forge some kind of plan to meet this emergency. We've been attacked, and we must assume we'll be attacked again, given the savagery these people have already demonstrated."

"I agree we must prepare for the worst, Your Majesty," Shamir Taje said. "At the same time, however, surely the possibility that this attack was a mistake, or that it was carried out by some rogue junior officer, must also exist. If we assume war is inevitable, may we not make it so?"

Most people would not have recognized the true question in the First Councilor's voice. But that was because most people hadn't known him as long as Zindel chan Calirath had. He recognized exactly how surprised Taje was to hear his emperor, of all people, sounding so ready to embrace war and so dismissive of the chance for peace.

"Old friend," Zindel said quietly, "I pray from the bottom of my heart that war is *not* inevitable. I would give literally anything, for reasons of which you cannot even dream at this moment, for that to be true. But," his expression was grim, his eyes dark, "for the last week—since, in fact, shortly before this message was sent upon its way to us—both Princess Andrin and I have been experiencing a major Glimpse."

The Council Chamber was deathly silent, for these were *Ternathian* councilors.

"Nothing I've Glimpsed at this time says war is absolutely inescapable," Zindel continued in that same, quiet tone. "But *everything* I've Glimpsed shows fighting, bloodshed, death on a scale Sharona hasn't seen in centuries."

Andrin's face was carved from ivory as she heard her father's deep, resonant voice putting the nightmare imagery of her own Glimpses into words that tasted of blood and iron.

"I've Glimpsed men with weapons I cannot even describe to you," the emperor told his silent Council. "I've Glimpsed creatures out of the depths of nightmare, and cities in flames. Not all Glimpses come to pass. No one knows that better than someone born of my house. But it is my duty as Emperor of Ternathia to prepare for the possibility that this one *will* come to pass."

"I . . . understand, Your Majesty," Taje said softly into the ringing silence when he paused. "Tell us how we may serve the House of Calirath."

"We must understand from the beginning that the other heads of state won't have shared my Glimpse," Zindel said. "Most of them will recognize the potential catastrophe looming before us, but none of them will have Seen what I've Seen, recognize just how serious a threat this has the potential to become. Some of them will want to procrastinate and try to dodge their responsibilities, and others will bicker about protocol, precedence, and political advantage. Some may urge that we do nothing to 'exacerbate' the situation, while others will *demand* action, especially when the details of what happened to our survey crew become known to them. Still others may hope—as I do, however unlikely I feel it to be—to find a means to defuse the crisis through diplomacy and restraint. But whatever our views, however much we may agree or disagree with one another, we'll still have to come to agreement on some unified response, and Ternathia is the oldest, largest, and wealthiest empire on Sharona. As such, we must plan to play a leadership role in shaping that response.

"I need recommendations for Ternathia's most effective role. I know my own thoughts on the subject, but I want to hear yours, as well. All of them, no matter how seemingly foolish. You may come up with something important that I haven't considered. And I need facts, my friends—data on Ternathia's preparedness for war. The Empire hasn't actually fought a war in centuries. Skirmishes with claim jumpers or pirates in new universes hardly qualify—that sort of fighting doesn't come close to what I fear we may find ourselves facing. We may need to mobilize every fighting man in the imperial forces. Indeed, we may even need to expand the size of our military. Drastically."

"But, Your Majesty," Nanthee Silbeth, Councilor for Education, protested, "we have the largest Army and Navy on Sharona!"

Zindel opened his mouth, but the First Councilor responded before the emperor could speak.

"Yes, Nanthee, we do. But look at the population distribution. Most of the universes we've discovered are still virtually empty, and we've been exploring for *eighty* years. If we put every fighting man from every military organization on Sharona into the field tomorrow, shipped them all out by rail and troop ship, we still wouldn't have the manpower to guard all those universes, let alone mass the strength needed to hold them in a sustained, pitched battle."

"That's true enough, Shamir," chan Gristhane said, "and I certainly agree that we're probably going to need far more military manpower than anyone on Sharona currently has. At the same time, there's not going to be any point trying to cover *all* of the universes we've explored.

"First, because unless new portals form in critical places at exactly the wrong time, there's not going to be any way for the other side to magically bypass the portals we already hold. Believe me, offensive action on fronts as restricted as those portals permit is going to be very, very expensive, unless one side or the other holds an absolutely crushing advantage in terms of the effectiveness of its weapons.

"Second, even if that weren't true, if we put every single man of military age into uniform, we still wouldn't have even a fraction of the men we would need to garrison every universe against attack."

"You're right, Thalyar," the emperor said. "And it's also true that the sheer distances involved in getting from here to the frontier, or the other way round, mean there's not much realistic possibility of either side scoring some sort of lightning-fast breakthrough. Not unless, as you say, it turns out that one of us has a decisive advantage over the other when it comes to our soldiers' weapons.

"At the same time, we don't know yet who these people are. Worse, we don't know how *many* of them there are, how many universes they hold, how much population density to expect in *their* colonized worlds. We could be facing a civilization two or three or even ten times the size of our own." Zindel shook his head. "Shamir is absolutely right in at least one respect. If this does turn into a real war, it's going to be a potentially long and nasty one, and I doubt very much that our existing military is going to be large enough for the job."

Dead silence greeted that assessment, until, finally, Brithum Dulan, Councilor for Internal Affairs, cleared his throat.

"Your Majesty, may the Council inquire as to your reasons for including Grand Princess Andrin in this meeting?"

Andrin abruptly found herself the focus of every worried eye. She couldn't breathe, waiting for her father's answer, for the words she feared would seal her doom. Even though she couldn't imagine what that doom might be, she was terrified of it. And then, to her surprise—and the obvious surprise of the Council, as well—her father rose from his thronelike chair and crossed the room to take her chilled hands in his own.

"I'm sorry, child," he said gently, "but you are heir-secondary, and Janaki's Marines are stationed only two universes from where our people were slaughtered. That's why I have no choice but to include you in our policy debates. If anything happens to Janaki . . ."

He watched her closely as his words sank in. Her cheeks were ice-pale, and her fingers flinched in his grip, but she didn't indulge in histrionics. Not that he'd expected her to. She was only a barely grown girl, not yet eighteen, who might well have been forgiven tears or impassioned denials that she might need to step into her brother's shoes as heir. But she was also a Calirath. She simply gripped his hands, swallowed hard, and nodded.

"Yes, Father." Her voice came out low but creditably steady. "I understand. I'll do my best to be prepared if—"

She faltered and swallowed again.

"I'll do my best, Sir." She met his gaze levelly. "If I might suggest it, I could organize a military widows and orphans committee. I'm afraid it may be needed." He looked into her eyes and saw the dark shadows of his own Glimpse. "And I could help Mama oversee the travel arrangements," she added.

"Travel arrangements?" he quirked one eyebrow.

"To Tajvana." She frowned at his expression of surprise. "We are going to Tajvana, aren't we? For the face-to-face Conclave after this preliminary one? It's necessary, and it just feels . . . right, holding it there. It's where the Portal Authority is headquartered, and we can't do a proper job of meeting this emergency just through the Voices."

She was stumbling over her words now, as if they were as much of a surprise to her as to anyone else. Yet there was no doubt in her tone, no question. It was obvious to Zindel that she was trying to logically frame what must have been a strong Glimpse. One that not only matched his, but dovetailed with the latest message he'd received from his Privy Voice, as well.

"No," he agreed, "we can't do this entirely through our Voices. But before we consider sailing to Tajvana or anywhere else, we must prepare for *this* Conclave. So, you'll join the Conclave with the rest of the Privy Council. And I want you to do more than listen as we prepare for it. Your suggestion about assisting widows and orphans is a good one. There are undoubtedly going to be more of them than any of us would wish, and they'll need more assistance than ordinary pensions, before this thing is over. So if you have *any* questions, or other ideas, I want to hear them. Is that clear?"

She nodded, eyes stunned.

"Good."

He led her to the table and seated her firmly, making it clear to everyone—including her—that she was now a formal member of the Privy Council of the Ternathian Empire. She took her seat gingerly, as though poised for flight, but she held herself straight and kept her chin up. He was so proud of her it hurt.

"Now then," he said, resuming his ornate seat, "shall we discuss our readiness to fight a multi-universal war for survival?"

CHAPTER TWENTY-THREE

"I'M SORRY, BUT Mr. Kavilkan is in a meeting and can't be disturbed."

Jali Kavilkan's private secretary spoke with more than a hint of frost, and when frost appeared in Linar Wiltash's voice, most men cringed. Davir Perthis didn't. He was SUNN's Chief Voice, and he was too busy resisting the compulsion to tear out his hair with both hands to waste time cringing. Instead, he leaned forward, planted both hands on her desk, and thrust his jaw out.

"If you don't disturb him for *this*, you'll be looking for another job by supper. *Move*, damn it!"

Wiltash's eyes widened. Then she stood, spine stiff with outrage, crossed her palatial office with obviously irritated strides, and tapped at the door of the *sanctum sanctorum* of the Sharonian Universal News Network.

"*What?*" The predictable bellow rattled the door on its hinges, and Wiltash eased it open just a crack.

"Voice Perthis says it's urgent."

"It had fucking well better be! Get in here, Perthis!"

The Voice scooted, and he felt a sudden spike of satisfaction as he stepped through the door. The meeting he'd interrupted was providential, because Tarlin Bolsh, SUNN's division chief for international news, sat across the ship-sized desk from the executive manager of the largest news organization on Sharona. Or, in the entire multiverse, for that matter.

Jali Kavilkan didn't seem to feel there was anything providential about the moment, however. Kavilkan lacked any kind of physical grace. Short and broad, with a square, heavy-child face, he moved as ponderously as a Ternathian battleship, overflowed any chair

Perthis had ever seen him sit in, and somehow contrived to loom larger than men a foot taller than him. And, at the moment, he had his patented bellicose, take-no-prisoners glare focused directly upon one Davir Perthis.

"Well? What the hell's so godsdamned important?" he demanded.

Perthis closed the door behind him, pulling until the latch clicked with reassuring solidity. Wiltash had ears in every pore of her anatomy, which she used to keep Kavilkan informed of everything that happened in SUNN's headquarters. For once, though, Perthis was privy to information she didn't have yet, and he wanted to keep it that way.

Once he was certain the door was closed, he met Kavilkan's angry stare with a level gaze of his own.

"Sharona's at war, Sir," he said flatly.

"*What?*" Kavilkan's bellow actually lifted him to his feet, jerked up like some immense marionette. It came out half-strangled, the oddest sound Perthis had ever heard from him, and he half-crouched across his desk.

"Just what the hell do you mean by that?" he demanded an instant later.

"Exactly what I said, Sir. We're at war. One of our survey crews has been slaughtered by soldiers from an unknown human civilization. The Portal Authority hasn't released the official word yet, and it won't release *details* until families are notified, but Darl Elivath's got confirmation from three of his best sources."

He paused briefly, and Kavilkan jerked a brusque nod for him to continue. Elivath was SUNN's senior Portal Authority correspondent. His strength as a Voice was much too limited for service in the long-range Voice network, but his *sensitivity* and ability to capture nuances was enormous. And his talent for cultivating inside sources was legendary. No one could remember the last time Darl Elivath had been willing to go on the record with one of his sources and been wrong.

"According to Darl, there were no survivors from our crew." Perthis heard the harshness, perhaps even the denial, in his own voice as he continued. "Orem Limana has blood in his eye, and he's already redeploying the PAAF. And that's not all. He's ordered a full Voice Conclave on his own authority. Every head of state on Sharona—and all of our inner-ring colony universes—got the word maybe twenty minutes ago. The Conclave's set for three-thirty, Tajvana time, over the EVN."

For three solid heartbeats, Kavilkan stood rooted in place, as if Perthis had just turned him into stone, and Tarlin Bolsh's jaw eddied towards the floor. Then the executive manager shook himself like a rhino heaving up out of a dust bath somewhere on the Ricathian plains.

"Darl is *sure* of this?" he demanded.

"I wouldn't be here if he weren't," Perthis replied. "And you know Darl."

"What about confidentiality?" Bolsh asked. Perthis looked at him, and the international news chief grimaced. "You know what the Authority will do to us if they think we've breached Voice confidentiality on something like this, Davir."

"This is *Darl* we're talking about, Tarlin," Perthis more than half-snapped.

"I know that," Bolsh replied. His tone wasn't exactly placating, but there was definitely a . . . soothing edge to it. Perthis' defense of his Voices was proverbial. "I'm not saying he *has* breached confidentiality; I'm just asking if we're in a position to *prove* he hasn't if the wheels come off."

"I'm sure he'll be able to demonstrate it for any Voice Tribunal he might have to face," Perthis replied, and Kavilkan nodded sharply.

"That's good enough for me," he pronounced. Then he frowned, finally straightening his spine while the acute brain behind his eyes spun up to full speed.

"Three-thirty, you said?"

"Yes, Sir." Perthis nodded. "And they're going to play hell getting a Conclave set up that quickly, too."

"You're telling me?" Kavilkan snorted. "But the question's how soon we break the story."

"I think we have to be a little cautious with this one, Jali," Bolsh said. The executive manager looked at him, and the division chief shrugged. "If it's big enough for Limana to call a Conclave, then it's really, really big. It's not just a question of pissing people off if we break the story sooner than they want; it's a question of knowing what the hell we're talking about before we splash a report like this over the entire planet. At the moment, all we've really got is Darl's heads-up, and with all due respect for his normal reliability, I think the possibility that the entire planet might find itself at war with an entirely new trans-temporal civilization needs to be thoroughly checked out before we go public."

Kavilkan scowled, but he didn't jump down Bolsh's throat, either. Instead, he squinted his eyes in deep and obvious thought for several seconds. Then he nodded to himself and refocused his attention on Perthis.

"Tarlin's right. We've got to doublecheck everything on this. Is there any sign anyone else's picked up on the same story?"

"Not yet," Perthis said a bit unwillingly. This was the biggest scoop of any newsman's career, and the thought of sitting on it for one second longer than he had to was almost more than he could stand. "It won't be long, if they haven't already, though," he pointed out. "Limana's used the EVN to set up a Conclave. The fact that he activated the EVN at all is going to become public knowledge pretty damned quickly. Once that happens, other people are going to be digging, too."

"Granted," Kavilkan agreed. "And I'm not saying we don't start setting up for it right this minute."

He yanked open a file drawer and hauled out a folder Perthis recognized as SUNN's crisis-communications tree—the list of names of every SUNN office on Sharona, the men and women who represented the first tier of people they would need to contact. Each of those people, in turn, had his or her own list of people to contact, comprising the second tier in the system that would send a priority message worldwide within minutes, via SUNN's own Voicenet.

"Pass the preliminary alert now," he instructed the Chief Voice, handing across the file. "And start roughing voicecast copy, too. Go with two versions. Number one assumes we have a clear scoop; number two assumes we're neck-and-neck with at least one of the minors."

Perthis grimaced but nodded. It wasn't like Kavilkan to play it this cautious, but by the same token, this was the biggest news story in at least eighty years. It wasn't too surprising that the executive manager was being a bit careful. And, when Perthis came right down to it, none of the other news services could compare with SUNN's coverage and penetration. Over seventy percent of the home universe's population—and closer to eighty-five percent of the home universe's Talented population—were SUNN subscribers, directly or through one of SUNN's many affiliates. Even if one of the minor services managed to break the story first, SUNN's massive, well-oiled organization would overwhelm the competition in short order with the sheer depth of its own coverage.

"Go ahead and work up both copy sets using everything Darl has," Kavilkan continued. "If there hasn't been any official release by three o'clock, Tajvana, then we break the story with whatever we've been able to confirm."

"Yes, Sir," Perthis said, with considerably more enthusiasm, and handed over a hastily scribbled sheet of paper. "I've actually made a start on that already. I thought we'd use this for the first announcement, then do a Voice patch to the Authority HQ. Darl's standing by there now, with a reporter, in case we want to use visuals. And I think we want a talking head standing by, too. Maybe a retired survey crewman who can give us an expert opinion on what's going on out there. It'll give us a good human interest angle, too."

"Who?" Kavilkan demanded, then answered his own question. "Gortho Sandrick," he said, naming the man Perthis had already chosen, and switched his forceful gaze back to Bolsh. "He's in your division, isn't he, Tarlin? Wasn't Gortho a survey crew chief before he joined SUNN?"

"For twelve years," Bolsh agreed with a nod. "Before he broke both legs so badly in that landslide and had to retire."

Kavilkan grunted in acknowledgment, his eyes scanning Perthis' copy.

"Yes," he muttered under his breath. "Good job, Davir." He handed back the sheet. "Put Grandma Sholli on to conduct the interview with Gortho. This story needs a woman's touch, and Sholli brings out the best in human interest elements. She's everyone's favorite grandmother. And use Nithan Dursh to anchor the main voicecast. He's got the physical presence it takes to keep people calm."

"As calm as we *can* keep people, with news like *that* to report," Bolsh growled, and Kavilkan swore.

"The last thing Sharona needs is a bunch of damned fools running around in a state of total terror. We've got to minimize panic as best we can, and Nithan's our best bet." He ran a hand through iron-gray hair. "Gods and thunders, who the *fuck* did we run into out there? Well, don't stand there trying to answer a question nobody can answer yet. Move it! And Davir—"

"Sir?"

"*Damned* good work. Tarlin, I'll want banner headlines on every newspaper SUNN prints. Go ahead and start setting that up now—we're not going to be able to get a special edition out before three, anyway, so we might as well get to it now. But tell everyone, down to the typesetters, that if *anyone* leaks a single word of this before I personally say to, he—or she—will never work in this business again."

"Understood," Bolsh said. And, like everyone else, he knew Jali Kavilkan wasn't given to hyperbole when it came to things like this.

"Drag as much information as we can out of the Authority. Use smart speculation on what they don't have—or won't give us—but make damned sure we distinguish clearly between official information and speculation. And, while you're doing that—"

Perthis didn't stay to hear the rest of Kavilkan's instructions to Bolsh. His job was the Voicenet, not newsprint, and he had one hell of a job on his hands.

He rushed across the dumbfounded secretary's office without so much as glancing at her. He'd spent forty-three years in the news business. In that time, *nothing*—not even the Juhali eruption—had even approached this one in sheer magnitude. He was already spinning out follow-up voicecast ideas as he ran through SUNN's hallowed corridors, planning which SUNN Voices to put at the disposal of reporters in imperial and national capitals to cover the political repercussions this was bound to have.

Under other circumstances, Perthis would have felt euphoric over the scoop they were about to grab. Instead, his mind ran in frantic circles, wondering—as Kavilkan had—just what it was they'd run into "out there." Not to mention how nasty the other side intended to get. Perthis wasn't accustomed to the hollow feeling in his stomach, a disquieting sensation that he finally identified as fear. Stark, raw, ugly *fear*. Fear of the unknown, of a human civilization that shouldn't even exist. He wasn't used to feeling fear, and he didn't like it. In fact, he *hated* it.

He vastly preferred the outrage simmering around the edges of that fear. Outrage that anyone would dare to attack Sharonians. Fury that marauding soldiers had slaughtered Sharonian *civilians* without a shred of pity or human decency. Such monstrously uncivilized behavior deserved nothing but the most hardfisted military response. Sharona needed to throw their violence right back into their teeth. He bared his own teeth, and his eyes were hard. Rage was an ugly emotion, but it was far better than fear or terror. People needed to demand justice and reprisals, not to cower in stunned panic like a pack of quaking rabbits.

He grimaced at the thought. He knew politicians. Knew them well enough to predict political disaster. He couldn't believe the governments of the world would voluntarily set aside their squabbles and do what had to be done. The Portal Authority's First Director was determined enough, but the Authority couldn't handle a crisis of this magnitude. It didn't have the authority it would need to commandeer men and supplies from every corner of the globe, every universe they currently possessed.

Sharona needed a world government—a *strong* world government. One headed by someone with the experience to run a massive group of diverse people. Someone with a tradition of strong military leadership, yet with an equally strong and unshakable tradition of justice. There

was only one name on Davir Perthis' short mental list of people qualified for that job. But there were two names topping his list of people
who would *want* that job—and one of them couldn't be trusted with
a child's milk money, let alone the reins of world power.

They'll be coming to Tajvana, he told himself. *They'll hash it out
amongst themselves, what to do with the crisis, what to do about who
makes the decisions when decisions have to be made fast.*

Tajvana was the logical location for such a meeting. Almost all the
international—and interdimensional—organizations were headquartered
there, not to mention the Portal Authority itself, and Tajvana had
the infrastructure to handle a gathering of that size. And it carried
the enormous weight of precedence, as well. What other city had
ever been the capital of an empire that had covered or colonized
two-thirds of the world?

And when they came to Tajvana, they would give Davir Perthis
his golden opportunity.

It was time to rouse the public to action, to hit the world's leaders
with a deluge of demands for prompt, forceful action *and* strong,
unimpeachably honest *world* leadership, and a cold smile touched
his mouth, displacing the grim set of his lips. As a SUNN division
chief, he had the power to *make* the public issue those demands,
without people even realizing he'd done it. Savvy SUNN executives
had used that power time and again over the decades. Perthis fully
intended to use it, as well—and for a far greater and far better cause
than it had ever been used before.

Then he turned the final corner and he was back in his own
domain, bellowing for his staff. People scurried like ants, and he
flung himself into the comfortable chair behind his own desk and
started jotting down hasty, time-critical notes while other people
came running toward his office.

His pen moved with furious speed as he focused his mind totally on
the project in hand . . . and very carefully didn't think about his sister's
only son, who was on a survey crew somewhere "out there."

*   *   *

Traveling by ETS was unnerving.

One moment, Halidar Kinshe was looking at the console where
the ETS Porter sat, eyes closed in fierce concentration as she prepared to teleport them from Tajvana to the ETS station in Sethdona,
fourteen hundred-odd miles away. And then there was a moment
of overwhelming dizziness, wrenching nausea, and an indescribable
sensation—as if he'd slipped between the empty spaces between one
thought and the next.

And then he was swaying, dizzy and shaken, on another platform, blinking into the eyes of a totally different person.

"No, don't try to take a step just yet," the young man said as he balanced Kinshe carefully on his unsteady feet. "Wait until your equilibrium returns. Your inner ear still thinks it's in Tajvana."

Kinshe didn't feel quite so bad when he saw Samari Wilkon. The big, strapping Faltharian Voice was almost a foot taller than Kinshe, and he looked decidedly gray-faced as he leaned heavily on another attendant's shoulder.

"That was, ah, very odd," Kinshe managed as he finally began to regain his balance and his breath, and the attendant propping him up smiled.

"That's what most of them say, Sir," the young man assured him.

"And the ones who don't?"

"Are usually on their knees, too busy throwing up and cursing to say *anything*." The attendant's smile turned into a grin, and Kinshe surprised himself with a genuine chuckle.

"Ready to try a few steps now?" the younger man asked, and he nodded. The attendant guided him carefully off the platform and down to the floor. His knees still felt rubbery, but they worked. By the time they'd reached the other side of the room, he felt almost normal again, and Wilkon was right behind him, looking sheepish.

"Your wife is waiting in the lobby, Mr. Kinshe, and there's a carriage waiting for you, as well, just outside," the young man said, finally letting go of him to see if he really could take a few steps on his own. He could. In fact, by the time he reached the door, he was actually convinced he could walk out of the ETS station unaided.

"Thank you very much," he said, gripping the attendant's hand in thanks. "I wish I could tell you why it was so urgent."

"These teleports usually are, Sir," the young man said with a smile.

Kinshe nodded, but his answering smile was more than a little forced. This pleasant youngster would be finding out soon enough, he thought grimly, and when he did, he would no longer be smiling, either.

"Ready, Samari?" he asked, turning to see if the Voice had recovered.

"Yes, Sir," the towering Faltharian nodded. "Let's get this over with, Sir. We may have time to get there first, yet."

Kinshe nodded, opened the door, and strode briskly through it into the station lobby. His wife, Alimar, was waiting for him there, her expression anxious. Alimar had decided not to accompany him to Tajvana this trip because her caseload was always so heavy this time of year. With the schools in session, Healers—even relatively minor Talents like his wife—were in high demand.

Alimar wasn't as skilled or powerful, in a purely physical sense, as some of the truly outstanding telempathic Healers. But she had an adept way with the normal bumps and scrapes that school children managed to acquire on a playground, and her sensitivity to emotional nuances made her exceptionally valuable working with children, who were seldom able to fully articulate their feelings. He'd sent word ahead by Voice, asking her to accompany him today, and warning her that her particular ability to soothe and comfort would be needed before this day was over.

She just didn't know how *desperately* it would be needed . . . or why.

He pulled her close and held her for a long moment, and his embrace tightened as images of destruction and devastation flickered through his mind. The thought of some rapacious horde of barbarians rushing through the portal in Tathawir and then spreading out across the face of the world in a ravening mass, killing and maiming everyone within reach, filled him with a sudden, icy fear that was all too real—and personal—as he felt his wife in his arms.

"What is it, Hal?" she asked in a frightened voice as she tasted his emotions, if not their cause, through her Talent.

"Not here, love," he murmured. "Only when we're alone."

She bit her lip, but nodded. She'd long since been forced to accept that his work in both the Portal Authority and the Shurkhali Parliament meant there would be things to which he was privy that he literally could not share with her. Not without violating his responsibilities to Shurkhal's independence.

But that, too, was about to change, Kinshe thought grimly. Unless he very much missed his guess, Shurkhal would no longer be an independent nation, once the dust settled and their world got down to the serious business of meeting this threat. But he couldn't say that, either, so he guided his wife across the lobby—and faltered to a halt.

Crown Prince Danith Fyysel was standing beside the door.

"Your Highness?" Kinshe said in surprise.

"My father felt it appropriate that I go with you, Sir," Danith said, and Kinshe drew a deep breath, then nodded.

"Thank you, Your Highness." He managed to smile. "I was afraid your father would insist on sending a whole retinue with us."

The crown prince's smile was fleeting—not surprisingly, given the grim business which had brought them both here—but it warmed his eyes for a moment.

"I talked him out of it," he said. "The ambassador will be distressed enough, as it is, without having to cope with a whole roomful of royal retainers fluttering uselessly about."

"Thank you," Kinshe repeated with another nod, then inhaled deeply. "I'm told there's a carriage waiting?"

"Indeed. And an express train, as well, at Fyysel Station."

Alimar Kinshe-Falis's eyes had widened in deep surprise at sight of the crown prince, and they'd grown still wider while Danith and her husband spoke.

"What is—?" she began, then closed her lips again, blushing painfully. "Sorry. I won't ask again."

"Let's get into that carriage," Kinshe said. "Once we're on the train, I'll fill you in. Both of you."

The crown prince inclined his head gravely and led the way outside. There was, indeed a carriage—one of the royal coaches, no less, with a section of ten Household Cavalry waiting as escort.

"I've arranged to bring it with us on a special car," he told Kinshe as they approached it, then paused as a footman opened the door. "No, Mrs. Kinshe-Falis. After you," he said as Alimar hesitated, waiting for the prince to enter first, as custom decreed. "I insist."

"Thank you," she murmured, and Kinshe handed her up.

The prince entered the coach next, then Kinshe climbed in, and Wilkon followed last. The moment the footman had closed the door, the coachman clucked to the horses. The beautifully matched team of four grays responded instantly, and the footman scrambled up onto the boot as they sprang into motion, accompanied by the cavalry escort.

The Sethdona ETS station was logically located in the heart of the capital city between the Royal Palace and the Parliament building. That placed it relatively close to the train station, as well, and traffic was thankfully light at this time of day. The journey was a short one, and when they reached the station, the carriage turned down a special drive reserved for conveyances that were to be shipped overland.

The commander of the mounted escort had obviously been briefed ahead of time, and they proceeded directly to the correct track, where the carriage paused alongside a private passenger car which bore the royal coat of arms on both sides. Three more cars were coupled behind it. One was the special car for the carriage Danith had referred to, while the other two were standard-looking passenger cars. The first of them was obviously for the use of the crown prince's security escort, and Kinshe suspected that the other contained a hastily assembled support staff.

The footman opened the carriage door, and Kinshe led the way out at the prince's gesture. He assisted Alimar down the steps, then stood waiting until Danith had joined them. As the crown prince led the way towards the royal passenger car, Kinshe found himself gazing at the quietly panting locomotive in something very like awe.

"It's one of the TTE's new Paladins," Crown Prince Danith said quietly. Kinshe glanced at him, and the young man gave him a true aficionado's smile.

"I'm afraid I'm not as well informed about locomotives as you, Your Highness," Kinshe admitted. "First Director Limana is a huge fan, but I've been more involved with personnel administration than the Authority's freight divisions."

"Actually, the Paladin's a bit too much engine for our purposes, but it was the best compromise available in a short time frame."

"Too much engine, Your Highness?"

"For four cars?" Danith chuckled, and waved one graceful hand at the maroon-and-black painted, steam-breathing behemoth. "This is a 4-10-4, Halidar. Eighty-inch drivers and something like six thousand horsepower. On reasonably flat ground—which describes a lot of Shurkhal, when you think about it—a Paladin is capable of sustained speeds well above a hundred miles an hour with complete passenger trains! Assuming, of course, that the *rails* are up to it."

Kinshe blinked. That did sound a tad excessive for a mere four cars.

"Father told the line supervisors speed was of the utmost importance," the crown prince continued more soberly. "There's not a locomotive on Sharona that will get us there more rapidly than this one."

Kinshe's jaw muscles knotted at the reminder of why they were here, and he nodded. Then they were climbing up into the plushest train car he'd ever seen. Attentive rail stewards showed them to their seats and offered refreshment while the carriage and team, along with the escort's horses, were rapidly loaded. Within ten minutes, the mighty Paladin gave a deep-throated "*chuff*" of steam, and the special train began to move.

They maintained a decorous speed through the city, but they began to speed up as soon as they reached the open desert. The acceleration was smooth, yet as he watched the eastbound rails and ties of the double-track blur beside them, Kinshe realized that the crown prince's speed estimate had been completely serious.

It was an astonishing and exhilarating sensation to move at such speed, and he was reluctant to pull his attention back to the business at hand. Partly, he knew, that was a form of cowardice. He didn't *want* to think about it, but Alimar needed to know why they were racing through the desert at such enormous speed.

So he told her.

"They did *what?*" His wife, normally a gentle and loving soul, stared at him with eyes of naked fury. "They butchered an *innocent girl?* What kind of monsters *are* these people? They must be punished! Tracked down like jackals and punished!"

"Yes." Kinshe nodded, his expression grim. "They must be—and they will. In fact, they may very well already have been. Don't forget, our information is a week old. A column has already been dispatched to confirm what happened and rescue any of our people who may have survived, and I imagine they've made contact with the other side by now . . . one way or another. But you have my word, Alimar; the people who could perpetrate this kind of atrocity won't escape justice."

As he spoke, he met Crown Prince Danith's eyes. The heir to the throne had not yet married, but he had sisters. The look that passed between them was a vow made in Shurkhal—the blood-debt honor: not another Shurkhali woman would die. *Not one.*

Kinshe couldn't help wondering what King Fyysel's ultimate vote in Conclave was going to be. The parliamentary representative knew the crown prince shared many of his own political convictions, but if Sharona ended up voting in a world government, Danith Fyysel would lose his opportunity to wear a crown.

"My father and I have already spoken about the most important aspect of Shurkhal's participation in this Conclave, Representative Kinshe," the crown prince said, as if he'd read Kinshe's mind, and his tone was as formal as his choice of titles. "He specifically instructed me to share our thoughts with you, since you are both a senior member of Parliament and a Portal Authority director. Both of us know Sharona must have a world government. At the same time, Father has already sworn on blood-honor that we will never tolerate a government run by Uromathia. His exact words were, ah, 'death before Uromathia,' I believe."

"That certainly sounds like your father, Your Highness. Rather mild for him, actually," Kinshe observed with a grimace, and the crown prince's lips twitched.

"You know him well. What I want to say, however, before this matter even comes to vote, is that I support Father's position absolutely. I hold the survival of Sharona far higher than any petty desire to sit on a fancy chair in Sethdona. We can't afford that kind of nonsense."

"Your Highness," Alimar Kinshe-Falis said softly, before her husband could speak, "you've just proven how worthy you would have been to sit in that chair."

Danith Fyysel blinked in surprise. Then the Crown Prince of Shurkhal actually turned red for a second or two before he finally managed a chagrined smile.

"Thank you, Mrs. Kinshe-Falis," he said. "That may be the greatest compliment I've ever received."

CHAPTER
TWENTY-FOUR

ANDRIN'S HEAD WAS throbbing by the time her father called a much-needed break. She sat, rubbing her temples, and watched servants carry an early luncheon into the Privy Council Chamber. Despite her father's forceful personality and Shamir Taje's skill as an organizer, they'd managed to accomplish only a fraction of what they really needed to do in the time they had. Hopefully, it was the most *important* fraction, and her father was undoubtedly correct about the need for all of them to eat before launching into a Conclave which would undoubtedly run for many hours.

And so they ate, sitting at the inlaid table that had been covered protectively with a crisp white linen cloth, while they continued to cover critical bits and pieces of business in side conversations. When they'd finished, the servants whisked away the remnants, then refilled wine cups and served hot tea, New Farnalian coffee, and steaming mugs of the New Farnalian cocoa Andrin and several other councilors enjoyed. They also re-stoked the coal fire on the hearth, which Andrin appreciated. The heat at her back was as delicious as the rich cocoa in her mug.

She listened to the side conversations and realized how little she truly understood about what the Councilors were saying. It quickly became clear to her that she simply lacked the critical building blocks of known facts to tie the other conversations together in any comprehensible fashion. Unfortunately, she couldn't exactly break into the discussions and request explanations and definitions—certainly not under this sort of emergency time pressure. Yet if she didn't ask now, how would she be able to remember the proper questions later?

She pondered the problem for a moment, then asked one of the servants—a girl perhaps three years older than she was—to find her a notebook and a pen. She also asked for a filled inkwell, in case the pen's internal reservoir ran dry. The servant hurried back with the requested items, and Andrin thanked her sincerely.

"That be my pleasure, Your Grand Highness," the girl murmured, almost too low to hear as she swept a deep curtsy that took her nearly to the floor. She glanced up, meeting Andrin's eyes for just a fleeting instant, then looked down again, almost fearfully.

"You see," she said, speaking in a rush as if it took all her courage for one hurried burst of words, "it's just *forever* I've been wanting a chance to serve you. If you be needing anything else, I'll be waiting just outside. Just you open that door a crack and ask. I'll go and fetch anything you'd be wanting."

She rose with a surprising grace and retreated from the room. Andrin watched her go in mild astonishment, then pulled her attention back to the ongoing discussion, sipping cocoa, listening, and jotting down occasional questions or ideas. At length, the mantle clock chimed the half-hour, and her father signaled for silence and turned to Alazon Yanamar.

The Privy Voice sat in a waiting attitude, eyes closed, clearly Listening for the incoming message from First Director Limana. Or, rather, from the chain of Voices between Tajvana and the Privy Council Chamber. The arrangements and coordination required for Voices to relay over truly lengthy distances could be unbelievably complicated, especially at a time like this, when individual, totally secure links had to be maintained between the Portal Authority in Tajvana and *every* national capital on Sharona. Not even the EVN could maintain a real-time link to the various colonial governments, since no Voice could communicate with another through a portal. But Andrin knew that there were other chains of Voices, stretching down the transit chains between universes, to provide the fastest message turnaround humanly possible.

Then Yanamar's eyes opened so suddenly Andrin actually twitched in shock.

"Your Imperial Majesty," the Privy Voice said, in a deep, rich voice filled with subtle tones, one so beautiful Andrin would have given all the silly baubles in her jewel box to possess its equal. "First Director Limana has begun the Conclave. The Portal Authority's Head Voice, Yaf Umani, is transmitting what he sees and hears."

Her voice shifted suddenly. It took on not simply a different timbre, but a different rhythm and accent as she repeated the words of a man a quarter of the world away. That was remarkable enough, but what stunned Andrin was the projection that abruptly appeared at the far end of the room. It was a three-dimensional image of a man standing at a podium in a room she'd never seen. There were others present, seated between themselves and the speaker, and a map of the newly discovered portals hung behind him. The man at the podium was looking right at them, even though he couldn't possibly have actually seen them.

Andrin had always known Voices could receive and transmit detailed images of actual events, but less than one Voice in ten thousand could actually project those images for nontelepaths to see. Despite her birth rank, she herself had seen that particular Talent used exactly once, when the universe-famed Projective Falgayn Harwal had visited the Imperial House of Music here in Estafel. She still shivered inside when she remembered how Harwal and his dozen highly trained, powerful assistant Voices, had filled the entire Opera House with a projection of the New Tajvana Choir's eight thousand singers and voices.

But Harwal was unique, the sort of Talent who arose perhaps once every two hundred years. Although Andrin had always known there were others with the same ability, if only on a far smaller scale, she'd never actually seen it done. Not this closely and intimately. No wonder Alazon Yanamar was her father's Privy Voice! Her Talent must be indispensable to a man who governed an empire that covered several major islands and most of a continent.

She wondered if the Portal Authority's Head Voice could do this, as well. Probably, she decided. Then Yanamar's voice dragged her attention back to the meeting underway.

"Honored heads of state of the sovereign nations and colonies of Sharona and the various advisory councils and board members with you. For those of you who have never personally met me, I am Orem Limana, first Director of the Sharonian Trans-Temporal Portal Authority. In that capacity, I thank you for joining this Conclave. May we have a roll call of official members of the Conclave, please?"

Yanamar's recitation didn't quite match the movement of Limana's lips, but it was incredibly close. It was almost uncanny watching the eerie projection and listening to Yanamar's voice repeating the words of the man speaking in a room three thousand miles away.

The Privy Voice repeated a seemingly endless list of names as First Director Limana proceeded alphabetically down the official roster of nations and colonies. Andrin watched the map of Sharona as he spoke, trying to fix the names of various heads of state in her mind, but she had to give up within moments. She uncapped her pen once more and made her first note of the Conclave: *Memorize the names of every head of state on Sharona and our colonies.* She looked down at it, and, after a moment's consideration, added, *And their heirs, if they're monarchies, and their seconds in command, regardless of what form of government they have.*

She managed not to groan as she contemplated the size of that task, but it wasn't easy.

Once the First Director had completed the daunting task of merely determining that everyone was listening, he turned to the reason he'd summoned the Conclave in the first place.

"I'll begin by reminding every person participating in this Conclave that the news of this attack is to be considered a level-one secret under the Portal Authority Founding Charter, at least until such time as the family members of those killed, wounded, or captured in it have been notified about what's happened to their loved ones. Official Portal Authority representatives are en route even now, taking word to the immediate families of each of the survey crew's members.

"I would further ask that this news not be made public until such time as this Conclave has formulated a plan to ensure Sharonian security in the Karys Chain and its approaches. The more we can do to reassure the public at the same time we finally break the news, the less panic is likely to ensue. Are we agreed on that point?"

Andrin's father nodded, and the Privy Voice transmitted his response. Again, a lengthy delay ensued before the Portal Authority's director spoke again.

"Thank you. I deeply appreciate your promised discretion in this matter."

He cleared his throat. It was the first sign of nervousness—if that was what was—he'd displayed, and Andrin was deeply impressed by his apparent *sang froid.*

"Very well," he said, "the purpose of this Conclave is to meet the current emergency. The Portal Authority will be intimately involved in that process, but the Authority is primarily an organizational tool, one which was never designed to handle *this* kind of emergency. Bearing that in mind, I'll begin the Conclave by bringing you up to speed on my responses and decisions to date. Once I've done that, I'll request specific guidance from the members of the Conclave on the best course of action until we can convene a face-to-face Conclave.

"And before anyone protests, please let me assure you that we *will* need a second Conclave. We must devise a permanent, long-range structure of governance to effectively mobilize, organize, and deploy Sharona's military and civilian resources. That's going to require lengthy, direct, pragmatic, and *flexible* decision-making, and we can't do that in a meeting format like this one. I would suggest Tajvana as the place to hold that face-to-face meeting. The Portal Authority is headquartered here, and Tajvana has been a world capital in the past. As such, the city is well equipped with the infrastructure to handle large diplomatic and security delegations.

"If there are no objections to Tajvana as the site of the second Conclave, I'll have my staff contact each of you to arrange a date on which as many of you as possible can attend. We'll work out the details, schedule the meeting, and arrange appropriate meeting space—perhaps in the old Calirath Palace—as rapidly as we can. I'll inform you of our final arrangements, work out travel schedules, and make Voice arrangements to give any of you who simply cannot personally attend the best access possible. Are there any objections?"

There were none, to Andrin's considerable surprise, and her father glanced at her and quirked one eyebrow.

"Well, it seems you were right, 'Drin," he said very quietly. "We will be traveling to Tajvana."

She nodded, rubbing her arms in an effort to smooth down the prickling sensation under her gown's sleeves, where the downy hair was trying to stand on end. She wasn't surprised, so much as unnerved by the swiftness with which her Glimpse had proven itself accurate.

"Once I've listed the specific areas in which I need interim guidance," Director Limana continued, "I will call for discussion by the members, asking that each of you bear in mind possible answers to those specific points. Both during my initial assessment of the current situation, and during the open discussion, we will observe strict parliamentary rules of order, simply to keep the discussion from becoming too unwieldy for the Voices to transmit.

"If you want to ask questions or share comments, ideas, or solutions—and I hope you will *have* solutions for various aspects of this crisis—please send your request through the Portal Authority's Head Voice, Yaf Umani. He will relay it to me in the order in which it was transmitted, so that you may speak in your turn. I realize this may be inconvenient, given the awkwardness of holding a meeting of this size through the Voice network. Indeed, that awkwardness underlines the necessity of direct, face-to-face meetings. For the moment, however, I can't think of a fairer way to handle the discussion. Is that clear to everyone?"

Andrin's father nodded once more, and the Privy Voice's eyes lost their focus for a moment as she sent out the response.

"Very well," Limana said again. "I'll begin with a review of the tactical situation and my decisions and actions to date.

"The situation, as it now stands, is both unclear and alarming. We've received two follow-on messages since the initial one arrived approximately four hours ago. Please bear in mind the extensive water gaps which have to be covered in several of these universes. Frankly, I'm astonished that we've received even these two messages so quickly.

"The first message was an expansion of Company-Captain Halifu's original report. As the commander of the nearest portal fort, here in New Uromath," Limana indicated the newly named universe on the map, "he dispatched a rescue party to do what it could. Due to the large number of portals recently discovered in this area, he—like all of the fort commanders in the vicinity—is badly understrength, and he was able to field only a single cavalry platoon.

"The second message, which was relayed to us simultaneously, was from Company-Captain chan Tesh, in command of the reinforcing column which was already en route to Company-Captain Halifu. He was also accompanied by a Petty-Captain Traygan, the Authority Voice assigned to Halifu, who received a relay of the original contact report while he was here, in Thermyn." Again, the First Director indicated the universe in question. "Chan Tesh reported that he was moving immediately by forced march to reinforce Halifu with several platoons of cavalry and infantry and at least some of his artillery.

"That's all the additional news we have at this time, and it will probably be at least several days before we hear anything else."

Limana paused again, looking up from his notes at the faces of those physically present, then continued.

"What we know right this moment is simply that our survey crew was attacked and that most or all of its members were killed. Company-Captain Halifu and Company-Captain chan Tesh are clearly acting as quickly and decisively as possible, given their resources, the distances involved, and the lack of improved communications. They have reported that they consider their immediate primary responsibility to be the location and rescue of any survivors. Although their messages and reports carry an undeniable undertone of great anger, they do not appear eager to provoke a general war. However—" Limana paused very briefly, sweeping his visible audience with his eyes "—it's quite evident from their dispatches that they intend to use deadly force not simply in self-defense but to *compel* the other side to release any prisoners they may have taken. By this time, they have almost certainly already made contact, which means it would be far too late to issue orders *not* to use deadly force under those circumstances, even if we desired to do so. Which, speaking for myself, I do not."

His voice went grim and harsh on the final sentence. Alazon Yanamar's beautifully trained and expressive voice transmitted his tone perfectly, and Andrin saw cold approval on the faces of at least half of her father's Privy councilors.

"We're fortunate that Company-Captain Halifu has both a qualified Whiffer and a qualified Tracer, which will give us the best possible forensic analysis of the site of the attack," Limana resumed after a moment. "Nonetheless, it may be weeks or even months before we have any definite information on the fate of our civilians.

"In the meantime, we have to be aware of the enormous challenges Halifu and chan Tesh face. All indications are that the Chalgyn Consortium crew's latest discovery is an entire cluster of portals in close geographic proximity. There's no way of knowing at this time which portal—or *portals*—of that cluster have already been explored by our opponents. In addition, the *entry* portal here—" he tapped the bland circle of a still-unnamed universe from which no less than six additional, question-mark-tipped transit lines extended "—is enormous. According to Chalgyn's measurements, it is thirty-seven miles in diameter."

Andrin inhaled sharply in surprise. That wasn't simply "enormous"— it was stupendous!

"It would take many times the troop strength Halifu and chan Tesh have to defend a portal that size," Limana continued grimly. "I've sent instructions, on my own authority as First Director, to reinforce them as quickly as possible with all of the troops available to the PAAF in that vicinity, but current indications are that everything available amounts to little more than a few battalions. We certainly don't have sufficient troop strength to hold what would amount to a seventy-four-mile front against heavy attack.

"Moreover, the lack of rail communications means troop move-ment will be slow as our personnel approach the contact universe, so I've also contacted Gahlreen Taymish at the TTE. He's been brought fully up to speed, and I've activated the emergency clauses of the Trans-Temporal Express's right-of-way agreement. As of this moment, the TTE is under the direct control of the Portal Authority, and will remain so until released. Director Taymish has already sent out instructions to redeploy all available TTE construction crews to the Hayth Chain, but it will take some weeks for him to get additional equipment and workers into place."

Limana paused again, as if for punctuation, then shook his head slowly.

"I'm sure most of you hope, with me, that this tragic and, yes, brutal attack will not lead to all-out war with another trans-universal civilization of unknown size, power, and capabilities. Unfortunately, we dare not assume that will be the case. Regiment-Captain Namir Velvelig commands Fort Raylthar, covering the outbound portal from Failcham." Limana indicated the universe in question. "Fort Raylthar is the closest properly manned portal fort, although even its garrison is more than a little understrength thanks to the sudden expansion along this chain. As you can see, Fort Raylthar is within two universes, and about eighteen hundred miles, of the point at which our crew was attacked. The regiment-captain has already sent some reinforcements forward, and—"

The First Director's voice disappeared into roaring chaos as sudden, wrenching terror swamped Andrin. She jerked upright in her chair, the breath frozen in her throat. Regiment-Captain Velvelig was Janaki's commanding officer, and something dreadful—formless and black and horrifying—was going to happen out there under Velvelig's command. There was fire everywhere, men were screaming, guns thundering, lightning stabbing and strobing impossibly, and something ghastly was in the air, rushing down upon them and—

Andrin bared her teeth, snarling in defiance and fury and terror. Something had seized her, was shaking her whole body, and she gasped and struck out with both fists, trying to fend off the attack. Then someone truly *did* seize her. Hands closed on her flailing forearms, capturing them with huge yet gentle strength. They immobilized her, pushed her arms down by her side, held her, and her eyes snapped abruptly back into focus.

She stared wildly into her father's face. The emperor gripped her arms, holding her, and his face was white as death, except for the large dark spot on one cheekbone which was already beginning to bruise. She stared at the mark, feeling the memory of the blow which had created it in the knuckles of her own right hand, and realized she was on her feet with no memory of when or why she'd stood up.

"Papa?" she whispered, shaken to the bone. Then she realized she'd disrupted the entire Conclave, distracting her father from the First Director's critical report, and her own cheeks blazed. She wanted to crawl under the table and die of shame.

"Andrin," her father's voice was low but iron command echoed in its depths, "tell me exactly what you Saw. *Everything* you Saw."

"I-I don't know." She began to tremble. "There was fire—fire everywhere. Fire in the sky. Raining down on us. And lightning. And something huge and black, diving down. I couldn't see what it was, where it was coming from. Men were shooting, people were screaming, *burning . . .*"

"*Where?*"

"I don't know! Director Limana was talking about Regiment-Captain Velvelig sending reinforcements, and it hit me like a runaway train." She was shaking violently, now, no longer trembling. "I'm sorry," she whispered, unable to dredge up anything more from the Glimpse. "All I know is Janaki is out there, but I don't know when, or where, or even if he'll be there, and—"

"Hush," her father said gently. Her teeth were chattering, and he drew her close, enfolding her in his powerful, infinitely comforting arms. He eased her back down into her chair and dragged it closer to the fire, then knelt beside her, chafing her icy hands.

"Send someone for brandy!" he snapped over one shoulder.

"It's already on the way," Taje said, just as the door crashed open. The serving girl who'd brought Andrin the pen and notebook skidded through the doorway and rushed forward, brandy decanter in one hand, cut-crystal tumbler in the other. Her eyes were huge with fear.

"Here it be, Your Majesty!" she gasped breathlessly. "I ran as fast as ever I did in my life!"

"Bless you, child," the emperor said, and took the decanter. He splashed brandy into the tumbler and held the rim to Andrin's lips.

"Sip it, 'Drin. Yes, that's good. No, don't push it away—sip it again. That's right. All of it, dear heart. You need it."

Andrin gulped again, choking on the liquid fire, as the dreadful shudders began to ease.

"Better?" he asked gently, and she nodded, surprised to discover it was true.

"Yes," she managed. "Much better."

"Thank Marnilay," he said reverently. Then he wrapped his own coat around her shoulders and told the hovering servant girl to fetch a blanket. As the girl ran from the room, the emperor turned back to his Privy Voice.

"Alazon, please send an urgent message to Director Limana. Ask him to warn Regiment-Captain Velvelig to expect trouble in the near future. I can't say when or where with any precision, but Grand Princess Andrin has just experienced a major Glimpse. Ask the First Director to relay all the details of what she's just told us to the regiment-captain."

One or two councilors looked a bit skeptical, and Andrin's cheeks heated again. Her father noticed, and his swift response stunned her—and his councilors.

"Let me make something perfectly clear," he said, in a far colder voice than Andrin had ever heard from him. "This was not a case of a girl's overactive nerves. If any of you doubt the validity of my daughter's Talent, I advise you to remember the Kilrayen forest fire. Moreover, I will remind you—*all* of you—that Andrin is heir-secondary. Given her youth, we have not, perhaps, made that status sufficiently clear in the past. But should *anything* happen to my son, Andrin will replace him in the line of succession. You *will* accord her the respect due her rank and station. And should any of you continue—unwisely—to cherish any doubts about the validity of her Glimpse, let me add one clarifying fact. I just experienced exactly the same Glimpse, but hers was clearer and more detailed. My daughter is strongly Talented, and a valuable asset to our war effort and this Empire. Does anyone on this Council wish to debate that point?"

No one spoke. Those whose glances had been skeptical now looked at her with contrition and apology, and, quite unexpectedly, Andrin felt sorry for them. It must be difficult for someone as highly placed as a Privy Council to take any schoolgirl of seventeen seriously, however imperial her blood. The thought gave her an unanticipated insight into them, and she found herself smiling back at them. Several gave her sheepish return smiles, which defused the tension so thoroughly that even her father was left blinking for a moment.

Then the Privy Voice cleared her throat.

"Your message has been sent and acknowledged, Your Majesty. Word will be passed to Regiment-Captain Velvelig."

"Thank you, Alazon," the emperor said quietly. He drew Andrin's chair back to the table, gave her shoulder a reassuring squeeze, and resumed his own seat.

"Very well, I suggest we return our attention to the Conclave."

Andrin was astonished to discover that Director Limana had halted the entire Conclave to await Ternathia's return. She was mortified by the thought that her outburst had kept every other head of state on Sharona waiting, yet at the same time, it gave her a major insight into the importance the First Director placed on Ternathia's participation. Which meant on her *father's* participation, which gave her something else to mull over as Limana resumed his system report.

"As I was saying, Regiment-Captain Velvelig is two universes away. In my opinion, sending forward any greater numbers of reinforcements would weaken his own command unacceptably. I believe it would be wiser to draw the additional troops we'll need from universes farther up the line. The entire chain, from Hayth to New Uromath, is overland, with the exception of an eleven-hundred-mile water gap here in Salym. The rail line is well established as far forward as Traisum, so troop movements from universes farther from the scene can be executed fairly rapidly."

Behind Limana, a dark-haired young woman had appeared beside the transit chain map. As Limana began discussing specific PAAF garrisons, where they were stationed, and how rapidly they could be moved farther forward, his assistant marked their positions on the master map.

As she did, it became painfully evident to Andrin that the authority's multinational military forces were even thinner on the ground than she'd feared.

Well, of course they are, she told herself scoldingly. *The PAAF is primarily a peacekeeping force! If you hadn't known it before, you certainly should have picked up on that from Janaki's letters!*

The thought of her brother sent a fresh, cold serpent of fear slithering through her, but she thrust it firmly aside. It didn't go easily, but it went, and when she looked back up, she saw Privy Voice Yanamar cock her head in a listening posture.

"A question from Emperor Chava Busar of Uromathia," she said. "He says, 'We have a large force of cavalry in the field for defense of our colony in Camryn, which is only four universes from Traisum. We could divert a thousand men—possibly as many as fifteen hundred—for duty at some of the new portal forts without leaving our colony unacceptably vulnerable. I would be honored to make those men available in this emergency, and my General Staff would be prepared to work with the Portal Authority in an advisory capacity to make most effective use of them.'"

Shamir Taje swore aloud. Andrin didn't believe she'd ever heard the First Councilor use profanity before, and the sizzling intensity of the one short, pungent phrase he permitted himself was an eye-opener. Then he glanced quickly at her, blushed, and shook his head in mute apology before he looked back at his older colleagues.

"I'll just bet Chava would be willing!" he said sourly. "Give that man a foot through the door, and he'll put an army in your bedroom!"

"Patience, Shamir," her father said gently. "Fifteen hundred extra men that close to the danger zone is nothing to sneeze at, whatever the source. And Orem Limana knows how to deal with heads of state who overstep their authority. Especially those who try to tread on *his*. Besides," he gave the First Councilor a cheerful grin, "under the provisions of the Founding Charter, no head of state may assume direct command of the Portal Authority's military forces without an authorizing majority vote by the rest of the Conclave's members. Do you *really* think Uromathia is popular enough to win that particular contest?"

Rather than the chuckles or smiles Andrin had expected, the Privy Council greeted their emperor's droll assessment with grim scowls and mutters of "Thank Marnilay." That was interesting. There had always been a certain traditional wariness on Ternathia's part where Uromathia was concerned, but the Council's reaction appeared far more pointed than she would have expected, and she made another entry in her growing list: *Find out why Uromathia isn't trusted.*

"Your offer is greatly appreciated, Emperor Chava," First Director Limana said. "I'll put Division-Captain Raynor in touch with your General Staff. And that brings up precisely the point I wished to discuss next. I'm a civilian administrator, not a military officer. Division-Captain Raynor is currently Commandant of the PAAF, and he has plenty of field experience, as well as a thorough familiarity with our current troop dispositions, forts, and supplies. His appointment, unfortunately, is due to expire in two months, at which time he will return to the Republic of Tathawir in New Farnalia. Division-Captain Inar Alvaru of Arpathia is scheduled to hold the commandant's post for the next two years. I mean no offense to Division-Captain Alvaru, or to the Septentrion, but it seems to me that replacing a man who is thoroughly familiar with our current military strengths—and weaknesses—with someone new, right in the middle of a major military crisis, would be . . . unwise. I believe Division-Captain Alvaru would add a valuable voice to our planning, but I strongly recommend keeping Division-Captain Raynor in place as commandant, at least until Division-Captain Alvaru can familiarize himself with our current troop dispositions."

"An extremely wise suggestion," Andrin's father murmured. "Orem Limana's no soldier, but he obviously understands the realities."

Captain of the Army chan Gristhane nodded his agreement from his place at the table, and Yanamar cleared her throat once more and continued Limana's transmission.

"And that brings up another important point," the First Director said. "I'm not at all comfortable making military or political decisions that may affect the very survival of Sharonian civilization. I don't have the training to deal with this kind of emergency. I'm an administrator. I run portals. That's a demanding enough job as it is, and it's going to get immeasurably tougher, trying to move enough men and war materiel to guard our frontier across thousands upon thousands of miles, through portals that will bottleneck our efforts, and through universe after universe of total wilderness.

"I hate to see the Portal Authority militarized, but there are some decisions I'm simply not qualified to make. I need your guidance, so that we don't fumble and open ourselves to the enemy's guns, or whatever it was they were using to blow our people to hell. Tubes that threw fireballs and hurled honest-to-gods *lightning bolts*. We must decide which portal forts to strengthen first, which universes may be safely left unguarded, what kind of equipment to move first, what our construction priorities should be—building railroads to transport weapons and men, building troop transports to cross the water gaps . . . or freighters to haul raw materials and freight across them. Felling timber or building cement factories to construct emergency forts. The list is endless, and, frankly, I have no idea what we should concentrate on as our immediate and long-range priorities.

"We need the sort of military expertise which can identify and assign those priorities. But that's only a *portion* of what we need, and this Conclave—or the next one—must decide how to operate the Portal Authority on a full wartime footing. Who will have the military—and political—authority to make the necessary decisions? Who will direct me—or whoever ends up running the Authority—in prioritizing the Authority's tasks? Who will give militarily and politically appropriate orders for the defense of our people in the field? Nothing in the Authority's existing charter or any of the enabling treaties which created and authorized that charter gives me or any of the Authority Board the power to exercise that sort of authority. Yet *someone* is going to have to do it, so I'm asking you to implement an emergency chain of command, as well as to suggest *long-term* solutions to the problems of command and control."

"My gods," Shamir muttered, running both hands through his silvered hair, and Andrin's father whistled softly.

"Now *there's* a can of worms, if ever I saw one," the emperor said.

"You're not just kidding," Taje growled. "He's talking about a fuc—"

The First Councilor caught himself—this time, at least—glanced at Andrin, turned even redder than before, and cleared his throat loudly.

Someone chuckled softly farther down the conference table, but Taje carefully didn't notice that as he returned his gaze to Zindel.

"He's calling for an honest-to-gods *world government*," he said. "And who the devil is going to head *that?*"

"Not Uromathia," Captain of the Army chan Gristhane growled. "I will be dipped in sheep sh—"

It was his turn to break off midsentence and glance sheepishly at Andrin, who tried very hard not to giggle at the harassed expression on the grizzled old warrior's face.

"I'll go to my grave before I take orders from the likes of Chava Busar," he said after a moment. "And I'm not exaggerating, Your Majesty. I won't tolerate that man giving orders to put *our* soldiers under *his* command."

The emperor's lips quirked.

"I rather imagine this exact same conversation is being repeated in every throne room and president's office in Sharona. 'Nobody but *us*, by the gods!' That," he added in a voice as dry as winter static, glancing at Andrin, "is why it's such a can of worms. As to the, ah, reluctance to swear in front of my daughter, a lady who stands in line for Ternathia's throne will certainly hear a good deal worse than a few off-color remarks. We do her no favors trying to shelter her, or by treating her as though she were delicate. It won't be easy for her, but she's a very strong young woman. I have every confidence in her ability to survive the occasional . . . burst of colorful self-expression, shall we say."

Several of the Privy councilors chuckled this time, and that gave Andrin the courage to ask her first question since the Conclave had begun.

"Thank you, Papa. But may I ask why everyone distrusts Uromathia so intensely?"

Chan Gristhane barked a humorless laugh.

"Give me about twenty years, Your Grand Highness, and I ought to be able to give you a fair basis for it."

"Now, now, Thalyar," her father said mildly, "just because Chava VII has violated every treaty he's ever signed, attempted to confiscate Ternathian shipping while trying to enforce illegal import duties and outrageously inflated harbor fees, been caught red-handed trying to bribe Portal Authority officials, and been linked repeatedly to shady business practices by Uromathian survey crews in half the universes so far discovered, is no reason to threaten *suicide*. You have my word that Ternathia will decline to sign *any* treaty on world governance if the nations of Sharona are temporarily insane enough to elect

Emperor Chava as Sharona's military or political commander during this—or any other—crisis."

Someone snickered farther down the table. Captain of the Army chan Gristhane glowered for a moment, then relented and gave his emperor a sour grin.

"Oh, very well, since you put it that way, Your Majesty." He met Andrin's wide-eyed gaze. "Young lady, if Chava Busar ever offers you a gift, do *whatever it takes* to politely decline it. His gifts have a way of attempting to destroy their recipients."

"I see," she said faintly. "Thank you for the warning, Captain."

Chan Gristhane gave her a tight smile, and her father leaned forward.

"I want to add one further, important point, Andrin. For the most part, Uromathia's subjects are honest, hard-working people who simply want to make a decent living and give their children a good legacy. Uromathia's banking industry has been utterly critical to the development of new universes, and on the whole, Uromathian banks are aboveboard and scrupulously honest. They use fair business practices, they don't discriminate against non-Uromathians, and they don't favor Uromathians over other clients. It's almost always a mistake to blame a whole society for the bad decisions of its rulers."

Andrin thought about that for a moment. Then—

"Even the society that slaughtered our survey crew?" she asked quietly, and her father frowned.

"That remains to be seen. Sharona's own past includes societies that were guilty of rabid xenophobia, which led them to commit what we would consider atrocities by today's standards. I regret to say that some of the worst examples of that xenophobia occurred long after the emergence of the Talents, too.

"We won't know what we're dealing with out there until we learn more. I've always tried to keep an open mind, but I have to admit things look pretty damning at the moment. Whether they remain so is a question only time and additional contact with them can answer."

His face tightened for just an instant with what she knew was an echo of the Glimpses of war and slaughter both of them had Seen. Then he inhaled deeply, harshly.

"My personal gut reaction is to wade into them, guns blazing in retribution." His voice was iron, yet he shook his head at the same time. "But that's precisely why I distrust that reaction. A ruler responsible for hundreds of millions of lives who indulges a personal desire for revenge is a disaster. That sort of response is a surefire recipe for killing a lot of our own people, and frankly squandering the lives of courageous men—and women—selfishly, often for no good or justifiable reason, makes *you* a mass murderer."

Someone down the table hissed through his teeth.

"If, on the other hand, I believed, really *believed*, Andrin, and had the hard evidence to prove to my total satisfaction that the *only* way to ensure the survival of Ternathia—or Sharona—was to wage *genocide*, I would do exactly that. It would rip my soul to shreds, but I would, by all the gods, *do* it. Just as I would fight to the death to stop *others* from committing genocide, if I believed them to be wrong morally and politically. That is what it means to rule. Don't *ever* forget it, Andrin."

His gaze was so intense she felt as if she were on fire. She met it through sheer willpower, scared to the bottoms of her stockings. Scared of the man inside her father's clothes—a man she'd never met before. A man capable of ordering the deaths of millions . . . and implacable enough to stand up to anything and anyone under the gods' heavens who opposed any decision he made.

I can't fill those shoes! her mind gibbered in terror. *I don't even understand the man* wearing *them!*

Then the blazing intensity in his eyes gentled, and he gave her a sad smile.

"I hate frightening you, 'Drin. But it's better for you to know the truth, however brutal, *now*, not months or years down the road, when a misstep on your part could bring catastrophe to the Empire. Janaki has already faced the weight of the crown I wear—that one of *you* will wear in the future. Would to all the gods that I could have let you remain a child just a little longer."

The terror in her breast turned into an ache that made breathing impossible and clogged her throat. The tears she couldn't hold back broke free, filling her with shame for letting them show, for her lack of control . . . for making her father's pain even worse. She wanted to say "I'm sorry," but her throat was too tight, too raw. So she only nodded, hoping he would understand, or at least stop looking at her through eyes filled with remorse she couldn't bear. It cut like a blade, that remorse, yet it came without a hint of apology for the necessity of what he'd said. He couldn't have not said it and continued to be worthy of his crown. She understood that, too . . . and couldn't find the words to tell him that, either.

She had never felt like such a wretched failure in her entire life.

Without a word, he pulled a handkerchief from a coat pocket and passed it down the table. She clutched the square of white linen as though it were a lifeline, drying her eyes and ordering the faucet behind them to stop leaking. Fighting her whole body, which ached with the need to put her head down and bawl like a lost child. Instead, she stiffened her spine, gulped several times, and got herself under control. She very carefully did not look at the distress and sympathy in the faces of the Privy Councilors, for her emotions were too precarious to risk seeing it. Instead, she met her father's gaze head-on once more, and as she did, she felt a new and special kinship with him.

He had experienced exactly this same moment, she realized suddenly, seeing the emperor inside the father ... and the boy who had become the man so long ago. He knew exactly what he was doing to her, what she was enduring—*must* endure—because *his* father had done the same thing to him, and that understanding made it infinitely worse for the father who loved her. And as she looked into his eyes, saw that memory and that pain merged in their depths, she loved him more deeply than she ever had before.

"I'm sorry for disrupting the Conclave yet again, Father," she managed to croak. "It won't happen again."

He didn't embarrass her further by assuring her that it was quite all right, because she knew it wasn't. She desperately wanted her mother ... and knew, without hope of regaining what she had lost, that she would never again be able to hide her face in her mother's shoulder and pretend the world wasn't waiting to hurt her again. In a roomful of people, she felt more alone than she had ever felt in her life as her father nodded and asked the Privy Voice to continue transmitting Director Limana's address.

CHAPTER
TWENTY-FIVE

THE TRAIN FINALLY cleared the congested city of Gulf Point,
situated at the base of the Finger Sea, where the Gulf of
Shurkhal connected that sea with the Harkalan Ocean. Even with the
crown prince's prized locomotive, the journey had required almost
ten hours, and the Voice Conclave had been over for over an hour
by the time they reached the city. Halidar Kinshe felt drained and
exhausted, although he'd actually said very little during the Conclave
itself. Wilkon had kept him and the crown prince fully informed,
and, if he was going to be honest, Kinshe had to admit that it
had gone far better than he'd feared. But the generally ugly mood
of the attending heads of state had not filled him with optimism.
Worse, they'd resonated with his own grinding sense of responsibility
and blazing need for retribution, and his mood was heavy as they
approached their destination at last.

The Gulf's busy shipping lanes carried freighters laden with goods
from around the globe, making Gulf Point one of the busiest ports
in the world. It took time to thread their way through the jammed
city, swinging around the southwestern-most point of land to head
east toward the little town where Shaylar had gone to school. It lay
only thirty miles farther down the coast, but the sun had settled
well into the west as the special train pulled into the small local
station at last and the prince's carriage was unloaded.

It took a little longer to get the cavalry escort's mounts off-loaded,
as well, before they could set out to the Institute, and they drew
curious stares from the townfolk, who recognized the royal crest on
the carriage. Kinshe could see excited conversations springing up in
their wake as people speculated about this unannounced royal visit,
but they rode in absolute silence as they followed the road through

town and out beyond it. The Cetacean Institute was visible now, another three miles ahead.

Kinshe hadn't visited this part of Shurkhal in years—decades, to be more exact. He'd stood on this shoreline as a very junior member of Shurkhal's Parliament, celebrating the opening of Shurkhal's own Cetacean Institute—the kingdom's sole cetacean translation facility. Part embassy, but mostly research station, the Institute had been founded by Dr. Shalassar Kolmayr-Brintal. Although Shalassar was not a native-born daughter of Shurkhal, she had built a legacy in which the entire kingdom could take pride.

Thanks to her work, the dolphins had led Shurkhali divers to rich pearl beds which might have lain undiscovered for centuries, otherwise. Shurkhali pearls fetched excellent prices on the world market, famous for their size and luster, and Shurkhali explorers had laid claim to those same pearl beds in other universes, as well, increasing the kingdom's prestige while providing income to establish Shurkhali colonies.

All of Shurkhal knew who they truly had to thank for that, and Shurkhalis had long since come to recognize Shalassar Kolmayr-Brintal as one of their own, even though she had been born on one of the tiny island chains scattered across the Western Ocean. The Western was Sharona's largest body of water, more than nine thousand miles long, north to south, and nearly ten thousand miles wide along the equator. Most of its islands were governed by the Lissian Republic, whose main landmass was the continent-sized island that was home to some of the strangest creatures on Sharona.

Shalassar had grown up on one of those Lissian-governed islands. She was a tremendously Talented telepath, whose childhood friends had been dolphins and the great whales that roamed the Western Ocean. She had come to Shurkhal to establish the Institute as one of a worldwide chain of embassies serving the sentient whales and dolphins.

They were close enough now to see the large dock and the enormous area which had been roped off around it to serve as the official embassy. A large bell hung from a pole on the dock, with a stout cable that trailed into the water. That bell was a necessary signaling device. Kinshe had heard that she'd had to replace it—and the dock—occasionally when an emissary from a new pod of whales approached to ask for assistance and gave the cable too hard a tug the first try. Shalassar Kolmayr-Brintal simply took it all in stride, as she had everything else in her life.

Until now, at least, he thought, biting his lip.

No one was at home in the house. A note on the door said: "We're at the embassy. Come on down, the water's fine!"

Kinshe's heart twisted as he read the cheerful words, and he looked at his wife. She was biting *her* lip now, and he took her hand as they climbed back into the carriage and followed the road around to the cluster of buildings at the water's edge, half a mile from the house. Outside the carriage, the silence was glorious, broken only by the wind and the heartbeat-rushing of the sea against the shore. Inside the carriage, the silence was oppressive, as heavy as a storm brewing on the horizon, broken only by the knife-sharp rattle of horses' hooves on the graveled drive.

"Hal," Alimar murmured, squeezing his hand. She started to say something more, then simply closed her lips and fell silent again. She'd tried to convince him on the train that this wasn't his fault. She'd tried hard . . . and she would still be trying when he lay on his deathbed.

The carriage clattered to a halt in front of the Institute's main administration building. The footman scrambled to open the door, and this time the crown prince climbed down first and handed Alimar to the ground. Kinshe followed, and Wilkon climbed out last.

The Institute's front door opened and Shalassar Kolmayr-Brintal herself hurried out into the sunlight, eyes wide with surprise as her glance flicked across the royal crest on the carriage door.

"Your Highness!" she said, clearly astonished to see the crown prince. "And Representative Kinshe," she added, as she dropped into the deep curtsy she had learned in the years since arriving on the shores. Shaylar was very much a miniature of this woman, whose Lissian island heritage showed in her honey-toned skin and the sleek black hair falling straight as a waterfall down her back. It was tinted here and there with strands of pure silver, but those were the only signs of age Kinshe could detect. It was obvious that their arrival had taken her completely by surprise, but she was trying not to show it, and her immense natural dignity helped.

"Forgive me for not sending word ahead to expect our visit," Danith Fyysel said gently. The final decision had been his, although Kinshe had been in total agreement. They could have asked Wilkon to alert her and her husband, but they'd chosen to remain silent rather than alarm and worry them hours in advance. Now the crown prince took her hand, lifting her from the deep curtsy, and made introductions.

"You know Representative Kinshe, I know," he said. "Allow me to present his wife, Alimar Kinshe-Falis, and Samari Wilkon, a senior

Voice of the Portal Authority." He finished the formalities, then inhaled deeply. "My father asked me to accompany Representative Kinshe and Voice Wilkon today. I must ask, is your husband home, Doctor?"

Shalassar's eyebrows rose, and she looked back and forth between Kinshe and the crown prince.

"Yes, he—" she began, then broke off abruptly. She stared into Crown Prince Danith's eyes, and the color seemed to drain out of her face.

"Something's wrong, isn't it?" she said tautly. "Something's happened."

Danith squared his shoulders, but Halidar Kinshe took a small step forward before the crown prince could speak. He wished profoundly that someone else could have brought this news, but it was his job, and no one else's.

"We've brought a message, Doctor. A very urgent and important message. We need to deliver it to both you and your husband."

Shalassar had pressed her hands against her cheeks. The long, slender fingers were unsteady.

"It's Shayl, isn't it? Something's happened to my little Shayl. . . ."

Her lips trembled, and her huge, expressive eyes were dark with shadows. It was a mark of just how distressed she was that she'd used the pre-marriage form of her daughter's name. She stared at Kinshe for several more seconds, then turned away, started for the Institute, stopped, and turned back to them.

"Come in, please," she said in a faint voice. "Come in out of the sun. You must be frightfully hot and thirsty from your journey. I'll have my assistant bring some cool water, some fruit . . ."

Alimar bit her lip again and tightened her fingers around Kinshe's as Shalassar tried desperately to cling to the proper conventions. They followed her into the Institute's main lobby, such as it was. The administration building was mostly office space, with a small antechamber where infrequent guests could wait for the two or three minutes necessary to track down the director.

Wide open windows caught the sea breeze, carrying the unmistakable scent of deep ocean water into the thick-walled room. It was pleasantly cool, despite the fierce heat outside. Just offshore lay the floating dock and the bell. The colorfully painted floats holding up the rope around the dock's reserved approaches hurt his eyes as the afternoon sunlight slanted fiercely across them. They hurt his heart, as well, as he contemplated his reason for being here. It was monstrous to bring such news to this beautiful place.

The promised assistant arrived with the refreshments while Shalassar went out to fetch her husband. She could have simply spoken to him with her mind, since both of them were strong telepaths who shared the even closer communication possible through their marriage bond, but she went to find him in person. No doubt, Kinshe thought, in hopes of regaining her shattered composure before she had to face them once again.

He sipped water gratefully, but he couldn't even nibble at the succulent orange slices or sweet palm dates on the platter. His stomach rebelled at the mere thought of food, and Wilkon didn't touch the fruit, either. The Voice's eyes showed his own inner agitation, which was far worse even than Kinshe's. Kinshe knew what message they were here to deliver, but he was no telepath. Wilkon was, and the Farnalian had actually experienced it himself already.

Then Shalassar returned with her husband in tow. Thaminar Kolmayr, like most full-blooded Shurkhali, was a slender man, neither tall nor short, but lean and tough as old leather. Despite his strong telepathic Talent, he had chosen to remain on his family's land as a farmer and livestock breeder, rather than seek a position as a registered Voice. His skin was the weathered, furrowed brown of those who spent lifetimes laboring in the fierce desert sun, and he was possessed of all his people's personal dignity and presence. He greeted his crown prince with a deep, formal bow; then met Kinshe's gaze head-on. Muscles bunched in his jaw under his dark, close-trimmed beard.

"Come into the office," he said, his voice rough. "We'll talk there."

They stepped into a room which reflected its owner's life as much as the work done here. Island artwork hung on the walls, reminders of Shalassar's girlhood home, but file cabinets took up most of the wall space, their wooden cases carefully oiled against the dry desert air. A desk in one corner looked almost like an afterthought, a concession to the need for orderly workspace to record the conversations with various cetaceans, the dissertations written by various transient students over the years, research data, published articles and books, even—and perhaps most important—treaties that governed Sharona's relationship with their sentient, aquatic neighbors.

Even as that thought crossed his mind, Kinshe saw several sleek, wet hides break the surface, visible through the office window, punctuated by the hiss of cetaceans surfacing to breathe. Given their size, he surmised that a pod of dolphins had come calling, although one or two might have been larger. It was hard for him to tell.

Then Shaylar's father closed the door, and Kinshe turned his attention to repeating the introductions. Thaminar Kolmayr and his wife stood together, arms wrapped around one another, even their free hands gripping one another's. Two strong telepaths, fused for the moment into one terrified personality staring at him with parents' eyes.

"What is it?" Thaminar asked, his voice even rougher than before. "What's gone so wrong that the king sends his heir and a royal representative to deliver the bad news?"

"There's been an incident—" Kinshe began, then paused, cursing his own cowardice, and amended his phrasing. "An act of war has been committed against Sharonian citizens. I'm desperately sorry to bring such news. The Portal Authority Director has asked Voice Wilkon to deliver the last message your daughter transmitted."

Shalassar's knees buckled at the dreadful word "last." She clutched at her husband, nostrils flared, eyes clenched shut, and he eased her into a chair. He crouched beside her, wrapping his arm around her while she shuddered, and lifted angry wounded eyes to meet Kinshe's.

"What you mean by that, Kinshe? *An act of war?*"

"Exactly that, Sir," Kinshe made himself reply as levelly as possible. "We don't have very many details yet, but Shaylar's team ran into an unknown human civilization—a violently hostile one, apparently. Her first message reported that one of their crew had been shot by an unknown assailant. They ran for the nearest portal. They didn't make it."

Shalassar began to weep, her breath ragged, her wet face twisted with grief, and Kinshe steeled himself to tell them the rest.

"Her second and final message was sent less than two hours after the first. Because of a transmission delay, it overtook the first, and both of them arrived at the Authority simultaneously this morning."

He cleared his throat.

"There might be survivors. It's not much of a hope," he added quickly, hating to crush the sudden wild hope in her parents' eyes, "but the nearest fort has sent out a rescue party. On the chance that somebody survived the second attack. It's—"

He had to pause, had to swallow hard. He wasn't a telepath himself, but even the secondhand description had been brutal.

"It's very unlikely that anyone lived," he said softly, levelly. "But we're going to find the people who did this, and we're going to find out whether or not they took prisoners. And there *will* be payment for it," he added in a voice which sounded like a stranger's. "We—the Portal Authority Director, King Fyysel and Crown Prince Danith,

Alimar and myself—we wanted you to receive your daughter's last message before we go public with this.

"Sharona's world leaders have already met in a Voice Conclave today, to decide how Sharona will respond to the crisis. That will be reported on, even if we tried to keep it quiet, and know that when reporters know there's been a Conclave, they're going to start asking why. We wanted to be certain that *you* were told before that happened."

Shaylar's mother lifted her face, and her voice was brittle.

"And how will Sharona's leaders respond?"

Halidar Kinshe drew a deep breath and told her. When he mentioned the high probability that Sharona's military would be drastically expanded, Shaylar's parents went pale again. He wasn't surprised. He knew very well that Shaylar's military-age brothers would shortly discover a burning reason to volunteer for combat.

"I'm sorry," he said gently. "I could introduce legislation barring enlistment of every single son from one family. It might well pass . . . but even that might not deter them from enlisting under false names."

Shaylar's father held his gaze for long moments, then shook his head.

"No, it wouldn't," he said gruffly. "My sons are too much like me to expect anything different of them. But thank you for considering our fear, for offering to help. It was a great kindness. What it would cost us if they—"

He halted, unable to go on, and a ghastly silence hovered until Crown Prince Danith broke it.

"My father begged me to bring you a personal message from His Majesty. With your permission, I'll deliver it now, not . . . after the Voice has given you the message he carries."

Dr. Kolmayr-Brintal's throat worked. She tightened her fingers around her husband's already firm grip and seemed to settle even deeper into the straight-backed chair.

"Go on," she said in a voice of gravel.

"His Majesty wants you to know that he will never stop the search for your daughter, will never rest until answers, at least, are found. Shurkhal is raising troops, as agreed upon in today's Conclave. Those troops will have one order, above and beyond all else: find Shaylar Nargra-Kolmayr . . . or the people who killed her."

Shaylar's mother flinched, and his face tightened.

"I'm sorry," he said in a voice raw with his own pain, "but we must face the likelihood that she's gone and act accordingly."

He drew a deep breath and continued.

"The people of our Kingdom will feel this loss deeply, as a wound not just to our national pride, but to our national heart. His Majesty begs you to remember that your daughter was loved by millions—and so you shall be, when this news is released. His Majesty knows how desperately private your grief will be, so he has made arrangements to send a small full-time staff to you, to handle the response when people are told. If there's some small office, perhaps here at the Institute, where they could work out of your way, they'll take charge of all that, giving you the privacy you need and dealing with the chaos for you. Is that acceptable to you?"

Shaylar's parents only stared at him, too shellshocked to respond. Perhaps, Kinshe thought, neither of them had fully understood until that moment how deeply proud of their daughter all of Shurkhal had felt—and how keenly the Kingdom would feel her loss. Even those who hadn't approved of her taking on a "man's job" in the first place . . . or perhaps, in their way, *especially* those who hadn't approved.

Her father unfroze first.

"That isn't—that is—Do you really think this is necessary?"

"Yes, Sir," Crown Prince Danith said quietly, putting the concern he felt into every word. "I *do* believe it will be necessary. So does His Majesty."

"I agree," Kinshe added quietly. "Your family will become the focus of all Sharona's shock and outrage. We—the king, Parliament, the entire kingdom—cannot leave you to face this alone, unprepared to deal with what will come when word of this is released. What we're offering to do, to handle the uproar for you, isn't much—not nearly enough, compared with the magnitude of your loss. But you will need someone who can deal with all of that. Please let us help, even in so small a way."

Shalassar nodded, her head moving like a broken marionette's. Thaminar simply looked lost, a strong man whose grief and anger had been punctured by something he couldn't understand. Something he feared. His gaze—which had gone to a place very far from this small room with its wooden file cases, its thick walls and open window, the scent and sight and sound of the sea—gradually pulled itself back and focused on the king's heir.

"Very well," he said, his voice low and hollow. "If more trouble must fall across our shoulders, it will be restful to have someone help us carry the weight." Kinshe sensed a gathering of strength within him, or perhaps merely a gathering of the shreds of courage. Then he turned to the Voice.

"You have a message from our child?"

"I do." Wilkon's voice was thick with pain. "I beg your forgiveness, both of you, for what I am about to show you."

Shaylar's parents' hands gripped tighter even than before, tight enough for knuckles to whiten and tremble.

"Show us," Thaminar said hoarsely.

They closed their eyes, and for an instant—perhaps two heartbeats, certainly no longer—nothing happened.

Then, as one person, they flinched violently back. Kinshe couldn't even begin to describe the sound that broke from Shaylar's mother. It was like cloth ripping, or a whimper . . . or something soft dying under the wheels of the train. He couldn't bear to look at them, yet couldn't wrench his gaze away from the sweat, the muscle-knotting agony, the—

A sudden scream ripped into his awareness, and not from Shaylar's parents. It came from outside—from beyond the window. From the sea . . .

Kinshe whipped around to stare out the window. The sea inside the floating ropes that marked the cetacean's embassy had gone mad. The dolphins surged from the water, fifty or sixty of them rising on their tail flukes, and the sound that broke from them turned his blood to ice. Then a deeper bellow broke across the chittering snarls, and a whale broached. Larger than the crown prince's train car, it roared out of the water, standing for just an instant on its own tail fluke, a mountain of glistening flesh spearing straight toward the desert sky. Sound exploded into the air, a shockwave of sound that struck Kinshe's bones through the open window like a fist. Water crashed outward from its massive weight as it came down again, and the dock and bell splintered under the impact.

A humpback, he realized through numb shock. *One of the singing whales.* Only that was no whalesong bursting from it. That was *rage*. Pure, distilled, and terrible rage.

Gods, Kinshe realized. Shaylar's mother was broadcasting what she saw. She probably didn't even realize it, but the cetaceans did, and he jerked his gaze back to her. She was shuddering, eyes clenched tightly shut, her sounds like those of some small, trapped animal. Then she stiffened, and her eyes flew wide.

"*Shaylar!*" she screamed, and her husband flinched so violently he nearly went to the floor. Then Shalassar collapsed. She sagged in her chair, her head falling forward in merciful unconsciousness.

Kinshe stared at her, his eyes burning, and took a single step forward.

"*Stay away from her!*" Thaminar snarled.

His eyes were burnt wounds in his face, and he bent over his wife, stroking hair back from her wet face and murmuring her name over and over. Fragile eyelids fluttered. Opened. For long moments, there was no sense in Shalassar's eyes at all. Then remembrance struck like a crack of thunder, and she began to weep. She sobbed, the sound deep and jagged, while her husband cradled her close, looking utterly bereft.

Kinshe could only stand there, feeling a tear trickle down his own cheek, wondering what to do. What anyone *could* do. And then—

"You men, out," Alimar Kinshe-Falis said firmly to her husband, her crown prince, and Samari Wilkon, and it was an order, not a request. "Go. Find something to do—I don't care what. Just go."

She didn't even look at them. She simply marched across the tiny office, gathered Shaylar's mother into her arms, and turned to Shaylar's father.

"Go and get some brandy, if you have any," she commanded. "Wine, if you don't. She needs it."

To Kinshe's infinite surprise, Thaminar rose without a sound of protest and left the office, like a ghost walking through terrain it can no longer see or touch. Kinshe watched him go, and then he understood.

He needed to feel useful. Needed to do something for his wife. He just didn't know how.

Halidar Kinshe's respect for his wife, already high, soared to dizzying heights, and he tiptoed very softly from the room, beckoning the others to follow.

Alimar clearly understood what needed to be done far better than he did, so he left her to do it.

CHAPTER
TWENTY-SIX

CHIEF SWORD OTWAL Threbuch moved through the darkness like a ghost.

He *felt* like a ghost must feel—cold, empty inside, and incredibly ancient. He shouldn't have been alive, and after what he'd seen, there was a part of him which wished he wasn't. He told himself that was exactly the kind of thinking he'd spent decades hammering out of raw recruits who'd heard too many stupid heroic ballads, but that did nothing to soften the pain. Or his sense of guilt.

He'd lain on that limb, watching, helpless to intervene as the portal defenders were cut to pieces. He'd been as surprised as anyone when the enemy artillery opened fire *through* the portal, and he had no doubt that the shock of that totally unanticipated bombardment explained how quickly Charlie Company—*his* company—had been slaughtered. But it wasn't the full explanation, and deep in his heart of hearts, Otwal Threbuch cursed Hadrign Thalmayr even more bitterly than he had Shevan Garlath.

He'd known what was coming the instant that idiotic, incompetent, *stupid* excuse for a hundred opened fire on someone obviously seeking a parley. He'd recognized Thalmayr, of course, and the moment he'd seen the other hundred, he'd also recognized the answer to his questions about Hundred Olderhan's apparent lapse into idiocy. Not that his relief over the fact that Sir Jasak's brain hadn't stopped working after all had made what had happened to Threbuch's company any less agonizing.

Every ounce of the chief sword's body and soul had cried out for him to *do* something as the debacle unfolded. But the steel-hard professionalism of his years of service had held him precisely where he was, because there'd been nothing he *could* do. Nothing that

would have made any difference at all to the men cursing, screaming, and dying in front of him. It might have made him feel a bit
better to try, might have spared him from this crushing load of guilt
at having survived—so far, at least. But that was all it could have
accomplished, whereas the information he already possessed might
yet accomplish a great deal, if he could only report it. Besides, as
far as he knew, he was the only uncaptured survivor from the entire
company, which meant he was also the only chance to report to Five
Hundred Klian what had happened.

He clenched his jaw, eyes burning, as he reflected on everything
he had to report, including the death of Emiyet Borkaz.

Borkaz had been unable to force himself to sit out the fight.
When the desperate survivors had launched their hopeless charge in
a despairing bid to get their own support weapons to this side of
the portal, Borkaz had left his cover and run madly towards them,
screaming and cursing. He'd managed to get most of the way through
the trees before he was spotted, and Threbuch thought he'd managed to kill at least one of the enemy on the way through (which
was more than *Threbuch* had managed), as well. And then at least
three of those hideous thunder weapons had struck him almost
simultaneously. He must have been dead before he hit the ground,
Threbuch thought grimly.

But at least the enemy could make mistakes, too. The fact that
Borkaz had obviously come from behind them ought to have set off a
search for whoever *else* might be behind them, as well. On the other
hand, perhaps he was being too hard on them. Given the nature of
the terrain, they might not realize where Borkaz had come from at
all. They might think he'd come from the swamp side of the portal
and simply gotten farther than any of the rest.

The chief sword froze abruptly. Something had moved, and he
stood motionless, straining his eyes and ears. There!

The enemy sentry hadn't moved very much at all. Probably nothing more than easing a cramped limb. But it had been enough, and
Threbuch slid silently, silently to his right, giving the other man a
wider berth.

Part of him was intensely tempted to do something else. His
arbalest would have been all but inaudible under cover of the night
wind sighing in the trees. For that matter, he probably could have
gotten close enough to slit the other man's throat. It was something
he'd done before, and the thought of managing at least that much
vengeance for Charlie Company burned within him like a coal. But
his job wasn't to kill one, or two, or even a dozen enemies, however

personally satisfying it might have been. His job was to get home with the most deadly weapon in any universe—information—and if he left any dead bodies in his wake, the enemy would *know* at least one Arcanan had gotten away. They'd also know how important his report might be, and a dead sentry would set off a relentless search he might well fail to evade.

He felt the moment of transition as he belly-crawled across the portal threshold, moving instantly from autumnal chill into steamy tropical heat, and he fought down a sudden sense of release, of safety. Any soldier with an ounce of competence—which, unfortunately, these bastards certainly appeared to have—would have sentries on *both* sides of the portal.

He kept going, easing forward, working his way cautiously through the dense swamp grass and mud at one edge of the portal and praying that he didn't startle some nesting swamp bird into sudden, raucous flight.

Somehow, he managed to avoid that, and to creep silently behind the one additional sentry he did spot on the swamp side of the portal, silhouetted against the moon. It took him almost three hours to cover a total distance of little more than another eight hundred yards, but he made it. And once the wrecked base camp was a quarter-mile behind him, he rose to his feet at last, got out his PC, activated the search and navigation spellware, took a careful bearing on Fort Rycharn, and started walking. The thought of hiking seven hundred-plus miles across snake- and croc-infested swamp, without any rations at all, was scarcely appealing, but he couldn't think of anything better to do.

*   *   *

Just over an hour later, Threbuch stiffened in astonishment. He froze instantly, listening to the night, and looked down at his PC. The crystal's glassy heart glowed dimly, its illumination level deliberately set low enough to keep anyone from seeing it at a distance of more than a very few feet, and the chief sword's eyes widened as he saw the small, sharp-edged carat strobing at one side of the circular navigation display.

He stood very still for several more moments, watching, but the carat was equally motionless. After a moment, the noncom turned towards his right, rotating until the strobing carat and the green arrowhead indicating his own course lined up with one another. Then he moved slowly, cautiously, forward through the currently knee-deep swamp.

The carat strobed more and more rapidly, and then, abruptly, it stopped blinking and burned a steady, unwinking green.

Threbuch stopped, as well, standing in a dense, dark patch of shadow in the lee of a cluster of scrub trees growing out of the swamp. The combination of moonlight, shadow, and swamp grass rippling in the wind created a wavering sea of eye-bewildering movement, and he cleared his throat.

"Who's there?" he asked sharply.

"*Chief Sword?*" a hoarse voice gasped. "Gods above, where've you *been?*"

"Great thundering bollocks—*Iggy?*"

"Yes, Chief."

Threbuch watched in disbelief as Iggar Shulthan crawled cautiously out of the scrub trees. The other Scout's silhouette looked misshapen, and Threbuch's eyes went even wider as he realized what Shulthan had strapped to his back.

"Gods!" the chief sword half-whispered in the reverent voice of the man who'd suddenly discovered there truly were miracles. "You've got the *hummers!*"

The company's hummer handler reached out. Threbuch extended his hand, and Shulthan gripped it so hard the bones ached. The younger noncom's face was muddy, and even in the uncertain moonlight, Threbuch could see the memories of the horror Shulthan had witnessed in his eyes. Or perhaps he couldn't, the chief sword reflected. Perhaps he simply knew they had to be there because he knew they were in his own eyes.

"I-I ran, Chief." Shame hovered in the javelin's voice. "I grabbed the hummers, like Regs said, and ran with 'em. I *ran*, Chief!"

Tears hovered in Shulthan's voice, and Threbuch released his hand to grip both of the younger man's shoulders hard.

"Son, you did *exactly* the right thing," he said. "Don't you *ever* doubt that! Those regulations were written for damned good reasons. You're the Company's link with the rest of the Army. When the shit hits the fan, and the bottom falls out, *somebody's* got to get word back. The hummer handler's the only man who can do it."

"But the hundred never gave me the order," Shulthan whispered, blinking hard. "He went down so fast, and they were dropping us like flies, and—"

"I know, Iggy," Threbuch said more gently. "I was trapped on their side of the portal. I had to sit there and watch it all, because my recon report for Five Hundred Klian is every bit as critical as yours." Threbuch found it abruptly necessary to swallow hard a few times. "That was the hardest thing I've ever had to do—*ever*. So don't think for a minute I don't understand exactly what you're feeling right now, Iggy."

The younger man nodded wordlessly, and the chief sword gave his shoulders another squeeze before he released them, stood back, and cleared his throat roughly.

"So, do you think anyone else got out?"

"No, Chief." Shulthan shook his head. "I haven't seen anyone. Not even *them*."

"I haven't seen any signs of pursuit, either," Threbuch said with a nod, although that wasn't exactly what he'd asked. He'd already known Shulthan was alone. Unlike the hummer handler's PC, the chief sword's carried specialized spellware which could give him the bearing to any of his company's personnel within five hundred yards. Bringing up the S&N spellware had automatically activated the locator function, thank the gods! But because of that, he'd known none of their other people were within a quarter mile of his current location. He'd simply hoped—prayed—that Shulthan might have seen someone else get out. Someone else who might be hiding out here, beyond the spellware's reach, trying to make his own way back to the coast.

"Where's Borkaz, Chief?" Shulthan asked after a moment, and Threbuch's jaw tightened.

"Didn't make it." He shook his head and started to explain, then stopped himself. Shulthan's anguish at having cut and run while his friends died behind him was only too obvious. He didn't need to be told how Borkaz had died running in the "right" direction. Not, at least, until he had enough separation from his own actions to realize just how stupid Borkaz's had been.

"All right," the chief sword continued after a moment. "Have you already sent back a hummer?"

"No, Chief." Shulthan shook his head. "I've just been running and hiding," he admitted in a shamefaced tone.

"Don't think I've been doing anything else since it happened," Threbuch said, shaking his head. The chief sword looked at the sky. The night was at least half over, he reflected.

"We need to send one back now, though," he continued. "It's going to take the rest of the night just to reach the coast, and we need to let Five Hundred Klian know what's happened. Come to that, we need to set up an LZ for them to pull us out of here, too."

"Yes, Chief."

Threbuch looked down at his PC again, trying to decide on the best spot. He didn't want a dragon within miles of the base camp. Gods alone only knew how far those bastards could throw whatever they'd used for artillery!

His empty stomach rumbled painfully while he was thinking, and he glanced at Shulthan again.

"You wouldn't happen to have anything to *eat* on you, would you, Iggy?" he asked, and blinked as Shulthan actually chuckled.

"Matter of fact, Chief, I managed to grab my whole pack. I've got a couple of blocks of emergency rats."

"Iggy, it's too bad you're not a woman," Threbuch said with the fervor of a man who hasn't eaten in well over twenty-four hours. "Or maybe it isn't. If you were, I'd have to marry you, and you're ugly as sin." The chief sword looked back down at his PC, picked the coordinates he needed, and then glanced back up at Shulthan. "Let's get that hummer on its way. Then lead me to those rations and stand back."

* * *

"Is a . . . unicorn," Shaylar said in slow, carefully enunciated Andaran.

"Yes, exactly!" Gadrial replied in the same language with a broad smile. She leaned closer to the breathtakingly lifelike image displayed above the gleaming crystal on her tiny desk and indicated the booted and spurred man standing beside the beast in an anachronistic-looking steel breastplate. "And this?"

"Is a war-rider," Shaylar said firmly. Gadrial nodded once more, and Shaylar smiled back at her. Then she glanced at Jathmar, sitting beside her on the unused bed in the quarters which had been assigned to Gadrial, and felt her smile fade around the edges as she tasted his reaction to the imagery Gadrial was showing them through the marriage bond.

The coal-black creature Gadrial had just informed her was called a "unicorn" was unlike anything either of them had ever seen before, yet it was close enough to familiar to make it even more disturbing than something as totally alien as a dragon. The beast was roughly horse-sized and shaped, except for the legs, which were proportionately too long, and the improbably powerful looking hindquarters. But no horse had ever had those long, furry, bobcatlike ears, or that short, powerful neck, or the long, deadly-looking tusks—like something from some huge, wild boar—and obviously carnivorous teeth. Or the long, ivory horn which must have been close to a yard in length. And then there were the eyes. Huge green eyes with purple irises and catlike slitted pupils.

Jathmar, she decided, had a point. Compared to that bizarre, opium-dream improbability, the half-armored cavalry trooper standing beside it with his lance and saber looked downright homely.

"Your words?" Gadrial asked, and Shaylar looked back at the images and shrugged.

"No word," she said, pointing at the 'unicorn' and grimacing. Then she pointed at the man standing beside it. "Cavalryman," she said, and watched the squiggles of Gadrial's alphabet appear briefly under the image.

"Good. Thank you," Gadrial said, and touched the small wandlike stylus in her hand to the crystal-clear sphere of her "PC." The image changed obediently, and this time it showed something Shaylar and Jathmar recognized immediately.

"This," Gadrial said "is called an 'elephant.'"

*   *   *

Gadrial watched her "students" studying the floating picture of the elephant and tried to keep her bemusement at their rate of progress from showing.

She'd almost forgotten that she had the language spellware package with her. It wasn't something she'd ever used before, but it had come as a standard component of the "academic" package an enterprising vendor had managed to sell the Garth Showma Institute a year or so before. Gadrial had been perfectly happy with the previous package's general capabilities—most of the spellware she used in her own work was the product of her own department at the Academy, or at least so highly customized that it bore very little relationship to its original form—but the Academy had insisted on providing the new and improved spellware to all its faculty members. She'd been more than mildly irritated at the time, since she probably would never use more than twenty percent of the total applications and the changeover had required her to become familiar with the new package's idiosyncrasies (which were, as always, many). But she'd long since learned not to waste energy fighting over the little things, and it wasn't exactly as if the bundled spells providing all the useless bells and whistles she'd never need were going to use up a critical amount of her PC's memory.

Over the last four days, though, she'd actually found herself deeply and profoundly grateful for the white elephant with which the Academy's administration had lumbered her. She'd thought she remembered something in the manual about language and translation spellware. After their arrival at Fort Rycharn, she'd hauled out the documentation and, sure enough, she had a comprehensive translation spell package, capable of both literal and figurative translations between any Arcanan languages. More importantly, under the circumstances, it also included what she thought of as a "Learn Ransaran in Your Spare Time" spell platform for people who preferred to master those other languages for themselves, rather than relying upon magical translations. Of course, it couldn't simply magically stick another language inside someone else's head, but it was well designed to introduce that language to a new student in a carefully structured format. The people who'd put it together had assumed—not unreasonably—that their students would speak at least one of Arcana's languages, which created quite a few problems of its own, but it had still provided her with an invaluable basis from which to begin teaching Shaylar and Jathmar Andaran.

She hadn't even considered teaching them Ransaran, for several reasons. First, even though it sometimes irked her to admit it, Ransaran wasn't an easy language to learn. There were those, especially in Mythal, who were wont to refer to Ransaran as a "bastardized mongrelization," and she couldn't really dispute the characterization. Ransaran was riddled with irregular verb forms, homonyms, synonyms, irregular spellings, nonstandard pronunciations, and appropriations from every other major language. One of her friends at the Academy had a T-shirt which proclaimed that "Ransaran doesn't *borrow* from other languages. It follows other languages down dark alleys, knocks them on the head, and goes through their pockets for loose grammar." Over the centuries, Gadrial cheerfully admitted, Ransaran had done precisely that . . . which was why it was unparalleled for concision, flexibility, and adaptiveness. Indeed, she'd heard it argued that the notorious Ransaran flexibility and innovativeness stemmed directly from the semantic and syntactic responsiveness of the Ransaran language.

But it *was* a difficult language to learn, even for another Arcanan.

Andaran, on the other hand, was a very *easy* language to learn, although she'd always found its tendency to create new words by compounding existing ones rather cumbersome compared to the Ransaran practice of simply coining new words . . . or stealing someone else's and giving them purely Ransaran meanings. It had virtually no irregular verbs and very few homonyms, and a completely consistent phonetic spelling. If you could pronounce an Andaran word, you could spell it correctly.

And it was the official language of the Arcanan Army. Not surprisingly, she supposed, given that seventy to eighty percent of the Arcanan military was also Andaran.

Gadrial had actually become quite fond of Andaran during her years in Garth Showma with Magister Halathyn. It might not be the most flexible language imaginable, but it was far more flexible than the various Mythalan dialects. Actually, Mythalan was probably the most precise of any of the Arcanan language groups, which lent itself well to the exact expression of nuance and meaning required by high-level arcane research. But its very precision made it inflexible. It didn't lend itself at all well to improvisation or adaptiveness, which Gadrial had often thought had a lot to do with the preservation of Mythal's reactionary, xenophobic society and its caste structure.

Andaran was much less . . . *frozen* than that, and she had to admit that it had a rolling majesty all its own, well suited to oratory and poetry. In fact, it was quite beautiful, and she'd become a devotee of ancient Andaran literature. There were still plenty of things about Andara that she found the next best thing to totally incomprehensible. The entire society was, after all, a military aristocracy—or perhaps it would actually be more accurate to say military *autocracy*—with strict codes of honor and lines of responsibility, obligation, and duty, while *she* was one of those deplorably individualistic Ransarans. Most of the Andaran honor code continued to baffle her, but the ancient heroic sagas often brought her to the edge of feeling as if she *ought* to understand Andara.

In this instance, however, the fact that it was the Union of Arcana's official military language carried more weight than any other single factor. Eventually, as she was certain Shaylar and Jathmar were well aware, the military was going to insist on talking to them.

Despite the unanticipated advantage the language spellware provided, Gadrial had expected the teaching process to be clumsy and time-consuming, at least at first. Shaylar, however, had an almost uncanny gift for languages. Her accent was odd, lending the sonorous Arcanan words and phrases a musical overtone that was as pleasant to the ear as it was unusual, but her ability to pick up the language was astounding. She was clearly much better at it than Jathmar, and although it was still going to be some time before she started building complex sentences and using compound verb forms, her basic ability to communicate was growing by leaps and bounds.

In fact, Gadrial had come to the conclusion that there was more than a mere natural ear for language involved in the process. It had become abundantly clear to her that Magister Halathyn had been correct in his initial assessment that Shaylar and Jathmar's people had never even heard of anything remotely like magic. And yet there was something about Shaylar . . .

Gadrial hadn't forgotten that bizarre moment on Windclaw's back, when she'd understood beyond any possibility of doubt that Shaylar was begging her to get the dragon "out of her head." When Gadrial added that to the tiny woman's obvious and exquisite sensitivity to the moods and emotions of those about her, plus Shaylar's breathtaking language skills, the only explanation she could come up with was that Shaylar truly did have some strange talent—almost the equivalent of a Gift, perhaps. Gadrial wasn't prepared even to speculate on how that "Gift" might work, and she'd kept her suspicions about it to herself, but she'd become more and more firmly convinced that whatever it was, it existed.

And she was taking advantage of it for more than one purpose. Not only was she teaching Shaylar and Jathmar Andaran, but she was simultaneously building up a vocabulary of *their* language, as well. They understood exactly what she was doing, and they clearly weren't exactly delighted by the thought, but they equally obviously understood—and accepted—that it was inevitable.

Somewhat to her own surprise, Gadrial had found the language lessons a soothing distraction while she and Jasak awaited Chief Sword Threbuch's return. What didn't surprise her a bit was that she *needed* that distraction, and not just because of Threbuch. She still couldn't stop fretting about Magister Halathyn and his obstinate refusal to show enough common sense to accept that he had no business at all that close to the swamp portal under the present circumstances. She'd told herself repeatedly that she was probably being too alarmist, but she'd also recognized the self-convincing tone of her own mental voice whenever she did.

"All right," she told her students, shaking herself free of her gloomy thoughts and bringing up the image of a slider chain and indicating the third car in it. "This is called a 'slider car,' and it's—"

She broke off as someone tapped on the frame of her open door. She turned towards the sound, and her eyebrows rose as she realized it was Jasak Olderhan who had knocked. Then she stiffened as his appearance registered. He was standing in the doorway like a man awaiting an arbalest bolt, and his face was bone-white, his shoulders rigid.

"Magister Kelbryan," he said in a desperately formal voice, "Five Hundred Klian begs a few minutes of your time."

"What's wrong?" She came to her feet, nearly dizzy with fear, her eyes on his face as his body language and expression sent spikes of apprehension hammering through her, but he shook his head.

"Not here," he said, and that was when she noticed the other men with him. The Gifted healer who'd healed Shaylar stood behind him, and behind *him* was an armed guard.

"What *is* it?" she repeated, and heard her own voice go thin, almost shrill. Jasak obviously heard it, too. She saw it in his face and eyes, and he swallowed.

"News from the portal," he said hoarsely. "Please, come with me," he added, making it a plea a rather than a command. "These gentlemen will stay with Jathmar and Shaylar."

She realized she was wiping damp palms against her trousers. She looked at him for a moment longer, then turned to Shaylar, who was proving the faster of the two at absorbing her language lessons.

"I go, Shaylar," Gadrial said, speaking carefully and slowly. "With Jasak. I'll be back soon. Understand?"

The other woman nodded, and her eyes were dark with concern.

"Gadrial?" She held out one hand, touched Gadrial's arm gently in that concerned, almost tender way that seemed habitual with her. "Is there . . . trouble?" she asked. She clearly had to search for a moment to come up with the second word, and Gadrial gave a helpless shrug.

"I don't know," she admitted. Shaylar bit her lower lip, then nodded. Jathmar was staring at the armed guard, eyes hooded and lips thin, and Gadrial turned to the healer . . . and the guard.

"If you don't mind, please leave the door open. It distresses them less, to leave the door open."

Something moved in the guard's eyes—something dark and dangerous, almost lethal. What in Rahil's name had happened at the portal? She felt a chill chase its way down her back as she asked herself the question . . . and remembered who had stayed behind.

"Please," she added, catching and holding the guard's eye. "They're *civilians*." She stressed the word deliberately. "Frightened, bewildered civilians whose lives we—" she indicated herself and Jasak "—smashed to pieces. Whatever's happened, none of this was *their* fault."

The guard's jaw muscles clenched, but he gave a stiff nod.

"As you wish, Magister. I'll leave the door open." *And I'll watch them like a gryphon looking for a meal*, his eyes and body language virtually shouted.

Gadrial held those hard, dangerous eyes for a moment, then nodded and followed Jasak into the corridor. A moment later, they were outside, where the stiff sea breeze ruffled her hair and carried her the clean scent of salt water while afternoon sunlight poured golden across the open parade ground. Then she noticed the gates; they were closed. The massive wooden locking beam had been dropped into its brackets, and sharp-eyed sentries manned the parapet, weapons in hand, while field-dragon gunners stood ready behind the relatively small number of artillery pieces Five Hundred Klian had retained when he sent the rest forward to Hundred Thalmayr.

What in hell had *happened*?

Jasak walked beside her in total silence, nearly as ramrod-straight as the sword at his hip. She studied his profile, trying to understand the complex emotions seething just below the surface of the rigidly formal mask his face and voice had become. There wasn't time to decipher it, though, before they had crossed the parade ground and entered the fort's central administrative block.

Sarr Klian's clerk practically leapt from his chair, coming to attention with a sharply snapped salute.

"Sir! The Five Hundred is waiting for you, Sir!"

The one, quick look the clerk shot at Gadrial left her insides quaking, and then Jasak rapped sharply on the five hundred's door.

"Enter!" Klian's voice called almost instantly, and Jasak opened the door, holding it for her as he gestured her into the room ahead of him. She started forward, then caught sight of Chief Sword Threbuch and the company's hummer handler, waiting for them.

"Chief Sword!" she cried, smiling and hurrying forward to grasp his hands in sudden delight. "We were so worried about you! I'm so glad you made it back safely."

The tall, powerfully built North Shalomarian was visibly taken aback by her greeting. His normally immaculate uniform was filthy, she realized, and his face was heavily stubbled. It was also gaunter and thinner than she remembered, and much older looking. The obvious signs of weariness and privation sent a pang of sympathy through her, but then his expression truly registered. He wore that same desperately formal mask which had transformed Jasak's features into marble. That was bad enough, but something flickered behind it as he looked back at her. Something that turned Gadrial's joy at seeing him into abruptly renewed fear.

"What's wrong?" Her voice was sharp, urgent. "Something dreadful's happened, hasn't it?"

Pain flared deep in Threbuch's eyes. His jaw tightened, but he didn't speak. He just turned back toward the five hundred and waited for Fort Rycharn's commandant to answer her terrified question.

"Magister Kelbryan," Klian said in a heavy, almost exhausted voice. "Please sit down. Please," he repeated.

He's afraid I'm going to collapse when he finally tells me what's going on, she realized with a pang of icy dread.

"It's Magister Halathyn, isn't it?" she whispered as she sank into the chair opposite the five hundred's desk. "Something's happened to Magister Halathyn."

The officer's eyes actually flinched. Then he drew a deep breath.

"Hundred Olderhan," he began, "urged me to recall our forces from the swamp portal to minimize the risk of another violent confrontation between our forces and Shaylar and Jathmar's people." He cleared his throat. "I should have listened, but I thought the risk was far less than it actually was. I also hoped—assumed—that any powerful military response on their part would take much longer to mount. But the chief sword has confirmed Magister Halathyn vos Dulainah's belief—and yours—that the portal our prisoners came through was at least a class seven. In fact, it's almost certainly a class eight, judging from the chief sword's reconnaissance . . . and there's an enemy fort smack in the middle of it."

Gadrial's breath caught savagely.

"It appears to be understrength, still under construction," Klian continued. "But the chief sword watched the arrival of a relief column which had evidently moved ahead by forced march. They had more of those weapons you and the hundred here, encountered. And other weapons, as well, with tubes that were—"

He glanced at Threbuch.

"How large again, Chief?"

"They were about six feet long, Sir," Threbuch replied. "Looked like they were probably four and a half or five inches across, with fairly thin walls. They had four of the damned things covering my aspect of the portal, but according to Javelin Shulthan here, there were at least two or three more covering the other aspect. And they had something else, too. I don't know *what* to call it. It was another tube, shorter and not as big across, mounted on a tripod, almost like an infantry-dragon. But it wasn't a dragon. It had a . . . crank on the side, and a long belt of those cylinder things we found at their camp went into it. When they turned the crank—" He swallowed, his lips tight. "It was like those shoulder weapons of theirs, Sir," he said, turning to look directly at Jasak. "But instead of firing just one shot at a time, it fired again and again, so fast together that it sounded like one, long, single shot. It must've fired *hundreds* of times a minute, Sir."

He stopped speaking abruptly, and a line of sweat trickled down his brow.

He saw it used, Gadrial realized, going even colder.

"They attacked the portal." Her voice was a thread. "*Our* portal—didn't they?"

"They did." Five Hundred Klian gave her a jerky nod. Harsh,

full of pain and anger. "After asking—asking by *name*, mind—for Shaylar."

Gadrial's breath hissed and she paled as she instantly recognized what he was implying. If they'd asked specifically for Shaylar, did that mean they somehow knew she'd survived the initial battle? It must! But if they did . . .

She turned to stare at Jasak.

"*How?* My God, how could they have gotten a message out? Your men searched for any sign of a runner, both at their camp and at the clearing."

"Yes," Jasak said through clenched teeth. "We searched—damned thoroughly. No messenger went out, unless he went up the river before he headed for their portal. But however it happened, they got a message through . . . somehow. And somehow damned quick, too. According to the chief, here, the head of their initial scouting column passed him long before anyone could have gotten back to their portal on foot to summon them even if they did manage to get a runner out."

Gadrial touched her own cheek with fingers which had gone icy chill.

"But that's—" She broke off. Clearly, it wasn't impossible, since they'd obviously done it. "They must have something like hummers," she said instead, aware her intellect was grasping at straws, seeking any excuse, any distraction, to avoid hearing the rest of the doom they were about to pronounce.

"Something," Klian agreed. "And we're hoping you can find out what. Shaylar, at least, seems to trust you, to a certain degree. If you can find out how they warned their people, you'll give us information that will save lives. Possibly a lot of lives. We need every advantage we can possibly get to deal with their people, Magister, because they've just demonstrated a frankly devastating military superiority.

"Granted," he added in a harsh voice, "we made mistakes which made it even worse. I did, for example, when I failed to listen to Hundred Olderhan's warning, and Hundred Thalmayr made several serious mistakes of his own that proved costly. At least one of those was probably my fault, too, because I'm the one who ordered him to position himself on our side of portal. I intended that to apply only to his fortifications and main position, not to his sentries. It's standard procedure to picket both sides of any contested portal in a threat situation, and I expected him to follow SOP in applying my orders. Apparently, however, he interpreted my instructions to mean he was to do otherwise."

Fort Rycharn's commander paused again, his face tight and grim.

"I'm afraid, though, that however much Thalmayr's mistakes—and mine—may have contributed to the disaster, there was an even more terrifying factor involved." He looked directly into her eyes, his own appealing, almost desperate. "Somehow, these people can fire artillery *through* a portal, Magister."

He stopped, and Gadrial stared at him. No wonder he was staring at her that way, pleading with her to explain how it might have happened. But she couldn't. *No* spell could be projected through a portal interface! That had been established two centuries ago. It was an absolute fundamental of portal exploration, and—

Her yammering thoughts stopped abruptly, as a truly terrifying possibility occurred to her. No, a spell couldn't be projected through a portal . . . but from Shaylar's reaction to Magister Halathyn, these people didn't even know what sorcery *was*! Their weapons obviously relied on totally nonarcane principles; she and Jasak had already figured that much out. But if that was true for their shoulder weapons, why shouldn't it be equally true for their artillery weapons? And if their artillery fired physical projectiles, like the ones their shoulder weapons fired, then—

"I don't have any idea what makes their weapons work, Five Hundred," she said frankly. "Not yet, at least. But one thing I do know is that they don't rely on any magical principles with which I'm familiar. Which means the *limitations* we're familiar with probably don't apply, either."

She saw fresh, even worse fear in his eyes, and shook her head quickly.

"Whatever they are, however they work, I'm certain they have limitations of their own," she said. "Any form of technology does. We simply have to figure out what limitations apply to theirs. For the moment, though, I think we're going to have to assume that instead of *projecting* a spell the way our weapons do, they launch a physical projectile which actually *carries* the spellware, or whatever it is they use. If that's the case, then they can fire them anywhere any physical object could pass. Like through a portal interface."

Klian and Jasak looked at one another, their faces tight, and then the five hundred looked back at her.

"However they did it, Magister, it was devastating. I'm sure Hundred Thalmayr never expected it, any more than I would have, and it turns our entire portal defense doctrine on its head. We're going to have to come up with some answer, whether it's a way to stop them from doing it, or a way of figuring out how to do the same thing ourselves."

Gadrial nodded, and a part of her brain truly was even then reaching out, looking for some sort of solution. But it was only a tiny part, for most of her mind refused to let her hide any longer from what she most dreaded.

"How badly—" She had to stop and clear her throat. "How badly did they hit us?"

For a moment, no one spoke, and she cringed away from their silence. Then Fort Rycharn's commander inhaled deeply.

"The only men left from the swamp portal detachment are in this fort, Magister." His voice was harsh with emotion that not even years of Andaran military discipline could disguise. "Of the men actually stationed at the portal at the time of their attack, including the wounded we hadn't yet evacuated, only Chief Sword Threbuch and Javelin Shulthan made it back. All the rest are either dead or prisoners."

Gadrial felt her hands clench into white-knuckled fists on the arms of her chair. Despite all they'd already said, all her own efforts to prepare herself because of what she'd seen in their eyes, the sheer scope of the disaster hit her like a hammer. And behind that was the regret, the *pity*, burning in Sarr Klian's eyes as he faced her squarely.

She couldn't speak, literally couldn't force the words past her lips to ask the question that would confirm what her heart and mind already knew. She tried, but nothing happened, and then it was no longer necessary.

Chief Sword Otwal Threbuch went to one knee in front of her chair. The man who was so strong, so professional, in such command of his own emotions that she'd privately concluded that he'd been chiseled from granite. *That* man knelt in front of her chair and took her icy fingers in his, and even through her pain she felt a distant sense of surprise as his own fingers actually trembled.

"My lady," he said in a choked voice, "I'm sorry. There wasn't anything I could do. Nothing at all. I was trapped on the wrong side of the portal, couldn't even get to our camp, let alone get to Magister Halathyn."

She started to cry, silently, because she was unable to draw a deep enough breath to sob aloud.

"How?" she whispered, the sound thin as skeletal fingers scratching on glass, and his eyes flinched.

"I wish to every god in heaven I could tell you the enemy killed him, Magister. One of their soldiers had pulled him out of his tent, was questioning him. About Shaylar, I think, because Magister Halathyn was pointing toward the coast, toward this fort. Then one of our field-dragon crews—"

"*No!*" The word was ripped from her. Jathmar's ghastly burns swam before her eyes, and the picture her mind's eye painted of Halathyn, caught in a dragon's fireball, was too horrifying to face.

"No, Magister!" Threbuch said urgently. The chief sword reached out, caught her chin in one hand, *forced* her to look into his eyes and see the truth in their depths. "I know what you're thinking, but it wasn't a fireball! The gods were at least *that* merciful. He didn't suffer, I swear that, My Lady! The lightning caught them both, killed them instantly—"

The sobs which had been frozen inside her broke loose. She sensed people moving, heard their voices, but couldn't make sense of the words. Threbuch's hands let go of hers, then someone else crouched in front of her, tried to hold and comfort her. But she jerked back in her chair, wanting to hate these men for not *forcing* Halathyn to leave the swamp portal with her.

"Gadrial, please." Jasak's voice reached her at last, hoarse and filled with pain. "Let me at least help you."

She opened her eyes, staring at him through the blur of her tears, and even from the depths of her own dreadful pain she saw the anguish in his ravaged face. And as she saw it, she realized that Sir Jasak Olderhan had just lost nearly every man of his command. Men he'd cared about, felt responsible for, had grown to know—even love—in that mysterious male way of soldiers: formal and distant, at times, yet as close as brothers. But he was also Jasak *Olderhan*, with all that name implied, captive to all those Andaran honor concepts she couldn't understand. Unlike her, he couldn't weep for his loss, for his dead. Shame stung her cheeks, punching through the wild rush of grief, and she shook her head.

"I'm sorry," she whispered. "You cared about him, too. About all of them . . ."

He merely nodded. The movement was jerky and stiff, but that was because there were witnesses, both men he had commanded and the man who commanded him.

"I'm sorry," she said again, louder, looking this time at Otwal Threbuch. "You must think I'll hate you," she continued, trying desperately to steady her voice. "I'm trying not to."

His eyes flinched once more, and she bit her lip.

"I'm trying not to blame any of you. Trying not to blame *myself.* He was so *stubborn*—"

She broke off, gulping hard to maintain control, and looked Threbuch squarely in the eye.

"You were on *their* side of the portal, Chief Sword. I know that, and I've *seen* what their weapons can do. You couldn't possibly have reached him." Her voice was hoarse, cracking, but she forced it onward. "Nobody could have, I know that. Not through that kind of fighting. It's just such a terrible—"

She did break down again, then, but this time she let Jasak put an arm around her shoulders. There was great comfort in leaning against the strength of his broad shoulder, in the warmth soaking into her, helping her rigid muscles relax. She was mortified, at one level, to have broken down so completely and deeply, having wept in front of these men like any other helpless female. But losing Magister Halathyn for any reason, let alone *this* way . . .

"Would you like to go back to your quarters?" Jasak asked gently.

She nodded, and he helped her stand up, steadied her, let her lean on his forearm. She tried to say something to Five Hundred Klian, but her throat was locked. She turned a helpless look on Otwal Threbuch, but her throat remained frozen, so she reached out one hand, instead, and gripped his fingers in silence. Then Jasak was guiding her across the room. He opened the door for her, slipped an arm around her shoulders when they stepped outside, and steadied her carefully as her knees went rubbery on the low wooden steps down to the parade ground.

They were almost to her quarters when she remembered and went stiff and stumbled to a halt.

"What is it?" Jasak asked urgently.

"Shaylar. And Jathmar. They're in my room."

She didn't think she could face them yet. They hadn't done anything themselves to kill Halathyn—or the others—but her mentor, the man who'd been her second father, was dead because soldiers from their universe had come looking for them. Gadrial couldn't—just couldn't—face them yet. Not while the shock was so raw.

Jasak swore under his breath, then changed direction and led her to his own quarters, in the building reserved for officers, not civilian technicians. His room was neat, tidy, and very nearly empty. The gear he'd brought back from the field was stored in orderly fashion, and his personal crystal sat on his desk, glowing lines of text visible where he'd obviously been interrupted in the middle of something when Chief Sword Threbuch had arrived with the news.

He guided her to the bed, rather than the chair.

"Lie down and rest for a while," he murmured, easing her down.

The bed, like all military bunks in frontier forts, was a simple cotton bag stuffed with whatever the regional commissary had been stocked with: feathers, cotton wadding, even hay. This one, like her own, had feathers inside, soft and comforting as she curled up on her side atop the neatly tucked-in blanket. He opened the window, letting in a cooling breeze, then looked back down at her.

"Just stay here for a while, Gadrial. I'll come back for you later, all right?"

His kindness in not mentioning the names of the people he was about to remove from her room left her blinking on salty water once more. She heard his feet cross the bare plank floor, then the door clicked softly shut behind him and Gadrial lay still, listening to the wind rustle through the room, the distant sound of men's voices, the occasional cry of seabirds high above the fort, and remembered.

She remembered a thousand little details. Her first day at the Mythal Falls Academy, an awestruck young girl from the windy empty plains of North Ransar, still short of her fourteenth birthday. How she'd gaped at the ancient stone buildings, stared in amazement at the thunderous roar of Mythal Falls, one of the two largest waterfalls in any universe, plunging into its deep chasm. The very air, and the ground under her feet, had been so pregnant with latent magic that her skin had tingled and her bones had buzzed, and yet even that had been almost secondary beside an even greater sense of wonder.

She—Gadrial Kelbryan—had scored so highly on the standard placement tests that Magister Halathyn vos Dulainah himself had offered her a place at the Academy.

It wasn't possible. She hadn't even known her Ransaran teachers had sent her exam results to the Academy, hadn't guessed how truly outstanding those scores had been. Not until the message crystal had arrived with Halathyn's personal invitation recorded in it. And then, impossibility piled on top of impossibility, he'd personally met her that first day, taken the unknown, timid teenaged girl from Ransar—the only non-Mythalan student in the renowned academy's entire student body, and one of the three youngest students ever admitted to it—under his wing. And he'd taken her out to the Falls themselves, shown them to her, and spoken quietly about the reason her body had buzzed so strangely there.

"Magic," he'd said in that almost childlike way of his, filled with wonder at the unending delights the universes—all of them—had to offer. "Magic gathers in places like these." He'd waved a dark-skinned, elegant hand at the roaring cataract below their feet. "Or, rather, magic bursts free at such places. There are other locations where the forces we call 'magic' well up in great concentrations: all great waterfalls, certain mountains, some deep caverns, places where lines of force cross. But this place, where the Mythal River plunges into this great chasm, where the entire continent is slowly pulling apart along the Rift—*this* is the most potent place in all Arcana."

Gadrial had stared at the tall, lean, imposing man she was actually going to be permitted to study with, if only she could overcome her own awe of him, and blinked.

"Mythal is pulling apart?" she'd asked. She'd felt incredibly stupid the instant the words were out of her mouth, but he'd only chuckled gently.

"Oh, yes. That's not common knowledge, mind you. Most people would be terrified to learn that the ground under their feet is actually moving. It's incredibly slow, of course—something on the order of a fraction of an inch a year. But it's definitely moving. Have you never wondered why the great continents, particularly Mythal and Hilmar, look like pieces in a child's puzzle? Pieces which obviously ought to fit together?"

"Yes, Sir." She'd nodded. "I had noticed it."

"Of course you had. You're bright, not just Gifted, or you wouldn't be here." He'd waved at the ancient stone buildings. "But it never occurred to you that those continents might look like that because they'd once been one solid piece of land?"

This time she'd simply shaken her head, and he'd smiled.

"Well, that's hardly surprising, either. Generally speaking, logic doesn't suggest that the ground under you is actually moving across the face of the planet, does it? But it is. We've confirmed it here." He'd cleared his throat. "Ahem. That is to say, my research unit confirmed it."

Gadrial had found herself grinning at his tone and his expression. Then she'd clamped both hands over her mouth, horrified at her slip in manners, but he'd just chuckled.

"Before your course of study is complete," he'd promised, "I'll teach you to sense it yourself."

And he had. He'd opened up her world to such wonders that she'd felt giddy most of the time, hungry in her very soul for new knowledge, new understanding of the world around her and the forces that only she and others with Gifts could sense and touch and use to accomplish the things that made Arcana's civilization possible.

Over the next three years, he'd given her the wondrous gift of teaching her how to really *use* her Gift. And then he'd stood like a fortress at her side when the other magisters—aided and abetted by her fellow students—had torn that precious gift of education from her shocked hands. Had expelled her on grounds so flimsy a sharp glance would have torn them to shreds. On the day when she'd stood wounded and broken, like a child whose entire universe had just been willfully, cruelly shattered.

On the day when Halathyn vos Dulainah had laid into his most senior, most renowned colleagues with barracks-room language in a white-hot furnace of fury which had shocked them as deeply as it had shocked her.

"—and shove your precious godsdamned, all-holy Academy—and your fucking, jewel-encrusted *pedigrees*—up your sanctimonious, lying, racist, hemorrhoid-ridden asses sideways!" he'd finished his savage tirade at length, and his personal shields had crackled and hissed about him like thinly leashed lightning. Sparks had quite literally danced above his head, and the Academy's chancellor and senior department heads—indeed, the entire Faculty Senate—had sat in stunned disbelief, staring at him in shock.

"We're leaving, Journeywoman Kelbryan," he'd said to her then, turning to face her squarely in the ringing, crackling silence singing tautly in his incandescent attack's wake.

"We?" she'd asked dully, her throat clogged with unshed tears. "I don't understand, Magister."

For just an instant, he'd glared at her, as if furious with *her* for her incomprehension. But then the anger seething in his brown eyes had gentled, and he'd taken both her hands in his.

"My dear child," he'd said, ignoring the Academy's still stupefied leadership, "the day this Academy expels the most brilliant theoretical magic adept it has ever been my privilege to train for 'insufficient academic progress' and 'attempts to violate the honor code by cheating' is the last day I will ever teach here."

Someone else had made a sound, then. The beginning of protest, she'd thought, but Magister Halathyn had simply turned his head. The fury in his eyes had roared up afresh, and the chancellor had shrunk back in his chair, silent before its heat.

"I resign from this faculty—immediately," he'd said.

"But you *can't!*" she'd cried, aghast. "You can't throw away your career over *me*! I'm just one more journeywoman, Magister, and you're ... you're—"

He'd laid a gentle fingertip across her lips, ignoring the men and women who had been his colleagues and peers for so many years.

"You are anything but 'just one more journeywoman,'" he'd told her, "and this ... this *farce* is only the final straw. I should have done this years ago, for many reasons. You're not to blame, except inasmuch as what these sanctimonious, closed-minded, willfully ignorant, arrogant, bigoted, power-worshiping, stupid *prigs* have just done to you has finally gotten *me* to do what I ought to have done so long ago. If they choose to wallow in the muck of their precious supposed *shakira* superiority to all around them, then so be it. *I* have better things to do than squat here clutching handfuls of my own shit and calling it diamonds! Besides," his sudden, delighted grin had shocked her speechless, "I've been offered a new position."

One of the other department heads had straightened in his chair at that, leaning forward with an expression of mingled suspicion, chagrin, shock, and anger. Magister Halathyn had caught the movement from the corner of his eye, and he'd turned to face the other man and his grin's delight had acquired a scalpel's edge.

"As a matter of fact, my dear," he'd continued, speaking to her but watching the other magisters' faces like a duelist administering the *coup de grace*, "I've been offered the chance of a lifetime. I'm going to set up a new academy of theoretical magic on New Arcana, under the auspices of the military high command. And you, Journeywoman Kelbryan, have just become its first student."

The protest had begun then. The shouts of outrage, the curses—the threats. But Magister Halathyn had ignored them all, and so had Gadrial, as she'd stared up into his eyes. Eyes so kind and so alive to the wonders of life, so passionate to see justice done. She'd met those eyes and burst into fresh tears, but not of despair. Not this time. Not ever again.

Until now, almost twenty years and God alone knew how many universes away from that moment.

Halathyn was gone forever. Stupidly. Cruelly. For *nothing*. A reckless, crazy shot by a dragon gunner too blinded by fear and the need to hurt the other side to notice that the greatest magister Arcana had ever produced was in his line of fire. Or—even worse, and just as likely—by a gunner who hadn't *cared* as long as his weapon's blast took down one of the men killing his company, as well.

Gadrial Kelbryan turned her face into Sir Jasak Olderhan's pillow and cried like a lost child.

CHAPTER
TWENTY-SEVEN

THEY LEFT THE fort at dawn.

Shaylar knew something terrible had happened, but no one would tell them what. No one even tried. Jasak had escorted her and Jathmar from Gadrial's quarters to their own the afternoon before, but he'd barely spoken, and Shaylar hadn't been able to touch him, so she had no idea what had happened. Whatever it had been, it had obviously been bad, because they'd spent the night locked in their quarters, with one armed guard at the door, another at the window, and for all they could tell, another on the roof.

Now they crossed the open parade ground in total silence and found Gadrial waiting for them at the fortress' barred water gate. Her haggard appearance shocked Shaylar. The circles under her eyes were so dark they looked bruised, her eyes themselves were swollen and red from prolonged weeping, and an exhausted, defeated look clung to her. It was one Shaylar recognized from her own recent, bitter experience.

"Who—" she started to ask, then realized she didn't know the word for "died." Not that it really mattered. Gadrial didn't answer her partial question, didn't even look at her. In fact, nobody was looking at them—not directly. People's glances sort of sidled past them, without ever coming to rest *on* them, and she and Jathmar exchanged baffled, worried looks.

The fort was built so that the wharf extending out into the harbor was a virtual extension of its walls. The only way onto or off of the long, narrow dock was through the fort itself, and other people were waiting at the water gate, as well. One of them was a tall man, with iron-gray hair. He stood ramrod straight, staring at absolutely nothing, and Shaylar vaguely remembered him from that first ghastly

450

day, after the battle at the clearing of toppled timber. She hadn't seen him since, though, and that made her frown.

If he'd been with Jasak Olderhan the day Jasak's men had slaughtered her crew, where had he been in the meantime?

The likeliest answer terrified her, because he had the tough, nononsense look of a professional soldier. A good one. The sort of experienced noncom a good officer might detach for some important independent duty . . . like a reconnaissance mission. Had he been to *their* portal? Shaylar knew nothing about Jasak's and Gadrial's people, nothing about the extent of their knowledge of this region. If they'd already known about the portal cluster, then the logical thing for Jasak to have done would have been to send someone to check the ones they already knew about the moment his men stumbled across Shaylar's crew, just to see if anything had changed. And if he had, that gray-haired man would have found plenty.

Like Company-Captain Halifu's fort. And if Company-Captain Halifu had sent someone to look for *them* . . .

She glanced at Jathmar, who'd picked up some of what she was thinking, or more precisely, feeling, through the marriage bond.

"I think they know about our entry portal," she said in a low voice.

"You may be right. Something big's happened, at any rate. If I had to guess, I'd say they've tangled with *our* military out there. And I don't think they enjoyed the experience."

"Then Company-Captain Halifu did send someone to look for us."

"Or to find out if anyone had survived what you transmitted." Jathmar nodded grimly. "You said they left most of their lightly wounded to walk the whole way back to their swamp base camp when they flew us out. That would have left a trail a child could follow, leading straight back to *their* portal."

Shaylar nodded, but fresh worry tightened her mouth. She had no doubt that Darcel Kinlafia would have accompanied any rescue force Halifu might have sent out. And if the other Voice had managed to make it to this side of the swamp portal, he would undoubtedly have done his best to contact her. But he hadn't succeeded, and neither had she managed to contact him, despite making the attempt again and again, especially at their normally scheduled contact times, since they'd Healed her head injury. Not that she'd ever had much hope that she'd be able to. She still didn't know exactly how fast a dragon could fly, but she was virtually positive that the long dragon flight from the swamp portal to their present location had taken her well outside her own contact range from the portal, and hers was much longer than his.

Without knowing about these people's flying creatures, and given the way the swampy terrain would hamper any sort of ground-based movement, Darcel wouldn't have any reason to believe that she could have been transported out of his range from the portal in no more than a week. Which meant that when he'd tried to contact her and gotten only silence—and hadn't heard anything from *her*, either—he'd undoubtedly assumed that it confirmed his worst fears.

But there was nothing she could do about that, and so she did her best to put the thought behind her. Instead, she considered what Jathmar had said from another perspective.

"Gadrial's in a state of shock," she said very quietly into Jathmar's ear. "She's lost someone—someone precious to her."

Jathmar glanced at her sharply, then his nostrils flared.

"That man at the camp," he said softly. "The one who looked Ricathian."

"The one with the words in the crystal, and the fire rose." Shaylar nodded. "Gadrial was close to him, emotionally. I could see it in her eyes, hear it in her voice. They'd known each other long enough for that easy bantering between good friends, and then she had that fight with him just before they left. Her and Jasak both, now that I think about it. You don't suppose . . . ?"

"I don't know," Jathmar said, still softly. "But I'd hate to think anything happened to that fellow."

Shaylar blinked, unable to conceal her surprise. The marriage bond made it impossible for her to be unaware of Jathmar's feelings where *all* of their captors were concerned. But that same bond made it impossible for him to misunderstand her surprise, and he shrugged.

"It's obvious he wasn't a soldier, any more than she is." He nodded slightly in Gadrial's direction. "Neither of them wore uniforms. And, well, I don't know how to say it. There was something about him . . ." He shook his head, unable to find exactly the right words. "I hope Grafin blew the rest of them into an Arpathian hell, but I'd be sorry to learn that that particular man had been killed. What was his name?" He frowned. "It started with an 'H,' didn't it?"

Shaylar glanced at the others, then leaned even closer to her husband.

"Halathyn," she said in a half-whisper, and he nodded.

"Yes. That was it." A regretful sigh escaped him. "I suppose they'll tell us, eventually. Or maybe we can ask. But not yet. I really don't think now's a good time at all."

Shaylar glanced from Gadrial's tear-swollen eyes to Jasak's thin-lipped, pale silence, and then at the big, gray-haired soldier's clenched jaw and strangely disturbed eyes.

"Right," she agreed firmly. "We ask later. *Much* later."

Then the massive wooden bar at the gate rattled and clanked as the sentries unfastened it and the gate creaked ponderously open. They didn't open it all the way—just far enough to let Jasak, Gadrial, and the soldier whose name she didn't know pass through the opening more or less abreast. She and Jathmar went next, followed by several other soldiers, including one in *chains*.

The sight of one of Jasak's soldiers in manacles and leg irons startled her into staring. She hadn't noticed him while standing at the gate, but she recognized him. Not by name, of course—she had no idea who he was, or what his duty might have been—but she'd seen him that first ghastly day, as well. He was dark-skinned, like Halathyn, and to Shaylar's eyes he looked like a Ricathian. But only physically. All resemblance to any Ricathian Shaylar had ever known ended with the color of his skin and the look of his hair.

Despite his chains, he walked with his spine ramrod straight, and he wore an expression of unmistakable aristocratic disdain. His lip curled in the way she'd seen occasional aristocrats sneer back home, particularly those from Othmaliz, who felt they were superior to pretty much everyone else on Sharona simply because their ancestors had retained possession of Tajvana. She'd had to deal with one or two of that sort, and she'd never enjoyed the experience, although not even the most haughty Othmalizi noble had wanted to cross swords with a fully accredited Voice of her stature.

But there was more than simple arrogance to *this* man. The look the chained prisoner sent Jasak Olderhan as Gadrial and the officer stepped past him contained such malice, such lethal hatred, that Shaylar's breath caught for just a moment. Then another soldier spoke sharply to him, and he stalked through the gate in turn, as though he were some great lord making his way through a gaggle of filthy beggars despite the jingle of his chains.

"I wonder who *he* thinks he is?" Jathmar murmured.

"Good question," Shaylar agreed.

"I'm not sure I like the idea of sailing on the same ship he does," her husband growled under his breath, gripping her hand tightly.

Since they didn't have much choice in the matter, Shaylar found herself hoping that these people had good locks on their doors. Then she shivered at the thought, since she and Jathmar would be held behind locked doors, as well. Gods' mercy, surely they wouldn't put her and Jathmar in the same cell as *that* fellow? She shivered again, wondering what he'd done.

The roughly built wharf looked almost rickety, but it was reassuringly solid underfoot, and Shaylar turned her attention to the ship tied up alongside it. Partly, she admitted, she was interested in anything which might distract her from the thought of being confined in the other prisoner's company. But the ship itself was more than enough to claim her attention in its own right, for it was, without reservation, the oddest vessel Shaylar had ever seen, and Jathmar was staring at it in just as much perplexity as she was.

"What on earth makes it *go?*" he wondered aloud.

Shaylar could only shake her head in bafflement. It wasn't a huge ship, although it was clearly large enough to tackle the open ocean. It was actually a bit bigger than she'd thought it was on the day of their arrival. Of course, she hadn't been in very good shape for making detailed observations at the time, not before their healers had gone to work on her.

This ship was somewhat smaller than the standard *Voyager*-class ships the Trans-Temporal Express had developed to cross the water gaps in its inter-universal transportation system, but not by very much. The *Voyagers* were about four hundred feet long and had a beam of about fifty-five feet, and Shaylar, like everyone who'd ever served in a portal survey crew, was thoroughly familiar with them. They were certainly serviceable craft, if not especially speedy, but they'd been designed primarily as cargo vessels, and their passenger accommodations left much to be desired. On the other hand, in the *Voyager*, the TTE had produced a design which lent itself to modular construction and mass production. The freighters were literally shipped across intervening stretches of dry land in pieces, carried on huge, special freight cars, and assembled once they reached their destinations.

But if this ship was of roughly the same dimensions, that was about all it had in common with the TTE design.

First, it appeared to be built of wood. That wasn't really all that surprising, in a lot of ways. Wooden hulls were more common than steel hulls for locally produced Sharonian shipping, after all. The TTE's modular designs were one thing, but for most people, it was far simpler to import a gang of shipwrights and the men needed to fell timber to build ships than it was to import enough infrastructure to build steel-hulled vessels in barely explored universes.

But the fact that this one was built of wood did seem odd considering the second obvious difference between it and the Sharonian ships with which she was familiar, because it was a far sleeker design. Whereas a *Voyager* had a straight, almost vertical stem, this ship's bow was sharply raked, and the hull flared gracefully as it approached deck level. Shaylar was no sailor, but she'd had the opportunity—or misfortune, depending upon one's viewpoint—to experience heavy weather aboard more than one of the TTE ships, and she suspected that this vessel would have provided much more comfortable transport under the same circumstances. It looked far more . . . modern, for want of a better word, which made its wooden construction one more of the endless anachronisms she'd observed since her capture.

The third thing she noticed was the size of the superstructure, and the fourth was the absence of anything remotely resembling a Sharonian ship's smokestacks. It had only a single mast, which carried no sails, so it had to have *some* sort of propulsive system, but she couldn't imagine what it might be.

But the *fifth* thing she noticed was a row of three-foot-wide ports which ran down the entire length of the superstructure right at deck level. At the moment, those ports were closed by hatches, but she didn't think they were access ways for ventilation or trash chutes. There were eight of them on the side of the ship closest to the wharf, and she assumed there was a matching row on the ship's outboard side.

She and Jathmar followed Jasak and Gadrial down the wharf towards the waiting ship, and she found herself wondering uneasily how far from Jasak's home universe they were . . . and what it might say about these people if this universe *wasn't* close to their home base. This vessel was obviously a warship, or at least armed for self protection, and no TTE design she'd ever seen had carried actual *weapons*. It was also far too large for any sort of coastal patrol craft. No, this was a ship designed for blue-water combat—at need, at least—which argued that it had been constructed by a fiercely militaristic society. Who else would send actual *warships* to a raw frontier?

That thought carried her clear to the boarding gangway, which proved to be much flimsier than she'd expected. Jasak said something to Gadrial, speaking much too quickly for Shaylar's very limited Andaran to follow. The other woman looked at him, managed a wan smile, and shook her head. Then she stepped onto the steeply inclined gangway, gripping its rope rail firmly, and started up it to the deck towering above them in the cool morning light. Jasak watched her for a moment, then turned to Shaylar and surprised her by producing a wry smile, despite the visible weight on his shoulders.

"Women go first," he said in careful, slow Andaran, holding out his hand, and Shaylar actually flushed, embarrassed that his courtesy had come as a surprise. Despite all of the obvious care he'd taken to protect her and Jathmar, she'd still allowed herself to expect a lack of consideration from him.

She hesitated for a moment, looking at him. Part of it was surprise at the offered courtesy, but there was more to it. She wanted—needed—to touch him, to use her Talent to acquire any information she could. But at the same time, she was almost afraid to. Despite his disciplined exterior, there was too much pain behind his eyes, too much pain waiting for her if she dared to sample it.

Gadrial had halted a few feet up the gangway, looking back with those bruised, swollen eyes, and Shaylar felt of fresh stab of confused shame. Despite Gadrial's own obvious anguish, she was still capable of worrying about the prisoners placed in her charge, capable of looking back because she sensed Shaylar's hesitation, even if she didn't begin to understand all the reasons for it.

That realization was enough to galvanize Shaylar, and she opened her Talent wide and reached for Jasak's waiting hand.

It was a mistake.

Shaylar knew that the instant she touched Jasak. She bit down on a hiss of shock and stumbled heavily, as if someone had just hit her in the back of the head with a hammer. Jasak's self-control was so rigid that she'd seriously misjudged the actual depth of his anguish, and she'd pushed her Talent hard, prepared to strain for any detail she might have been able to pick up.

What she got was death. Massive amounts of violent death, coupled with a sense of desertion, a tidal wave of helpless guilt. The fact that Jasak had been relieved by the other officer, the one who'd wanted to hurt her and Jathmar, had already been obvious to both of them, but that wasn't enough to absolve Jasak of that terrible, crushing sense of guilt. Or, perhaps, of responsibility. It didn't matter what she called it; what mattered was the raw, bitter poison of its strength.

She felt herself falling—falling physically, as she stumbled, and falling psychically, as she toppled into the dreadful abyss of Jasak Olderhan's pain—and she gasped as Jasak's powerful arms caught her before she could tumble to the dock's splintery planking. It was all she could do to keep from crying out as he lifted her, as if she were a child, and his genuine concern for her cut through the churning vortex of his darker emotions.

Shaylar fought her way up and out of the darkness, frantically shutting down her own receptiveness, backing away from the contact she'd sought as a means to gather information. It took her two or three heartbeats to pull far enough back to regain her own sense of self, and even as she did, she sensed Jasak's consternation and worry over her reaction.

She managed to shake her head, smile up at him with a mixture of apology for her "clumsiness" and thanks for his quickness in catching her. And then Gadrial reached out, as well.

The other woman's gesture was oddly hesitant, almost halfhearted, unlike anything Shaylar had seen from her before. It was almost as if she were fighting a war with herself, *making* herself offer that token of assistance.

Warned by her experience with Jasak, and again by Gadrial's uncharacteristic hesitation, Shaylar braced herself for the contact shock before she reached out for the offered hand. Instead of opening herself wide, she buttressed herself, and even so, her nostrils flared and her face went white as her fingers closed on Gadrial's.

Jasak's pain had been terrible enough; Gadrial's was worse, and Halathyn's name burned so hotly through her chaotic, grief-torn emotions that Shaylar actually *heard* it. She'd never done that with a non-telepath before, and she had to bite down hard on an impulse to fling both arms around the other woman. Gadrial had done so much to comfort her, had somehow kept Jathmar alive long enough to reach this fort. Now her agony cried out to Shaylar, and the Sharonian woman felt a desperate need to repay some of that comfort. Yet she couldn't, not without risking the revelation of her Talent, and for now, that must remain secret. And so she managed not to, managed to simply take Gadrial's hand as the two of them made their way up the steep, swaying gangway together.

They reached the ship's deck, and Shaylar released Gadrial's hand. She stood beside the other, grieving woman, looking back across the wharf at the land they were leaving, and wrapped both arms around herself to hold in the shivers while she tried to make sense of what she'd just sensed.

Halathyn was dead.

She was utterly certain of that individual death, but there were others, too. So many others. That was clear from Jasak's churning emotions, not to mention the way she and Jathmar were being treated. Company-Captain Halifu must have attacked their base camp at the swamp portal, and it was obvious he'd blown it straight to hell when he did.

Which Shaylar found a terrifying thought. She and Jathmar were helpless, prisoners of war in a society that would undoubtedly see

Sharonians as far more warlike than they really were after this second violent contact.

She didn't believe Jasak would retaliate against her and Jathmar, despite the fact that it was *his* men who had just become the latest casualties. She couldn't believe he would, not after the other things she'd already sensed out of him. But Jasak Olderhan was only one officer, and a relatively low ranking one, at that, unless she was seriously mistaken. Shaylar had been around enough military units since joining the field teams to develop a fairly good sense of the military pecking order, and Jasak clearly wasn't at the top of his. In fact, she suspected she was actually older than he was, given his apparent rank and assuming that his military worked at all like the PAAF and other Sharonian armies.

If events were escalating even remotely as quickly as she feared they were, it was unlikely that an officer of his junior rank would be able to protect them. Even if he was inclined to make the effort after his own men had suffered such brutal casualties.

The commandant of the fort—which looked strangely small from here, silhouetted against the endless miles of virgin swamp that stretched to the horizon—was obviously of much higher rank than Jasak, and considerably older, as well. He'd visited her and Jathmar in their quarters in his fort only once, and he hadn't spoken to them at all when he had. He'd simply looked at them for long, silent moments—studying first Jathmar, then Shaylar. Whatever he'd been looking for, it hadn't shown in his face. And whatever conclusions he'd drawn would remain a mystery, because he'd merely nodded to them once, then departed.

Shaylar would not—dared not—assume that other officers would show equal leniency. Especially not now. So she stood, holding in the shivers until Jathmar joined her on the deck. He wrapped a protective arm around her shoulders, and she turned toward him, wrapping both her own arms around him and holding on tight while the rest of the passengers passed them.

A half-dozen men who were obviously members of the ship's crew sorted out the new arrivals as they reached the deck. Like Jasak and the other soldiers, the sailors were uniformed, although their uniforms—composed of red jerseys for most of them, although one wore a red tunic with gold braid, over white trousers—were quite different from Jasak's. The one in the tunic was obviously a junior officer or petty officer of some sort. He and Jasak exchanged salutes, and the naval officer said something to one of his own men, then nodded towards Shaylar and Jathmar. The sailor started towards them, but Jasak said something, and the sailor stopped, looking back at his own officer. Again, the conversation was too quick for Shaylar's embryonic Andaran to follow, but it wasn't hard to guess what was being said.

Once again, Jasak was intervening on their behalf, asking the ship's officer to let them remain on deck at least a little longer before they were sent below to whatever quarters or confinement awaited them. After a moment, the other officer nodded in agreement and turned his attention back to more immediate duties.

The last few passengers trooped up the gangway, and the officer gave an order to one of the sailors. An instant later, the gangway began to rise. The sailors didn't haul it up. They didn't use a winch or a crane to lift it. It simply *rose*, detaching itself smoothly from both the side of the ship and the wharf below, turning until it was parallel with the centerline of the ship, and then rising still higher. It lifted until it was a good ten feet higher than even Jasak's head, and then nestled itself neatly into what were obviously waiting mounting brackets on the side of the ship's superstructure, one deck level above them.

Shaylar stared at it in disbelief as it drifted across above them, and she heard Jathmar's gasp of surprise when its shadow fell over them.

"How in all the Uromathian hells did they do *that*?" he demanded as a pair of sailors made the gangway fast in its new position. Shaylar was as startled as he was, but her memory flashed to that ghastly moment in the toppled timber when they'd first lifted Jathmar's stretcher.

"It's more of that levitation of theirs," she said wonderingly. "Remember your stretcher, or the ones they used for their own wounded?"

"Those little glassy cubes you were talking about?" Jathmar looked at her for a moment, then twitched his shoulders in a half-shrug. "I suppose if you can levitate stretchers, there's no reason you couldn't levitate gangplanks, as well, at that," he admitted. Then he snorted with a grimace. "Probably explains why they don't have any cargo derricks on this ship of theirs, for that matter. Why bother with cranes when you can just stick a little glass bead on your cargo pallets and *fly* them to where you want them?"

He shook his head wonderingly, then turned away as Jasak called his name quietly.

"Go to quarters now," Jasak said.

*   *   *

The quarters to which they were led were a pleasant surprise . . . and a far cry from the damp, dark, undoubtedly rat-infested cell Shaylar's imagination had pictured.

The cabin to which she and Jathmar were assigned lay one deck up in the superstructure, above the ship's weapons ports, on the outboard side and directly between Jasak's assigned quarters and Gadrial's. The older man with the iron-gray hair was given quarters on the other side of Jasak's, and the man in chains disappeared somewhere below—probably to the cell she and Jathmar weren't in after all.

It was a small cabin, but that was true of every shipboard cabin Shaylar had ever used. It might be even a bit smaller than what they might have received aboard one of TTE's *Voyagers*, but if she was right, and this *was* a warship, that was probably inevitable. At any rate, she'd always assumed accommodations would be more cramped aboard a man-of-war than aboard a civilian-crewed vessel.

It was also heartlessly utilitarian, but that didn't matter. It was clean, reasonably comfortable, with white-painted bulkheads and neat built-in storage compartments under its pair of bunks, and it had a porthole. It wasn't large enough to wiggle through, even for Shaylar, but it allowed them a view of the sea and—more important—it let in *daylight*, which was even more welcome for its contrast with the windowless cell she'd feared.

At night, they would even be able to see the moon.

She held back a sigh as she settled herself on the nearer bunk. It wasn't the softest bed she'd ever sat on, but it was softer than a sleeping bag on the ground. Then she looked up again at the sound of a cleared throat.

"Stay," Jasak said from the open doorway. "I come soon."

Shaylar nodded, knowing what came next. Then their door closed, but not before she'd caught a glimpse of the armed guard who'd taken up his station outside. A lock clicked, and Jathmar crossed his arms over his chest and glared at the door.

"We're in a room on a ship that will shortly be in the middle of the ocean," he growled. "That's a remarkably solid looking door, and it's locked tight. And that window isn't big enough for *you* to crawl through, let alone me! Why the *hells* do they bother with a guard?"

Shaylar felt the worry, fear, and frustration beating like a ragged headache under his sour mood. She went to him, brushed her lips against his, circled his chest with her arms, and rested her head against his heart.

"We must have hurt them badly," she murmured.

"I hope so!" he snarled.

"Shhh." She leaned far enough back to gaze up into his wounded eyes. "What's done is done. We have to live with the consequences. That means we'd better figure out what we're going to say when they ask how we got a message out. I'm learning their language, Jathmar, and even though it's maddeningly slow without another telepath to help, it won't be long before I know enough for them to ask that question—and expect an answer."

Muscles bunched along his jaw, but he didn't speak.

"Jathmar," she said gently, "you have to let go of at least some of the hatred and put your energy into figuring out ways to keep them guessing without making them suspicious enough to treat us worse than they have so far."

She thought for a moment that he would flare up at her, but he didn't. Instead, he bit back the surge of anger beating through him.

"They have treated us . . . decently," he muttered grudgingly, reluctantly. "All things considered."

"Yes," she murmured, "they have."

"But I can't stop hating, Shaylar. They've smashed everything we had, everything we ever wanted. Killed our friends, nearly killed us . . ."

He sucked down a deep breath, fighting to bring himself under control, but it was hard. Hard.

"I don't even dare try to love you," he whispered finally, miserably. "We don't even control the lock on our own door, can't know when someone's going to open it, drag us out of here! And what if you got *pregnant*?" He shook his head, teeth gritted. "Before, it would've meant dropping out of the survey crews, and that would have been bad enough. But now, what would they do with—or to—our child if they thought it would make us tell them things they want to know?"

He squeezed his eyes shut, tightened his grip on her, and buried his face in her hair. His aching need for her burned hot as lava through the bond, shot through with ripples and tremors of anger, fear, and despair, and she had absolutely no answer for him. She could only hold him, blinded by tears. They stood in the center of their comfortable little prison, and just held on while the awareness of their total helplessness and vulnerability burned through them.

Shaylar never knew exactly how long they stood there. Without their confiscated watches, it was difficult to gauge the passage of time, and so she didn't even try. She simply leaned against Jathmar, her cheek nestled against his chest and the strong steady beat of his heart, while she listened to the dim sounds beyond the locked door and the even more distant sounds drifting through the opened porthole.

Then the ship began to move, and once again she was reminded of the yawning gap between any previous experience and their present reality. There was no deep rumble of machinery, no throbbing vibration from engines. There wasn't even the flap of canvas, or the creak of masts and cordage. In fact, there was nothing at all except steady movement as the ship backed silently away from the wharf.

It halted once more, and she looked out the porthole as it rotated smoothly in place, swinging its bow away from the land. The motion swung the fort back into the porthole's field of view, giving her a last glimpse of the land, and tears stung Shaylar's eyes again. She gave Jathmar another squeeze, then wiped her eyes impatiently and moved to the window to look back at the vast sweep of marsh that ran along the coastline.

The ship began to move again, forward this time, still silently. Its speed built steadily, quickly, and there was sound at last—the ripple and wash of water and the creaking sound of wooden timbers flexing as they moved, but still not so much as a whisper to betray whatever power sent it slicing through the waves.

The fort where they had stayed for such a short time grew smaller by the minute as the ship accelerated quickly and smoothly. They were already moving faster than any of Trans-Temporal Express's freighters. It was hard for Shaylar to estimate, but they had to be moving at least as quickly as any of the great high-speed passenger ships, maybe even as fast as the new turbine-engined warships she'd heard about. Yet still there was that eerie lack of vibration, that silence. No funnel smoke, no noise, just this smooth, effortless sense of speed.

She pressed a hand to her lips, staring back through the porthole. That vast marsh and that tiny log fort looked inexpressibly lonely, kissed by the rising sun and populated only by great clouds of water birds and a tiny handful of people. Or perhaps it was only she who felt such unbearable loneliness.

Then Jathmar's arms tightened about her from behind.

"I'm here, love," he murmured. "Whatever else, I'm here."

She pulled his arms more tightly around herself and held onto them silently, her throat too constricted to speak. At the moment it was hard—so very hard—to remember that they'd come out here to see new sights, new places. Things no other Sharonian had ever seen, or even imagined. Tomorrow, perhaps, she would be able to remember that, but not just yet.

For the moment, she could only grieve . . . and hold tight to those loving arms which were all she had left in any universe.

CHAPTER
TWENTY-EIGHT

BALKAR CHAN TESH looked up as someone tapped lightly on the small gong hanging from the peak of his tent. He recognized the towering, youthful Marine officer instantly, although they'd never met. The youngster looked exhausted, as well he might after what had to have been an even longer forced march than chan Tesh's own, but he was also the spitting image of his father. Even if he hadn't been, the blue-gray peregrine falcon on the far-from-regulation leather pad covering the left shoulder of his uniform tunic would have been a powerful clue. The bird was huge even for a peregrine—easily over twenty inches long, with a wingspan which must have been well over four feet—and it was neither hooded nor jessed, which was . . . unusual, to say the very least. Its powerful talons gripped the shoulder pad securely, but it was obvious they were also delicately aware of—and restraining—their own strength. Its dark eyes were bright and alert, and they focused on the company-captain with unnerving intensity.

It was, chan Tesh thought, quite possibly the most magnificent predator he'd ever seen, and well it should be, given the millennia-long breeding program which had produced it.

"Yes, Platoon-Captain?" he said, giving absolutely no indication that he'd recognized the newcomer.

"Platoon-Captain chan Calirath," the Marine introduced himself. "Company-Captain Halifu told me to report to you as soon as I arrived."

"I see." Chan Tesh laid down his pen and leaned back in his folding canvas chair. "In that case, I suppose you'd better come in . . . assuming you'll fit," he added with a small, wry smile.

"Thank you, Sir," the Marine said politely, and chan Tesh gave a small mental nod of approval.

Platoon-Captain His Highness Crown Prince Janaki chan Cali-rath, heir to the Winged Crown, stood at least eight inches over six feet, with his dynasty's powerful shoulders, but imposing size wasn't enough to explain the sense of presence he projected. Chan Tesh had been curious about how the crown prince would introduce himself, and he was pleased by the way Janaki had actually done it. Of course, in an odd sort of way, that simple "Platoon-Captain chan Calirath" had only emphasized that the young man introducing himself was actually the future ruler of the oldest, most powerful empire in human history.

Well, in our *branch of humanity's history, anyway,* chan Tesh reminded himself.

"Wait for me, dear heart," Janaki murmured to the falcon, and shooed her gently off his shoulder. She launched with a soft cry, and chan Tesh watched her disappear into the overhead foliage. The crown prince watched her go with a smile, then maneuvered himself into the tent cautiously but smoothly. It was apparent that he'd had plenty of experience moving his substantial bulk in and out of the tents the PAAF provided for field use. He seated himself rather gin-gerly in the folding chair chan Tesh indicated, and the chair creaked alarmingly under his weight. Fortunately, it held.

"I hope you won't take this wrongly, Platoon-Captain," chan Tesh said, "but I could wish you hadn't turned up for duty *here* at this precise moment."

"Sir—" Janaki began, but chan Tesh's raised hand stopped him.

"Platoon-Captain," he said, "I'm Ternathian. I know the tradition of your family, and I honor it. But there's no point in our pretend-ing you're just one more platoon-captain. I don't wish to belabor the point, but you must be aware that who you are—and, even more importantly, who you someday *will* be—is going to play a part in the thinking of any of your commanding officers."

"Yes, Sir, I know." Janaki didn't quite sigh, but he came so close that chan Tesh was hard put not to smile.

"And you wish it didn't," the company-captain said, instead, as sympathetically as possible. "As it happens, however, in this particular instance I think I'm in a position to kill two birds with one stone. To be devastatingly blunt, Your Highness," he used the imperial title deliberately, "any sane CO would order you to the rear the instant he saw your face. Especially when the situation is as riddled with uncertainties and complete unknowns as this one is. In this case, though, the duty I have in mind for you could have been tailormade for someone with your experience."

"Sir?"

"We've got prisoners, Platoon-Captain," chan Tesh said much more grimly. "Several of them were pretty badly wounded in the fighting. Our Healers have done what they can for them, of course, and they're all at least stabilized now, but we need to get them transferred to the rear and better medical facilities. Even if that weren't the case, we'd need to get all of them—wounded and unwounded alike—moved to the rear for proper interrogation as quickly as possible. The only officer we took alive appears to have been their commander—he's one of the wounded I mentioned, and it doesn't look like he'll ever walk again—but we've captured several men who seem to have been senior noncoms. They're our best, and only, source of information, and we need to get them into the hands of someone who can at least start figuring out how to *talk* to them. Not to mention the fact that we need to move them farther back as a security measure against escapes or rescue attempts."

He paused, and Janaki nodded very slightly.

"I can't spare very many men as prisoner escort," chan Tesh continued. "I'm thinking that using your platoon for the job would make the smallest hole by avoiding pulling somebody out of my established units for the job. In addition, you're not exactly a typical platoon-captain. You've grown up in the palace. I'm quite sure you have a better ear than most junior officers for possibly significant political and military details.

"What I'd like to do is to send at least some of them all the way back to Sharona, and I'd prefer to keep the same officer in command of the escort detail the entire way. Some of these people appear badly shocked and demoralized by what's happened to them; most of them, though, are obviously prepared to resist divulging any important information. I suspect that spending two or three months with them could help engender a sense of familiarity which might get inside that defensive mindset of theirs. It certainly couldn't hurt. And if that does happen, I want the best attuned ears available to pick up anything they might drop.

"And, to be frank, I'd like the officer in command of the escort detail to have a certain stature—official or unofficial—to help discourage any of the intervening COs from poaching prisoners on the grounds that they ought to be interrogated closer to the front. In short, I think you'd make an excellent first filter for the analysts . . . and that you may have enough clout, despite your relatively junior rank, to actually get them all the way back *to* those analysts."

"With all due respect, Sir, mightn't there be some point to keeping them closer to the front, where whatever we learn can be gotten to the sharp end quickly?"

"Of course there is," chan Tesh agreed. "And I expect the bulk of the prisoners will be. At the moment, I'm assuming Regiment-Captain Velvelig will hold the majority of them—and probably all the more seriously wounded—at Fort Raylthar. That's far enough towards the rear to satisfy most security concerns, and big enough to have a capable Healer Corps detachment. But it's going to be equally important to get at least some of these people clear back to Sharona where the government and the staff's intelligence experts can gain a firsthand impression of them. Your job is going to be to expedite their delivery to Tajvana."

"Yes, Sir."

"In addition," chan Tesh said quietly, "there's the political situation back home to consider, as well. I have no idea how that's going to sort itself out, but I do know that some sort of unified military and political policy is going to be necessary. I don't think the Authority can handle that job as it's presently constituted, which means the politicians are going to have to come up with some new mechanism. I can't imagine that your family isn't going to be deeply involved in that process, and having you there couldn't hurt. Especially if you've just returned from the front, escorting the first prisoners we've taken."

The Marine looked back at chan Tesh without any expression at all for several seconds. The company-captain simply sat there, waiting. He very much doubted that anything he'd just said hadn't already occurred to the crown prince. As far as chan Tesh knew, there weren't any stupid Caliraths, and only an idiot could fail to recognize the sort of political catfight this situation was going to make inevitable back home. Nor could Janaki possibly be unaware of the role his family—and he himself—was going to have to play in that fight.

"Very well, Sir. I understand," the crown prince said, after a moment. He did *not* say that he *approved*, chan Tesh observed, but the company-captain was prepared to settle for that.

"In addition to all the rest of those considerations," he said, "there's one other job I'd like you to undertake for me."

"Sir?"

"Darcel Kinlafia—Voice Kinlafia—is the only survivor of the Chalgyn Consortium team." Chan Tesh's expression was grim. "Frankly, I'm . . . worried about him."

"May I ask why, Sir?"

"He was *there*, Platoon-Captain. He was linked with Shaylar throughout the entire battle. He *Saw* his friends being butchered all around him, and he couldn't do a single godsdamned thing about it. He blames himself for that. I think he may actually hate himself for it. It's . . . poisoning him, and he's a Voice. I'm sure it's inadvertent, but anyone with a hint of telepathy is picking up his leakage, and it's affecting our people. I don't need anything which might push our men towards atrocities in the name of vengeance if it comes to more fighting. Almost equally important, I think we need to get him away from here for his own good, as well. He needs a little space, a little time, if he's going to heal, and he's too close to where it all happened here."

"I see, Sir." Janaki nodded again. His sea-colored eyes held a small but unmistakable flicker of approval, but he also cocked his head to one side. "At the same time, Sir, can you afford to send him back? I understand that he's a Portal Hound, as well as a Voice."

"Yes, he is," chan Tesh agreed, impressed by how quickly the crown prince had picked up that particular bit of information. "But he's already been able to give us the bearing of the nearest portal—apparently the only other portal—in this universe. We know it's somewhere to the northeast, probably in Esferia or New Ternath. Of course, we don't know how far away it is, or whether or not they've got bases closer than that. And we sure as hell don't have any idea how they managed to get their people in and out of this godsforsaken swamp! But we know where to start looking for their portal if it comes to that, and that's about the best we could hope for from any Portal Hound. Frankly, we don't *need* any of the services he could still offer us, and we do need to get him out of here."

"And away from all of the memories," Janaki said slowly. "Somewhere he can start healing inside."

"Exactly," chan Tesh replied. "I'm not thinking just about Darcel, though. He *was* linked with Shaylar. I'm pretty certain there are more details still locked up in his memory than he's aware of, but he's . . . not very supportive of efforts to dig them out. I don't blame him for that. It must be pure hell to go back in there and relive it over and over again, especially for someone with a Voice's perfect recall. But I need someone who can convince him to do just that—someone who can wring every detail out of his experience.

"The information itself might be of enormous military value, but, to be perfectly honest, it may not be particularly significant, either. Not from the perspective of future operations, that is. But I've discussed it with Petty-Captain Yar, my senior Healer. He thinks it's important for *Darcel* to get it out, deal with it. Frankly, I suspect that he's a lot more likely to open up if someone like you presses him on it than he is if I do. And if you can convince him of the importance of his reporting his impressions firsthand back in Tajvana, we may actually manage to get him away from the front before I have to place him under arrest to protect any additional prisoners from him."

"It's that bad, Sir?" Janaki asked, eyes widened slightly, and chan Tesh shrugged.

"I may be worrying too much. He's a good, decent man. In fact, I think that's part of the problem. He's not used to carrying this kind of hate around with him, and he doesn't know what to do with it. But I'd like to *keep* him a good, decent man, if we can, Your Highness."

"Point taken, Sir," Janaki said respectfully, and chan Tesh nodded.

"In that case, Your Highness, why don't I take you around to the POW cage?" The company-captain smiled without any humor at all. "We'll probably find Darcel somewhere in the vicinity."

* * *

"I think this is going to be the most ticklish case, Sir," Petty-Captain Delokahn Yar said. He stood at Janaki's elbow at the foot of one of the cots under the canvas tarp arranged to shade a clean, breezy open-air hospital ward. The tall, powerfully built man on the cot lay still—not simply motionless, but rigidly, harshly *still*—staring up at the sun-patterned canvas above him.

"This was their commanding officer?" Janaki's voice was cold.

"We believe so, Sir."

"I see."

Janaki gazed at the man in question with cold, contemptuous eyes. Company-Captain chan Tesh had briefed him fully on the portal battle . . . and how it had begun. Platoon-Captain Arthag seemed rather more philosophical about it than chan Tesh, and Janaki supposed the septman was probably right. It was very unlikely that these people used the same sort of banner to indicate the desire to parley, after all. Still, the idiot had to have recognized that Arthag wanted to *talk*, not fight, and no officer worth his salt could overlook the way the sheer incompetence of his tactics—and his own peerless stupidity—had gotten the vast majority of his command slaughtered.

"What appears to be the problem?" the Crown Prince of Ternathia asked after a moment.

"The physical damage is bad enough, Sir. He took a hit—from one of the Model 10s, I suspect—right through the body just above and behind the hips. It was a clean in-and-out that somehow missed the major internal organs, but it clipped the spine on the way through. He's paralyzed from the waist down, and there's nothing we can do about it. On top of that, though, he's clearly suicidal."

Janaki nodded, although he couldn't avoid the thought that perhaps, in this case, *not* intervening to prevent a suicide might be the better course. Even aside from the man's stupidity, and all the deaths it had already caused, there was something else about him. Something Janaki couldn't quite put a finger on . . . but which resonated uncomfortably with the Glimpse he'd experienced in the mountains east of Fort Brithik.

"As nearly as I can tell, Sir," Yar went on, "none of these men even understand what Talent is. That's fair enough, I suppose, since *we* don't have a clue how in all the Arpathian hells they do some of the things we already know they do. But because of that, none of them understands what my corpsmen and I are trying to accomplish. They don't know how to help us, and at least some of them are so busy being frightened of us that they're actively blocking us, making it a lot harder for us to do them any good. And this man here is the worst of the lot. I think part of the problem may be that he actually has at least a trace of Talent. He's more aware of what I'm doing than most of the others, but he doesn't understand it any better than they do, and his own Talent, even untrained, is producing a lot of . . . interference that makes even pain management really difficult."

"I see," Janaki said again. "Which means, of course, that he's going to suffer a lot more discomfort when we transport him."

"Which is going to tie into the entire depression/suicidal cycle," Yar agreed. "In fact, to be brutally honest, Sir, I doubt he'll survive the trip unless we take some fairly drastic action."

"Such as?"

"I'm afraid the only thing I can think of to do at this point is to shut him down completely, Sir," the Healer said. He clearly didn't like the suggestion very much, but he made it unflinchingly, and Jasak forced himself to step back and consider it before he reacted.

"You really think that's necessary?" he asked after a moment.

"Sir, my Talent's strength lies more in repairing physical damage than emotional or psychological damage," Yar said frankly. "That's one reason I'm forward deployed, where physical trauma is more likely, and usually more immediately life-threatening when it turns up. But it's going to take someone with a lot more strength on the *non*physical side to get through to this man and keep him from simply withdrawing deeper and deeper into himself until he finally just goes out like a light. I don't think you're going to get him to that kind of care in time if we don't shut him down for the trip."

Janaki nodded yet again, his expression somber. The techniques for disengaging a patient's consciousness from his body and surroundings were fairly straightforward, but it was a major breach of medical ethics to apply them without the patient's informed consent. Unfortunately, there was no way this man could even have understood the question, far less make an informed decision. Yar's Healer's oath required him to seek the patient's agreement, and forbade him to apply the techniques without that agreement from a conscious patient. Yet the same oath required him to keep his patient alive.

And there's another factor, here, Janaki thought grimly. *Of all the prisoners chan Tesh took, this one undoubtedly has the most useful information of all. We need to keep him alive ... whether he makes my skin crawl or not.*

"If you 'shut him down,' will we be able to feed him and care for him properly all the way back to Fort Raylthar?" he asked.

"That shouldn't be a problem, Sir. Or, at least, not any more of a problem than dealing with any other patient with his spinal injury would present."

"In that case, write up your recommendation. I'll endorse it and ask Company-Captain chan Tesh to approve it."

"Thank you, Sir." Yar shook his head. "I hate to do it, but I just don't see a way to avoid it. Gods, I wish at least one of their Healers had made it!"

"None of them did?" Janaki frowned. "How did that happen?"

"It was just one of those godsdamned things, Sir," Yar said heavily. "It looks like they'd set up an emergency aid station in that pathetic redoubt of theirs, and one of the four-point-fives landed right on top of them." The Healer shook his head, his eyes dark. "One or two of them survived for a while, but they were too badly wounded for us to pull them through. I hate to lose any Healer, but I have to wonder what would have happened if they'd made it. Or if even just one of them had made it!"

"Why?" Janaki was surprised by the Healer's obviously genuine frustration. It showed, and Yar gave him a very crooked smile.

"Let's just say their Healers obviously know at least a few tricks we don't, Sir."

"Such as?" Janaki quirked an eyebrow, and Yar chuckled harshly.

"Once we'd taken their encampment, we discovered that most

of their wounded from the previous fighting seemed to have been evacuated before this round. Or that's what we thought at first, at least. We captured less than half a dozen people who were still undergoing treatment, and all of them seemed to have only minor wounds. But then Junior-Armsman Hilovar and Petty-Armsman Parcanthi went to work. They'd managed to Trace quite a few of the enemy's most badly wounded from Fallen Timbers, and it turned out a lot of them were still here. The very worst hurt obviously really were evacuated—somehow; we still haven't figured that part out. But the next most badly hurt were still right here, and they'd already been returned to duty. The ones still undergoing treatment were the ones who were *least* badly hurt in the earlier fighting."

"Excuse me?" Both of Janaki's eyebrows went up this time, and Yar chuckled again.

"Believe me, Sir, you aren't any more surprised—or confused—by that than I was when they told me! But as nearly as we can tell, these people's Healers can literally *force* healing. Some of our strongest Healers can work what seem like miraculous cures, don't get me wrong about that. But as nearly as I can determine from what Hilovar and Parcanthi have been able to pick up, these people must have some technique which promotes extraordinarily rapid healing of physical traumas. I'm guessing that it's either very expensive or somehow debilitating to the Healer, because it looks to me as if they applied it first to the most badly injured—the ones who might not have made it at all without intervention—and then worked their way down the list through the men with the next worst wounds. The ones who weren't in danger, or who were injured lightly enough to recover fairly rapidly with less drastic treatment, were the ones still in their sick tents when we took the camp."

"You think one of these . . . magical Healers of theirs might have been able to repair this man's injuries?" Janaki couldn't quite keep a hint of incredulity out of his voice, and Yar snorted.

"I doubt that, Sir. Neither Hilovar nor Parcanthi is a Healer, of course, so they can't give me the kind of information another Healer could, however good their Traces or Whiffs are. From what they've told me, though, it sounds as if what these people were doing was forcing the accelerated healing of wounds which would have healed anyway, in time. I'm not saying they weren't serious, life-threatening injuries. Don't get me wrong about that, either. But we're talking about tissues healing and bones knitting—things that would have happened with the passage of time, assuming the patient survived at all. Actually . . . *regenerating* something like destroyed nerve tissue, or treating a serious brain injury—" for a moment, Yar's voice darkened and his eyes met Janaki's grimly, dark with the memory of who had apparently suffered a serious head injury at Fallen Timbers "—would require an entirely different order of ability. I'm not prepared to say it's flatly impossible, but I'd say it's very unlikely. Unfortunately."

He was silent for a few seconds, brooding on what might have been if the other side's Healers *had* been capable of that sort of true miracle, then shook himself and continued.

"At the same time, though, if we had one of *their* Healers, we could probably get this man as recovered from his physical injuries as he's ever going to get before we started trying to transport him. In that case—if *all* we had to worry about was his mental and emotional state—I wouldn't be anywhere near as concerned as I am about his prognosis."

"I understand. And, like you, I hate to lose any Healer, whoever's uniform he's wearing." Janaki shook his head. "For that matter, to be honest, if they really do have that sort of a healing technique, we need to figure out what it is and learn to duplicate it as quickly as we can—for a lot of reasons."

"Agreed, Sir." Yar sighed. "Agreed."

The Healer stood a moment longer, gazing down at the stone-faced, totally nonresponsive man in the cot, then shook himself.

"Most of the rest of their wounded are in far better shape for transport," he said more briskly. "If you'll follow me, I'll show you what I mean, and then we can discuss—"

He led the crown prince towards the other side of the hospital tent, and Janaki followed after one more glance at the rigid, dead-eyed man responsible for so much suffering and death.

*   *   *

"Darcel Kinlafia?"

Kinlafia jerked as the unfamiliar voice spoke from directly behind him. He whipped around, and found himself staring at a man who was decidedly on the tall side, even for a Ternathian, in the uniform of an Imperial Marine platoon-captain.

Jumpy as a flea on a hot griddle, Janaki thought, reaching up one hand to reassure Taleena as the falcon bridled on his shoulder. Then he realized why the other man was that way. Post combat stress burned in the haunted eyes of the sun-browned man with shaggy hair that needed a barber's shears. Kinlafia was probably no more than ten years or so older than Janaki himself, but he looked far older than that at the moment.

"Yes." Kinlafia cleared his throat, easing his elbow back from its desperate clamp on the butt of his holstered pistol. "I'm Kinlafia. And you're . . . ?"

"Platoon-Captain chan Calirath," Janaki said, and the Voice's eyes widened.

"Good gods." He swallowed. "How can I help you, Sir? Your Highness? Your Grand Highness?"

His face had gone red as he stumbled over the correct form of address for a Ternathian imperial crown prince, and Janaki grinned.

"Platoon-Captain chan Calirath is fine. In fact, in light of how closely the two of us will be working together on this project, you might even opt for Janaki." Kinlafia gaped at him, and Janaki shrugged. "I don't stand on a lot of formality out here. In fact, I hate it. And, let's face it—I'm a pretty damned junior officer when all's said and done, after all."

Kinlafia's jaw was still scraping the ground, and Janaki sighed. It was always the same, although at least the military seemed to have figured out how to take it more or less in stride. No doubt because the military had its own chain of command and rules of seniority, which gave it a convenient pigeonhole marked "officer, junior, one" rather than "ruler after the gods, future, one." Still, he'd had more than enough experience even with fellow Marines, much less civilians, to understand how it worked. Occasionally, though, he wished his conversations with people he hadn't met before could be as ordinary as everyone else's conversations seemed to be.

"Look, just think of me as the officer assigned to escort our prisoners to the rear while simultaneously cleverly extracting politically and militarily critical information from them. Try to forget about the rest of it, would you? It's a damned nuisance, frankly, having people trip over their feet and stumble over their tongues every time I show up somewhere or run into someone new. And bad as it is *here*, it's even worse back home. I've just about made up my mind to stay in the Corps as long as they'll let me hide out here."

Kinlafia blinked at him. Then, all at once, he relaxed and actually managed a grin. It wasn't much of a smile, not on that grief- and anger-grooved face, but it was genuine. And, as he saw it, Janaki also had a Glimpse of the warmhearted, humorous man who'd once lived behind that face . . . and how important that man might prove to be. And not just to Sharona, the prince realized as his sister's features wavered through the same Glimpse. What in the names of all the gods, he wondered, did this man have to do with *Andrin*? But the Glimpse had vanished almost as quickly as it had come. Its

echoes hummed and quivered down inside him, with a deep, burning sense of true urgency and buzzing about in his bones with a
familiar sense of frustration. He couldn't pin it down, couldn't take
it by the throat and *make* it make sense, yet he knew it had been
a true Glimpse. Something that *would* come to pass, not merely
something which *might*.

"Really?" Kinlafia said, obviously oblivious to Janaki's Glimpse. "I
guess I hadn't thought of it that way. All right, I'll do my best to
forget who you are—and who you're related to."

"Thanks," Janaki said dryly, suppressing any outward sign of his
Glimpse with the thoroughness of long practice. "Actually, if the
Corps would let me, I'd probably go ahead and trade on a bit of
that familial fame after all, if it would let me spend an extra day
or so right here instead of heading straight back. Trust me, even a
Calirath's imperial arse gets *damned* tired of a saddle after a week
or two! Unfortunately, they want these people—and you—back up
the chain as quickly as we can get you there."

"Me?" Something almost like suspicion flared at the backs of
Kinlafia's eyes.

"Of course you." Janaki snorted. "I'm almost positive that a direct
order for you to report to First Director Limana ASAP is headed
back down the Voice chain to you right this minute. You're the
closest thing we've got to an actual eyewitness of the original attack,
and you accompanied Platoon-Captain Arthag's column all the way
back here. *And* you were part of the fight here at the portal; you
were one of the first men into their encampment; and you're the
only Voice—and the only observer of *any* sort who also happens to
have perfect recall—who was here for all of that. You think, perhaps,
the Powers That Be might be just a *little* interested in your offhand
impressions of those events?"

Kinlafia blinked again, and his expression changed from one of
suspicion to one of comprehension . . . and fear.

"I don't—"

"Stop," Janaki interrupted. "Don't say it."

"Don't say it?" Kinlafia repeated, and Janaki shook his head.

"You were about to say that you didn't see how your impressions
could be all that important," he said almost gently. "You were about to
point out that you're not a trained military man, that Company-Captain
chan Tesh and Platoon-Captain Arthag are much better information
sources on the actual fighting here, and on the enemy's tactics. And
you're about to say that Petty-Captain Yar's had much more contact with
the prisoners, especially the wounded ones, than you have. Right?"

"Something along those lines," Kinlafia said slowly, and Janaki shrugged.

"All of which is beside the point," he said. "As, I'm afraid, is how much I know it's going to hurt to answer all the questions people have for you."

This time there was no mistaking the gentleness in his voice. Yet it was a stern, inflexible gentleness. One that admitted that the owner of that voice understood how much pain even the most gentle interrogation would inflict, yet never backed away from the *necessity* of that interrogation. And one which somehow managed both to acknowledge the pain and Kinlafia's fear without in any way diminishing them. To sympathize with them in a way that offered the strength to overcome them rather than simple commiseration.

Kinlafia stared at the young officer who'd asked him to call him by his first name and realized that whether Janaki chan Calirath recognized it or not, that endless line of imperial ancestors stood behind him. There was, Kinlafia realized, not an ounce of arrogance in the young man who would one day wear the Winged Crown in the imperial throne room in Estafel. But the blood of Erthain the Great still flowed in his veins, and the mysterious magnetism which had led men and women to follow the Caliraths straight into the fire—and into the pages of legend—for over five thousand years glowed inside him.

Balkar chan Tesh and Delokahn Yar had been trying to get Kinlafia to face the inevitable for almost a week now, ever since the portal attack, and they'd failed. Now, in two short sentences, Crown Prince Janaki had succeeded.

And he's not even my *crown prince*, the Voice thought with a strange mix of despair, amusement, and surrender.

"All right, Your Highness," he said finally. "You're right. I know you are. But it's not going to be easy. Not at all."

"I realize that," Janaki acknowledged, then glanced up at the afternoon sun. "Look," he said, "it must be about time for supper. Why don't we let this rest until after we've eaten? If you're agreeable, we'll drop by my tent after we eat, drag out a bottle of Bernithian whiskey, and get down to it."

"Of course," Kinlafia said. And to his credit, Janaki thought, he actually managed to sound as if he thought it was a good idea.

CHAPTER
TWENTY-NINE

"I NEED TO know everything," Janaki chan Calirath said.

He sat crosslegged on his bedroll, having surrendered his single camp stool to his guest, despite the visitor's obvious discomfort at accepting it. But that discomfort over seating arrangements disappeared abruptly, devoured by something far worse, as the civilian's eyes met his, dark with memory.

"Everything?" Kinlafia asked hoarsely, and Janaki nodded.

"Believe me, I'm not asking this lightly. I've read Company-Captain chan Tesh's reports. I've spoken to Company-Captain Halifu, and Voice Traygan. I know *what* happened out here, but I can't begin to imagine what it must have been like to live through it, and—"

"No," Kinlafia agreed harshly. "You can't."

"I know that. But if we're going to protect others," Janaki said very gently, "we have to understand these people."

"What's to understand?" The demand was bitter, full of gritty rage, the pain feeding the white furnace of his hate. "They blew my crew to hell without a shred of mercy. They shot down Ghartoun chan Hagrahyl while he stood there with his hands empty, in plain sight. They attacked an unarmed man under a parley banner! They're butchers. You want to protect our people? Then send in a division or six and wipe '*these people*' off the face of the earth. Off every frigging earth we find them on!"

Janaki sipped air slowly. This man was even more bitter than he'd feared, and the prince wondered if he'd been wise after all to wait until after supper. Perhaps if he'd charged straight ahead earlier, before Kinlafia had had time to anticipate this moment—to finger through his dreadful memories and cut himself on their sharpnesses all over again—it might not have been so painful.

But Janaki had wanted time to chew on the strange little flash of Glimpse he'd had earlier, and so he'd waited. He hadn't been able to refine what he'd Seen, but he was even more convinced that it had been a true Glimpse. That narrowed his own options considerably, and while the Voice had every right to be bitter, he had to be made to see the larger picture, as well. And not just because of the information he might provide.

"Voice Kinlafia," he began again, "I understand—"

"No, you don't!"

"If you would be so good as to let me finish speaking before assuming you know what I'm about to say," Janaki said levelly, "we'd get through this agonizing conversation faster."

The man seated on his camp stool glared at him, breathing hard for a long, dangerous moment. Then Kinlafia's shoulders slumped suddenly. He sat back with a weary sigh and pinched the bridge of his nose.

"I'm sorry, Your Highness. That was . . . out of line."

"Yes, it was," Janaki agreed calmly. "What I was going to say is that I understand that you've been through a very personal hell which no one else—certainly no one who isn't himself a Voice and can't experience it directly himself—will ever be able to fully comprehend. I recognize that, and I regret the necessity of dragging you back through it all over again. But *you* have to understand that you're going to *have* to go back over it again and again. Not just for me, but for all of the analysts waiting to debrief you, to try to get some feeling about, some handle on, just what in all the Arpathian hells we're really up against out here.

"And what that means for you, is that somehow you've got to move forward. Not 'put it behind you.' Not 'let go of it.' I'm neither coldhearted nor arrogant enough to tell a grieving man something like that."

Suspicious brilliance touched Kinlafia's eyes. Eyes which blinked rapidly while their owner looked briefly away.

"But you do need to move forward," Janaki continued with that same gentle implacability, drawing Kinlafia's gaze back to him. "You have to decide what you're going to do about it. Not what the Army or the Corps is going to do. What *you're* going to do."

"What *can* I do?" Kinlafia lifted his hands in a helpless, frustrated gesture. "Other than join the Army and shoot as many of the bastards as I can line up in my sights, that is?"

Even to himself, that carried an edge of something that was almost . . . childish. Petulant, perhaps. Somehow, he felt vaguely ashamed to be sitting here in front of the heir to the throne of Sharona's most powerful and ancient nation whining about his own sense of helplessness. As if the entire multiverse revolved around or depended upon his personal exaction of vengeance for his dead.

But even as that thought crossed his own mind, Janaki surprised him by smiling.

"You'd be wasted in the Army, Kinlafia!"

"I beg your pardon?" Kinlafia blinked, and Janaki shrugged.

"Think about it. What would you accomplish, in the Army? You'd be just another soldier, and you're a Voice. That means you'd be stuck using your Talent, not your rifle. One more messenger, passing other people's orders through the Voice chain. Going where you were told to go. Shooting when you were told to shoot . . . and *not* shooting when you were ordered to hold your fire. Vothan! Voices are way too valuable for the military to risk in combat if it can possibly be avoided—you *know* that. So if you were to enlist, your chances of actually shooting anyone would go down, not up!"

That drew a scowl, and the crown prince chuckled a bit grimly.

"I didn't think you'd thought about that aspect of it," he said.

"No," Kinlafia muttered. "I hadn't."

"Then there's probably another thing you haven't thought about, either. Frankly, the *last* thing we can afford to do is to repeat what Company-Captain chan Tesh and Platoon-Captain Arthag managed to accomplish here."

"Why?" This time, the question wasn't belligerent, just baffled.

"Because we don't know how many of them there are, for one thing. How many universes do they occupy? How big is *their* army? Their navy? What the hells *do* they use for technology? Most of what we've seen doesn't make any sense at all yet—you know that even better than I do, because you've actually seen it. And Seen it, for that matter."

Janaki paused, holding Kinlafia's eyes levelly with his own, and wondered if the Voice saw the ghosts hovering within them. A part of him hungered to tell the Voice—tell anyone—what he'd Glimpsed that night in the mountains. But he couldn't. The visions of death and destruction, of flame exploding across the night, of bizarre weapons spitting devastation . . . those were his alone, for now at least. He was desperately afraid that they were going to become the property of other Sharonians, but they hadn't yet.

The thought flickered through his mind once again that he really ought to consider sending word to his father by Voice of what he had Glimpsed. Yet, what could he truly tell the emperor? That he'd Seen images of war and slaughter? That he'd felt the foretaste of his own terror? That he was afraid? His father's Talent was much stronger than Janaki's—almost as strong, Janaki suspected, as his sister Andrin's. He'd probably already Glimpsed everything Janaki had, and even if he hadn't, the Calirath Glimpses weren't something to be discussed through any intermediary, even that of a Voice. They had to be discussed face-to-face, where Talent could speak directly to Talent.

I wish my Glimpse had been clearer, *just this once, at least,* he thought far from the first time, with familiar frustration. But it hadn't been clear . . . only vast, powerful, and terrifying.

Well, at least if chan Tesh is sending me all the way home with these people, I'll be seeing Father in person for that little chat a lot sooner than I'd expected. That's something.

"We punched right through them here," he continued, still holding Kinlafia's gaze captive with his own. "Punched through so quickly and easily it wasn't even a contest. But this time we had the advantage of surprise, since they presumably don't understand *our* technology any better than we understand theirs. And armies, unfortunately, tend to learn more from failure than they do from success. Do we really want to assume we're looking at an endless succession of walkovers? They obviously didn't expect anything like Platoon-Captain chan Talmarha's four-point-fives. What if it turns out that they've got weapons *we* haven't even seen yet? Weapons that make mortars look like damp firecrackers by comparison? Do we want to send in 'a division or six' to wipe out every post they have in this region, then discover they've got *six hundred* divisions, with heavy weapons support, poised to wipe out every man, woman, and child from here to Sharona?"

"No." Kinlafia bit his lip, and his voice was low and reluctant. "No, we don't."

He sat slumped on the camp stool, gazing at nothing and seeing something that made his eyes go bleak, and for two long, endless minutes, he said absolutely nothing more. But then, finally, his eyes refocused on Janaki, deep, dark . . . and lost.

"What I never told anyone," he said in a terrible whisper, "was how much I loved her."

Janaki didn't speak. He couldn't.

"You're not a Voice," Kinlafia said softly. "You don't understand what it's like to communicate with another Voice. When you're linked, deeply linked, the way we were during that ghastly attack . . ."

His voice trailed off for another long moment, and his hands twisted themselves together in his lap.

"You *become* the other person, for a few minutes. For however long you're linked. Voices try to avoid going that deep. No matter how voluntary the link is, it's almost a . . . violation. It doesn't happen with normal message relays, but when the psychic impact is this deep, hits this hard, you *fuse*. Everything she felt, everything she saw, and heard, and smelled happened to *me*."

A shudder rippled visibly through him.

"For those few minutes, I *was* Shaylar. I could Hear and See more than just the thoughts and sights she was transmitting. I could taste her terror. Her love for Jathmar. The realization that she would never see her parents again, never have children, never leave that tangle of broken trees alive. Yet she stayed linked with me, deeper than I've ever linked with another Voice. And she kept shooting at them, when anyone else would have been cowering on the ground with both arms over his head. Hell, some of the others were doing just that! But not her. No, not *her*. She heard the rifle fire dying, knew our friends—our family—were being killed all around her, and she never stopped. Never quit *once*. She burned all her maps, all her notes, *everything*, and then she reached for her gun again, because there was no one else still up and shooting, No one but Jathmar, and the bastards killed him right in front of her! Gods! She was so beautiful, so brave . . . and I couldn't get to her, couldn't reach her, couldn't be *with* her, and then I *felt* her go. . . ."

His voice shattered.

Janaki's own eyes burned, and his vision blurred, but his hands were steady as he drew the cork from a bottle of highland single malt whiskey. He'd suspected from the beginning that it was going to be required, but even his darkest estimate had fallen short of how badly it would be needed. Now he poured some into a glass and thrust it into the shaken Voice's hands.

Kinlafia wrapped himself around the liquor and gulped at it, his hands unsteady as he struggled to regain control. Janaki was wise enough to say nothing. He simply refilled the glass when it emptied, then sat down on his bedroll again and waited until Kinlafia finally mastered himself sufficiently to meet his gaze one more.

"Thanks," the Voice said then, hoarsely, gesturing with the empty glass in his hand. Then he wiped wetness from his face with a brusque sleeve and cleared his throat, roughly.

"I still hoped, you know," he said. Janaki raised an eyebrow, and the Voice grimaced. "I still hoped she was alive. Parcanthi and Hilovar Saw her still alive after the fighting. Saw her being taken back to that camp of theirs. I hoped so hard that after we hit those bastards, we'd find her. But we didn't."

"But there were those glimpses of some sort of transport animal," Janaki said gently. "And we didn't find her body, either."

"Do you think I didn't think about that?" Kinlafia demanded harshly, half-glaring at Janaki. "But you've seen that swamp. My maximum range for reaching her was over *six hundred miles*. Sure, I had to trance to do it, but even if her own Voice had been completely shut down by some head injury, like Hilovar described, I'd have been able to sense her at up to four hundred, maybe even five, after linking that closely during the fight. I'd be able to *feel* her presence the same way I can feel the direction to the closest portal, and there was *nothing*. What kind of 'transport animal' could have taken her across four hundred miles of this kind of swamp in less than thirty-six hours?"

"I don't know," Janaki admitted. "I can't think of one."

"Neither can I. But we already know she was critically wounded, probably dying, just from what Hilovar and Parcanthi could tell us. So they put a dying woman on what ever *'transport animal'* they had and dragged her off to die somewhere out there in the middle of all that mud and water."

The Voice's jaws clenched again, and his hands tightened around the whiskey glass.

"They were probably trying desperately to keep her alive, you know," Janaki pointed out quietly. Kinlafia glared at him again, and the crown prince shrugged. "I didn't say they were doing it out of the goodness of their hearts, Voice Kinlafia."

"No, they weren't," Kinlafia grated. Then he drew a deep, shaky breath. "And whyever they were doing it, they were the ones responsible for what happened to her and all of the rest of my friends in the first place. They were the ones who chased them down like animals, then slaughtered them around her. The ones who did *all* of that to her before she died."

He shook his head, his eyes harder than obsidian.

"I will never, *ever* forgive them for that," he said quietly. "Maybe Shaylar could have done that. I can't. But you're right about what would happen if I enlisted. So what can I do, really?"

"You can start by telling me everything," Janaki replied. "Every detail you can recall, no matter how trivial. I won't lie and tell you this won't be painful, because it will. I intend to take you through every moment of contact you've had with these people, both directly and through Shaylar, over and over again."

"Why?" Dark emotion flared in Kinlafia's shadowed eyes.

"Because you need to get back to Sharona as quickly as possible, where what you know will do the most good for the people responsible for deciding how we respond. But before you go, the people at *this* end of the multiverse need the same information. I'm going to get that for them before we pull out, and the more times you go through it, step-by-step, the more you'll remember."

"Voices have perfect recall," Kinlafia objected harshly. "You said that yourself."

"Yes, they do. And at the moment, yours is shrouded with severe emotional shock. That's why it's imperative that we take you through it repeatedly—now, while it's still as fresh as possible. To be honest, this should have been done right after the initial attack, not after this long a delay's had time to cloud details."

Kinlafia winced, and Janaki shook his head.

"I'm sorry, but that's the way it should have been done, and it wasn't. We can't afford to let those experiences get any more distant. It's going to be hell going back through them, but there's no way of knowing what tiny bit or piece may prove to be vitally important before this is all over. Even her emotions could give us important information, and it's all there. Everything you Saw, Heard. Everything she touched or smelled. Everything she did, even everything *you* thought while you were linked. All the ideas, the impressions, the unconscious judgments—they're all in there, simmering away in the back of your mind. What we have to do is extract them, pull them out past the barriers of emotional reaction. And, for what it's worth, *I* have perfect recall, too, which is one reason I get to be the coldhearted bastard who drags you back through it all."

"Yes." Kinlafia was biting his lip again, but he nodded slowly, manifestly unhappily. "I see your point—all too clearly. I don't want to relive any of that, but I don't have a choice, do I?"

"No. Not if you really want to help us understand these people. And I don't have a choice, either, I'm afraid. I imagine you'll hate my guts before we're done."

"Probably." A humorless smile touched Kinlafia's mouth. "At the time, at least. But not permanently. I hated my third-level teacher while she was drilling multiplication tables into my head, when all I wanted to do was spend the day outside with a fishing pole or a hiking trail. But I didn't hate her for long. Not once I figured out how useful math is."

Janaki smiled back at him.

"That's hopeful sounding. I was rather looking forward to the chance to get better acquainted. I don't have much opportunity to talk with civilians, let alone Talented ones. Not just out here, either. Generally, people seem sufficiently in awe of my title to produce conversations that are a bit . . . stilted. If not downright impossible."

"I can't imagine." Kinlafia gave him a wan smile. "Be fair, Your Highness. It *is* a little unnerving talking to the Crown Prince of Ternathia."

"Who occasionally puts his socks on inside out in the dark, the same as any other man jolted awake in the middle of the night."

Kinlafia actually grinned. Then he sat back with a sigh.

"All right. I'll go through it all as many times as it takes, but what then? It sounded like you had something specific in mind for me to do, beyond helping you learn what I know."

"I have." Janaki nodded. "Tell me, Voice Kinlafia. What are the best ways a man—or woman—can have a really big impact on civilization?"

"Civilization?" Kinlafia echoed, and Janaki nodded.

Rather than answer off the cuff, the Voice took time to think about it. Janaki was glad. That was a good sign, considering what he wanted this man to do. Finally, Kinlafia pursed his lips.

"You can invent something really important," he said slowly. "Like a new form of transportation, or a new weapon or a new medicine."

Janaki nodded again.

"You can write something that influences the way people think," Kinlafia continued. "Or you could report the news in a way that changes how people think and act."

"That's true, all of it," Janaki agreed. "But tell me—who tells an army what to attack?"

"The generals."

"But who tells the generals?" Janaki pressed. "Who *sends* the generals?"

"The politicians, of cour—"

Kinlafia broke off, and his eyes widened.

"You can't be serious! I'm not a politician. I'm just a survey crew Voice!"

"You are *not* 'just a survey crew Voice.' Not any longer," Janaki told him. "You're the sole survivor of the crew that was wiped out by the greatest threat our civilization has ever faced. You were *there*. As close to there as any Sharonian anywhere. People will want to hear your story, and how you tell that story will have enormous impact on what people think about this crisis and how government leaders respond to it."

"But—"

Janaki's raised hand halted the automatic protest.

"If I were in your shoes," the crown prince said, "I'd run for the very next seat in the House of Talents of whatever government you call home. For that matter, by the time you get home, there may be just *one* government. The gods only know how all of this is going to play out in the end, but if we're not alone out here in the multiverse after all, then Sharona *needs* a world government, and that government will have a House of Talents. Make no mistake about that. And if I were you, I'd move heaven and earth and half the Arpathian hells, if necessary, to get myself into it."

"Gods, you're serious." A fire had kindled in Kinlafia's stunned eyes. "Do you really think I'd have a chance to get elected to something like that?"

"I can't name anyone with a better shot at it," Janaki said frankly. "You'd have instant name recognition. By the time you get back to Sharona, you'll be so famous the news media will flock to you, turn you into a major celebrity. If you tell them you're running for office on a platform of protecting other innocents, they'll give you so much free coverage you won't have to buy ad space in anything—newsprint or Voice network.

"And speaking of the Voice network, you're one of their own. They'll adore you, Kinlafia, and they'll champion your cause. You couldn't ask for better advocates than the Voice Guild and the Voice News Association. Play your cards right, and they might even bankroll your campaign. Yes, yes. I know they can't do that directly. That's illegal in most nations." He snorted. "The only one I know of where it *isn't* is Uromathia, which is hardly the sort of example we want to be following, I suppose. But the point is that they'll bend over backwards to publicize your *need* for funds. The money will come. Never doubt that. You may even find schoolchildren taking up donations for you."

Darcel Kinlafia stared at him. Then he drew in a deep breath, released it again with a sound of perplexed astonishment, and finally found his voice once more.

"Why are you doing this, Your Highness? Why would you tell me these things? Especially after telling me why what I want to do to eradicate these bastards from the face of the multiverse is a bad idea?"

"For several reasons, really," Janaki said.

He considered telling Kinlafia all of them, but decided—once again—against it. People tended to get . . . nervous when they found out a member of the imperial family had experienced a Glimpse which convinced him it was absolutely vital for them to do something. Especially when the Calirath in question couldn't explain *why* it was vital, since he didn't know yet himself. No, better to stick with all of the other perfectly valid reasons Janaki had been able to come up with.

"First," he said, "public outrage over this is going to be incredibly high. Sharona needs a focal point for that outrage. Something or someone people can support to feel like they're doing something to help.

"At the moment, you're a very angry man. That's inevitable, given what you've experienced, and I accept that you'll never be able to forgive what happened. But you're also an honest, conscientious man. And, if you'll forgive me for saying so, a compassionate one. In fact, it's that very compassion which *makes* you so angry right now. I don't know how all of that anger will work out in the end, but I do know there are all too many unscrupulous men who are going to try to take advantage of everyone else's anger and fear without giving one single, solitary damn about compassion or conscience. They're going to use it to put themselves into positions of power for their own selfish ends. I'd far rather see public support behind someone like *you*. Behind someone who genuinely cares—who's driven by a need for justice, not a desire to put public office into the service of personal gain.

"Don't misunderstand me. The snakes are going to come out of the shadows whatever else happens, whether you run for office or not. It's simply part of human nature. But if you declare your candidacy, you'll rivet a huge chunk of the public's attention to *your* campaign. Hopefully, that will eclipse some of the other, more manipulative campaign messages, and that would be a very good thing for Sharona."

"I suppose that makes some sense. But the fact that it's a good thing for Sharona won't keep it from making some mighty powerful men hate me," Kinlafia pointed out.

"Probably. That's all part of the game of politics, too. But don't underestimate the power of a man who's been wronged, appealing to the world for justice. Some of the men—and women—whose plans you spike might just fall under the spell themselves, and support you. Others will try to hitch themselves to you for gain, try to find a way to use you, and you'll want to watch out for that, too.

"Because that's really the most important part, when you come right down to it. Exercising a moderating effect on the rhetoric and fury of the campaign in the first place would be worthwhile all by itself, but the real object of the exercise is to put you into a position where you can actually accomplish something. A position which lets you kick the arses of the carrion eaters out to twist this entire crisis around to their own personal advantage."

"I see."

"Actually," Janaki smiled, "I doubt you do. Not the same way I do, anyway—not yet. But I've had politics bred into me for five thousand years. Coming out here," he waved one hand at the entrance to the tent, where the chill stars of a northern autumn were beginning to prick the sky, "was part vacation from my political education, and part necessary political foundation for the job I'll have to do some day."

Kinlafia blinked in surprise, and Janaki shrugged.

"A man who commands armies and navies tends to do a better job of it if he's spent time *in* the army or navy in question. Not always, I'm sorry to say, but on average. And people have greater confidence in a man who's been at the pointy end himself, as it were. Maybe even more to the point, someone who's had personal experience of what 'sending in the troops' can cost the troops has a tendency to stop and think really hard before he sends them into harm's way . . . and has more moral authority when he decides he has to do it anyway. Those are just a few of the reasons why emperors of Ternathia are almost always *chan* Calirath. We're military veterans, nearly all of us.

"But that's beside the point I'm trying to make. I truly believe Sharona needs the job you'll do, Voice Kinlafia. And," he added softly, "you'll need that job, too, won't you? Badly, I think. Not just for something to do, either. You've got to decide exactly how you want to confront Shaylar Nargra-Kolmayr's life . . . and death. Is it vengeance you want, or justice, and what price are you—and all our people—prepared to pay for whichever they choose to purchase in the end?"

Kinlafia's tightened-down fingers locked together. He couldn't speak at all, just gave Janaki a jerky nod, and Janaki nodded back.

"That's all I'll say for now, then. We'll talk about this again, if you're half as interested as I think you are. Or will be soon. We'll be traveling together at least as far as Fort Brithik, and I can probably teach you a fair bit—or give you some pointers, at least—along the way. And I can send letters of introduction ahead with you, as well. Hook you up with people who can help you in all kinds of useful ways."

Kinlafia gazed at him very thoughtfully for several seconds, then produced an off-center, lopsided smile.

"If Ternathia were a democracy, and if I were a Ternathian, I'd vote for you, Your Highness, in every election you ran in," he said, and Janaki blinked.

"Why?"

"Because you care about the people you'll rule one day. And you don't just care about Ternathians. You care about Sharonians—*all* of us. Hells, Your Highness, if you'll pardon my language, you even care about *me*, and I'm not even one of your subjects! From where I sit, that's pretty damned rare."

Janaki frowned in surprise. First, because Kinlafia was surprised. And, second, because he realized Kinlafia might just be right. Perhaps the Caliraths really were a rarer breed than he'd actually realized and he'd simply been too close to see it.

"Maybe you're right," he told the Voice with a smile even more lopsided than Kinlafia's had been. "I'll have to remember to thank my father, the next time I see him, for pounding that into me. Trust me, it wasn't always a particularly easy job!"

He chuckled, and Kinlafia chuckled back. But then the crown prince's expression sobered once more.

"Either way, that's probably enough said on that subject, for now, at least," he said. "Which, unfortunately, brings us to the more immediate reason for this conversation. Do you want another whiskey before we begin?"

CHAPTER THIRTY

ANDRIN'S FASHIONABLE COIFFURE streamed out behind her in a mass of flying, golden-shot black silk, shredded and ruined by the wind, as she stood at the forward edge of the thirty-thousand-ton steamer IMS *Windtreader*'s promenade deck. She paid her hair's careful arrangement's destruction no heed; she had far too much on her mind to worry about that, although her lips twisted wryly in anticipation of her lady-in-waiting—and protocol instructor's—reaction. Lady Merissa was nearly three times Andrin's age and profoundly conscious of her charge's social standing. She would undoubtedly be properly horrified . . . if she could bring herself out of her seasick misery long enough to notice. Andrin felt genuinely sorry for Merissa, even if she did find it unfathomable how anyone could be *seasick* aboard such a large vessel. Personally, she would vastly have preferred her father's racing yacht, *Peregrine*, where the motion would have been truly lively, but Lady Merissa's misery was too obvious for anyone to doubt.

Yet sympathy or no, this morning was far too glorious for Andrin to spend cooped up in the cabin, holding Lady Merissa's hand solicitously. And so she had climbed out of bed the moment the rising sun sent its golden light streaming into her cabin's scuttles. She'd thrown on an appropriate gown and a warm woolen coat, lifted her hawk Finena from her perch to her gauntleted arm, and headed for the cabin door with indecorous haste. Lady Merissa was far too well-bred to protest sharing her cabin with both a grand princess and her favorite falcon, but Andrin knew her seasick mentor would rest easier with Finena out of the room. So she'd carried her companion up into the sunshine with her, which had delighted the hawk as much as it had her.

And they'd needed that delight. Needed it badly.

The news of the slaughter of the Chalgyn Consortium survey crew had broken, as everyone had known it must. And the impact on public opinion had been even worse than anyone had feared.

The print coverage, and the editorials were bad enough. The non-Talented majority of Sharonians might not be able to share the Voicenet reports, experience the events directly, but they understood what had happened. They might not understand *why* it had happened—in which, Andrin admitted, they were not so very different from their emperors and kings and presidents—but they knew in excruciating detail what had happened to that survey crew. They knew because one courageous woman had held onto her Voice link through hell itself to be certain that they would . . . and they knew that, too.

But for those who could See the Voicenet reportage, it was even worse.

Andrin had forced herself to See the SUNN Voicenet report. She had only an extremely limited telepathic Talent, but it was more than enough to follow Voicenet transmissions. After witnessing that report, however, she found herself wishing passionately that she'd had no telepathic Talent at all. Not even the nightmares she'd experienced in her own Glimpses had been enough to prepare her for the sheer horror of what Shaylar Nargra-Kolmayr had endured before her own death.

The events themselves had been horrible enough, but the sheer power and clarity of Shaylar's Voice had stunned a universe. Everyone had known that she'd been one of Sharona's top Voices, but the intensity of her link with Darcel Kinlafia had been staggering. *Every* nuance of her emotions, her suspicions, her observations—every spike of terror, every gut-wrenching spasm of grief, every glorious, white-fire instant of courage—had hit every telepath on Sharona squarely between the eyes. The horror of those fiendish fireballs and lightning bolts. The massacre of her team leader, standing there without even a weapon in his hands when they shot him down. The dauntless determination of one young woman, burning her priceless records, her deadly charts, while their friends screamed and died and *burned* around her.

It was all there. It had happened to *them*, to *their* sisters, and *their* brothers. They knew precisely what she had experienced, because they had experienced it with her. And because even as they Saw it through her eyes, they had Seen it through the Darcel Kinlafia's, as well. He had relayed Shaylar's thoughts and emotions with agonizing fidelity, but they'd been too deeply linked for him to separate his own from the message when he passed it up the Voice chain.

And so, in addition to their own reactions to Shaylar's raw experiences, they saw them through the eyes of a man who had obviously loved her. And that added still more poignancy—and horror—to the nightmare which had devoured her.

No single event in the entire history of Sharona had *ever* hit home like this one. Andrin knew that it worried her father deeply. Zindel chan Calirath was no more immune to outrage and fury than anyone else, but he was Emperor of Ternathia. He *had* to think beyond the outrage, beyond the madness of the moment, and the blast furnace anger and hatred—and fear—sweeping through his home universe threatened to severely limit his own options and choices. As he'd told Shamir Taje he feared before the Voice Conclave, and as Andrin had seen in her own horrible Glimpses, the chance of somehow evading the cataclysmic possibility of open warfare with these people, whoever they were, was growing less and less likely by the day.

And that was the true reason—little though Andrin was prepared to admit it to anyone, especially her father—that she'd felt such a need to race up to the promenade deck and submerge herself in life and the input of her physical senses. To at least temporarily escape the conviction that some huge inescapable boulder was grinding down the mountainside of history towards her, crushing everything in its path.

And for the moment, at least, it was working, she thought gratefully in the corner of her mind still focused on analysis. It was a very small corner, because she was nearly drunk on the sensations of sunlight on seawater, of wind hammering past her face, the deep-seated vibration of *Windtreader*'s powerful engines underfoot, and the rhythmic wash and rumble of water, piling away from the ship's stem in a great, white furrow as the liner cut through the whitecaps. *Windtreader* was slower than *Peregrine*, the imperial yacht, but she'd been built for the trans-Vandor run between Ternathia and New Farnal, with emphasis on speed and comfort. She was easily capable of a sustained twenty knots, and her furnishings rivaled those of the finest hotel ashore. Designed to transport better than five hundred first-class passengers, four hundred and fifty second-class, and up to six hundred third-class, she had more than enough internal space for the huge staff which had to go everywhere the Emperor of Ternathia went. Which was fortunate, since this time there were several hundred important politicians and *their* staffs, as well.

And while *Windtreader* might be slower than oceanic greyhounds like *Peregrine*, it was unlikely she'd be called upon to outrun anyone on this voyage.

Andrin looked to starboard, where one of *Windtreader*'s guardians plowed steadily through the swell. IMS *Prince of Ternathia* was an armored cruiser—twelve thousand tons of sickle-prowed armor plate, with four twin nine-inch turrets, two each fore and aft, and a broadside of fourteen six-inch guns. Her sister ship, IMS *Duke Ihtrial* cruised watchfully to port of the liner, interposed between her and any threat, and Andrin wondered just how anxious Master-Captain Farsal chan Morthain, the escort commander, was feeling this fine morning as *she* stood here, enjoying the exuberant wind. It wasn't often, after all, that the emperor, the heir-secondary, the entire Privy Council, the speakers of all three of the Ternathian Houses of Parliament, a sizable chunk of the most senior members of the Ministry of Foreign Affairs, the most senior lords justicar of the Emperor's Bench, over seventy members of Parliament, *and* the Imperial chiefs of staff were all packed aboard a single ship.

Officially, chan Morthain and his cruisers were out there to guard *Windtreader* against "pirates," but there hadn't been a single pirate operating in the waters between Ternath Island and Tajvana in centuries. The possibility of some lunatic in a fast boat loaded with explosives probably figured far more prominently in chan Morthain's thinking. Personally, Andrin felt quite certain that the cruisers were intended much more as a precaution—and possibly a somewhat pointed hint—designed to get the attention of some of Ternathia's less scrupulous "allies" than as a defense against any sort of criminals.

Finena, perched delicately on Andrin's forearm, cocked her sleek head. She eyed the cloud of seabirds overhead with hungry interest, and Andrin laughed as the movement pulled her out of her own thoughts.

"Perhaps you should breakfast up here, love," she told the falcon. "Poor Merissa would lose the contents of her tummy—again—if you broke your fast in the cabin."

Finena tipped her head to gaze across at Andrin. Like Janaki's Taleena, Finena was an imperial Ternathian peregrine, but she looked like no other hawk which had ever broken shell in the imperial aviary. She'd hatched from the final clutch of Emperor Zindel's beloved falcon Charaeil, and though she wasn't quite a true albino—her eyes were as dark as any other peregrine's—she showed none of the bold bluish-gray plumage of male peregrines, nor even the browner tones of the females of the species. *Her* plumage was a dazzling white, and she showed mere shadows of gray where other peregrines' underparts would have been marked with sharply visible black bars. And while she wasn't a true sentient, like the dolphins and whales or the great apes, she came very, very close. Unlike any other longwings in the world, imperial Ternathian peregrines were never hooded, even after the completion of their training. Like other falcons, their natural prey was other birds, not ground game, but imperial Ternathian hawks like Finena were intelligent enough to know when it was time to fly. They required no blindfolds to prevent them from seeing other birds passing overhead, nor did they require jesses to keep them from leaving their human companion's fists without permission. Finena might not be a true sentient by most people's standards, but she *was* an extremely smart bird—one Andrin had hand-raised from an eyas.

Now Andrin ran a feather-gentle fingertip down Finena's strongly hooked beak. That dangerously sharp weapon pressed back equally gently, and Andrin's lip curled disdainfully at the thought of the Uromathian kings and princes who would—without the slightest doubt—bring their own falcons to the conclave. Finena wore no jesses and was never tethered, whether to her perch or to Andrin's gauntleted hand. Finena stayed with—and returned to—Andrin from love of her chosen human companion. Andrin respected the bird's freedom, and Finena was fiercely devoted to her. Uromathian kings and princes carried falcons as status symbols; that much of the traditional Ternathian practice they'd adopted. But unlike the Ternathian imperial house, they left their birds' routine daily care to hawk handlers and were always careful to fasten the birds securely to their wrists when they carried them—and to hood them, whenever they weren't actively hunting. It was true that none of their birds were Finena's intellectual equal, and Andrin was prepared to admit—if pressed—that carrying other, lesser breeds bareheaded under all circumstances might be . . . less than prudent. But she still considered hooding them simply for the falconer's convenience a barbaric and cruel practice, and her lip-curl of disdain turned into a sinful smile as she anticipated the expressions of the Uromathians when they caught their first glimpse of a Ternathian grand princess with a white Ternathian imperial peregrine.

And it would be up to the two of them to represent Ternathia's traditions, she reminded herself with a hint of sadness. Charaeil had died two years ago, and her father had never had the heart to partner with another bird. *I wish he would,* she thought wistfully, *but I understand why he hasn't. After all, how would I feel if it came to 'replacing' Finena?* The very idea sent a shudder through her, and she caressed Finena's beak again.

Finena preened on Andrin's arm as she caught her companion's emotions. They didn't share true telepathy, the way a cetacean or a chimpanzee shared with a translator, but their bond was very real, nonetheless, and Andrin felt it glowing between them as she turned and started for the external stair—which the sailors insisted on calling a "ladder"—from the promenade deck to the boat deck, above.

"You're going to be the envy of every Uromathian male in Tajvana, love," Andrin half-crooned. "For now, though, why don't you go ahead and bring down a bird for your breakfast? Just be a dear and eat it up there somewhere." She pointed to the lookout's fat pod on *Windtreader's* foremast. "After all, it wouldn't do to irritate Captain Ula or the crew by scattering blood and feathers all over the deck."

The glowing white bird, whose name meant "White Fire," let out a scolding *"rehk,"* and Andrin laughed.

"No, that's not an insult to your table manners, dearest. But that deck is clean enough for a baby to eat on, and I'd hate to make extra work for the crew. They're nervous enough as it is, with royalty aboard."

Someone snorted at her shoulder, and she glanced mildly back at her personal guardsman, who followed the regulation two paces behind her.

"Laugh if you will, Lazima chan Zindico," she said severely. "But it's true, and you know it."

"Oh, aye, that it is," chan Zindico agreed solemnly, but a devilish glint lurked in his eyes. "I'm just thinking how surprised they'd be to hear a grand princess of the blood worrying about the condition of their decks."

"You could be right," she acknowledged, then grinned. "You generally are, after all."

"Why, thank you, Your Highness. It's nice to be appreciated."

Chan Zindico's return smile was easy, but even here, on a Ternathian ship with a loyal and thoroughly vetted Ternathian crew, his constantly sweeping eyes remained sharp as flaked obsidian. He was pledged to guard her against all dangers . . . and at *any* cost. It was a pledge he'd taken voluntarily on the day of her birth, and that sometimes appalled Andrin. She might have turned out to be a raging, spoiled brat, and still chan Zindico would have honored that oath, thrown himself between her and any weapon that threatened her. She couldn't keep him from doing that, much though the thought secretly terrified her, and so she'd worked hard, almost from the day she could walk, in an effort to be worthy of that kind of commitment.

She was unaware that chan Zindico and her other personal guards, who traded off the twenty-four-hour-a-day job of keeping her alive, took a fierce pride in their young mistress. Or that they looked with pity on the guards who'd pledged their lives to young Anbessa. The emperor's youngest daughter had developed quite an imperial little temper—one Empress Varena was grimly determined to correct or die trying. Anbessa's guardsmen vehemently hoped their empress succeeded. Soon.

"Still and all," chan Zindico continued, smiling at Andrin as they stepped off the ladder onto *Windtreader*'s uppermost deck, "if Lady Finena wants to scatter feathers, I'm sure the crew won't begrudge her."

The grand princess laughed and flung her gauntleted arm aloft, launching the glowing white falcon. Finena rocketed upward, slashing high against the crystalline blue skies like a white flame. She circled the ship one, twice . . . then wheeled and streaked down through the flock of gulls like a gleaming thunderbolt. Feathers flew as the fisted talons struck, then snatched their prey out of the air, and chan Zindico knew his wasn't the only eye on deck drawn to that stunning flight.

"It's the grand princess' falcon!" one of the pair of lookouts on the starboard bridge wing said, nudging his fellow, as Finena perched on the yard spreading the foremast stays and began devouring her breakfast with typical messiness.

"Isn't she a fine sight, now?" his companion replied.

"The finest I ever did see, and that's no lie. Did you see her fly, man? From a ship's deck, no less! Triad's mercy, that's what an *imperial* Ternathian falcon can do!"

"Very nicely done, indeed, Your Highness," another voice said, and Andrin turned in surprise as a burly man in a captain's uniform stepped out of the wheelhouse. Captain Ula looked at her just a bit quizzically, and she found herself blushing.

"I beg your pardon for interrupting the routine of your crew, Captain," she apologized. "I hadn't realized Finena would prove to be such a distraction."

"No harm done, Your Highness." He swept her a low bow, then turned a scowl on the suddenly very intent-looking lookouts and raised his voice into a booming roar fit to carry through any gale. "But if I catch another man gawking at Her Highness' bird instead of attending to his duties, I'll feed his liver to the falcon, myself! Do I make myself clear?"

"Aye, Captain!"

The lookouts whipped back around to their assigned sectors, and Ula scowled at their backs for just a moment, but his eyes still twinkled. He waited another few seconds, then turned back to Andrin.

"I'll leave you to enjoy the air and sunshine, Your Highness," he said with another bow.

"Thank you, Captain. I know our voyage will be a great pleasure. You have a lovely ship."

A flush of pleasure touched his cheeks as he recognized the sincerity of her compliment. Then he touched the brim of his hat and left her to enjoy the morning.

Andrin pulled her coat collar up around her neck, leaned against the boat deck rail, and smiled to herself. The view was even more spectacular from up here, and she abandoned herself to sheer, sensual pleasure while Finena finished eating, then launched herself once more to drift effortlessly on the wind above the ship, staying well clear of the smoke trailing from the liner's tall funnels.

It was too good to last indefinitely, of course. She'd been there for perhaps a half-hour—certainly not much longer—when a movement on chan Zindico's part drew her attention. It wasn't much of a movement; most people probably wouldn't even have noticed it. But Andrin knew her guardsman well, and she recognized the signs. Someone was about to enter potential threat range of her.

She turned to see who it was, and her eyes widened in astonishment so great that she had to forcibly order her jaw not to drop.

"Marnilay preserve us," chan Zindico murmured, just loud enough for her to hear through the sound of wind and wave. "It's Earl Ilforth coming to pay his respects."

Andrin had never had the pleasure of meeting the Earl of Ilforth, Speaker of the House of Lords, in person. Her mother tended to avoid his company, which meant Andrin and her sisters had also avoided it, simply because they'd always accompanied the empress in her headlong flight from whatever wing of the palace his presence happened to threaten at the moment. Everyone had *heard* of him, though, and she knew he was considered the epitome of the term "court dandy."

Now she watched him coming towards her, and her mind busily sorted out first impressions even as she continued to dredge up everything she'd ever been told about him.

He might have possessed a certain wiry grace if he hadn't moved with such studied languor, she decided, and he was also short for a Ternathian. A good head shorter than Andrin herself, and built on narrow-shouldered, slender lines. And he was said to be quite sensitive about his relatively diminutive stature, among other things, she remembered. Rumor suggested that he compensated for it with a viperish tongue, and his biting setdowns of social inferiors (which, in his opinion, included virtually every other Ternathian ever born) and anyone who roused his ire were proverbial.

He was also wealthy enough to indulge his every wardrobe whim, and reputed to be inordinately fond of such indulgences. That much, at least, Andrin now knew was entirely accurate, for Mancy Fornath, fifty-first Baron Fornath and forty-fifth Earl of Ilforth, was resplendent in morning attire.

Or he would have been, if this had been Hawkwing Palace, rather than the deck of a passenger liner under full power.

His coif had been as elaborate as Andrin's own when he started out, and it was in just as many shreds as hers before he'd come halfway across the deck. The ornate quetzal feather in his hat would never be worth its weight in silver again, either, she judged, and his coat had so many layers and flutters and silken tassels that it looked alive in the stiff wind. In fact, it looked as if it were trying to devour him.

"Dear Marnilay, does he dress that way *all* the time?" she demanded under her breath, and chan Zindico snorted.

"That, Your Highness, is *conservative* for Earl Ilforth."

Whatever she might have replied to that went unspoken, for the distinctive—she couldn't possibly call such a spectacle distinguished—personage had reached his quarry and bowed sweepingly.

"My dear Grand Princess! How you've grown!"

Andrin could never decide later whether it was his patronizing tone or the ironic, languidly malicious look he swept up her tall, admittedly sturdy figure as he straightened his spine which did the most to leave her white-faced with fury. Not that it really mattered, she eventually concluded. Either one would have been more than enough, and if *they* hadn't done it, the lazy, mocking glitter in his light-colored eyes—the self-congratulating amusement of an adult making clever remarks which would sail right over a mere child's head—would have accomplished the same thing anyway.

Unlike Uromathia, Ternathia had outlawed the custom of dueling generations ago—which, she found herself reflecting, was a pity. Or perhaps not. Chan Zindico, who hewed to the millennia-old tradition of Calirath guardsmen, had begun her tutoring in self-defense when she was twelve, and seven words from the Earl of Ilforth left her with a sudden, passionate longing to see him on the firing range with his pasty face centered—briefly—in the sights of her favorite Halanch and Welnahr revolver.

Which might not be precisely the best way to stay on the House of Lords' good side, however satisfying it might be, she admitted regretfully. *On the other hand . . .*

"My dear Earl," she said, in tones fit to freeze lava, looking down her nose at him from her towering inches, "how nice to see someone of your . . . imposing stature this morning."

He blinked, and his face went blank. She wondered whether his confusion stemmed more from the evidence that she hadn't missed his mockery after all, or from the sheer disbelief that any snip of a schoolgirl would *dare* to cut him off at the knees.

"Ah, ahem, well—"

She turned her back on him in mid-stammer and whistled sharply. Finena wheeled high above her, then came hurtling down with the speed of a striking snake. Peregrines could attain velocities of over two hundred miles per hour in a stoop, and the smack of talon against leather as the hawk flared her wings at the last moment sounded shockingly loud above the wind. The white falcon turned a baleful eye on Earl Ilforth and hissed. Andrin had never heard such a sound from *any* hawk, let alone Finena, and Ilforth actually stumbled backward a step as she turned back to survey him through icy eyes.

"You were saying, My Lord?"

"Er . . . I . . ." He stared, apparently mesmerized, at the hawk for several seconds before he managed to tear his eyes away with a supreme effort. "A thousand pardons, Your Grand Highness. I hadn't realized how large your bird is."

"Really?" Andrin narrowed her eyes. "As a matter of fact, Finena's not particularly large for an imperial falcon, My Lord. Was there some urgent business you wished to discuss?"

He cleared his throat.

"I just wanted to say what an honor it is, to share a voyage of such importance with His Imperial Majesty and Your Grand Highness."

"I see. I *was* rather looking forward to the voyage myself."

She didn't actually emphasize the verb all that strongly, but it was enough to bring an angry scarlet stain to his cheeks. Clearly, he was more accustomed to setting down others than to receiving the same treatment himself, and his eyes flashed. He started to open his mouth, but then something else happened behind those angry eyes, and the red of his cheeks faded abruptly into something far paler.

"Your Grand Highness, I humbly beg your pardon." His voice was suddenly different as well. Lower, more hurried, without the polished confidence which had sneered through his tone before. "I . . . seem to have made hash of this conversation, and it was never my intention to be offensive. If I have caused you grief in some fashion, I sincerely beg your forgiveness."

Andrin managed to keep her own eyes from widening, but it was hard, as she saw sweat start along his upper lip. She'd never actually seen anyone do that before. *She'd* certainly never had that effect on anyone, and she found herself wondering a little frantically what a mere seventeen-year-old girl could have done to so thoroughly unnerve him. Simple surprise kept her silent, and that only made it worse.

And then, as she watched his face lose even more color, she realized with an insight like a thunderclap that it wasn't so much because of what she'd done or said, as because of who she was. Who she might yet become. He truly had expected his nasty little barbed comment to go right past a "mere girl." He'd never anticipated that it wouldn't, and it was the sudden realization of the truly colossal blunder he'd made which had rattled him so thoroughly. Ridiculing the physical size of a person who might one day occupy the imperial throne wasn't the very wisest political move a man could make.

Part of her was childishly delighted by his terror. She'd never before experienced anything like this sudden, visceral understanding that she could reduce grown men to quivering protoplasm merely by displaying her displeasure, and it was a heady sensation. But if part of her was delighted, the rest was quite abruptly shaken to the core. She had a sudden vision of just what sort of disaster she could unleash if she succumbed to the habit of using that power to gratify her own petty emotions, and it terrified her.

One corner of her lips tried to quirk as she contemplated this oaf's probable reaction if she *thanked* him for his unwitting assistance in her imperial education. She was sorely tempted to do just that, but decided to settle for a slight nod, instead.

"Very well, My Lord. I accept your apology," she said coolly, and he swept off his hat to give her the most elaborate bow she'd ever witnessed.

"I am eternally grateful for your mercy, Your Grand Highness."

Just when she was about to suggest that he'd kept his forehead on the ship's deck long enough, he rose with an elegance that was somewhat spoiled by the ship's motion. He overbalanced and nearly landed flat on his face, but recovered admirably, and gave her a rueful smile that was more genuine than anything else she'd seen from him.

"I fear I haven't yet found my sea legs, Your Highness."

"At least you're on yours, My Lord. I fear Lady Merissa is entirely too ill from seasickness to rise from bed at all."

"I'm sorry to hear that," he said softly. "Lady Merissa is a true jewel of the Court, and much beloved by all. I hope she recovers quickly."

Andrin wondered why such a simple statement left her wondering what the earl's marital status might be, and if he had any intention of altering it. She thought she remembered that he'd been married for several years, but she wasn't certain. And if he *was* married, was he ambitious enough to set aside his wife in favor of the mistress of protocol to his emperor's daughter? Such back-stair avenues to political influence and power had been used often enough in the Empire's past. Was Ilforth inclined in that direction? Or—her eyes narrowed suddenly—did he have his sights set somewhat higher?

In that moment, Andrin wished fiercely that her mother had come on this voyage, rather than choosing to remain for the present in Estafel with the younger girls. That was *not* the kind of question she could ask her father.

"I'll relay your well wishes to Lady Merissa when I see her again," she said after a moment.

"You're too kind, Your Grand Highness."

Yes, I am, she thought uncharitably. *Especially since I'd rather dump you overboard and let you* swim *to Tajvana. Or perhaps hand you an anchor first.*

"Did you have something else to discuss, My Lord?" she asked, determined to be polite, even as she found herself wondering a little frantically how to extract herself from a conversation she didn't want to continue. "Something to do with the Conclave, perhaps?"

"Ah, yes, the Conclave."

He was fiddling with his hat brim, gazing forlornly at the wreckage of the expensive New Farnalian feather he'd foolishly brought out onto a wind-swept deck where the biting wind off the North Vander Ocean came whipping around the southern tip of Ternath Island.

"You're probably wondering what instructions I carry from the House of Lords," he said with a last heavy sigh for his damaged headgear.

Andrin blinked mentally. She hadn't wondered anything of the sort, actually, but she suddenly—and belatedly—realized that she probably should have.

"Are you at liberty to share them?" she asked after a moment, and he looked up from his hat at last, his glance sly.

"Ordinarily, no, Your Grand Highness." He gestured elaborately with one hand, apparently attempting to convey the intricacies with which a man in his position must deal on a daily basis. Unfortunately, he ended up looking merely ludicrous. "However, as your position has, ah, *shifted*, shall we say, due to the current crisis, I feel it would be remiss of the Lords to endeavor to keep such an important member of the imperial family in the dark."

She only looked at him, waiting for something besides empty flattery, and he cleared his throat.

"Yes. Well. The Lords have made it quite clear that under no circumstances shall we yield so much as a fingertip's worth of Ternathian sovereignty over this business!"

"I see." Andrin pursed her lips thoughtfully. "I should imagine most of the other governments on Sharona share exactly the same sentiments, shouldn't you, My Lord? That wouldn't appear to leave a great deal of room for progress toward a practical governing system to deal with the crisis, would it?"

He blinked.

"I beg your pardon, Your Grand Highness?"

"Clearly, something must be done, administratively, to meet the crisis, or all Sharona could be at risk of attack, My Lord. Possibly even destruction. It seems to me that refusing to yield a fingertip's worth of anything at this particular moment is an exceedingly poor way to handle the worst international crisis in Sharonian history."

An odd, choking sound behind her left shoulder distracted Andrin for a moment. She actually turned to see if her bodyguard had been stricken ill, but though chan Zindico's face was slightly red, he seemed unharmed. Reassured, she returned her attention to the forty-fifth Earl of Ilforth.

"Well, My Lord?"

"Ah, well, ahem. There may be a great deal of merit in your argument, Your Grand Highness. Which I must say is remarkably cogent for a girl barely out of the schoolroom, if you'll pardon me for speaking bluntly."

She wanted to shout her irritation to the sky, or else—preferably—hit him over the head with something large and heavy. Instead, she favored him with a frosty gaze.

"My schoolroom is hardly noted for its incompetent schoolmasters," she observed, and Ilforth reddened.

"No, of course not. I hardly meant to imply—"

"Then perhaps you will be so good as to consider my argument's merit, regardless of the chronological age of its source."

She left him standing, hat in hand, gaping after her as she stalked clear across the broad, windswept deck to the opposite rail. She paused fractionally there, not sure she knew where she meant to go. But a moment later, she knew exactly what to do as the first Lord of the Privy Council appeared on deck, sensibly attired in a practical morning suit with nary a feather nor a geegaw in sight.

"My Lord! How delightful to see you! Would you join me for a stroll?"

Shamir Taje stared at her for a moment. Then he caught sight of Ilforth, still standing frozen on the far side of the deck, and a sudden, impish grin burst forth like sunlight.

"Your Grand Highness, I would be delighted to accompany you."

He held out one arm gallantly, and she laid her hand on his dark, sober sleeve and gave him a brilliant smile.

"I can honestly say I've never been so relieved to see you in my life," she said earnestly, and he chuckled.

"His Lordship has been his usual ingratiating self, I see. What diplomatic crisis has he engendered now?"

Finena, perched on Andrin's other forearm, let out an improbable squawk that lifted Taje's eyebrows and left Andrin laughing.

"I think she wants to eat his tongue for lunch," the princess said. "And, I must say, she'd make better use of it than *he* does if she did!"

"Marnilay preserve us, how badly did he offend you?" Taje asked, only half-humorously, and her eyes flashed.

"Have you a brace of pistols about you, My Lord?" she asked in reply, and he winced.

"That bad?"

"How in heaven's name did *he* ever get to be Speaker of the House of Lords?"

To her surprise, Taje met her gaze squarely, and his voice was completely serious.

"He's the Speaker because he's the most senior earl in the House of Lords, and because he has sufficient money, and therefore political influence, to sway an unfortunate—one might almost say unholy— alliance of extreme conservatives, status-conscious popinjays, and ambitious men who know better but find his money exceedingly useful. Never, *ever* underestimate the damage Ilforth can do in—or from—the House of Lords. Thank Marnilay Herself that the power of the imperial purse rests in the Commons, Your Highness, or that blue-blooded, damnfool-tongued disaster would be able to sit back on his undeserved laurels and dictate to the Throne whenever he felt like it. Which would be every minute of the day."

Andrin stared at the man who held, on a daily basis, more power than anyone in the Empire except her father. She'd never heard such venom from the eternally unflappable First Councilor in her life. Nor, she realized a moment later, had anyone—including her father—ever given her such a crystal-clear glimpse into the machinations of governance.

"My father has tremendous faith in your judgment, First Councilor," she said quietly after a moment. "I would be honored if you would teach me what you can in the limited time you have available."

The glow in his eyes warmed her to the soles of her feet.

"Young lady, I do believe that may be one of the highest compliments I've ever been paid." He cleared his throat, then continued gruffly. "I should be honored to act as your tutor. And I pray to all the gods who watch over our Empire that my tutelage will never be needed."

She slid her hand down his forearm to cover his.

"Amen, My Lord," she said softly, squeezing his fingers briefly. "No one could hope that more than I do. But," she continued with a grim fatalism new to her own experience, "I would far rather be prepared for something I never face than be caught wanting when it comes, no matter how unpleasant the preparations may prove. Should Janaki die and *anything* happened to my father—"

She couldn't even finish. The vision was too unrelentingly horrifying for that. She'd never forgotten the earthquake which had rocked her family when her grandfather had been killed in a completely avoidable accident in the middle of an utterly ordinary afternoon in the center of his own capital city. She'd been just five years old, but that memory would be with her until the day she died.

Shamir Taje, First Lord of the Privy Council, didn't move at all for several long moments. He just stared into her eyes. Then he made a tiny move with his free hand, hesitated, and finally finished the motion anyway. He brushed a wild strand of raven-black hair from her brow and tucked it behind her ear.

"You are your father's daughter in so many ways it takes the breath away," he said quietly. Then he drew a deep breath. "Very well, Your Grand Highness. Shall we begin with an analysis of the political situation in the House of Lords?"

"I would be most grateful for anything you could say to clarify that for me."

"In that case," he said, his voice dry as desert sand, "perhaps it's fortunate I hadn't made any specific plans for the balance of the morning."

She gulped, then gave him a brave smile. He nodded almost absently, tucked her hand back into his elbow, and began strolling aft in the shadow of *Windtreader*'s funnels as he started the morning's lesson.

CHAPTER
THIRTY-ONE

IT WAS ALMOST sunset of the third day of their voyage when Andrin spotted the sight she'd been waiting for all day and discovered that her breathless anticipation had been more than worth the wait. With Finena on her arm, her father beside her on the left, and Shamir Taje standing on her right, Andrin stared out at her first sight of the massive rock that guarded the narrow Bolakini Strait.

The Fist of Bolakin was the largest natural fortress on Sharona. It was also the longest continuously occupied fortress, and under the provisions of an ancient treaty, it was garrisoned jointly by Ternathia and Bolakin. That treaty, and the others between Ternathia and Bolakin which had been signed at the same time, were the second oldest in the Empire's history. Only its treaties with Farnalia predated them, and those were five thousand years old, cemented by intermarriage and the continued mutual interest of close neighbors.

The Bolakini treaties were the result of the shrewdest political move any of Ternathia's more distant ancient neighbors had ever made. The Queens of Bolakin, watching the Empire's expansion across the continent north of the Fist had accurately predicted Ternathia's intention—its need—to expand its naval presence into the Mbisi Sea to secure the southern shores of its new acquisitions. Aware that Ternathia would want control of the Fist, and that the Empire would tolerate no piracy, the Queens of Bolakin had approached the Emperor of Ternathia with a proposition: a joint garrison and shared sovereignty for the Fist, duty-free passage for both Ternathian and Bolakini vessels past the Fist, and the equal division of all duties collected on non-allied shipping through the Straits and bound for Ternathian or Farnalian ports of call, coupled with an ironclad guarantee that no Bolakini shore-runner would harass

Ternathian shipping. In exchange, Bolakin offered to open her ports to Ternathian ships, giving Ternathia access to the vast wealth being carried north from the Ricathian interior, both by overland caravan across the vast Sarthan Desert and by Bolakini merchant ships plying the long western shore of Ricathia.

The emperor had been impressed. Certainly, the proposal had represented an excellent deal for Bolakin, but it was also pragmatic and eminently fair to Ternathia, as well. Not only that, but his own naval commanders and merchants had been suggesting for some time that the Fist had to be either neutralized or taken under imperial control. He'd vastly preferred the treaty approach, which had the enormous advantage of avoiding the need to maintain armed garrisons to defend against Bolakini efforts to retake conquered territory . . . or rebel against an imperial oppressor.

So the treaties had been signed, the marriages of alliance had been arranged, and four and a half prosperous millennia later, Andrin carried a trickle of Bolakini blood and both sides were well content with a long-standing pact.

The Fist was an immense, crouching lion of stone, a sharply sloped mountain planted solidly to protect the sheltered waters of Bolakin Bay, carved out of the southeastern edge of the Narhathan Peninsula. The Fist was three miles long and three quarters of a mile wide, connected to Narhath by a low, sandy isthmus which had been steadily expanded over the years behind its advancing seawalls as land was reclaimed from the sea and used for wharves, warehouses, taverns, and—in recent years—luxury hotels. The ancient passage duties on shipping through the Strait were long gone these days, but Bolakin Bay remained a vitally important service port for the traffic sweeping in and out of the Mbisi every day, and it had also been one of the Empire's most critical naval bases for thousands of years. The original bronze-age forts had long since disappeared, although archaeologists had recently exhumed one of them, and the curtain walls and catapults and ballistae of a later age, and the muzzle-loading smoothbore cannon which had followed them, had disappeared in turn. Now armored gun turrets, their barbettes and magazines blasted deep into the Fist's stony heart, boasted rifled artillery capable of reaching entirely across the Straits to the shore of Ricathia.

Beside that huge, ancient crag, *Windtreader* was a child's toy tossed into the sea. The immovable mass of stone caught the westering sunlight with a deep golden glow. Stark black shadows marked the locations of the powerful batteries, their turrets protected by tons of armor plate and reinforced concrete, capable of sending any battleship ever built to the bottom at a distance of over twelve miles.

Two flags snapped and cracked in the wind above that mighty fortress, representing the two nations who shared sovereignty over it to this day. One was the black field and golden lion of Bolakin, rippling and wavering as it streamed out from its staff. The other was the eight-rayed golden sunburst of Ternathia on its deep green field, and as Andrin watched, both of them started down their staffs in perfect unison.

She couldn't have explained to anyone why sudden tears filled her eyes. It wasn't just pride in her people, wasn't just the honor that salute accorded to her father, her family, and all they represented to their people. There was something else. Through some strange alchemy, born of the eerie light of the dying sun and the black shadows that marked those immense guns, of the threat which pulled this ship and its passengers towards a fateful meeting in Tajvana, that simple salute—the dipping of two flags as the emperor passed by—became something more. Became a reminder of all the ancient Empire had endured . . . and an ominous portent of what was yet to come.

Men in Ternathian uniform were already on their way to fight. To rescue any survivors, and to prevent the deaths of more innocents. But Sharonians had already died, and that simple salute brought home with painful clarity the fact that still more would die tomorrow—for an unknown stretch of tomorrows. She felt the weight of those deaths pressing down on her soul, crushing her until it was a struggle simply to breathe. The enemy had no face, beyond the indistinct images transmitted by a woman unable to clearly see the men killing her, yet Andrin was suffocating under the weight of the more and more deaths to come. Her throat was locked. She wanted to promise the memory of Shaylar Nargra-Kolmayr that she would be avenged. She wanted so *badly* to make that promise, to give in to the need to strike back in an outraged demand for justice, but the terrible weight on her chest wouldn't let her.

She could see the men on the fortress walls, waving and cheering, and however hard she tried, she couldn't lift her arm to respond. They would literally go to their deaths, if ordered to do so by her father . . . or by Andrin, if she ever came to the throne. The terrible prescience, if that was what gripped her, left her chilled and frightened, alone despite her father at her side, despite Lazima chan Zindico at her back. She had never felt smaller, less heroic or less capable, in her life than she did as she contemplated the kinds of decisions an empress would have to make in time of war.

She swallowed once. Twice. And then she made a silent vow—not to Shaylar's shadow, but to the men in that fortress, and to all the other men in uniform scattered across the known universes.

She would do her best—the very utmost best she could—to prepare herself to lead them. And if the time ever came that she must, she would not risk them lightly. She was the daughter and granddaughter and great-great-granddaughter of emperors and empresses. Throughout the millennia of the Empire, its rulers had sent Ternathian fighting men out to die again and again, sometimes for good reasons, and sometimes for bad. She knew that, just as she knew emperors and empresses would send them out to die in the future, as well. She knew that, too. But if those men in that fortress must die under *her* orders, she would spend them well. Not on a whim, not capriciously, not to satisfy her own anger or out of her own fear. She would spend them as if their blood were more precious than gold, more precious than her own . . . because it was.

The thought burned through her, and then, without warning, Finena launched unexpectedly from her wrist. The silver falcon arrowed skyward, drawing the eye as white wings flashed red in the glowing sunset. She wheeled once, high above the fortress flags, then folded her wings and dove, streaking earthward like a meteor plunging down the sky.

She snapped her wings wide again, fanned her tail, and whipped across the deck at more than a hundred miles an hour. Sailors ducked out of sheer instinct, and Andrin lifted her wrist as Finena's piercing call shrilled against the wind. The falcon banked into a wide, sweeping turn, then floated back down the crystal depths of air like a dream of beauty until her talons slapped against Andrin's gauntleted wrist.

The magnificent bird perched there for an endless, breathless moment—a living sculpture, carved from silver and ash-pale ivory, wings spread wide, ready to fly again and strike at a moment's notice. Fierce, proud, defiant, protective . . . The adjectives and emotions tumbled through Andrin, too many and too rapidly to name them all.

Then the wings folded, the head tilted inquiringly up to meet Andrin's shaken gaze, and Finena was just a bird again. Only a falcon, sitting peaceably on Andrin's arm, and no longer an avatar of fate itself.

Andrin drew a single, shallow breath and turned her gaze from her falcon to her father. Her eyes met his, and she recognized the look in them. It was the same look she'd just given the soldiers in the fortress—the look of a man who knew his word would send other men to their deaths on a world so far away the message would travel for days, even at the speed of thought, just to reach it. Men who would go willingly, trusting him to send them for good reason, for a cause that was worthy of their sacrifice. The look of the man who knew the terrible weight of that responsibility . . . and feared that one day it would be transferred from his shoulders to *hers*.

Andrin wanted to weep. Then her father looked into *her* eyes . . . and did.

"I'm tired, Papa," Andrin murmured, trying to hide how desperately shaken she was. "I'll say goodnight now."

"Of course, 'Drin," he replied.

He kissed her brow, squeezed her hand for a moment, then let her go, and she fled to her cabin, where Lady Merissa was lying in her bunk, pale and asleep, thank all the gods. Andrin settled Finena on her perch, pulled off her own heavy coat and embroidered gown, and wrapped herself in the comforting softness of a silk night dress and a thick robe woven from Ternathian wool and exotic cashmere.

Her head ached fiercely, and she curled up in her own bed. She started to light the lamp as the sun sank toward the sea, but then she changed her mind. Instead, she simply gazed out the scuttle for a long, long time while the sea turned golden and the sun balanced on the rim of the world.

She couldn't actually see the sun slip beneath the waves. The sunset lay astern as *Windtreader* forged steadily onward, deeper and deeper into the Mbisi. But she watched the light on the water, watched the clouds overhead turn orange and crimson and deep wine-red, then fade into soft shades of purple. The cabin was chilly as the light finally disappeared and the heavens came to life, glittering with thousands upon thousands of autumn stars beyond the drifting banners of cloud. She pulled the thick woolen blankets up around her shoulders and leaned her aching brow against the cool glass. She didn't want to think about what would happen in Tajvana. She didn't want to think at all.

It was comforting to simply sit in the darkness, watching the stars and thinking of nothing while the ship moved beneath her and the throb of the powerful engines enveloped her. It was past time for supper, she realized distantly, but her stomach rebelled at the mere thought of food, and she swallowed queasily. Her head ached, and she closed her eyes, thinking longingly about an icepack, not food.

A quiet tap sounded at the door.

"Go away," she called, softly enough to avoid disturbing Lady Merissa.

Silence fell once more, but then, five minutes later, the tap sounded again. And again, five minutes after that.

Andrin wanted to scream at whoever was out there, interrupting her solitude. She sprang from the bed and crossed the cabin with long, angry strides, then snatched the door open—and closed her mouth over the furious words on the tip of her tongue. The servant girl who'd brought her the pen and paper in the Privy Council Chamber was standing in the passageway, literally wringing her hands, her eyes enormous with fright.

Andrin hadn't even realized the girl had come aboard the ship, far less expected to find her outside her cabin door with a covered tray of food on a serving cart. But she was obviously supposed to be there, since Brahndys chan Gordahl, Andrin's regular night bodyguard, was simply standing there watching her.

"Your Grand Highness," the girl got out in a rush, "I was ever so terrified. Are you all right, please? Your supper's getting cold, and I was afraid you'd took ill, which would be my fault, as it's my place to look after you on this voyage, and—"

"I beg your pardon?" Andrin interrupted the spate of words, staring at her in astonishment. The girl paled, and Andrin shook her head. "I only meant I don't understand," she said more gently. "Why is it *your* place to look after me?"

The girl swallowed sharply.

"Well, it's just that Your Highness' maid, Miss Balithar, she slipped and fell climbing up the staircase from the kitchen with your dinner. She broke her leg, pretty badly they say. She's with the ship's Healer now, having it looked after. Between Miss Balithar's broken leg and Lady Merissa ill with the seasickness, you've got no one to look after you. To make sure you're warm and comfortable and well fed."

"Oh, poor Sathee! She must be in agony!" Andrin's eyes widened in distress. Sathee Balithar had been her lady's maid since her fifth birthday—she was literally one of the family.

"When they came to fetch me, they said the Healer had already stilled the pain, before doing anything else. She's being looked after well, I promise you that, Your Grand Highness."

But the girl was still wringing her hands, and Andrin still had no idea why *she* was standing in the corridor with Andrin's dinner and a serious case of nervous distress. The princess forced herself to collect her rattled wits, feeling stupid and slow from the headache pounding at her temples from the inside.

"I'm glad to hear she's being taken care of. But why are you here? Who sent you?"

She glanced at chan Gordahl, and his eyes flicked to meet hers.

"She was thoroughly vetted, Your Highness, before setting foot aboard ship. Ulthar brought her up fifteen minutes ago, when she came with your dinner."

Andrin felt better immediately. Ulthar chan Habikon was another of her sworn bodyguards. There was no way anyone who wasn't completely above suspicion would have gotten past both him and chan Gordahl. She drew a deep breath, gave her guardsman a nod of thanks for the information, then met the girl's worried gaze again.

"Who are you?" she asked curiously. "And how—why—were you asked to take Sathee's place?"

"When the choosing of the staff was done, I got the chance of my whole lifetime, to help with the fetching and the carrying between the cabins and the cooks," the girl said. "They assigned me to you, Your Grand Highness, on account of my already being trusted to help with the Privy Council, which is a job not just every servant is allowed, you see. My father, he's been a footman of the Privy Council his whole life, and my mother, she's been maidservant to your grandmother, which is where I learned my trade, fetching and carrying for her. Please, Your Grand Highness, will you have some supper now?"

"I—" Andrin closed her lips and put a hand to her brow. "I'm afraid I have a frightful headache," she admitted. "I couldn't possibly eat a single bite."

To Andrin's astonishment, the girl's eyes lit with obvious pleasure.

"I can help you with that, Your Grand Highness. Honestly, I can! It's a Talent from my mother. Just sit you down, there, and let me help."

Andrin glanced at chan Gordahl again. The guardsman evidently knew a great deal more about this girl than Andrin did, because he simply nodded permission. Given her guardsmen's fierce suspicion of any possible threat to her safety, that said a great deal. Even so, she wasn't entirely certain about all this. Still, her head throbbed relentlessly, so fiercely even the light in the passageway hurt. And so she gave a mental shrug, willing to try whatever the girl had in mind, and sat down in the chair beside her writing desk.

"What's your name?" she asked as the girl entered the cabin timidly. She gazed at the gown Andrin had discarded with something like awe, and stared at Finena in open amazement.

"Relatha, Your Grand Highness," she all but whispered, mesmerized by the white falcon. "Relatha Kindare."

Andrin's thoughts were slower than usual because of her headache, but she blinked as she suddenly realized that Finena was completely at ease with the girl. That surprised her. The falcon didn't like very many servants, and was particular about the nobility, as well. The bird detested a fair number of courtiers on sight—the Earl of Ilforth came to mind—but she liked Relatha. Liked the girl enough to preen and angle her head for a caress.

"Would you like to pet her?" Andrin asked.

"Oooh, I wouldn't dare!" Relatha protested, and Andrin stood and moved closer to the perch.

"She likes you. Here, give me your hand."

Relatha's fingers trembled in Andrin's grasp as she held the girl's hand gently in front of the bird for a moment, then guided her to stroke Finena's silver back. The bird arched against the touch, all but crooning with pleasure, and Relatha gasped. Then a smile of utter enchantment lit her face.

She petted the falcon for several delighted moments, then turned back to Andrin.

"She's just the most beautiful thing I've ever seen, Your Grand Highness! But here, now. Your head's still aching, and I'm standing here petting a bird, selfish as can be! Sit you down again, now, and let me take care of that headache."

The instant Relatha touched Andrin's head, the princess knew she was in the hands of a master Healer. An untrained one, perhaps, but powerfully Talented. The headache simply drained away to nothing under the gentle ministration of Relatha's fingertips, and Andrin leaned back, eyes closed, and let the magic in the girl's fingers soothe her frayed nerves. Her breathing steadied, slowed, and when Relatha finally let her hands drop away, Andrin breathed a deep sigh and opened her eyes.

She turned in her chair and peered curiously up at the girl.

"Why have you never taken formal training, Relatha? Your Talent for Healing is profound."

"*Me?* A Healer?" Relatha goggled. "I'm a *servant girl!*"

"And what's that got to do with anything?" Andrin frowned. "There are plenty of women Healers from all classes of society. Talent isn't confined by social bounds. Have you ever even been tested?"

Relatha shook her head, struck literally dumb.

"Well, would you *like* to be tested? To be trained as a Healer?"

The very notion appeared to overwhelm Relatha.

"I—I don't know . . . I never even thought such a thing would be possible—"

"Well, there's no need to decide this instant," Andrin told her. "But think about it. If you want to be tested at the Healers' Academy, I'll arrange it."

"But—why?" Relatha asked, obviously still shaken, and Andrin smiled.

"Why not?" she challenged in return.

"But I'm just—"

"Don't you dare say 'just a servant' again!" Andrin ordered tartly. "You just cured a savage headache with a simple touch. If you can do that, when you've never even been *tested*, far less trained, then you're wasted fetching and carrying anyone's dinner, even mine. Was your mother ever tested?"

Relatha shook her head.

"No, Your Grand Highness. She said servants are servants, and there's an end of it. Her task is to care for your grandmother, which is quite enough for anyone, she says."

"Hmph!" Andrin folded her arms. "Maybe in my grandmother's day that was so, but I'm not my grandmother, and I positively *hate* the idea of seeing someone with this kind of Talent wasted running errands between the kitchen and *anyone's* cabin. Or even fetching and carrying for the Privy Council. Think about it, Relatha. Do you want to spend your life fetching my dishes? Or would you rather try to earn a position as an Imperial Healer?"

The girl's mouth fell open.

"*Me?*" she squeaked. "Imperial Healer? *Me?*" But her eyes had begun to glow. "Do you really think—?"

She broke off, staring at Andrin with those glowing eyes, and the princess shrugged ever so slightly.

"We'll never know if you're never tested," she pointed out reasonably, and Relatha swallowed hard.

"I'll . . . think on it, then," she whispered.

"Good! Now, about that supper you mentioned . . ."

Relatha grinned.

"It's in the passage, Your Grand Highness. I'll just fetch it in for you. Sit you down at the table."

Andrin wasn't sure why, but her own Talent hummed strangely in her ears as Relatha wheeled her supper into the room. She couldn't imagine why, but Caliraths learned early to pay attention to "feelings" when other people crossed the tracks of their lives.

She hoped Relatha would decide to be tested. It was more unusual than it ought to be for a girl from the serving classes to make that big a transition, into the upper reaches of the Talented professions, but it was scarcely unheard of, either. In fact, the whole reason the House of Talents existed in the Ternathian Parliament in the first place was to make sure girls like Relatha *could* improve their lives by making full use of their gods-given abilities. The fact that no one had even noticed the startling power of Relatha's Talent bothered Andrin, and she decided to find a quiet moment to speak with the Speaker of the House of Talents before they reached Tajvana.

That thought seemed to close some switch deep in Andrin's brain. She could almost physically feel it, and she was abruptly glad Relatha was aboard *Windtreader*.

Of course, it remained to be seen *why* her presence seemed so suddenly important.

CHAPTER THIRTY-TWO

SHAYLAR SAT CROSSLEGGED in Gadrial's cabin while the two of them—the only women aboard the warship—enjoyed what she thought of as a quiet "girls' day" together. She was bent over a project very dear to her. Using a borrowed needle and thread, some shears the ship's doctor had provided, and some cloth the captain had asked the purser to locate in storage, she was making a dress for herself.

It wouldn't be a fancy dress, not given the cloth she had to work with—military-issue gray cotton twill—but it would be a *dress*, and it would be *hers*. The only other clothing she had was what Gadrial had given her and some navy-issue pajamas she'd contrived to make into slacks and shirts which almost fitted her.

Gadrial was no seamstress, but she'd admitted to some skill in fancy needlework, so she was using the voyage time to decorate some of her own shirts and slacks. The style and patterns were lovely, unlike anything Shaylar had ever seen. While they worked, they talked. Not about anything important—just easy conversation that allowed Shaylar to practice her steadily growing command of Andaran.

Shaylar had come to realize that the speed with which she was mastering Andaran had aroused Gadrial and Jasak's suspicions. No Sharonian, accustomed to telepaths' "ear" for languages, would have been surprised, but she wasn't *in* Sharona any more. Unfortunately, by the time she realized Gadrial had never seen anyone from Arcana (which was what she and Jasak called their home universe) learn a completely foreign language so quickly, she'd already demonstrated her abilities. The best she'd been able to do was to appear to slow down, to stop and obviously fumble for a word more frequently and emphasize her "foreign accent." She had no idea whether or not it had done any good. For that matter, she wasn't even certain that trying to hide her language-learning ability was a good thing in the first place! It was so *frustrating* trying to envision what a civilization which apparently had never heard of the Talents would expect . . . or find frightening or threatening.

On the other hand, the speed with which she'd been able to acquire at least a usable command of Andaran worked both ways, she reflected, setting small neat stitches in the sunlight streaming through the bulkhead scuttles. It would allow Jasak's superiors to ask pointed questions much sooner, but by the same token, it had permitted Shaylar to probe for additional information about Arcana before she and Jathmar had to face those pointed questions.

Much of what she'd learned had been frightening. Other bits and pieces, however, had seemed to offer at least some grounds for cautious hope.

For example, she'd learned that Jasak came from one of several Andaran kingdoms which dominated the landmass she and Jathmar had known as New Farnalia. Andara, it appeared, provided the bulk of the Arcanan army, and it was a culture with a long, deep, highly developed military tradition. However poorly Arcana might appear to have performed in its initial encounters with Sharona, what Shaylar had learned so far discouraged her from hoping things would stay that way.

On the other hand, what she'd learned about Ransar was more encouraging. As nearly as she could tell, Gadrial's home region of Arcana corresponded to the region of Sharona encompassed by the Kingdom of Eniath, the Kingdom of Dusith, and the northern portions of the Empire of Uromathia. Unlike the monarchies of the various Uromathian states, however, Ransar was a democracy. Shaylar wasn't particularly interested in politics, but she was trying to learn what she could, and it was quite obvious to her already that Ransaran notions were much less militaristic—more "humanistic," she was tempted to say—than those of Andara.

And then, of course, there were the people called "Mythalans," but for some reason, neither Gadrial nor Jasak seemed to want to talk about *them*.

Despite the situation in which she and Jathmar found themselves, Shaylar was fascinated by the bits and pieces about Arcana she'd so far been able to fit together. It was frustrating to have so incomplete a picture, however, and not just where politics was concerned. In fact, there was something else which continued to puzzle her even more, and she looked up from her sewing.

"Gadrial?"

"Hmm?"

"What moves this ship?"

Gadrial glanced up in obvious surprise. She gazed at Shaylar for a moment, then used a word with which Shaylar wasn't yet familiar.

"What does that word mean?" she asked, and Gadrial laid her needlework in her lap and folded her hands, her expression thoughtful as she clearly considered how best to answer.

"It's what powers our whole civilization." She spoke slowly, choosing her words. "Not everyone can use it," she added. "You must be born with a Gift for it."

A small thrill of astonishment ran through Shaylar. Whatever it was, it sounded a little like Talents, except that no Talent had ever powered a *ship*. Then Gadrial stood up and retrieved a small leather case from her luggage. She opened it and extracted a familiar crystal.

"This is my PC," Gadrial said. "My personal crystal. You've seen me use it in our language lessons, but I also use it to store my other work—my notes, my calculations. Anything I need to record. It's—" she used the unfamiliar word again "—that makes it possible."

"Gadrial, it's just a stone."

Even as Shaylar said it, she knew she sounded foolish. Certainly Gadrial had already given more than sufficient proof that that "just a stone" was capable of remarkable things. It was just that the very notion continued to offend Shaylar's concept of how the physical laws of the multiverse worked. In fact, she realized, the real reason she'd said it was that a part of her desperately wanted for it *not* to work after all.

"Don't be silly, Shaylar," Gadrial chided, as if she were the telepath and she'd read Shaylar's mind. "You've seen it work before. But it won't work for just anyone. It takes someone born with a Gift to build a PC or compile the spellware to make its applications work. But each crystal can hold immense amounts of data, if you know how to encode and retrieve it, and someone with a Gift can even program it so that non-Gifted people can use it. Here."

She began to murmur. Whatever she was saying, it wasn't in Andaran, and despite the number of times she'd already seen it, Shaylar's scalp prickled as the crystal began to glow. Squiggles of light appeared within it, recognizable as writing, although the words weren't in the same script as the signs aboard this ship.

"Here," Gadrial repeated, extending the crystal towards Shaylar. "This time I've powered it up for *you*."

Shaylar accepted it very gingerly. It was heavier than she'd expected. It still looked like nothing so much as absolutely clear quartz, yet it was clearly denser than quartz from the way it weighed in her hand. The squiggles glowing in its depth shifted slightly as the crystal settled into her palm. The unintelligible words moved, as if to present themselves to her for easier reading.

"What do you mean, powered it up for me?" she asked.

"I mean I've . . . turned it on for you. Activated its spellware in non-Gifted mode and released my password so that you can enter and retrieve data if you want to."

"But *how*?" Shaylar demanded in frustration. "This isn't a machine—it's just a lump of rock!"

"Of course it's a machine," Gadrial replied.

"No, it isn't. It's not—" Shaylar shook her head, searching for the Andaran word for "mechanical." Unfortunately, that wasn't one she'd learned yet. "There are no switches," she said instead. "Nothing to provide power."

It was Gadrial's turn to blink in apparent surprise. Then she shrugged.

"*I* provided the power," she said.

"But *how*?"

"By saying the proper words. Here, try this." Gadrial handed Shaylar a stylus or wand which appeared to be made out of the same transparent not-quartz as the crystal itself. "Write something on it," she encouraged.

Shaylar looked at her for a moment, then pressed the tip of the stylus hesitantly against the "PC." A spark of light—a bluish-green light, quite different from the color of the words already floating in the crystal—glowed to life at the point where stylus and crystal made contact. As she moved the stylus, the spark became a line, following the stylus tip as she slowly and carefully wrote her own name. She finished and lifted the stylus away, and her name floated instantly to the glassy center of the crystal, displacing the words which had been there before.

Shaylar stared at it, half-delighted and half-terrified by the implications, then shook her head.

"I don't understand!"

"That's because you don't have a Gift," Gadrial explained. "A non-Gifted person can use most of our machines if the spellware is set up that way and someone who *is* Gifted charges them first. But if you don't have a Gift yourself, you're completely dependent on someone else to write the spellware and power the system."

They were speaking the same language, but no communication was taking place, and Shaylar drew a deep breath.

"You can't run a machine by just talking to it," she said slowly and patiently, and Gadrial's brows drew together.

"Of course I can! I told you—I'm Gifted."

"But—" Shaylar wanted to tug at her hair. "You keep *saying* that, but what does Gifted *mean*? What is it you can do—that someone without a Gift can't—that makes hunks of rock light up this way?"

"I can tap the field," Gadrial said, exactly as if that actually explained something.

"*What* field?"

Gadrial used the same word that had started this conversation, and Shaylar let out an exasperated howl.

"Why are you upset, Shaylar?" Gadrial asked, starting to frown.

"Because your words make no sense!" Shaylar pointed to the ominously glowing rock in her own hand. "This piece of stone makes no sense. This *ship* makes no sense! Nothing *about* you people makes any sense!"

She realized she was breathing hard, teetering on the edge of a genuine panic attack. She was afraid—terribly afraid—and she didn't quite know why. She felt as if she were standing on the edge of a cliff, and if Gadrial kept talking, she would tip right over the edge and fall.

Gadrial reclaimed her "personal crystal" and set it carefully on the blanket to one side. She let her left hand rest lightly on it while she regarded Shaylar steadily, and then she shook her head slowly.

"Your people truly don't have anything like this, do they?" she finally said, her voice filled with wonder and what sounded like *pity*.

"No," Shaylar admitted, and Gadrial inhaled deeply.

"Magister Halathyn told me that," she said. A flicker of pain went through her eyes as she mentioned Magister Halathyn's name, but those eyes never left Shaylar's face, and she continued steadily.

"I didn't really want to believe him," she admitted. "It suggested a universe so different from ours that I can't really wrap my mind around it. Not yet, anyway. But everything I've seen from you since has only confirmed it, and now this."

She shook her head again.

"No wonder you're so lost. Let me try to explain."

She sat back, once again obviously thinking, looking for the best way to explain something complicated using the still limited vocabulary they had in common.

"There is a force in the universe," she began finally. "People with a Gift can sense it, can touch it—use it to do certain things. Some Gifts are very weak. People born with them can do only little things, because they can touch only a little of that force. It's like . . . like a field of energy. Of sunlight. A sea of energy that lies *between* things."

Gadrial's frown of concentration was deeper, more intense. Shaylar had the feeling that the other woman was attempting to explain color to a blind person, and she didn't like it. She was a telepath, a Voice; communication was her speciality, what she'd been born to do, and she'd never felt blind before. Not until now.

"Other people," Gadrial continued, "have very strong Gifts. My Gift is a strong one, for instance. The only person I ever knew with a stronger one was Magister Halathyn. He taught—"

Her voice caught suddenly, raggedly, and her eyes filled with tears.

"I'm sorry," Shaylar said softly, touching Gadrial's hand. The other woman's emotions were a chaotic whirl of love, grief, and empty, aching loss.

"I know you are," Gadrial said, and her voice was a small sound in the silence of the cabin.

Shaylar could sense, as well, that Gadrial was struggling not to blame her and Jathmar for Halathyn's death. She wished she knew a way to comfort the other woman's grief, but she couldn't—not given the circumstances. And so she could only wait until Gadrial dashed the tears from her eyes and straightened once more.

"I know you are," she said again, her voice firmer, then cleared her throat. "Anyway, Halathyn's Gift was profound. No one, I think, understood the field better than he did. He taught me everything I know about it. What I've learned on my own is built entirely on the platform he gave me."

Once more the agony in her eyes and voice tore at Shaylar, but this time she refused to yield to them.

"He taught me," she said more steadily, "and he wouldn't want me to fall to pieces like this now. So . . . This field can be tapped, manipulated—harnessed. It's power is immense. That's what moves the ship." She gestured. "Someone with a Gift speaks the proper formula to tap the field, which allows them to channel that power into the ship's storage cells. When that energy is released, it drives the ship forward through the water. It also powers other machines, all kinds of machines."

She dug through her luggage again, and pulled out another case.

"This is a machine Halathyn and I developed together. It helps us find portals. That's what we were looking for when we stumbled across you. Looking for a portal nearby."

She murmured to the gadget, which began to glow. Several colored indicators came to life in what looked like a rectangular window on the front of the device.

"Here. See these displays?" Her index finger indicated its several small glowing arrows and columns of light. "We'll be docking sometime tomorrow morning at the island we call Chalar back home. That's where our next portal is. See how the arrow points to it?"

Shaylar nodded slowly, but deep inside she was stunned. This single small device in Gadrial's hand was more effective—and efficient—than any Portal Hound she'd ever heard of! If they could do this, what *else* could they do? Then she realized that Gadrial was still talking.

"—still experimental, of course. That's what we were doing that day in the forest, when your people killed Osmuna—"

"Osmuna?" Shaylar asked. "Who is Osmuna?"

"The soldier your people killed," Gadrial replied in a surprised tone.

"*Our* people killed?" Shaylar demanded. "*Your* people killed Falsan! Gods, Gadrial—he died right in my arms! He'd staggered for *miles* with that arrow in his chest, trying to reach our camp—"

"I didn't know he'd died in your arms," Gadrial said quietly. "I'm sorry about that. As sorry as I can possibly be."

"But that didn't keep your people from killing the *rest* of us, did it?" Shaylar replied, more harshly even than she'd intended to. Gadrial winced, but she refused to look away.

"That wasn't what we wanted," she said. "Jasak realized what must have happened sooner than anyone else. Two men met in the forest. Just the two of them, and no one will ever know which one of them shot first. *We* certainly didn't. We couldn't even figure out *how* Osmuna had died. All we knew was that someone had killed him, and we trailed that person back to your camp. But you'd already headed toward the portal we'd come to find, and—"

"And then you ran us to ground like *dogs!*" Shaylar jerked up off the bed, her face twisted as the words she'd acquired—the words that finally freed the pain so deep inside—poured out of her. "We were *terrified!* Someone had murdered Falsan—that was all we knew. And they were *chasing* us. We couldn't run fast enough!"

"Of course we were." Gadrial stared at her. "What would one of *your* army officers have done if one of his men was dead? If he'd been responsible for controlling the situation?"

"*Controlling the situation?*" Shaylar barked a harsh, ugly laugh. "Is that what you call it? You were only 'controlling the situation' when Ghartoun tried to talk to you, without even a weapon in his hands, and you *shot* him?"

"*Garlath* shot him," Gadrial snarled, and even without touching her Shaylar realized that the other woman was genuinely angry. No, not angry—she was *furious*. And not, Shaylar realized in shock, at her.

"That stupid, cowardly, arrogant, incompetent son of a—" Gadrial was abruptly using words Shaylar hadn't heard before, but they hardly needed translating. Whoever this Garlath was, Gadrial had despised him. *Still* despised him.

"I wasn't close enough to see it happen," Gadrial said finally. "Jasak wouldn't let me get that close. But I heard him shouting at Garlath. Only that *idiot* shot anyway, and then unholy hell broke loose. I'd never heard *anything* like that."

Shaylar was trembling. Her perfect Voice's memory replayed the shouted command she'd heard when Ghartoun stood up. The words which had meant nothing at the time, which she'd assumed all this time had been the order to attack. But now she'd learned at least some Andaran, and in her memory, she heard the voice once more. The voice she recognized now as Jasak Olderhan's.

"*Hold fire, Fifty Garlath!*"

The words rang through her mind like a jagged lightning bolt, and she stared at Gadrial.

"Jasak ordered him not to shoot," she said slowly, softly. "He ordered him *not* to shoot."

"Yes, he did!" Gadrial's expression was tight with remembered anguish. "I heard him say it. Heard that crossbow's slap and twang *after* he'd shouted that order. Then that horrible, thunderous roar—"

Shaylar felt nothing but truth in Gadrial Kelbryan, and she began to weep. Silently at first. Then she covered her face with both hands and began to sob.

They'd died for nothing. *For nothing!* And Company-Captain Halifu had come looking for them, with no way to know Jasak had never meant for anyone to die, and *more* blood had been spilled. Halathyn had died, and so had a lot of others. And all anyone in Sharona would know was what *she'd* transmitted to Darcel. The images of fire and blood. Of intentional murder and deliberate slaughter, because that was what she'd thought—*known*—was happening!

There would be a war, she realized. She could see it as clearly as she had ever seen anything in her life. As if she'd been a Calirath experiencing a Glimpse. There would be a terrible, monstrous war, and more people would die, stupidly, on both sides, because no one back home knew the first massacre had been a *mistake*.

Gadrial had put both arms around her, was making helpless sounds, trying to comfort her. And then, suddenly, the door between the sleeping cabin and the tiny sitting room of Gadrial's quarters crashed open and Jathmar was there, white to the lips.

"*Shaylar!*"

She turned blindly toward him. Then she was in his arms, clinging to him, weeping helplessly.

"What happened?" he demanded raggedly. "What did she *do* to you?"

"Nothing." Shaylar hiccuped. "Nothing, Jathmar. Oh, Jath—the whole thing was a terrible *mistake!*"

She tried to tell him, although her explanation wasn't nearly as coherent as Gadrial's had been, and he listened to her words, to the emotions churning through the marriage bond. When she finally got the ghastly truth Gadrial had just revealed through to him, he sat in silence for long moments, jaw muscles clenched tightly. Then a deep sigh shuddered out of him.

"All right. I believe it. Because *you* believe *her*. Gods, what a stupid, monstrous waste!"

Shaylar just nodded, and he tipped her chin up, smiled into her eyes, and wiped tears from her cheek with his index finger.

"You need a handkerchief, sweetheart, only I haven't got one."

She sniffed, then flashed a grateful look at Gadrial when the other woman pressed a scrap of cloth from her sewing into her hand. Shaylar dried her eyes, blew her nose, and gave Gadrial a watery smile.

"Thank you," she said, then realized Gadrial was watching both of them closely, her brow furrowed in puzzlement.

"Shaylar?" she said slowly, almost uncertainly.

"Yes?"

"How did Jathmar know you were upset?"

Shaylar and Jathmar exchanged mortified glances.

"Oh, hells," Shaylar said, but Jathmar shook his head.

"My fault," he muttered in Shurkhali (which was *not* the Ternathian they'd been teaching Gadrial), rubbing the bridge of his nose. "You just scared the daylights out of me, honey. I caught your fear, then your emotions went so crazy I just—"

"Hush." It was Shaylar's turn to shake her head, and then she shrugged with a crooked smile. "It had to happen sometime. And it's no more your fault you responded than it's my fault for having felt that way in the first place!"

"But why *did* you? You were already headed that way before she dropped that little bombshell about what's-his-name, Garlath. That's what set off the explosion, but you were already under a *lot* of pressure, Shaylar. What in all the Arpathian hells has been going *on* in here?"

"Gadrial's been explaining something important to me, Jathmar. Something about the way their technology works. We joked about Halathyn using magic, but, Jathmar, I think that's exactly what it *was*. Magic. I don't know what else to call it."

She drew a deep breath and tried to explain. On the one hand, she was handicapped by the fact that she simply didn't understand it all herself by any stretch of the imagination. On the other hand, she had the advantage that she and Jathmar shared a far more complete command of their language—not to mention the marriage bond—plus a common base of reference. It took a while to get the fundamental concept across, and longer for Jathmar to accept it. But then he nodded abruptly, choppily.

"You're right," he said. "Manipulating energy with special words? Spells and incantations? Magic rings—well, those little cube things—to store the spells inside? It's utterly fantastic, *impossible*, but how else could they be doing it?" He sighed. "And now I've blown our cover. We've got to tell her *something*."

"Yes, we do," Shaylar agreed. "Let me think."

Her thoughts raced as she tried to figure out how to word it without giving *too* much away. Finally, she faced Gadrial, who sat watching them through narrowed, suspicious eyes.

"I'm sorry," Shaylar sighed. "Jathmar was very confused. He wanted to know why I was upset, so I had to explain. Everything. He, too, is very distressed by the mistake that was made."

"But how did he *know*?" Gadrial asked, and Shaylar gave her a crooked little smile.

"You said you have a Gift. Something you were born with. On Sharona, our home world, we have . . . not the same thing. We don't have your . . . magic." She wasn't sure she was using Gadrial's word properly, but it was as close as she could come at the moment. "Not anything like it. But some people are born with something other people don't have. We call it . . ."

She hunted for the word, only to discover she didn't have exactly the right one in her still limited vocabulary.

"What do you call it when a great artist, or a great singer, has something other people don't? The thing that lets him do what he does so much better than anyone else can?"

"A talent?" Gadrial suggested, and Shaylar nodded vigorously.

"Yes. A talent. Some people in my world have special Talents. They're—" she wrinkled her brow trying to find the way to say it. "They're in the mind." She tapped her temple. "Jathmar and I are married. We both have a small Talent, nothing very special, really," she said as smoothly as she could, grateful that Gadrial was no telepath to sense her departure from the truth. "But when two people with Talents marry, a bond forms. A bond of the mind. The emotions. Jathmar always knows when I'm afraid or upset. And I always know when he's worried or angry. It's stronger when we're closer together, but we don't have to be in the same room to feel it. Don't your people have anything like this? A mother who just *knows* when her child's been injured, for example?"

"No." Gadrial shook her head, eyes wide, and Jathmar and Shaylar exchanged startled glances.

"*Nothing* like it?" Jathmar's astonishment showed even through his slower, more labored Andaran.

"No."

The three of them stared at one another, thunderstruck for entirely different reasons.

"Well," Gadrial finally said, "it's clear we come from very different people. *Very* different."

"Yes," Shaylar gulped. "Even more different than we'd realized."

"Which brings up another question." Gadrial held Shaylar's gaze. "What *are* your . . . Talents?"

Shaylar had known it was coming. It was, after all, the next logical question. She just wished she'd thought to come up with an explanation for it before this. Lying, even by withholding information, did not come naturally to a Voice. For that matter, she wasn't certain exactly *which* lies she should tell! Should she understate what Talents could do in an effort to lull these people into a false sense of security? Hope they would take Sharona and the Talented too lightly? Or should she *exaggerate* the Talents? Hope she and Jathmar could make the Arcanans nervous enough that they'd move slowly, cautiously? Possibly create enough nervousness to buy time for their own people to mobilize in response to the threat?

"Jathmar is a Mapper," she said finally. "He . . . Sees the land around him. Not very far," she added. "For a few miles in any one direction, at most."

Gadrial's mouth had fallen open. She stared at Jathmar for a moment, then back and Shaylar.

"And you?"

"Oh, my Talent isn't very much," Shaylar prevaricated. "Mostly, I sense Jathmar through the marriage bond. It helps me know if he's in trouble, when he's out Mapping. And I help draw the charts, too."

"We didn't find any maps," Gadrial said, studying them with hooded, wary eyes. Shaylar met those eyes forthrightly and shook her head.

"No, of course you didn't. I burned them."

"You *burned* them?"

"What would *you* have done?" Shaylar challenged. "Would you have just handed them over? To people you didn't know? People who'd murdered one of your friends, who'd chased you down like animals, who were shooting and killing the rest of your friends all around you? Trying to kill *you*? Would you have let people like that get hold of maps that showed the way to *your* home?"

"No," Gadrial said softly, after a moment. "I don't suppose I would."

"Neither would I. Neither *did* I."

Gadrial nodded slowly, but another deep suspicion showed plainly in her expression. She started to ask a question, paused, then closed her lips. Shaylar waited, meeting her gaze levelly. It was one of the hardest things she'd ever done, but she held that gaze steadily, as though she had nothing further to hide.

"Shaylar," Gadrial said at last, sounding unhappy, "we think—Jasak thinks—your people got a message out. One that warned your people about what had happened. *Did* someone on your crew get a warning out? Using this Talent of the mind?"

Continuing to meet Gadrial's gaze was agony, but Shaylar did it anyway.

"I don't know, Gadrial."

"Don't know? Or won't tell me?"

"What do you want of me, Gadrial?" Shaylar's eyes filled. "We're your *prisoners*."

"Not *my* prisoners." Gadrial shook her head, biting her lip. "You're Sir Jasak Olderhan's prisoners."

"Don't you mean the army's?" Jathmar asked harshly in his accented Andaran.

"No, I don't. I don't understand all of it, because I'm not in the Army, either. And I'm not Andaran. The Andarans are a military society, and they have a lot of complicated rules I don't understand. But one of those rules is about prisoners, and about responsibilities toward them. You'll have to ask Jasak about it, if you want to know."

"I do want to know," Jathmar said in a voice full of iron. "And I think we have a right to know. Don't you?"

Gadrial bit her lip again, more gently this time, looking at him levelly. Then she drew a slightly unsteady breath.

"Yes, I do. If you'll wait here, I'll go find him and ask him to explain. Explain to *all* of us, actually. I'm caught in the middle of this thing, too, and I don't understand it as well as I should."

"Thank you," Shaylar said softly, and Gadrial nodded. Then she left the cabin, and Shaylar began to tremble.

"They're going to figure it out, Jathmar," she said, once again in Shurkhali.

"Eventually," he agreed heavily. "Probably sooner than we'd like. And it's my fault. I should have realized you weren't really in danger—not with Gadrial."

"Don't blame yourself." She laid a hand against his cheek, and his lips quirked.

"There's no one else *to* blame, sweetheart. It certainly isn't your fault." He captured her hand, kissed her fingers, and tucked them against his heart. "I know how hard that was, lying to Gadrial just now. I don't think I could have done half as well as you did. She's half convinced you don't know for sure if a message went out."

"Only half," Shaylar muttered, "and Jasak Olderhan won't be so easy to fool."

"No, he won't. Still, you're right. What else should they expect from us? If they were in our shoes, do you think they'd have volunteered that information about magic powering their whole civilization?"

"Probably not," Shaylar agreed dryly. "It would be interesting to know how much information our side's managed to gather from *their* prisoners." She shivered. "I'm not sure I want to know how we're treating their soldiers, though. We've been so fortunate . . ."

His arm tightened around her. He didn't need to speak; she could taste his fear for her, his fear about what lay ahead. When Jasak came into the room to explain, Shaylar would know he was telling the truth, if only she could arrange to touch him. But having said as much as she had already, he would undoubtedly be doubly suspicious if she tried anything so obvious. Up until now, their captors had viewed her penchant for touching people as a simple personal habit. She'd been careful to be just as "touchy-feely" with Jathmar as she was with them, but now—

She might never be given another opportunity to touch them again. She faced that probability squarely. And as she did, she also realized that lying to them now and being caught in that lie later would not do them a great deal of good down the road. It might well damage their circumstances, worsen their treatment, incur all sorts of unpleasantness.

The thoughts flowed through her, but before she could discuss them with Jathmar, it was too late. The door opened again, and Jasak Olderhan filled the frame, his eyes hooded as he stared down at them.

CHAPTER
THIRTY-THREE

HE KNOWS, SHAYLAR realized with a jolt of pure terror. *He already* knows. . . .

The cold anger in Jasak's eyes was bad enough, but what lay *under* that anger had Jathmar moving abruptly, thrusting her behind him, facing Jasak with nothing in his hands but courage.

"If you hurt her," Jathmar said softly, each word enunciated precisely, carefully, "I will do my best to kill you."

Something lethal stirred in Jasak Olderhan's eyes. Then he drew a long, slow breath through his nostrils and let it out again, just as slowly. The glittering threat left his eyes. He was still angry—deeply angry, with a cold, controlled fury—but homicide no longer stared them in the face. Jathmar stayed where he was, anyway.

"Gadrial," Jasak said heavily, "please stay in the passage. I don't want you walking into this cabin."

Shaylar wanted to tell him Gadrial wasn't at risk, but what she felt from Jathmar held her silent. If anything threatened her, Jathmar would use whatever was at hand to keep Jasak away from her. Even Gadrial, the closest thing either of them had to a friend in this entire universe. Her breath sobbed in her throat. This was madness. . . .

Jasak stepped fully into the cabin and closed the door carefully behind him. He didn't lock it—not that there was much reason to on a ship in the middle of the ocean—but he stood with his back still against it, staring at them for several more seconds. Then he drew another deep breath.

"Gadrial tells me you want to know your status as my prisoners?"

"That's right."

"Well, *I'd* like to know how you sent a message to your soldiers."

Icy silence lay between them. It lingered, chilling despite the sunlight through the scuttle.

"Do you have any idea," Jasak asked softly, "what your people did to my men?"

"From what I've gathered, about the same thing *they* did to my crew," Jathmar said in a flat voice.

Jasak's eyes flashed. That murderous look glittered in them again for a moment, but then his nostrils flared.

"All right. I suppose there's a certain justice in that view." He very carefully unknotted his hands, then scrubbed his eyes in a gesture that combined weariness, frustration, and almost unbearable tension in one.

"Do you remember Hadrign Thalmayr?" he asked finally, abruptly.

"The man who replaced you? The one who hated Shaylar and me?"

"Yes." Jasak's voice was as dry as a Shurkhali summer wind. "He was a very...." He paused, clearly searching for words Jathmar's limited Andaran would allow him to understand. "He thought in narrow terms. I tried to convince him to pull out, to abandon that portal at least for a time. We'd already made one mistake, and I didn't want anyone making another one that led to more shooting. But he wouldn't listen. Neither would Five Hundred Klian at Fort Rycharn. They thought it was unlikely there was a body of your soldiers anywhere near our portal. And they thought it was unlikely you'd gotten a message out. But they were wrong on both counts, weren't they?"

"Were they?" Jathmar countered.

"You tell me," Jasak said softly. "And before you do, think about this. I've been adding things up. Puzzling things. We've been holding you for barely two weeks, yet you speak Andaran astonishingly well. How? *Nobody* learns languages that fast—not in Arcana.

"Then there's your wife's ability to know things about people. She's a very sensitive creature, your wife. Always touching someone. Always concerned. Always so understanding. She understands too much, Jathmar. It's almost like she knows what you're thinking."

He looked past Jathmar, staring directly into Shaylar's eyes, and her insides flinched. But she forced herself to meet his gaze, the way she'd met Gadrial's. It was harder—much, *much* harder—to simply meet Jasak Olderhan's gaze, let alone lie to those cold-steel eyes. When those eyes tracked back to Jathmar, she nearly sagged in relief. It felt as if someone had turned off the blowtorch they'd been holding on her.

"Then there's the dragon," Jasak added softly.

"The dragon?" Jathmar echoed, genuinely baffled this time.

"Oh, yes. The dragon. You were still unconscious, but Shaylar remembers. Don't you?" The glance he flicked into her eyes felt like a lance driven through her. Then he clicked that glance back onto Jathmar. "We had to airlift you out to save your life. When the transport dragon arrived, we loaded *you* on with no trouble. But when we tried to load Shaylar, the dragon went berserk. He hated her on sight, and I want to know why. What did the dragon sense about her that *we* couldn't?

"Stranger still, the dragon's rage seemed to hurt her. Not just terrify her; *hurt* her. She clutched at her head, and she screamed. Not just once, either. Not just the first time we tried to put her on the dragon's back. It happened again, right after we got airborne. The dragon actually tried to buck us off in midair, tried to reach her with his teeth. But your wife didn't even see that, because she was clutching her head again, screaming in pain. Gadrial had to put her to sleep, knock her unconscious with her healing Gift, just to stop the pain she was in. And to—how did Shaylar put it? To 'get the dragon out of her mind.'"

This time, Shaylar flinched. She couldn't help it. Her memory of that dreadful night was too chaotic, too confused, for detailed recollection, even for a Voice. But she remembered that moment. Remembered her desperate plea to Gadrial. Yet she'd never suspected Gadrial might actually have *understood* her. The deadly implications of that revelation stabbed through her and she felt the same awareness resonating through the marriage bond with Jathmar.

"Would you care to explain all of that, Jathmar?" Jasak said. "If I hadn't known such things were impossible, I'd have said she was doing something with her mind—something that enraged our dragon, and that the dragon's rage was somehow spilling over into her mind. But that was impossible. Absurd. Except that it isn't impossible, after all, is it? You people have these *Talents*." He spat the word out like poison. "You do things with your minds. Just what kind of game are the two of you playing with *our* minds?"

He's scared, Shaylar realized abruptly. *He's scared to death of something he doesn't understand.* She knew exactly what that felt like; she'd just gone through the same experience herself, with Gadrial's explanation. But his fright ran much deeper than hers had, much deeper than simple fear of something he didn't understand.

He's terrified that we'll put thoughts into their minds, control them somehow. What else could *he think, if they don't have anything like telepathy? And he feels* responsible. *He's not just afraid for himself. It's not that simple for him. He's a military officer, responsible for others, for making certain we don't do something to* them.

"It doesn't work that way, Jasak," she heard herself say.

"*Shaylar!*" Jathmar twisted around to stare at her, his eyes dark with protest, but she shook her head.

"No, Jathmar. I need to say this. Trust me, please." She'd deliberately spoken in Andaran, and her husband searched her eyes even as he searched her feelings through their bond. He bit his lower lip, taut with fear for her, and yet in the end he nodded and turned to Jasak once more.

"I'll say it again, Jasak Olderhan. Hurt her, and I will do my best to kill you."

Their gazes locked for a long, dangerous moment. Then Jasak let out an exasperated sigh.

"For people with 'Talents,' you can be amazingly unobservant, Jathmar! I don't kill women. Not if I know they're in the line of fire. And I don't *hurt* women, either. When I discovered Shaylar in those trees . . ."

The agony reflected beside the anger in his eyes was plainly visible, and not just to Shaylar, and she felt a little of the tension drain from her husband. Just a little, but it was enough to take them all one step back from the killing edge of danger. Jathmar still wouldn't let her move closer to Jasak, not even to stand at his own side, which was where she desperately wanted to be—held in his arms, not cowering behind his shoulder. But there was no point in making the tension worse.

She did reach forward, needing contact with him, even if that contact was as slight as interlacing her fingers through his, and he reached back to squeeze her hand.

"Please open the door, Jasak," she said then. "I know you're afraid. You're worried Jathmar might try to use Gadrial as a hostage, out of fear. But she needs to hear what I have to say."

Jasak stared into her eyes for long moments, trying to see past them into her mind. She could feel the attempt battering at her, and wondered abruptly if perhaps he did have at least a trace of Talent himself. But even if he did, he didn't have the slightest idea how to use it, and so he ended up with nothing but intense frustration and no real answers. In the end, he finally turned and opened the door.

Gadrial's eyes were wide and worried. She started to step forward, but Jasak lifted a hand.

"Don't come in," he cautioned. "Not yet. But Shaylar wants you to hear this, too. It ought to be . . . interesting."

He turned that cold-steel gaze back onto her and waited.

"I am Talented," Shaylar said, speaking very quietly, very steadily. "A Talent is a little bit like a Gift. You're born with it. But we don't use Talents to control some energy field outside ourselves. We use our minds to do different kinds of work. We call someone with my Talent a 'Voice.' I can use my mind to talk directly to another Talented Voice. I can't do that with anyone else, not even Jathmar."

Jasak stood rigidly in the open doorway, clearly not believing it, but Shaylar kept going, because she didn't have any other choice. She released Jathmar's hand just long enough to reach up and brush fingertips across her husband's temple. Then she moved her hand from his temple to her own.

"Jathmar and I share a special bond. When Talented people marry, there's such closeness, such sharing, that a deep and permanent bond forms. But it isn't the same as a full Voice. He can feel my emotions; I can feel his. And I can feel Jathmar's mind. Not hear it, exactly, but *feel* it—like I'm touching something solid. And he can feel mine, even across a distance of several miles. We can often *guess* what the other is thinking, because we know each other so well, but I can't read his mind.

"And I can't read yours or Gadrial's, either. I can't hear your thoughts. I can't put thoughts into your mind. You noticed how often I touch people." Her rueful smile startled him. "I knew one of you would, eventually, but I didn't know who would see it first. Gadrial spends more time with me, but you're more suspicious." She shrugged. "You're a soldier. It's your job."

He glowered at her, but then, to her vast relief, he seemed to unbend the tiniest bit.

"Yes. It *is* my job," he said gruffly, then drew another deep breath and forced the steel burr out of his voice.

"All right. I'll try to listen with a little less suspicion. I need to understand this, for a lot of important reasons. And while I'm listening," he met her gaze, "I'll remind myself that despite what your soldiers did to my men, despite the threat to my people they represent, neither you nor Jathmar tried to kill my men until *we* fired on *you.*"

"No," Jathmar said stiffly. "We didn't. *We* weren't stupid. We were good enough woodsmen to notice panicked wildlife rushing ahead of a wide line of men driving through a forest to surround us. We guessed right then that we were outnumbered. That's why we found a hiding place. And when we finally saw your people, it was obvious we faced soldiers. Less than twenty civilians against enough men to cut off our escape from every direction? We'd have been crazy to shoot first! But that didn't help us in the end, did it—because you had to come in shooting anyway! Maybe Gadrial is right and you didn't order your people to shoot, but you were in command. *You* were the one who pushed it—chased us—until it was inevitable!"

His accent was more pronounced even than usual, and he had to pause several times to find the words he wanted. But his anger came through with perfect clarity, and Jasak studied him for long silent moments.

"Let me tell you what *I* see about that day," he said finally. "You had personal weapons more terrifying than anything we'd ever seen—certainly more terrifying than anything we 'soldiers' had. Something that killed with horrifying violence, something we couldn't even identify. And when we tracked the man who'd killed one of *my* men to your camp, we discovered that you hadn't made the sort of open encampment we 'soldiers' made when we bivouacked. Oh, no, you'd built a palisade, well placed on commanding ground, with good fields of fire. An obviously *military* palisade. One of my men was already dead, I had no idea who you were, where you'd come from, who'd shot first, what other weapons you might have, how close other *military* forces might have been, what your intentions were, what sort of people you were. And when we finally did catch up with you, you were holed up in the best *military* position we'd seen anywhere on that side of our portal! Yes, you *turned out* to be civilians, but how was I supposed to know that *then*? I knew *nothing* about you—except that you'd already killed one of my people—and every member of the Arcanan military forces has standing orders where contact with another human civilization is concerned. We're to make it a *peaceful* contact if we possibly can. *But*, if there's already been blood shed, especially by what appears to be an organized military force, then those same standing orders *required* me to *control* the contact. Given all of that, Jathmar, how would you have reacted differently up until the instant fire was opened?"

It was his turn to hold Jathmar's gaze challengingly, and he did. Yet even Jathmar could see it was a *challenge*, not simple anger, and he felt his own anger waver.

He didn't want to feel that. The sudden realization that he wanted—*needed*—to cling to his anger shook him badly, but it was true. He didn't want to take a single step toward understanding what Jasak had known, what *Jasak's* options had been, because understanding might undermine his hatred.

Yet he couldn't afford to clutch that hatred to him, either. And so, finally, he shrugged.

"I don't know," he said shortly. "I'm not a soldier. I'd like to think I wouldn't have run down a civilian survey crew, but if I'd thought *they* were soldiers?" He shrugged again. "I don't know."

"I appreciate your honesty in coming that far," Jasak said. "But there was another side to it, as well. Something I'd already recognized even before the shooting started. You were trying to keep the situation under control, too. You didn't want a bloodbath any more than I did, and I knew it."

"How?" Shaylar asked, totally astonished.

"You could have opened fire without warning. I was sure you'd gone into those fallen timbers. If you'd wanted a fight, you could have dug in in your palisade, tried to set up an ambush when we followed your man back to your camp. You hadn't done that; you'd run for your portal, instead, tried to break contact. There could have been a lot of reasons—*military* reasons—for that, but you didn't open fire when we started closing in on your position out in those fallen trees, either. You had concealment and cover—you could have killed a lot of my men before we even knew where to shoot back—and you didn't. Not until someone on our side killed someone else on your side who was trying to talk, not shoot."

He shook his head again, slowly, heavily.

"I'm not prepared to second-guess all my decisions that day, and we'll never know what happened when your man—Falsan—met Osmuna. But the bottom line is that my people shot first, whether I wanted them to or not, in the *second* encounter with you. However it happened, that was the outcome. And that means you deserve for me to at least listen with as open a mind as I possibly can."

Shaylar started to speak, but he raised one hand. The gesture stopped her, and he smiled without any humor at all.

"Don't misunderstand me. I'm still a soldier, and my duty is still to protect my people. After what happened at our portal—after what your soldiers did to us, when they came looking for you—I'm very much afraid that an ugly, brutal war is waiting for all of us." He spoke with dark and bitter honesty. "Even if we, the four of us, could figure out a way to stop it, it may be too late already. Military people on both sides are obviously already beginning to react to what's happened as the reports go up the chain of command, and the gods only know where *that's* likely to go. And once the politicians get their hooks into this, it may be impossible to stop.

"All we can do is this; try to convince me, Shaylar. Convince me your mental Talents aren't super weapons. That you can't use your minds to destroy Arcana at any time you choose. Whether you believe it or not at this moment, I am absolutely the closest thing to a friendly judge you're going to find. If you can't convince *me*, you'll never convince the Andaran High Commandery, let alone the politicians who govern the Union of Arcana."

"I know that," she whispered. "And that terrifies me."

"It should."

The dark thing riding his shoulders left Shaylar trembling. She was more than afraid for herself; she was afraid for Sharona. For every Talent alive. But then Jasak went on.

"Whatever else you say or don't say, before I come to a final decision about whether or not I believe what you're telling me, answer me this. Why *do* you touch people, if it isn't to read minds?"

He still sounded suspicious, although less unbelieving, and she met his gaze unflinchingly.

"Most people, even those without Talents, can tell a great deal about a person's emotions. When you look at a person, Jasak, you can see emotion in him, can't you? In his expression, his eyes, the way he stands or walks. You learn a great deal about a person that way, don't you?"

He nodded, clearly unsure where she was going.

"Well, I can see all that, too, visually. But when I *touch* a person, I can sense their emotions directly. Not their thoughts, just their feelings. If they're terrified, I feel waves of terror, as though I'm terrified of something, too. If they're angry, it's like being hit with a fist. If they're grieving, it's like drowning in the need to weep."

She turned to look at Gadrial, who still stood in the passage beyond Jasak.

"The day we came onto the ship, Jathmar and I knew something terrible had happened. That was obvious, because Gadrial had been crying. Her deep emotional shock showed in her eyes, in her face, in her posture—*anyone* could see that. But," her gaze moved back to Jasak's face, "when *you* took my hand to help steady me on the gangway . . ."

Shaylar shut her eyes, shivering involuntarily.

"I almost fell down, your grief was so terrible. I know now it was for what had happened to your men, but I didn't know that then. And I didn't even have time to block it out. It just smashed into me like a club. It literally knocked me off my feet. I would have fallen, if you hadn't caught me, and then *Gadrial* took my hand, and that was almost worse. It felt—"

She cast through every nuance of that memory, trying to be as accurate as possible.

"There was terrible loss. Personal loss, even worse than yours for your men, Jasak. Like when a family member dies. It felt . . . as if you'd lost a father?" she finished uncertainly, reopening her eyes to meet Gadrial's.

"Yes." Gadrial's breath caught on a ragged half-sob. "That's exactly what it feels like. Halathyn *was* a father to me."

"I'm sorry he was killed," Shaylar said softly. "I touched him that first day." She had to blink to clear her eyes. "I trusted him instantly. He was very gentle inside. It felt like he loved everything."

"Yes." Gadrial wiped away tears. "He did. I still can't believe he's gone. That he died so horribly . . . so *stupidly*."

"They *all* died horribly," Shaylar said, her voice suddenly harsh. "They all died stupidly. There was no *need* for any of it! I bleed for you and Halathyn, Gadrial—but who bleeds for *us*? Who bleeds for Ghartoun, who stood up to talk to you with empty hands? For poor, maddening Braiheri, who studied plants and animals? For Barris Kasell, who kept me sane when Falsan died in my arms? Who died trying to keep *me* alive? We had *boys* with us, too. Young men, barely out of school, who took care of our pack animals, the supplies. Boys with dreams and their whole lives to live. And they *all* died horribly. Stupidly. For *nothing*."

Gadrial bit her lip, and Shaylar looked directly into Jasak Olderhan's eyes.

"That first day, that horrible first day . . ." She didn't even try to fight the tears. "You can't ever know how terrified I was. How deep the shock was, even before you cremated the dead. I was badly injured—your own Healers have confirmed that. My husband's life hung by a thread, with burns so terrible I couldn't even bear to look at them. And then you *burned* the dead."

She shuddered. Her mind wanted desperately to shy away from that particular memory, but there was a point she needed to make, and she couldn't do that without facing the memory herself.

"When you burned them, I started to fall. You caught me—just like you did on the gangway. Do you remember that, Jasak?"

He nodded slowly.

"When you touched me—" She paused, swallowed sharply, wrapped both arms around herself. "My Talent was badly damaged because of my injury, but I could still feel your regret. Your *horror*. It shocked me. I didn't expect it, and I was too dizzy, too sick, to understand fully. But I felt more than enough to realize you'd actually intended to *honor* my dead."

His own memories of that dreadful day floated like ghosts in his eyes as she stared into them.

"And under the regret there was a sense of desperate sorrow—one I finally understood when Gadrial told me today, in this cabin, that you'd ordered your man not to shoot Ghartoun. I didn't want to believe it when she did, but a Voice has perfect recall, Jasak. I can shut my eyes anytime I want and *hear* you shouting not to shoot. And when I learned that, it hurt me, terribly, to finally know for certain that my friends had died for absolutely no reason except one scared man's *stupid* mistake. But it also confirmed what I'd felt inside you that day."

He looked down at her, his eyes still hooded, still suspicious, and her temper snapped.

"Gods' mercy, Jasak! Why else do you think I was able to *trust* you that day? To let you touch me? To not jerk back in horror every time you even *looked* at me? You've talked about how frightening our weapons were to you—what about *your* weapons to *us*? You'd just butchered my dearest friends—burned them *alive*, curse you! My gods, I'd never seen anything so barbaric in my life! You claim to be civilized people, but you build weapons designed to roast an enemy alive!

"You can't possibly know what you did to me that day! What you're still doing to me, every single day I spend trapped in a room with guards staring at me if I even try to look out a window. I can't go for walks in the moonlight anymore. I can't go for walks anywhere! I can't even take a *bath* by myself, without having to ask Gadrial to order some musclebound guard not to shoot before I step outside that cabin door without permission!"

She stood glaring at him, bosom heaving with emotion she could barely contain. She wanted to scream, wanted to hit him with her fists to make him see what he'd done to them, what he was still doing to them. And buried in her anger, making it burn even fiercer, was the knowledge that he *did* know. That he understood, and deeply regretted it. That he would have done *anything* to undo it . . . and that he was still unflinchingly determined to do whatever his "duty" required of him. That unless she could convince him their Talents did not present some deadly danger to his nation and the men in his army, he would take whatever steps seemed necessary to eliminate that danger.

"It was my *Talent*—the Talent you're so worried about right now—that let me understand what you were feeling. I wanted to hate you. Gods, I wanted to *kill* you! I was in deep shock, and the shocks just kept coming and coming, and it was all *your* fault. I didn't want you to touch me, not then, not ever, but you did.

"And because you did, and *because* I'm Talented, I *knew* you hadn't wanted it to happen. I knew how terribly you regretted it, and how determined you were to protect me from still more harm. And when that happened, I couldn't keep hating you. I *couldn't*. I'm a Voice—I was born to understand people. I can't *help* understanding people. Even," she sobbed in rage, "when I don't want to!

"I wanted to hate you, and my Talent wouldn't let me. I'm not a weapon—I'm a *Voice*. A bridge between people. A living tool to help people communicate and understand one another. It's in my blood, my bones, my very *skin*. If you would just stop holding onto your suspicion with both fists and all your teeth, you'd see the truth, Jasak Olderhan."

She drew a deep breath, scrubbed the angry tears from her face, then shook her head.

"I can't *prove* to you that my Talent is no danger to you," she said quietly, almost softly. "But if it were, don't you think I'd already be using it? All I've done is use it to learn your language. If there *were* something I could do to strike back at you after all of the agony, fear, humiliation, and helplessness your people have inflicted on us, you can be certain that I would." She met his eyes levelly, challengingly. "You'd deserve that, and I'm sure you'd expect it. But there isn't, and I can't, and you're not a Voice, don't have a scrap of telepathy. So words are all I have to convince you I'm telling you the truth."

He continued to gaze down at her, then turned to look at Jathmar again, and she wanted—more than she'd ever wanted anything in her life before—to touch him. To see what emotions were streaming through him behind that expressionless mask of a face. But that was the last thing she could do, and so she simply stood, waiting.

* * *

Jasak looked at the tiny woman standing in front of him. Looked at the face of that woman's husband and read Jathmar's desperate fear for Shaylar, and the horrible, debilitating knowledge that there was no way he could protect her from whatever Jasak decided to do.

And that was the crux of the problem, wasn't it? Jasak had to decide what to do, and Shaylar was right. He had no "Talent" of the mind, no yardstick to measure the truth of what she'd said, or to sense what *her* true emotions might be. He had to choose whether or not to take her unsupported word for it.

Despite all she'd just said, it was entirely possible that she could be—and had been—subtly influencing his judgments, his decisions, his very thoughts. The very passion with which she'd presented her argument had only driven home the fact that he had no way of knowing what other hidden abilities lurked within her. Not only had she admitted that she could sense the emotions of others, but the way she'd described herself—as a "Voice"—had told him *exactly* how they'd gotten a message back to their own side. And she'd forgotten to try to disguise her fluency in Andaran. Jathmar's progress in learning Jasak's language had been phenomenal enough, but the command of it which Shaylar had just demonstrated was little short of terrifying.

Yet that was the entire point, wasn't it? *Should* it be terrifying, or did it simply feel that way because he didn't understand? Because it was a simple, everyday ability of her people which simply lay so far outside his own experience that he couldn't recognize it as such?

"Sit down, Shaylar. Please," he said finally.

She stared at him for a few more seconds, then stepped back behind Jathmar and settled gingerly on the foot of Gadrial's bed. Jasak waited until she'd seated herself, then pulled the straight-back chair back away from the small desk in the cabin's corner and placed it for Gadrial. He waited until the magister was seated, as well, then drew a deep breath.

"First," he said quietly, "I acknowledge that I was in command of the troops who killed your companions and wounded the two of you. That's a significant point, which I'll return to in a moment."

Jathmar was watching his face even more intently than Shaylar. Now he reached out and took his wife's hand once more, and Jasak realized he was also clinging to that "marriage bond" Shaylar had mentioned. That he was using it to help himself follow what Jasak was saying with his own, more limited Andaran.

"Second," he continued, "whatever concerns I might have over the threat your 'Talents' might or might not pose to the other people on this ship, or to the Union of Arcana as a whole, I wouldn't blame you for using them any way you could. Indeed, I'd expect no less out of you, just as I would expect no less out of Gadrial and her Gift under similar circumstances.

"And, third, I believe you." He saw both of his prisoners' taut spines relax ever so slightly, and shook his head. "I believe what you've told me is the truth. That doesn't mean I believe you've told me the *entire* truth."

They stiffened again, but he continued calmly.

"In your places, *I* certainly wouldn't tell my captors anything which would help them against my people unless I absolutely had to. I've seen enough of both of you by now to realize you won't, either. But you're also both highly intelligent. That means you know that sooner or later you're going to be very thoroughly questioned. Questioned by professional interrogators who know how to put bits and pieces together and learn things you never even realized you were telling them. For the moment, however, and speaking for myself, I'm going to operate on two assumptions. First, that what you've told me up to this point is true. Secondly, that I have your parole."

Not even Shaylar recognized the last word, and he smiled crookedly.

"Your 'parole' is your word—your promise—that you won't attempt to escape, that you won't hurt anyone else except in direct self-defense, and that you will refrain from hostile actions so long as you're treated humanely and with respect. And—" he continued, looking directly into Jathmar's eyes as the Sharonian stiffened with an expression of borning outrage "—I believe that if you're honest with yourselves, you have no choice but to acknowledge that you have been treated both humanely—and with respect—by both Gadrial and myself. I can't undo what happened that day in the forest, but I've done the very best I could to see to it that you were treated well afterward."

Jathmar inhaled, but before he could speak, Shaylar squeezed his hand hard. He turned and looked into her eyes for several heartbeats, then turned back to Jasak.

"You want us to promise to be . . . obedient prisoners," he said in his slower, more halting Andaran. "What about our duty to escape?"

"Escape to where, Jathmar?" Gadrial put in gently from her chair. He looked at her, and she smiled sadly. "Even if you could escape custody, where could you go? How could you ever possibly hope to get home on your own?"

"Gadrial is right," Jasak said as Jathmar looked at her mulishly. "Trust me, however much any of us may regret it, you aren't going to be able to escape, no matter what you do. Unless, of course," his smile turned even more crooked, "your 'Talents' are quite a bit more . . . useful than I've just agreed to assume they are."

"If escape is so impossible, why should we promise not to?" Jathmar challenged.

"Because it will affect the precautions I have to take as the officer responsible for you," Jasak replied unflinchingly.

"But how much longer will you be the officer 'responsible' for us?" Shaylar asked. "I said I trust you, Jasak, and I do. As much as I'll ever be able to trust any Arcanan, at least. But what about that other man—that Hundred Thalmayr? What about all of the other soldiers and officers I've seen glaring at us? Sooner or later, someone senior to you is going to be the one 'responsible' for us. How do we trust him? And why should any promise we make to you affect how *he* treats us?"

"Because of that point I told you I'd come back to," Jasak said. "Because I was in command when your people were killed. That makes *me* responsible for what happened to them, and for everything that's happened to you since."

"But I know you ordered that other officer *not* to shoot!" Shaylar protested.

"Yes, I did. And I doubt very much that even with your Talent you can understand how much it means to me that you realize that. But the officer who opened fire was one of my subordinates. I ought to have ignored the letter of the regulations and relieved him before we ever caught up with your people. I didn't, and after he was killed, after the shooting had become general and I had men down all over that clearing—wounded, dying, dead—I assumed tactical command of the battle. *I* fought that battle, not Shevan Garlath. And I'd do it again, exactly the way I did it then, under the same circumstances and given what I knew at the time."

He met the Sharonians' eyes levelly.

"I had no choice at that point, but that doesn't change the fact that it was my command which attacked you, or that you were civilians who were simply defending yourselves. My men destroyed your lives as surely as they killed your companions, and that leaves me with an honor obligation towards you."

"Honor obligation?" Jathmar repeated carefully, and Jasak nodded.

"Among my people—Andarans, not Arcanans as a whole—there's something called *shardon*. It's the term we use to describe the act of taking someone under your own and your family's shield. You and Shaylar are my *shardonai*. As the commander of the troops who wronged you and yours, I'm obligated to protect you as I would a member of my own family. In fact, under Andaran law and custom, a *shardon* is legally a member of the family of his *baranal*."

"Which means what?" Jathmar asked.

"Which means I'm honor-bound to refuse to surrender you into any other officer's custody, regardless of our relative ranks. It means my family and I are obligated to see to it that you're treated well, that no one abuses you, and that you're assured of all the personal safeguards any other member of our family would receive. It means that even though you and Shaylar are Sharonian, not Arcanan, any children born to you on Arcanan soil will be Arcanan citizens and entitled to all of the rights and protections of citizenship. No one can take them from you, no one can use them against you, and no one can violate their civil rights. The sole difference between you, as my *shardonai*, and my sisters or my parents is that the protections which we can extend to you continue to apply only so long as you voluntarily remain under my protection."

"In your custody, you mean." Jathmar's tone was more cutting than it had been as he made the correction, and Jasak nodded.

"For all practical purposes, yes," he said unwaveringly. "I'm sorry, but no one can change that. Not now."

"And how long is your government going to be willing to leave us in your custody?" Shaylar asked tautly.

"For as long as I, any member of my family, or either one of you is alive," Jasak said flatly.

The two Sharonians looked at him in obvious disbelief. Then Gadrial cleared her throat.

"I've lived among Andarans for years," she told them. "There are a lot of things about them and about their honor code that I still don't pretend to understand, but I do know this much. If Jasak tells you his family will protect you, they *will* protect you."

"From the entire army? Your entire government?" Jathmar couldn't keep the incredulity out of his voice . . . assuming that he'd tried to.

"I think you may not fully realize just who Jasak's family is," Gadrial said with a slightly crooked smile. They looked at her, and she shrugged. "Jasak is *Sir* Jasak Olderhan. His father is Thankhar Olderhan, who happens, among other things, to be the Duke of Garth Showma . . . and the planetary governor of New Arcana. There may be one other Andaran nobleman with as much personal political and military power as His Grace. There couldn't possibly be *two* of them, though. And under the Andaran honor code, the entire Olderhan family and every one of its dependents and liegemen will die before they allow *anyone* to harm an Olderhan *shardon*."

"And the rest of your government, of your politicians, would allow them to do that?" Shaylar demanded as she and Jathmar looked at Jasak with completely new expressions.

"Some of them won't like it," Jasak admitted. "Some of them will try to get around it, probably especially among the Mythalans. And there may well be some—especially among the Mythalans—who attempt to step outside the law and justify it on the basis of 'national security.' But," he added in that same flat, inflexible, rock-ribbed voice, "they won't succeed."

Shaylar and Jathmar looked at one another, then back at him, and as he looked into their eyes, he realized that at last they believed him.

*   *   *

"All right," Jathmar said finally.

He tried to keep his voice level, his tone normal, but it was hard. Partly, that was because of the enormous relief flowing through him. He'd had no idea Jasak might come from such a prominent, powerful family, nor had it even crossed his mind that the protection of that family might be extended to him and Shaylar. But relieved as he was, grateful as he might be, he couldn't forget that the price tag of that protection amounted to a lifetime as prisoners. He told himself that they'd have been prisoners under any circumstances, that this *shardon* relationship offered them the chance to live as human beings, anyway. He even knew it was true. But that didn't change the fact that its protection had been extended to them by the very man who acknowledged he was responsible for the massacre of their friends and their own capture in the first place.

He could feel Shaylar's reaction through the marriage bond, and knew her emotions were far less . . . conflicted than his own. But Shaylar was Shurkhali. She'd been brought up in that culture, that society, and its acceptance of an honor code which had obvious resonances with the one Jasak and Gadrial were describing. Jasak had finally found something Shaylar *understood*. A rock she could grasp, use as an anchor, and Jathmar was grateful for that, as well. Yet he couldn't quite suppress his resentment of *that*, either. Of the fact that it was Jasak, her captor—and not her husband—who had provided her with that almost painful sense of an understood security at last.

"All right," he said again. "We accept that we're . . . *shardonai*, and that you—and your family—will protect us to the very best of your ability. On that basis, we're willing to give *you* our 'parole,' but only as long as we are to remain with you and under your protection."

"Thank you," Jasak said softly.

He sat without saying anything more for the better part of a minute, then he gave himself a shake and looked at Shaylar intently.

"As a part of your parole, Shaylar," he said, "I need to know how close you have to be to another Voice for him to hear you."

Shaylar froze. Then she darted an agonized glance at Jathmar. Her husband looked just as startled as she felt, and she kicked herself mentally. They'd already known Jasak was keenly intelligent. Obviously, he'd put two and two together and come up with exactly the answer she'd hoped he wouldn't reach, and she should have realized he would.

She started to say something. She didn't know what, and it didn't matter, because Jasak's raised hand cut her off before she began.

"I know you're tempted to lie," he said. "I don't blame you for that. And I won't try to compel you to tell me if you refuse to. But honor obligations cut both ways, at least in Andara. Refusing to answer is one thing; lying to your *baranal* is another."

"And if she doesn't answer?" Jathmar asked, bristling with fresh suspicion.

"If she doesn't answer, then I'll be forced to assume the worst. In that case, my responsibility as an officer in the Army of the Union of Arcana will be to ensure that she isn't in communication with anyone from Sharona. Or, at least, that she has no access to information useful to Sharona. In accordance with the first possibility, I'll ask Gadrial and her colleagues at the Institute to attempt to devise spellware which will permanently shut down Shaylar's 'Voice.' Frankly, I don't know if that would be even remotely possible, however, or how we could test to be sure it was actually working if they did. In the absence of that sort of guarantee, my responsibility then would become preventing her from learning anything useful about Arcana. I'd do so as gently as I possibly could, but the consequence would be effectively close confinement. You would be almost totally isolated. I would vastly prefer to avoid doing that, but the obligations of my officer's oath would leave me no alternative."

Jathmar began a hot answer, but Shaylar touched his shoulder.

"Wait, Jath," she said softly in Shurkhali. He looked at her, and she grimaced. "I'm the one who let the cat out of the bag," she said. "I didn't mean to, but he's obviously even sharper than we were afraid he was. And, be honest—is what he's saying really all that unreasonable? If you had a prisoner who had the potential ability to communicate—tracelessly, silently—with an enemy, would you give her access to potentially useful information?"

"Well . . ." he began, and she shook her head.

"These people don't have Voices at all, Jath. That means they can't have anything like our Voice Protocols to cover a situation like this. Even if I wanted to tell them how to temporarily disable my Voice, they wouldn't have anyone who could *do* it!"

"So you want to tell them the truth? All of it?"

"They've obviously already figured out I was the one who got word back to Darcel. That's going to give them a minimum range figure, no matter what. But should we try to exaggerate my range or to minimize it?"

Jathmar thought furiously, trying to keep his expression from showing the depth of his concentration. He wished passionately that they had longer to think about this—or that he'd been smart enough to insist that they think about it in advance. But they hadn't, nor did they dare to hesitate too long before they came up with some sort of answer now. Given what Jasak had said about the difference between lying and simply refusing to divulge information at all, the security offered by the *shardon* relationship might well disappear if Jasak decided they were lying.

And, he thought unwillingly, *Jasak's right about honor obligations cutting both ways. If we're prepared to accept the protection this relationship offers, then we should damned well accept that we're duty-bound to meet our obligations under it. Besides, if we don't, it might just go away completely, and then what happens?*

"Tell them the truth," he said after a long moment, this time in Andaran.

"All right," Shaylar said in soft Shurkhali, and kissed him lightly on the cheek. Then she looked at Jasak.

"We're well outside my maximum Voice range," she said unflinchingly, admitting that she was the one whose warning to Darcel Kinlafia had brought the savage counterattack down on Jasak's men. She saw his recognition of that fact flicker in his eyes, but he only nodded, and his voice remained calm, almost gentle.

"How great is your range?" he asked. "And what sorts of messages can you send?"

"Range varies with the Voice," she replied. "*My* range is a bit over eight hundred miles, but even if it were greater than that, no Voice can transmit through a portal. As for messages—" She shrugged. "I can send—*could* send, if another Voice were in range—any message you could give me. Or, I could link deeply enough with another Voice that he or she could literally see through my eyes, hear through my ears. In that sort of link, the two Voices . . ."

Shaylar Nargra-Kolmayr sat back on the bed in Gadrial Kelbryan's cabin, holding her husband's hand, looking into the eyes of the man whose honor was all that stood between her and a hostile universe's enmity, and willed for him to recognize her honesty as the ship about her carried her towards a lifetime of captivity.

CHAPTER THIRTY-FOUR

"SO, HAVE YOU considered my suggestion?"

Darcel Kinlafia turned his head and cocked one eyebrow at the towering young man riding beside him. He had to admit that Prince Janaki had become steadily more impressive, not less, in the days they'd spent together. It wasn't just the young man's magnetic personality and obvious intelligence, either. He *looked* like a crown prince—improbably tall (even for a Calirath), athletic, broad shouldered, and handsome—and the magnificent horse under his saddle and the hawk riding on the frame attached to it only added to that perfection of imagery. With that new sense of awareness, that self-image of himself as a possible political animal, Janaki's suggestions had awakened within him, Kinlafia had come to realize that Janaki chan Calirath was an imperial publicist's dream come true.

Of course, the prince's horse had never come from a standard PAAF string of mounts, the Voice thought. No doubt the crown prince's sheer size would have made him difficult to mount under any circumstances, but the House of Calirath had been dealing with that particular problem for centuries. Janaki's blue roan—one of a matched pair whose full sibling was trotting along with the column's remounts—was a Ternathian Shikowr, a breed that had been carefully, lovingly developed in the lush, green paddocks and meadows of Ternathia in a breeding program whose stud book had been opened well over two thousand years ago.

Named after its founding stallion—who, in turn, had been named for the ancient Shurkhali cavalry saber the Empire had adopted for its own mounted troops following their resounding initial defeats at the hands of Shurkhali horsemen—and with careful infusions of Shurkhali bloodlines, as well, the Shikowr was a large, powerful breed.

545

It had a characteristic stance, with the front end thrust forward and the hindlegs straight out behind, and a remarkably smooth gait for a horse which could reach seventeen hands in height. In fact, the Shikowr was unique in that it had no trotting gait at all. Instead, it had two four-beat gaits which allowed it to cover a huge amount of ground in a short time, and instead of trotting, it simply moved directly from its fast marching gait into a smooth canter. The Shikowr was as tall as most heavy draft horses, though it was less heavy, and it was renowned for its combination of speed, intelligence, and sheer endurance.

It was even up to the formidable task of carrying male members of the Ternathian imperial family.

All of that had made it the Empire's first choice as a cavalry mount for centuries, although Janaki's roan, a truly superb example of the breed, hugely outclassed the horses which might be found in the typical cavalry or dragoon regiment.

It was said that when the Empire ran into the Arpathians, the most prized booty any septman raider had been able to claim had been Shikowr stock to be incorporated into their own world-famous breeding programs. Having seen Platoon-Captain Arthag's Palomino alongside Prince Janaki's Shikowr, Kinlafia believed it.

"Which suggestion was that, Your Highness?" the Voice replied finally, gazing up at Janaki.

"The one about seeking a career change."

"Oh." Kinlafia smiled. "*That* suggestion."

"I see you're already practicing the fine art of evading direct answers," Janaki observed. "Is that a good sign, or a bad one?"

"That depends on a lot of things, I imagine, Your Highness," Kinlafia said in a much more serious tone, turning his attention back to the muddy trail before them as it began to climb once more.

"Janaki," the crown prince corrected yet again, but Kinlafia shook his head.

"Your Highness, I deeply appreciate your invitation to use your first name. And perhaps one of these days, if I do go into politics, and if my career prospers the way you seem to feel it might, I may even take you up on the offer—in private, at least. But I don't feel comfortable doing it yet. For that matter, it probably wouldn't be a very good habit for me to get into. I imagine there are quite a few sticklers, not all of them in Ternathia, who'd hold that sort of *lesse majesty* against me at the polls."

"There might be, at that," Janaki agreed after a moment. "And the fact that you're thinking that way suggests to me that you are indeed considering seeking a seat in whatever new parliament comes out of this situation."

"Yes, Your Highness." Kinlafia sighed. "I am." He shook his head, his expression rueful. "I can't believe I am, but I am. And it's your fault."

"Guilty as charged," Janaki conceded cheerfully. Then his smile faded. "There's a reason I've been pressing you about it, though."

"A reason, Your Highness?"

"Yes. It's going to take us quite a while to reach Fort Brithik with these ambulances. The going's better after that, but we're still not going to set any speed records through the mountains, especially if they decide to send the wounded clear to Fort Raylthar instead of holding them at Brithik. If you're seriously contemplating taking my advice, then I think you should also consider going on ahead of the column. You'd make a lot better time on your own. In fact, if you think your backside is up to it, I have the authority to authorize you to use remounts from the PAAF liveries along the way."

"Why?" Kinlafia looked back across at the prince. "I mean, why is it important for me to rush ahead that way?"

Janaki didn't reply immediately. Instead, he turned in his saddle and looked back down the trail behind them. For a wonder, it wasn't raining for once here in New Uromath, not that anyone expected that to last. Fortunately, Sharonians in general and the PAAF in particular had amassed an enormous amount of experience in how to move people and material through even highly unprepossessing terrain.

Each party which had passed through on its way to Company-Captain Halifu's fort and the portal which had acquired the so-far informal name of Hell's Gate had done at least a little to improve the going for whoever might come after. Company-Captain chan Tesh's main column had done the lion's share of the work, in no small part because it had been accompanied by freight wagons (which had to get through somehow). No one in his right mind would call the trail a "road," but at least the worst of the ravines and gullies had been crudely bridged, the worst of the unavoidable swampy bits had been corduroyed with felled trees, and a right-of-way of sorts had been hacked out, just wide enough for two of the standard Authority freight wagons—or one of its ambulances—to pass abreast.

Unlike the freight wagons, the ambulances had broad, fat pneumatic tires, made out of the relatively newly developed heat-treated rubber, and the best shock absorbers and springs Sharona could design. Given the nature of the terrain, even the best sprung vehicle was going to jolt a wounded man agonizingly from time to time, but overall, the ride was remarkably smooth. The ambulances were also far lighter than the freight wagons, which, coupled with their wide tires, gave them a much lower ground pressure and made them far easier for their mule teams to haul.

Despite all of that, the four ambulances attached to Janaki's POW column were undeniably slowing it down. Kinlafia understood that perfectly. What he didn't understand was why Janaki was worried about it. Personally, the Voice would be just as happy if it did take him a little longer to get back to Tajvana. He dreaded the inevitable encounters with reporters, once he got there, almost as much as he dreaded the visit he already knew he was going to have to pay to Shaylar's parents.

"I don't know exactly what's happening back home any more than you do," Janaki said finally, turning back to him. "I do know things are going to have to move quickly, though, and the railhead was most of the way to Fort Salby before all of this began. Even going ahead without us, it's going to take you at least the better part of two months to reach Salby, which means that by the time you get there, the line will certainly be completed. So from there, you can get all the way home in another two or three weeks. But that's still close to three months, Darcel. Three months for the political situation to change and elections to be scheduled. I want you home before that happens, if we can possibly manage it."

Kinlafia frowned ever so slightly. He'd come to accept that Janaki truly believed that Darcel Kinlafia actually had something to offer to his home universe's political leadership at a time like this. And he'd also come to realize that, despite a certain inevitable trepidation, he wanted the job. Yet he couldn't quite shake the suspicion that there was more than simple political calculation behind the crown prince's ardent desire to get him elected to office. Like any Voice, Kinlafia was acutely sensitive to the emotions of those about him, though he would never dream of violating Janaki's privacy by deliberately probing the prince's. But because he was sensitive to them, he knew the other man's focus on his own possible political future carried with it an almost physical (and highly personal) sense of urgency.

He considered asking what lay behind that urgency, but decided—once again—that it would be presumptuous. So instead of worrying about the question he couldn't answer and wouldn't ask, he focused on the rest of Janaki's argument. And the more he thought about it, the more he realized that Janaki, as usual, had a point.

Janaki chan Calirath watched the thoughts moving behind Kinlafia's eyes. He was pretty certain Kinlafia was aware that he hadn't shared *all* of his reasons for urging the Voice to seek office, and he was grateful to the other man for not pressing him on the point. If Kinlafia had asked, Janaki would have answered, as best he could; the problem was that he still couldn't come up with anything he would consider even remotely satisfactory as an explanation. The Glimpse he'd experienced several times now simply refused to clarify. That was frustrating enough for Janaki, who'd had no choice but to grow accustomed to the fragmentary nature of the visions his Talent presented. It would have been far more frustrating, and probably more than a little frightening, for Kinlafia. Especially since even though it had refused to clarify, it had become even more urgent feeling. And especially given the fact that while having Kinlafia there would be good for Andrin, that didn't necessarily mean it would also be good for *Kinlafia*.

Whatever it was that the Voice was going to do for Andrin, though, it was *important*, and Janaki loved his sister. Which meant Parliamentary Representative Kinlafia was as good as elected, as far as Crown Prince Janaki was concerned.

"All right, Your Highness," Kinlafia agreed finally. "I'll take you up on your offer. *Both* your offers." He looked at his watch, then glanced up at the sun sliding steadily westward overhead. "I'll stick with the column for the rest of the day and bivouac with you tonight. Then I'll move on ahead tomorrow."

"Good." Janaki managed to keep his relief out of his voice as he smiled at the other man. "That'll give me time to dash off a couple of more notes of introduction for you before you disappear. One of them—" he smiled wickedly at the Voice "—will be addressed to my father. He has a little political influence of his own, you know."

*   *   *

Shaylar and Jathmar stood on the Arcanan ship's foredeck as the vessel moved steadily towards another wooden pier. This one extended out from a considerably larger fort, built on the southeastern curve of a bay which, according to Jathmar's Mapping Talent, was over thirty miles wide from north to south and over sixty from east to west. Shaylar was almost positive that it was on the southern coast of the big island of Esferia—the same island Jasak and Gadrial called Chalar—which dominated the New Farnal Sea and the Gulf of New Ternathia. On Sharona, Esferia was a prosperous transshipment point for commerce between Chairifon and New Ternathia and New Farnal, but on Arcana Chalar was the home of the greatest maritime empire in the planet's history.

They could see the broad arc of a portal well inland, beyond the river that meandered down out of the hills to the raw-looking town clustered against the fort's eastern face. It was hard even for Jathmar to judge distances, but it looked as if the portal was perhaps fifteen miles inland, in which case it must have measured about ten miles across. It was easy enough to see the portal's boundaries, though. The sky on this side was a cloudless, scorchingly hot tropical blue; on the other side, it was night . . . with a violent thunderstorm raging. Even as she watched, she could see the crackling flare of lightning lashing the stormy bellies of the clouds on the far side, and an outrider of thunderheads thrust through the portal to *this* side. Where she stood, the sun was hot and warm, the breeze gentle; along the fringe of the portal, powerful gusts of wind swept treetops into dancing fury on a tempest's breath, and rain born in an entirely different universe came down in sheets.

Shaylar shivered at the sight, but it was one of the bizarre juxta-positionings one got used to traveling between universes. Which didn't make the thought of venturing into it any more pleasant.

Actually, she was much more interested in what she could see closer to hand as their vessel slid alongside the pilings.

This fort—Fort Wyvern, Jasak had called it—was considerably larger than the one they'd left behind. That didn't make it huge, by any stretch of the imagination, but it was clearly a more substantial, longer established structure. It had to have been here for a while, judging by the size of the town nestled up against its inland perimeter, but there was much less of the sense of bustle and frontier energy which would have clung to most Sharonian settlements.

At first glance, the entire town looked like some primitive farming village, with no sign of the steam- or water-powered local industry which would have sprung up in any Sharonian-explored universe. But as she and Jathmar continued to study it, they quickly realized just how deceiving first appearances could be.

They were close enough to get a decent look at what was obvi-ously the local shipyard, for example. It wasn't very large, and there were only three vessels under construction, but Shaylar felt her eyes opening wide as she studied it. She'd seen enough Sharonian boat-yards located in equivalent settlements to know what to look for, but there was no sign here of the steam- or water-powered sawmills and forges she would have found in one of them, nor did she hear or see any axes or adzes.

Instead, she saw big timbers levitating themselves effortlessly into the air, hovering there while some unseen force slabbed them into neatly trimmed planks which stacked themselves to one side. Tearing her eyes away from that fascinating sight, she saw workmen engaged on an entire series of equally improbable activities.

Two men were shaping what were obviously framing timbers for the largest of the vessels under construction, but they were doing it without any tools Shaylar could recognize. Instead, each of them held what looked like simple hand grips at either end of a shaft of shining crystal. The grips were mounted at right angles to the shaft, which was about eight feet long and an inch in diameter. It swelled into a thicker cylinder—perhaps a foot long and seven or eight inches across—at its central point, and the workmen were moving that thicker cylinder carefully across the timber they were shaping while chips and sawdust flew away from it in bizarrely silent clouds.

Other pairs and small groups of workmen were dealing with other jobs—jobs which would have been accomplished with snorting steam or raw muscle in Sharona. Here, though, they were done with more of that eerie "magic" of Gadrial's, and the implications were frightening. There couldn't have been more than thirty men working in that shipyard, but the biggest of the three vessels they were constructing was probably three hundred feet long. That was smaller than the ship on which she and Jathmar presently stood, but it was still a substantial hull, and unlike the smaller ships being built beside it, it was *not* sail powered. Back in Sharona, the construction crews working on a project that size would have been far bigger. If Arcana's "magic" allowed that much greater productivity out of its workforce . . .

"We'll be going ashore shortly," Jasak announced, walking up behind them. "I'll have to report to Five Hundred Grantyl, the base commandant. I'm sure he'll want to . . . meet both of you. I don't imagine we'll stay long, though."

"That doesn't look very pleasant," Shaylar offered, waving one hand at the violent storm raging across the portal threshold.

"No, it doesn't," he agreed. "The other side of the portal is in what I believe you call Uromathia in your home world. The temperature's not too bad there, but we'll have some mountains to cross to reach the next portal. We'll have to wait for the weather to clear before we can leave, and we'll have to bundle up for the flight."

"Flight?" Jathmar repeated, and Jasak nodded.

"We're going to be spending a lot of time on dragonback," he told them. "That's one reason I hope Windclaw's reaction to you had something to do with your head injury, Shaylar."

"So do I," she replied, just a bit tremulously, although she'd come to the conclusion that Windclaw had probably reacted less to her head injury than to her efforts to use her damaged Voice Talent to communicate with Darcel. Those efforts had coincided with both of the transport dragon's determined efforts to eat her, and she was just as grateful, in a guilty sort of way, that there couldn't be anyone within her range now.

"In case it didn't have anything to do with the concussion, though," she offered with a wan smile, "I'd personally vote for traveling on horseback!"

"Oh, no, you wouldn't," Gadrial told her. Shaylar looked at the other woman, standing beside her with the hot breeze stirring her hair, and Gadrial made a face. "Believe me, I've already made this trip, and it's going to be a pain. They haven't extended the slider rail beyond Green Haven, and that's something like twenty thousand of your miles from here. And it's sixty thousand *more* miles from Green Haven to New Arcana, so even with dragons to get us as far as the sliders, it's going to take something like four months to get to Garth Showma. You don't even want to *think* about making that trip on horseback!"

"No, I don't imagine I would," Shaylar replied, trying to hide her shock at what Gadrial had just said. It was less than *forty* thousand miles from New Uromath to Sharona. She and Jathmar had already realized that the Arcanans had clearly been exploring the multiverse longer than Sharona had, but still . . .

"Well," Jasak said as the boarding gangway once again lifted itself out of its brackets and settled into place between the ship's deck and the pier, "I suppose we might as well tell the captain good-bye and get ourselves ashore."

*   *   *

Division-Captain Arlos chan Geraith broke off his conversation with Division-Captain chan Manthau as the conference room door opened. They turned away from the snowcapped mountains, visible along the northern horizon outside the window, and stood respectfully silent as Corps-Captain Fairlain chan Rowlan, commanding officer of the Fifth Corps of the Imperial Ternathian Army came through the open door, followed by his chief of staff and his senior logistics officer.

Chan Rowlan headed directly for his chair at the head of the conference table. The corps-captain was of little more than moderate height for a nativeborn Ternathian, and he normally moved with a certain deliberation, as if to compensate for his lack of height. There was no sign of that today, however. His movements were quick, almost urgent, and his expression was grim.

Which doesn't exactly come as a tremendous surprise, now does it, Arlos? chan Geraith told himself sardonically. There was real, if trenchant, humor in the question, but he was entirely too well aware of his own grim worry—and anger—simmering away beneath it.

"Good morning," chan Rowlan said to chan Geraith and his companions. "I'm glad you were all on the base this afternoon, but time's short. So let's get seated and get to it."

Chan Geraith crossed to the table and took his own seat. Fifth Corps' other two division-captains—Yarkowan chan Manthau of the Ninth Infantry and Ustace chan Jassian of the Twenty-First—seated themselves to his left and right respectively, and he reflected (not for the first time) on how different the Ternathian military was from that of its only true rival, Uromathia. Uromathians were much more addicted to flashy uniforms, rank insignia, and salutes—not to mention bowing and scraping properly to one's superiors. Ternathians, by and large, preferred to get on with the job in hand. They'd been doing it for a very long time, after all. There weren't very many current-service units in any army which could trace their battle honors in unbroken line of succession for over four thousand years.

The Third Dragoons was one of them . . . which made chan Geraith's division substantially older than the entire Uromathian Empire. Or, for that matter, the Uromathian *language*.

With that sort of history behind them, Ternathian officers felt no particular need to emphasize their own importance and prestige. Even division commanders like chan Geraith, with the next best thing to nine thousand men under his command, normally eschewed dress uniform in favor of the comfortable, practical field uniform he wore at the moment. And while there was no question about chains of authority and military discipline, the Ternathian tradition was for senior officers to discuss military problems and strategy like reasonable adults. Unlike certain other empires whose relative youth caused them—and their senior officers—to act like touchy adolescents whose insecurity had them playing the bully on a playground somewhere.

Chan Geraith knew he was being at least a little unfair to the Uromathians, but he didn't really care. The fact was that he didn't *like* Uromathians. He was always scrupulously polite in his dealings with them and in his public comments about them, but he saw no reason to waste fairness on them in the privacy of his own mind.

"I'm sure you're all as well aware as I am of events in the Karys Chain," chan Rowlan said.

For just a moment, the corps-captain's face twisted with a spasm of intense pain mingled with something far darker and uglier. Unlike chan Geraith, who wasn't Talented at all, chan Rowlan's wife was a Voice, and the corps-captain had a fairly powerful telepathic Talent of his own. Chan Geraith hadn't often seen raw hatred on his corps commander's face, but he was seeing it now, and he didn't blame chan Rowlan one bit.

"What you don't know yet," the corps-captain went on a moment later, with a certain forced briskness, "is that I've just received orders from Captain-of-the-Army chan Gristhane, placing Fifth Corps on immediate notice to deploy forward."

Chan Geraith felt his fellow division commanders coming upright in their chairs with him as if they'd rehearsed the choreography ahead of time.

"There are several reasons we were selected," chan Rowlan continued. "One of them is purely political, and not to be discussed outside this room. Specifically, Chava Busar has already placed the better part of two cavalry regiments at the Authority's disposal. They're being given absolute priority for transport forward on the basis that they're the closest non-PAAF force available. We don't want to see Chava get his military toe any further into that door than we can avoid, hence the offer of our own troops.

"Among the purely military reasons, we're the closest Ternathian corps HQ to Larakesh. For that matter, Fort Erthain is closer to Larakesh than any major *non*-Ternathian—" he very carefully did *not* say "Uromathian," chan Geraith noted "—military base, as well. We can entrain and get to the portal more rapidly than anyone else, and with a lot more combat power when we go. In addition, at the moment the railhead hasn't quite reached Fort Salby in Traisum. That leaves us almost four thousand miles—four thousand *unimproved* miles, all of them overland—from Hell's Gate."

He used the new, unofficial name for the contact portal without hesitation, chan Geraith noticed, and the division-captain raised two fingers in a request for attention.

"Yes, Arlos?"

"Should I assume that, for my sins, the Third gets to take point?"

"Yes, you should," chan Rowlan replied, and chan Geraith nodded.

Fort Emperor Erthain, on the mountain-ringed plains of Karmalia, was one of the Imperial Ternathian Army's largest military bases. In fact, it was by most measures the largest military base in the entire multiverse. *Well, in our part of it, anyway*, he reminded himself. It was also home to the Empire's major military proving grounds, and the place where the Imperial Army played with its newest toys to see what they could do.

For the last two years, Fifth Corps in general—and the Third Dragoon Division, in particular—had been experimenting with a radically new approach to military logistics. The basic concept had suggested itself following the improvements in heavy construction equipment produced by the Trans-Temporal Express's insatiably expanding rail net. There were those who believed the newfangled "internal combustion engine" was going to be the powerplant of the future because it was so much lighter and more efficient than steam, and chan Geraith wasn't prepared to tell them they were wrong. But those noisy, oil- and gasoline-burning contraptions were still taking the first, hesitant steps of infancy, and out in the field, where the TTE did most of its heavy construction work (and where the army might be called upon to maneuver), refined oil products might not be available. So TTE had specialized in developing ever more efficient steam-powered excavators, bulldozers, and tractors. Designed to burn just about any fuel which could be shoveled into their fire boxes, they'd grown steadily more powerful, lighter, and more reliable for over fifty years now.

In fact, they'd grown reliable enough for the Imperial Army to take a very close look at them. Chan Geraith was one of the general officers who continued to nurse serious reservations about their maintainability in the field, but he'd seen enough over the past twenty-odd months to become convinced they were, indeed, the future of military transport.

Plans had called for the entire Fifth Corps to be provided with the new personnel carriers and freight haulers, but as was always the case (especially with peacetime budgets) procurement rates had run far behind schedule. Third Dragoons, tasked as Fifth Corps's quick-response division, was the smallest of the three divisions (horsed units always had lower manpower totals than infantry units), as well as the most mobile. It was also the only one which had received anything like its full allotted transport, although even it was still a good twenty percent below the intended establishment. On the other hand, chan Geraith's mounted troopers wouldn't require anywhere near the personnel lift one of the infantry divisions would have demanded.

"In order to make Arlos up to strength," chan Rowlan went on, looking at chan Manthau and chan Jassian, "we're going to raid you two pretty heavily. In fact, we're going to focus on putting him as far over establishment as possible. All of us know we're going to have maintenance problems and breakdowns once we've got the steamers out there under real field conditions, so we're going to have to try to make up for lack of reliability with redundancy."

The two infantry commanders nodded. It was obvious neither of them was happy about the prospect, but, equally obviously, both of them understood it.

"Captain-of-the-Army chan Gristhane has also informed me that the procurement and development of additional steamers—and the alternate program, looking at the gasoline-powered versions—is about to get a brand new priority. In fact," the corps-captain produced his first genuine smile since Seeing the Voicenet reports from Hell's Gate, "the Navy's already been informed that it won't be getting two of those new battleships it wanted. It seems the Army's finally going to get first call on the Exchequer."

The smile vanished as abruptly as it had appeared as all four commanders remembered why that was. Then chan Rowlan cleared his throat.

"Arlos, your division is going to move out ASAP. Dust off your mobilization plans."

Chan Geraith nodded without mentioning that he'd done that over thirty-six hours ago. Third Dragoons had been checking equipment, shoeing horses, drawing ammunition and supplies, and combat-loading its steamers since dawn yesterday.

"Can you move out within twenty-four hours?" chan Rowlan asked, which made it clear he was well aware chan Geraith had begun his preparations long since. "It's going to take almost that long for the railroad people to assemble the cars you're going to require."

"I can have my lead brigade ready to entrain in another twelve hours," chan Geraith promised. "It's short about fifteen percent of its assigned steamers, but if we're going to make up the shortfall from Yarkowan and Ustace, I can strip what First Brigade needs out of Second and Third. It'll probably slow Third down, since I'm guessing we'll get a ripple effect into its transport when I send Second out in the next echelon, but I suspect we can still have everybody ready to go by the time the quartermasters can put together the trains to get all of us on the rails, anyway."

"Good!" chan Rowlan said. Then he straightened his shoulders and inhaled visibly.

"At this time, we don't know what we're going to be called upon to do when we finally get to New Uromath," he said. "Arlos, we'll do our best to keep you informed of policy changes and strategic intentions via the Voice chain, but the time delay is going to mean you'll have to use your own discretion—a lot. I'll come forward to join you as soon as we've got at least one of the infantry divisions *en route*, but until then, you're going to be the man on the spot, in more ways than one."

"Understood," chan Geraith said.

"Then understand this, too. Our primary responsibility is the protection of Sharonian civilians and the recovery of any of our people who may be still in enemy hands. I know we all hope we're talking about Shaylar Nargra-Kolmayr, but there are other civilians—and quite a few military dependents—in proximity to this point of contact, as well. Their safety is our first concern.

"Having said that, however, Captain-of-the-Army chan Gristhane has pointed out that there's a very important secondary consideration here. Specifically, Hell's Gate is a cluster, and according to the Authority's best guess, several of the portals in the Karys Chain are of relatively recent formation. That suggests this is an unusually active chain, which may be expanding even as we sit here talking. We cannot afford to leave a hostile—and these bastards have certainly demonstrated their hostility, I believe," chan Rowlan showed his teeth in grim amusement "—in possession of that cluster. Particularly not if it *is* expanding rapidly and might double back into one of our own chains at some point."

"So my orders are to secure control of that universe, as well?" Chan Geraith wanted to be very certain he was clear on that point, and chan Rowlan nodded.

"It may be that eventually some sort of diplomatic solution can be arrived at. For that to happen, it will have to include severe punishment for the people responsible for this . . . assuming Company-Captain chan Tesh hasn't already taken care of that in full. But at this time, the very least we would find acceptable would be some form of shared control of this cluster. If it takes a mailed fist to accomplish that, then so be it. It's always possible that whatever comes out of this new Conclave in Tajvana may change those instructions, but I consider that highly unlikely. You'll have formal written orders to cover as many contingencies as we can envision, but the bottom line is that you *will* secure control of that cluster and hold it."

It was chan Geraith's turn to nod again. The thought of taking a single division of dragoons off to face the massed fighting power of a totally unknown trans-universal empire was daunting, to say the least. Especially in light of the uncanny weapons the other side had already displayed since, unlike some of his fellows, chan Geraith strongly suspected that so far they'd seen only the surface of the other side's technological iceberg. There were more, and nastier, surprises waiting for them, although it seemed quite obvious that Sharona had had a few surprises for the other side, as well. The confidence, almost exuberance, he'd seen out of some of his junior officers as news of chan Tesh's successful attack on the other side's portal forces reached home worried him, and the fact that they had no idea of what sort of logistical constraints the enemy faced—or didn't face—was another concern.

But despite any of those worries, chan Geraith felt confident of his ability to secure and hold the portal cluster if he could only beat the enemy there in the first place. At the moment, chan Tesh controlled the enemy's access portal, and it was only a few miles across. Third Dragoons could hold *that* much frontage even against an army of Arpathian demons.

"I understand, Sir," he said. "When you get there, that cluster will be waiting for you."

*   *   *

"You wanted to see me, Gahlreen?" Olvyr Banchu said politely as the secretary opened the office door and bowed him through it.

Gahlreen Taymish, First Director of the Trans-Temporal Express looked up from the paperwork on his desk and nodded sharply.

"Damned right I did," he said briskly. He shoved his chair back and walked around his immense desk to shake Banchu's hand, then jerked his head at the huge window overlooking the Larakesh Portal.

Banchu took the hint. Taymish was renowned for his wealth, his capability, his tough mindedness, his temper, and his arrogance, yet deep inside him was the little boy who'd grown up on a hardscrabble farm right outside Larakesh, dreaming about the huge portal which dominated the city and its entire universe . . . and his own future. That little boy had never tired of the marvelous view connecting him to the mountains over four thousand miles—and a universe away—near the southern tip of Ricathia. Taymish did his best thinking standing in front of that window, looking at that view and pondering the promise of all the other universes which lay beyond it.

"I imagine you know why you're here," the First Director said after a moment, darting a sharp sideways look at Banchu.

"I can think of two possible reasons," Banchu replied. "First, I'm here so you can tell me I'm fired for not meeting that insane schedule you gave me. Or, second, I'm here so you can tell me that you never believed I'd meet it anyway, and that you want to congratulate me on how well I've actually done."

"Close, anyway," Taymish said with a tight grin. "Yes, I never believed you'd meet the schedule. I've discovered over the years that demanding the impossible from someone quite often gets him to do more than he *thought* was possible before he started trying to satisfy the idiot screaming at him. And, yes, I'm more than pleased that you've done as well as you have. However, I've got a new little task for you."

"Oh?"

Banchu regarded his superior warily. In the fifteen years since Taymish, then the executive head of TTE's Directorate of Construction, had lured him away from his position in the Uromathian Ministry of Transportation, Olvyr Banchu had learned that Taymish's idea of the proper reward for accomplishing the impossible was almost always a demand to accomplish something even more preposterous.

"Exactly." Taymish smiled broadly at the Trans-Temporal Express's chief construction engineer. It was only a brief smile, however, and it vanished quickly. "I want you to go out to Traisum and take personal charge."

"I see."

Banchu could hardly pretend it was a surprise. The rail line creeping steadily down the Hayth Chain towards Karys had been progressing satisfactorily enough before the murderous attack on the Chalgyn Consortium survey crew. Enormous as the task was, it had also been essentially routine for TTE. And the fact that every planet the Authority had opened through the portal network was a duplicate of Sharona itself helped enormously, of course. By and large, the routes for rail lines could be surveyed here on Sharona—or even simply taken directly from already existing topographical maps. Getting the men, material, and machinery forward to do the actual construction work was more of a straightforward logistics concern, than anything else, and the TTE building teams were the most experienced, efficient heavy construction engineers in human history. They'd laid well over two million miles of track across forty universes, and along the way they'd developed the techniques—and machinery—to take crossing an entire planet in stride.

But what had been a more than acceptable rate of progress in an essentially peaceful and benign multiverse was something else entirely when there was a vicious, murderous enemy at the far end of the transit chain.

"You want me to ginger them up, is that it?" he asked after a moment.

"That's part of it," Taymish agreed. "You're invaluable here in the office, but let's face it, you were born to be a field man yourself. If anyone can get a few more miles a day of trackage out of our people, it's you. But, frankly, the main reason I want you out there is because of your seniority."

"Ah?" Banchu raised one eyebrow, and Taymish chuckled. It was not an extraordinarily pleasant sound.

"We've got heavy equipment, rails, and work crews pouring down the Hayth Chain right this minute. We've pulled in entire crews, from other projects all over the net. For that matter, we've shut down operations completely in the Salth Chain to divert everything we have into pushing the Hayth railhead to Karys and New Uromath. That means we've got some very senior field engineers all headed for the same spot, and we don't have time for any stupid headbutting over who's got the seniority on *this* project. With you out there on the spot, that sort of frigging stupidity can be nipped in the bud.

"Possibly even more to the point, we're going to have some really senior military personnel moving into the region, as well. I want someone with equivalent seniority from our side of the shop there to coordinate with them. Someone who can speak authoritatively about the realities of what we can and can't do and explain exactly what sort of priorities we need from them."

"And the fact that I'm Uromathian and I'll be in charge of the most critical single infrastructure project in Sharona's history won't hurt anything, either, will it?" Banchu said shrewdly.

"Never has yet," Taymish admitted cheerfully. "Hells, Olvyr! I never could decide whether I recruited you in the first place more to poke Chava in the eye by luring you away from him or to make you my token Uromathian to satisfy the Ternathian liberals! The fact that you turned out to be at least marginally capable was just icing on the cake."

Banchu shook his head with a laugh. Given Gahlreen Taymish's penchant for killing as many birds as possible with every stone, there probably really was at least a grain of truth in that. Not that Taymish would have hired *anyone*, regardless of his origins, if he hadn't been convinced that that person was the very best available.

Still, the First Director often showed a degree of sensitivity to human interactions and dynamics which would have startled most of his (many) detractors. Having a Uromathian of Banchu's seniority out there in charge of the critical rail-building project really might gratify Emperor Chava—or, at least, placate his pride and hunger for prestige. And it was unfortunately true that many other Uromathians shared their emperor's resentment of the way Ternathia's towering reputation as Sharona's only true "superpower" continued to linger, despite Uromathia's population and power. Having "one of their own" out there at the sharp end would play well with them, as well, and the Uromathian press would love it. And if some of the PAAF military officers in the area happened to be Uromathian themselves, Banchu's presence could turn out to be extremely valuable in terms of reduced friction and amicable relations.

"All right," he said. "I've got two more construction trains moving out tomorrow. I can assign myself to one of them. For that matter, I may even have time to kiss my wife goodbye!"

CHAPTER
THIRTY-FIVE

TAJVANA STUNNED THE senses.

Andrin was accustomed to vistas on an imperial scale, but even the approach to the city was nothing sort of amazing. She knew the map, of course, and she'd seen pictures—both paintings and the new photographs, as well. But it was a far different matter to sail down the Ibral Strait's long, finger-thin strip of water, with the long peninsula known as the Knife of Ibral on the left and the northwest shoulder of the ancient kingdom of Shurkhal on the right. The thirty-eight-mile long stretch of water was barely four miles across at its widest, and less than one at its narrowest, yet the volume of shipping streaming through it at any given hour, night or day, boggled the imagination.

Buoys, lighthouses, pilot vessels, and units of the Royal Othmaliz Customs Patrol managed to keep things more or less under control in the rigidly policed traffic lanes, and the fines for any violation of the Ibral Maritime Regulations were enough to ruin most shipping lines. Andrin knew all about that, just as she knew about the multitracked railroads which had been built paralleling the Strait to relieve some of the congestion. Yet for the last two days, they'd seen—and passed—a steady throng of merchant ships of every size and description making steadily for or sailing out of the Strait. Seeing that mass of merchant shipping with her own eyes had brought home just how vital Sharona's exploitation of the multiverse on the far side of the Larakesh Gate truly was.

Both coastlines were visible along the entire sword-straight length of the Strait as *Windtreader* started down the narrow passage. They were lined on either side with fortresses, many of them almost as old as the Fist of Bolakin. They had been built and rebuilt, modernized, or merely replaced, as weapons technology and methods of warfare changed, and their harsh faces underscored yet again how vitally important this stretch of water had been throughout Sharona's history. The Ibral Straits had not been taken by force since before the advent of gunpowder, and before the Empire's voluntary withdrawal, no one had ever even dared to challenge Ternathia's hold on the iron gauntlet leading to its one-time imperial capital.

Most of the fortresses were little more than tourist attractions these days, but not all of them were entirely empty, even now. The Kingdom of Othmaliz, which had reclaimed Tajvana after Ternathia's withdrawal, kept the approaches manned. The garrisons were small, of course, since war hadn't broken out in earnest anywhere on Sharona for so long. But they were manned, and *Windtreader* had to obtain official clearance from the Othmalizi government before passing them. The actual procedure had taken only seconds to accomplish via Voice transmission to and from Alazon Yanamar, but the seriousness behind the formality hadn't been lost on Andrin.

Nor had the consequences of *Windtreader*'s arrival. As the liner approached the Strait's western terminus, the massive flow of commercial shipping had slowed to a trickle, and then ceased completely. Andrin hadn't understood why that was, at first—not until *Windtreader* started up the long, suddenly lonely strip of water, preceded by *Prince of Ternathia* and followed by *Duke of Ihtrial*.

The entire Strait had been cleared of all commercial shipping.

The only vessels in sight were Customs Patrol cutters or light warships of the Othmaliz Navy, and as she watched, *Windtreader*'s escorting cruisers dipped their flags in formal salute. The two powerful Ternathian ships undoubtedly outgunned every Othmalizi vessel she could see, but they were the ones who rendered first honors, and she looked up at her father.

"Wondering why *we're* saluting *them*, 'Drin?" he asked with a slight, teasing smile.

"Well . . . yes," she admitted.

"Othmaliz is a small nation, true," he said. "On a per-capita basis, it may well be the wealthiest kingdom in the entire multiverse, but it's tiny compared to the Empire. For that matter, it doesn't even really have a king, even if it is technically a 'kingdom.' But this—" he pointed up at the dipped flag flying from *Windtreader*'s foremast, then at the Othmalizi flags descending in a return salute "—is important. Not because Othmaliz wants to flaunt its power, but because it's our duty as foreign nationals to extend the same courtesy to them that we'd expect from someone entering *our* sovereign territory.

And don't overlook the fact that they've cleared the entire Strait for our passage. We're moving well above the normal speed limit, but even so, it's going to take over three hours for us to complete the passage. Three hours in which they've completely shut down what's undoubtedly the busiest waterway in the world in order to ensure our security."

Andrin nodded soberly. The same thought had already occurred to her.

"No one believes for a moment that Othmaliz, despite all the importance of Tajvana and the Kingdom's control of the Straits, is the equal in wealth or power of Ternathia," Zindel said. "But the Kingdom is just as entitled to be treated with respect in its own territory as we are. One country may go to war with another, but in time of peace, a wise nation—or ruler—treats all other nations with respect.

"Courtesy seldom costs anything, and the willingness to extend it can be its own subtle declaration of strength. There are times it may be taken as a sign of weakness by some more belligerent nation or head of state, and one has to be aware of that, as well, but the Empire's tradition has always been to remember and recognize the acceptable protocols and international courtesies, even to our enemies. To fail to show courtesy is to demonstrate arrogance and contempt. In some cases it also demonstrates envy, fear, or belligerence, but whatever it stems from, such diplomatic slights are serious business, 'Drin. They form the basis for anger, distrust, and dispute, and they're seldom quickly forgotten. It's our duty as representatives of our nation to be open, aboveboard, and courteous to our neighbors. Violating that duty opens the door to the sort of international discord which could lead very quickly to misunderstandings, rancor, short tempers, or even violence."

She thought about the prevailing opinions of Uromathia's emperor, and understood exactly what he meant. But she had a further question.

"Don't our Voices help us avoid that kind of misunderstanding in most cases?"

"In theory—and generally in practice—yes. But once hostility begins to grow, simple clarity of communication isn't enough to make it magically disappear. If two nations have a tradition of dislike, if they treat one another to public displays of discourtesy or petulance, if they get into the habit of denigrating one another in efforts to sway international diplomatic opinion to favor their side in some dispute, misunderstandings and flares of temper can occur quickly, particularly during times of increased stress. If they're lucky, the diplomats and the Voices can step in to control the situation before it spirals out of control, but that isn't always possible, and when it isn't, the consequences can be terrible for all concerned."

"You're thinking about what happened at Hell's Gate," she said quietly, and he nodded heavily.

"Yes, I am. It's not the same thing, of course, since in this case there *were* no proper diplomatic channels or protocols available to either side, but it's highly probable the entire incident stemmed from nothing more sinister than surprise, fear, and lack of familiarity. I could be wrong about that, and we may never know exactly what sparked it, or how it happened, but we're all going to be dealing with the consequences for a long, long time. Which, I suppose, drives home just how important it is for us to avoid misunderstandings *here*, in Sharona. Especially at a time like this."

"Yes, I can see that, Papa. Thank you."

"It was a good question, 'Drin. See that you go on asking more like it. That's *your* current duty."

"I will, Papa."

Silence had fallen—a quiet, thoughtful silence—and they'd stood together, watching the coast slip by on either side, for the entire three hours it had taken to transit the Ibral Strait and reach the sea of the same name.

It took much longer to cross the Ibral Sea, which stretched a hundred and seventy five miles from northeast to southwest and was nearly fifty miles across at its widest. Despite its small area, Andrin knew it was over four thousand feet deep in the center, and the long lines of merchant vessels waiting to enter the Strait *Windtreader* had finally cleared stretched as far as she could see.

Andrin left the deck only long enough to eat and endure an exhausting hour or so undergoing Lady Merissa's ministrations. Then she returned, trailing Lazima chan Zindico—and Lady Merissa—to resume her place at the promenade deck rail and watch the dark waters of the Ibral Sea flow past. The merchant shipping gave *Windtreader* and her cruiser escorts ample elbow room, but there was still plenty to see, and she didn't really care if people thought she was gawking like a teenager. After all, she *was* a teenager, she thought with a grin.

It was well into afternoon when the city finally began to rise from the waves. A gray smudge appeared on the horizon and thickened, grew steadily higher and wider, until details began to emerge.

Tajvana straddled the southern end of the nineteen mile-long Ylani

Strait, and it was indisputably the wealthiest, most culturally diverse crossroads on the face of Sharona. History lay thick as fog on those dark waters, and so many cities had existed along those banks that they'd piled up in layers of silt and ancient foundations, each of them laid over even older foundations. Walls built and rebuilt until the layers were more than a hundred feet thick in places.

Andrin longed to explore not only the living city, but also the ancient ruins historians had excavated here. There were structures in Tajvana older than the Ternathian Empire itself, which counted five full millennia. She'd read about the ancient ruins beneath Tajvana, had seen the old engravings of the early excavations, and the modern photographs as more of the ancient city was progressively uncovered for study. But not even the marvel of photography could equal the impact of walking through the actual ruins. Andrin had already told her father how much she longed to go, and he'd promised to arrange a tour.

"We won't be the only sightseers wanting to gawk at the city, after all," he'd said. "Most members of the Conclave will want to explore at least a little. I rather doubt that many of the Conclave's delegates have ever had the opportunity."

"Thus proving that even an inter-universal crisis can have *some* benefit." Andrin had smiled, and her father had laughed aloud.

"Fair enough. And don't worry, I'll be gawking right alongside you, 'Drin. Unlike you, I may have been here before, but you're not the only Calirath intrigued by ancient ruins and monuments."

Now her father appeared beside her at the rail as she saw high spires rising from the temples of two dozen or more faiths. Gilded domes caught the sunlight with mirror brilliance, scattering diamond points of light into the sky. And then, ahead of them, a faerie arch rose like a golden thread. It joined a second delicate arch, then another and another, as span after span marched across the wide Ylani Strait, and Andrin's breath caught at the sight of that eldritch bridge, spanning an impossibly wide gap.

"How?" she breathed softly. "Who could build such a bridge?"

"I wish we Ternathians could take the credit, but we can't," her father said with smile. "That honor goes to His Crowned Eminence, the Seneschal of Othmaliz. It's been finished for seven months, I believe."

Andrin glanced from the bridge to her father.

"But *how*, Papa? Surely a bridge that long ought to collapse under its own weight! Or as soon as a heavy wind hits it!"

"Well," Zindel's eyes twinkled, "some say he made a pact with the devils of the Arpathian Hells—all eleven of them. Hells, that is," he amended. "I don't think anyone could possibly count the number of devils Arpathians fear. Not even the Arpathians. *I* gave up trying several years ago, since they seem to invent new ones each time the moon changes phase or the wind shifts. Others say the seneschal pledged his immortal soul to obtain the plans and that he'll have to spend the rest of his life building temples, trying to earn it back." He chuckled. "It's less colorful, perhaps, but the simple truth is that he put out a call to the greatest engineering geniuses on Sharona and promised a dukedom and half the lifetime earnings from the bridge traffic to the engineer who could design and build it."

"It's . . . astonishing," she said, inadequately.

So it was, and the closer they came, the more astonishing it grew. The pilings were massive towers of concrete and stone. The spans were made of steel, but not the solid steel she'd expected. Instead, they were made of steel cables, which gave the bridge its gossamer appearance, like a bridge made of thread. She frowned, trying to reason it out, as the wind whipped past in crosswise gusts.

Then she understood.

"It really *is* sheer genius!" she cried aloud in pure delight. "Using cables, not rigid beams, means the entire structure can flex just enough to keep from cracking!"

Her father grinned from ear to ear.

"Bravo, 'Drin! That's precisely why it worked. And don't forget, this part of the world is subject to relatively frequent earthquakes. I'm sure that was another factor in the final design." He laughed. "If you ever grow bored enough to entertain thoughts of an ordinary career, you might consider engineering."

Lady Merissa, who'd finally recovered from her seasickness, gasped behind Andrin's shoulder.

"Your Majesty! What a ghastly suggestion! Her Highness is a *Calirath*! Not a . . . a tradesman!"

The guardian of Andrin's reputation was glaring at her father, her expression scandalized, but the emperor turned to meet that outraged stare calmly.

"My dear Lady Merissa, I didn't mean to shock you. But as a Calirath, if Andrin wants to build bridges between her comportment lessons, her sessions with the dancing master, and her studies with Shamir Taje—among other distinguished tutors—" he said, his eyes twinkling, "then by all means, she may build as many bridges as Ternathia has need of, with my blessing. We Caliraths have taken up any number of interesting occupations, just for the challenges involved. Besides," he added smugly, "engineering isn't a *trade*. It's a *profession*."

The distinction, alas, was lost upon Lady Merissa, and Andrin had to clap both hands over her lips to keep from laughing out loud at her protocolist's apoplectic look. Lady Merissa, clearly horrified by the emperor's answer, turned a savagely repressive glare on Andrin . . . whose father *did* have the temerity to laugh.

"Lady Merissa," he said with a chuckle, "you're a hopeless aristocrat."

Lady Merissa was clearly torn between squawking in indignation and the deference due the most powerful single human being on Sharona. While she tried to make up her mind which to do, the human being in question turned back to his contemplation of the Ylani Strait Bridge, and gave Andrin a solemn wink. Zindel chan Calirath thought the whole notion of Andrin shocking the bluebloods by taking up engineering was wickedly funny. Yet there was a bittersweet edge to his amusement, for Andrin's future was crushed under far too many restrictions, and he feared that even more were coming.

She was a vibrant, intelligent young woman whose natural enthusiasms were all too frequently curbed by the political realities of her birth rank. For other girls, the choice to study engineering might have surprised people, including the engineers who taught their discipline to new generations, but at least it would have been *possible*. For Andrin, that door was almost certainly closed, and her father deeply regretted that. He looked back down at her and brushed hair back from her brow.

"You do understand, Andrin, don't you?" he asked softly.

Her eyes were as gray as the wind-chopped water of the Ibral Sea. No guile lived in those forthright eyes, but there was a depth of reserve, a sense that they looked steadily at a thing, measured it carefully against a host of complex factors, and sought to understand it within its many shifting contexts. They were eyes too old for a girl of seventeen, yet strangely vulnerable and young.

"Yes, Papa," she said equally softly, and the smile that touched her lips was sad. "I understand. I have to be too many other things to think about indulging a passing fancy."

Or even a serious one, he added silently.

"I wish it weren't so," he said aloud. "But we can change neither the world, nor our place in it. And that's enough said on the subject. Look—" he pointed to the left-hand bank "—isn't that the most beautiful Temple of Shalana you've ever seen?"

Andrin looked, then let out a long "Ohhhh!" of appreciation. A tall needle-shaped tower rose from the top of a soaring dome. The needle was gold—genuine gold filigree—and the dome was a patchwork of gold and blue in a swirling, striped pattern that boiled intricately down its curved surface. The gold portion, like the needle tower, really was genuine gold, applied as a thin foil in layer upon successive layer by thousands upon thousands of pilgrims, and the blue swirls were brilliant lapis, a mosaic of thousands upon thousands of tiles cut from the semiprecious blue stone that was sacred to Shalana. The strips of lapis were, in turn, inlaid with other stones—blue stones that caught the sunlight with a fiery dazzle of light. Faceted sapphires by the thousands encrusted the dome in a breathtaking display of the wealth controlled by Shalana's ruling order of priest-esses, and the Grand Temple's walls were white marble, inlaid with still more lapis in an intricate geometric pattern of sunbursts and stylized waves. The Order of Shalana was reputed to be the most powerful religious order in the world, with temples—and banks—in nearly every country in Sharona, and Andrin could believe it as she gazed at that gloriously beautiful structure.

"I've never seen anything so lovely in my life!" Andrin breathed softly. "It's more beautiful than *any* of the temples in Ternathia. *Anywhere* in Ternathia."

Then she gasped and pointed to the right-hand bank.

"What's *that*?" she demanded, but understanding dawned almost instantly as she recognized the vast structure dominating the right-hand bank, rising high on a hill overlooking the Ylani Strait.

"*It's the Palace!*" she squealed, and for just that moment, she sounded exactly like the young girl she really was beneath the layers of poise, caution, and politically necessary reserve.

It was, indeed, the Great Palace of the ancient Ternathian Empire. And it was also still a residence, occupied by the Seneschal of Oth-maliz and his vast staff, but *not* his family.

The Kingdom of Othmaliz was not ruled by a dynastic kingship, but it was far from a democratic republic. The title of seneschal had originally been held by the official who had governed the day-to-day affairs of Tajvana in the name of the emperors of Ternathia. After the Empire had withdrawn, the title had become a theocratic one, for Othmaliz was ruled by a priest—an unmarried priest, as the holy laws of Othmaliz decreed. He wasn't celibate, far from it, but he didn't marry, and his many offspring could not inherit his title or the wealth which went with it. Nor did they live in the palace with him. When a seneschal died, the new seneschal was chosen from the highest ranking priests in the Order of Bergahl. More than one seneschal *had* been succeeded by a son or a grandson, but only when the successful candidate had attained sufficient seniority within the order to stand for election in his own right.

It had always struck Zindel as a ridiculous waste of space to use the entire vast Great Palace to house one man and his staff. The palace covered fifty acres of ground, and that was only the roofed portion; the grounds were even larger. Now he stood beside his daughter, savoring her delight as she beheld the ancient home of her ancestors at last.

The Great Palace's walls were a glittering sight, inlaid with sheets of mineral mica that sent sparkles of light cascading and shimmering across its surface. The roof was an astonishing fairyland of glittering domes and steep-sided slopes that were covered not with the ubiquitous tiles prevalent throughout the region, but with imported slabs of slate. The slate glittered golden in the brilliant sunshine, like the scales of some fantastic fish sent as a gift by the god of the sea, for every slab had been edged in gold leaf, so that the entire vast structure shone with an unearthly brilliance.

The effect was stunning against the backdrop of bone dry stone walls and sundrenched rooftops whose homely red clay tiles had faded into a dusty, washed out shade of pink. The light shimmering around the sparkling, mica-flecked walls and the incandescent rooftop made the entire, fifty-acre edifice appear to be floating above the city. The optical illusion was so strong that Andrin kept blinking, trying to clear her dazzled vision to see what was really there, the solid stone that anchored the building to the hot and thirsty soil of Tajvana. It didn't seem possible mere human hands could have built it.

She felt numb as she tried to take in the fact that her own family, her direct ancestors, had walked its rooms, run through its corridors, lived in it, laughed and played and hated and loved within its walls and beneath its glittering roof. They'd ruled half the world from that floating palace. But the world they'd ruled was gone. It had vanished quietly down the corridors of time, a world not so much lost as relinquished with passing regret, and gazing at what her family had given up, Andrin was devastated.

Yet even as those thoughts tumbled through her mind, another thought blew through her like a chill wind. The world *Andrin* lived in had changed just as completely as the world of her ancient ancestors, and far more abruptly. Hers was a new and frightening place, and everything—and everyone—in it was threatened with destruction by a faceless enemy. For one ghastly moment, she saw the Great Palace spouting flames against a night sky, with smoke pouring from it, and people rushing towards the inferno—or perhaps running headlong away, trying to reach safety. She gasped and clutched the ship's rail, unsure whether the vision had been a true Glimpse or merely the product of an overactive imagination giving shape and form to her fear for the only world she knew.

She drew down a gulp of air, trying to steady her badly shaken nerves, and glanced up at her father. She was surprised by the thoughtful frown which had driven a vertical slash between his brows. Whatever his thoughts were, they were as brooding and disturbed as her own, so she turned uneasily away and studied the harbor, instead. Or, rather, Tajvana's *harbors*. There were several, split between both banks, but the massive docks on the left-hand bank were clearly for utilitarian commercial purposes, whereas the docks on the right bank appeared to be equipped for the passenger trade, handling small personal yachts and the larger passenger liners and ferries plying the routes to some of the world's most popular resorts and business destinations.

Captain Ula steered *Windtreader* clear of the cargo wharves, thick with gantries where cranes unloaded huge crates and pallets from the holds of scores of ships. As they entered the Ylani Strait proper, Andrin saw that the commercial docks swept around the perimeter of the vast bay that led inland, curved like a golden horn that ran through the heart of Tajvana's business district. Farther up the slopes were the villas and palaces of the wealthy, both rich merchants and the nobility of Othmaliz, some of whose lineages were almost as long as Andrin's own. She could see carriages and wagons in the streets, and hundreds of sweating stevedores hauling cargo to waiting wagons which would carry it out to dockside warehouses.

But *Windtreader* was bound for the right bank as Captain Ula reduced speed and conned his ship through clearly marked channels towards the passenger docks under the attentive watchfulness of hovering tugboats. Andrin could see beyond the Ylani Strait now, to the vast Ylani Sea, whose chilly, dark waters met the placid waters of the Ibral Sea in a turbulent, silt-laden chop. There was always a powerful current flowing out of the Strait, and flurries of foam rose as *Windtreader*'s graceful stem cut through it.

Finena, riding the jeweled, white leather gauntlet on Andrin's arm, shifted her wings a bit uneasily, as if the sudden proximity of Tajvana after so many days alone on the empty sea made her nervous. Andrin soothed the falcon, stroking those glossy silver wings, and found herself reflecting that Finena's splendid coloring was far better suited to the Great Palace than hers was. She knew only too well that her own appearance was rescued from hopeless, oversized coltishness only by Lady Merissa's skill with cosmetics, hairdressing, and wardrobe. Indeed, at the moment, she wore a close-fitting bonnet designed to keep the wind from totally destroying the gemmed coiffure Lady Merissa had spent more than an hour coiling around her head after lunch, preparing her for their landing at Tajvana.

Andrin would have been lost without such guidance, and she knew it, which helped her to overlook Lady Merissa's sometimes tedious mannerisms and cloying attention to social etiquette. Especially now. The one thing Andrin wanted desperately to accomplish on this trip was to bring credit to her father and her Empire. She would die of shame if she brought embarrassment to her father's name, instead.

Fortunately, Lady Merissa had taken great pains with her appearance this morning, with a great deal of giggling help from Relatha, who had become Merissa's indispensable right hand and Andrin's indispensable companion. *Windtreader*'s galley had, perforce, lost one of its assistants, but Andrin didn't feel at all guilty for the appropriation of Relatha's talents. Among other considerations, it was a genuine comfort just to have another girl her age aboard.

"Oh, Your Grand Highness," Relatha had sighed when Lady Merissa had finished buttoning her into a gown of ivory and silver brocade, trimmed with ermine and pearls. "You look a picture, so you do, just like your beautiful falcon. You ought to have a portrait done, just like that!"

Lady Merissa had paused and tipped her head to one side, considering.

"You know, Your Highness, she's right. You *should* have a portrait done with that gown and Finena on your arm. Ternathia's imperial grand princess and her imperial peregrine, symbol of the Empire for five millennia. Yes, I do believe we'll have to arrange that, when we return to Hawkwing Palace."

"If you insist," Andrin had muttered, thinking privately that her bird would outshine her.

A light cloak covered the brocade gown at the moment, protecting it from the brisk wind, although it was scarcely needed for warmth. It might be autumn, but it was warmer here than back home in Estafel, and the temperature had to be in the sixties. Palm trees grew along the hillsides, and the wind was merely brisk and cool, not chill. The cloak was enough to shield her elaborate gown from the capricious breeze, and it hid her nervous movement as her free hand smoothed the brocade unnecessarily under its cover.

She knew there was to be a formal reception and dinner once all the Conclave's delegates had arrived, and she had every intention of making one of Lady Merissa's carefully crafted political statements for the occasion. She simply didn't know yet what that statement would be. That would be determined largely by the mood and tenor of the preliminary—yet scarcely less formal—social occasions which must be endured before all of the official delegations arrived. She shivered under her cloak, not from cold, and leaned against her father, who wrapped an arm around her and gave her a gentle smile.

"We're nearly there, poppet," he said softly.

"Yes," she said simply. He hadn't called her that since her fifth birthday, and she smiled up at him, then lapsed back into silence and watched their final approach to Tajvana's passenger docks.

The captain rang down "Finished with Engines," and the chuffing paddlewheel tugboats moved in, pushing with bluff bows to ease *Windtreader* alongside an ornate, marble-faced quay aflutter with official flags of every nation on Sharona. A mob of carriages and people dressed in elaborate finery cluttered the long pier, well back from the longshoremen waiting for the ship's lines.

Paddlewheels churned white froth, *Windtreader* quivered as her thirty thousand-ton bulk nuzzled against the massive fenders, and steam-driven windlasses clattered as mooring cables went over the waiting bollards and drew snug. Crisp orders and acknowledgments went back and forth, and more steam hissed as it vented through the funnels.

And then, for the first time in almost a week, the deck under Andrin's feet was motionless once more.

CHAPTER THIRTY-SIX

MUSIC DRIFTED ACROSS the pier from a surprisingly large band, as the Ternathian imperial anthem floated to their ears in an appropriate salute to the arriving delegation. The imperial sunburst crackled from every mast as the longshoremen ran out the boarding gangway which would allow them to disembark, and Andrin's father lifted his arm from her shoulder, then offered her the crook of his elbow, instead.

"My dear, shall we greet Tajvana?"

She gave him a brave smile and nodded, placing her gloved hand on his coat sleeve with careful precision. Lady Merissa removed Andrin's bonnet, so that her dark hair, with its strands of gold, shone in the elaborate hairstyle she'd worked so hard to perfect. Jewel-headed pins and clasps flashed in the afternoon sunlight, like a crown of living fire, and Andrin thanked her softly. Then the grand princess lifted her other arm, crooking her arm and raising her glittering white gauntlet so that Finena rode at the level of her breast as she walked at the emperor's side.

When they reached the gangway, Andrin released her father's arm to manage her skirts, concentrating carefully on the placement of her feet. The last thing she wanted to do was to trip and fall flat on her face in front of Tajvana's waiting dignitaries. She made it safely to the quay, shook out her heavy skirts, and placed her hand back on her father's waiting arm with a serene smile that belied the tremors in her knees.

The band was swirling and skirling its way through the fourth verse of the imperial anthem as she and her father stepped onto a long, purple carpet that ran from the side of their ship to the center of the quay, where an immense crowd waited. A veritable sea of faces peered toward them, leaving Andrin's fingers damp inside her formal gloves. When they'd crossed the carpet, they came to a halt before a semicircle of elegantly attired dignitaries. One of them, a short broad man in the elaborate robes of the Order of Bergahl, was obviously the Seneschal of Othmaliz himself.

Andrin gazed at him thoughtfully as Finena shifted on her gauntleted wrist. The falcon opened her beak but didn't—quite—hiss, which surprised Andrin, given what she could could sense of her companion's emotions. It was obvious Finena didn't much like him, but Andrin hoped the bird's agitation would be put down to the crowd about them, and not to her reaction to the seneschal. It would never do to begin their visit here by insulting Othmaliz's ruler, yet, Finena's reaction left Andrin wondering just what it was about the man the falcon disliked.

She knew the history of the Order of Bergahl, although not in the sort of detail she suddenly wished she could command. Bergahl had been the patron deity of Tajvana before Ternathia had arrived. He was a war god, and a god of judgment, whose followers had been pledged to the militant pursuit of justice. The Empire, with its long history of religious toleration, had accepted the religious beliefs of its new capital's people, although the emperors had insisted that civil law was now the business of the imperial justicars, and not Bergahl's priesthood. The Empire had made no objection to the Order retaining its position as the administrator of *religious* law, however, and with Ternathia's withdrawal from Tajvana, it had gradually reemerged as the dominant force in secular matters, as well. That was really all she could recall, although she also seemed to remember reading somewhere that the Order had been none too scrupulous about how it went about regaining its previous power in the wake of the Empire's withdrawal.

A functionary standing in front of the seneschal bowed low and greeted them in fluent Ternathian.

"His Crowned Eminence, the Seneschal of Othmaliz, bids greeting to the Emperor of Ternathia and the Grand Princess Andrin. Be graciously welcome in this city. It has been many fine centuries since Ternathia last stood upon its shores."

Her father's arm turned to stone under Andrin's hand, and she heard someone gasp behind them. She didn't know why that phrase had drawn such a violent reaction, but it was quite obvious her father had just been profoundly insulted, and it had to have something to do with that last sentence. After all, this *wasn't* the first time the emperor had visited Tajvana, and everyone knew it. For that matter,

Ternathia had withdrawn from Othmaliz less than three hundred years ago, which scarcely qualified as "*many* fine centuries." So why include the phrase in a formal greeting? What sort of point or message could the man be trying to deliver?

She didn't have any idea, but she didn't have to understand the insult to realize one had just been offered. Rather than go hot, her cheeks drained white, and her eyes went cold as gray ice as she stared through the seneschal as though he didn't exist. Neither she nor her father spoke, and an uneasy stir ran through the crowd behind the seneschal. Even the functionary, who was doubtless repeating verbatim a speech he'd been carefully instructed to deliver, seemed to realize his seneschal had blundered gravely, and *his* face did darken . . . with embarrassment, not anger.

Shamir Taje stepped in front of Andrin and her father and cast a scathing glance at the stammering official. The functionary's face blazed red as he tried to hold the First Councilor's gaze. He wasn't very successful.

"Your greeting is received in the spirit in which it was given. Please tell your seneschal," Taje's words could have been shards of ice, and the title came out as very nearly an insult, "that His Imperial Majesty, Zindel chan Calirath, Emperor of Ternathia and Warlord of the West, requires immediate conveyance to quarters appropriate to his rank and station."

Taje's icy tone made it clear that he seriously doubted the seneschal was capable of producing either. Even the seneschal flushed. But then he lumbered forward, a ponderous man in jeweled robes that made him look like a decorated egg.

"A thousand pardons for my herald's clumsy greeting! You are warmly welcome, of course, to the city of your ancestors. Please, my own carriage is waiting to take you and your lovely daughter to the Great Palace. Suitable chambers have been made ready for you there."

Andrin bristled silently. She was no more a "lovely" daughter than the seneschal was a polite host; but she gave him a chilly smile and a gracious nod, answering his offer as her mother would have, had Empress Varena been there.

"Your hospitality will, I'm sure, be admirably suited to our needs," she said in flawless Shurkhali, the official language of Othmaliz.

The seneschal's eyes widened. Then his gaze was drawn almost hypnotically to Finena, and those same eyes nearly popped. His Adam's apple bobbed with alarm under his ornate, jeweled collar, and Andrin's smile widened as she realized he was *afraid* of her bird! She found that thought quite comforting and hoped the seneschal's carriage was a deliciously cozy affair that would allow him an up-close look at the falcon during the whole drive from quayside to palace.

"May I present Finena," she said sweetly, still speaking in fluent Shurkhali. "She's a Ternathian imperial peregrine falcon and my devoted and constant companion."

The seneschal gave her a weak smile.

"Such a handsome and unusual creature, my dear Grand Princess." It was obvious the man would avoid Andrin's company with all the religious fervor of his holy office. "Ahem. My carriage is this way."

He gestured elaborately, and Andrin inclined her head graciously. As she did, she caught her father's eye and realized it was twinkling wickedly, which made it a bit difficult for her to maintain her own decorous solemnity as they set out side by side. They had to run a gauntlet of Othmalizi dignitaries, and Andrin did her best to memorize as many as possible of the names and faces. Any she forgot, Lady Merissa would be sure to remember. One of Merissa's most useful talents—it very nearly qualified as a Talent—was an eidetic memory. Lady Merissa never forgot *anything*. It made her utterly priceless as a protocol instructor for a grand princess of the blood. Tiresome at times, but priceless.

Beyond the dignitaries waited a sea of common folk, including a double line of reporters—dispatched to Tajvana from every nation on Sharona, judging by their attire. Andrin's eyes were dazzled by flash powder long before they reached the seneschal's ornate carriage, which proved to be an antique closed coach, literally dripping with gold.

"Still using the Ternathian imperial coach, I see," someone muttered behind Andrin's shoulder. "You'd think he could have ponied up the money for his own carriage, at least. He's wearing enough cash to *buy* several carriages."

Andrin's lips twitched as she recognized the voice of the Earl of Ilforth. In that moment, she very nearly adored the pompous ass. Only Mancy Fornath would have been so crass as to comment on the seneschal's carriage, but his observation gave her another insight into their host . . . and not a flattering one.

The seneschal started to offer Andrin his hand to assist her into the carriage, but this time Finena did hiss. He jerked his hand back with unceremonious speed, and Andrin bit her tongue, composing her expression as she allowed her father to hand her up the step into the ornate carriage, instead.

The conveyance certainly *smelled* as if it were several centuries old, she thought tartly. The leather seats, while ornately tooled, should have been replaced at least a century ago with something less . . . musty. She was intensely grateful for her cloak, and she was very careful to make sure it lay between her brocaded skirts and the odiferous, ancient leather.

Another calculated insult? she wondered. Or simply a host unwilling to spend his own money on fancy coaches when the imperial "leavings" were still serviceable? The coach certainly looked grand from the outside, and given the outrageous expense of the garments he wore, he clearly believed he deserved the grandeur he aped, regardless of *whose* grandeur it had originally been. Or how musty it had grown since they'd abandoned it.

Her father sat beside her, and the seneschal took the seat opposite theirs. Other carriages conveyed the rest of their delegation, falling into line behind the one-time Ternathian imperial carriage as they set out with a jolt through the streets of Tajvana. Her father began to chat easily with the seneschal, discussing the sights they passed. Andrin listened with half an ear, but it was the sights themselves which absorbed the lion's share of her interest.

Tajvana, unlike its seneschal, was more than worthy of that absorbed interest. The main avenues were broad, paved with stone and lined with palm trees. Narrow gardens ran down the center of each avenue, dividing the lanes of traffic, which had apparently been rerouted to make way for the official procession, and spectators lined the streets. They were probably there to gawk at the arriving Emperor of Ternathia, Andrin thought . . . and that was when she received the biggest shock of the day.

Roars of welcome greeted them along every city block for miles. Children waved ribbons in the green and gold of the Ternathian imperial flag. Women threw armfuls of flowers. The city's wildly enthusiastic greeting overwhelmed Andrin, who hadn't expected anything like this outpouring of visible joy. The seneschal remained silent, apparently unaware of the tumult, but his eyes were hooded and dark as he watched his own people greet a foreigner, an emperor whose family had ruled the seneschal's homeland for thousands of years.

Andrin could almost feel sorry for him.

So many people were waving in such wild delight that she found herself waving back. It was a purely spontaneous response, and she was astounded when her simple gesture caused grown women to burst into tears and toss still more flowers her way. Uniformed police, many of them mounted, were very much in evidence, apparently to keep the crowd's enthusiasm from spilling over into a headlong rush toward the carriage. As she watched, however, she noticed that not quite everyone along the route was openly delighted. Here and there she saw young men of military age whose glances were hostile and suspicious. She saw older men whose eyes were cold, without the fire of youth, but equally suspicious. She even saw a few people carrying signs whose words she couldn't read, since other people in the crowd invariably snatched them out of the air almost before their owners could unfurl them.

She glanced at her father, whose keen gaze had also noticed those scattered signs of protest, and decided her best course would be to emulate him. He, too, was waving graciously to the crowd through the other window of the ancient carriage. She followed his example, continuing her own greetings, although the first thrill of the moment had faded into a more sober consideration of the deep currents running through Tajvana's society. She wanted very much to find someplace private to discuss the situation with her father and Shamir Taje. Andrin hoped the anti-Ternathian sentiments were a distinct minority, but her eerie vision of the Great Palace in flames drew a shiver down her back.

Surely no one would be insane enough to burn down a palace full of innocent people?

The child in her hoped not; the budding imperial heiress, who was beginning to understand that *anything* was possible when politics came into play, wasn't so sure. She was abruptly glad that her personal guardsmen—and her father's—rode in the carriage directly behind theirs, less than twenty feet away, and that the entire security retinue would be housed in the same palace wing they were. She wasn't accustomed to thinking that way, but she had a sudden depressing vision of spending the rest of her life taking such dark factors as the very real necessity for full-time security into consideration.

*   *   *

Davir Perthis stood at the window on the seventeenth floor of the Mahkris Shipping Corporation Building and watched the procession winding its way through the streets of Tajvana. He'd been in this building, at this window, for the arrival of every delegation to the impending Conclave. He'd watched all of them rolling down the city's avenues towards the Great Palace. Some had been greeted by curious crowds. One or two—like Emperor Chava's Uromathian delegation—had been greeted with near-silent, cold-eyed suspicion. None of them had been greeted by anything like the roaring sea of people who had turned out to welcome Emperor Zindel back to his family's ancient capital.

Perthis smiled, just a bit smugly, at the thought. He never doubted that thousands would have crowded the sidewalks no matter what he or SUNN had done. But he did doubt very much that as *many* thousands would have been there, or that the welcome would have been quite so frenzied.

His smile faded. Whether or not he achieved his goal remained to be seen . . . as did the interesting question of whether or not he'd still have a job when it was all over. No matter how Perthis looked at it, his last few weeks of effort were a clear violation of both SUNN's internal code of conduct and its official editorial policy against taking sides on political issues. Jali Kavilkan had never specifically said so, yet Perthis strongly suspected that the executive manager knew exactly what he was up to. That probably made Kavilkan's silence either a good thing or a very, very *bad* thing, but whatever happened to his career, Perthis had no regrets.

His smile was a distant memory now, as he allowed the horrific images of Shaylar Nargra-Kolmayr's final Voice transmission to play through a corner of his mind. He'd convinced Kavilkan to transmit those images raw, without the normal process of editing out the emotions and surface thoughts of the originating Voice. Kavilkan had wavered back and forth for an hour or two, well aware of just how horrible that transmission would be. In the end, he'd shown the moral courage to authorize it anyway. Not because of its titillation value—although SUNN was no more immune to the need to maintain high viewership than anyone else—but because it was important for Sharona's people to know what had really happened out there. Not to be fed some sanitized version, but to *experience* the terror and the anguish—and the raw, blazing courage—of Shaylar Nargra-Kolmayr.

And so, every SUNN Voicenet subscriber, which meant effectively every Sharonian with even a scrap of telepathic Talent, didn't just know what had happened. They'd *been* there. They knew, with absolute fidelity, exactly what Sharona faced. And they knew exactly who had fired first. Who had shot down an unarmed man, holding out his empty hands in an effort to open some sort of dialogue.

The print accounts had pulled no punches, either, and Perthis was privately prepared to admit that the print journalists as a group had actually done a better job of analysis. But the sheer, raw, punch-in-the-gut impact of the Voicecast transmissions were what had truly awakened the white-hot fury sweeping across the entire explored multiverse.

And it was also the Voicecasts which had first emphasized the need for a planet-wide government to meet the emergency. Not some temporary lash-up designed to deal with the immediate crisis. Not even some international military alliance to coordinate the forces of existing nation states. No. What Sharona needed—*required*—was a functioning *government*. One which could give orders to anyone's military in its own name. One with no need to debate strategies and accept limitations because it was forced to cajole its "allies" into cooperating with it. One with the force of law behind its decisions. One which could speak for all Sharonians . . . and which could wage deadly war in their name.

Whether or not Kavilkan had recognized what Perthis was up to, Tarlin Bolsh certainly had. The international news division chief had chosen his "talking heads" well, and he'd shaped his entire division's editorial policy to point subtly in the direction Perthis wanted to go. For example, the guest lists for all of the various Voicenet discussion shows his division produced had seemed to somehow feature distinguished statesmen and foreign-policy experts who all just happened to have very favorable views of the Ternathian Empire and its current emperor.

Bolsh's people had also produced both a series of print articles and a Voice documentary on Tajvana's millennia-long history. They'd made the direct link between the scope of the present crisis and the innumerable crises which had already been met, coped with, and—for the most part—hammered into submission here in Tajvana. And in the process—quite accidentally, of course—they had pointed out exactly which dynasty had done the hammering.

The documentary had been a superlative historical survey. It had also been scrupulously accurate, which had only made it even more effective for Perthis' purposes. By now, everyone in Tajvana had either viewed the Voicecast version, or read the print version, and been reminded of their city's glory days under the Caliraths.

Inevitably, there'd been some backlash. Much of it, Perthis admitted, was completely justifiable. Tajvana—and Othmaliz—were independent once more. They had better than two hundred years of independence and achievements in their own names of which to be proud. The thought of being once more submerged into someone else's massive embrace, losing that regained individuality as part of some vast, corporate whole, wasn't going to find a ringing welcome in every heart.

But against that stood the Calirath reputation for honor and responsibility. For the administration of impartial justice, and for fairness. And Perthis had been quietly astonished by how many

Tajvanis—and how many people of other nations—had turned in their moment of greatest fear and uncertainty not to their own governments, but to the Calirath legend. The life of Emperor Halian had been recalled from the dusty archives, and with it the memory of his death, personally leading his army in the defense not of his own people, or his own Empire, but of their Bolakini allies. He and his army had been hideously outnumbered, but they had been all that stood between a Bolakini city and the barbarian horde which had slaughtered its way across half of Ricathia.

The Ternathian Navy had been waiting, just offshore, prepared to whisk Halian and his troops safely out of the path of destruction. And Halian had refused.

Refused not simply to withdraw his army, but to have himself taken to safety. And so three quarters of his army had died, and him with it . . . but the walls of that Bolakini city still stood today, and the statue of the dead emperor lay before the Halian Gate, exactly where his hideously hacked and hewn body had been found on the field of battle, surrounded by every member of his Imperial Guard.

Halian was not the only Calirath who'd made a similar decision. Oh, there'd been the occasional Calirath coward, even the occasional Calirath treacher or tyrant. At least one emperor had clearly been insane, and there were persistent (unproven) rumors that he'd eventually been assassinated by his own bodyguards. But there'd been remarkably few of those over the endless, dusty centuries of the dynasty, and people had remembered that, too. Two hundred and thirty years of freely granted independence had not been long enough to erase the memory of *millennia* of just government and protection, and the ground swell not just here in Tajvana, but all across Sharona, was building steadily, exactly as Perthis had hoped.

No doubt that explained why the seneschal had made such an unmitigated ass out of himself, Perthis thought with a wry grin. He'd never thought much of the seneschal at the best of times, and the man's current conduct had knocked any respect Perthis might have had for him right on the head. Obviously, he was terrified by the notion that the Caliraths might, indeed, return to Tajvana—and not, Perthis suspected, simply because of the power and authority he would lose if they did. There'd been rumors for quite some time of serious abuses of office on the current seneschal's part. Most probably, those rumors represented only the tip of the reality's iceberg, and the seneschal must be sweating bullets at the thought of what an impartial investigation of his conduct as the Othmalizi head of state might reveal.

It was hard to think of anything the seneschal could have done to improve his case, but the course he'd adopted had done exactly the reverse. Perthis had heard about the odd greeting the seneschal's herald had produced . . . and Taje's response to it. He had no idea what that had all been about, but he fully intended to find out.

What mattered at the moment, however, was that everyone knew that whether *they'd* understood the subtext or not, the seneschal had offered some deep and personal insult to the Emperor of Ternathia upon his arrival. Zindel's response to that insult (or, perhaps, his *lack* of response) had only underscored the pettiness and stupidity of the man who'd offered it. And, Perthis' grin turned into a broad smile, Grand Princess Andrin's response—like her falcon's—had been magnificent.

Perthis had never seen the grand princess with his own eyes before. In fact, he'd discovered that there was remarkably little press coverage of Andrin or either of her younger sisters. All he'd really known about her was that she was about seventeen years old, tall, reputed to be both quiet and intelligent, and that she had already demonstrated that she possessed the Calirath Talent.

He hadn't been prepared for the perfectly poised, elegantly groomed, ice-eyed young woman who had inspected the rotund, squat, undeniably *oily* seneschal as if he were some particularly loathsome slug she'd discovered on the sole of her sandal. She'd been perfect—*perfect*—standing there like a tall, slender statue of ivory flame, crowned in the fiery sun-glitter of her jeweled hair, and the seneschal's obvious terror of her falcon had only made it better. Her father had made the seneschal look petty; *she'd* made him look ridiculous, and that was far, far more deadly.

Perthis raised one hand in salute to the raven-haired young woman waving from the window of the hideously overdone, antique carriage rolling past below him. He hadn't counted on her, but he'd already set his research staff to work on her. She might just prove almost as effective for his purposes as her father.

Not, Perthis' smile vanished, that she was likely to thank him for it once she realized what he'd actually done to her and her family.

*   *   *

The approach to the Great Palace was lined with cheering crowds all the way to the ornate palace gates, which were guarded by men in Othmalizi uniform. They carried the same Model 10 as the Ternathian Army, something Andrin was proud of herself for recognizing. Her father had not allowed her to skip that portion of her education, just because she wouldn't be serving in Ternathia's armed forces.

The officers in charge of the guard details saluted sharply as the seneschal's carriage passed through the gates, and their men presented arms crisply, but there was a taut professionalism under that military theater. Their eyes were sharp and intense, obviously screening the passengers in each of the carriages behind them in the long procession, as well. Andrin found that rather reassuring as she thought of the protesters she'd seen along the way.

The palace's drive ran down a short avenue of palm trees, then ended in a circular space before the glittering building's ornate main doors. Those doors, Andrin knew, were panels of solid, burnished silver, more than twice her father's impressive height. Her study of the Grand Palace's history had already told her that, but nothing could have prepared her for the reality of their mirror-bright magnificence, and she swallowed a silent gasp of amazed delight as she finally beheld them with her own eyes.

If the emperor was particularly impressed by the sight, he gave no sign of it. He simply exited the carriage first and handed her down. Then he stepped courteously aside for the seneschal, and waited for their host to precede them across the stone-paved drive to the main steps. Those steps were of polished white marble, lined by liveried servants who bowed or curtsied nearly to the ground as they passed.

The enormous doors swung open as they approached. Each panel was a *bas relief* masterwork, illustrating key scenes of Ternathian history that Andrin recognized at a glance. She lifted the hem of her skirts as she stepped across the raised threshold—a curious architectural feature she'd never seen before—then paused as a servant bowed low and slipped her cloak from her shoulders. Other servants were taking the coats and cloaks of other members of their delegation, which followed discreetly behind, and Andrin stepped forward once again. Her footsteps clicked on the marble floors, and she managed to keep her lips closed against a powerful urge to gape.

It wasn't easy. The Great Palace put Hawkwing to shame.

Andrin had never witnessed such opulence in her life. The huge entry hall alone was stunning, a glittering marble room filled with the finest art treasures of Sharona. She'd seen illustrations of at least half the marble and bronze statues they passed along the way in textbooks on art history and the masterworks of antiquity, but she didn't have time to admire them the way she wanted to. There was too much to do, and too many people to see, and she forced her attention back to the task at hand.

Othmalizi courtiers bowed low as they passed. Great ladies in

gowns as elaborate as Andrin's curtsied, graceful as flowers and jeweled more splendidly than most reigning kings and queens. It was a
daunting experience for any seventeen-year-old, but Andrin refused
to let anyone see that. And it helped enormously, she discovered,
that—due entirely to Lady Merissa's efforts—she could rest secure in
the knowledge that her own attire at least matched that of the court
ladies, while Finena's silver feathers shone as brightly as any jewels
in the sunlight streaming through tall windows and skylights.

And my great-grandmothers lived *in these rooms,* she found herself
thinking again and again as they passed from one stunning chamber to another. She quickly lost track of the rooms they'd crossed,
a seemingly endless maze of corridors and vast, echoing chambers.
It seemed to go on forever, but they finally ended their journey at
last in what was clearly an audience hall. One which was filled at
the moment with a glittering array of people whose widely varying
skin and hair color—not to mention their garments—proclaimed
them to be official delegates to the pending Conclave.

Andrin stiffened internally at the sight and scalding anger flared
through her. Their host had brought them straight from the docks
to an official function, without even offering them the chance to
rest or wash the salt from their skin, or even the slightest warning
that this reception awaited them.

Another calculated insult? Or just gross insensitivity?

Then another thought flickered through her anger. Had these
people already been assembled here for some other event? Or
had everybody come to this room specifically to greet her father's
arrival? She didn't know of any discreet way to find out, and there
was little time to think about it as a waiting functionary called out
their names in a piercing voice.

"His Crowned Eminence, the Seneschal of Othmaliz! His Imperial
Majesty, Zindel chan Calirath, Emperor of Ternathia! Her Imperial
Highness, Grand Princess Andrin of Ternathia!"

Polite applause greeted them, and Andrin gave the assembled crowd
a brief, decorous courtesy, carefully balancing Finena on her arm.
Her father gave an equally brief bow, and a ripple of conversation
ran through the room, much of it focused on the falcon riding her
arm. And then the inevitable round of introductions and greetings
began.

The first face Andrin saw belonged to a Uromathian prince, several years her senior. The young man's almond eyes had gone wide
with stunned envy and shock when he saw that Finena wore neither
hood nor jesses. Another Uromathian prince standing beside him

was gasping something to his older companion, but she wasn't close enough—or sufficiently fluent in Uromathian, yet—to catch what he was saying.

Unlike Finena, the falcons both princes carried wore jeweled and tasseled hoods. Strong leather jesses bound each bird's taloned feet to its owner's gloved wrist, and Andrin flicked a cool glance across the bound birds and inclined her head to the princes as she swept past on her father's arm. Another Uromathian prince farther down the line caught her glance and startled her by grinning and sweeping an ornate bow to her, balancing his own falcon carefully on one wrist. He was not a handsome young man, but his eyes sparkled with open delight as he took in the stunned gazes of his fellow Uromathians.

Andrin committed his face to memory, determined to find out who he was, where he came from, and why he was so pleased by his peers' dismay. If she asked Lady Merissa—and she fully intended to do so—her protocol instructor would doubtless have his name, rank, family pedigree, and net worth to the last decimal place by the time they sat down to supper tonight.

But first they had to endure an endless receiving line. It was rapidly apparent that at least two thirds of the delegations had already arrived, and each member of every single delegation was waiting with bated breath to meet the Emperor of Ternathia and his overly tall daughter. And she *was* overly tall, she thought glumly. In fact, she towered over most of the men and *all* the ladies, until the Farnalian delegation reached them, at which point she wanted to throw her arms around the Dowager Empress of Farnalia with a gasp of pure thanks for standing taller than she did. The elegant, silver-haired dowager empress flashed a conspiratorial smile as Andrin greeted her formally, then dropped a wink that cheered the girl immensely.

"You probably don't remember me, my dear," the empress said, her voice quiet but surprisingly deep with emotion. "You were only a baby the last time I was in Estafel, but your grandmother and I were dear friends as girls. I stood beside her at her wedding, and she stood with me at mine. You must come and see me at dinner this evening."

"Grandmama has spoken often of you," Andrin replied, smiling in genuine delight. "I should adore a chance to visit with you, at dinner or any time at all."

"You're kind to humor an old lady. I'll see you this evening." The empress pressed a socially correct kiss to her cheek, but her hand was warm and strong when she gripped Andrin's fingers.

The only other good thing to come out of that interminable receiving line was the chance to discover the name of the Uromathian prince with the infectious grin. When he reached Andrin and her father, she discovered—to her secret delight—that while he might be Uromathian by blood, he was no subject of Emperor Chava.

"Junni Fai Yujin, King of Eniath, and Crown Prince Howan Fai Goutin," the Othmalizi functionary handling the introductions intoned.

Like many of the seminomadic people he ruled, Junni Fai Yujin was a large man for someone of Uromathian blood. He was shorter than Andrin, but only by half a head, and his shoulders were actually broader than any part of her. That was a distinct first for any of the men she'd so far met from the other Uromathian delegations, and he bowed over her hand with fluid grace, despite his size. He spoke no Ternathian, and her Uromathian wasn't up to the radically different dialect spoken in Eniath, which shared almost as much linguistic heritage with Arpathian as it did with Uromathian.

She curtsied deeply, indicating her respect for his kingdom and his people—and for their renown as falconers. To her amusement, the king was staring at Finena more rapturously than he was at her, and she angled her arm to bring the white-winged falcon to a better viewing angle.

"Finena," she said softly, stroking the glossy white feathers.

"Finena," the king breathed in response. He glanced up at her, his dark eyes filled with questions he lacked the words to ask. Then he turned to his son and rattled off something Andrin couldn't begin to catch. Crown Prince Howan Fai Goutin, whose family name—like those of all men of Uromathian descent—was traced through the middle name, not the last, spoke in halting Ternathian.

"Name of silver one is . . ." he paused a moment, mentally translating. "What for meaning?"

"What does her name mean?"

"Please?" he nodded.

"White Fire," she said, and Prince Howan's eyes glowed.

"Ahhhhh . . ." The sound was almost reverent, and then the prince turned and spoke formally to his father. Andrin caught three whole words of the rapid exchange. Then King Junni asked another question, which Howan relayed.

"Please, why Finena no corded?"

Andrin glanced at the jesses on both the king's falcon and Prince Howan's. They were magnificent birds, and she longed to see both of them flying unhindered through the bright sky as free as Finena herself.

Then she looked up and met Prince Howan's gaze for a moment before she turned and spoke directly to King Junni himself.

"Does one chain the wind?" she asked simply. "Finena is free. She stays for love of Andrin."

Prince Howan hissed softly. When Andrin risked a swift glance in his direction, she found not the censure or displeasure she'd half-expected to see, but a look of such respect it stunned her. He spoke briefly to his father, and King Junni made a sound almost precisely like his son's. Then he lifted Andrin's free hand and drew her fingers forward, resting them briefly against his own heart. He turned to her father, still holding her hand, and bowed with deep formality. Then he spoke again, and Prince Howan once again translated.

"My father says Ternathia grows wise daughters. He must talk with you. Soon. Before Conclave."

"Ternathia is honored." Her father bowed. "It will be my pleasure to speak with Eniath, whenever King Junni Fai Yujin chooses."

King Junni bowed again, still with that deep formality, and departed with great dignity. The crown prince gave Andrin a piercing glance and an equally formal bow, then followed his father down the receiving line, and Zindel leaned close to stroke Finena's wings.

"Well done, indeed, 'Drin," he murmured in a low tone, for her ears alone. "That was as nice a piece of diplomacy as I've seen in many a year. I need Eniath's support in Conclave, and I wasn't sure I could get it. Now there's at least a piece of common ground—and mutual respect—to build from."

She went nearly giddy with pleasure and wanted to give him a radiant smile, but contented herself with a small upturn of her lips, acutely conscious of the crowd of people watching her every move. Controlling her face was difficult, but she managed it, and his eyes lit with an approval that made her feel as if her feet were floating ten inches above the marble floor.

CHAPTER
THIRTY-SEVEN

SHAYLAR AND JATHMAR sat in their quarters in Fort Wyvern, talking quietly with Gadrial, and listened to the wind.

It was dying down at last, and they were glad. The thunderstorms on the far side of the portal had raged with only occasional periods of relative calm for better than twenty-four hours after their arrival here, and the violent weather seemed to have spread to this side. At least, that was what it had felt like for the next two days, as rain and strong winds pummeled Fort Wyvern. None of the transport dragon pilots had been at all happy about the prospect of taking off under such conditions, and Jasak had decided not to push the issue. Instead, they'd settled down to wait out the weather on *both* sides of the portal before proceeding.

It had not been a comfortable wait. Five Hundred Grantyl, Fort Wyvern's commanding officer, was very different from Five Hundred Klian. There'd been none of the sympathy, none of the awareness that what had happened certainly wasn't their fault, that they'd seen in Klian. Instead, there'd been suspicion, hostility, and more than a little fear. It had been obvious to Shaylar that Grantyl would have been far more comfortable locking them up in a dungeon somewhere, and preferably losing the key.

The fact that he hadn't gone ahead and done exactly that underscored the accuracy of what Jasak and Gadrial had told them about the institution of *shardon*. Shaylar had been too far away to catch more than a few fragments of the "discussion" between Jasak and Grantyl, but she hadn't needed her Talent to recognize how disgruntled—and angry—Grantyl had been. Yet despite his anger, and despite the fact that he outranked Jasak substantially, the five hundred hadn't even attempted to put them into close confinement. He'd insisted on stationing sentries outside their quarters, but aside from that, they'd been treated almost as guests. Not *welcome* guests, perhaps, but still guests.

"You know," she said now to Gadrial, "I don't think I'd truly realized—not deep down inside—just how lucky we are that Jasak is basically a decent man."

Jathmar stirred, sitting on the bed at her side, and she reached out and took his hand. Her husband's attitude towards Jasak remained far more ambivalent than her own.

"I don't think this fort's commander," Shaylar went on, "was all that happy about not throwing us into chains the instant we got here."

"You're right, Grantyl did want to lock you up in the brig beside vos Hoven," Gadrial said. "But he's an Andaran himself, which didn't leave him much choice but to accept Jasak's position. Of course," she smiled thinly, "he also knows who Jasak's father is, which may have had a little something to do with it."

"I'll settle for that," Jathmar said with a slightly grim answering smile.

"So would I, in your place." Gadrial nodded, but there was an edge of unhappiness, or concern, perhaps, in her tone, and Shaylar arched her eyebrows.

"You don't seem entirely satisfied about something," she observed, and Gadrial grimaced.

"It's just that I'm not too happy about the commander of the *next* fort," she admitted.

"Why?" Jathmar demanded, his eyes suddenly intent.

"Two Thousand mul Gurthak most definitely *isn't* Andaran. In fact, he's a Mythalan, and although he hasn't chosen to flaunt it, he comes from a fairly prominent *shakira* clan-line. He's also a long way away from any authority which might overrule him . . . or punish him. Frankly, if anyone's likely to try to violate Jasak's role as your *baranal*, it's going to be a Mythalan."

"Why do you and Jasak hate Mythalans so much?" Shaylar asked. Gadrial simply looked at her, and Shaylar shrugged. "You said Magister Halathyn was a Mythalan, and from what I saw and sensed about him, he was a wonderful man. But I've never heard you or Jasak say a positive thing about any other Mythalan, aside from Sendahli. And that other soldier of Jasak's—that vos Hoven—almost sets himself on fire with his own hatred every time he looks at Jasak."

"It's a long, complicated situation," Gadrial said slowly. "And I take the point you're trying to make. In fact, it's probably true that the mere fact that mul Gurthak is Mythalan would be enough to make me . . . wary of him. But if the question you're really asking is whether or not our opinions of Mythal and its society are war-ranted, you might think about the fact that Jasak and I come from extremely different backgrounds ... and neither of us can stomach the way Mythalans think societies should work."

"Why?" Jathmar asked, and Gadrial sighed.

"In our universe, Mythal—what you call Ricathia—has the oldest civilization of any of our major cultures. It's also where almost all of the techniques for handling magic, tapping the energy field, were first worked out. A lot of that development stemmed from pure trial and error in the early days, but Mythalans have been studying magic for a *long* time, and they began working out the theory behind those early brute force applications well over two thousand years ago. The true scientific method only evolved in the last few hundred years, but most of their original theoretical work has stood up extremely well. Even today, they dominate in the field of theoretical sorcery. They're not as good at devising practical applications of their own research as, say, my own people are, but the most prestigious of all of the academies of magic is still the Mythal Falls Academy, where Magister Halathyn used to teach."

Pain flickered through the magister's dark eyes. More pain than mentioning Halathyn usually caused her, Shaylar thought. But whatever its cause, she brushed it off quickly, almost angrily, and continued in that same level tone.

"No one—especially a magister like me—can fail to respect the work Mythal Falls has carried out over the centuries. But it's unfor-tunately true that Mythal developed a very different society from the rest of Arcana, one based almost entirely on whether or not the members of that society are Gifted. In fact, I've often thought that they developed their society as a result of their single-minded focus on the principles of magic.

"If you're Mythalan and Gifted, then you belong to the *shakira* caste, or perhaps to the *multhari* caste; if you aren't Gifted, then you belong to the *garthan* caste. There are some exceptions, but not very many."

"Castes?" Shaylar frowned at the totally alien word, and Gadrial sighed.

"The best way to think of it is that the Mythalans divide their society into three distinct groups, what we call 'castes,' each of which has a specific place. The relationships between castes—and what's permissible behavior *within* a caste—are defined by ironbound tra-dition and, in most cases, statutory law, as well. For the most part, the caste you belong to—*shakira, multhari,* or *garthan*—depends on whether or not you were born Gifted, and there's nothing you can do about that.

"As I say, the *shakira* are the Gifted caste. They're the small percentage of the total population, no more than twenty percent or so, at best, who form the tip of the social pyramid. They control the wealth and political power of the entire society, and they think of themselves as extremely enlightened because they practice a form of direct democracy no other Arcanan nation practices. Of course, the only people who get to vote are members of the *shakira* and traditional *multhari* families. That's one reason they can use direct democracy; they've got so few voters that the system actually works.

"Next in power and prestige after the *shakira* are the *multhari*, the traditional Mythalan military caste. You might think of them as the Mythalan equivalent of Andarans, although there are tremendous differences between them. Not least because one of the *multhari*'s primary responsibilities is to keep the *garthan*'s neck firmly under the *shakira*'s heel. Some of the *multhari*—many of them, in fact—are also *shakira*, and the enlisted ranks of the Mythalan military have always contained quite a lot of *garthan*, although all of its officers are *multhari*.

"In Mythal, most *garthan* who end up in the army are conscripts. Traditionally, the *shakira* who entered the army could usually expect to attain high rank, especially if their families were also part of the traditional *multhari* hierarchy. Since the creation of the Union, there isn't any official Mythalan Army these days, and the integration of the *multhari* into the Union armed forces hasn't always gone smoothly. They've tended to carry a lot of that traditional *shakira* sense of superiority and automatic privilege around with them, and they seem to resent the fact that they have to compete with the non-Gifted—and non-Mythalans—on an equal basis for promotion. Their resentment when they don't get it has had a tendency to be . . . fairly evident, let's say, and that's created a lot of friction between them and, say, Andaran or Ransaran personnel.

"For the last forty years or so, Mythal appears to have been trying to overcome some of those problems. More *multhari* have been attending the Army Academy at Garth Showma before joining the army, which appears to have smoothed down at least some of the rough edges. For that matter, some of the younger *shakira* from outside the *multhari* have actually been signing up for at least a tour or two in the enlisted ranks. They're being encouraged to do so by their caste-lords, on the grounds that whether their caste *agrees* with the rest of us or not, they're stuck with the terms of the Accords, and they have to learn to get along with those restrictions if they ever want to reduce the traditional friction between their own people and the rest of us.

"It's at least a pragmatic idea," Gadrial admitted a bit grudgingly, "and I suppose they may actually be sincere. Unfortunately, their 'solution' doesn't come without problems of its own. For example, the soldier you were talking about, Shaylar—vos Hoven—belongs to the *shakira*. That's what the 'vos' in his name indicates. But Sendahli belongs to the *garthan* caste. He fled Mythal and enlisted in the *Union* Army as a way to escape the limited, second-class future which was all he could expect at home. And the reason vos Hoven is under arrest is that Jasak caught him brutally beating Sendahli to extort Sendahli's pay out of him."

Jathmar frowned deeply and quickly. He opened his mouth, but before he could say anything, Gadrial continued.

"The reason he was doing that—and the reason Sendahli was *letting* him do that, despite the fact that he could have broken vos Hoven's neck any time he wanted to—is that under Mythalan custom and law, *garthan* have *no* legal rights in *any* dispute with a *shakira*. They can't even testify in court against a *shakira* defendant. Up until the formation of the Union of Arcana, *garthan* were legally property. They were required to belong to someone from the *shakira* caste, and they were denied the right to own property, the right to vote, or the right to choose their own trades and professions . . . or to any income they might have earned from that trade or profession. In many cases, they were denied even the right to choose who they married, and even today, Gifted children of *garthan* parents are taken from their birthparents by the courts and placed for adoption by *shakira* families."

"That's *barbaric*!" Shaylar burst out, and Gadrial nodded.

"That's exactly what it is," she agreed grimly. "I'm Ransaran. *My* people believe in the fundamental equality of all human beings. We're the dangerous, humanistic, *liberal* part of the Union, and there's been a fundamental hostility, almost a hatred, between us and the Mythalans for as long as anyone can remember on either side. Jasak, on the other hand, is an Andaran, and they're as different from us as the Mythalans are. Their entire culture is bound up in concepts of mutual obligation and duty, of responsibilities that define who they are. They believe in the rights of the individual, but they also believe that those rights have to be earned by meeting all of those obligations and responsibilities, and they have no sympathy for anyone who fails to measure up to their standards of honor.

"Yet they despise the Mythalans as much as we Ransarans do, because of the Mythalan attitude towards the *garthan*—that the mere fact that people like Sendahli aren't Gifted makes them less than human in the eyes of their own rulers. It turns them into something which exists solely for the convenience of their natural superiors, the *shakira*. If an Andaran like Jasak considered the non-Gifted as truly inferior—which he never would—his cultural obligation would be to protect and defend them, not to abuse them. When he came across vos Hoven beating Sendahli, he ordered vos Hoven off ... and vos Hoven tried to kill him."

Jathmar shook his head in a combination of dismay and disbelief, and Gadrial smiled humorlessly.

"I'm sure there are people back home in Sharona you wouldn't exactly be proud to be associated with, Jathmar. Maybe not anyone as bad as the Mythalans, but I can't imagine your people are that different from ours, Talent or no. Unfortunately, we Ransarans and Andarans had no choice but to include Mythal in the Union. Partly, because whether we like them or not they do live on the same planet we do, which I suppose gives them at least some inherent right to share in the exploitation of the portals. But, frankly, mostly because when the first portal appeared on Arcana, it sparked the most terrible war in our history. The weapons that were developed were devastating, so terrible we barely managed to stop short of our own complete destruction."

Jathmar and Shaylar froze, their faces suddenly tight with fear.

"Andara and Ransar realized the situation was about to spin totally out of control," Gadrial continued grimly. "*We* proposed the creation of the Union as a world-government to ensure that every Arcanan nation had the same opportunities to profit from the exis- tence of the portals, and the Andarans supported us strongly. It was only our united front which *forced* Mythal to accept the proposal, and the Mythalans held out for a much greater degree of local autonomy—essentially the protection of their own social system within their own territory—than any of the rest of us wanted to give them. Unfortunately, they'd been the leading researchers for the weapons which had been used in the Portal Wars. They had more of them, and better ones, than the rest of us, and they refused to destroy them unless we accepted their terms in that regard."

Shaylar's face was white as she absorbed the implications of magical weapons capable of destroying an entire planet's civilization. Jathmar looked equally horrified, and Gadrial faced them squarely.

"I know what you're afraid of, and I don't blame you. But I will tell you there are severe limitations on even the most deadly weapon, when it's applied to inter-universal warfare. For one thing, no spell can be cast *through* a portal, so you'd still have to physically assault each portal and establish a bridgehead on the other side before you could deploy any sorcerous weapon. That wasn't a factor in the Portal Wars, because they were fought entirely on Arcana, over who'd end up with possession of the portal in the first place.

"For a second thing, those weapons were outlawed two hundred years ago. As part of the Union Accords, all signatories were required to destroy all weapons of mass destruction and the spellware and research which had supported them. Several other particularly nasty spells were outlawed at the same time, and an inspection process was set up to ensure that there were no holdouts and that no one was doing fresh research in the proscribed areas."

"But if things get nasty enough, your people could always change the law, couldn't they?"

"Yes, Jathmar, we could," Gadrial said very, very quietly. "And the people most likely to push for doing just that are going to be the Mythalans. They're xenophobic to an almost crippling degree, even with their fellow Arcanans. I don't even want to think about how they're going to react when they find out about your people. Especially," she smiled wanly, "because they're going to think they're looking at an entire worldwide civilization of Ransarans."

Shaylar and Jathmar looked at one another, and Gadrial leaned forward in her chair to take Shaylar's hand. Shaylar's eyes stung with tears as she realized the other woman was deliberately giving her the opportunity to read her emotions, her honesty.

"The Andarans and Ransarans would never stand for the resurrection of those hideous weapons," she said flatly. "Not unless your people were foolish enough to convince us that our only other alternative was our own complete destruction. From what I've seen of the two of you, I don't think that's ever going to happen. I can't promise that, obviously, but I truly, truly believe it."

She decided—again—not to mention the fact that she'd already received specific instructions from mul Gurthak to program all available data on the Fallen Timbers cluster into the other three prototypes of the portal detector she and Halathyn had come out here to field test. She could think of only one reason he might want those, and while she had to agree, however unwillingly, with the logic, she doubted that Shaylar or Jathmar would find the news reassuring.

"Still, you need to be aware that Mythalans share neither my own people's belief in the inherent rights of the individual—especially not of non-Gifted individuals—nor (to anyone outside their own caste, at least) Jasak's people's ironclad belief in honor obligations and an individual's overriding obligation to meet them. You need to be careful—very careful—what you say to any of them, and you have to be aware that if one of them thinks he sees an opportunity to get around Jasak's protection, he may well try to seize it.

"That's the bad news. The *good* news is that seventy or eighty percent of the entire Arcanan army is Andaran, just like Five Hundred Grantyl. Even if they don't like what Jasak's done, they'll respect it, and they won't like it one bit if some Mythalan dishonors all of Andara by harming you in any way."

*   *   *

Shaylar thought about that conversation three days later as their transport dragon circled above yet another fortress. This one was even bigger than Fort Wyvern, and unless she was very much mistaken, it lay in what would have been east Farnalia back home in Sharona. Endless ocean waves of coniferous forest spread out in every direction, and the flight over the sharp-spined mountains between Fort Wyvern's portal and this new fort—Fort Talon—had been just as freezingly cold as Jasak had warned them that it would be.

It had also required them to fly so high that the dragon's pilot had issued each of his passengers a small cylinder of oxygen attached by a tube to a tightfitting mask which had covered mouth and nose. Shaylar had huddled down in her thick, fur-lined flying garments and leaned against Jathmar's back as the dragon carried them through the ice-cold, crystal-clear gulfs of the heavens. Despite her protective clothing (and another one of those unnatural seeming little spells which had actually heated her furs), she'd never been so cold—nor felt so far from Shurkhal's beloved, sunstruck warmth—in her entire life, and she'd been almost prayerfully thankful when they landed on the western side of those towering mountains.

The total flight from Fort Wyvern had taken almost a full three days. She and Jathmar had been rather relieved to realize there were some real physical constraints on the Arcanans' uncanny capabilities. Dragons could fly at preposterous speeds, but their endurance clearly wasn't unlimited. They appeared to be capable of perhaps a thousand miles or a bit more in a single day, but the greater exertion of crossing those high mountains had taken its toll. Their dragon had required additional rest after they finally landed, and Jasak and the pilot had agreed to take an extra day at the small, bare-bones dragonfield.

But they were here at last, descending through a drizzling rain towards their next destination. Their next *interim* destination, she reminded herself grimly, smearing moisture away as she wiped her protective goggles and recalled what Gadrial had said about the distance between them and New Arcana.

Fort Talon's portal rose out of the forests behind it. It was larger than Fort Wyvern's, and the terrain on the other side of it looked like the flat sweep of Jathmar's native New Ternathia's midwestern plains. She could see a small river, but it was late night on the far side, and she didn't have much time to consider details before the dragon planed gracefully down. She was still trying to get used to how suddenly and abruptly the huge beasts decelerated when they landed, and her arms tightened around Jathmar's waist as they hit the ground.

Then they were down—once again in one piece—and she drew a huge breath of relief.

I'm going to have to get over this fear of landing, she told herself firmly. *Of course, given how far we've got to go, I should have plenty of time for it.*

The thought made her chuckle sourly, and then they were once again climbing down for yet another brief stay.

Aside from her, Jathmar, Jasak, and Gadrial, they were accompanied only by Jugthar Sendahli, Otwal Threbuch, Javelin Shulthan, and Bok vos Hoven. That left a lot of unused passenger space aboard the dragon, and Shaylar was just as happy that it did. Vos Hoven was a brooding, hate-filled presence, and she was relieved that there was enough room for him to be kept well away from her and Jathmar. Not that the Mythalan was likely to pose much of a threat, given his manacles and the eagle eye Threbuch kept trained upon him. Shaylar was reasonably certain that nothing would have pleased Threbuch more than for vos Hoven to try something which, regrettably, ended up with the prisoner plunging several thousand feet to his doom after a brief, desperate struggle with his guard. From vos Hoven's attitude, he probably thought the same thing.

A uniformed reception committee waited for them on the edge of the dragonfield hacked out of the virgin forest which rose like green walls around it. None of them were Mythalans, and all of them looked remarkably young, certainly not much older than Jasak. Apparently the fort's commander couldn't be bothered to greet the new arrivals in person, and she saw what looked like a hint of irritation far back in Jasak's eyes.

"Hundred Olderhan," their *baranal* said, with one of his people's crisp, clenched-fist salutes, "*en route* to New Arcana with Magister Kelbryan and party."

"Commander of One Hundred Neshok," the officer Jasak had greeted responded in a cool voice. "You're late, Olderhan. Five Hundred Klian's hummer message told us to expect you three days ago."

"We had a weather delay at Fort Wyvern," Jasak replied in a level voice. "And the pilot and I agreed that the dragon needed some extra rest after clearing the mountains."

"I see." Neshok's tone made it perfectly clear he did nothing of the sort, Shaylar thought, holding Jathmar's hand tightly. The Fort Wyvern hundred gazed at them for a second or two, then looked back at Jasak.

"The Commander of Two Thousand will see you shortly. Follow me."

Neshok turned on his bootheel and started toward the fort without another word.

"If there'd been any more warmth in that greeting," Shaylar murmured to Jathmar in Shurkhali, "the air would've frozen solid."

"I'd say that was a bit of an understatement," Jathmar agreed. "And frankly, after what Gadrial told us about this mul Gurthak, I find that disturbing. I hope she was right about how hard it would be for anyone to take us out of Jasak's custody!"

"Yes. Mother Marthea, yes," Shaylar replied fervently, but her attention wasn't on Neshok. She was looking at two men who stood well back in the little crowd beside the hard-packed dirt road leading from the dragonfield to the fort's gates. Most of the men in that crowd were soldiers, but not the two who'd drawn her attention. They stood out because they weren't in uniform, and because they were also older than the soldiers standing around them.

Jathmar followed her eyes and frowned.

"Wonder who they are?" he muttered under his breath.

"So do I." The edge in Shaylar's voice surprised Jathmar. She'd wrapped both arms around herself as though still warding off the chill of flying across the mountains, and her reaction worried him.

He turned his attention back to the two unknowns. Both were in their forties or fifties, at a glance, and although Jathmar knew nothing of Arcanan fashions, their clothing was clearly made of high-quality material. It looked custom-tailored, too. That kind of garment wasn't what he'd expected to see in a frontier fort, and they looked even more out of place than he felt.

According to Jasak and Gadrial, Arcana's exploration of virgin universes was conducted by the military. So who were these two civilians? And what were they doing out here among the trees, mosquitos, and swamps, wearing tailored garments made of what looked like silk?

Government functionaries of some kind, perhaps. Or could they be independent businessmen intent on opening trade routes? He knew there wasn't much point in speculating in the dark, but something about them compelled his curiosity. There was a hardness in their eyes, or perhaps a hooded look of speculation, that made him intensely uncomfortable. He'd grown used to seeing fear, or at least anxiety, as the rumors of the Sharonians' "demonic weapons" traveled up the transit chain ahead of them. But these men weren't looking at Shaylar and him fearfully. There was something measuring, watchful . . . calculating about them.

He couldn't put his mental finger on just what it was about them that bothered him any more accurately than that, but it was enough to raise his hackles, and he put his arm around Shaylar as they walked past the silently watching civilians.

Neshok led them up the road toward the new fort, and Jathmar abruptly found the two civilians displaced from the forefront of his concerns. The landing field was literally ringed with dragons. There were dozens—possibly even scores—of the beasts, and their path led them directly past half a dozen of them.

Skyfang, the dragon which had transported them here from Fort Wyvern, had shown no sign of Windclaw's ferociously hostile initial reaction to Shaylar. Jathmar had concluded that she'd been right in her suspicion that it was her attempt to use her Voice which had set the original transport dragon off. Now, as they headed across in front of *six* of them, he found himself hoping fervently that they'd both been correct after all.

Most of the beasts ignored them completely, but one of them raised its head abruptly. The predominately crimson and gold beast was smaller than any of the dragons Jathmar had previously seen, but that scarcely made it tiny. Its head was still longer than Jathmar's body, much less Shaylar's, and the spikes protecting its throat and head were sharper looking, and proportionately longer, than Windclaw's had been.

It cocked its head, like some huge falcon, turning to fix its knife-sharp gaze upon Shaylar, and its mouth opened, showing carnivore fangs the size of serving platters and a long, shockingly red forked tongue. Then its forefeet thrust at the rain-slick ground, shoving it half-upright, and it hissed like a Trans-Temporal Express locomotive venting steam.

Shaylar went white. She closed her eyes, trembling, and Jathmar felt her desperate effort to completely close down any hint of Talent. Even the marriage bond was abruptly muted, almost impossible to feel, and his arm tightened around her.

The dragon's reaction hadn't escaped Jasak or Gadrial. As if *they'd* been the telepaths, the two of them moved as one, in perfect coordination, to interpose their own bodies between the clearly agitated beast and Shaylar. And Gadrial, Jathmar realized with sudden shock, was abruptly outlined by a literal corona of light. Fire seemed to crackle in midair, three inches from her skin, her hands rose in an odd, intensely graceful posture which reminded him of some sort of martial artist, and he felt a sudden, ominous, ozone-breathing pressure radiating from her. It was like knowing he was standing directly in the path of a lightning bolt, a corner of his mind gibbered, and for the first time since they'd met, he was actually afraid of her.

Neshok, on the other hand, didn't even seem to have noticed. He'd halted, but he was staring with obvious perplexity—and what looked like quickly growing suspicion—back and forth between the dragon and the two Sharonians, not at Jasak or Gadrial.

"What—?" he began, but Jasak overrode his questions savagely.

"Get us out of here—now!" he barked. Neshok turned his head to glare at him, and Jasak snarled. "*Now*, godsdamn it! Unless you want a massacre on your hands!"

Fury tightened the other hundred's expression, but then he glanced at Gadrial, and his eyes widened. He'd opened his mouth as if to say something more, but it snapped shut as more fire began to crackle at the tips of her fingers. That and the look on Jasak's face—and the fact that a *second* dragon was beginning to rouse—seemed to get through to him. He barked orders to the escort, and the entire party moved into a half-run.

The agitated dragons began to calm once more as soon as Shaylar was forty or fifty yards away. The one who'd roused up first looked after her with one last almost querulous hiss. Then it, too, settled back into its original position and laid its fearsome head on its forelegs.

"It wasn't me, Jasak! It wasn't! It *couldn't* have been me! I wasn't *doing* anything!" Shaylar cried, and Jasak looked down at her as she hastened along between him and Jathmar.

"I believe you," he said, laying his own hand on her shoulder, but he also shook his head. "I just wish I knew why those two reacted that way, when none of the transport dragons have since Windclaw."

"What are you talking about?" Neshok demanded harshly. He was glaring at Shaylar, his eyes flinty, and he didn't seem to be very much happier than that with Jasak. "What does she mean, she 'wasn't doing anything'?"

"The transport dragon that airlifted my wounded out reacted violently to Lady Nargra-Kolmayr's presence." Jasak's voice was level, his expression calm, but Shaylar could sense his emotions through the hand still on her shoulder. He wasn't at all happy about broaching this entire subject, she realized. "We didn't have any problems with the dragon from Fort Wyvern, though. I'd hoped it was just a fluke the first time."

"That still doesn't answer my question," Neshok said flatly, stopping in the road now that they were far enough away from the dragons and glaring at Jasak. "What did she mean about not doing anything?"

"Lady Nargra-Kolmayr," Jasak said, and Shaylar realized he was deliberately stressing the Andaran title he'd suddenly assigned her rather than use her first name, "has what her people call a Talent. It's an ability to communicate with others using her mind, and we think some of the dragons may be reacting to it."

Neshok's eyes flared wide in sudden alarm, and Jasak shook his head quickly.

"It's very much like our Gifts, Hundred," he said. "In fact, you could just think of it as a different sort of Gift. It doesn't turn her into some kind of magic mindreader, nor can she influence your thoughts or communicate with her own people from this far away."

"And just how do you *know* that?" Neshok demanded, his face dark with anger.

"I know because she told me so," Jasak said flatly. "And because if there'd been any way for her to use her Talent effectively against us, she'd certainly have done so, and she hasn't."

"Because she *told* you so!" Neshok repeated in a scathing tone, completely ignoring Jasak's second sentence. "The woman's a prisoner of war, and you expect her to tell you the *truth*? Are you a *complete* idiot? She's going to lie with every breath she takes! I ought to put a bolt through her right now—or throw her back to the dragons!"

Jathmar stiffened, his hands closing into fists. Neshok was speaking too rapidly, and too angrily, for Jathmar to completely follow the conversation, but he'd understood enough. He started to step in front of Shaylar, but before he could move, Gadrial's hand—no longer limned in fire, thank the gods!—closed on his elbow. He looked down at her, then looked back up ... just in time to see *Jasak* step in front of his wife.

Jasak was a good three inches taller than Neshok, and much broader across the shoulders, but it was his expression and his body language, not his size, which made the other hundred abruptly step back a pace.

"I'm getting tired of explaining this to pigheaded, pea-brained, bigmouthed excuses for Andaran officers who frigging well ought to know better," Sir Jasak Olderhan said very, very softly. "But I'll try one more time, and I advise you to listen to me very carefully, because I'm not going to repeat myself again. Lady Nargra-Kolmayr and her husband are my *shardonai*. Any insult, any injury or threat, offered to them is offered to a member of my family. Perhaps you'd care to reconsider that last sentence of yours."

His hand hovered in the vicinity of the short sword at his hip, and Jathmar's tension clicked up yet another notch as Jugthar Sendahli and Otwal Threbuch quietly stepped out on either side of Jasak, facing Neshok and his detail. The Second Andaran Scouts, Jathmar abruptly remembered from Gadrial's explanations, were the hereditary command of the Dukes of Garth Showma. Apparently, he realized, that relationship extended rather further than he'd assumed it did.

None of them actually touched a weapon. But none of them had to, either.

"Very well," a white-lipped Neshok grated after a moment. "I withdraw the last sentence. But *shardonai* or not, how can you be so sure they're telling you the truth? For that matter, how can you be sure you didn't decide to make them *shardonai* in the first place because she somehow influenced your mind?"

"Because she was three-quarters unconscious with a concussion when I made my decision," Jasak said almost contemptuously. "And because after three weeks in their company, I've discovered that unlike certain Arcanans I could mention, these are both people of honor who understand the mutual obligations of a *baranal* and his *shardonai*. They may not volunteer information, and they may even refuse to answer questions, but they won't lie to *me*, Hundred."

Neshok's angry, frightened expression didn't change. He was obviously not convinced, but equally obviously he couldn't think of a way to continue the argument without edging back into potentially dangerous waters. That was when Gadrial spoke up unexpectedly.

"Lady Nargra-Kolmayr is as clear as glass, Hundred Neshok. It's not in her nature to lie! God above, man—all you have to do is *look* at her to know that!"

Gadrial's outburst had drawn Neshok's angry eyes back to her. Now those eyes softened with an expression of pity.

"Magister Kelbryan, your work with Magister Halathyn vos Dulainah is renowned, even out here on the frontier. I can't imagine the grief and shock you must have experienced after his murder by these—" his glance flicked once more toward Shaylar and Jathmar, hardening again "—barbarians."

White-hot fury exploded suddenly inside Shaylar, made even worse by the lingering echoes of the terror she'd felt when the dragons began to hiss, and she jerked free of Jathmar's arm. She took a long, angry stride towards Neshok, stepping around Jasak. The Fort Wyvern officer towered above her, but the mantle of her anger made her a giant.

"*Barbarians?*" she hissed in his face. "Don't you dare call us barbarians! Don't you *dare* use the word 'murder' after what your soldiers did to *us!* We were civilians, damn you—*civilians!* And if you don't believe that, look what happened when your soldiers finally had to face *ours*. You kill civilians—use weapons that burn civilians alive!—but you call *me* a barbarian?

"My country is *four thousand* years old—four thousand years of civilization, art, science, and literature! Sharonian civilization is over *five* thousand years old. Five thousand years of recorded history—how many do *you* have?"

Neshok looked like a man who'd picked up his boot and suddenly discovered a cobra in it.

"We're not the ones who've acted like barbarians, but don't think for a moment that we don't know how to *respond* to barbarians! My mother is a Shurkhali *ambassador!* Do you think she, or any of our countries, will ever forgive you for what you've done? They think—*she* thinks—that I'm dead, curse you!"

She stood there in a puddle of utter silence, glaring up at Neshok, and naked shock had detonated behind his eyes. Even Jasak seemed stunned.

"Your mother is an *ambassador?*" he asked hoarsely, and she turned on him with flaming eyes, too shaken by the encounter with the dragons to contain the pain and rage Neshok had roused.

"Yes! What? You thought our people were too primitive, too violent for something that civilized?"

"No, Shaylar," he said, deliberately taking both her hands in his so that she would *know*. "I never thought that. Any civilization that could produce you is worthy of respect. But your mother's status makes this whole situation even more difficult, more complicated."

Shaylar bit down on a hysterical laugh as it tried to break loose in her throat.

"You don't have the slightest idea how much more," she told him. "You don't have any *concept* of how the Shurkhali honor code is going to react to what's happened."

"No, but I'm trying to understand, for your sake, as well as because it's my duty. And it's also," he flicked a cold glance at Neshok, "just one more reason to treat Lady Nargra-Kolmayr and her husband with courtesy."

His eyes locked with Neshok's, and a muscle jumped in the other man's jaw.

"The two thousand is waiting," he half-snapped after a moment and turned on his heel once more to march toward the fort.

Some people, Shaylar thought, couldn't be forced to see reason, even at gunpoint. But Neshok's reaction to Halathyn's death—not to mention his instant, unthinking attitude towards her and Jathmar—only underscored how dark the future had become.

She could scarcely imagine how Sharona must have reacted to the belief that she was dead. She'd never been a vain person, but she'd been embarrassedly aware for years of the way the Portal Authority had used her face, her image, in its public relations campaigns. She knew how all of Shurkhal, even the men who'd harbored the most reservations about her choice of career, had taken a fierce and possessive pride in her accomplishments. If Darcel had relayed everything she'd transmitted over their link before she was injured, then all of Sharona had probably been swept by a fury it hadn't seen in centuries, if not longer. As for how Shurkal must have reacted—!

Now Neshok's attitude gave her some idea of how *Arcana* was going to react to news of Magister Halathyn's death. And the fact that he'd been killed by an Arcanan soldier, not by Sharona, wasn't going to matter a bit.

Her shoulders slumped as an abrupt, crushing weariness crashed down across her. She wanted to curl up someplace sheltered and private, someplace she could hide. Someplace where men like Neshok didn't exist, where monstrous weapons didn't threaten Sharonian lives, and where no unnatural creatures could crawl inside her mind.

"We'll settle you into your quarters and let you rest," Jasak promised her quietly. "I can see how shaken you are. Jathmar will help you, all right? It shouldn't be too far now."

She just nodded, and he released her hands. Jathmar slid his arm back around her, taking some of her weight, and met Jasak's gaze levelly.

"When we leave this place," he said in a low voice, "would it be too much to ask to have those murderous beasts moved someplace else?"

"That's a very reasonable request," Jasak said, and turned a cool glance on Neshok. "And a damned good idea from a security standpoint. Not only is it my duty to protect my *shardonai*, but I somehow doubt the Commandery would appreciate losing Lady Nargra-Kolmayr to dragon attack."

"They'll be moved," Neshok snapped without even turning his head. "Satisfied?"

"For now," Jasak said coldly. "In the meantime, if you'll escort us to our assigned quarters, I'll see my *shardonai*—" he emphasized the noun deliberately "—settled in, and then pay my compliments to the two thousand. Will he want to debrief Magister Kelbryan or Lady Nargra-Kolmayr and her husband?"

"If he does, he'll send for them. This way."

If anyone thought the confrontation between Neshok and Jasak was over, they were speedily disabused of the notion when they reached the fort and Neshok tried to lock Shaylar and Jathmar into the cell beside vos Hoven's.

It was not a wise decision on his part. The exchange between him and Jasak was short, ice cold, and bitter, with Neshok taking spiteful refuge in the instructions he'd received from Two Thousand mul Gurthak. He insisted that he was merely following mul Gurthak's explicit orders—orders he lacked the authority to countermand.

"Two Thousand mul Gurthak doesn't have the authority to order the arbitrary incarceration of any civilian member of my family without specific charges under Arcanan law," Jasak told him savagely. Neshok started to open his mouth again, but this time Gadrial interposed before the situation could get totally out of hand.

"Fine!" she snapped, glaring up at Neshok as furiously as Shaylar had. "If those are your orders, obey them. Lock them up in your filthy jail. But you'll do it with me locked in the same cell with them!"

"Magister Kelbryan, you can't be serious!" Neshok protested.

"I've never been more serious in my life," she told him icily, and her lip curled. "I wouldn't want to suggest that they might have some sort of . . . accident locked up here in your jail, Hundred. But I think we'd all feel better with a senior magister who's fully trained in combat magics—who's *taught* combat magics at the Garth Showma Institute for the last ten years—between them and any unfortunate little episode. Don't you *agree*, Hundred Neshok?"

Neshok's troopers, Jathmar noticed, seemed to stiffen into statues at the phrase "combat magics." After what he'd seen down by the dragonfield, he found he could understand their attitude perfectly.

Shaylar, on the other hand, was watching Neshok, and the sudden, dark flush which spread down his neck told her everything she needed to know about the intentions of this fort's commander. Or—just as possible—about *Neshok's* intentions. A man who extracted information from recalcitrant prisoners for his superiors might just find it easier to climb the rank ladder. And if he succeeded in getting information, it was unlikely anyone would quibble too strenuously with his methods, however ... unpleasant they might have been for the prisoners in question. She shivered in Jathmar's arms at the thought.

"Very well," Neshok bit out. "I'll escort you to other quarters."

The room the Sharonians ended up in was small and utilitarian, and Jasak made a point of assigning Jugthar Sendahli to deal with any of their needs. Neshok flushed angrily again at Jasak's none-too-subtle provision of a guard he knew he could rely upon. More than that, their room was next to Gadrial's, and the guard Neshok posted at their door was fully cognizant of Gadrial's open door.

"I will hear any attempt you make to have them removed by force," that door said, without a word spoken aloud. *"And if anyone tries it, they'll wish they had never been born ... briefly."*

Neshok looked as if he wanted to chew live snakes, but he choked it down raw and accepted the situation. That satisfied Jasak, who saw them settled in before he disappeared in the direction of the commanding officer's office.

Shaylar sank down onto the bed and simply looked at her husband.

"He intended to hurt us," she said, and Jathmar nodded silently.

"It's going to get worse," she said even more quietly, and her husband nodded once more.

"I'm scared, Jath," she whispered, and he wrapped his arms about her and held her very, very tightly.

CHAPTER
THIRTY-EIGHT

COMMANDER OF TWO Thousand Nith mul Gurthak sat his chair like a throne. He was one of the small but growing number of Gifted Mythalan officers who'd chosen a career as a line officer rather than to serve in one of the specialist slots most Gifted soldiers—Mythalan or otherwise—usually preferred. Jasak didn't know how strong mul Gurthak's Gift might be, although the fact that the two thousand chose to go by "mul Gurthak" rather than the "vos and mul Gurthak" which a *shakira* officer was entitled to claim could be an indication that it wasn't extraordinarily powerful.

That was only one of the things Jasak didn't know about mul Gurthak, for they'd never met before. The Mythalan officer had been away from Fort Talon on an inspection trip when Jasak had passed through on his way to Mahritha and Five Hundred Klian's command. He hadn't met Rithmar Skirvon or Uthik Dastiri before, either, although he'd noticed the two civilians down by the dragonfield. The chestnut-haired, green-eyed Skirvon was obviously of Andaran descent, although the last name sounded more Hilmarian. Dastiri, younger, darker, almond-eyed, much shorter, and slimmer, with an evident abundance of nervous energy, was obviously Ransaran.

"We just arrived last night, ourselves," Skirvon told Jasak as the hundred settled into the chair at which mul Gurthak had rather brusquely gestured. Neshok stood just inside the office door, a brooding, still angry presence, and Otwal Threbuch stood behind Jasak's shoulder with his hands clasped behind him in a stand-easy position. "We came in response to the hummer message Commander Five Hundred Klian sent out."

"Master Skirvon and Master Dastiri are field representatives of the Union Arbitration Commission," mul Gurthak put in. "We were fortunate they were in Ilmariya on another matter when Five Hundred Klian's hummer message arrived. They arrived by transport flight at about two o'clock this morning."

Jasak nodded with an undeniable edge of relief. The UAC reported directly to the Union Senate. It was a quasi-diplomatic organization charged with resolving inter-universal disputes between both local governing entities and private individuals. Skirvon and Dastiri might not be formally accredited as Union ambassadors to extra-universal civilizations, but they were certainly the closest anyone was going to be able to come to that, and at least they did have diplomatic training.

"I'm very glad to see you, gentlemen," he said. "And I've learned something else today which may be of interest to you. Lady Nargra-Kolmayr is the daughter of a Sharonian ambassador."

Skirvon and Dastiri twitched in visible surprise. They looked at one another, then back at Jasak.

"I heard there'd been some . . . disturbance down at the dragonfield," mul Gurthak said after a moment. "Something about the female prisoner." His eyes flickered briefly toward Neshok, and he grimaced in obvious distaste. "I understand she made quite a scene."

"I suppose someone might put it that way, Sir," Jasak said just a bit coolly, never even glancing at Neshok. "For myself, I believe that almost being attacked by a battle dragon and then treated with obvious contempt by her escort would probably constitute justification for losing her temper."

Mul Gurthak's lips tightened.

"I've read Five Hundred Klian's dispatch, and I know all about your decision to declare them *shardonai*, Hundred," he said frostily, and something ugly glowed in his eyes for just an instant. But then he drew a deep breath and shook his head slightly.

"That's part of your people's culture, not mine," he continued in a somewhat less chilly voice. "I don't say I agree with your decision, but I understand its implications. At the same time, however, both you and your *shardonai* need to understand that they *are* prisoners—prisoners of *war*—and the only intelligence resource we currently possess. If they continue to refuse to cooperate with us, it's going to place everyone in a very . . . difficult position."

"Refuse to cooperate, Sir?" Jasak arched one eyebrow. "I fail to understand how anyone could accuse them of refusing to cooperate. Obviously, as you've just observed, they're the prisoners of people who killed all of their companions, and they aren't going to voluntarily disgorge information which might help us kill more of their people. But they've been working as hard as anyone could possibly ask in their efforts to learn to communicate with us. In fact, Lady Nargra-Kolmayr has learned to speak fluent Andaran in less than two weeks, and she's been able to teach her husband how to speak it amazingly well. And—"

"Excuse me, Hundred, but did you say they're *fluent* in Andaran?" Skirvon interrupted.

"Lady Nargra-Kolmayr is, certainly," Jasak confirmed. "Frankly, the speed at which she's mastered it is astonishing."

"And has she reciprocated?" mul Gurthak asked, his brows furrowed in an expression that practically shouted mistrust.

"Taught us Sharonian, you mean, Sir?" Jasak asked. Mul Gurthak nodded, and Jasak gave a tiny shrug.

"Like us, Sharona has many languages, Sir. Between themselves, they normally speak one called Shurkhali. That's Lady Nargra-Kolmayr's native language, but not her husband's. Just as Magister Kelbryan has concentrated on teaching them a single one of our languages—Andaran—we've been learning one they call Ternathian. According to Lady Nargra-Kolmayr, it's the language of Sharona's most powerful nation."

"You say you've been learning it?" Skirvon pressed.

"Not nearly so quickly as they've been learning Andaran," Jasak assured him with a wry smile. "But Magister Kelbryan has been working with them using the translation spellware programmed into her PC. Every time she taught them a word in Andaran, they gave her the equivalent word in Ternathian. Magister Kelbryan's spellware stores the words both in written phonetic form and in audio, and it's been analyzing and deriving the Ternathian rules of grammar, as well. For all intents and purposes, it's produced a primer for Ternathian, and it's capable of running audio translation, as well. I'm sure there are still holes in what we've got, and I'm equally sure that it wouldn't give one of our people anywhere near the fluency Lady Nargra-Kolmayr has attained in Andaran, but it's a very substantial beginning."

He reached into the breast of his uniform tunic and extracted a sheaf of neatly printed pages.

"Magister Kelbryan generated this from her PC last night," he said, and handed the pages to Dastiri, the nearer of the two diplomats.

"Incredible," Dastiri muttered, flipping through the pages. He shook his head and handed it to Skirvon, who was senior to him in the UAC.

"Very impressive," Skirvon agreed. "Could you arrange for Magister

Kelbryan to download a copy of this to our PCs? And of her translation spellware. The UAC would find it of incalculable value."

"And I'll want a copy, as well, Hundred," mul Gurthak said.

That was fine with Jasak. As the senior military officer at this end of the transit chain, mul Gurthak was definitely in a need-to-know position. Indeed, the more Ternathian-fluent officers they could produce, the better. There was going to be additional contact with the other side, no matter what happened, and having some means of communication besides shooting at one another struck Jasak as a very good idea, indeed.

"I'm sure Magister Kelbryan will be happy to download copies for both you and Master Skirvon and Master Dastiri, Sir," he said. "And if you'd be so kind, Master Skirvon, you could download a copy for Five Hundred Klian's use when you reach Fort Rycharn, as well."

"That's an excellent idea," Skirvon said. "We'll be sure to do that."

He looked back down at the hard copy for a moment, then tucked it away in his briefcase and extracted his own PC. He activated it and tapped the menu with the stylus to switch it to audio recording mode, then leaned back in his chair.

"We're scheduled to depart for Fort Rycharn tomorrow," he said. "Obviously, I'm not going to have time to acquire a great deal of fluency before we arrive there, although this 'primer' of yours will be an enormous help. But if we're not going to be able to indulge in complex discussions with them at first, it's vital that we have as much background knowledge as we can get. So what can you tell us about these people we've encountered, Sir Jasak?"

"Quite a bit, actually, Master Skirvon. That's one reason why I said it would be difficult to legitimately accuse Lady Nargra-Kolmayr and her husband of refusing to cooperate. They've been extremely reticent about military matters—and, frankly, I believe they truly are civilians and probably not all that conversant with the details of their military, in the first place—but they've been very forthcoming about their home universe and its political and social structure."

"Indeed?" Skirvon's eyebrows rose.

"We've learned a great deal about how Sharona is organized," Jasak said. "Most of the details are recorded in Magister Kelbryan's PC, along with the notes on the Ternathian language. I think you'll be astonished at how ancient their civilizations are, and although they don't have the sort of world government we do in the Union, most of their nations appear to share an amazing degree of common values and beliefs. According to Lady Nargra-Kolmayr, the Ternathian

Empire, their oldest state, is over five thousand years old. At one time, it ruled more than two thirds of the then-known world, and it apparently left its cultural imprint behind when it gradually disengaged from its high-water mark."

Skirvon nodded, although Jasak had the distinct impression the diplomat didn't really believe him. Or, rather, that Skirvon suspected Shaylar had deliberately exaggerated the antiquity and strength of her home civilization.

"You'll be able to review her comments for yourself, Master Skirvon," Jasak said. "Personally, I believe what she's told us is substantially accurate, but I'm sure you'll form your own opinion."

"I'll review them very carefully, Sir Jasak," Skirvon promised. "In the meantime, however, there's a more immediate point I'd like to address. Five Hundred Klian's reports state that these people's technology is very different from our own."

"That probably ranks with the most severe understatements I've ever heard, Master Skirvon," Jasak replied with a twisted smile. "We've brought the captured equipment with us, and with your permission, Sir," he glanced at mul Gurthak, "I'd like to leave a representative selection of it—especially of their weapons—here with you. I'm sure the Commandery will want us to transport most of it back to New Arcana where it can be thoroughly examined, but as close as you are to the point of contact, I'd like you to be able to form some idea of its capabilities for yourself."

"An excellent idea, Hundred," mul Gurthak said with the first unqualified approval Jasak had sensed from him.

"But in answer to the point you've raised, Master Skirvon," Jasak turned his attention back to the diplomat, "they have a great many devices and tools we don't begin to understand yet. They're remarkably good engineers and artisans, and their metallurgy and textiles are every bit as good as our own, but they don't appear to have any equivalent of our arcane technology."

"So I understood from Five Hundred Klian's report," Skirvon said, yet he was frowning heavily. "I find that very difficult to accept, however. Obviously, I haven't spent as much time in these people's company as you have, Sir Jasak. But they certainly appear to be just as human as we are, so presumably they ought to have the same basic genetic heritage. The same Gifts."

"I can't debate that point with you," Jasak said. "At this point, we know too little about them for me to be comfortable making any sweeping assumptions, even if I had the medical or technical background to make that sort of judgment in the first place. But

I can tell you that any magic-based technology clearly astonishes them. *Anything*, no matter how simple. Magister Halathyn conjured a simple light-rose, something any four-year-old with a decent Gift could do, so that he could give Lady Nargra-Kolmayr a flower. When it blossomed from his fingertips, it shook them both to the core. Both of them reacted exactly the same way, spontaneously: with astonishment so deep it bordered on terror."

"*Terror?*" Skirvon's frown deepened. "Great gods, *why?* What's to be afraid of? It's just magic!"

"Because Sharonians don't use magic. In fact, they have nothing at all even resembling magic, let alone our technology. They didn't even believe it was possible until they were shown ordinary tools that use it."

"That's ridiculous," Dastiri muttered. Then he seemed to realize he'd spoken aloud and waved one hand. "I'm sorry, Sir Jasak, but it just sounds too . . . bizarre for words."

"Oh, I certainly agree with you there," Jasak said feelingly. "Nonetheless, it's true. Magister Kelbryan and I have discussed it with them at considerable length, and they're very emphatic. The Sharonian civilization isn't built around the laws of magic at all."

Skirvon was sitting bolt upright in his chair now, staring at him. So was mul Gurthak, but there was something besides simple astonishment in the two thousand's eyes.

"But—" the senior diplomat sputtered. "But how in the gods' names does anyone build a civilization *without* it?"

He glanced around mul Gurthak's office, an austere frontier room which nevertheless boasted more than a dozen magic-powered appliances, from his own PC to the lighting to the insect-repelling spell to the quietly turning blades of the ceiling fan, all in plain view, and doubtless many others in storage in the various cabinets.

"I'm sorry, Sir Jasak, but Uthik is right. It sounds . . . *impossible.* They'd live under appallingly crude conditions. People in a place like that would be little better than barbarians!"

"With all due respect, Master Skirvon, I wouldn't use that term within their earshot," Jasak said mildly, and heard a smothered sound from behind him. Mul Gurthak looked past him and raised an eyebrow.

"You had something you wished to add, Hundred Neshok?" he asked in a deceptively mild voice.

"I was just going to say, Sir, that no one should say it around that girl, for sure. The little bitch has quite a temper."

"That's quite enough, Neshok!" The mildness had vanished from mul Gurthak's voice, and his face was hard. "You insulted the lady and her people, and you threatened her, and the fact that she's fluent in your own language only made it worse. Whatever else we may think about her and her people, it's difficult to condemn her for becoming angry in the face of such boorishness and discourtesy. Consider yourself fortunate that only *she* has reprimanded you so far."

"Yes, Sir." Neshok's voice sounded strangled, and Jasak could almost feel the heat radiating from his flushed face.

"Don't repeat that mistake, Hundred."

"No, Sir."

No one, Jasak mused, enjoyed eating crow. Neshok appeared to hate it more virulently than most . . . which was just fine with Sir Jasak Olderhan.

Silence lingered for several seconds. Then Jasak cleared his throat, looked back at Skirvon, and continued.

"I was saying that I wouldn't assume their civilization is either crude or simple just because their technology isn't magic-based. We manufacture mechanical things ourselves, but there's a huge difference between an arbalest that fires a steel bolt and one of their weapons. Jathmar field-stripped one of their shoulder weapons—a 'rifle' he calls it—for me at Fort Wyvern. Frankly, it's a complex nightmare of tiny, precisely machined parts. They serve interlocking functions, designed to load and fire the projectile, but even the projectile has multiple parts. The most fascinating part, to be honest, is the granular gray powder inside what he calls the 'cartridge.' It's the powder that performs the 'chemical'—that's another one of his words we're still trying to figure out—operations which actually fire the projectile. As nearly as I can picture it in my own mind right now, they basically set off something very like one of our infantry-dragon fireballs *inside* the cartridge, and that expands with enormous speed and drives the 'bullet' down the hollow barrel of the 'rifle' and through its target."

"An arbalest sounds far more practical and reliable," Skirvon observed with another frown.

"They're reliable enough, Sir." Jasak almost blinked in surprise as Otwal Threbuch inserted himself into the conversation. "And practical, too, begging your pardon. Have you ever seen an arbalest quarrel punch clean through a man three hundred yards away? Have you ever seen an arbalest mow down thirty men in three seconds? A whole *line* of men, forty feet across? They went down like one man—like they'd run into an invisible wire.

"Only it wasn't a wire. The things hitting them were blowing holes straight through them—big holes. Big enough to put your thumb through in front and your *fist* through in back. And that doesn't even begin to describe what their *artillery* can do. They fired it *through* the portal and dropped it *behind* Hundred Thalmayr's fieldworks." The big noncom shook his head grimly. "Believe me, Sir, an arbalest may be less complicated, but it's definitely *not* more practical or reliable."

Both diplomats were ashen, and mul Gurthak looked more than a little shaken himself. Another brief silence fell, until Skirvon shook himself again.

"I'm not a military or a technical man myself, Sir Jasak," he admitted. "I still find the entire concept of a civilization without any magic at all extremely difficult to accept, but for now, I don't think we have any choice but to accept that your description—yours and the chief sword's—is accurate.

"Still, if I'm not particularly well versed in technological matters, I *do* have a bit of experience in diplomatic affairs. You say they don't have a world government. In that case, how do they manage their portal exploration?"

"There's some sort of central authority, an organization that operates their portal forts and apparently runs the actual portals. It sounds like the equivalent of our UTTTA, and it has some sort of authority over their survey crews, but it's also some kind of private entity, I think. I'm not very clear on it yet. It sounds to me as if it's some sort of government-approved or supervised private company. But whoever sponsors it, their 'Portal Authority' decides who's permitted to work on their survey crews. Lady Nargra-Kolmayr says she's the first woman ever approved to join a team; she anticipates being the last, as well."

The diplomats exchanged thoughtful glances. Then they looked back at Jasak.

"So it would probably be this 'Portal Authority' we'd be speaking to, not the representatives of an actual government?" Skirvon mused aloud.

"I'd guess so." Jasak nodded. "But let me emphasize that it would be only a guess on my part. One thing we haven't been able to discover is how extensively the Sharonians have explored. My distinct impression from several things they've let drop is that they were operating on the leading edge of a very extensive frontier when we encountered one another. If that's so, then I'd think it would be difficult for them to get diplomats to the front much more quickly than we could. And that completely ignores the fact that if they don't have a world government, the first thing they'd have to do is decide *which* government should be talking to us."

"A very well taken observation, Sir Jasak." Skirvon nodded vigorously, then cocked his head to one side.

"I know I'm jumping around a bit," he said, semi-apologetically, "but it's just occurred to me that if they don't have anything like magic, then presumably they don't have anything like our hummers, which should give us a substantial advantage in response time."

"I wouldn't count on that if I were you, Master Skirvon," Jasak said, a bit grimly. "No, they don't have hummers. But that's because they don't *need* them."

"Why not?" mul Gurthak asked sharply, and Jasak grimaced.

"We only discovered after we left Fort Rycharn that while these people don't have Gifts, they do have what they call Talents," he said heavily.

His own reluctance to mention the matter surprised him. It also made him realize just how protective he truly felt where Shaylar and Jathmar were concerned. Yet he was an officer of the Union of Arcana. It was his duty to pass the information along, and so he told them everything Shaylar and Jathmar had told him about their own Talents and how those Talents had served the survey crews and Sharona in general.

"Obviously," he concluded, several minutes later, "the military applications of this . . . living technology are enormous. And, frankly, the civilian applications must be equally staggering."

His audience looked stunned. Then mul Gurthak leaned forward over his desk, his body language and expression angry.

"When," he asked icily, "did you discover *this* little bit of information?"

"About one day out from Fort Wyvern, Sir," Jasak said coolly. "Since we were coming through by dragon ourselves as soon as possible, I decided not to send it by hummer. I thought you'd probably prefer to hear about it in person, and with as little chance for it to leak as possible."

"I see." The two thousand sat back in his chair again, toying with a stylus, and the anger slowly ebbed out of his expression. But he still didn't look precisely satisfied, and he frowned at Jasak. "What prompted them to make such a revelation? They have to know how seriously that knowledge will compromise their side in any conflict."

"I'm not certain they are aware of *all* the implications," Jasak said reluctantly. "As I say, they're civilians, not soldiers. As to why they admitted it, partly it was because they didn't have much choice. I confronted them over something that had shaken Magister Kelbryan pretty badly, which pressured them into making a partial explanation. They volunteered the rest, though."

"But why?" Skirvon sounded as baffled—and skeptical—as mul Gurthak.

"I think it's because they're trying desperately to find some grounds for mutual understanding, Master Skirvon," Jasak said slowly. "They're fully aware of how different we are from one another—in fact, they're probably far more aware of it than we are, since they're the ones trapped inside *our* culture. I think they believe that the more we know about them—the more completely we understand that they aren't monsters, just *different*—the greater the chance for establishing some sort of trust between us. And I also think they have a point. When you get right down to it, the implications of these Talents of theirs aren't a lot different from the implications of our own Gifts. Just as we've done with our Gifts, they seem to have concentrated their Talents through specific family lines, and everything we've been able to learn from Shaylar so far suggests their Talents are probably much less useful for what Magister Kelbryan calls 'macro effects' than magic is. That's probably why they rely so heavily on complex mechanical devices.

"But however frightening or threatening this capability of theirs may seem—for that matter, however dangerous it may yet actually prove to be—one fact remains. Sharona has also produced two individuals from very different Sharonian nations who share similar traits which are important to our understanding of them. They're honorable, courageous, and—under the circumstances—surprisingly honest and forthcoming."

One again, the diplomats exchanged glances. Jasak wasn't at all sure he cared for their expressions.

"Most helpful, indeed, Sir Jasak," Skirvon said after a moment.

"There's another point I'd like to make, as well, if I may," Jasak said. "We know Sharona has many countries, and we also know Lady Nargra-Kolmayr and her husband don't come from the same one. You only have to look at them to see that they're obviously from different genetic stocks. Yet their ideas, their values—what they believe at the deepest core level—are remarkably similar. And when you stop to think about it, how many Arcanans actually choose to marry outside their birth cultures? Not very many, yet we've been a united world, under one government, for two centuries."

The mention of cross-cultural marriages tightened mul Gurthak's lips in visible disapproval. Despite that, it was the two thousand who first grasped the point Jasak was trying to make.

"What you're trying to say is that even though they may not have a world government, their culture—their civilization—may be much closer to monolithic than we'd assume?"

"Exactly, Sir," Jasak said with a nod.

"One wonders," Dastiri said thoughtfully, "how common this marriage pattern of theirs truly is?"

"That's certainly something to be curious about," Skirvon agreed. "It's possible that it's not actually very common at all, but I'm inclined to trust Sir Jasak's instincts on this matter. He doesn't have any formal training in diplomacy, I know, but as the heir to Garth Showma, he probably has a better sense of political and cultural nuances than most people. Certainly a better one than most officers of his seniority," the diplomat very carefully did not glance in Neshok's direction, "and he's spent a great deal of time with his prisoners. Excuse me, with his *shardonai*." The diplomat smiled apologetically at Jasak, then looked back at Dastiri. "If he believes we're dealing with a cultural monolith, regardless of their political organization, I'm inclined to trust that judgment."

Neshok's nostrils flared, and mul Gurthak's eyes went a shade frostier, but only for a moment. Then the two thousand drew a slow, deliberate breath.

"A well-taken point," he said. "It appears we're fortunate to have your insight into these matters, Hundred Olderhan."

He studied Jasak with opaque eyes for several seconds, then shrugged.

"Given the role the late Shevan Garlath played in the disaster at Fallen Timbers," he finally said, "I'm forced to revise my first, overly hasty assessment of your judgment as a field officer. Five Hundred Klian's evaluation of Fifty Garlath's fitness as an officer makes it clear you were saddled with a . . . difficult situation, even before you made contact with these Sharonians."

He produced a wintry smile.

"One is always tempted to blame messengers who bear unpalatable news, particularly when military and political disasters are involved. But Chief Sword Threbuch's report on the second encounter with these people makes it clear—to me, at least—that you did a brilliant job of containment."

Jasak bristled silently at the use of the word "containment." It was accurate enough—he'd certainly "contained" the Sharonians, at least physically—but something about the word, or perhaps the way it had been delivered, set him on edge. That surprised him, but he didn't have time to ponder it now, for mul Gurthak was still speaking.

"I may never forgive Hadrign Thalmayr," the two thousand said in a bitter tone, "for promptly throwing away all you'd accomplished and losing the men you'd managed to bring safely back. Not to mention losing control of the *portal*."

He shook his head, leaned far back in his chair, and steepled his fingers across his chest.

"I realize your primary concern will be sending reports ahead as you make the return trip to New Arcana. The Commandery has to know everything you learn as soon as possible. The time lag is immense, as it is. Even at the speed hummers fly, this is a *long* transit chain."

"Yes, Sir. I know that only too well." The initial message that there'd been a contact with another civilization was still winging its way—literally—back to New Arcana. "No one even knows the Union has new neighbors, Sir. Let alone that battles have already been fought. No one in the *Union*, that is."

His eyes met mul Gurthak's, and the two thousand nodded, his expression grim. Skirvon and Dastiri's ears seemed to prick up, as if they realized something they didn't understand had just been said, and mul Gurthak favored them with a hard, thin smile.

"You gentlemen weren't listening to the hundred," he said. "What was it he said? They don't *need* hummers, I believe."

Skirvon stared at him, then blanched visibly.

"Gods! They already know, don't they? They've probably known for *weeks*!"

"Lady Nargra-Kolmayr's effectively confirmed that," Jasak agreed unhappily. "I don't know exactly how long it took their message to get home, but given the structure she described, with official Voices stationed permanently at every single portal they've discovered, and at relays in between, as necessary, their home world may have known within hours. I'd bet that someone in their Portal Authority knew by the time we airlifted out the wounded. And something she said this afternoon confirms that her family thinks she's dead. She used the present tense, and I don't think it was a slip of the tongue. She knows that whatever message she was sending out when she was knocked unconscious at Fallen Timbers has already reached her home world."

Both diplomats had turned a sickly shade of yellow-green.

"This is a first-class disaster," Skirvon groaned. "They've had time to move in whole *divisions* of troops!"

"It's not quite that bad," mul Gurthak disagreed. They looked at him incredulously, and he shrugged. "I've been operating on the assumption that word might have gotten back to their high command ever since I received Five Hundred Klian's initial dispatches. The force which attacked Hundred Thalmayr was undeniably stronger than anyone anticipated, however it scarcely represented the kind of troop strength I'd have expected from a major base. And we know these people don't have dragons, or, apparently, anything else that flies. Neither, according to the chief sword," he nodded at Threbuch, "do they have enhanced cavalry mounts like our own. So what we're probably facing is a situation in which their high command can receive reports and dispatch new orders much more rapidly than we can, but our *forces* can move much more rapidly than theirs can."

Jasak nodded. He'd already reached the same conclusion himself, and it should have been reassuring to know that the senior officer in the area agreed with his own assessment. And it was . . . mostly. Still, there was something about mul Gurthak's eyes. . . .

"Hundred Olderhan," the commander of two thousand continued, turning his attention back to Jasak and smiling much more warmly than before, "I want to thank you for a first-class briefing. I'm very impressed by the amount of information you've been able to obtain from the prisoners. I suppose it's another case of that old cliché about catching more flies with sugar than with salt," he added, giving Neshok a speaking glance.

"I also concur that it's critical that we get our diplomatic presence as far forward as we can, as quickly as we can. *And* that you continue to New Arcana with all dispatch. Indeed, I'm coming to the conclusion, based on what you've said here, that we could scarcely have acquired a more valuable source of intelligence if we'd been allowed to choose who to capture ourselves."

One again, something bristled deep inside Jasak. It was his protective instinct, he knew. His *shardonai* had become personally important to him, not just an honor obligation, and that might not be a good thing, from the perspective of the Union of Arcana. Mul Gurthak was undoubtedly correct about Shaylar and Jathmar's value, and Jasak ought to place the same priority on squeezing them for every bit of information, as long as they weren't mistreated in the process.

"I'm sure you're fatigued after so long on dragonback, Hundred," mul Gurthak went on after a moment. "Moreover, given the . . . unpleasant episode down by the dragonfield, I'm certain both your *shardonai* and Magister Kelbryan are rather anxious to discover just how well this debriefing went. With that in mind, I'll let you go find your own quarters and reassure them that no one at Fort Talon has any intention of changing their status or attempting to remove them from your custody."

"Thank you, Sir."

Jasak recognized his dismissal and stood, although leaving that office at that particular moment was the last thing he wanted to do. Unfortunately, whoever his father might be, Jasak was only a commander of one hundred. There was no way he could insist upon remaining for the additional discussion he knew was about to begin.

"Chief Sword, Javelin, you're also dismissed," the two thousand continued. "Hundred Neshok will see to it that you're quartered."

Threbuch and Iggy Shulthan braced briefly to attention, then turned and followed Jasak and Neshok out of the office.

The sound of the door closing behind them wasn't really a thunder-crack of doom . . . it only sounded that way to Jasak.

CHAPTER
THIRTY-NINE

THE MAN WHO thought of himself as Nith *vos* Gurthak only
when he was totally alone, watched the door close behind Sir
Jasak Olderhan and his noncommissioned officers, then swiveled his
eyes slowly across Rithmar Skirvon and Uthik Dastiri.

"A passionate young fellow, Hundred Olderhan," the commander
of two thousand observed with a thin smile.

"No doubt," Skirvon said. "But he seems to know his job. After
the initial contact blew up in his face that way, he did very well
indeed, in my opinion. It's a pity he wasn't still in command when
the Sharonians hit our base camp."

"Indeed it is," mul Gurthak agreed. *And for more reasons than you
can possibly know*, he added silently. "However, I'm afraid he may
have allowed himself to get a bit too close to his prisoners since
then. He's obviously very protective of them, and I'm not convinced
they aren't using that against him."

"Playing on his sympathy to convince him of how saintly their
own people are, you mean?"

"Something like that. And quite possibly the reverse, you know."
Mul Gurthak tipped back in his chair once more. "If they can convince us they have a truly unified, militarily powerful culture when
they really don't, we may end up grossly overestimating the amount
of combat power they could commit to any shooting war. I can certainly see how they might think that inspiring . . . excessive caution,
shall we say, on our part could be very useful to their side."

"That's true enough, Sir," Dastiri said. "At the same time, though,
aren't we effectively constrained to assume the worst, anyway?"

"To an extent, Master Dastiri," mul Gurthak said. He and Skirvon
exchanged a glance Dastiri didn't notice, and the commander of two

thousand continued. "The problem is that as we all just agreed during our conversation with Hundred Olderhan, nobody back home in New Arcana has any hint of what's going on out here. They won't for a long time, either, and once they *do* find out, it's going to take even more time for them to get any instructions out here for our guidance. Which means that, as the senior local commander, *I* have to decide what to do about these people."

"Without instructions from Parliament or the Commandery?" Dastiri looked horrified, and mul Gurthak raised one hand, palm uppermost, in an eloquent gesture of fatalism.

"We're at the pointy end of an incredibly long transit chain," he pointed out. "The nearest sliderhead is twenty thousand miles from here, and this chain hasn't exactly been packed to the heavens with combat power." Mul Gurthak chuckled sourly. "If it had been, there'd be someone far senior to a mere two thousand in command out here. Under those circumstances, I don't have any choice but to act on my own initiative while praying that I get comprehensive instructions as quickly as possible."

"That's certainly true," Skirvon said, his expression thoughtful. "Under the circumstances, as you say, and given that there have already been at least two military clashes, I think there's no question but that the decisionmaking authority has to rest with you, as the senior military officer. How can Uthik and I help?"

"Hundred Olderhan's entirely correct in his belief that we need to get diplomats involved in this as soon as possible," mul Gurthak replied. "Obviously, the best solution would be a peaceful, diplomatic one, with no more deaths on either side. Failing that, however, we need to at least keep these people talking long enough for me to assemble what forces are available to me."

"Excuse me, Two Thousand," Dastiri said, "but didn't you just say there *weren't* very many forces available to you?"

The younger diplomat, mul Gurthak reflected, had that annoying Ransaran habit of asking questions whether or not their answers were any of his business. Still, the man had been partnered with Skirvon for almost a year now, which said a lot. Obviously, Dastiri wasn't *too* Ransaran in his attitudes, so mul Gurthak might as well be polite.

"What I said was that the chain hadn't been packed with combat power, Master Dastiri," he corrected in as pleasant a tone as possible. "That doesn't mean there aren't a lot of individual Army battalions and Air Force combat and transport strikes scattered around it. As soon as I got Klian's initial dispatch, I sent out orders for as many of those scattered units as possible to report to me here, at Fort Talon, as quickly as transport can be arranged. The first few infantry companies have already arrived. Others are on their way, and they're bringing more transport dragons—and cargo pods—with them as they come in."

"I see." Skirvon studied the commander of two thousand's expression thoughtfully. His own professional diplomat's expression was almost impossible to read, but, then, mul Gurthak didn't *have* to read it to know exactly what was going on behind it.

"How confident do you feel about your ability to hold against a serious attack, Two Thousand?" the civilian asked after a moment.

"That's difficult to say." Mul Gurthak rocked his chair gently from side to side, his lips pursed in thought. "I suppose it depends on a lot of factors. As I pointed out to Hundred Olderhan, the other side has the advantage in terms of communications speed, given these Voices of theirs, and any strategist could tell you how huge an advantage that constitutes. But *we* have the advantage in terms of tactical and strategic movement speeds, and that's just as big an advantage. Remember, gentlemen, these people not only don't have magic—assuming our prisoners are, in fact, telling us the truth—but they also don't have dragons. And if they don't, then they can't begin to imagine how rapidly we can transport military forces across even totally unimproved terrain.

"As for these weapons of theirs, I'm entirely prepared to admit that they appear to be powerful and dangerous. But the real reason Thalmayr managed to get himself captured or killed, and all of Hundred Olderhan's company along with him, was the simple fact that unlike us, they can fire artillery through a portal. In a straight-up firefight in the open, between his infantry and field-dragons and their artillery, I strongly suspect that Thalmayr would have massacred them. What happened to him was, in the final analysis, the result of a totally unanticipated tactical advantage of the other side.

"We know, now, that they can do that. It won't be a surprise next time—assuming, of course, that there *is* a next time. They, on the other hand, have yet to see what our weapons can really do. And if they're truly as ignorant about magic and arcane technology as they seem, they're in for a whole series of equally nasty surprises of their own."

"Forgive me, Two Thousand," Dastiri said, "but it sounds to me as if you think there *will* be a next time."

"I'm a soldier, Master Dastiri," mul Gurthak replied, just a bit more frostily. "It's my job to think in worst-case scenarios. And it's also my job to have the forces under my command as advantageously positioned as possible to meet any contingency. Obviously, no one wants a war. But if we have one on our hands, anyway, it's my responsibility to see to it that *we* win the opening engagements."

"Quite so," Skirvon murmured. "And there's another point to consider, as well. If Magister Kelbryan and Magister Halathyn are correct, if this really is a genuine cluster of portals in close proximity to one another, it would scarcely be in the Union's best interests to leave a demonstrably hostile power in control of it. I expect they probably feel the same way about us, too. Which means," he glanced at his civilian subordinate, "that it's our job to convince them to see it our way, Uthik. And if Two Thousand mul Gurthak can provide us with a significant force advantage, it will strengthen our bargaining position substantially."

"Precisely," mul Gurthak agreed, nodding vigorously. "Whether we want a war or not, there are a huge number of reasons for us to position ourselves to be ready to fight if we have to, and no reason not to."

"Unless they decide we're threatening them, Sir," Dastiri pointed out respectfully. "Or unless we're wrong about how quickly they can bring up forces of their own, after all."

"There's no reason why they should feel the least bit threatened, Master Dastiri." Mul Gurthak made himself smile again. "The logical staging point for any deployment against this cluster would be Fort Rycharn. That's over seven hundred miles from the swamp portal, and unlike us, these people don't have any aerial reconnaissance capability. If we move in enough troops and transport dragons, we'll have the flexibility to conduct a mobile defense against any invasion attempt they might decide to mount, or to execute a lightning offensive of our own, if that should prove necessary. Our aerial units could be right on top of them before they even had a clue we were in the same universe with them."

Dastiri's eyes had widened slightly as he listened to the two thousand. Now he looked at his civilian colleague, and his eyes were dark with speculation. He sat that way for a moment or two, then turned back to mul Gurthak.

"I think I understand, Two Thousand," he said, and let his eyes drop briefly—significantly—to the PC in Skirvon's lap, still operating in recording mode. "You're right, of course, that no one wants this thing to escalate any farther than it already has. I'm sure Rithmar and I will both do our best to see to it that it doesn't. But it clearly is your responsibility to prepare for the possibility that we'll fail."

"Exactly." Mul Gurthak smiled at Dastiri yet again—rather more warmly, this time—then glanced at the digital time display on the corner of his desk.

"I see it's approaching time for supper, gentlemen, and I still have a few administrative chores to deal with this evening," he observed. "I suggest we adjourn this meeting until after everyone's eaten."

"Of course." Skirvon nodded and deactivated his PC.

Dastiri stood, then paused as he realized Skirvon had made no move to climb out of *his* chair. He glanced back and forth between his civilian superior and the military officer still sitting behind the desk, and, for just a moment, he seemed to hover on the edge of saying something more. But then he gave his head a little shake, bestowed a half-bow upon mul Gurthak, and smiled at Skirvon.

"I have a couple of minor errands of my own I need to deal with before supper, Rithmar," he said easily. "I'll see you then, shall I?"

"Of course, Uthik," Skirvon said, and watched the other man walk out of mul Gurthak's office and close the door behind him.

"So, what do you really think of Olderhan?" mul Gurthak asked the diplomat as soon as the latch clicked.

"An ardent and reasonably intelligent young officer," Skirvon replied. "I'm not prepared to evaluate his military capability, beyond what I've already said—I'll defer to your judgment, in that area—but he's obviously observant, and he's done surprisingly well not just in extracting information from these people, but in developing insights into them, as well. Into how they organize themselves, how they think."

"But—?" mul Gurthak prompted when the diplomat paused.

"As you say, 'but.'" Skirvon sat back in his chair and rested his elbows on the armrests. "He'll probably make a good Andaran duke, one day, but he really doesn't understand diplomacy."

The two men smiled thinly at one another. Skirvon might be of Andaran descent, but his family had been Hilmaran for centuries, and there was still that lingering tradition of hostility between Hilmarans and the northern kingdoms which had once conquered and ruled so much of their continent. The diplomat didn't much care for any Andarans, and particularly not for the Duke of Garth Showma, the most powerful of them all. Most people didn't realize that, largely because Skirvon *was* of Andaran descent himself, on his mother's side. But mul Gurthak and his . . . associates had been aware of the man's true leanings for quite some time.

Then Skirvon's expression sobered.

"Quite aside from any other considerations," he said, "young Olderhan doesn't seem to realize that there's only a vanishingly small chance of averting war with these Sharonians. I suppose he has a powerful motivation to find one before still more people get killed, but there honestly wasn't much hope of that even before his own discovery about the things they can do with their minds. Given what we know about them now, about what they are, I'd say the chances of avoiding war are virtually nonexistent. As a Mythalan, you'll appreciate better than many how this news will play at home."

"An entire universe filled with people—*non-Gifted* people—who read minds and turn thoughts into weapons?" mul Gurthak snorted. "The *shakira* lords will *froth*."

"Precisely." Their eyes met, and then Skirvon shrugged. "It's clear Olderhan believes his prisoners are honest and decent people. And they may very well be. On a person-to-person basis, justice and fair play and equality with others are concepts most of us value, after all, particularly as applied to ourselves."

His smile was so tart it could have soured milk, and mul Gurthak snorted a chuckle. "Fair play" and "equality with others" were nasty habits indulged in by dangerously unstable and degenerate societies. Societies whose chaotic habits were a serious threat to the properly regulated, orderly political and religious structure that kept the world in its proper alignment. Not to mention keeping the *shakira* lords precisely where they belonged: in charge, at the top of a very steep and very narrow ladder of power.

It was so very fortunate that Rithmar Skirvon had been the closest senior diplomat available when this entire catastrophe began to unravel. Of course, there'd been a reason mul Gurthak had requested Skirvon for the arbitration assignment with which he'd been dealing when Klian's first reports arrived. Men who understood the realities of diplomacy—and also where their own best interests lay—were always useful.

"How . . . pragmatic do you think your young friend Dastiri is going to be about this?" the two thousand asked after a moment.

"Well, he *is* Ransaran," Skirvon observed with a slight grimace. "On the other hand, he prides himself on being a realist. And he's from Manisthu."

"Ah." Mul Gurthak nodded.

The Kingdom of Manisthu dominated the Manisthu Islands off the eastern coast of Ransar. They'd retreated into a self-imposed isolation for several centuries at one point in their history, and even today, they remained somewhat out of step with the rest of Ransar. They were just as irritatingly insistent on individual rights—especially their *own* individual rights—but they also labored under a sense of being looked down upon by their mainland neighbors. Of being considered rubes, without quite the same degree of sophistication and philosophical superiority to all those other, more backward, irritating, non-Ransaran people the gods had unfortunately and thoughtlessly scattered around the globe. Perhaps as a result, Manisthuans had a pre-Union historical tradition of practicing *garsulthan*, a Manisthuan word which translated roughly as "real politics." On more than one occasion, they'd proven as pragmatic—and at least as ruthless—in international affairs as any Andaran warlord or Mythalan caste-lord.

Mul Gurthak and Skirvon gazed at one another for several moments, while the two thousand considered the implications of what the diplomat had just said. Then Skirvon cocked his head to one side.

"How do you really want us to play this?" he asked, getting down to serious business at last.

"That's the difficult question, isn't it?" Mul Gurthak frowned thoughtfully, toying with an antique dagger he used as a paperweight. Not many people would have recognized it as a Mythalan *rankadi* knife. More modern *rankadi* knives were far simpler and more utilitarian. "There's no way the *shakira* lords are going to support some sort of 'peaceful coexistence' with these people, whatever those lunatic Ransarans want. I'm not sure where the Andarans are going to come down, though. If it weren't for the fact that Garth Showma's son is right in the middle of this, I'd expect them to be closer to agreement with us, for a change. As it is, I think it's going to depend on how the story plays out in public opinion back home.

"For the moment, we really do need to keep a lid on this situation, at least until we can completely redeploy our own forces. And we also need someone who's a bit older and wiser—maybe even a bit more cynical—" he smiled quickly at Skirvon, "to make a firsthand analysis of the other side. Someone not quite so blinded by the . . . intricacies of the Andaran honor code."

"I've always been considered a pretty fair analyst," Skirvon observed.

"Yes, I've heard that about you." Mul Gurthak smiled again, but his eyes were very serious as he continued. "Still, don't forget that you're dealing with a complete unknown here. These prisoners of Hundred Olderhan can insist all they want to that their people don't know anything at all about magic. *I'm* not going to take that as a given without some additional, *independent* confirmation."

"And if it turns out that they really *don't* know anything about magic?" Skirvon asked delicately.

"Why, in that eventuality," the two thousand half-drew the dagger, turning it to let the light gleam wickedly on its razor-sharp edge, "our menu of choices would change quite radically, wouldn't it?"

* * *

Mul Gurthak leaned back in his chair again, once more alone in his office, and grimaced at the ceiling.

Rithmar Skirvon was almost as smart as he thought he was, the two thousand reflected. But only almost. He'd been perfectly happy to enter into certain subsidiary business arrangements with various Mythalan financiers and banks, and he'd always held up his end of any arrangements. But by and large, he seemed to think money and *personal* power were all that were at stake. He knew he was involved with *shakira*, but he thought they were acting as individuals, in their own self-interest. He didn't have a clue about the bigger picture . . . which was fortunate for him. Men who knew too much about the Council of Twelve and its plans inevitably had accidents.

Which didn't do a thing to simplify mul Gurthak's present nasty situation.

The two thousand sighed. As he'd said to Skirvon, he couldn't begin to forecast how the Andarans were going to react to this. The Ransarans—aside from Dastiri's Manisthuans, perhaps—were far easier to predict. They'd want to *understand* these Sharonians, because Ransarans, for reasons only they could fully comprehend, wanted to understand everything and everyone. It was the second most maddening thing about them, after their obnoxious conviction that everyone else should agree with their mad notions about the total equality of everybody everywhere with everyone.

Mul Gurthak managed not to shudder at the thought only because he'd spent so many years dissembling. Ransaran democracies were just short of mentally aberrant, and their citizens—who were usually as vocal about their absurd beliefs as they were lunatic—frequently left him feeling queasy. He hadn't been at all distressed to learn that Magister Kelbryan had chosen to stay with the prisoners in order to reassure them.

That choice of hers told mul Gurthak everything he needed to know about Kelbryan's views on Jasak Olderhan's precious *shardonai*. It was scarcely a surprising position for her to take, given her pedigree and history, and if she wanted to spend time with them, so much the better. The woman represented one of the greatest public relations disasters in the history of Mythal, after all, not to mention a staggering affront to anything approaching decent behavior. And at least this way, he wouldn't have to clench his teeth against nausea while listening to her expound her thoughts about these Sharonians. If it should happen that she developed any genuine insights, they'd undoubtedly show up in Olderhan's reports, anyway, so he wasn't overly concerned about depriving himself of critical military intelligence.

The problem was that, aside from the regrettable power of her Gift, Kelbryan was *typical* of Ransarans, and there were a lot of them. An appalling number of them, as a matter of fact, when it came to seats in the Union Parliament. Unlike Mythal, which was experiencing a steady decline in population, thanks to the current massive *garthan* exodus (which had the caste-lords howling in outrage and threatening to impose emigration quotas—as if the Accords would have permitted them to do any such thing), the Ransaran population on Arcana Prime was growing steadily. Not just in absolute terms, but as a percentage of the total planetary population, as well.

Despite their much vaunted individualism and the depressing technological advantages it had given them, however, Ransarans as a group tended not to relocate as much as other Arcanans. In part, that was simply because they preferred the creature comforts of home. Given the almost universally high standard of living amongst Ransarans, higher than that of any other group in the Union, outside a few dozen *shakira* ruling families, Ransarans simply preferred to stay home.

Roughing it in a cabin in the wilderness, with no hospitals, no universities, no theaters or museums, no banks or stock exchanges, and no shopping emporia stuffed with luxury goods from every Arcanan universe, was simply too crude for most self-respecting Ransarans. That was one Ransaran attitude mul Gurthak understood perfectly. *He* missed the comforts of home, as well. Bitterly, at times.

But sacrifices had to be made. That was a concept he'd embraced long ago, although it clearly continued to elude most Ransarans. Of course, one of these fine days, those same Ransarans would wake up to discover that a few *changes* had been made. Nith mul Gurthak took great personal satisfaction in being part of the mechanism which would make that moment inevitable.

The world would be a far safer—and vastly more stable—place when that day finally came, but that wasn't something he could discuss even with Skirvon. He had allies, to be sure, and the diplomat was one of them. But Skirvon wasn't part of the inner circle, and never would be, for the simple reason that however *useful* he might be, he wasn't Mythalan.

Mul Gurthak grimaced again at that thought, then pushed his chair back and stood, reviewing the string of unutterably bad news he'd received over the past few weeks. One hand clenched itself around his belt dagger's hilt, and he managed—somehow—not to swear. This whole nasty business had thrown a serious spanner into a very delicate piece of machinery, and he had so many piles of pieces to pick up that he hardly knew where to start. He could perceive—imperfectly, as yet, but perceive—certain strands of opportunity running through the chaos which had engulfed so many years of effort. But even the best of those opportunities were problematical, and it had taken all of his formidable self-control not to curse out loud during the past few hours.

Dissembling was a game which had long since palled. He'd grown weary of presenting a calm and measured face to the world, hiding his true opinions in order to accomplish his mission. But it had never been as difficult as it had while he listened to Olderhan—*Olderhan*, of all people—spouting his goodness-and-light interpretation of the current situation. He'd *needed* to curse someone, starting with the incomparably incompetent Shevan Garlath and ending with the *next* problem on his list.

He glowered out his office window at the rapidly settling evening and reached a decision. Then he turned his back on the dusk and his eyes hardened as he looked down at the antique *rankadi* knife on his desk. *That* problem he could safely vent spleen on to his heart's content, he decided. And by all the gods of his grandfathers' fathers, the stupid little bastard had earned every ounce of spleen mul Gurthak intended to vent.

He opened his office door and looked at his clerk.

"Send someone to the brig. I want to see Bok vos Hoven."

"Yes, Sir." The clerk snapped a salute and stepped out to arrange for the brig's sole occupant to be escorted to the commandant's office. Eight minutes later, there was a tap at mul Gurthak's door.

"Come!" he called, and the door opened six inches.

"The prisoner and escort have arrived, Sir."

"Good. Have the escort wait in your office, but send the prisoner in."

"Yes, Sir."

The clerk disappeared again, briefly, and Nith mul Gurthak reseated himself behind the desk and assumed the stern guise of a thoroughly disgruntled *shakira* caste-lord. A moment later, the door opened once more to admit a single person.

Bok vos Hoven was all starch and swagger as he entered. Clearly, he was confident mul Gurthak would get him out of the trouble he'd gotten himself into, and the two thousand shook his head mentally. *This* was what the caste was coming to?

The clerk closed the door with a sharp click. Vos Hoven smiled and started to step closer to mul Gurthak's desk, then paused. His smile seemed to falter as mul Gurthak simply sat staring at him through narrow eyes and said nothing at all. The younger *shakira* looked around, uncertainly, and mul Gurthak waited until the first few beads of sweat appeared on his forehead.

"Would you kindly explain," the two thousand said then, suddenly, coldly, chopping the first hole in the icy silence he'd so carefully built, "which variety of dragon shit you use for brains?"

"Sir?" Vos Hoven's eyes shot wide in shock, and fury exploded through mul Gurthak. It was the depth and genuineness of the swaggering jackass's confusion that did it. Did the blundering idiot expect mul Gurthak to *congratulate* him for his conduct?

Pure rage jerked the two thousand explosively out of his chair. He snapped to his feet and slammed both fists against his desktop.

"*Imbecile!*" he snarled. "How *dare* you risk everything we've accomplished for your *petty personal convenience?*"

The prisoner stumbled backward, almost falling as he flinched from mul Gurthak's wrath.

"Mightiest Lord," vos Hoven whispered in Mythalan, using the form of address the most groveling supplicant used to address the highest caste-lord of his birth line, "how have I erred so grievously? I thought—"

"You *thought?*" Mul Gurthak hissed. He stepped around his desk and snatched vos Hoven up onto his toes by the front of his suddenly sweat-stained uniform blouse. "If you'd *thought*, you wouldn't be chained and awaiting trial! Did you honestly think I'd lift a fingernail to save you? When you've proven yourself to be the stupidest fool ever born in Mythal?"

He released the fool in question with explosive energy, shoving him away, and vos Hoven went to his knees, shaking. Weeping. Mul Gurthak glared at him, then slapped him hard enough to send him sprawling all the way to the floor.

"You're so proud and conceited you can't even *grovel* properly!" the two thousand grated. "A man in your shoes should be on his belly begging not to be ordered to commit *rankadi!*"

The words struck home—and finally pierced the armor of vos Hoven's inflated self-worth. He went rigid for a long, horrified instant, then rolled onto his belly, where he belonged, moaning and covering his head with his chained hands to hide his shame.

"Better!" mul Gurthak hissed.

"M-may I plead with My Lord?" Vos Hoven's voice quivered with the tremors running through him.

"Plead for what? Your miserable life?"

"N-no, Mightiest Lord. That is yours, to end, if you demand it," vos Hoven whispered, then gulped and waited.

"It's good to see that at least a few basic facts continue to rattle around inside that empty skull of yours. What do you plead for?"

"Understanding. I have failed the caste, and I don't know *how!*"

There was genuine anguish in that confused cry—the anguish of a spoiled, selfish child taught poorly by careless, empty-headed adults. A child now caught in the jaws of a genuinely vicious trap. If he could see and admit that he'd erred without knowing how, there might—just might—be some hope of salvaging something from the ruins.

"What fool raised you?"

Vos Hoven cringed under the withering scorn of that question. There was no more profound insult than to openly denigrate a Mythalan's family line. In the world of the *shakira*, there was nothing more important than family line. The family determined one's position in the caste, just as the caste determined one's position in the world of men and the realms of the gods. Without caste, a man was nothing to the gods. Without family line, a man was nothing to the caste. To be born of a line of fools was to serve the forces of chaos . . . and to well deserve one's inevitable divine destruction.

Mul Gurthak listened to the desperate weeping of the man whose place in the eternal cosmos he'd just ripped so totally and unexpectedly into shreds. The two thousand felt no pity at all. Mithanan's bollocks! That terrible deity, God of cosmic destruction, would wreak vengeance on the entire caste for the utter *idiocy* of this worm at his feet. Such awe-inspiring stupidity was beyond belief.

"Please, Mightiest Lord," vos Hoven cringed, "will you not instruct me? How have I sinned? How have my teachers failed me and caused me to fail the caste?"

Mul Gurthak paced thoughtfully around the creature on his office floor, trying to decide how best to go about attempting to salvage something out of it.

"Explain the purpose of the *garthan*," he commanded finally, and for just a moment, vos Hoven lifted his face off the floor, staring up at him in total confusion.

"My Lord?" he said, and mul Gurthak reached for patience.

"What is the purpose of the *garthan*?" he repeated. "Of their entire caste?"

"To serve the *shakira*," the prisoner managed to get out as he pressed his face back where it belonged: on the floor.

"To serve the *shakira*?" Mul Gurthak glowered down at the prostrate body. "How?"

"As our slaves." Vos Hoven's voice was low, tentative. Obviously he wondered why he was being taken through this basic nursery school catechism. "To do whatever we demand."

"Fools." Mul Gurthak shook his head almost pityingly. "Triple-cursed fools have had the raising and teaching of you."

"B-but . . . why are they fools?"

"*Garthan* exist to make it possible for the *shakira* to carry out the most critical work in the cosmos: the study and mastery of magic. To understand magic, at all its levels, in all its nuances, is to touch the minds of the gods themselves. To gain admittance into the Divine's sacred presence. To bring one's *yurha* to a point of growth worthy of Divine notice, as a first step toward achieving oneness with the Divine.

"If the *shakira* had to plow the ground and grow food out of it, if *shakira* had to weave cloth and cook and raise the cattle that provide leather for shoes, if *shakira* had to haul the freight and clean the latrines, no one in all of Arcana would understand magic. No one would be able to use magic. It was Mythal that tapped the Divine spirit and won the Gifts for the human race. It was Mythal that set down the laws of magic, mapped the dimensions of magic, discovered what magic could do when properly harnessed. It was *Mythal* that built Arcanan civilization, spell by spell, and Mythal did it through the *shakira* caste's tireless efforts across millennia of study.

"But none of that would have been possible without the *garthan*. Without the magicless masses—unwashed, untutored, unlettered, inferior in every possible sense of the word. Yet without them, Arcana—and the glories of Arcanan civilization—would be nothing more than a collection of illiterate laborers and herders. *That* is the purpose of the *garthan*. That is their *sole* purpose. They don't exist to polish your boots and pop the zits on your worthless arse because you're too godsdamned lazy to do it yourself!"

Vos Hoven flinched under the whiplash of that caustic voice, and mul Gurthak snorted harshly.

"Next question. What does caste law say of the man who beats his children in a public place?"

"The Law Giver's holy command is that such a man be punished by his caste-lord in kind, for the disciplining of children is a private matter, to be carried out in the domain of the family line, the privacy of the home. To beat children in public shows lack of judgment, lack of patience, and lack of sufficiently wise instruction of the young entrusted to the family line. These things bring shame to the family line and to the caste."

He was parroting the words by rote, without the slightest understanding of their meaning, mul Gurthak thought disgustedly.

"Under caste law—*true* caste law, not the bastardized, compromised version forced upon Mythal when the Union formed—what were a family's *garthan*?"

"Its property."

"A narrow reading. Give me the ancient reading of that law—its *full* meaning."

Mul Gurthak could practically see vos Hoven's mind searching through the texts memorized by rote, repeated recitations spanning one's entire childhood.

"The oldest text I have heard mentioned, although I was never shown a copy of it, Mightiest Lord, mentioned *garthan* as our ... children. . . ."

Vos Hoven's voice trailed off, and he gulped.

"But I didn't discipline the *garthan* in public!" he protested. "I was careful to do it in private! Away from the eyes of others."

"And that is precisely why you are a fool!" mul Gurthak hissed. "Because you understand *nothing*. You can parrot back the words, but your brain is full of sand and your *yurha* is as devoid of understanding as the gulfs between the stars. The words have no meaning in your emptiness, and so you make mistakes—stupid mistakes. *Costly* ones. Mithanan's balls, do you have *any* idea of the cost of this mistake? Out here, outside the borders of the homeland, we are all under scrutiny—we are all *in public*, fool! Is it so impossible for you to understand that there *is* no privacy? Now, because of what you've done, every Andaran officer will watch every *shakira* in uniform, looking for evidence of *garthan* abuse! And what will any evidence of the 'abuse' of *garthan* do? It will taint *all* of us. It will cause these honorbound Andarans to watch our every move. And what will that do to the cause you and I are here to serve? What will that do to *our mission*?"

The prisoner whimpered, and mul Gurthak sneered.

"Oh, you see it now, do you? A *shakira* who's watched too closely can't function as we need him to function, can't acquire the seniority we need. You've jeopardized everything the Council of Twelve has spent the last *thirty years* putting into place. Our whole timetable must come to a screeching halt while we try to make certain that no one's stumbled across what we're doing because of the way *you've* made all of them look so much more closely at all of us. I'll have to send messages, you utter, cursed moron, warning others to stop. To lie low. Messages that will put *me* at risk of exposure!"

Vos Hoven trembled violently, whimpering once more. Mul Gurthak was so angry he wanted to kick the idiot's ribs until something broke, but he couldn't—not without risking even more probing questions than vos Hoven had already set in motion. Yet his fury was too great not to do *something*, so he crouched beside the other *shakira*, seized his hair, jerked his head up off the floor by the long braids. Dark eyes rolled in abject terror, and mul Gurthak leaned close to hiss into his face.

"I've worked too hard, swallowed too many insults from socially and spiritually inferior louts, to attain my present position. I've gone without too many creature comforts to see everything I've struggled to achieve come crashing down in ruins. And why is it falling apart? Because you used your fists to bruise a *garthan* for not licking the mud off your feet! I should feed your worthless carcass to the *dragons*."

Vos Hoven shuddered violently. No court in Arcana had actually ordered that court-martialed soldiers or other prisoners be fed to dragons in the last two centuries. But the actual law had never been repealed, and there were a handful of *shakira* lords in Mythal who *did* still feed the damned to their dragons. In strict and careful privacy, of course . . .

Mul Gurthak straightened, letting let the stupid worm stew in his own juices for long, silent moments, and the stink of vos Hoven's sweat was sharp and foul, the smell of terror.

"I had plans for you," the two thousand said at last, coldly. "Plans that must now be scrapped. Why do you think I transferred you to Jasak Olderhan's company in the first place? Or is your memory so short you've already forgotten the private mission I assigned you to carry out?"

"Mightiest Lord, I-I tried! But I couldn't. He never comes right out and says it, but he hates us—hates *shakira*. You should have seen him fawning over that *garthan*. Praising him—recommending him for promotions. But he hated the rest of us Mythalans, the *shakira* in the Company. He shunned and loathed us. You could see it in his eyes whenever he looked at us."

"He hated *shakira*?" mul Gurthak asked softly. "Even Halathyn vos Dulainah?"

"Vos Dulainah," vos Hoven all but spat the dead magister's name, "was a filthy traitor. He abandoned his caste, even his wife and son. Yes, Olderhan doted on the old man. And why? Precisely *because* vos Dulainah had shunned and betrayed the rest of us. The rest of the *shakira*."

"So you say he treated the *shakira* in his company badly?" Mul Gurthak glared sternly at vos Hoven. "Be certain of your answer, fool. If you lie, I'll know, and I do not tolerate lies from a subordinate. Not in my command, and not in my caste."

Vos Hoven gulped. For several seconds, he kept his face pressed firmly into the floor, silent. But then, finally, he answered in a low, reluctant voice.

"No. He didn't treat us badly. If a *shakira* kowtowed and obeyed like a good little *garthan*, Olderhan treated him like anyone else. It was a double insult. First he demanded that we act like *garthan*, and when we did, he treated us *equally*, as if *he* were just as good as we."

Mul Gurthak was genuinely appalled.

"How in Mithanan's name did someone with your awe-inspiring stupidity get chosen for the great cause?" he demanded.

"My family line is one of the oldest and greatest in Mythal." Pride had crept back into vos Hoven's voice, despite his plight. "My mother's brother is a caste-lord. My father's father is a caste-lord. That's two caste-lords in the near-kin family!"

Nepotism. Mul Gurthak wanted to rend something—preferably Bok vos Hoven—into very small, bleeding pieces. This fool had been sent out on a mission that called for guile and dissimulation, the acting skills of a professional stage player, not because he was *fit* for it, but because his relatives were politically powerful!

"So you're superior to Olderhan, are you?"

"Of course I am!"

"Did it never occur to you that you'd joined the *Army*? That in an army, officers give orders to men of lower military rank—regardless of their respective birth ranks? That you are required to give your commanding officer your respect, your instant obedience, be he ever so low-born? Even if that man were a *garthan* from your own family's fields, you would still be required to obey him and show him respect!"

"*Never!*" vos Hoven gasped, fiery rebellion burning in his eyes, and mul Gurthak slapped him. Jerked his head up off the floor and slammed a backhanded blow across his mouth.

"Silence!"

Rebellion fled. Vos Hoven stared wide-eyed at mul Gurthak, unable to believe even now that he'd just been struck.

"You were supposed to get close to Olderhan. To win his confidence, his trust. To learn things from him—about his father. Things we can't find out any other way. To become the one who could deliver him to us at the proper time, in the proper place. You say he didn't trust you, but he doted on vos Dulainah. Did it never occur to you that the way to win his confidence would be to act the way vos Dulainah did? To mimic his attitudes, his professed beliefs? No matter what you really felt about them?

"No, it didn't, did it? And because you were too infernally stupid to use the means at your disposal, we've now lost all hope of getting anyone close to him. Not just because he's going back to New Arcana, where it would be difficult to get close to him under the best of circumstances, but because you've made him doubly wary of us. Do think he'll trust *any* Mythalan now?"

Vos Hoven tried to make himself as small as possible while mul Gurthak glared down at him, still looking for some way to salvage something.

Garth Showma was the key, the linchpin of Andaran political power. If Garth Showma could be brought down, it would be far easier to pick off the other Andaran noble houses, and that had to be done. Parliament trusted the Andaran aristocracy to run the military for it, because Andarans were good at it. Because they liked to do it, and everyone knew they were sufficiently honorbound to be worthy of others' trust.

Which meant that the only way to replace the Andaran military leaders was to destroy that faith in them. The Council of Twelve had spent thirty-plus long, patient years getting *shakira* officers into the field army, where they could work their way up the command-grade ranks. The plan remained some years short of fruition, but the necessary cadre of highly ranked *shakira* officers, men with "Arcana's best interests" in mind, who had distanced themselves from the stereotypical *shakira* arrogance and cultural chauvinism by choosing to serve the mainstream of Arcanan society, would be ready when—*if*—the time came for them to step into the gap left by Andara's disgrace and take charge.

But for the plan to work, Andara had to *be* disgraced, starting with Garth Showma, and the imbecile on mul Gurthak's office floor had botched one of the most critical components of the entire plan. Jasak Olderhan had been supposed to be the chink in his father's armor. A source for useful information, true, but even more the tool who could be led into the carefully prepared trap with all the exquisitely devised "evidence" to prove to all of Arcana that the heir to the most powerful Andaran aristocrat of them all had disgraced himself through his gross violation of the honor code he and his fellow aristocrats were supposed to hold so dear.

But Olderhan was out of his reach, now. Out of *Mythal's* reach. It was entirely possible he would be cashiered over this business, but mul Gurthak had learned a great deal about the way the Andaran mind worked. Whatever happened to Jasak's military career, his fellow Andarans—and the critical members of Parliament—would recognize that his performance throughout had actually been exemplary. Klian's report already made it blindingly obvious that if Jasak's advice had been followed, the entire portal attack would never have happened.

That might not be enough to prevent him from being cashiered, but it would certainly prevent him from being *disgraced*. And if Jasak left the Army, he would have to find another career worthy of Garth Showma, which meant just one thing: politics. An Andaran might actually turn a disaster like being cashiered, despite having done all the right things, into a political asset, if he were clever enough. And if Jasak Olderhan wasn't, *Thankhar* Olderhan certainly was.

But what if it turned out that he *hadn't* done all the right things?

Nith mul Gurthak stood very still, thinking furiously.

If future conflict with these Sharonians was avoided, it would be obvious to almost anyone that a great deal of the credit for it went to Hundred Olderhan. After all, he would be the one who'd saved the lives of the two Sharonian prisoners—made them his own *shardonai*—who had provided the critical insight into who and what Sharona truly was. Not to mention the prisoners who had taught Arcanan diplomats how to speak the Sharonians' language.

But if future conflict *wasn't* avoided, then young Jasak would get no credit for preventing it and still have to face the consequences of having *started* it. And if it turned out that it had all started out of his own incompetence or cowardice, and that he'd then falsified his report, knowing it couldn't be challenged because every man of his company had been killed or captured by the enemy as a direct *consequence* of his incompetence while he himself was safe in the protection of Fort Rycharn ...

It wouldn't be easy to sell, but it wouldn't be impossible, either. Not with the proper groundwork, and not with the elimination of so many witnesses who might have corroborated Olderhan's version of what had happened. There were only three survivors from the company, beside vos Hoven and Olderhan himself, and if they couldn't be suborned, there was always the possibility of securing obedience by taking hostages. That had worked often enough in the past. Or they could simply be eliminated. Klian would have to go, too, of course. But with *all* of them gone . . .

Mul Gurthak drew in several breaths, then, finally, looked back down at the chained *shakira* on his office floor.

"All right, there may be one way out of this mess you've made. Listen *closely*, do you understand me? Because if you bungle this, I will personally hunt you down, put the *rankadi* knife in your hands, and watch you cut your own throat with it. Have I made myself perfectly clear on that point?"

"Y-yes, Mightiest Lord."

"Good. See that you remember, because you're not going to enjoy this process. I don't give a rat's ass about that, either, do you understand me? You'll do exactly what I tell you. You'll swallow the stigma, the shame, and the punishments you've earned, and in the end, you may well fail anyway. But if you succeed, I won't issue the order to commit *rankadi*. That's the only bargain you'll get; is it one you can live with, or shall I hand you the knife right now?"

Vos Hoven lay trembling under the two thousand's cold, implacable stare for a small eternity. Then, finally, he gulped and nodded convulsively.

"Yes, Mightiest Lord," he whispered. "I understand."

"Good!" mul Gurthak repeated. "Now shut up, and for once in your worthless life, *listen!*"

CHAPTER
FORTY

ZINDEL CHAN CALIRATH's head ached.

So did his back. And after twelve murderous hours in the instrument of torture some sadistic furniture joiner had managed to pass off as a chair, his backside had gone from aching to screaming to numb, with occasional needles and pins that ran down the backs of both thighs.

Whoever designed these chairs should be shot, he groused. *Or chained to one of them for a month or two.*

His mood, he thought, wouldn't have been quite so sour if his fellow world rulers hadn't been so utterly, pigheadedly, invincibly, *blissfully* parochial. All their insufferable demands, excuses, obstructionist arguments, and refusals to simply get the job done were driving him rapidly mad. They needed to suck down their petty personal concerns and vote in a government—even a *temporary* one—so they could get on with the urgent business of preparing Sharona for war.

Didn't *anyone* see the dire risks they all faced?

It took time to gear up for a military campaign—especially one of this magnitude. No Sharonian nation had ever fought a war that stretched across multiple universes. The logistics problems alone would be the stuff of nightmares. This Conclave needed to be thrashing through that, not arguing over who would have the right to install traffic signs and draw school zones in local towns and villages.

When the Limathian prince regent stood up and started demanding that any planetary governing authority must have the power to grant guarantees on deep-sea fishing rights, something snapped inside Zindel. It jerked him to his feet. Sent his fists crashing down upon his delegation's table in the vast Emperor Garim Chancellery which had been chosen as the Conclave's initial meeting site.

"Mr. Director! Ternathia lodges a formal protest!"

The prince regent's mouth fell open. Every head in the chamber swiveled, like so many marionettes on strings, as their owners stared at him. Orrin Limana, visibly drooping against the presiding officer's lectern after twelve hours on his feet, straightened abruptly.

"Emperor Zindel," he said crisply, "what is the nature of your protest?"

"Mr. Director, I protest the utter waste of our time into which shortsighted members of this Conclave are forcing us! This is the second day we've met. We sat here for fourteen hours yesterday. We've been sitting here for twelve and a half *more* hours today, and we've decided exactly *nothing*. Not one, solitary, blessed thing! The troop movements arranged unilaterally by Emperor Chava and myself, with your cooperation, are the *only* military preparations anyone outside the Portal Authority has managed to carry out, even though three *weeks* have passed since the attack on our survey crew."

He glowered around the huge, marble chancellery's gorgeous precincts, as if daring any person present to dispute what he'd just said.

"This Conclave has one purpose. Just *one*. We aren't here to decide where to put traffic signs. We aren't here to decide which school our children should attend. While we sit here bickering over inconsequential trivia, Sharonian men and women—Sharonian *children*—are in mortal danger.

"We have colonies—not just forts with garrisons of soldiers, but *colonies*—within four transits of New Uromath, and by my conservative count, there are no fewer than twenty-three survey crews in that region. The Chalgyn Consortium crew was less than two days away from a portal fort, yet every member of it was massacred. Ternathia's Third Dragoons are *en route* to Fort Salby, but they won't arrive there for more than another full month, although Uromathia's cavalry regiments, fortunately, will reach Salby in two weeks, and the remaining divisions of Fifth Corps will entrain over the next several weeks.

"I'm sure we're all relieved to know troops are moving towards the front. But those troops are *all* we have moving towards the threat, and it's another *five thousand miles* from Salby to New Uromath," he said grimly. "It will take them almost a month and a half just to reach Salby, and then *another* two and a half months to reach the front, and we have no idea what sort of attacks they may face along the way. No way of knowing what numbers of troops we'll *need* at the front. And *still* we haven't taken a single step towards organizing our planet for the sort of war we may face. Not one . . . *single* . . . step."

His voice echoed in a dead silence.

"It's obvious the other side knows about multiple universes and portals, since Company-Captain chan Tesh found them camped right in the middle of one. I shouldn't have to point out that we have no idea how large their territory is, how many universes they've already occupied. How *long* have these people known about portals? How many universes have they explored? How many have they colonized?

"How *big* are they?"

He paused again, sweeping them with his eyes before he resumed.

"We've been exploring for eighty years. That seems a long time, my friends, but it isn't. Not really. It certainly hasn't been long enough for us to build a large population base out there. Most of our colonies have been established in the last thirty or forty years, directly from Sharona. That leaves our out-universe populations stretched thin. We're strung out, like beads on a broken necklace, and *none* of our colonies have the manpower, out of their own resources, to hold against a powerful attack. None of them is capable of self-defense, yet there are far too many people living in them for evacuation to be a practical option even if we decided to pull them all back to Sharona.

"Our enemies *might* have just discovered portals in their backyard, but it's just as likely they've been exploring and colonizing for *centuries*. We could be facing a population two, or ten, or even a *hundred* times our size. Yes, the point of contact is forty thousand miles from here. Yes, the thought of someone being able to successfully project military power along an invasion route that long boggles the mind. But think about the troop movements rail lines and steamships make possible. We can get troops from here to Fort Salby, even allowing for water crossings, in less than two months. That's how long it took Captain-of-the-Army chan Baraeg to march an *infantry* army from the Bernith Channel to the Janu River *three thousand years ago*. Does anyone in this chamber wish to suggest that we haven't fought wars—terrible, destructive wars—over greater march distances and despite far greater logistical challenges than that?

"With modern transport, wars *can* be fought at distances that great. Never think they can't! I pray that we can avoid fighting any war at all, that diplomacy and sanity can still stop this situation from lurching into an all-out military confrontation with someone we know *nothing* about. But what if they can't? If diplomacy fails, we *do* have a war to fight, and however long it might take for that fighting to reach Sharona itself, it will sweep over our colonies far, far sooner unless *we* prevent that. Are we going to sit here, secure in the safe insulation of distance, and try to use this Conclave to settle long-standing, purely Sharonian problems while combat marches towards those colonies? Are the people who live there somehow less important than where we put our *traffic signs*?

"We have *lives* to save, godsdamn it! Do you honestly believe the mothers in the colonies closest to the people who've massacred an entire survey crew of civilians give a single solitary *damn* about who catches fish off the coast of Limathia? They're too busy wondering when their children will be shot down before their eyes, or burned to death in a fireball!"

He glared at them, and all of his frustration, anger, and driving need to save Sharonian lives, boiled up in a bullthroated challenge roar.

"We don't have *time* to argue about the godsdamned *fish*!"

Somebody in a high gallery behind him cheered. An instant later, what seemed like every gallery in the chancellery—and at least a third of the delegates on the chamber floor itself—had broken into thunderous applause. The Prince Regent of Limathia had gone crimson. Reporters were snapping photographs so fast the flash powder half-blinded Zindel, and Orem Limana wasn't even trying to gavel the crowd of spectators to order. He just stood there, watching it roar its approval, while a strange half-smile flickered across his face.

The tumult eventually wound down, and when Limana finally raised his hands for silence, the last of the applause died away. People settled back into their seats at last, but Zindel remained standing. Not only could he not abide the thought of sitting back down in that hateful chair, but he intended to *finish* this business.

"Emperor Zindel," the Portal Authority's First Director said into the restored silence, "thank you for lodging your protest. It is well taken—very well taken, indeed. If more Sharonian lives are lost because we fail to act swiftly enough, their blood will be on our hands, and no one else's."

"Will the Emperor yield?" another voice asked, half-lost in the enormous chamber, yet firm. Zindel turned his head until he saw the speaker, standing in the midst of the Shurkhali delegation.

"Master Chairman," the emperor said to Limana, "Ternathia yields temporarily, and without prejudice, to the Honorable Parliamentary Representative from Shurkhal."

"Representative Kinshe, you have the floor," Limana said, and actually managed to sound as if he had absolutely no idea what Halidar Kinshe was about to say.

"Your Majesty, I thank you," Kinshe said simply, then turned to face the rest of the assembled delegates.

"As Emperor Zindel has just so . . . eloquently pointed out, we've sat here today for twelve and a half hours—over twenty-six hours, in all—listening to what amounts to no more than opening remarks," he said into the ringing silence. "I suppose that's inevitable, to some extent. This is the greatest gathering of heads of state in Sharona's history. Of course every nation represented here has some problem, some dispute, some need which it wishes to place upon the record, and for which it wishes to seek resolution.

"Yet the fact is, that those very desires, and the very fact that they are so natural, so inevitable, underscore the true nature of the challenge we all face. We are gathered here as representatives of scores of independent nations, yet we face a menace—a danger—to *all* of our citizens. One which we cannot possibly meet unilaterally, out of our own national resources.

"Every person in this chamber knows of Shurkhal's loss." Kinshe's voice was suddenly harsh, his expression bleak. "Thousands of Shurkhali men have already flocked to the colors, already sworn themselves to blood vengeance for Shaylar Nargra-Kolmayr and her husband. Yet Shurkhal recognizes that she cannot seek justice by herself. We must act together, we must act as one, and above all, we must *act*."

He paused, and silence hovered, unbroken by so much as the rustle of feet or a single cough.

"My friends," he said finally, "we need a system of world governance, and we have no time to thresh out all the details of some new and splendid system with which we will all be content. And since we have too little time for that task, it seems to me most fortunate that we don't have to undertake it."

He paused once more, and this time the silence was so intense it seemed to hurt his audience's ears.

"We already have a working model of governance to draw upon," he said quietly. "A model which has endured the test of time, war, natural disaster, and adversity of every kind. The model of a government which has administered a region spanning half the globe. Governed diverse peoples from dozens of different cultures and languages, and done it justly and well. A government which has fought more successful wars than all the other nations of Sharona *combined*, and yet one which has never embraced militarism for its own sake. One whose subjects enjoy great personal freedom, and perhaps the highest average standard of living in the world.

"Sharona has no better model for a world government. Indeed, Sharona *cannot* have a better model. Rather than thrash around creating something new and untested, something whose strength we cannot know and whose stability we cannot trust, let us turn to one all of us know, most from our own history. There is too much at stake for us to settle for anything less. And, perhaps most important of all, its current ruler has already demonstrated the ability to see very clearly the most important tasks ahead of us. The nature and magnitude of the risks we face, and what must be accomplished to meet them.

"I move that we create a united Empire of Sharona, based on the model and institutions of the Ternathian Empire."

Zindel's jaw tried to drop, but before he could do more than draw breath to protest, another voice called out.

"Farnalia seconds the motion, provided that we also adopt the current Ternathian emperor, Zindel chan Calirath, as the new Emperor of Sharona!"

"The Queens of Bolakin second the motion as amended!"

Zindel stared hard at his longtime allies, who merely gazed back at him as if the motion—and its amendment—were truly spontaneous. And, despite his own sudden suspicion, he knew he would never be able to prove they hadn't been.

But if it was a put-up job, the well-organized steamroller wasn't allowed to proceed to its destination unchallenged.

"Uromathia protests!" Chava Busar, Emperor of Uromathia, was on his feet, his face livid, and another uproar swept the chamber.

It took several minutes for Orem Limana to gavel the chaos back to order once again. He managed it in the end, not without a bit of shouting of his own, then looked very formally at the Uromathian ruler.

"What protest do you wish to lodge, Emperor Chava?"

"I protest the unseemly and improper haste with which certain parties wish to call for a vote on two critical issues at once, without open debate or formal nominations for each separate issue!"

"Those two issues being—?"

"The first being the motion to adopt the Ternathian Empire as the model for a world government, as if Ternathia's were the only great empire in Sharonian history," Chava bit out. "And the second being the question of who would *head* this proposed Empire of Sharona. They are separate issues. They must be voted on separately!"

"They are not separate issues!" the Emperor of Farnalia bellowed, surging to his feet in furious disregard of the formal rules of parliamentary procedure. Ronnel Karone, a bigger man even than Zindel, towered two feet and more taller than the Emperor of Uromathia, and his expression was not pleasant. "We're not adopting Ternathia as a *model*. We're adopting Ternathia as our *government*, and Ternathia *has* a ruler. A capable, intelligent, *honest* ruler."

Zindel winced; Chava went purple; Karone didn't even pause.

"We're voting to place all of Sharona under the rule of the Ternathian Empire, so we don't need a separate nomination and vote, because there *is* no separate issue. Ternathia *has* an emperor; Sharona will have the same one!"

"Uromathia will never tolerate you, or anyone else, shoving an emperor we don't trust down our throats without so much as the courtesy of open debate, let alone open and honest nominations!" Chava bellowed back, and pandemonium erupted once more.

Shouts and threats flew thick as hailstones while the First Director banged his gavel again and again, shouting for order. No one even seemed to notice for what seemed like hours, but finally, slowly, the raucous uproar began to wane.

"We have a motion on the floor," Limana announced firmly, once order had finally been restored. "It has been seconded. We also have a serious protest on the floor. In the interest of justice, I cannot in good conscience allow the vote to go forward until the protest has been addressed."

"Master Chairman!"

"The Chair recognizes the Emperor of Ternathia."

"Thank you." Zindel stood once more and faced the other delegations, shaking his head.

"My friends, First Director Limana has a point. Technically, I suppose, we should proceed to debate the motion as stated and vote upon it. Any protests would, obviously, form a part of that debate.

"But Ternathia didn't seek this proposal, and Ternathia's emperor has no wish to rule the people of Sharona under a vote whose propriety is in any way questionable. We cannot afford to create a situation in which *any* nation feels it was coerced or pressured into accepting what amounts to foreign rule. That, my friends, is the very definition of tyranny, and I will *not* play the part of tyrant, be the emergency we face ever so great.

"With all due gratitude to the Emperor of Farnalia and the Queens of Bolakin for their confidence in me," he bowed formally in their direction, "I must insist that this protest be honored. It's one thing to spend twelve hours arguing about trivia; it's quite another to ram through a vote of this magnitude without open debate and the opportunity for nominations from all of Sharona's sovereign rulers."

Chava's triumphant smile was very nearly a gloating sneer. Zindel knew perfectly well that if anyone had been mad enough to nominate Uromathia as a government to rule all Sharona, Chava Busar would never have insisted on a fair and open debate as to who should do the ruling. Zindel understood that. Indeed, it had taken all of his own determination to insist upon scrupulous honesty, and that decision on his part might yet cost him and all of Sharona dearly.

But as he'd said, he would not rule under what amounted to a fraudulent nomination, no matter how attractive it might be in ensuring that Uromathia's current emperor didn't end up in power. Karone looked at him for a moment, then shot a glowering look at Uromathia's gloating ruler—a glare which said all too clearly, *Every hell in Arpathia will freeze solid before I see you on the imperial throne of Sharona!*

"Ternathia moves—indeed, insists," Zindel said, "that the current motion and nomination be withdrawn and replaced by two separate motions. The first, that Sharona adopt the model and institutions of the Ternathian Empire as the basis for a worldwide government. The second, that nominations be opened for who shall serve as emperor—or empress—of a united Sharona."

"Second both motions!" Chava called instantly.

"Very well," Limana said. "It has been moved, and seconded, that the current motion and nomination be withdrawn and replaced by two new motions. First, that Sharona adopt the Ternathian Empire as the basis for a worldwide Empire. Second, that nominations be opened for emperor or empress."

He paused just long enough for a profoundly respectful half-bow to Zindel, then gazed back out across the enormous chamber.

"The Chair will now entertain debate upon the first motion," he announced.

CHAPTER
FORTY-ONE

"SOMETHING'S BOTHERING YOU," Gadrial said quietly.

Jasak twitched in surprise at the sound of her voice. He hadn't noticed her walking up behind him as he stood on Fort Talon's fighting step, weight balanced on his crossed forearms while he leaned forward against the parapet and gazed out into the gathering evening. It was unusual for anyone to be able to approach him that closely without his noticing. He'd always had a particularly well developed case of what his father called "situational awareness" and his mother called "that damned, nervous cat Olderhan paranoia," and he'd been paying even more attention than usual to his built-in warning system since his encounter with vos Hoven.

And, he thought wryly, *since I started worrying as much about my superiors as about potential enemies.*

Now he turned toward the magister, arching one eyebrow.

"What makes you think something's bothering me?" he asked mildly.

"I'm not developing Shaylar's 'Talent,' if that's what you're afraid of," she replied with a tart smile. "Mind you, it would probably come in handy trying to understand you inscrutable Andarans! But the explanation is actually a lot less exotic than that. You've been standing here staring at the dragonfield for the better part of thirty minutes without even moving. Which suggested to my powerful intellect that either something was bothering you or else you'd chosen a remarkably uncomfortable spot for an after-dinner nap."

"I see." He smiled back at her, but there was more tension in his smile than in hers.

"It's all right, Jasak," she said more gently. "Chief Sword Threbuch is standing in the hallway right outside their door. And—" she studied his expression for a moment, as if considering whether or not to tell him something, then shrugged "—I might as well admit that I'm not quite as trusting as I ought to be."

"Meaning?" His eyes narrowed, and she shrugged again.

"Meaning I've tagged both of them with magister-level security spells. If anyone whose personae I didn't include in the original spell comes within four feet of them, I'll know. And if anyone tries to hurt them or drag either of them off against their will . . . Well, let's just say whoever it is won't enjoy the experience one bit."

She studied his expression far more anxiously than her own expression might have indicated. Sir Jasak Olderhan was Andaran, after all, with an Andaran's faith in the honor of the Arcanan Army and its officer corps.

"Is that legal?" he asked after a moment.

"As long as the enforcement aspect of the spell is nonlethal, it's not *illegal*," she replied. "It's a gray area, in a lot of ways. Under the circumstances, and given our shared commitment to see to their personal safety and the importance of the intelligence asset they represent, I don't think there could be any objection. Not any *legitimate* objection, anyway."

"Except, of course, from the people who try to do the dragging," he observed lightly. He smiled, but it was a fleeting smile, and his eyes turned bleak. "Which, Magister Kelbryan, won't bother me one tiny bit. Thank you."

"You're welcome," she said quietly, and laid one hand on his forearm. "I said it was 'our commitment,' Jasak. It is. I may not understand everything about your people's honor code, but what I do understand, I respect. I even admire most of it, although it's all very unRansaran. But even if I didn't, Shaylar and Jathmar have suffered enough. If anyone wants to hurt either of them ever again, they're going to have to come through *both* of us, not just you."

"Thank you," he repeated in a much softer tone, and patted the hand on his forearm once, lightly.

She looked into those dark, brown eyes of his and felt a twinge of surprise. She kept her expression serene, but her pulse seemed to have speeded up unaccountably, and she scolded herself for it. That was the last thing either of them needed at this particular time!

"So," she said more lightly, "what's bothering you?"

He snorted. It should have sounded amused, but it didn't, and then he turned back to the fort parapet and pointed at the forest-walled dragonfield with his chin.

"What do you see out there, Gadrial?"

"What?" Gadrial blinked in surprise, then stepped up beside him to gaze out over the same vista for several seconds. "Just the dragon-field," she said finally.

"'Just the dragonfield,'" he repeated softly, almost musingly.

"Obviously you're seeing something I'm not."

"No." He shook his head. "It's just that I know what we *ought* to be seeing. I know you've spent a lot of time in Garth Showma, but you're still basically a civilian, Gadrial. I'm not."

"So tell this poor 'civilian' what she's missing."

"Sorry." He flashed her a grin, acknowledging her tone's exagger-ated patience. "I didn't mean to be mysterious. It's just that there are an awful lot of dragons out there, Gadrial. A *lot*."

Gadrial frowned, gazing out over the field once more, and then nodded slowly. She'd noticed when they arrived that the field seemed unusually crowded, but her mind had been on other matters at the time. Now that Jasak had called her attention to it, she realized that the number of dragons out there actually exceeded the field's designed capacity by a substantial margin. Each dragon was supposed to have its own assigned nesting place, with overhead cover against the ele-ments, but there were too many of the huge beasts for that to be possible. At least a quarter of those she could see were housed—if that was the word for it—in hastily improvised wallows the recent rain had turned muddy, giving them a bedraggled, down-at-the-heels look she was unaccustomed to seeing from the Air Force.

"You're right," she acknowledged. "I hadn't noticed."

"That's not all," Jasak said soberly, and nodded towards the flatter area to the south of the dragonfield.

The area to the north was given over to paddocks and holding pens filled with the imported cattle and locally rounded up bison which provided the dragons' primary food supply. Now that Jasak had drawn her attention to the number of beasts actually thronging the field, she realized that the holding pens were unusually full, as well. But he was pointing in the opposite direction, and she felt her forehead furrowing as she saw the neat rows of white tents.

"That's at least a two-company bivouac," he told her. "And that's the next best thing to five hundred men."

Gadrial nodded slowly. Once upon a time, she knew, the Andaran rank titles which the Union's military establishment had adopted had been literal descriptors of the size of an officer's command. Over time, however, as armies grew and evolved, that had changed. Jasak was a commander of one hundred, and one hundreds had always commanded infantry companies. But a company consisted of almost two hundred and fifty men these days, not the hundred men it had once contained. And Five Hundred Klian's battalion consisted (or should have, assuming it had been at full strength) of almost eleven hundred men, not five hundred, while a commander of two thousand's regiment was over three thousand men strong.

None of which explained what five hundred men were doing living in tents outside Fort Talon's barracks.

"Mul Gurthak's calling in reinforcements," she said.

"That's exactly what he's doing," Jasak agreed. Then he inhaled deeply. "We shouldn't be surprised. After all, he's the most senior officer this side of the Ucala sliderhead, and that's still over twelve thousand miles from here. It's his responsibility to concentrate as much combat power as he can, just in case. It's just . . ."

His voice trailed off, and he shook his head. Not that he needed to complete the sentence for Gadrial's benefit.

She stood beside him, gazing at the innocent looking white tents which housed the men mul Gurthak couldn't squeeze into his available barracks space and at the transport dragons ringing the field. There were at least a dozen battle dragons, like the two which had reacted to Shaylar so strongly, as well, and Gadrial's blood ran cold at the thought that dragons might actually be used in battle once again.

And if we're prepared to use dragons for the first time in two hundred years, she thought with a bone-deep shiver, recalling a conversation with Shaylar and Jathmar, *what* else *are we prepared to do for the first time in two hundred years?*

It was a question she couldn't answer, and she felt like a coward for being grateful that she could not.

*   *   *

"Well, gentlemen," Nith mul Gurthak said, tipping back his chair and smiling at Rithmar Skirvon and Uthik Dastiri, "I suppose it's time that you were on your way."

The sun had barely risen over Fort Talon, but the two diplomats were already packed and ready to go. Their beautifully tailored civilian clothing had been exchanged for utilitarian Air Force flight suits, and neither of them looked any more enthralled by the prospect of a five thousand-mile journey than mul Gurthak would have been in their place.

"I'm afraid so," Skirvon agreed with a grimace. "I wish we were eligible for flight pay!"

"Understandable, I suppose," mul Gurthak conceded with a slight smile. Then his expression grew more sober. "A great deal depends upon you gentlemen—on your judgment and your efforts. I won't belabor that point further, since I know we're all already aware of it. I wish there were time for us to seek formal guidance from Parliament and the Commandery. There isn't."

"Understood, Two Thousand," Skirvon replied somberly. "I assure you that we'll do our best."

"I never doubted it." Mul Gurthak rose behind his desk and extended his right hand. "Good luck, gentlemen."

"Thank you, Two Thousand," Skirvon said very seriously. Then mul Gurthak shook hands with both of them and watched them walk out of his office.

*   *   *

"How far did you say it was to the next portal?" Shaylar asked as she and Jathmar followed Jasak and Gadrial towards the dragon-field.

"About nine hundred miles," Jasak replied. "One day's dragon flight."

"Assuming, of course," Shaylar forced an edge of humor into her voice, "that the dragon in question doesn't just decide to eat me and be done with it, instead."

Jasak stopped. The rest of their small procession—including a still obviously irked Hundred Neshok and half a dozen soldiers from his company—stopped as well, and Jasak turned to face her.

"That isn't going to happen, Shaylar," he told her firmly. "We're taking Skyfang, and we haven't had any problems with him."

"No, we haven't," Shaylar agreed. She couldn't keep her intense relief from showing, not that she tried particularly hard. The Fort Wyvern dragon Skyfang and his pilot, Commander of Fifty Daris Varkal, were a well oiled team. They'd obviously been together a long time, possibly as long as Muthok Salmeer and Windclaw. Unlike Windclaw, however, Skyfang—who was even larger than Windclaw—had shown no inclination to take large, messy bites out of her. In fact, she'd almost felt as if the dragon actually *liked* her, although she wasn't about to invest any great confidence in that possibility.

"As a matter of fact, Shaylar," Gadrial said with a slight smile for Jasak, "Jasak's requested that we stick with Skyfang and Fifty Varkal as long as possible. We may have to change dragons in Rycarh or Jylaros—we have fairly long sea voyages crossing each of those universes, and we may not have enough room aboard ship for Skyfang—but if we can, we'll hang onto both of them all the way to Ucala."

"Is that likely to be possible?" Jathmar asked.

"It depends on the available shipping," Jasak said. "That's one reason I hadn't mentioned the possibility to you. Not all of our ships are configured as dragon transports, so we may not be able to. I'd say the odds were probably slightly in our favor, but I can't guarantee it."

"Whether we can or not, I truly appreciate the thought, Jasak," Shaylar said. "Thank you."

"I told you, Shaylar," Jasak said quietly, taking her delicate hand in one of his and squeezing it gently, "you and Jathmar are members of my family, now. However deeply I may regret the circumstances which make that so, I'm honored to have you as a sister, and I look out for *all* my sisters. And—" he looked across her head at Jathmar "—my brothers, too. Now that I have one."

Jathmar looked back at him, more than a little uncomfortably. Then the Sharonian grimaced.

"Like Shaylar, I appreciate the thought," he said. "On the other hand, has anyone suggested why some of the dragons seem to react so much more strongly to her? Or why they *don't* react to me the same way?"

"As to why they react to her, the only logical explanation is that it's something about her particular Talent," Gadrial said. "My best guess is that a 'Voice's' abilities produce some sort of . . . signature, or emission, dragons are sensitive to. And, obviously, one they don't much like."

She smiled without any humor at all, and Jathmar snorted.

"I believe you could safely say that," he agreed.

"As for the reason some of them respond more strongly than others," Jasak took over as they began walking towards the field once again, "I've got the beginnings of a theory."

"You do?" Jathmar glanced sideways at his Andaran "brother" as they headed down the dirt road. He was relieved to see that all of the field's dragons had been moved back from the roadway for a safe distance.

"Yes," Jasak said. "I want to ask Daris a couple of questions before I say anything more, though. And even if I'm right, it only changes the question, it doesn't really answer it."

"We're supposed to be the ones concealing sensitive information from *you*," Jathmar said dryly, and Jasak chuckled.

"I'm not really trying to be mysterious, Jathmar. It's just that I didn't want to get anyone's hopes up for what may turn out to be the wrong reasons. Besides—"

He broke off as they reached the field itself. Fifty Varkal and

Skyfang were waiting for them, and the dragon's head rose, turning towards them, nostrils flaring. As always, Jathmar was acutely uncomfortable when any of the huge beasts showed an interest in Shaylar, but Skyfang gave no sign of hostility. Indeed, something suspiciously like a deep, subterranean purr seemed to rumble in his enormous chest.

"Good morning, Hundred. Magister Kelbryan." Varkal greeted Jasak and Gadrial, then looked past them. "Good morning, Master Nargra. Good morning, Lady Nargra-Kolmayr."

"Good morning, Daris," Jasak replied for all of them while Shaylar and Jathmar smiled at him. Unlike most of the Arcanan officers they'd encountered, Daris Varkal had been genuinely and naturally courteous from the moment they met.

"We're cleared and ready to go as soon as we're all on board, Sir," the fifty told Jasak.

"Good," Jasak replied approvingly. Varkal reached out a hand to Gadrial, preparing to assist her in mounting to Skyfang's back, but Jasak's raised hand stopped him.

"Sir?"

"I've been wondering about something, Daris. How well do you know Squire Salmeer and Windclaw?"

"Pretty well, Sir," Varkal said just a bit cautiously. "Muthok's a good man—one of the best. I've learned a lot from him, and Windclaw's one of the most experienced transports you're ever going to see."

"That was my impression of them, as well." Jasak nodded. "What I was wondering, though, is how much you know about Windclaw's pedigree." Varkal looked surprised, and Jasak chuckled a bit sourly. "The first time Windclaw met Lady Nargra-Kolmayr, he wanted to eat her," he reminded the pilot, "but Skyfang here actually seems to like her."

"He does, Sir." Varkal seemed a little surprised that Jasak had noticed and turned to smile at Shaylar. "The hundred's right about that, My Lady," he said earnestly. "Skyfang's smart. He's not as old as Windclaw, but he's been around, and I've had him for a long time now. I know him pretty well, and he *does* like you." He shook his head, his expression turning more than a little chagrined. "I should have told you that already, I guess. After all, Muthok warned me about how Windclaw reacted. I should have realized you'd be worried."

"I thought he liked her," Jasak said with a hint of satisfaction. "That's what started me wondering about pedigrees. I'm no Air Force officer, but I've seen quite a few dragons over the years. I hope it won't offend you if I say that Skyfang here looks a bit bigger and . . . less agile than Windclaw."

"No offense taken, Sir," Varkal said with what certainly looked like a genuine grin. "Old Skyfang's a transport to the bone. All of his ancestors—clear back to the first egg in Ransar, as far as I know—have been transports." He reached higher than his head to pat his dragon's massive foreleg with affectionate pride. "Windclaw's a fine beast, but Skyfang can out-lift him any day. We can haul half again the weight Muthok and Windclaw can, although, to be fair, you were lucky you drew them for your medevac. Like you say, Windclaw's quite a bit more agile. From your description, I don't think we could have gotten in and out again where he and Muthok did."

"Because Windclaw's line is a transport-battle dragon cross, isn't it?"

"Yes, Sir. I couldn't say exactly how far back, but it's easy enough to see if you know what to look for." Varkal shrugged. "A pure transport like Skyfang is bred for strength, stamina, and range before anything else. He's a . . . strategic transport, I guess you'd say—bred for moving the maximum loads well behind the front line. Windclaw, now, he's more of a *tactical* transport, bred to support the air-mobile outfits. He can't carry as much, but he's fast and maneuverable—for a transport. That counts when you're trying to get troops or supplies into a hot LZ, and a lot of mission planners like to have at least some breath weapon capability in their frontal area tac transports."

"That's what I thought." Jasak looked at Shaylar and Jathmar. "As nearly as I can tell, all of the dragons who have reacted so negatively to Shaylar have been either battle dragons or, like Windclaw, a transport-battle dragon cross. So whatever it is about you, it would appear that it only bothers the combat types, and we should see less and less of those as we get further to the rear."

"That's a relief—assuming you've got it right," Jathmar said. "On the other hand, I'd still like to know exactly what causes the reaction in the first place."

"So would I. I'm not sure we ever will, though. And at the moment, I'll settle for anything that lets us keep Shaylar safely away from dragons that won't like her."

"Me, too," Shaylar said firmly.

Emboldened by Jasak's theory, she reached out and patted Skyfang's huge, scaly, tree trunk of a leg the same way Varkal had. The huge dragon raised his head once more, cocking it to one side and looking down at her. Then he lowered it—not with the quick, angry motion the other dragons had shown, but slowly, almost gently.

Shaylar heard Jasak inhale sharply and felt Jathmar's sudden spike of fear through the marriage bond, but she stood her ground as that enormous head hovered just above her. The gigantic right eye considered her thoughtfully, reassuringly calmly, and then Skyfang's vast forked tongue flickered out and touched her on the shoulder. The tongue alone—narrow as a serpent's, in proportion to the dragon—was as broad as her torso, and she felt its enormous weight . . . and strength. But its touch was gentle, and she smiled delightedly as she sensed something at the very edge of her Talent.

She'd always known she had at least a trace of her mother's Talent. She'd felt it quite often, swimming with the dolphins at her mother's embassy, although compared to her Voice Talent, it had been far too weak to bother trying to train. Now she felt Skyfang, the same way she had felt those dolphins and whales, and unlike Windclaw's angry, almost savage aura, Skyfang was a calm, relaxed presence. Her impression of him lacked the . . . brightness, the sharpness, of true sentience, but it came much closer to fully developed self-awareness than she'd expected. And without the other dragon's fury, the big transport suddenly felt no more threatening to her than the huge whales with which she had swum since childhood, and she patted his leg again in simple delight.

Jathmar exhaled explosively as he tasted her emotions through his own bond with her, and she smiled at him before she turned back to Jasak.

"I think you may be onto something," she said. "I can't feel Skyfang's emotions the same way I could a person's, but I am getting at least a little something from him, and it's a lot different from what I felt from Windclaw."

"Good," Jasak sighed, then grimaced. "I'm glad to hear we may not have to worry about the way other transports react to you, Shaylar. All the same, would you *please* not do things like that?" He jerked his head at the hand she still had on Skyfang's leg. "I'm sure Jathmar would feel better if you'd at least consult with him before you rush in to test one of my theories, and—" he looked at Jathmar again across her head and grinned crookedly "—I know damned well that *I* would."

CHAPTER FORTY-TWO

"NOW *THAT'S* IMPRESSIVE."

Division-Captain chan Geraith stood with his hands on his hips, watching as one of his Bisons snorted up the loading ramp onto the massive flatcar under a floating banner of black smoke and the careful direction of the loadmaster. The Bison—technically, the Transport Tractor, Mark I, Model B—was based on the same powerplant as the next to largest of the Trans-Temporal Express's bulldozers, although its suspension and caterpillar tracks had been substantially modified in an effort to allow for greater speed over even rougher terrain. It wasn't an actual transport unit itself, but rather designed to tow a capacious wheeled or tracked trailer, and despite its funnel, it was sleek, low-slung, and powerful looking.

It was also dwarfed by the flatcar it was busily climbing onto. Indeed, two more Bisons were already in place on the same car. TTE employees were tightening the tie-down chains on the second of them even as the third clanked into position, and there was still going to be almost enough room for a *fourth*, he realized.

"You think so, Division-Captain?"

Chan Geraith turned his attention from the flatcar to the man standing beside him. Train Master Yakhan Chusal of TTE's Directorate of Operations was the sprawling transportation giant's senior train master. He'd been overseeing the loading of TTE freight trains for almost thirty years, and his eyes were rather more critical than the soldier's.

"Yes, I do," chan Geraith said. "I never realized you had flatcars that size. Oh, I've seen pictures of the special, articulated cars you use to transport ship hull sections, but I'd never realized you had standard cars this big."

"I wish we could make them even bigger," Chusal replied with a grimace. "They're just barely large enough for our biggest steam shovels as it is, and you can't put a shovel on an articulated car and get it through some of the mountains we've got to transit on this run. Some of the curves are way too sharp, not to mention the little question of whether or not the trestles would stand the weight. In fact, I understand Engineering had to turn down a new shovel design because we couldn't guarantee that we could transport it."

"You mean you need a flatcar that size for *one* steam shovel?" chan Geraith demanded in an almost shaken tone.

"That's right." Chusal shrugged. "In fact, we have to break them down into two loads, even with cars that size. Which, of course, means we need big damned cranes—which we *also* have to ship out—to put them back together again at the other end. When you've got to dig your way through a godsdamned mountain range, or dig a frigging canal, you need a really big shovel. Well, we've got them."

Chan Geraith shook his head with a bemused sort of expression. Before his own recent experiences with the experimental mechanization program, he probably wouldn't have been as impressed as he was. Now, though, he'd had far more firsthand experience with incredibly powerful and yet sometimes frustratingly fragile heavy machinery.

"I guess we're lucky TTE's got as much rolling stock as it does," he said after a moment, and Chusal snorted.

"Depends on how you look at it, Division-Captain. Our charter from the Portal Authority requires us to maintain a fifteen percent reserve over and beyond our normal operational and maintenance requirements. Frankly, it's always been a pain in the ass for the bean-counters, and I've got to admit that there have been times when I was royally pissed to have that many cars—and engines—basically just sitting in sheds somewhere. But there wasn't much *luck* to it. And," his expression darkened, "I don't think the reserve's going to be big enough after all."

"You don't?"

Chan Geraith's eyes narrowed. Short of TTE's Director of Operations, Chusal was undoubtedly the most knowledgeable person, where the Trans-Temporal Express's rails were concerned, in any of the many universes Sharona had explored. If he thought there were going to be bottlenecks, then chan Geraith was grimly certain that there were.

"Well," Chusal looked away, shading his eyes against the afternoon sun with one hand while he watched the loading activities under the sky of autumn blue, "I can't say for certain, of course. But unless this new government does go through, and unless it budgets one hell of a lot more money for the line after it does, there's no way we're going to be able to meet the transport requirements we're facing. We're transferring engines and cars from every other trunk line to the Hayth Chain, but just getting them where we need them is going to be a royal pain. I've been sending them out basically empty, or half-empty, at least, just to get them where we're going to need them down the road."

"How bad is it, really?"

"Honestly?" Chusal looked up at the considerably taller Ternathian officer with a thoughtful expression, as if considering whether or not chan Geraith really wanted to know the truth, then grimaced. "The biggest problem's going to be the water gaps. There's a six thousand-mile voyage to cross Haysam to get to Reyshar, and another nine hundred-mile cruise between Reyshar and Hayth. Then there's another eleven hundred miles of water between Jyrsalm and Salym. We're going to have to detrain all of your people, all of your horses, all of your equipment, at each water gap, load it onto ships and sail all of it across the gap, then load it back onto *another* set of cars, and haul it to the *next* water gap. Then repeat the process."

It was chan Geraith's turn to grimace, although he wasn't really all that surprised. He could read a map, after all.

"I can't say I'm looking forward to the process," he said after a moment, "but surely it's one you've had to deal with before."

"Oh, yes. Of course we have." Chusal nodded. "We have to deal with it constantly, in fact. Unfortunately, we've never had to deal with it on quite this *scale* before, Division-Captain. Moving whole armies, not to mention all the ammunition and other supplies they're going to need—and all the coal our *engines* and steamships are going to need, if we're going to go on moving all that other stuff—simply *devours* rail capacity. And, obviously, shipping capacity between ports.

"Haysam and Reyshar are pretty well provided with freighters and passenger liners we can conscript for the military's needs, since everything moving in and out of the home universe has to pass through both of them. But we haven't needed anything like this sort of transport capacity in the Hayth Chain before. Sealift's going to be a real problem in the move between Salym and Traisum, and then there's the rail ferry across the Finger Sea in Traisum itself to consider, at least until they get the bridge built.

"That's all bad enough, but we've never had to assign the Hayth Chain anywhere near the rolling stock we're going to need now on the outbound side of Hayth. That's why I've been sending so many perfectly good engines and freight cars out empty. And it's also why every heavylift freighter in both Haysam and Reyshar has been withdrawn from regular service and assigned to hauling those engines and cars across the water gaps. Which," he added sourly, "has created a monumental bottleneck in commercial cargo service."

"I see." Chan Geraith frowned. "I hadn't realized it would impose quite that much of a strain."

"Division-Captain, you haven't even begun to see 'strain' yet," Chusal said grimly. "We're building up as much capacity as we can, but basically, we're looking at at least three totally separate rail lines, for all intents and purposes. That's what those water gaps do to us, since we've got to have the rolling stock we need between *each* of them. Worse, in Reyshar and Salym, we've got two *separate* rail legs divided by water too wide to bridge. So we can't just load you onto one set of cars and send you all the way to the end of the line. We can do a lot to economize if we plan our turnarounds on the shorter legs carefully, but it's still going to be a nightmare keeping everything moving. And so far, we're only looking at moving one division at a time. What happens if we have to start sending entire corps down the same transit chain simultaneously? For that matter, the line's only double-tracked as far as Jyrsalm! We're working on that, too, and that's another logistical consideration we have to juggle somehow."

The train master sounded both weary and frustrated, and chan Geraith couldn't blame him for either emotion. On the other hand, he'd known men like Chusal before. Yakhan Chusal hadn't become TTE's senior train master by accident, and chan Geraith suspected that he was going to prove much more capable of doing that logistical juggling than he thought he was at the moment.

None of which invalidates a single thing he's said, of course.

The division-captain shook his head. He'd known going in that managing his logistics down a single supply line as long as this one was going to be a . . . challenge. No one in history had ever before even considered attempting such a thing, far less planned for it, and the urgent need to get his division loaded up and moving in the right direction had kept him from giving it the sort of attention and preplanning any peacetime maneuver would have permitted. He'd been painfully aware of that, but he'd also known he and his staff were going to have literally weeks in transit to work out the details.

"Train Master," he said after moment, "would it be possible for you to assign someone from your operations staff to me on a temporary basis? My staff and I are reasonably competent when it comes to planning moves around the Empire, or across a single planet. I'm beginning to think, though, that we need someone with a better feel for genuine trans-universal movements. Besides, we're accustomed to simply telling the quartermaster how much lift capacity we need. This time around it looks like we're going to need an expert just to tell us how much capacity there *is*!"

"Now that, Division-Captain, is a very good idea," Chusal said warmly. "And, as it happens, I think I have just the man for you." Chan Geraith arched one eyebrow, and Chusal chuckled. "I've assigned Hayrdar Sheltim as your train master. He just happens to be one of our more experienced train masters . . . and he also just finished a three-month assignment to operations right here at Larakesh Central. If you've got questions, Hayrdar can answer them as well as anyone I can think of."

"Thank you, Train Master. I appreciate that—a lot."

* * *

"It doesn't look like much, does it?" Second Lord of Horse Garsal grumbled.

"Perhaps not," Lord of Horse Jukan Darshu, Sunlord Markan replied quietly as they watched the first of his Uromathian cavalry troopers climb down from the passenger cars which had carried them as far as Fort Salby.

They were moving slowly, stiffly, and the sunlord's lips quirked in a wry sympathy he would never have admitted to feeling. The last twelve days had been a severe jolt to their systems, he thought. The rail trip from Camryn to Salym hadn't been all that bad, but then there'd been the move to the hastily improvised transports in Salym for the voyage from Barkesh to New Ramath. The horses had hated it, the heavy weather they'd encountered *en route* had left half the men miserably seasick, and at the end of it, they'd had to climb *back* into the rail cars for the trip from New Ramath to Fort Tharkoma covering the portal between Salym and Traisum.

New Ramath was only a few hundred miles from Tharkoma, but they were mountainous, inhospitable miles, and the slow, swaying trip along the steep tracks which twisted like broken-backed serpents between the port city and the fortress had been exhausting, especially for the men who hadn't yet fully recovered from their seasickness. Yet even that hadn't been the end of it, for the Traisum side of that portal was located in the equivalent of the Kingdom of Shartha.

Shartha lay on the west coast of Ricatha, which lay thousands of feet lower than—and three thousand miles south of—the Salym side of the portal, and it had been snowing hard in Salym. The change as their train wheezed through the portal from sub-freezing Tharkoma to the brutal, brilliant heat of the Shartha Plain had been stunning even for hardened trans-universal travelers. The cold, insufficiently heated passenger cars had gone from icebox to oven in what had seemed mere minutes as the ice and snow which had encrusted them turned abruptly into water. Indeed, Markan rather thought that most of it had probably gone straight to vapor without even bothering with the intermediate liquid stage. The shock to the system had been profound, and the day and a half it had taken to get from there to Salby had offered insufficient time for men—or horses—to adjust.

"Impressive or not," Markan continued now, "it will serve neither the need of the moment nor the emperor to reflect upon that fact too loudly."

He glanced levelly at his second-in-command. The two of them stood on the front platform of the palatial passenger car which had been assigned to Markan's senior officers for the move, and a flicker of what might have been mere irritation or might have been anger showed in Garsal's eyes. Whatever it was, it was gone as quickly as it had come, however, and he nodded.

"Point taken, Sunlord," he said.

Markan nodded back. There was no need to do more, for several reasons. First, Jukan Darshu was a sunlord, what a Ternathian would have called a duke, whereas Tarnal Garsal was only a windlord, or earl. Second, despite Garsal's fastidious, finicky dislike for frontier conditions (and his undeniable arrogance), he truly was a highly competent officer. And third, because Garsal was a distant relative of Chava Busar, and knew better than to disappoint his imperial cousin.

Not to mention the minor fact that our entire multiverse—Ternathia and Uromathia alike—is at risk this time, Markan reflected.

It felt . . . unnatural to think of the Empire and the long-resented Ternathians facing a common threat. For as long as Markan (or any other Uromathian) could remember, Ternathia had been if not precisely the *enemy*, the next closest thing available. And, he admitted, since Chava had come to the throne, the long-standing rivalry between the two great Sharonian empires had once again grown both more intense and nastier.

I suppose it's a little silly of us, the sunlord reflected. *Or, at least, it was in the beginning. By now, it's taken on a life of its own.*

Markan knew he was rather more sophisticated, in many ways,

than most Uromathians, including all too many members of the high aristocracy. Despite that, however, deep down inside, *he* still suffered from that ingrained Uromathian sense of . . . not *inferiority*, really, but something close.

The truth was that Uromathia could never quite forgive Ternathia for being almost four millennia older than it was. Ternathia had made Tajvana its capital thirty-three centuries ago, and the Caliraths had stayed there until less than *three* centuries ago. In the interim, their empire had lapped as far east as the Cerakondian Mountains, in the south, and eventually as far as Lake Arau, in the north, until it finally stopped against the Arau Mountains in far eastern Chairifon. It had reached the Araus just under nine hundred years ago, and on the far side of that mountain barrier, it had finally encountered another empire almost as large as it was.

That empire had been Uromathia, which had controlled everything beyond the Cerakondians and the Araus as far south as Harkala. In terms of territory, Uromathia had been the smaller of the two; in terms of population, they'd been very nearly evenly matched. But Uromathia had been far younger, hammered together only over the previous three or four centuries as the various Uromathian kings and, eventually, emperors had watched the Ternathian tide sweeping steadily and apparently unstoppably towards them.

There hadn't really *been* a Uromathia until that steadily approaching Ternathian frontier—and example—had created it. In fact, Markan's ancestors had been too busy fighting and slaughtering one another in the service of their innumerable nobles and kinglets to pay the notion of "civilization" a great deal of attention. The threat of being ingested by Ternathia had concentrated the minds of the more powerful Uromathian kingdoms marvelously, however, and they'd begun cheerfully eliminating one another by conquest in an effort to build up a powerbase sufficient to remain uningested. Strictly, of course, out of a patriotic sense of their mission to resist foreign occupation. Perish the thought that personal power could have had anything to do with it!

They'd succeeded. In fact, they'd built a very respectable empire of their own by the time Ternathia arrived on their doorstep. They'd actually been even more centralized, since they had deliberately constructed their imperial bureaucracy for streamlined, military efficiency, whereas the Ternathian bureaucracy had been the product of millennia of gradual evolution and periodic bouts of reform. Their military capability had been impressive, as well, and they'd already acquired most of the Talents by intermarriage. Taken altogether, it had been an enormous accomplishment, one of which anyone could have been proud, and they had been.

But the thing which had stuck in the Uromathians' collective psyche was the lingering suspicion that Ternathia had stopped where it had not because Uromathia's power had given the Winged Crown pause, but because Ternathia had *chosen* to stop. The two great empires had sat there—coexisting more or less peaceably, with occasional, interspersed periods of mutual glaring—for the better part of six hundred years. Until, in fact, the Calirath Dynasty had begun its long, steady disengagement from the Ternathian Empire's high-water mark borders. And in all that time, there had been only three true wars between them . . . each of which Ternathia had won quite handily.

Ternathia had never made any effort to conquer Uromathia. That had never really been the Ternathian way, as Markan was prepared to admit, at least privately. But Uromathia had never quite been able to forgive the Ternathians for never—not *once*—letting the Uromathians beat them. The Uromathian Empire had fought its own wars, established its own prowess, but always in the Ternathian shadow. Never as Ternathia's equal. The fact that Chava Busar's was the fourth dynasty to rule Uromathia while the Caliraths were only the second dynasty in Ternathia's history (and that they had ruled Ternathia in unbroken succession for over *four thousand years*) didn't exactly help the situation, either. Uromathia had become the perpetual younger, smaller, *weaker* brother who deeply resented his older brother's patronizing attitude . . . even—or perhaps especially—when that older brother didn't even mean to be patronizing.

And that attitude lingered, even today.

Of course, Fort Salby didn't belong to Ternathia, the sunlord reminded himself. It was a Portal Authority base, which—theoretically, at least—meant it was a multinational installation, belonging to neither empire. The fact that the Portal Authority Armed Forces had seen fit to adopt Ternathian rank structures, weapons, tactical doctrines, and even military tailoring might, perhaps, explain the fact that it didn't *feel* that way.

But this time, we were the ones close enough to respond when the lightning struck, Markan thought with a certain grim satisfaction. *I only wish the emperor had seen fit to send us more detailed instructions.*

Part of Chava's vagueness was undoubtedly due to the emperor's suspicions of the Voice network. Unlike Zindel of Ternathia, Chava of Uromathia was completely unTalented, and he cherished a deep and abiding distrust for those who were. Despite all evidence and experience to the contrary, he was absolutely convinced that the Portal Authority Voices would violate their sworn confidentiality any time it suited their purposes. And, of course, their purposes—*whatever in all the Arpathian hells they might be*, Markan thought waspishly—were inevitably hostile to Chava's own.

In this case, however, it was at least equally probable that the emperor's failure to provide detailed instructions had as much to do with the totally unprecedented nature of the threat as with his undeniable paranoia. It was certainly enough to strain *Markan's* . . . mental flexibility, at any rate.

The sunlord wasn't especially fond of Shurkhalis, whether as individuals or corporate entities, like the Chalgyn Consortium. While he might sometimes feel his emperor took his hatred for all things Ternathian to unnecessary extremes, the fact remained that Shurkhal had been a part of the Ternathian Empire for almost three thousand years and that it had stubbornly aligned its national interests and foreign policy with its one-time imperial masters, rather than its much closer neighbor in Uromathia, since regaining its nominal independence. As a consequence, it was normally a bit difficult for him to work up a great deal of sympathy for any minor misfortunes which might befall the desert kingdom.

Then there was the fact that this particular survey crew had included Shaylar Nargra-Kolmayr. Markan had never met the woman, and had nothing against her personally, but her exploits had been a direct affront to his own notions of proper female behavior, and he was scarcely alone in that. Not in Uromathia, at least. Nor did the fact that the Portal Authority had been using her so heavily in its own propaganda leave him feeling much more cheerfully inclined towards her, given how unfond of the Authority he was.

Like most Uromathians, Markan had always resented the Portal Authority. His resentment was less pointed than that of many Uromathian aristocrats, especially those closest to the emperor, but it was nonetheless real. No Uromathian could quite forget that the Authority stemmed directly from a *Ternathian* demand (although courtesy had required that it be called only a "proposal," of course) for the internationalization of the Larakesh portal. Nor could any Uromathian forget that the then-Emperor of Uromathia's efforts to assert control over the portal and the proposed international authority had been stymied by a direct threat of Ternathian military action. Or that it was Ternathia which had insisted that the Authority's board of directors must represent all major nations yet remain completely and rigorously politically independent of any of them.

If pressed, Markan was prepared to admit—grudgingly—that Ternathia had no more direct control over the Authority than Uromathia did. Unfortunately, it didn't *need* direct control. Not when the "independent" Authority had fallen all over itself adopting Ternathian models for everything from its internal organization and exploration techniques to its military forces. Including, probably, the way they wiped their arses.

Stop that, the sunlord told himself sharply. *You're letting your* own *paranoia get the better of you again!*

He snorted in wry amusement, then shook his head when Garsal looked at him inquiringly.

"Just a thought, Tarnal," he said. "Just a thought."

He looked around for a moment longer.

It was appropriate, he supposed, that Fort Salby was located in what would have been Shurkhal on Sharona. At the moment, they stood on a plateau in the rugged Mountains of Ithal, which fringed the western coast of Shurkhal along the Finger Sea. Back home, the location was the site of the city of Narshalla, built around an oasis and bounded by an extensive lava field to the east and by the arid hills of the Ithal Mountains on the other three sides. In Traisum, where thousands of years of human habitation hadn't completely deforested the Shurkhali Peninsula, those hills were less arid than their Sharonian equivalent. They weren't what Markan would have called lush or luxuriant, even here, but they were far less forbidding and desolate than the ones Shaylar Nargra-Kolmayr must have known.

Despite any improvement in the local climate, driving the rail lines from Traisum's entry portal on the flat coastal Plain of Shartha to Salby had been a gargantuan task. The straight-line distance between Fort Galsar and Fort Salby was over fourteen hundred miles; the *actual* distance imposed by the terrain was at least half again that far. To reach the rail ferry across the southern terminus of the Finger Sea while avoiding the rugged, tangled mountains of the Shartha Highlands, the engineers had been forced to run their lines clear up and around both sides of the Horn of Ricathia. The route from the ferry's western terminus through the Ithals hadn't been any picnic, either, he reflected, although at least they'd been able to make up some of the lost time in the fast, fairly straightforward run along the coastal plain at the Ithals' feet until they had to turn inland to reach Fort Salby.

He'd been impressed, as always, by the accomplishments of the TTE construction crews. Especially by the fact that they'd already more than half completed the construction of a multitrack bridge across the Strait of Tears which connected the Finger Sea to the Gulf of Shurkhal. The coral-encrusted Strait of Tears was shallow and constricted—back home, it required constant blasting and dredging to keep it open for deep-draft shipping, and the span across the narrower, two-mile-wide eastern channel was already complete. They were well advanced on the longer, sixteen-mile length required to cross the western channel, as well, and work on it was proceeding twenty-four hours a day.

No doubt, he thought sardonically, *recent events farther down-chain have something to do with all the overtime TTE is accumulating at the moment. I wonder who'll get the final bill for that?*

"I suppose you'd better look after getting our people off the train while I go find this Regiment-Captain chan Skrithik," he said finally.

"Better you than me," Garsal muttered, but quietly enough Markan could pretend he hadn't heard. Then the windlord saluted. "I'll see to it, Sir," he said much more crisply.

"Good," Markan replied, and climbed down from the platform.

Actually, "go find" was scarcely the correct choice of verbs, he admitted as a tall Ternathian officer—*and aren't they* all *tall?* Markan thought wryly—stepped up to greet him.

"Lord of Horse," the Ternathian said in barely accented Uromathian. "Welcome to Fort Salby. I'm delighted to see you."

"Regiment-Captain," Markan responded in Ternathian, offering his right hand for a Ternathian-style handclasp. He was impressed by chan Skrithik's command of Uromathian, which was actually better than his own Ternathian. Nonetheless, there were appearances to maintain. A Uromathian lord of horse—and a pedigreed sunlord, to boot—could scarcely permit a Ternathian to be more cosmopolitan than he was, after all, he told himself sardonically, and rather suspected that he saw a matching flicker of amusement in chan Skrithik's eyes.

"We got here as quickly as we could," Markan continued. "Indeed, I was rather astonished by how quickly the TTE was able to arrange things once our troop movement was authorized."

"TTE's always been good at improvised movements," chan Skrithik agreed. "And just so we get off on the right foot, let me say that I'm as grateful as I am delighted to see you. I realize there's always been a certain degree of friction between Ternathia and Uromathia, and I don't imagine your men are going to be any more immune to that tradition than the Ternathians in my own garrison are. However, this isn't about Ternathia or Uromathia—it's about *Sharona*, and I've seen to it that everyone under my command understands that. As one *Sharonian* to another, then, welcome to Fort Salby."

"Thank you," Markan replied. He was impressed by chan Skrithik's willingness to confront the situation so openly. And pleased, as well. And the Ternathian had shown considerable tact in suggesting that the "friction" existed only between his own empire and Uromathia, he thought. Any Arpathians and Harkalans in the Fort Salby garrison were probably torn between welcoming Markan's troopers with open arms and shooting them in the back at the first opportunity.

"I've stressed the same points to my own personnel," the sunlord said, and indeed he had. "I'm sure there are going to be at least some incidents, anyway, of course. But my officers have been instructed that if—when—such incidents occur, they are to be reported first to you, as the base commander and the senior officer in the PAAF chain of command. They've also been instructed to warn their men that any breach of discipline will be severely punished under our own regulations *after* any penalties you may see fit to award under the Authority's."

He showed his teeth in a tight smile.

"That's good to hear," chan Skrithik said. "Of course, your troops' internal discipline is your own affair. I'm sure any difficulties which arise can be dealt with expeditiously."

"As am I," Markan said with a slight bow.

He didn't add that he'd told chan Skrithik about his instructions to his officers for a specific reason. Markan's own rank was the equivalent of the Ternathian rank of brigade-captain, which made him senior to chan Skrithik. But chan Skrithik was the ranking *PAAF* officer present, and this was a Portal Authority post. More to the point, one instruction Emperor Chava *had* made crystal clear was that Markan was not, under any circumstances, to do anything which might be construed as attempting to undermine the Authority chain of command. In fact, Markan had been specifically ordered to obey chan Skrithik's orders, regardless of who might technically be senior to whom. Clearly the emperor wanted no unfortunate incidents in the field while the Conclave back home was still debating what sort of political arrangements were going to emerge out of all this.

Markan doubted there was any need to be more explicit with chan Skrithik. The man was obviously intelligent, and the quality of his spoken Uromathian suggested a certain degree of familiarity with Markan's native culture. He would recognize Markan's message—that Markan intended to obey the spirit, not just the letter, of the orders subordinating him to chan Skrithik's command—without the sunlord having to be more direct.

"In that case, Sunlord," chan Skrithik said after a moment, "let's see about getting your people settled in."

"I think that's an excellent suggestion, Regiment-Captain."

*   *   *

"About damned time!" Hardar Jalkanthi announced with profound satisfaction as the signal arm swung into the upright position and the signal lamp glowed green.

"Try to be at least a little patient, Hardar," Charak Tarku grunted with a laugh. "*I'm* supposed to be the impatient barbarian around here."

Jalkanthi chuckled. Tarku was his regularly assigned senior fireman, and he knew he'd been lucky to hang onto him under the present chaotic circumstances. The burly, broad shouldered Arpathian was a rarity in TTE, given the usual Arpathian attitude towards technology, and Jalkanthi was glad to have him. He knew better than most just how sharp a brain lurked behind the typically Arpathian façade Tarku chose to present to the rest of the multiverse. The engineer wasn't quite certain why Tarku had decided to play to the Arpathian stereotype, and it often irritated Jalkanthi, but the two of them had been together for almost four years now. That was more than long enough to cement a solid friendship, despite their very different backgrounds, and Tarku knew him better than just about anyone else.

"I always thought Arpathians were supposed to be deadly nomadic hunters, patient as the very stones," he said now, as the two of them swung up the high steps to the footplate of TTE's Paladin 20887.

"Nothing but a fairytale," Tarku said, waving one hand airily. "Just another baseless exaggeration we put about to bolster our fearsome reputation and mystique."

"Well, I think it's about time your mystique settled down and started doing its job," Jalkanthi told him.

"Orders, orders. *Always* orders," Tarku grumbled with a grin. Then he caught hold of the vertical handrail and leaned well out to peer back past the bulk of 20887's integral tender, the auxiliary sixteen thousand-gallon water tender, and the second Paladin and tenders coupled in behind 20887.

"See him?" Jalkanthi asked.

"No, not—Ah! *There* he is!" Tarku leaned a bit further out, waving to show Train Master Sheltim he'd seen him. The train master waved back from his place on the station platform, but the green flag was still tucked firmly under his arm.

"Well?" Jalkanthi pressed.

"No point fretting at *me*," Tarku told him. "Sheltim will waggle his little flag at us when he's good and ready to."

Jalkanthi grimaced, then tapped the glass face of the pressure gauge pointedly. Tarku only grinned, and Jalkanthi produced an oily rag and carefully wiped the already gleaming bronze of the burnished throttle lever. He was always inordinately proud of his big Paladin's speed and power, but today he had a special reason for his impatience to be off.

Jalkanthi was Ternathian, from the city of Garouoma in the Province of Narhath, but his wife was Shurkhali. In fact, it was almost frightening how much like a taller version of the murdered Shaylar Nargra-Kolmayr Jesmanar Jalkanthi-Ishar looked. Jalkanthi might not have been born Shurkhali, but he'd absorbed more than enough of his wife's culture to feel the same fury which had swept across her native kingdom. Worse, Jalkanthi had just enough Talent to have Seen SUNN's Voice broadcast of Shaylar's final message. He didn't really care what the assembled heads of state decided in their precious Conclave. He'd been gratified by his own emperor's attitude, and he wasn't very happy about even the most remote possibility of winding up with Chava of Uromathia running things, but he didn't have time to waste worrying about either of those things just now. He knew what *he* wanted to happen to the bastards responsible for the Chalgyn Consortium crew's massacre, and he was impatient to deliver the first installment of Sharona's vengeance.

He'd been prepared to pull every string in sight when he heard about the decision to send the Third Dragoons forward to Fort Salby. He'd *wanted* that train, and he'd been determined to have it. But he hadn't had to pull any strings in the end, because Yakhan Chusal knew who TTE's best engineer was. So at least—

"Green flag!" Tarku announced suddenly.

"At last!" Jalkanthi replied, and cracked the throttle.

Steam hissed, and the enormous, powerful engine shuddered, trembling like a living creature. The ten huge drivers, each of them almost seven feet high, began to move—slowly, at first, with a deep, strong chuff, spinning on the steel rails as they fought the incredible inertia of a train over two miles long. Then, behind 20887, the second, identical engine hissed into motion as well, drive rods stroking, and the massive drag began to creep slowly forward. Jalkanthi propped one elbow on the window frame as he leaned out of the cab and felt the incredible mass of the train behind him. Thirteen *thousand* tons, Train Master Sheltim had told him. Most people would have found that hard to believe, but this was the TTE. It routinely hauled loads that massive—or even larger—down the ribbons of steel which stitched the endless universes together.

The vast semicircle of the Larakesh Portal loomed ahead of him. Beyond it, he could see the high mountain plateau of South Ricathia and the thriving city of Union.

He'd always thought calling it "Union City" was more than a little silly. For one thing, Union was really no more than an extension of the vast sprawl of Larakesh into the universe of New Sharona. At the time it had been founded, the newborn Portal Authority had felt it was imperative to establish a new, independent city with its own government beholden to no existing Sharonian government, even a purely local municipal one.

Since then, practices had changed—most other portals the size of Larakesh had spawned single cities, with quite efficient unified governments, which sprawled across their thresholds—but Union City had been a special case on several levels. Not only had it been the first extra-universal city Sharonians had ever established, but the Portal Authority, at Harkala's suggestion (although it was widely rumored that the original idea had come from Ternathia), had been granted ownership of the massive South Ricathian gold fields. The vast majority of the authority's operating revenues over the ensuing eighty years had come from the exploitation of those gold deposits—whose location, of course, had been easy to project from Sharona's own experience—which had neatly absolved the governments which had established it from any requirement to provide it with long-term funding. And, Jalkanthi knew, it had also avoided a situation in which those governments which made disproportionate contributions to the Authority's budget would have acquired an equally disproportionate amount of clout with the authority Board of Directors. That was why he tended to believe the rumors about Ternathia's behind-the-scenes involvement in creating the arrangement in the first place.

Rather than develop and mine those deposits itself, however, the Authority had chosen to lease the mining rights for a percentage. Union City had been built largely for the specific purpose of overseeing and accommodating that exploitation.

Still, "Union City" had been a silly choice of names, whatever the Authority's reasoning, given the fact that the one thing exploration of the multiverse *hadn't* done was to unite all of Sharona. When Jalkanthi had been much younger, his grandfather had told him how so many people had hoped that the abrupt appearance of the Larakesh

Portal truly would bring their own world together at last. The old man had cherished the dream of a restored Ternathian Empire as a worldwide bastion of freedom and just governance, both welcomed back to the many lands it had voluntarily freed and extended beyond them, as well, and he'd scarcely been alone in that.

Unfortunately for those dreams, Sharonians had been too attached to their nations and their national identities. And, his grandfather had grudgingly admitted, the Portal Authority had done too good a job of administering the portals in everyone's name. There'd been no *need* to create a true world government, and so "Union City" had remained no more than a name. No more than an unfulfilled promise, in the eyes of people like his grandfather, at least.

But maybe that's going to change at last, Grandpa. And it looks like we may even get the Empire back, just the way you wanted, Jalkanthi thought as the endless train of passenger cars, freight cars, and flatcars loaded with the tools of war moved steadily forward. Thick black smoke plumed from the funnels of both Paladins. Steel drive wheels flashed, and the trucks of the cars behind banged, grated, and squealed with ear-stabbing shrillness, then began to sing as they moved faster. Buffers rattled and banged thunderously as the double-headed train crossed the switches, swinging onto the mainline.

Jalkanthi watched the familiar landmarks, watched the front end of his own streamlined engine cross the portal threshold. Unusually for portal connections, Larakesh and Union City, although they were almost six thousand miles "apart" in their respective universes, were in the same time zone. Of course, what was fall in Larakesh was spring in Union City, and the sun was at a totally different angle, whatever clocks and watches might say. But Jalkanthi was accustomed to that. He was more concerned with getting through the vast Union City side of the enormous Larakesh Central yard and its innumerable sidings—the biggest and busiest rail terminal in the entire known multiverse, by any standard of measurement—and out into the Ricathian countryside, where he could open 20887's throttle wide.

Not much longer now, he told himself, caressing the smooth bronze lever like a lover. *No, not much longer.*

CHAPTER
FORTY-THREE

SARR KLIAN TRIED not to swear out loud.

It wasn't easy.

"So, Master Skirvon," he said instead, "as I understand it, then, my instructions from Two Thousand mul Gurthak are to defer to your judgment where any contact with these people is concerned?"

"I suppose you could put it that way," the senior of the two civilians who'd arrived at Klian's fort that morning replied. "Obviously, Five Hundred, no one is going to try to take away or undermine your *military* authority," he hastened to add, which softened Klian's frustration quite a bit. "But, as you yourself so cogently suggested in your dispatches to Two Thousand mul Gurthak, it's clearly essential that we get a *civilian* diplomatic presence established here as quickly as possible." He smiled. "Men in civilian suits and carrying briefcases are much less threatening than men in military uniforms carrying arbalests," he pointed out.

"I couldn't agree more," Klian said. It was, after all, as Skirvon said, exactly what he himself had asked for. But mul Gurthak's orders seemed to imply that Skirvon *did* have authority, even in purely military matters. Klian didn't like that a bit. Besides, there was something about this Skirvon and his sidekick that . . . bothered the five hundred. He couldn't quite put a finger on what it was, and he couldn't help wondering if a part of it wasn't that he resented having any of his own authority supplanted by a "mere civilian." He hoped it wasn't, but he couldn't be certain.

And I truly don't think that's what it is, either, he thought grimly. *In fact,* he looked back down at the message crystal from mul Gurthak, *I'm pretty damned sure it's at least as much the tone of mul Gurthak's orders and dispatches as anything about these two.*

"Well, gentlemen," he said aloud after a moment, looking back up at them, "how soon do you want me to arrange transport forward? And how big a military escort are you going to require?"

"I don't see any reason to be in a blazing hurry at this point," Skirvon replied. Klian's eyebrows rose, and the civilian shrugged. "Master Dastiri and I are still studying this language primer Magister Kelbryan was able to put together. Fortunately, we both have good ears for foreign languages—frankly, his is better than mine—but both of us could still use a few more days of study before we get dropped into the deep end. And since there's no present contact between our forces and theirs, it would probably make more sense for us to do just that rather than rush forward with incomplete preparation and risk some overly hasty contact that could have additional unfortunate consequences."

Klian nodded. His instincts all shouted to get the two sides talking to one another as quickly as possible, yet Skirvon had made at least two very telling points.

"As for military escorts," Skirvon continued thoughtfully, "I don't know that one's going to be required at all, at least initially. It seems to me that, so far, both sides have been reacting militarily to immediate, perceived threats. I don't think either side's gotten much beyond that so far, and it occurs to me that making the next move from our side by sending in two unarmed, civilian diplomats without any military presence at all, might help us pour a little water on the flames."

Klian frowned. What the man had said made sense, but the professional officer in the five hundred wasn't at all happy with the thought of sending out an official embassy without any military protection at all.

"You don't think that leaving everyone behind—not taking even a token honor guard—might be misconstrued as a sign of weakness?" he asked.

"Not everyone is automatically impressed by the presence of soldiers armed to the teeth," Dastiri, the junior diplomat, said, speaking up for the first time. "And not everyone will automatically interpret their absence as a sign of weakness. Under the circumstances, I think it would be best all round for us to proceed as cautiously as possible. In fact," his tone was cool, "part of the reason the situation is as bad as it is at the moment is that we've had military people on both sides who were too close to things, too unwilling to give ground, to back off and deescalate the situation."

Klian bristled. He couldn't help it. It was possible Dastiri hadn't

intended to sound insulting—or at least dismissive—in his analysis of
the Army's actions to date. Unfortunately, it didn't sound that way.

"Contrary to what you may assume, Master Dastiri," the five hundred
said in an equally cool tone, making no particular effort to hide the
dislike in his eyes, "not every military man wants to charge into every
situation, sword in one hand and arbalest in the other. As I indicated
in my report to Two Thousand mul Gurthak—which you and Master
Skirvon have obviously had an opportunity to read—I concur with
Hundred Olderhan's view that we would have been far wiser to simply
pull back to Fort Rycharn in the first place. I allowed myself at the time
to be convinced by Hundred Thalmayr, which I deeply regret, given
what happened to Charlie Company when these Sharonians attacked.
Or counterattacked, or whatever. I'm in favor of anything that allows
us to—how did you put it? 'Back off and deescalate the situation.' My
only concern is how best to go about doing that."

Dastiri flushed and his almond eyes hardened, but Skirvon laid a
hand on his subordinate's shoulder and smiled at Klian.

"I apologize if it sounded as if either of us intended to denigrate
the Army or your legitimate concerns, Five Hundred. That certainly
wasn't our intent. All the same, I think my colleague here has a
point. Two Thousand mul Gurthak is mobilizing all available forces
to support us if and as required. We'll have quite a lot of firepower
available, very shortly, if we need it. In the meantime, however, I'd
very much prefer to keep this a completely civilian contact from
our side, initially at least. After all," he smiled again, more broadly,
but there was a faint, unmistakable tang of iron in his voice, "this
is what we do. I'd never try to tell you how to conduct a military
operation, because I wouldn't have the least idea where to begin.
But with all due respect, I believe Master Dastiri and I are probably
rather more experienced at diplomacy than you are."

"No doubt," Klian conceded, yet deep down inside, he wasn't
fully convinced. After all, the Union of Arcana hadn't really needed
diplomats for the last two hundred years. With the emergence of
the Union, traditional international diplomacy had been replaced by
what were effectively bureaucratic administrators. Or perhaps "facili-
tators" would have been a better choice of word: arbitrators, with
full authority to issue binding decisions and full access (officially,
at least) to all information on both sides of any issue which had
to be settled. There wasn't a single living "diplomat" in the entire
Union who'd *ever* had to sit down across a bargaining table from a
completely separate and sovereign entity, far less one about which
the "diplomat" in question knew absolutely nothing.

That's what bothers me, he realized. *These two keep talking about diplomacy and diplomatic judgments, but they don't really seem to understand that they're dealing with something completely outside their experience. They really do think they understand what's going on, and I suppose it's possible they do. But what if they* don't?

"Very well," he said, standing behind his desk to signal an end to the meeting, "please let me know if there's anything I can do for you during your stay. And whenever you're ready to move forward to the swamp portal, I'll be happy to arrange transportation."

"Thank you, Five Hundred," Skirvon said.

He and Dastiri departed, and Klian sat back down, toying with the message crystal from mul Gurthak and considering the two thousand's dispatches and their implications.

He couldn't say he was particularly surprised by them, except, perhaps, for how quickly the two thousand was moving. He could hardly disapprove of *that*, of course, although he didn't much look forward to finding himself superseded by someone else.

Come now, Sarr, he told himself. *Mul Gurthak specifically says you'll remain in command of Fort Rycharn whatever happens. Surely you didn't expect anything else?*

No, of course he hadn't. On the other hand, he hadn't exactly expected to find himself superseded by Commander of Two Thousand Mayrkos Harshu, either.

Of all the officers it could have been, why did it have to be Harshu? Klian demanded of his office's silent walls.

There was nothing at all wrong with Two Thousand Harshu's military credentials, but the man had a reputation within the Union Army. Worse, he knew he did. In fact, he'd deliberately cultivated it.

Harshu was a throwback, one of those who bemoaned the fact that he'd been born into such "boring" times. He embraced what he believed was the true Andaran tradition, although Klian had always suspected that men like Thankhar Olderhan were truer keepers of that tradition. Harshu's version of it was heavily laden with the trappings of military glory, which there'd been precious little of in the two centuries since the Union was formed, and he seemed remarkably oblivious to just how much that "military glory" had cost in lives, as well as money. It might not be precisely fair to call him a hothead, but Klian was unable to come up with a better term, and that worried him.

Of course, he's always been a top performer in every maneuver, too, the five hundred forced himself to concede. *However full of himself he may be, he didn't earn that reputation by sitting around being stupid. And if he's the next most senior officer in the area, mul Gur-thak doesn't have much of a choice about putting him in command, unless he wants to come forward and take the field command himself. Which, now that I think about it, presents an interesting question of its own, doesn't it? Why* isn't *mul Gurthak moving himself closer to the point of contact, since he's ultimately responsible for whatever happens out here?*

Klian frowned. There could, of course, be all sorts of reasons for mul Gurthak to choose to remain in Erthos. For one thing, his lines of communication were substantially better, and he might well feel that he needed to keep himself available to browbeat anyone who wanted to drag his feet when the two thousand ordered him to send all of his available fighting strength forward. But judging from mul Gurthak's message crystal, he was going to be sending at least the equivalent of a full air-mobile brigade—possibly even a division—to Fort Rycharn. With cavalry support, no less.

A brigade was a commander of five thousand's billet, and a division was properly commanded by a commander of ten thousand—neither of which, unfortunately, Arcana had available at the moment. And this was the first time in the Union of Arcana's entire history that its army had confronted the possibility of open combat with another power. So why was the officer with the ultimate responsibility for what happened—not to mention the opportunity to command the most important troop deployment in the Union's history—staying behind and sending someone junior to him forward to assume operational command?

Klian tipped his chair back, arms crossed, and thought about it. And the more he thought, the less he liked it.

You're just being paranoid because he's Mythalan, he scolded himself. *After all, he didn't say he intended to stay behind in Erthos forever, did he? Harshu's in command of the immediate deployment; there's no reason mul Gurthak can't come forward and relieve him as soon as he's convinced he's got everything running smoothly in the rear areas.*

In fact, that actually made more sense than rushing forward would have made. As long as mul Gurthak stayed in Erthos, where he had his own command staff well broken in (not to mention far better hummer and dragon lines of communication than he could possibly expect from Fort Rycharn), he was well placed to see to it that the troop movements went as smoothly as possible. And that was at least as important as—if potentially much less glamorous than—actually commanding in the face of the enemy.

Maybe it's because he is *Mythalan,* Klian thought, then shook his head with a wry snort. *You're worried about Harshu because he's a throwback to what he thinks were the good old days of Andaran militancy. And you're worried about mul Gurthak because he isn't acting like a throwback to the good old days of Andaran militancy! Not very consistent of you, Sarr.*

He grimaced and let his chair come back upright. Whatever might or might not be going through mul Gurthak's head, Klian's immediate responsibilities were unpleasantly clear.

The voyage between Fort Rycharn and Fort Wyvern was completely unacceptable from a logistical viewpoint. There were only two true "transports" in Mahrithan waters, and only one of them was configured to carry dragons. Even that ship could transport only two dragons at a time, for that matter, and that wasn't even a fraction of the sealift required to move or supply the troop strength mul Gurthak was talking about.

There was a way around that, of course, but it came with its own price. No dragon, not even one of the long-range heavylift transports, could make the flight from Fort Wyvern to Fort Rycharn in one hop. But any dragon—even one of the shorter-ranged battle dragons—could make the hop from Fort Wyvern to the long isthmus connecting the continents of Andara and Hilmar. From there, they could proceed southward overland, which would permit them to make it clear to Fort Rycharn in a four-day flight rather than a five-day voyage.

They'd have to delay their flight at least once to permit the dragons to hunt, but this universe's Hilmar teemed with game animals which had never heard of dragons and could be expected to be relatively unwary—for a time, at least. And by flying the transports forward instead of sending them by ship, mul Gurthak could send in as many of them simultaneously as he could lay hands on . . . and take advantage of the beasts' airlift capacity, as well. Whereas a medium-weight transport like Windclaw could carry perhaps half a platoon of infantry and its personal weapons, the heavy transports could lift much bigger loads, even before the Quartermaster Corps' spell engineers got into the act.

With the proper levitation spells added to the equation, a pair of heavylift transports could easily tow a freight pod capable of transporting an entire company of infantry, its support personnel and weapons, and enough rations for several days of operations. Cavalry units devoured transport volume at a much higher rate than infantry outfits, of course, but with the cargo pods and levitation spells, even heavy cavalry could be airlifted to within striking range of the enemy. The spells were difficult—more because of the power levels involved than because of their technological complexity—and they didn't last long. The same accumulator that could power a surface ship for a week would support levitation spells of that level for less than twenty-four hours, although freight pods were routinely fitted with multiple accumulators to give them more endurance.

Even with the pods, though, transporting the numbers of men mul Gurthak's message crystal suggested were en route was going to be a massive undertaking. And it was going to tie up an incredible number of transport dragons. In fact, the availability of transports was probably going to prove at least as big a limiting factor as the availability of manpower, when all was said and done. Which probably explained why mul Gurthak was busy gutting the air transport network for at least half a dozen universes rearward from Erthos—thus neatly illustrating one of the many unpleasant costs involved in getting significant numbers of troops forward deployed in a hurry.

It explained Klian's rapidly approaching problems, as well, because there was no provision in mul Gurthak's orders for all of those transport dragons to turn around and fly back to Erthos. Instead, he wanted them held at Fort Rycharn, available to Two Thousand Harshu in the event that military operations became necessary, after all. That, too, made sense, Klian supposed, but Rycharn had never been intended to support that many men and—even more difficult—that many dragons for any length of time.

Fortunately, dragons were quite willing to eat fish or whale meat, and the water between Fort Rycharn and Fort Wyvern was just as rich with life as the continent. The entire Fort Wyvern fishing fleet—such as it was, and what there was of it—was already on its way forward to help feed the dragons once they arrived. And, also fortunately, it was going to take at least four waves to get all of mul Gurthak's earmarked troop strength forward.

According to the two thousand's tentative movement orders—which were undoubtedly going to suffer considerable revision as the realities of moving that many men impinged upon them—he'd have the first two Air Force strikes and the first battalion of infantry at Fort Rycharn within the next week. A strike was a standing formation which consisted of three four-dragon flights (*and why*, Klian wondered, not for the first time, *can't those Air Force pukes use the same names for their formations everyone* else *uses?*), which meant he was going to have to figure out how to feed twenty-four battle dragons, with their notoriously overactive metabolisms, in addition to all of the transports necessary to get the rest of Harshu's force forward.

Worse, according to those same orders, mul Gurthak would have an entire three-strike Air Force talon—thirty-six battle dragons, not twenty-four—at Fort Rycharn within a month. In fact, he might have as much as twice that many.

Feeding seventy-two battle dragons and their supporting ground crews would be a gargantuan task, all by itself. Adding in the two hundred or so transports mul Gurthak was projecting (and *their* ground element), plus the reconnaissance and strike gryphons, *plus* the fodder for the unicorns and heavy cavalry mounts on the movement list, not to mention all of the men he was going to have to feed, was only going to make things incomparably worse. And the responsibility for managing all of those "minor" housekeeping details was going to land squarely on Sarr Klian's shoulders.

No wonder mul Gurthak is staying safely in Erthos! he thought with another snort. *He knows damned well what kind of nightmare he's about to dump on me.*

It was the first truly amusing thought the five hundred had entertained since Skirvon and Dastiri had turned up in his office.

He didn't expect to have a great many more of them over the next few weeks.

CHAPTER
FORTY-FOUR

"YOU LOOK TIRED," Regiment-Captain Namir Velvelig observed dryly, tilting back his head to regard the enormous young officer who'd just dismounted from the magnificent blue roan Shikowr.

"Thank you, Sir," Platoon-Captain chan Calirath replied with exquisite politeness. "Somehow that had escaped my notice."

Velvelig's lips twitched. For the hard-bitten Arpathian, that constituted the equivalent of anyone else's deep belly laugh, and Prince Janaki smiled. He'd been attached to Velvelig's command for just over six months before being sent forward to New Uromath when Company-Captain Halifu appealed for help covering the vast new frontiers the Chalgyn Consortium had been so unexpectedly opening up back in those ancient days—all of two months ago—before everything had gone straight to hell. During that time, he'd developed a deep respect, even admiration, for the shorter, squarely built regiment-captain, and in turn, Velvelig had made it clear that he intended to treat young Platoon-Captain chan Calirath like any other junior officer ... within limits, of course.

"I didn't expect to see you back so soon, Platoon-Captain," Velvelig said now, his voice lower, as Janaki handed his reins to an orderly and stepped up onto the wooden veranda which fronted the administrative block of Fort Raylthar.

No, he reminded himself, *it's* Fort Ghartoun *now.*

He'd noticed the new name on the signboard outside the fort's main entrance, and he wondered whose idea it had been to rename Raylthar. From what he knew of Velvelig, he rather suspected what the answer was. The regiment-captain was as immune to fear and as implacably determined as any Arpathian stereotype, but there was a warm and caring human being down inside all that armor.

The fort itself lay on the eastern flank of New Ternathia's Sky Blood Mountains, barely ten miles from the deep, beautiful waters of Snow Sapphire Lake and within twenty miles of the legendary Sky Blood Lode, probably the biggest silver deposit in history. The discovery of this portal was going to make the Fairnos Consortium, which had first surveyed it, unbelievably wealthy once the railhead steadily advancing from Fort Salby reached it. Although the portal and the fort which covered it were located at little more than forty-five hundred feet of altitude, the Sky Bloods' higher peaks between Ghartoun and Snow Sapphire rose to almost ten thousand snowcapped feet. Their lower flanks were heavily forested, although Ghartoun itself got precious little rain or snow, even in the winter, and the lower mountains and foothills east of the fort were drier and far less hospitable. Still, Janaki preferred Fort Ghartoun's normal climate to the soggier environs of Company-Captain Halifu's post. This late in the year, the temperature was dropping close to freezing at night, but it was no more than pleasantly cool during the day, with just enough nip to make a boy from Estafel feel refreshed and vigorous. For the last two weeks, Janaki had been looking forward to spending at least a day or so out on the lake, but Velvelig's remark reminded him of why he'd really returned to Ghartoun.

"I didn't expect to *be* back so soon, Sir," he said now, his expression turning grimmer. "Then again, a lot of things no one expected have been happening lately, haven't they?"

"That they have, Platoon-Captain," Velvelig agreed. He looked up at Janaki for another few seconds, then twitched his head at the admin block door. "Come into my office."

"Yes, Sir."

Janaki followed Velvelig into the administration building, down the short, rough-planked corridor to the regiment-captain's office, and through its door. He closed it behind himself and started to brace to attention, but Velvelig shook his head impatiently.

"Forget that nonsense," he said briskly. "Consider yourself already reported on-post."

"Yes, Sir. Thank you."

"Don't start thanking me yet," Velvelig snorted. Janaki quirked an eyebrow, and the regiment-captain seated himself in the swivel chair behind his desk with a grimace.

"May I ask *why* I shouldn't thank you, Sir?" Janaki asked after a moment.

"Because I'm pretty sure you were hoping to spend at least a day or two resting up before heading on up-chain to Failcham."

"Ah." Janaki nodded slowly. "I take it that's not going to happen, Sir?"

"You take it correctly . . . Your Highness."

Both of Janaki's eyebrows went up at that, and Velvelig leaned back in his chair and sighed.

"I know you specifically asked not to receive any special treatment when you reported to me eight months ago, Janaki," he said, "and overall, I thought you were right. Still do, in fact. I'm not Ternathian myself, of course, but I've always thought the Ternathian tradition that the heir to the throne ought to have military experience—*real* military experience, not just a token version of it—makes a lot of sense. That's why I went ahead and deployed you forward to New Uromath when Halifu needed reinforcements. But I'm sure you're aware of how things have changed out here in the last month or so."

He paused, his head cocked slightly to one side, and Janaki shrugged.

"Of course I am, Sir," he said quietly. "And I also understand why I was detailed to escort these prisoners to the rear. I don't say I *like* it, but I understand it. But if you'll pardon me for saying so, you sound as if you've got something even more specific in mind."

"I do." Velvelig turned his chair just far enough to one side to be able to gaze out his office window at Fort Ghartoun's parade ground. "You don't have a Voice assigned to your platoon, do you?" he asked.

"No, Sir." Janaki was a bit puzzled by the question. "Company-Captain chan Halifu considered sending one along with us, given the prisoners we're escorting. But we're short along this entire chain, especially with all the troop movements going on. Certainly too short to start assigning Voices to mere platoons. Besides, the company-captain knew Darcel Kinlafia was coming with us, so we were covered. Until he . . . went on ahead, of course."

"I know." Velvelig chuckled slightly. "Kinlafia came through here a week and a half ago like his horse's tail was on fire. For that matter, he looked like a man whose *arse* was on fire, too! But he didn't even stay to soak his saddle sores." The regiment-captain appeared to be studying something on the empty parade ground with great intensity. "Seemed to be in quite a hurry, now that I think about it. Had a note from you, too, I believe."

"Yes, Sir. I, ah, felt it was advisable to get him home to make a firsthand report as quickly as possible."

"You did, did you?" Velvelig glanced back at the crown prince. "Well, maybe you were right about that. But my point is that you've been more or less out of communication since you left Brithik."

"Yes, Sir."

The long overland march from Fort Brithik had taken the next best thing to three weeks. He'd been able to make better time (until, at least, he'd hit the mountains between Brithik and Salby) after leaving the majority of his wounded prisoners, in no small part because there were actual roads between Brithik and Fort Ghartoun. Several small towns—little more than a handful of roughly constructed buildings clustered around Portal Authority remount stations and Voice relay posts—had been strung along those roads like beads when Janaki and his platoon originally deployed forward from Fort Raylthar. On the journey back, many of them had been deserted, except for the Voices and Authority personnel still manning the remount stations.

Although he'd left the majority of the wounded at Brithik, he was still accompanied by half a dozen ambulances. It was far simpler to load the prisoners onto the vehicles rather than try to find individual mounts for them . . . and accept the additional security problems which would have gone with it. A single mounted Marine with a Model 10 at the ready could guard an entire ambulance full of prisoners quite handily, and none of them was in the position to make an individual break for freedom. And, because he'd had to bring the ambulances along anyway, he'd also brought along Commander of One Hundred Thalmayr.

He hadn't wanted to do that, for several reasons. One was the fact that he continued to hold the idiotic Arcanan officer responsible for the massacre of Thalmayr's own command. Janaki had had more time now to think over what Thalmayr had done, and the more he'd thought about it, even after allowing for the unknown nature of Company-Captain chan Tesh's weapons, the stupider he'd realized the man had to be. But he was honest enough to admit that the main reason was that Thalmayr reminded him entirely too much of a zombie in his present state. Petty-Captain Yar had, indeed, "shut him down" completely, and Janaki hadn't made sufficient allowance for how . . . creepy he was going to find that totally expressionless, blank-eyed face whenever he was forced to look at it.

Unfortunately, Petty-Captain chan Rodair, the Fort Brithik Healer, had insisted that Thalmayr be taken on to what had been Fort Raylthar. From his own examination of the captured Arcanan officer, chan Rodair believed that Thalmayr's paralysis might be the result of pressure on his spinal cord, rather than actual damage to the cord itself. If that were the case, then surgical intervention might restore the Arcanan's mobility, but chan Rodair wasn't trained as a surgeon. Company-Captain Golvar Silkash, Velvelig's post Healer, *was* a school-trained surgeon, and a good one. In addition, Silkash's assistant, Platoon-Captain Tobis Makree, was not only a trained surgeon in his own right, but also a powerfully Talented Healer. Given that—and especially given Makree's unusual combination of skills and Talent—chan Rodair had argued that Thalmayr's best chance for an actual recovery lay at Fort Raylthar.

Personally, Janaki had decided that he didn't give much of a damn one way or the other whether or not Hadrign Thalmayr ever walked again. He didn't much like admitting that, but there was no point lying to himself about it. And whether he cared about it or not didn't affect his duty to see to it that the man had the best chance for recovery he could provide, even if rank stupidity was one of the two most unforgivable sins of which any officer could be guilty. So, rather against his will, he'd delivered Thalmayr to the renamed Fort Ghartoun.

"I did manage to check in once, about . . . eighteen days ago, Sir," he said now. "May I ask why the fact that I couldn't do so more frequently is significant?"

"Because," Velvelig said with a crooked smile, "about *twelve* days ago, your father stood up on his hind legs at the Conclave and informed the assembled heads of state of Sharona that they were sitting there with their thumbs up their arses while people were being shot at out here. He, ah, *suggested* that they might have better things to do than debate fishing rights on Sharona. Suggested it rather *forcefully*, as a matter of fact. If you'd care to hear what he had to say for yourself, I believe my senior Voice could replay the Voice broadcast of the session for you."

"Oh . . . my," Janaki said after a moment, and, Arpathian impassivity or no, this time Velvelig laughed out loud at the crown prince's expression.

"I'd heard rumors about the emperor's temper before," the regiment-captain said, shaking his head, once he'd stopped laughing. "Apparently they actually fell short of the reality."

"Father is one of the most patient people in the universe . . . as long as the people around him are at least trying to do their jobs," Janaki replied. "He drives himself harder than he ever drives anyone else, too. But may the gods help anyone he thinks is shirking his responsibilities to others."

"That's about what I'd gathered. In this case, according to the SUNN reports we've been getting over the Voicenet, he was more than justified. In fact, most of the Conclave seemed to feel that way. Which explains why he's been nominated as the first planetary emperor of Sharona."

For a moment, Janaki just looked at the regiment-captain. He'd known from the beginning that his father and his family were going to have a prominent part to play in whatever decisions the Conclave ever came to, but he'd never expected anything remotely like what Velvelig appeared to be suggesting.

For several seconds, it simply refused to sink in. Then it did, and his first reaction was that he couldn't think of anyone on Sharona who could possibly do the job better than Zindel chan Calirath. His second reaction was that it had been extraordinarily thick-witted of him not to see this coming. And his *third* reaction was a stab of sheer, unmitigated terror as he realized who would someday have to *succeed* his father in that role, if it was confirmed.

Which, he thought a moment later, *might just explain why I wasn't about to let myself think about this particular possibility!*

Velvelig watched the implications sink home in the broad-shouldered youngster sitting across his desk from him, and he was impressed by what he saw. Very few people would have realized what the sudden, slight widening of Janaki chan Calirath's eyes represented. Velvelig did, and he watched those broad shoulders come a fraction of an inch further back as Janaki's spine straightened and he drew a deep breath.

"That's . . . quite a bit to take in, Sir," he said.

"Oh, it gets even better," Velvelig assured him. "You see, there were two candidates for the nomination. Your father . . . and Chava Busar."

The eyes which had widened a moment before abruptly narrowed and went very cold, Velvelig observed. That, too, pleased him immensely. There were very few Arpathian septs which didn't have at least one bone to pick with Emperor Chava, and Velvelig's sept—what was left of it—nursed long and homicidal memories of the debt *it* owed the Busar Dynasty. Which, although he'd never actually explained it to Janaki, was one of the reasons Namir Velvelig had been so pleased when Platoon-Captain chan Calirath reported to him for duty.

"I can see where that could get ugly, Sir," Janaki said after a moment. "Still, I suppose it was inevitable. Who else could possibly put together an opposition candidacy?"

"It wasn't much of a 'candidacy,'" Velvelig demurred. "As nearly as I can tell from the reports we've gotten so far—and remember, they're a week old—your father buried him in the voting. It wasn't even close. Unfortunately, Chava's refused to accept that the Conclave's decision is binding upon him. Which, since the Conclave is a purely voluntary association, is probably a not unreasonable position," the regiment-captain conceded unwillingly.

"He's flatly refused to accept the outcome of the vote, then?"

"No, not quite. But he's put forward an incredible shopping list of demands which he insists have to be met before he'll even contemplate the possibility of 'surrendering Uromathia's sacred sovereignty to a foreign crown.'" The regiment-captain made a face. "The Conclave is considering those demands now. Personally, I don't see any way he can genuinely expect to get ninety-nine percent of them, but he seems perfectly prepared to go on arguing about them forever."

"Which means he *is* going to get at least some of them," Janaki said grimly. "*He* may be willing to go on burying his head in the sand while the tide comes in, and he may be perfectly willing for everyone else to drown with him rather than give in, but the rest of the Conclave isn't going to be that capricious."

"That's my reading of the situation, too," Velvelig agreed. "Since the only two options are to give him at least some of what he wants or to start a second war between Uromathia and the rest of the planet to force him to submit, I'm guessing he'll probably end up settling for two or three concessions. Which, I'm sure I hardly need to point out to you, are going to be the ones he figures are best calculated to hamstring your father's ultimate authority over him."

Janaki nodded, and Velvelig shrugged.

"That's why you're not going to get a rest stop here after all, Janaki," he said quietly. "I'll take the rest of the wounded off your hands, and we'll provide you with additional teams for your ambulances so that you can make better time with the unwounded prisoners, but I want you back in Sharona as quickly as I can get you there. Whatever Chava's up to, your father doesn't need his heir universes away at a time like this. In fact," he looked sympathetically at the younger man, "I'm afraid your days in uniform are over. We can't afford to have anything happen to you now."

Janaki wanted to protest. In fact, he started to, then stopped as an echo of the Glimpse he'd had of Kinlafia and Andrin rippled through the back of his mind. It remained frustratingly unclear—probably because he himself wasn't in it—but something about what Velvelig had just said had waked that echo. He knew that much, even if he had no idea at all what it had been. And whatever it was, Velvelig was undoubtedly correct. What had been an acceptable risk in peacetime for the heir to the Winged Crown was *not* an acceptable risk in wartime for the man who might be about to become heir to the crown of all Sharona.

"I understand, Sir," he said finally, and Velvelig nodded in approval. He'd seen the protests fluttering in the backs of Janaki's eyes, and he'd also seen the Calirath sense of duty which kept those protests silent.

"I know you do," the regiment-captain said quietly. "And for what it's worth—and it may not feel like it's worth very much at this particular moment—I think it's a damned shame. About the uniform, I mean. There are some people who simply wear it without ever learning what it really means. You already knew that when you arrived. I think you would have been one of the really good ones."

"Actually, that means quite a lot coming from you, Sir," Janaki replied. He inhaled again, then stood. "With your permission, Sir, I'd better go and alert the platoon that we won't be staying over after all. At least everyone ought to have time to get a hot bath and a sitdown meal in a proper mess hall before we hit the road again."

"Of course." Velvelig stood as well, then reached across the desk to offer his right hand. "Good luck, Your Highness. And I hope you won't object if a heathen Arpathian spends the odd night hour praying for you and your father." He smiled crookedly as the prince clasped his hand firmly. "After all, it could hardly hurt, could it?"

*   *   *

Petty-Armsman Harth Loumas sat in the hot patch of shade cast by the small canvas tarp and tried to ignore the insects whining around his ears. He told himself that, despite the bugs' irritation quotient, he couldn't really object to his present duty. Or, he *shouldn't*, anyway; obviously he *could*, because he was. All the same, he knew that most of his fellow PAAF troopers would willingly have exchanged places with him. For one thing, he did get to sit in the shade, which was more than they got to do. He knew that, and in an intellectual sort of way, he actually agreed. But that wasn't exactly the same thing as saying that he actively enjoyed sitting here sweating.

He checked his watch, then closed his eyes again and reached out with his Talent. Loumas had extremely good range for a Plotter, but he was still limited to no more than four miles, and he had to concentrate hard, at any range beyond about two miles, if he wanted to separate human life essences from those of other animals. It took him a good twenty minutes to sweep the total area he could See from his present location, and the portal itself created a huge blind spot in his coverage. Since no Talent could operate through a portal, he had to move physically around to its far aspect in this bug-infested swamp if he wanted to See around it. That was why he was parked at one end of the portal with Tairsal chan Synarch, Company-Captain chan Tesh's senior Flicker. They were outside both the sandbagged outer picket posts and the main defensive position chan Tesh had thrown up on the Hell's Gate side of the portal, but they could shift to the other aspect of the portal by simply walking around it in this universe, which took all of fifteen minutes.

It also meant that if anything did turn up, chan Synarch could nip around to the Hell's Gate side of the portal and Flick a message straight back to chan Tesh and Company-Captain Halifu in a handful of seconds.

Loumas and chan Synarch changed positions every hour on the hour, moving around to the far aspect, in order to maintain a three hundred sixty-degree watch. It was, quite frankly, boring as hell, but it was also necessary. No one had any idea where the enemy troops—the "Arcanans," as they called themselves—had come from. Platoon-Captain Arthag had led sweeps a full fifteen miles out in every direction without finding any sign of human habitation. He'd lost one man and two horses to the local crocodiles in the process, and Company-Captain chan Tesh had decided there was no point in sweeping farther out. No officer worth his uniform liked losing men for no return, and if there'd been any evidence of where these people had come from, or how they'd gotten here, some indication of it should have turned up inside that thirty-mile circle. Besides, he hadn't wanted Arthag and any of his men that far out from the field fortifications he'd thrown up here at the portal itself.

Frankly, Loumas was beginning to wonder if there might actually be anything to the wild rumors about flying beasts. He wasn't certain where they'd started. The Arcanan prisoners had all been sent farther back, safely beyond the possibility of any attempt to rescue them. Loumas would have preferred for at least some of them to have been kept closer to hand, where the local garrison might have been able to begin learning their language and possibly conduct some useful interrogations. On the other hand, he understood just how vital an intelligence resource those prisoners were, and he could hardly blame Company-Captain chan Tesh or Company-Captain Halifu for wanting to make sure nothing happened to them.

But if none of the prisoners had been spreading ridiculous stories about huge, winged creatures, Loumas had no idea where they might have come from.

Probably a combination of sheer boredom and the fact that we don't know diddily about these people—except that they've got some fucking dangerous weapons!

He snorted in what he wanted to be amusement but which was tinged with something entirely too much like fear for comfort. He reminded himself that the other side obviously didn't know anything more about Sharona and the capabilities of Sharonian weapons than he did about *their* weapons. The way they'd tried to defend this very portal was proof enough of that! But that didn't make him—or anyone else—any happier about confronting the completely unknown, and the eerie way these people had somehow managed to establish their base camp here without anything remotely like roads or leaving a single boat behind didn't make it any better.

Well, at least they won't be sneaking up on us, he told himself firmly. *It may be boring, but I'm damned sure not—*

His thoughts froze and he stiffened, focusing in tightly. Then he swore aloud.

Damn! I wish we had a decent Distance Viewer! he thought.

His Talent would let him spot living creatures, but what he Saw of them was always . . . fuzzy. The creatures themselves were clear enough, but exactly what they might be doing, or exactly what their surroundings were, was often almost impossible to discern. Half the time, he had to extrapolate, and like most Plotters, he was fairly good at that. But extrapolation depended on some sort of familiarity with what the people he was Plotting were likely to be doing, and who the hells knew what *these* people were likely to be up to? If he'd had a Distance Viewer to team with, he'd have been able to coach the other Talent into finding the proper distance and bearing, and the Distance Viewer would have been able to See exactly what was happening.

Loumas closed his eyes, concentrating hard, then punched chan Synarch's shoulder.

"Huh?" The wiry Marine snorted awake. His head snapped up, and his eyes cleared almost instantly as he looked a question at Loumas.

"We've got an incoming contact," Loumas said crisply. "I think it's a small boat, headed in from the east."

Chan Synarch nodded sharply and reached into the cargo pocket on his right thigh and extracted a pad of paper and pencil.

"Shoot," he said tersely, pencil poised.

"It's not as clear as I'd like," Loumas admitted, knowing chan Synarch would understand why that was. "They're about four miles out. I can't get much of a feel for the boat, but it's moving *damned* fast—I make it at least twenty-five or thirty miles an hour, whatever that is in the 'knots' or whatever it is you Ternathian swabbies use."

The two of them grinned tensely at each other, and he continued.

"There's three of them. One of them's in some kind of uniform, but it doesn't look like anything we saw here. I don't think he's wearing a helmet, and his tunic or jacket is red, not the camouflage pattern they had." His hand stabbed in the direction of the wrecked Arcanan fortifications and camp. "I think the other two are in civilian clothes. Doesn't look like any uniform I ever heard of, and they aren't dressed alike. I don't See any weapons on any of them. None of those tube things, and no crossbows anywhere I can See, either." Loumas grimaced. "A Distance Viewer could probably tell us more, but that's all I've got right now."

"Understood." Chan Synarch had been writing quickly and clearly in the shorthand every Flicker was trained to use while Loumas talked. Now he read back what he'd written, and Loumas listened carefully, then nodded.

"That's it," he agreed.

"Then I'd better get it off," chan Synarch said. He ripped off the sheet on which he'd written, folded it, put it into one of the metal carrier cartridges on his belt, and trotted briskly around the edge of the portal until he crossed over into the cool, forested depths of Hell's Gate and had a clear line of sight to Company-Captain chan Tesh's HQ bunker. As soon as he did, he Flicked the message cartridge directly to the company-captain's orderly.

"Sent," he reported laconically to Loumas as he jogged back around to the swamp side, and the Plotter nodded. He was still tracking the incoming boat. In the three minutes it had taken him and chan Synarch to get the message off, the boat had covered almost another mile and a half. It was going to be here in another three minutes—four, tops—and—

A bugle awoke suddenly from the far side of the portal, sounding the "Stand-To," and Loumas exhaled the breath he hadn't realized he was holding. He watched men double-timing towards their assigned actions stations, and his lips skinned back from his teeth in a tight smile.

I might have missed some kind of super weapon in their frigging boat, he thought, *but they aren't going to take us by surprise with whatever it is.*

CHAPTER
FORTY-FIVE

BALKAR CHAN TESH lowered his field glasses with a thoughtful frown. He'd gotten to Platoon-Captain Parai chan Dersal's forward observation post from the Hell's Gate side of the portal while the boat Loumas had detected was still a good mile out. He'd stood beside the Marine and watched it during its final approach, and he hoped his perplexity was less apparent to his men than it was to him.

How the hell do they make the thing move? he wondered. There was no sail, no oars, no paddle, and certainly no steam launch's tall spindly funnel or plume of smoke. Yet the boat—not more than fifteen feet long, at most—came sliding through the deeper channels of the swamp fast enough that its stern squatted and its bow planed across the water.

It's not natural ... and isn't that *a silly thing to be thinking after everything that's already happened out here?*

He slowly and deliberately cased the field glasses, then folded his arms and stood waiting while the boat slowed abruptly as it slid the last few dozen yards to the raised hillock before the portal.

As Loumas had reported, there were three men in it. Two of them wore what was obviously civilian clothing of some sort, although—not surprisingly—chan Tesh had never seen garments cut that way. They were much more tightly tailored, more formfitting, than any current Sharonian fashion, and the civilian jackets were long-tailed, with broad, cutaway lapels and outsized silver buttons. Both jackets were dark colored—the larger, chestnut-haired fellow in the bow, who looked to be the older of the two, wore one that was the color of port wine, while the younger, Uromathian-looking one on the midships thwart wore one of a dark, rich green—but the tight trousers were light-colored, and tucked into pointy-toed dress boots which rose to midcalf. All in all, chan Tesh couldn't imagine a less practical outfit for wading around in swamps.

The man sitting in the stern of the boat and managing the simple rudder—*at least I know what* that's *for*, chan Tesh thought wryly—was obviously in uniform, although as Loumas had already informed him, it didn't match anything they'd seen yet. There was something about him which suggested a noncommissioned officer, chan Tesh decided, and his red jerseylike tunic reminded the company-captain vaguely of naval uniform, for some reason. Possibly, he thought, because the man seemed to be doing what one might expect a sailor to do.

The boat drifted gently and silently through the reeds in the shallower water, then nosed into the mud with a soft slosh of swamp water and a muddy slurp. Its occupants sat very still, their hands in plain sight. Even the man at the rudder was very careful to make no sudden moves as he released the tiller bar and placed his open hands palm-down on his thighs, and chan Tesh smiled humorlessly at the sight. He'd be doing exactly the same thing if twenty Model 10 rifles and at least one machine-gun (that he could see) were aimed at *him*.

The older of the two civilians had busy eyes, chan Tesh observed. They swept back and forth across the waiting Sharonians, and the company-captain had the distinct impression that they weren't missing much. Then the moving eyes seemed to narrow slightly as they settled on chan Tesh himself.

"Hello!" the stranger said, in oddly accented but perfectly intelligible Ternathian. "We come talk?"

Chan Tesh stiffened. Despite everything, he was shocked to be addressed in his native tongue, and he hoped his astonishment didn't show. Nor was he the only one who reacted strongly. He heard someone inhale sharply behind him, and then someone else snarled in what he obviously thought was a whisper, "Those bastards have a live prisoner!"

The talkative civilian started to stand up in the boat, then froze as half a dozen rifles tracked him. He obviously knew what the weapons were, and he swallowed hard, sweating more heavily than the swampy heat alone could explain. But he didn't panic; chan Tesh had to give him that much.

"No shoot," he said in a commendably level voice. "We talk, please? Much killing mistake. You send word? Say we talk. Important."

"You think they really want to parley, Sir?" chan Dersal said softly behind chan Tesh.

"I'd sooner parley with a fucking cobra!" Platoon-Captain chan Talmarha half-snarled, and the Marine grunted.

"We hit them hard, Morek," chan Dersal pointed out to chan Tesh's mortar commander. "Twice. In their shoes, *I'd* think about talking truce. Hard."

Chan Tesh made a very slight gesture with his right hand, and the two platoon-captains shut up instantly. The company-captain gazed back at the Arcanan in silence for several seconds. Although he'd cut off the conversation behind him, he realized that he found himself favoring chan Talmarha's position. Unfortunately . . .

"Master-Armsman chan Kormai," he said quietly.

"Yes, Sir?" his senior noncommissioned officer replied from behind his right shoulder. Frai chan Kormai was a typical Ternathian, unlike chan Tesh. He was a good foot taller than the company-captain, with shoulders broader than an icebox, and if he carried more than two ounces of excess weight anywhere about his person, chan Tesh had never noticed them. The master-armsman had enlisted in the Imperial Ternathian Army when he was sixteen, and he would be celebrating his forty-sixth birthday in two months. Over those thirty years he'd seen just about everything, and chan Tesh found his unflappable professionalism more comforting than he cared to admit. Especially at this moment.

"I think we need to make certain these . . . gentlemen aren't carrying anything we'd prefer for them not to be carrying, Master-Armsman."

"Understood, Sir." Chan Kormai's cool green eyes surveyed the boat. "You want it polite, or thorough, Sir?"

"After what they've already done, I think I can stand it if their feelings get a little bruised, Master-Armsman," chan Tesh said dryly. "Let's just try not to leave too many *physical* bruises, shall we?"

"I think we can handle that, Sir."

"Good." Chan Tesh looked back at the man in the boat. "We'll talk," he said, speaking slowly and carefully and wondering how much the other fellow actually understood. "First, though, we're going to take a few precautions."

" 'Pre-cautions?' " the civilian repeated, obviously not understanding the word.

"First we search you," chan Tesh told him, and pantomimed slapping his own pockets with his hands. The civilian cocked his head to one side for a moment, then grimaced.

"Understand," he said in less than enthralled tones. "You—" He paused again, obviously trying to find the word he wanted, then used one in his own language. Chan Tesh looked politely blank, and the civilian puffed out his cheeks in apparent frustration. Then he twitched his shoulders in an obvious shrug and said something to his companions. Chan Tesh recognized the language their prisoners had spoken, but he hadn't had the opportunity to learn to understand it, and so he simply waited until the civilian turned back to him.

"Understand 'precautions,'" he said, speaking the new word carefully.

"Good," chan Tesh said, and nodded to chan Kormai.

The master-armsman had been quietly picking his assistants while the company-captain explained to the ignorant foreigner. Now he moved forward, followed by four more men. All of them were Marines, chan Tesh noted, and they were also older, more experienced men.

"Get out of the boat," chan Kormai told the talkative civilian, speaking as slowly and carefully as chan Tesh had. "Slowly. Put your hands like this."

He demonstrated lacing his fingers together behind his head, and this time a flash of anger showed in the civilian's eyes. That was fine with chan Tesh. Frankly, he didn't give a damn how angry they got.

The younger civilian said something sharp in their own language, but his superior shook his head. Then, as chan Kormai had instructed him, he stepped slowly and carefully ashore. His boots sank to the ankle in the mud, and he grimaced in obvious distaste as suction tried to pull them off his feet. He managed to reach solider ground without losing them, then put his hands behind his head as chan Kormai had demonstrated.

The master-armsman stepped around behind him, and the civilian's jaw set hard as the noncom proceeded to search him very thoroughly, indeed. Chan Tesh was impressed as the master-armsman demonstrated a previously unsuspected talent. The company-captain had seen very few police—civilian or military—who could have frisked a man so competently . . . and thoroughly. Chan Kormai wasn't especially gentle about it, either, although it was obvious to chan Tesh that he wasn't being deliberately rougher than he had to be, and the civilian winced once or twice. By the time the master-armsman was through, however, it was quite obvious that the civilian couldn't have anything hidden away outside a body cavity.

Chan Tesh was tempted to insist that *those* be searched, as well, given the bizarre things of which these people appeared to be capable. There were limits to even his paranoia, however, he decided. If these people were equipped with some sort of super weapon so small that it could be hidden someplace like that, then they had no need to send anyone out to talk to them in the first place. Besides, if this really was an effort to establish some sort of diplomatic contact, there was probably some professional code of conduct which ought to be followed. He didn't have a clue what it might insist that he do, but he was pretty sure it existed and that ordering a foreign envoy to bend over and spread his cheeks wasn't very high on the list of approved greetings.

Chan Kormai finished and stood back. The civilian turned to face him with what struck chan Tesh as commendable aplomb, and raised his eyebrows.

"Finished," the master-armsman told him, and pantomimed lowering his hands.

"Are satisfied?"

"For now . . . Sir," chan Kormai replied, and gestured for the man to move further away from the water. Two of the master-armsman's Marines kept a careful eye on the civilian without being particularly unobtrusive about it, and chan Kormai turned to the second civilian.

His search was just as thorough this time, and the younger man lacked his older companion's self-control. His face flushed with anger, and his jaw muscles bunched in obvious humiliation as he was searched. Chan Kormai was no rougher than he'd been with the first man, but neither was he any gentler, and it was obvious that the ire in the younger civilian's eye left him totally unmoved.

"Finished," he said eventually, for the second time. The younger man wasted no effort on conversation. He simply stamped across the damp ground to his companion, and chan Kormai glanced at chan Tesh. There was a slight, undeniable twinkle in the master-armsman's eyes, the company-captain observed, and felt his own lips twitch as they tried to smile.

The man who'd managed the steering on the way in was calmer and more phlegmatic about it than either of the two civilians had been. Unlike them—or, unlike the younger of them, at least—he clearly understood there was nothing personal about it, which suggested to chan Tesh that his original estimate that the man was a long-term noncom had probably been correct.

Once all three of the Arcanans were safely ashore under the watchful eye of chan Kormai's Marines, the master-armsman turned to the boat itself. As with his search of the passengers, he took his time, proceeding with methodical thoroughness.

Each of the civilians had come equipped with what was obviously a briefcase, and chan Kormai went through both of them carefully.

He took pains not to damage or disorder any of the indecipherable documents he found inside them, but he examined each folder individually. Then he paused, halfway through searching the first case, and held something up.

"Look at this, Sir," he said to chan Tesh.

The company-captain crossed to the boat and frowned as the master-armsman held out a rock. That was certainly what it looked like, anyway. A big chunk of clear quartz crystal, larger than chan Tesh's fist. For that matter, it was larger than *chan Kormai's* fist, which took considerably more doing.

"What do you make of it, Sir?" chan Kormai asked as chan Tesh accepted it just a bit gingerly. It wasn't quartz after all, he decided. It was too heavy, too dense, for that. In fact—

"Well, Master-Armsman," he said dryly after a moment, "I doubt they brought it along just to use as a paperweight. It reminds me of the stuff those artillery pieces of theirs are made of, which suggests at least a few unpleasant possibilities, doesn't it?" He grimaced. "It's not the same thing—not quite. But it's got that same . . . feel to it."

"I think you're right, Sir. And—" chan Kormai's eyes flicked sideways at the envoys, if that was what they were "—they're watching you like hawks."

"Really?" chan Tesh murmured, never looking up from the piece of crystal as he rotated his wrist to catch the hot sunlight on its polished surface. "Do they look nervous, Frai?"

"Don't know as I'd call it 'nervous,' Sir," the master-armsman replied softly. "Curious, though. And maybe a *little* worried. Hard to say. But I'd say they're at least as curious about your reaction to it as we are about what the hell it is."

Chan Tesh snorted in amusement. He wondered how the Arcanans would react if he suddenly tossed the piece of not-rock as far out into the swamp as he could. He was actually quite tempted to do just that, if only to see how they responded. But he didn't. Instead, he handed it back to chan Kormai.

"Put it back in the bag," he said. "And I'll bet you you'll find another one in the other briefcase."

"Sorry, Sir. I don't take sucker bets—even from officers."

As both of them had expected, there was, indeed, a second, almost identical crystal in the other briefcase. Those two enigmatic artifacts made chan Tesh a bit nervous—more nervous than he wanted to let on, at any rate—and he carefully didn't immediately return the briefcases to their owners. Instead, he set them to one side while chan Kormai finished with the boat.

In addition to the briefcases, there were three canvas knapsacks which contained food and water and what looked—and smelled—like some sort of insect repellent. Aside from what were obviously eating utensils, there was nothing even remotely resembling a blade or any other recognizable weapon.

Once the boat had been emptied, chan Kormai waved a half-dozen more troopers forward and had it hauled completely out of the water. Chan Tesh wasn't sure whether the master-armsman was taking caution to its logical conclusion, or whether he was simply as curious as chan Tesh himself about how they'd made the boat move. Whatever it was, neither of them found his question answered. There was nothing at all out of the ordinary about the boat, aside from the fact that it was obviously designed for a higher rate of speed than most boats its size which chan Tesh had ever seen before. Well, nothing besides that and the small, dense, glittering block of crystal fastened to its keel near the stern.

Unlike the lumps of not-quartz in the briefcases, the block clearly *was* made of exactly the same material as the rod-like weapons they'd captured from the other side and the perplexing bits and pieces Soral Hilovar and Nolis Parcanthi had turned up. Which clearly suggested that it was the source of the boat's motive power. It just didn't do a thing to explain how it *provided* that power.

Finally, chan Kormai straightened with a reasonably satisfied expression.

"That's it, Sir," he said. "Aside from those rock-things, and this," he waved at the glittering block, "I don't see anything they could be planning on using as some sort of weapon."

"I just wish we knew whether or not they *were* weapons," chan Tesh said dryly, and the master-armsman shrugged.

"If you want, Sir, I'll see how this block stands up to a forty-six," he said, tapping the butt of the Halanch and Welnahr holstered at his hip.

"And would you be willing to fire at the fuse of a twelve-inch naval shell, Master-Armsman?" chan Tesh inquired in an interested tone.

"Depends, Sir," chan Kormai replied with a slow grin. "Wouldn't be willing if it were a Ternathian shell, but if it was one of those Uromathian pieces of shit, I might take a chance."

"Well, I don't think we'll do that this time," chan Tesh told him.

"Yes, Sir. In that case, begging the Company-Captain's pardon, but what *are* we going to do with them?"

"Now that, Master-Armsman, is the pressing question, isn't it?"

*   *   *

"I'm going to get that bastard," Uthik Dastiri muttered, glaring at the big, red-haired Sharonian who'd searched them.

His voice was soft, but he was unable to suppress the bitter hatred in its depths. Rithmar Skirvon understood his reaction, although he didn't share it. After all, he'd understood the reason for the search, as well, and he couldn't hold it against the soldier. It hadn't been personal, merely professional, which was obviously something Dastiri hadn't quite grasped yet. But personal or not, it had been brutally thorough, and because Skirvon understood Dastiri's distress he only shrugged and refrained from reprimanding him for his anger.

"I've had warmer welcomes in my life," he observed instead.

"Is that all you've got to say?" Dastiri demanded, his face heating, and Skirvon patted his shoulder.

"I understand you're a little upset, and I can't blame you for that. But remember this—the longer you hold onto your anger, the longer you'll spend at a disadvantage in this situation. The angrier you are, the less clearly you'll be able to see or think, notice important details about these people."

"How can you be so calm about it?" Dastiri asked, his expression wavering between contrition and bitter hatred. "When he shoved—"

"He was doing his job, Uthik," Skirvon said gently but firmly. "In his boots, I'd have done exactly the same thing, for exactly the same reasons."

The younger diplomat chewed on that in silence for several uncomfortable moments. Then, finally, he sighed.

"I'll try to remember that, Rithmar. But as Torkash is my witness, I'd sooner put an arbalest bolt between his eyes than smile at that bastard for *any* reason."

"Yes," Skirvon said dryly. "I gathered that."

The older diplomat started to say something more, then changed his mind. There wasn't much point, at this stage, and Dastiri had to learn someday. In the meantime, he had other things to think about.

They'd been careful in their approach to deny the Sharonians any additional militarily useful information. Including, especially, any hint of the existence or capabilities of their own dragons. It was always possible, perhaps even probable, that the Arcanan prisoners these people had taken had already revealed the existence of the beasts, but there was no point in giving the other side any better feel for what they could do. So Five Hundred Klian had ordered the transport dragon to fly them and their boat to within forty miles of the swamp portal. They'd made the rest of the trip the hard way, and Skirvon devoutly hoped that the Sharonians would be thinking solely in terms of other boats for the future.

There wasn't anything else he could do about that at this point, so he'd concentrated on the Sharonians' reaction to his and Dastiri's PCs. Their curiosity had been obvious to someone with Skirvon's training, although he wasn't prepared yet to venture a guess as to exactly what had spawned their curiosity. It was always possible, he supposed, that Olderhan and Kelbryan's preposterous theories about a civilization which didn't use magic at all were accurate, but that still seemed so—

His thought broke off in mid-sentence as the man who was clearly these people's commanding officer said something to the man—probably a chief sword or something of the sort, Skirvon had decided—who'd conducted the search. The hulking noncom said something back, then the officer nodded, turned, and walked across to Skirvon.

"I am Company-Captain Balkar chan Tesh," he said. "Who are you, and what do you want?"

Well, Skirvon thought. *That's certainly blunt and to the point.*

"Rithmar Skirvon," he said, speaking slowly and carefully. Then he introduced Dastiri, as well.

Chan Tesh—whose name indicated he was Ternathian, according to the information Magister Kelbryan had assembled for them—didn't look particularly happy to see them. His expression was controlled, but Skirvon had been a diplomat for a long time. He didn't need any "Talent" to recognize the anger crackling around in the back of chan Tesh's outwardly calm eyes.

"How did you learn Ternathian?" the company-captain demanded, as soon as the introductions were over, and Skirvon nodded mentally. He'd been reasonably certain that was going to be the first question, and he'd prepared his answer carefully.

"One person live. Short time," he said. "Bad hurt. Spoke words, recorded. Try to save, but Arcanan healer die in fight. Long days to new healer. Many, many days. Bad hurt. Talk words, but not live. Die before see healer," he ended sorrowfully. "Arcanan grief. We talk?"

Chan Tesh's expression never wavered, but his eyes were cold, suspicious.

"Who was it?" he asked. "Who survived?"

Skirvon and Dastiri had argued repeatedly over how to address that particular point. Thanks to the girl, Shaylar, they had a complete list of names for the dead crew, not that he intended to admit that, even if this chan Tesh held him over hot coals. But they did know everyone's names, and they even knew which men she'd personally seen die. The Sharonians would have that same list, as well, since the little bitch had sent out her report—her *visual* report, no less!—right in the middle of the fighting.

Dastiri had wanted to select a name from the list of Sharonian men Shaylar hadn't seen die, rather than admit that she herself had survived. Skirvon had waffled back and forth over that choice, but he'd finally decided that they couldn't afford to take chances, given the number of Arcanan soldiers these people had taken prisoner. They'd had the survivors of Olderhan's company in custody for a month now, and if they'd had another of those damned "Voices" available to help interrogate them, gods alone knew how much they'd managed to learn. Shaylar had insisted she couldn't "read minds," and she might even have been telling the truth. However . . .

Skirvon found it disturbing that *both* survivors from a crew as small as the one Olderhan had encountered had "Talents" of the mind. They weren't even the same Talents, for that matter, which meant there was no way to know what else these people could do with their minds. Skirvon wasn't quite willing to risk *everything* by getting himself caught in an easily detectable lie this early in the negotiations, so he'd decided to play the hand cautiously.

"Arcana much, much grief," he said sadly. "Girl bad hurt. Try hard to go healer. Far, far walk. She die," he added, and actually managed to summon a few tears.

"*Shaylar?*" Shock exploded in chan Tesh's face. The man's hand dropped to the butt of the weapon—the "pistol"—holstered at his side, and his fingers curled around the polished wooden grip. "Shaylar *survived*? And you let her *die*?"

The sudden violence seething in chan Tesh's eyes was a terrifying shock, especially given the obvious strength of the man's self-control. Nor was he alone in his reaction. Every Sharonian soldier in sight mirrored the same sudden, explosive rage.

"Try hard save life," Skirvon insisted, dredging up more tears. "But bad, bad hurt. Hard talk. Long, long walk go healer. Arcana big, big grief. Arcana, Sharona, no shoot. Ne-go-ti-ate," he said with exaggerated care. "No shoot."

"If she was so badly hurt," chan Tesh demanded coldly, "how did you manage to get enough of our language out of her to learn to talk to us?"

Skirvon saw the man's knuckles whiten around the pistol grip and realized abruptly—emotionally, not just intellectually—that his own life hung by the proverbial thread. Obviously, Olderhan's estimate of Shaylar's importance in these people's eyes had been on the mark. In fact, Skirvon was beginning to think Olderhan had *underestimated* it.

He managed (he hoped) to keep his thoughts from racing across his expression, but it suddenly occurred to him that his strategy of insisting Shaylar was dead might have been a mistake. Returning her and her husband before they'd been thoroughly interrogated back in Arcana or New Arcana was clearly out of the question, of course. He'd figured that insisting they were both dead—and he knew from Olderhan's report that Shaylar had believed Jathmar was dead even while she was busy sending her accursed report back home—would be the simplest and neatest way of keeping their return off the table. Now he was suddenly confronted by the fact that because he'd claimed she was dead he couldn't put her return *onto* the table even if he wanted to. Which, given the hatred looking at him out of all those Sharonian eyes suddenly seemed as if it might have been a very good idea, indeed.

Unfortunately, there was no going back now.

"She hurt bad," he said instead. "Head hurt—inside." He tapped his own temple, where—again, thanks to Olderhan's invaluable report—he knew the little bitch actually had been injured. "Not . . . work right," he continued, deliberately searching for words. "She talk. Not to us—to her. We recorded it."

He intentionally used the Andaran verb for "recorded," and chan Tesh glared at him right on cue.

"That's the second time you've used that word—'*record*,'" he said. "What does it mean?"

"It mean—" Skirvon paused and rolled his eyes in obvious frustration. "Not know words. Can show. Please?"

He managed not to heave an overt sigh of relief as chan Tesh's eyes narrowed. The company-captain's anger didn't disappear, but he was obviously forcing it back under control.

He even managed to take his hand away from his pistol.

"Show how?" he asked skeptically.

"Please, bag," Skirvon said, pointing to his own briefcase. Chan Tesh cocked his head for a moment, then nodded and said something to the big chief sword. Although Skirvon's Ternathian language skills were far better than he was prepared to admit, they weren't good enough to follow the rapidly spoken sentence. On the other hand, they didn't need to be, as the noncom handed him the briefcase.

Skirvon opened it cautiously, then withdrew his PC. To his surprise, chan Tesh tensed obviously, and the diplomat found it less than easy to ignore the half-dozen rifles which were suddenly pointed in his direction once again.

"What is that?" chan Tesh asked sharply.

"Is only personal crystal," Skirvon said soothingly, once again using the Andaran words and holding the crystal up. Chan Tesh looked blank.

"What does it do?" he demanded.

"Rock hold talk. It *records* talk."

"What?" chan Tesh blinked.

"Hold talk," Skirvon said again, and murmured the activating incantation. The PC's glow as he initiated the spellware was lost in the brilliant sunshine, of course, but it was angled so that *he* could see its display. He tapped the menu with the tip of his stylus, calling up the special, limited word list they'd manufactured from Magister Kelbryan's primer specifically for this exchange. Then he touched the playback command.

"Shaylar," a woman's voice said.

Putting together that word list had required days of careful work. He and Dastiri had deliberately limited the audio recordings Magister Kelbryan had downloaded to them, choosing individual words on the basis of how clear Shaylar's voice had sounded when they were recorded. All of them were recognizably her voice, but distorted by fatigue . . . or pain. In some cases, he knew, the pain had been purely emotional, but that didn't matter for his purposes. What *mattered* was that the chosen words sounded like someone who'd been severely injured. Like someone who was muttering to herself, wandering through her own injury-confused thoughts.

He'd expected a powerful emotional reaction, but not the one he got.

Chan Tesh's jaw fell. Literally.

Skirvon stared at him and experienced a sudden epiphany. Despite everything Olderhan had told him, despite his study of the notes Kelbryan had meticulously recorded, despite even chan Tesh's obvious reaction when his chief sword had found the PCs in the first place, he hadn't really believed until that moment that Sharonians had no experience with magic. He *couldn't* believe it, because no one could possibly build a real civilization without it. He'd been absolutely convinced that Shaylar and Jathmar had been shamming in a successful effort to confuse and mislead their captors.

But chan Tesh wasn't shamming. The company-captain was clearly a disciplined, confident officer, and what his forces had done to Hadrign

Thalmayr's command was brutal evidence of his competence. Yet his astonishment at hearing a simple recorded word played back from a completely standard personal crystal was total. Indeed, it appeared to border on superstitious terror, and deep inside, Rithmar Skirvon grinned like a kid with his daddy's jar of accumulators.

Olderhan had been right. *They had no magic!*

Why, they weren't nearly as formidable as he'd first believed. If they couldn't do something this simple, they were babes in an adult world—a mean and nasty one. Mul Gurthak had been right, too. All they had going for them was their machines, the "guns" they'd used—used by surprise—in both violent encounters. And, as mul Gurthak had pointed out, it was only that surprise, that totally unanticipated ability of theirs to throw not a spell, but a physical projectile, through a portal which had defeated Thalmayr.

Skirvon had been convinced these people must actually have their machines and their "Talents" in *addition* to the magic which was the necessary foundation for any advanced civilization. But they genuinely *didn't have it*, and that reordered everything he'd thought about them.

But first things first, he told himself firmly. *First things first.*

He waited until chan Tesh shook himself.

"How did you do that?" The Sharonian's voice was ever so slightly hoarse, Skirvon noted with carefully hidden satisfaction.

"Rock is *personal crystal*," he repeated the Andaran phrase carefully. "Shaylar talk, it *record*—" again he used the Andaran "—her word. Then *spellware*—" yet another Andaran word "—work words. Make . . . list our words, your words."

He tapped the menu again, bringing up the Andaran and Ternathian words for "word" side by side in the display, then angled it so that chan Tesh could see it. The company-captain's eyes narrowed once again. Clearly, the phonetic spelling of the Ternathian word meant no more to him than the totally unknown characters of the Arcanan alphabet floating beside it. Equally clearly, he was intelligent enough to realize what he was seeing. He stared into the crystal for several seconds, then shook himself and looked back at Skirvon.

"So you say this . . . 'personal crystal' of yours let you capture Shaylar's words and then analyze our language?"

"Please," Skirvon said, summoning up a pained expression, "too many words. Not have big number."

Chan Tesh scowled in evident frustration.

"If you could do *that*," he gestured at the PC, "why couldn't you save Shaylar?"

"Tried. Tried *hard*," Skirvon insisted soulfully. He remembered Olderhan's account of the prisoners' reaction to magic healing. Given these people's total ignorance about magic, it would undoubtedly be even simpler than he'd expected to convince them that Shaylar had died of her injuries. Especially since she undoubtedly *would* have without the healers' intervention.

"Head hurt bad," he said once more. "Our healer killed in fight. Tried walk to *second* healer, but many, many days. She die before we reach. She very brave," he added sadly. "Arcana much grief."

"Yes," chan Tesh said harshly, glowering at him. "She *was* very brave. And my people will demand punishment for whoever killed her."

"Please," Skirvon said again, earnestly. "Too many words. Must learn more. But now, come talk Sharona. No shoot, *talk*."

"A truce?" Chan Tesh sounded massively skeptical, but that was a distinct improvement over the white-hot fury of a few moments before. "You want to negotiate a truce?"

"Truce is no shoot?" Skirvon said, and chan Tesh nodded. "A truce is a time to talk, yes. A time to talk, not shoot. That's what you want? To talk about not shooting us again?"

"Sharona no shoot, Arcana no shoot. Yes."

"I can't authorize a truce. You understand? I must talk to someone higher than me. With more power, more authority. Understand?"

"Yes. Send talk?"

"I'll send a message."

"Ah . . . *message*." Skirvon tapped the crystal's menu again, dutifully recording the "new" word into it. The word "message" was already in its *real* vocabulary list, of course, but these yokels would never know that.

Chan Tesh watched as the word appeared in both Andaran and phonetic spelling. Then Skirvon looked back up at him expectantly, and the company-captain frowned.

"You understand you can't talk to *me* about a truce?" chan Tesh pressed. Skirvon only looked at him and said nothing, and the Sharonian tried yet again.

"I'm not a diplomat. I'm a soldier—a 'diplomat' is someone who speaks for a government. You understand?"

Skirvon nodded sharply, busily coding the "new" words into his crystal.

"I'll have to send for a diplomat," chan Tesh continued. "I'll send a message, and the diplomat will come here."

"Ah!" Skirvon nodded again, more enthusiastically. But then he stopped nodding and shook his head instead. "No," he said. "Not here."

"What?" Chan Tesh's eyes narrowed once more, and Skirvon knelt in the mud with a silent apology to his tailor as he contemplated what it was going to do to the knees of his trousers.

"Sharona portal," he said, using a dead twig to draw a circle in the mud. Then he drew another circle, about two feet from the first. "Arcana portal," he said, and indicated the portal soaring high above them.

Chan Tesh scowled and opened his mouth, but Skirvon held up one hand, gesturing for patience. Chan Tesh looked at him, then shrugged and nodded.

"Go on. Say the rest, I mean."

"Arcana, Sharona di-plo-mats meet here."

Skirvon drew an "X" in the mud between the two circles he'd already drawn and tapped it to indicate the approximate spot of the slaughter. He let his face fall into a deeply sorrowful expression which Dastiri mimicked beautifully. Even the Navy petty officer who'd managed the boat for them contrived to look sad.

"Great grief," Skirvon said. "Much hurt." He touched his chest to indicate his heart, then patted the "X" again. "Diplomats talk here." Then he pointed to the portal overhead and said, "Sharona stay here. Arcana want Sharona stay here." He pointed at chan Tesh's soldiers and their sandbagged positions. "But diplomats go, talk here."

He pointed to the "X" again, and chan Tesh cocked an eyebrow at him.

"You mean you're willing to accept that we keep this portal? You just want your diplomats to meet our diplomats here?" It was chan Tesh's turn to point at the "X" in the mud.

"You stay—soldiers stay," Skirvon said, very carefully not answering chan Tesh's first question directly, then indicated the "X" once more. "Diplomats talk here. Me. Dastiri. Sharonian diplomats."

"Under a flag of truce?"

"No shoot, yes. Talk. Negotiate."

Chan Tesh gazed thoughtfully at the muddy diagram, then studied Skirvon and Dastiri carefully before he finally spoke once more.

"I'll send a message to bring a diplomat here." He pointed at the "X." "To Fallen Timbers."

"Fall En Tim Burr?" Skirvon asked, this time genuinely puzzled, and chan Tesh pointed at the massive trees behind him on the Sharonian side of the contested portal.

"Trees," he said. "Also 'timber.'" He pantomimed a tree with his arm, positioning his forearm vertically with his fingers outstretched as branches. "Timber." Then he blew hard at his hand and lowered it as if his arm were a falling tree. "Fall. So we call the site where you murdered our civilians 'Fallen Timbers.'"

"Ah . . . grief place." Skirvon nodded. "We walk, negotiate Fallen Timbers."

"Why?" Chan Tesh's eyes were cold again, the soul-deep anger back again, burning coldly in their depths. "Why at Fallen Timbers?"

"Sharona fight hard. Arcana grief. Arcana want see, want re-mem-ber—" Skirvon spoke the Ternathian word carefully "—brave Sharona."

Chan Tesh's eyebrows soared. Then he frowned thoughtfully.

"You want to meet where they were murdered? To do them honor?"

"'Honor'?" Skirvon repeated.

"If someone does a brave thing and dies doing it, we feel respect. We feel honor. We say they were good and brave and should be remembered with a good feeling here." Chan Tesh touched his own heart, and Skirvon nodded emphatically.

"Yes. Meet at Fallen Timbers, honor brave Sharona." Then he gave the soldier a concerned look. "No bad anger, meet at Fallen Timbers?"

"Will we be so angry we won't negotiate?" Chan Tesh shrugged. "I can't say. I don't have the authority. Meeting there to *honor* our murdered civilians will help, but it won't be easy to set aside our anger. *We* didn't start this."

Skirvon cocked his head and smiled gently.

"Arcana no start," he said. "*Who* start? Two men dead, no man see. Who start?"

Chan Tesh blinked, then grimaced.

"So *that's* your story? You didn't start it because no one saw who killed Falsan? I find that profoundly interesting."

He gazed at Skirvon thoughtfully, but, to Skirvon's surprise, the uneducated rube didn't continue. He neither badgered Skirvon in an attempt to forcibly change his mind, nor pointed out—as they certainly could have—that it was Arcana who had run a party of civilians to ground and then slaughtered them. Skirvon kept smiling, gently, and revised—just a tad—his opinion of this particular provincial rube in uniform. At least the man was intelligent enough to leave that chore to the diplomats.

"When meet?" Skirvon asked.

"Stay here," chan Tesh replied. "We'll send a message. Wait here until the answer to that question comes back."

Either chan Tesh didn't know where the nearest diplomat was, Skirvon reflected, which was an interesting piece of information. Or he didn't want to admit how far away he was, which would be another interesting piece of information.

"We'll feed you while we wait," chan Tesh added stiffly. "We'll give you water and loan you blankets, if they're needed."

If they were needed? Could these thought messages, which Skirvon still found almost impossible to credit, really travel that fast? Or was a diplomat that near? The lack of information was maddening, but at this stage in the negotiations, their best was all they could do.

"We wait," Skirvon agreed.

Chan Tesh nodded sharply and turned on his heel as smartly as any Andaran aristocrat on a parade ground. That was interesting, as well. Out in the middle of the godsforsaken wilderness, this company-captain—the equivalent of a mere commander of one hundred, assuming Kelbryan's primer had gotten it correct—was as spit-and-polish formal as some self-important, blue-blooded Andaran.

Either these people were as virulently militant as Andara itself, or else he was putting on a show for them, exaggerating his militancy for effect. Either answer would present its own possibilities, once Skirvon managed to figure out which one applied. It would, he realized with a slowly building emotion almost akin to relish, be a very interesting little exchange all around, wouldn't it?

The possibilities, he thought, licking his mental chops, were boundless.

CHAPTER
FORTY-SIX

DORZON BASKAY, VISCOUNT Simrath, had dropped the "chan" from his name for his new role. It was possible that the Arcanan diplomats had discovered that the word indicated military service, and Platoon-Captain Simrath wasn't being a member of the military just now. After all, a diplomat as young as he was wouldn't have had time to become a military veteran, as well, so he couldn't be one, either, because right this minute he had to be a diplomat. A very *convincing* diplomat.

He wasn't at all happy about that, but he didn't have much choice. Sharona didn't *have* a real diplomat within less than three months' travel, and no one was prepared to admit that to the other side. They'd already delayed for the better part of two days while Company-Captain chan Tesh had conferred by Voice with Regiment-Captain Velvelig, but chan Tesh and Velvelig had both been aware that the possibility offered by the Arcanan contact might well be fleeting. If it wasn't seized *now*, it could slip away and never be offered again. Neither of them wanted to lose any possibility of avoiding an all-out war, and so Velvelig had finally made the decision which had led to chan Baskay's present unhappiness.

"We don't have an official diplomat, and we don't have time to get one," chan Tesh had told chan Baskay bluntly. "I don't have any idea whether or not these people are sincere. Even if they are, they've made it fairly clear that they're at the end of a long—and slow—communications chain. So whatever *they* may want doesn't necessarily mean a damned thing about their superiors' or their government's ultimate intentions. But I agree with Regiment-Captain Velvelig that we can't afford to let this possibility slip away if they *are* sincere. That means we don't have time to sit around, literally for months, with our thumbs up our arses while we wait for a 'real' diplomat—from whatever government we finally wind up with—to get all the way out here to Hell's Gate. Which brings us to *you*, Platoon-Captain."

Chan Baskay had nodded, although he hadn't cared at all for where chan Tesh was obviously headed. Chan Baskay was no diplomat; he was a cavalry captain, even if he had been born into the aristocracy, and a cavalry officer was all he'd ever wanted to be. He might be the son of an earl, with a lineage of political service to the Ternathian Empire that could have stretched from Hell's Gate clear back to Estafel, but *he'd* never wanted that part of the family tradition.

He'd hoped that he'd managed to dodge it when he'd been assigned to the PAAF. Unfortunately, it appeared his bloodline had caught up with him after all.

"According to your personnel file," chan Tesh had continued, "you've served in the House of Lords. Is that right?"

"Not exactly, Sir," chan Baskay had replied. "My father holds a seat in the Lords. As his eldest son, I've deputized for him on a few occasions, mostly while I was still at the Academy." He'd smiled a bit tartly. "Frankly, I think it was his way of trying to convince me to change my mind and go into the Foreign Service instead of the Army. It didn't work."

"I see." Chan Tesh had sat back in his camp chair, considering the young cavalry officer for several seconds. He'd wondered why the platoon-captain went by "chan Baskay" instead of the "Viscount Simrath" to which he was certainly entitled.

"I suppose it's ironic—at least—that I should wind up talking to you about this, if you never wanted Foreign Service in the first place," he'd said then. "At the same time, I hope you can understand why I'm glad to have someone with your background available. Frankly, Platoon-Captain, there's no one else out here with *any* background in diplomacy or high-level politics. I suppose the ideal person for this would have been Crown Prince Janaki, but just between you and me, I'm delighted that he's no longer available."

"You won't get any argument from me about that point, Sir," chan Baskay had said fervently. The mere thought of having the heir to the throne hanging out here at this particular moment had been enough to make the platoon-captain shudder.

"But with him gone, you're our next best choice," the company-captain had pointed out. "On the other hand, I don't suppose this is something we can simply order someone to do."

Chan Tesh had paused, looking at him with a waiting expression, and chan Baskay had heaved a deep and mournful mental sigh. He would vastly have preferred to be able to decline, but that was impossible, of course. For a lot of reasons—not least that endless lineage of service to the Winged Crown. A Ternathian noble simply did not refuse when duty called. Not if he ever wanted to face the scrutiny of his revoltingly dutiful ancestors. Or, chan Baskay had conceded, his own conscience.

And at least if he had to do this, he had the proper background for it. Chan Tesh was right about that, too. He'd imbibed a basic understanding of political realities almost with his mother's milk, whether he'd wanted to or not. And he'd also had those dozens of generations of blue-blooded ancestors—not to mention his observations of several hundred currently carnate fellow aristocrats—upon which to draw for role models. He'd been reasonably confident he could act the part.

What he hadn't been confident of was whether or not he could do the *job*. He'd been crushingly aware of the responsibility looming before him, and it had terrified him. This wasn't a job for someone pretending to be a seasoned diplomat—it was a job for the most experienced diplomat Sharona had ever boasted. And what Sharona actually had was . . . him.

"It's all right, Sir," he'd finally sighed. "I understand, and I'll give it my best shot. How exactly do you and Regiment-Captain Velvelig want me to handle it?"

Which was how he came to find himself riding steadily through the breezy woods under a dancing drift of blowing red and gold leaves towards his first meeting with the representatives of another trans-universal civilization.

A civilization, he reminded himself, *with which we're effectively at war, at the moment. Vothon, please don't let me screw this up!*

At least he'd had two genuine strokes of luck. The first was his baby sister's idiocy. Charazan Baskay was enrolled in one of those ghastly finishing schools that specialized in turning young ladies' brains into mush, and it appeared to be working just fine, in her case. She'd decided, on the basis of logic so . . . unique that chan Baskay hadn't even tried to follow it, that it would be a good idea to send him a dress suit and cloak to wear at "cotillions and military balls." Exactly where she'd expected him to find either of those out here on the bleeding edge of the frontier eluded him, and he'd rolled his eyes heavenward and stuffed the ludicrous outfit into the bottom of a trunk the day it arrived. He'd intended for it to languish there until the day he finally returned to Sharona, and he certainly hadn't realized that his batman had packed the contents of that trunk into his duffel bags when he'd been ordered forward with the rest of Company-Captain chan Tesh's column.

But there it was, and he was inclined to see the hand of fate in his batman's apparent lapse into lunacy. Thanks to that, and Charazan, he actually had the proper civilian attire to pull off this charade. He'd blessed his harebrained baby sister fervently when he realized that he did.

The second stroke of good fortune was the presence of Under-Captain Trekar chan Rothag. The dark-haired and dark-eyed chan Rothag was a Narhathan who'd grown up almost in the shadow of the Fist of Bolakin. Where chan Baskay had the fair hair and gray eyes so common among the Ternathian nobility, chan Rothag's hair was so dark a brown it was almost black, and his swarthy complexion and powerful nose could almost as well have been Shurkhali. Unlike chan Baskay, chan Rothag had no connection whatsoever to either the aristocracy or the Foreign Service. What he *did* have was a Talent which police agencies and military intelligence organizations had always found extraordinarily useful.

Chan Rothag was a Sifter. He couldn't read minds, wasn't actually a telepath at all. But he knew, instantly and infallibly, when someone lied. He couldn't magically—chan Baskay shuddered at his own choice of adverb, under the circumstances—divine the truth they were lying to conceal or distort, but knowing they'd lied at all was almost as useful. Most commanders above the platoon level in any Sharonian army tried to get at least one Sifter assigned to them. More often than not, they failed; Sifters were too useful for senior officers to be willing to turn the limited supply of them loose. Balkar chan Tesh, however, had what amounted almost to a Talent for scrounging the personnel he wanted, which was how chan Rothag had ended up attached to his column.

Chan Rothag had also spent several days in company with their Arcanan prisoners before Crown Prince Janaki carted them off. As a trained interrogator, he'd found his complete inability to communicate with them frustrating, and chan Baskay knew that chan Tesh had been tempted to send chan Rothag along with Janaki. But the company-captain had decided not to in the end, because there'd been plenty of equally well-trained interrogators further up the chain, while chan Rothag had been the *only* interrogator at this end of it. Under the circumstances, chan Baskay had decided to regard chan Rothag's continued presence, like that of Charazan's gift, as another example of the hand of fate in action.

"Well," he said now, his voice low pitched as the tangle of fallen and broken trees where the Chalgyn Consortium survey crew had died came into sight, "here we go."

"Be brave, Viscount," chan Rothag replied with a slight smile, using the title by which every member of their party now addressed chan Baskay. "You'll do just fine."

"Easy for *you* to say," chan Baskay growled back.

"Just play the part, Viscount, and remember our signals." Chan Rothag sounded revoltingly calm, chan Baskay thought. Which might be because, unlike chan Baskay, he was about to spend the next several hours basically saying nothing at all. They had no proof at this time that the Arcanans' command of Ternathian was as limited as it appeared to be. If they were concealing a greater fluency, then trained diplomats might well be able to recognize that chan Rothag had about as much diplomatic expertise as a pig on roller skates. Chan Baskay had done his best to get some of the rudiments, at least, through to the under-captain, then given up in despair.

"Just keep your mouth shut," he'd advised finally. "We'll work out some sort of signal system so you can tell me whether or not they're lying. And at least we both speak Farnalian. We'll use that, if we have to talk to each other without—hopefully!—the other side understanding us. And . . . hmm . . ."

He'd regarded chan Rothag thoughtfully.

"I think you've just become Shurkalian," he'd said finally. The Narhathan had raised one eyebrow, and chan Baskay had shrugged. "If we can convince them you're related to Shaylar, then we'll have an excuse for you to break in—as emotionally as possible, in Farnalian, of course—if we twang something sensitive and you need to warn me about it. Right?"

"Right," chan Rothag had agreed, not even trying to hide his relief at being denied a speaking part. Which was what made his current breezy confidence particularly irritating. On the other hand, it was also the best advice chan Baskay was likely to get, and he let his mind run back over the cover story one last time, like an actor settling his stage character comfortably into place.

According to what chan Tesh had told the senior Arcanan diplomat, Viscount Simrath was a middle-ranked Ternathian diplomat, who'd been visiting his sister in the last (carefully unnamed) civilian city in this transit chain (*also* carefully unnamed), to which she'd emigrated after her marriage. When the Chalgyn crew had been slaughtered, the viscount had sent a Voice message back to Sharona, asking the emperor if he should try to reach the contact universe.

On the emperor's subsequent orders, he'd set out immediately, reaching Company-Captain Halifu's fort—now formally named Fort Shaylar—almost simultaneously with the Arcanan message requesting a truce and negotiations for a genuine cease-fire.

Chan Baskay would have felt much better if the emperor truly had authorized his mission—and this ruse—but there hadn't been time for any message to reach Sharona and come back down the chain. As a result, he didn't even have an official set of conditions acceptable to the emperor or the Portal Authority. He hoped chan Tesh and Velvelig were right—that approval would definitely be forthcoming. In fact, he was almost certain they *were* right, but part of his job was going to be to keep talking until somebody in authority sent him a real set of terms.

They reached the agreed upon conference site, and chan Baskay felt his jaw muscles tighten. It wasn't the first time he'd seen the lingering burn marks and other scars left by the brief, vicious battle, and a familiar hatred kicked him in the gut. He kicked it right back.

Your job is to put together a negotiated cease-fire and stop something like this from ever happening again, he told himself. *Besides, you just got here after traveling down-chain. You've never seen it before, and you're a frigging* diplomat, *not a soldier. Act like one—they're watching you.*

He did allow his face to harden slightly as he surveyed those telltale signs, then glanced at the waiting Arcanan contingent with exactly the right edge of aristocratic hauteur. They were, indeed, watching him closely, he noticed, and wondered if they'd deliberately insisted on meeting at this spot to push Sharona's diplomats into a state of rage.

On the face of it, the idea was silly. Why ask for talks at all, if they only meant to sabotage them by enraging the other side? On the other hand, they might have done it in hopes of keeping the Sharonians sufficiently distracted by anger and hatred to give them an edge in the talks. To win extra points for themselves because the Sharonians were too busy being furious to notice that they were giving up important concessions.

It sounded paranoid, even to him, he realized. It sounded devious. It even sounded insane, perhaps.

But it *felt* accurate.

The Arcanan negotiating party had arrived early. As stipulated by the initial agreement, the two men in civilian clothing—who had to be the Arcanan diplomats, Skirvon and Dastiri—were escorted by no more than twenty-five of their own soldiers. Company-Captain chan Tesh had accompanied them—ostensibly as a mark of respect; actually to make sure they didn't get up to anything of which Sharona would have disapproved—along with Petty-Captain Arthag and the Arpathian officer's cavalry platoon. When the twenty men of Viscount Simrath's escort were included, that gave Sharona a man-power advantage of over two-to-one, and none of those troopers were taking any chances.

My, chan Baskay thought mordantly as he watched the various military contingents not quite fingering their weapons as they glared at one another, *isn't* this *a soothing atmosphere, well suited to the dispassionate negotiation of an inter-universal cease-fire?*

Petty-Captain Arthag's "honor guard" acknowledged the arrival of Viscount Simrath's party, and Company-Captain chan Tesh gravely and respectfully saluted one of his more junior platoon commanders.

"Viscount," the company-captain said formally. "Welcome to Fallen Timbers."

"Thank you, Company-Captain," chan Baskay replied with a pleasant, if somewhat distant, smile. Then he allowed the smile to fade. "I could wish that none of us had to be here," he continued, deliberately pitching his voice loudly enough for the Arcanan diplomats to hear. "I've Seen the reports, of course, including Shaylar's message." He shook his head, allowing his expression to turn a bit bleaker. "The personal messages I've received from home are as furious as anything I've ever heard before, and the official correspondence isn't much better."

"I don't doubt it, My Lord." Chan Tesh shook his head. "Still, according to these people, it was all a mistake."

"So I've been told." Chan Baskay glanced at the Arcanans again. "I would dearly love to find that that's the truth, and that we can end all of this without still more bloodshed."

"Well, My Lord, I suppose that's largely up to you. And to these ... gentlemen, of course."

"True enough, Company-Captain," chan Baskay agreed. "True enough. So I suppose we'd best get started. Could you perform the introductions for us, please?"

"Of course, My Lord."

Chan Baskay dismounted, handing his reins to one of Arthag's troopers. Then he and chan Rothag accompanied chan Tesh across to the waiting Arcanans.

The Arcanans in question had set up a conference table at which the deliberations were to take place, and that "table" was sufficiently startling to capture chan Baskay's attention for several seconds. It was made from several narrow slats of wood which had been hinged together to form a folded up bundle that could fit onto a pack saddle. When it was unfolded, crosspieces slid into place across the bottom, stiffening it and locking it in the open position.

That much was fairly unremarkable, but it did have one small feature guaranteed to arrest his attention instantly: it had no legs.

The tabletop simply floated there, perfectly level despite the rough terrain, hovering in midair at the ordinary height of a standard table, and chan Baskay's scalp crawled at the sight. It wasn't natural, he thought, and the back of his brain even whispered the word "demonic," before he squelched it back down where it had come from.

Not demonic, he told himself. *It's just* different. *Very different, perhaps, but only different.*

He told himself that rather firmly, and he knew—intellectually—that it was true. That this was merely a form of technology his own people had never seen before, assuming that anything which caused a ten-foot-long tabletop to float thirty-six inches off the ground under a canopy of flame-shot autumn leaves could be called "merely" anything.

It was the obvious solution to their need for a portable table, of course, but it was sufficiently alien to distract chan Baskay from the business at hand. It took him a heartbeat or two to realize it had. Then he glanced up, swiftly and without moving his head from its "gosh-look-at-the-table" position, and saw the faintest hint of smug satisfaction in the Arcanans' eyes.

That satisfaction vanished instantly when they realized he was watching them closely without seeming to do so. Their own eyes narrowed, and they stood up straighter, put on notice that they weren't dealing with a total babe-in-swaddling. He noticed that, too, and gave them a polite little smile which, he was pleased to observe, replaced their satisfaction with an edge of speculation, instead.

Chan Baskay managed to keep his smile from growing and very carefully concealed his own flicker of satisfaction. He'd also noticed—and ignored—what looked remarkably like a half-dozen chairs whose legs had been amputated. They were tucked underneath the floating conference table, as if the Arcanans had hoped they wouldn't be immediately spotted, and he carefully paid them no attention at all even as he filed away their presence for future consideration.

"Viscount Simrath," chan Tesh said formally, "this is Rithmar Skir-von and Uthik Dastiri, the diplomatic representatives of something called the Union of Arcana. Master Skirvon, Master Dastiri, this is Sir Dorzon Baskay, forty-sixth Viscount Simrath, of the Ternathian

Foreign Ministry, acting in behalf of the Portal Authority and the Emperor of Ternathia, and Lord Trekar Rothag, his associate and adviser."

Everyone bowed gravely to everyone else, and chan Baskay raised one aristocratic eyebrow.

"I understand you gentlemen speak our language?"

"Speak some," the older of the two Arcanan civilians—Skirvon—said. "Learn more with PC while talk. Can show?"

He indicated the large lump of quartz sitting in the center of the floating table, and chan Baskay allowed his other eyebrow to rise.

"By all means," he invited.

Skirvon bowed slightly, then murmured something in his own language. The lump of quartz glowed briefly, and then the floating words chan Tesh had already described to chan Baskay appeared within it. Skirvon leaned over it, touching it with a crystal stylus, then said something else, much longer and considerably more involved, in his own language.

"The PC can help learn languages," another voice said suddenly. It sounded a great deal like Skirvon's, but not exactly, and it was coming not from the Arcanan, but from the glowing lump of rock. "When we talk, it listens. Learns. It will turn words in my language into your language, and your language into my language."

The words coming from the "PC" were much clearer, smoother, than anything Skirvon had produced in Ternathian. Even chan Tesh, who'd already seen multiple examples of the Arcanans' astounding technology, was clearly taken aback, and it took all of chan Baskay's self-control not to show his own astonishment. But he managed it somehow, and looked at Skirvon levelly.

"So, if I speak to your rock, it will translate whatever I say into your own language?" he said, and heard a voice which wasn't quite his saying something in a language he'd never spoken.

*   *   *

Skirvon watched the Sharonians' response to his newest ploy and managed not to smile like a fox in a henhouse. Despite their best efforts to conceal it, they were clearly impressed by this fresh manifestation of magic. Of course, they didn't know the PC had an unfair advantage. *They* thought it was still learning the language as it went, and he had no intention of suggesting otherwise. In fact, he'd loaded the same translation spellware Magister Kelbryan had used with Shaylar into his own crystal. It contained the complete vocabulary the magister had acquired from her prisoner, as well, and Skirvon had to remind himself to phrase his comments in Andaran rather more simply than he would have normally. It would never do to inadvertently reveal the fluency in Ternathian which he already possessed.

On the other hand, he thought, *it won't hurt a bit to impress these yokels with how quickly the "learning spellware "improves its grasp of Ternathian in the course of our little chats.*

"Is this acceptable?" he asked earnestly in Andaran.

*   *   *

"Is this acceptable?" the crystal on the table said in Ternathian, and chan Baskay nodded.

"Indeed. And quite convenient, too," he said calmly.

*   *   *

Skirvon was impressed. This Viscount Simrath obviously had been just as surprised as chan Tesh and the others, but there was remarkably little evidence of it in his expression or his voice. The man's title—*forty-sixth* Viscount of Whatever?—indicated an incredibly long aristocratic pedigree, which was entirely in keeping with the preposterous age Shaylar had imputed to this Ternathian Empire. That was impressive enough, but his obvious self-control and total self-confidence was even more impressive. Clearly, the man was an experienced diplomat, as well, despite his apparent relative youth, and Skirvon wondered what stroke of luck had put him far enough down the transit chain from Sharona to get him to this place at this time.

Perhaps I'm better matched than I expected, he thought almost cheerfully. After all, it was always more satisfying to match wits with a fellow professional, rather than simply steal candy from unwary babies. Not that the end result was likely to be any different.

"In that case," he gestured casually and spoke the word which activated the spell accumulators on the camp chairs he'd had a member of his military escort arrange around the conference table. The comfortably cushioned chairs rose immediately, floating levelly at the exactly correct height.

"Be seated, please," he invited blandly.

*   *   *

This time, chan Baskay didn't even turn a hair. He'd expected nothing less, and he simply smiled, handed his cloak to one of Platoon-Captain Arthag's troopers, and seated himself. The pit of his stomach felt just a bit hollow as he parked his posterior on the unnaturally floating chair. A part of him couldn't quite help expecting it to collapse under his weight, but no sign of it showed in his expression, and he laid his forearms on the conference table, folded his hands neatly, and gazed at them with a politely attentive expression.

Like the comfortably padded chair underneath him, the conference table didn't even quiver under the weight of his arms. It was
as rock-steady as any table he'd ever sat at before, which his intellect
had known would be the case. It would scarcely have worked to the
Arcanans' advantage for it to be anything else, after all.

*   *   *

Definitely a professional, Skirvon thought ungrudgingly, giving the
Sharonian diplomat points for composure.

He glanced at Dastiri as the junior Sharonian diplomat, Rothag,
seated himself somewhat more gingerly at Simrath's right. Then they
took their own seats, facing the Sharonians across the conference
table. Skirvon opened his mouth, but Simrath spoke before he could
say anything.

"This translating rock of yours will be most convenient," he
observed. "On the other hand, words are only tools, are they not?
What truly matters are the answers to two simple questions. Do
you plan to end your acts of violence against Sharonian civilians?
And do you intend to stop attacking soldiers attempting to negotiate
under flags of truce?"

Skirvon's eyes widened. Despite his own many years of experience,
he couldn't quite conceal his surprise at the other man's directness.

"With all respect, Viscount," he said after a moment, "those questions are not as simple as you suggest. You say your people were
civilians. Our soldiers did not know that, and many of them were
killed in the same fight. Arcana deeply regrets what happened, but
how it came about is not at all clear to us at this time."

"It is very clear to *us*," Simrath said with a pleasant smile. "Your
soldiers attacked our civilians. When one of our officers—Platoon-
Captain Arthag, I believe—" he gestured at one of the officers who
had accompanied the Arcanans and their escort from the swamp
portal "—attempted to approach your soldiers under a flag of truce
to inquire as to the fate of our people, he was fired upon. From
our viewpoint, it's quite clear who fired the first shot in each of
those incidents."

Skirvon ordered his expression not to change. Clearly, Simrath
intended to cut right to the heart of things, and it was equally
obvious that his plan was to place Arcana squarely on the defensive.
To some extent, that would work out very well for Skirvon's chosen
strategy, but it would never do to allow the Sharonians to feel *they*
were driving the negotiations. Or, rather, to allow them an expec-
tation of a quick resolution to those same negotiations. He had to
keep them talking for at least a couple of weeks, and allowing this

Simrath's forcefulness to push him into premature concessions or admissions could make that considerably more difficult. What he needed was something that could keep them "negotiating" without reaching any premature final agreement.

"Excuse me, Viscount," he said, "but I am afraid you are speaking too quickly and using too many new words for my crystal to translate them correctly. It will get better as we continue to speak to each other, but it has not yet learned enough words for long, complicated talk."

*   *   *

Chan Baskay laced his fingers together atop the conference table as he considered what the Arcanan had just said. It made sense, he supposed. And *he* certainly had no way to judge what the glowing hunk of rock's true capabilities might be.

"So," he said with a thin smile which would have done his most arrogant ancestor proud, "your . . . crystal isn't up to the task after all?"

"That is not what I said," the crystal translated a moment later. "What I said is that it will take time. We wish to talk, wish for there to be no more shooting, but it is important that we understand what is said. That we are clear when we talk. And that you understand what we think happened while we understand what *you* think happened."

Chan Baskay cocked his head to one side and pursed his lips thoughtfully. He suspected that the Arcanans' marvelous hunk of rock was doing a better job of translating than this Skirvon wanted to admit. At the same time, he had to concede that the man had a point. If they were going to talk to each other at all, they had to at least listen to the other side's view of the events which had led them to this point.

"Very well," he said after a moment. "You asked us to meet with you. What does Arcana wish to say? Sharona is willing to listen."

*   *   *

That's better, Skirvon thought. *Get him tied up in formal exchanges and we can kill lots of time without actually saying a damned thing we don't already both know anyway.*

"Arcana is grateful that Sharona is willing to listen," he said aloud, and arranged himself into what he thought of as "formal discourse posture" to make it clear that what he was about to say was a formal position statement.

"Arcana is shocked by the violence that has taken place between our people and yours," he continued. "It caused us great grief to discover that the sole survivor was a young woman. We do not allow women to serve in our military, so we were not expecting to find one."

"She was not serving in the military," Simrath said in a voice chipped from solid ice. "They were civilians."

"Yes," Skirvon said. "We know that now. We did not know that then, however. And we did not expect to find a girl in the middle of such combat."

*   *   *

Chan Baskay considered pointing out that the Arcanans had gone into that same battle with a woman of their own in tow, but he chose not to play that particular card just yet. So far, the other side had given no indication that there were any Talented Arcanans. It was difficult for him to conceive of a human civilization in which that was true, but, then, he'd never seriously conceived of one which routinely used magic to float tables in midair, either. So it was entirely possible the Arcanans were as ignorant of the possibilities open to the Talented as Sharona was—or had been—to the possibilities of magic. If that was the case, the less the Arcanans knew about the capabilities of Sharonian Whiffers and Tracers, the better.

"Very well," he said instead, after a moment. "I will accept that you were not aware our people were civilians . . . at first, at least. Continue."

"Thank you, Viscount," Skirvon replied, then drew a breath.

"We were horrified to find her," he resumed after a moment. "We tried hard to keep her alive. But the healer attached to our soldiers was killed in the fighting. They had a magister with a minor arcana for healing, but nothing even remotely close to an actual healer. So they tried to carry her to a real healer."

Chan Baskay frowned, then unlaced his fingers and leaned back in his floating chair, tugging at the lobe of his right ear in one of his prearranged signals to chan Rothag. The Narhathan petty-captain didn't appear to notice, but he sat back himself and crossed his legs.

So, chan Baskay reflected, *not exactly a lie, but not the entire truth, either. Well,* that's *hardly a surprise from a diplomat, now is it?*

"A moment," he said. "Your crystal failed to translate two of the terms you just used. What is a 'magister'? And what is a 'minor arcana'? Isn't Arcana the name of your world?"

Skirvon blinked in what certainly looked like genuine surprise. Then he smiled.

"Ah, I see the problem. First, Viscount, a 'magister' is someone with a Gift, an ability to use magic." He tapped the floating table.

"Like this. Some people with Gifts can make things float or perform other similar actions. Others—what we call 'magistrons'—are able to use healing magic. The only magister our soldiers had with them immediately after the fighting was not a magistron.

"Second, we use the word 'arcana' to mean a specific Gift or magical ability. The tradition among my people is that the same word is used to mean the entire world because the world is a gift from the gods to all men. That is where the confusion about 'minor arcana' came from.

"What I tried to say was that the magister who was with our soldiers had only a minor, weaker, Gift for healing. It was not a strong, trained Gift, which could have healed the young woman's injuries."

"I see." Chan Baskay nodded, then glanced at chan Rothag. The petty-captain's posture was unchanged, but he rubbed the tip of his right index finger gently across the cuff of his left sleeve. Which meant that this time, at least, the Narhathan was confident that pretty much everything Skirvon had just said was the truth.

"Very well," he said. "You say you were horrified to discover a woman among your victims." He allowed his eyes to harden slightly. "How and when did Shaylar die?"

"She had suffered a terrible head injury," Skirvon said. "She was burned, as well. Not as badly as some of the others, but the burns made her other injuries worse. We transported her as quickly as we could to our nearest base with a fully trained healer, but we were unable to get her there in time. She lived for six days."

Chan Rothag sat up, uncrossing his legs, and chan Baskay's nerves tightened abruptly.

"A moment, please," he said courteously, and glanced at chan Rothag. "Look sad," he said in Farnalian. "Then tell me what he's lying about."

"He's lying through his teeth about the burns, and about the six days," chan Rothag replied in the same language. He looked as if he wanted to weep. "The rest of it is pretty much true. Do we want to call him on the part that isn't?"

"Not yet." Chan Baskay leaned towards the other man, laying a hand on his shoulder with a concerned, sorrowful expression. "There's no point letting them know you can tell when they're lying," he said softly, gently. "Besides, let's see how much rope he'll give himself."

Chan Rothag nodded, still looking stricken, and chan Baskay patted his shoulder comfortingly, then turned back to Skirvon.

"Lord Rothag is Shurkhali," he lied with an absolutely straight face. "The confirmation that his countrywoman suffered such horrible wounds and lingered for so long is very painful to him."

He watched Skirvon's expression carefully without seeming to. Presenting such a bald-faced lie would have been unthinkable if he'd faced other Sharonians, since both sides knew the other one was bound to bring its own Sifters to any negotiations. But he'd done it deliberately, as a test, and he saw no sign Skirvon could tell that *he'd* just lied. Which was something to bear in mind. Clearly, Skirvon and Dastiri came from a totally different tradition, one which used no equivalent of Sifters.

I'll bet they're used *to being able to lie to each other*, he thought. *Which means they'll do it at the drop of a hat. That's something else to bear in mind.*

"I am sorry to have caused him grief," Skirvon said. "But there is great grief in Arcana, as well. We had never met you or any of your people before. We did not mean for the original battle to take place. The officer in charge of the soldiers in that battle was removed from command as soon as his superiors heard what had happened. Yet before we could learn your language, or make any new, peaceful contact with you, you attacked our camp without warning and killed still more soldiers." He allowed himself a slightly aggrieved expression. "The officer you attacked was not even the one responsible for the attack on your civilians, but you did not attempt to learn that before you attacked."

"When we attacked your camp without warning?" chan Baskay repeated flatly, shaking his head. "*We* did not do the attacking. Your officer may have been 'innocent' of the carnage you'd already committed, but he gave a deliberate order to fire on a single officer who had approached him under a flag of truce to ask for the return of our wounded. *You* attacked *us*. Again."

He met Skirvon's eye very levelly, his expression cold.

"It's one thing to state your position, Skirvon. It's quite another to twist the truth out of all recognition, and to insult our intelligence in the process."

Skirvon and Dastiri conferred briefly in a language that wasn't Andaran and which the crystal didn't translate into Ternathian. Then Skirvon turned back to him.

"This is very difficult," he said. "We have one view of these things; you have another view. We are trying to apologize for the violence, but you are so suspicious, we cannot even finish a thought. And while we understand how angry you must be, there is—or will be, once the news gets all the way to our home universe—great pain and anger in our world, as well. Not only have we lost many of our soldiers, not only have we killed civilians, but we have lost a civilian, as well.

"The civilian killed in your attack on our camp was one of the most important research magisters our civilization has ever produced. Magister Halathyn vos Dulainah was in our camp. He did not even try to fight, but he was killed without pity. The whole of Arcana is or soon will be in an uproar. Magister Halathyn was beloved by millions, *hundreds* of millions. The shock of his death, the anger felt over it, is very terrible."

"So now you say one of your civilians has been killed as well?" Chan Baskay frowned.

"Indeed, a most important and very beloved one."

"Perhaps," chan Baskay said coolly, "one as beloved as Shaylar Nargra-Kolmayr was among *our* people?"

Skirvon appeared to wince slightly, and chan Baskay shook his head.

"Lord Rothag is Shurkhali," he said, repeating his earlier . . . misrepresentation. "A moment, please, while I discuss this with him. I'll be . . . interested in his perspective on our relative losses."

He turned to chan Rothag and cocked his head.

"I think we may actually be looking at something important here, Trekar," he said, once again in Farnalian. "The problem is, I don't know what—or how important it may be—and I've got the feeling he's about to try selling me a used horse. Can you give me any guidance on how many lies he's telling this time?"

"Actually he's telling the truth about this fellow being killed," chan Rothag replied in the same language. "And about how popular he was and the sort of reaction he anticipates. But you're right that something funny's going on, as well. I notice he's not saying anything about why this important researcher was out here in the middle of all this nowhere. And he's being careful not to say that we actually killed him."

"I caught that, as well," chan Baskay replied, managing to keep his frustration out of his tone or his expression. "I wonder what these twisty bastards are up to this time?"

He turned back to Skirvon. The Arcanan's expression remained attentive, leavened with exactly the right degree of sorrow and regret, but chan Baskay saw the curiosity in the backs of the man's eyes. Obviously, Skirvon was simply dying to know what he and chan Rothag had just said to one another. The thought gave chan Baskay a certain amount of amusement, but he produced a dutifully sad frown of his own.

"Sharona grieves to learn that another civilian has died, and especially one who was so beloved that his death can only add to the anger and fear between our peoples," he said, meaning every word of it. "But that only underscores the urgent need for us to negotiate a cease-fire. Sharona does not want any more innocents to die."

"That is exactly Arcana's position, as well," Skirvon said earnestly. "We want an end to the shooting while we talk with you about a permanent settlement." It was his turn to smile sadly. "It may take a long time for us to agree as to where guilt and innocence truly lie. And I am sure it will take even longer for us to reach agreement on the terms of any final settlement, and on how best to manage further contacts between our peoples. For example, there is the question of who holds ultimate possession of this entire universe."

"Hell's Gate is Sharonian territory." Chan Baskay's tone was flat.

"Hell's Gate?" Skirvon repeated, and chan Baskay smiled coolly.

"Given what your soldiers did to our civilians here, it seemed an appropriate name to us," he said. Then he allowed his expression to soften very slightly. "And, I suppose, given what happened to your troops, it may seem appropriate to your people, as well."

"Indeed, it may," Skirvon agreed. "Still, whatever we may call it, the question of who *controls* it must be of vital importance to both your world and mine."

Chan Baskay allowed his eyes to narrow once more, and Skirvon shrugged with an open, honest expression.

"Surely, My Lord, your people realize as well as my own that this—" he waved at the trees about them and the steady drift of bright colored leaves sifting downward whenever the breeze blew "—is what we call a 'portal cluster.' There are many portals close together, giving access to many universes. However much we may regret the violence which has already occurred, your emperor and your Portal Authority must recognize that the control of so many portals is not something either of us will gladly give up, especially to someone we do not fully trust because of the violence which has already occurred.

"At the moment, each side desires complete control of the entire cluster, if only to provide for its own security, and neither side will be willing to concede that to the other. In the end, some sort of agreement—possibly some compromise, under which control is shared, or under which certain portals are ceded to either party—would have to be worked out if we were to have any real hope that our natural desires and fear of one another will not push us into additional conflict. Working out any such agreement would certainly be difficult, and would without doubt take much time and patience. But surely, it is always better to talk rather than to shoot."

Beside chan Baskay, chan Rothag crossed his legs once more, and chan Baskay sighed inside, wishing chan Rothag could tell him exactly *which* parts of what Skirvon had said this time were "mostly true."

Part of him wanted to stand up and call Skirvon on his lies about Shaylar right then and there. In fact, the cavalry officer in him wanted to choke the truth out of the bland-faced Arcanan. If Shaylar hadn't died the way he said she had, then how *had* she died? What had they *really* done to her in their quest for information like the words stored in their crystal? He could think of several reasons why her stored voice might sound slurred, confused, even broken. Reasons which had nothing at all to do with any wounds she might have suffered here at Fallen Timbers. Had they done those things to her? Was *that* how she'd died—in some grim little cell somewhere? And if so, did this smiling bastard across the table from him *know* she had?

The questions burned inside him, demanding answers, but he kept his expression under control. He couldn't give in to the anger he felt, couldn't call them cold-blooded murderers, even if he did know that an innocent, courageous young woman had not died the way they'd told him she had. And the fact was that Skirvon also had a perfectly valid point about the question of who would hold eventual sovereignty over the Hell's Gate Cluster. Certainly, no one in Sharona would be at all happy about the thought of abandoning the cluster—which the Chalgyn crew had clearly discovered before the Arcanans ever ventured into it—to a bloodthirsty, murderous lot of savages whose uniformed soldiers had slaughtered its original surveyors. And whatever he thought of Skirvon, or his unknown superiors, the man was right that Arcana would be no happier at the thought of conceding all of those portals to Sharona. Especially not with the spilled blood which already lay between them.

The sovereignty issue was going to *have* to be dealt with. That much was painfully obvious, as was the fact that he must not do anything at this point to prejudice Sharona's position on the issue. It would be another five days before Company-Captain chan Tesh's message that the Arcanans had asked for talks could even reach Sharona; it would take another week after that for any response to reach Hell's Gate. He could not allow his own emotions to erupt and sabotage any possibility of a diplomatic solution—especially not when he'd never actually been authorized to represent the Authority or his own emperor in the first place!

"Of course it's better to talk than to shoot," he said, smiling at the lying bastard across the table from him. "Is that your formal position?"

"We wish for there to be no more fighting while we talk," Skirvon said, nodding vigorously, and chan Rothag touched his left cuff once more.

Well, that's certainly something I can agree to in good faith, chan Baskay thought with a distinct feeling of relief. *And he's right, I suppose. Talking is better than shooting. I just wish I knew what else is going on inside that twisty brain of his. And I suppose the only way to find out is to go ahead and talk to him.*

"Very well," he said. "Sharona will agree to talk, instead of shooting."

CHAPTER
FORTY-SEVEN

"I HAVE TO say that this is a heavenly relief." Shaylar sighed, leaning back in her deck chair. "Don't get me wrong," she cracked one eye, glancing at Gadrial as the magister reclined in the deck chair beside hers. "I've gotten very fond of Skyfang, and I'm delighted they were able to fit him aboard, but dragon riding is still pretty . . . strenuous. Especially for Jathmar and me."

"Especially for you?" Gadrial looked back at her.

"Well, at least you and Jasak have more experience with the entire process."

"We've done it before, if that's what you mean. But if you think having made the same trip on the way out is making it any more restful to make the trip on the way back *in*, I'm afraid you're mistaken." The Arcanan woman grimaced. "Believe me, I'm not particularly enjoying all those endless hours with the wind whistling around my ears any more than you two are."

"I suppose not," Shaylar conceded with a smile. "And I have to admit, it *is* fascinating to watch the world rolling by underneath. Jathmar's always had dreams about wanting to fly. I think it has something to do with his Mapping Talent. The fact that his dreams had to come true *this* way's put a pretty heavy damper on his enjoyment, of course, but there's still a 'little kid in a fairy tale' excitement to it. Of course, it starts to wear a little thin after the first five or six hours in the saddle."

"Oh, you noticed that, did you?"

Shaylar grimaced at Gadrial's teasing tone, and the magister chuckled. Then, reminded of Jathmar by Shaylar's comments, she turned her head, glancing up at the fat lookout pod on the ship's single mast. Jasak and Jathmar were both up there at the moment, gazing out across the endless blue waters of the southern Evanos Ocean. She doubted that they were going to see anything significant from up there, but that wasn't really the point.

Jathmar's emotions remained much less . . . resolved than Shaylar's where Jasak was concerned. That was undoubtedly inevitable, for at least two reasons, Gadrial admitted unhappily.

First, Jathmar lacked Shaylar's ability to directly sense the emotions of those around her. Shaylar was a Voice. As she'd said, she'd been born and bred to communicate. She couldn't *help* communicating, even when she didn't want to. That meant she had a much more direct grasp of Jasak's feelings about what had happened. And from several things she'd said, Gadrial also suspected that the Shurkhali honor code was probably quite a lot closer to that of Jasak's native Andara than the one Jathmar had grown up with. Which was particularly ironic, given that it sounded as if Jasak and Jathmar had probably grown up within a few miles of one another on their respective home worlds.

But, second, and possibly even more important, Jathmar was also male. Gadrial tried not to sigh in exasperation, but there it was. There was a zoologist's term one of her friends at the Garth Showma Institute had explained to her. It was "alpha male," and from the moment her friend had explained what it meant, Gadrial had thought it was a great pity that the Andaran military hadn't been required to take courses in zoology. If she'd ever met an "alpha male," it was that paragon of all Andaran virtues, Sir Jasak Olderhan. And if she'd ever met a second "alpha male," it was Jathmar Nargra.

Which just goes to show you that truly irritating male characteristics are inter-universal in scope, she thought grumpily. *Rahil! What did I do to deserve* two *of them at a time like this?*

Jathmar knew that Jasak was completely—one might almost say fanatically—dedicated to protecting him and Shaylar from additional harm. But he was also Shaylar's husband, and he loved her, which meant that primitive male wiring of his demanded that he protect her. That *he* protect her. Which, of course, he couldn't do. The fact that he was totally reliant upon Jasak (the officer whose men had slaughtered all of his and Shaylar's friends, whatever Jasak might have wanted to happen) to provide the protection he couldn't, only made his own sense of frustration and failure even worse. And the fact that Shaylar, as deeply as she loved Jathmar, was comfortable with the notion that Jasak's honor code required him to protect her—and that *she* looked to Jasak (who was *not* her husband) as the protector for both of them probably punched more than a few male jealousy buttons, as well.

Then there was the fact that Jasak, in his own invincibly "alpha male" fashion, couldn't conceive of any circumstances which could possibly absolve him of his responsibility to protect his *shardonai*. That left him with a protective attitude not just towards Shaylar, but towards *Jathmar*, as well. Which, despite the fact that Jathmar's intellect knew better, struck his raw-edged and bleeding emotions as . . . patronizing. Not to mention insulting, diminishing, and infuriating.

That was why Gadrial and Shaylar had effectively packed the two of them off to the lookout pod where they could—hopefully—spend a little time getting over the worst of their mutual prickliness.

Of course they can, the magister thought dryly. *And the Evanos is only a little damp.*

"Do you think they've said three words to each other the whole time they've been up there?" Shaylar asked, and Gadrial blinked as the other woman's words broke in on her thoughts.

"What?" she asked, and Shaylar snorted in amusement.

"I asked if you think they've said three words to each other the whole time they'd been up there," she repeated, waving one hand at the lookout pod.

"I'd like to think so," Gadrial said after a moment, grinning as they both admitted what was really going on. "I'm not holding out a lot of hope, though."

"Me either." Shaylar's slight smile slowly faded, and she drew a deep breath. "Not that I can really blame either of them. It's an . . . ugly situation, isn't it?"

"Very," Gadrial agreed with a heavy sigh of her own. "If there were *any* way we could undo it, we'd—"

"Don't say it," Shaylar interrupted. Gadrial's eyes widened, as if with an edge of hurt, and Shaylar shook her head. "What I mean, is that you don't *have* to say it. I know it's true, and so does Jathmar, however . . . uncomfortable he may still be around Jasak. It's just that there's not any point. Saying it won't change anything, and there's no good reason why you should keep beating yourself up over it, apologizing for things that weren't your fault and that no one can change, anyway."

"I suppose not. But in that case," Gadrial smiled crookedly, "what *can* we talk about to wile away this pleasant little ocean voyage?"

Shaylar chuckled. As nearly as she could figure out, they were traveling from the eastern coast of the great island-continent of Lissia across the Western Ocean to the western coast of New Farnalia. That was almost five thousand miles, which was going to take them around nine days, even aboard one of the Arcanans' marvelous ships. Still, as she'd told Gadrial, she was profoundly grateful for the break in their arduous travels, even if every mile of seawater they crossed did remind her of her mother's embassy back home.

"Actually," she said, after a moment, "I've been thinking about what Fifty Varkal and Jasak had to say about the difference between Skyfang and Windclaw."

"Yes?"

"I got the distinct impression that there are more significant differences between 'battle dragons' and what Fifty Varkal calls 'transports' than just their size and maneuverability." Shaylar ended on an almost questioning note and raised both eyebrows.

"Oh, there are," Gadrial agreed. "Mind you, I'm no magistron, and what I know about dragons—or, for that matter, any other augmented species—isn't much more than any other layman would be able to tell you. Well," her lips quirked, "maybe a *little* more than that, given what I do for a living, but not a lot. Still, if you'd like, I'll tell you what I know."

"By all means, please," Shaylar said, sitting up a bit straighter in her deck chair and rolling slightly up on one hip as she turned to face the other woman more squarely.

"Well," Gadrial began, "as Daris suggested back at Fort Talon, battle dragons are deliberately designed to be faster and more maneuverable than transport dragons."

"'Designed'?" Shaylar repeated. Gadrial looked surprised by the question, and Shaylar gave her head a little shake. "I haven't had much choice but to accept that your people can do all sorts of 'impossible' things, but I guess I'm still just feeling a bit . . . uncomfortable over the notion of 'designing' a living creature."

"As I said, I'm not a magistron, so it's not remotely my area of specialization," Gadrial replied, "but the actual techniques have been around for a long time. As matter of fact, it's one of the few areas in which Ransar actually led the way in both theoretical and applied research for something like three hundred years."

"Over Mythal, you mean?"

"Exactly." Gadrial looked away, gazing out across the endless, steady swell as the passenger ship sliced through it with a graceful, soothing motion. "It was a Ransaran magistron who first perfected the spells for examining what he called the genetic map of living creatures."

"And what's a 'genetic map'?" Shaylar inquired with an air of slightly martyred patience.

"Sorry." Gadrial looked back at her and smiled. "The word 'genetic' is derived from the Old Ransaran word for race or descent. And the reason Hansara—Rayjhari Hansara, the magistron who developed the original concept and spells—called it that was that it's basically a symbolically congruent representation of the physical characteristics of the creature. It's a fundamental principle of magic that the map is the territory, and once Hansara came up with a way to represent a living organism's characteristics in a fashion which could be visualized and manipulated, it really did become possible to 'design' creatures to order."

Shaylar shivered as if a sudden icy wind had found its way up and down her spine. And, in fact, one had, in a metaphorical way of speaking.

"And does that include *people*?" she asked after moment.

"No," Gadrial said firmly. Shaylar looked both relieved and skeptical, in almost equal measure, and Gadrial shrugged. "There's no arcane reason it *couldn't* include people," she conceded. "Human beings' codes can be visualized just as well as those of any other creature. But from the very beginning, any efforts to tinker with humanity were outlawed."

"Even in Mythal?" Shaylar said, with rather more skepticism, and Gadrial surprised her with a harsh bark of laughter.

"*Especially* in Mythal! The last thing any *shakira* would want to do is come up with a way to turn *garthan* into *shakira*. Given their religion, they'd see it as blasphemous, at the very least. And from a practical perspective—which I personally happen to think is even more important to them than their ludicrous religious concepts—if they were to turn all of the *garthan* into Gifted *shakira*, what happens to the existing *shakira*'s slave class? It's been my observation that their 'religious principles' serve their more worldly ambitions much more than the other way around."

"But what about turning *garthan* into even more obedient slaves?"

"Now *that* probably would be something that would appeal to the caste-lords," Gadrial admitted with a grimace of distaste. "These days, at least. But at the time the rules and laws which prohibit tampering with humans were being put into place, no Mythalan *garthan* had any hope of ever managing to escape or defy his overlords. There was no need to turn them into 'more obedient slaves,' because it was impossible for them to be *disobedient* under the existing system."

"And why did everyone else feel it should be outlawed?"

"Because, at the time, it was all a process of trial and error," Gadrial said. "In fact, that's still the case whenever anyone begins mapping a new species, in a lot of ways. Hansara had found a way to produce a congruent map, but it's an incredibly complex chart, Shaylar, and initially, he had no way of establishing the congruency between a particular section of the map and *specific* characteristics of the creature it represented. So he and his fellow magistrons not only had to come up with techniques to modify the chart, they also had to figure out which parts of it they *needed* to modify to achieve a specific objective. Most of their initial efforts—for decades, literally—produced creatures which couldn't possibly survive on their own. Or, at best, which were far, far cries from what they'd *wanted* to produce. No one was willing to allow them to experiment on humans when they might as readily produce a three-headed monster as an improvement on the original model. And, of course, Hansara and his colleagues were almost all Ransarans."

"Which was significant why?" Shaylar asked, and Gadrial paused with an arrested expression.

"You know," she replied after moment, "you speak Andaran so well that I keep forgetting how little you actually know about Arcana. Like all of the reasons, aside from the purely personal, of course, a Ransaran like me would have for disliking a Mythalan."

"Should I take it that one or more of those reasons would have a bearing on all of this?"

"Oh, I think you could probably take it that way. You see, one of the primary causes for the hostility between Mythal and Ransar is that we have totally different religious beliefs. Mythalans believe in something they call reincarnation. They believe that each individual human soul—they call it a 'yurha'—experiences dozens, possibly thousands, of lives, and that the purpose of those lives is for each *yurha* to become more completely realized—a 'higher being'—in each incarnation. Ultimately, the individual *yurha* reaches a state of actual divinity, in which it becomes one with the entire universe. That's what they visualize God to be: the entire universe. He's not an individual entity, not a creator, but a sort of . . . confluence of all of the magical energy bound up in all of creation. That's why the *shakira* are 'obviously' the highest of the Mythalan castes. Because they're the ones with the Gifts which allow them to manipulate that magical energy, they're clearly much closer to attaining the godhead than anyone else, since they as a caste *must* consist solely of people with highly evolved *yurhas*.

"It also justifies their treatment of the *garthan* on several levels. The function of the *garthan* is to do all of those dirty, demeaning, physically exhausting jobs the *shakira* couldn't possibly take the time to do, since it would draw them away from their mastery of magic and thus separate them from the godhead. It would actually be sinful for them to *allow* themselves to be diverted, since that might cause their *yurhas* to move *downward* through their 'great chain of being.'"

"That sounds a little bit like a really distorted version of what some Lissians believe," Shaylar said cautiously. "But the Lissians are among the gentlest, most compassionate people on Sharona."

"Well, Mythalans certainly aren't gentle *or* compassionate," Gadrial said tartly. Then she sighed.

"I suppose my own experiences with them really do color my reaction," she admitted. "But part of the problem I have with their entire culture is that once you accept their religious beliefs, and the mindset they've developed to go with them, then their treatment of the *garthan* is perfectly logical and reasonable. They really and truly simply don't understand why the rest of us can't just *see* that and admit that Mythal's been right all along . . . which is one of the reasons both Ransar and Andara simply can't stand them.

"As they see it, the whole object of the human race, the whole reason we exist—according to the Mythalans—is for all of us eventually to obtain oneness. And, since they believe in reincarnation, each of us has an effectively limitless number of lives in which our *yurha* can advance. So no matter what they do to an individual *garthan*—or to all *garthan*, as a caste—they aren't *really* harming that individual, are they? After all, this is only one brief stop in an endless journey, and eventually all *garthan*—aside, of course, from the inevitably willful or evil ones—will become *shakira* themselves. In fact, some of the greatest cruelties the *shakira* have traditionally practiced upon the *garthan*, like the law codes which take Gifted children away from *garthan* parents and give them to *shakira* to raise, are justified on the basis of *helping* their victims attain enlightenment sooner."

Shaylar looked at Gadrial for several seconds, reminding herself that, by her own admission, Gadrial hated Mythalans. But she'd also come to know Gadrial Kelbryan. If the magister hated Mythalans, it was probably because she despised their beliefs, rather than a case of her despising—or distorting—their beliefs because she hated them.

"So how do Ransaran beliefs differ from Mythalan beliefs?" she asked finally.

"In just about every conceivable way," Gadrial snorted. "First, every Ransaran—with the exception of the Manisthuans—is monotheistic. That is, we all believe there's only a single God, since God is, by definition, infinite and since, equally by definition, there can't be *two* infinite beings. All of our theologians agreed long ago that if two beings are separate from one another, then neither can be truly infinite, since they have to *stop* somewhere if there are going to be two of them in the first place. Unfortunately, we're Ransarans. While we may all agree that there's only one God, we don't all agree on who He—or She—is."

The corners of her eyes crinkled with amusement at Shaylar's expression, and she chuckled.

"In fairness to the Mythalans," she said, "and much as it pains me to even *consider* being fair to them, I can't conceive of anyone who could possibly be more profoundly . . . irritating to them than Ransarans. It's almost as if God deliberately designed us to drive them crazy. And *vice-versa*, of course.

"There are three major Ransaran religions, Shaylar, and quite a few subsidiary sects floating around the fringes. I personally belong to the Fellowship of Rahil, and we Rahilians follow the teachings of Rahil, the Great Prophetess. By all accounts, she was a magistron of truly phenomenal ability back in the days before the theoretical basis for magic was at all understood. We believe her abilities in that regard were directly inspired by God as a sign of His favor, and her writings about God constitute the seminal text of our religious beliefs. In the Rahilian view, God is infinite, and as such infinitely unknowable, but a benign and loving Creator who progressively reveals to us as much about Him as finite mortals are capable of understanding.

"Like the Mythalans, Rahilians believe that the purpose of a physical, mortal existence is for the individual soul to live and grow—to 'evolve' upward, to use the Mythalan term—by making choices and acquiring experience. But we also believe that God is separate from the universe around us, that He extends beyond and transcends it as an individual distinct from it, and that He seeks an individual relationship with each of us. That was what Rahil taught, at any rate.

"Over the centuries, the Rahilians and the other two major Ransaran religions have spent quite a lot of their time massacring one another over various points of religious disagreement," Gadrial admitted. "We stopped doing that about, oh, nine hundred years ago, I guess. Not that we all turned into sunshine and light where our differences are concerned, of course. But at least all of us got to the point where we agreed that whoever was right, God would probably be fairly irritated with His—or Her—worshipers if they insisted on slaughtering everyone else in job lots simply for being mistaken.

"At any rate, there are three things that all three of our major religions have in common. First, we believe there's an individual God, an all-powerful being who exists *outside* the material universe, rather than being bound up in it.

"Second, none of us believe in reincarnation, although all of us do believe in the immortality of the human soul. And we believe that each soul has a single mortal existence in which to establish its relationship to God. There's some disagreement among us about what happens to the souls that don't manage to establish the *right* relationship with God. In fact, that's one of the points we used to kill each other over, back in the good old days.

"Third, we believe each individual must have the greatest possible opportunity to become all that he or she *can* become. Not simply because all of us agree God wants us to love one another, but because in the process of becoming all a person can be, that person is brought closer to God and so to the ability to establish that 'right relationship' we all believe in . . . even if we're not quite in total agreement over what it ought to be."

She stopped again, gazing at Shaylar, and the Voice nodded slowly. Gadrial was right, she reflected. Assuming that the magister had described the Mythalan and Ransaran viewpoints as accurately—or, at least, honestly—as Shaylar was confident she had, it was scarcely surprising that the Mythalans would hate, despise, and fear everything Ransar stood for. And she could think of nothing someone with Gadrial's religious and philosophical values would find more revolting and cruel than the Mythalan caste system. Which only made the deep and obvious love which had existed between Gadrial and Magister Halathyn even more remarkable.

"At any rate," Gadrial continued, "given the Ransaran views on the preciousness of each individual life, the possibility of any of our major religions—most of which were still quite cheerfully chopping up the adherents of their Ransaran coreligionists at the time—signing off on the notion of trial-and-error experiments on *humans* was . . . remote, shall we say. So both the Mythalans and the Ransarans, each for their own very different reasons, outlawed that sort of experimentation on humans from the very beginning."

"But not on other creatures," Shaylar said, and managed not to grimace when Gadrial shook her head.

The more Shaylar heard about the Mythalans, the more she preferred the Ransarans. Yet it was obvious to her that even the humanistic Ransarans were very, very different from her own people. Most Sharonians would have found it exceedingly difficult to "sign off on" that sort of experimentation upon *any* creatures, not just humans. There were exceptions, of course, as she was well aware, but the existence of those like her mother, whose Talent allowed communication with sentient nonhuman species, made them rare. Very few Sharonians would have been prepared to suggest that a cow, or a chicken, was intellectually or morally equivalent to a human being. But, by the same token, very few Sharonians would have been prepared to *deny* that the great apes and the cetaceans had attained a very high level of intelligence which, if not equal to that of human beings, certainly approached it very closely. In some ways, that same Talent kept them from over-anthropomorphizing the lesser animals, with whom no meaningful contact was possible. Still, by and large, they tended to regard themselves as the stewards of the worlds in which they lived, and the notion of creating experimental monsters would have been highly repugnant to them.

Not that she had any intention of discussing that with Gadrial just now. Especially since, so far, she'd managed to conceal the existence of that specific Talent, despite her mother's life work.

If they ever ask me exactly who Mother's an ambassador to, keeping that particular secret a secret is going to get sticky, she thought. *So let's not go there just now, Shaylar.*

"So, how does all of this relate to transport dragons and battle dragons?" she asked, instead.

"Well, it was Ransaran magistrons who built the first dragons," Gadrial said, as if she were discussing how to go about baking a cake, Shaylar thought.

"'Built' them out of *what*?" the Voice demanded.

"There's some dispute about that," Gadrial admitted. "According to at least one tradition, there were still some of the great lizards living in Ransar at the time." She shrugged. "I've always had problems with that particular explanation, myself, since the fossil record seems to indicate that all of the great lizards had died out—rather abruptly, in geological terms—long before dragons were ever developed. Still, there are undeniable similarities.

"At any rate," she continued, as if blithely oblivious to the way Shaylar's eyes were bugging out ever so slightly, "the original dragons were developed in Ransar strictly as beasts of burden. As a way to move cargo quickly from point to point, for the most part, although there are still some wingless dragons in Ransar, where they've been used for centuries instead of horses or unicorns as really heavy draft animals. For the most part, though, their military applications were limited strictly to improving transport. Until the Mythalans got into the act, that was."

"And why did I see *that* one coming?" Shaylar demanded rhetorically.

"Because you're so clever," Gadrial told her with a wry chuckle.

"I've always rather suspected that Mythalan resentment that we primitive Ransarans had produced something *they* hadn't played a part in what happened," the magister continued. "After all, to be brutally honest, most of us *were* pretty primitive compared to Mythal, at that particular point. Hansara was a Tosarian, and Tosaria had evolved a much higher level of civilization than most of the rest of us. *My* ancestors, for example, were still painting themselves blue and yellow and pickling their enemies' heads as door ornaments at the time. As far as Mythal was concerned, though, *all* Ransarans were still doing that, and yet the Tosarians had produced not just dragons but Hansara's basic work. Given *shakira* arrogance, I'm sure they felt an enormous temptation to prove they could do it better than we had. But they weren't interested in simply improving transportation capabilities; they were looking for direct military applications."

Gadrial's amusement of only moments before had vanished.

"Skyfang is a pure transport type. As Daris says, he probably goes clear back to the first egg. Which means he's bigger, stronger, and less maneuverable than a battle dragon, but that he has more endurance and basic lift capability. And, aside from his teeth and claws, he has no natural weapons."

"You mean battle dragons *do* have other weapons?" Shaylar's eyes widened.

Mother Marthea! she thought shakenly. *Surely the things' fangs, claws, and horns are vicious enough! How could even Mythalans want to add still* more *weapons to their nightmare?*

"They certainly do." Gadrial's voice was as grim as if she'd actually Heard Shaylar's thought . . . and shared it. "The weapons Jasak's men used against your people are called 'infantry-dragons' because they replicate the 'natural' weapons the Mythalans built into their real dragons, Shaylar. Some battle dragons breathe fire—or, rather, spit fireballs. Others throw lightning bolts. And still others, despite periodic efforts to ban the breeds in question entirely, project poisonous gases and vapors."

Shaylar gazed at her in horror, and the magister shrugged. She was obviously sympathetic to Shaylar's reaction, but there was something more than simple sympathy behind that shrug, and she returned Shaylar's gaze levelly.

"I can understand that you find the thought frightening and unnatural, Shaylar," she said. "And I don't disagree with you that

building something like that into a living creature is a typically
Mythalan sort of thing to do. In fact, I've always thought battle
dragons are probably the most horrific battlefield weapons—short
of the mass destruction spells which were banned when the Union
was formed, at least—that Arcana's ever deployed. But I can't believe
your people are that much different from ours when it comes to
fighting wars. You've thrown the fact that Jasak's troopers' infantry-
dragons burned your people to death into the face of every Army
officer you've confronted, and I admit that that's a horrible way to
die. But war is *full* of horrible ways to die, isn't it? Are you going to
tell me your people never poured flaming oil onto someone trying to
storm a castle wall? That they never blew someone's abdomen open
with those artillery pieces of yours—those "mortars"—and left him
to bleed slowly to death on the field of battle, screaming in pain?
Never used fire as a naval weapon that gave men the choice between
burning to death or drowning when their wooden ships went up in
flame around them?"

Shaylar started to open her mouth in a quick response, then paused
and closed it once more. Gadrial was right, she realized. When it
came to the organized slaughter of combat, there were countless
horrific ways to die. No one had a monopoly on ghastliness.

"I'm not saying you don't have every right to regard what happened to your survey crew as an act of barbarism," Gadrial said
more gently. "If nothing else, your people were civilians, and all you
were doing was defending yourselves. But when you think about all
the horrors Arcanan weapons could unleash against your people,
you need to remember that our people are worrying about horrors
just as great coming from *your* people. Both sides are terrified, and
both sides think the people on the other side are barbarians. I pray
to God every night that we're both wrong, that Master Skirvon and
Master Dastiri are going to sit down with your people and somehow negotiate an end to all of this without one more single person
being killed.

"But if Skirvon and Dastiri don't pull that off, then Jasak's father
is one of the men who are going to decide what happens next, how
Arcana goes to war against Sharona. You already know what Jasak's
going to tell him, but it's going to be almost as much up to us—to
you, Jathmar, and me—to convince the duke that prosecuting the
war with every weapon at our disposal is the wrong thing to do.
And if you're going to help convince him of that, you've got to be
able to be brutally honest about just how much barbarism there
really is on both sides."

She stopped speaking, and there was no sound except the noise of wind and water for several seconds. Then Shaylar gave a tiny nod.

"You're right," she said. "Or partly right, at least. I'm sure being caught in the explosion of an artillery shell is just as terrible as being killed by one of your lightning bolts. And, yes, my people have used flaming oil and set their enemies' ships on fire with what we call 'Ternathian Fire.' I suppose the only real difference is how we go about inflicting our mutual atrocities, isn't it?"

"I'm afraid so," Gadrial agreed sadly.

"Maybe it's only the fact that I *am* a civilian," Shaylar continued. "I'd never seen anyone actually killed in front of me before, never even thought about how horrible and terrifying and ugly that would be. And," she managed something that was almost a smile, "something about being on the receiving end of something like that does tend to give you a somewhat biased opinion of just how ... humanitarian it is.

"But I'll try to think about what you've said. Especially the bit about helping to convince Jasak's father Sharona isn't simply a pit of horrors waiting to consume Arcana."

"From what I've heard of the duke, he's not likely to think that, anyway," Gadrial said. "But there are going to be others, as well, and some of them very well may."

"I understand." Shaylar nodded. Then she inhaled deeply and squared her shoulders.

"But you were saying about the dragons?" she said.

"I was saying that they call the infantry support weapons 'dragons' because of the way they replicate dragons' natural weapons," Gadrial said. "But they aren't anywhere near as deadly as an actual battle dragon. The artillery's field-dragons are many times more powerful than the infantry-dragons Jasak's men had with them that day, and much longer ranged. But even the heaviest field-dragon is much less powerful than the weapons built into battle dragons. All of the infantry and artillery weapons rely on charged spell accumulators, but battle dragons *are* spell accumulators. They charge *themselves* from the magic field after every shot."

"I'm trying very hard to remember what we were just saying," Shaylar told her a bit wanly. "It's a bit difficult, though, when you tell me about something like *that*."

"I never said it would be easy. Just that we've got to do it, anyway."

"I know, I know." Shaylar shook her head. "But are you saying that you think it's something about the ... magic the Mythalans used to graft those horrible capabilities into their battle dragons that causes them to hate me where transports like Skyfang don't?" Shaylar asked, deliberately trying to step back from the horrendous vision of dragons flying over Sharona belching death and devastation.

"Probably," Gadrial said, leaning back in her deck chair as if she, too, was grateful to back away from the same vision. "Although, actually, I think it probably has less to do with the weapons themselves than with the changes in the dragons' . . . personalities, for want of a better word, that went with it. The original Ransaran dragon breeding lines had deliberately emphasized docility. The breeders didn't *want* something that size which would suddenly decide it ought to be eating its handlers. The Mythalans, typically, decided to 'improve' upon that when they set out to create dragons for combat. So they spliced in several of the characteristics of a Mythal River crocodile." She grimaced once more. "You might say that their personalities are just a *little* more aggressive than those of a pure transport, like Skyfang."

"I see," Shaylar said slowly, and, in fact, she rather thought she did. She'd sensed a similarity between Skyfang and the huge whales who sought out her mother when they needed an interface with humanity. The dragon wasn't as intelligent as the great whales—or, at least, she certainly didn't think he was—yet there was that undeniably familiar "feel" to his personality. But if Skyfang was somehow similar to whales, then the battle dragons were more akin to the great sharks . . . or, perhaps, to barracudas.

"That's very interesting," she said after several seconds. "It's a lot to take in, of course . . . even without your well-deserved little lecture." She smiled crookedly, then she yawned. It wasn't completely feigned, and her smile turned lopsided. "In fact, if you don't mind, I think I'm going to take advantage of the sun until lunchtime and sleep on it."

"By all means, get as much rest as you can," Gadrial advised her with an equally crooked smile. "We won't be getting much of it over the next half-dozen universes or so."

"In that case . . ."

Shaylar settled back in her deck chair and tucked the light blanket around her legs. Then she gave Gadrial a smile, closed her eyes, and dreamed nightmares of Sharonian nights filled with the ghastly pyres of dragon breath.

CHAPTER FORTY-EIGHT

"SO, DAVIR. WHAT kind of effect do you expect these negotiations to have?" Darl Elivath asked.

It was late as he and Davir Perthis sat sipping tea. They were in the Sharonian Universal News Network's green room, in the wing of the Great Palace set aside for the press, waiting for official word that the Conclave's Committee on Unification had finally managed to report out draft language for the proposed amendment to the initial Act of Unification.

"On the Conclave and the Unification? Or on whether or not we go to war with these people?" Perthis asked.

"Both, I suppose," Elivath said. "It took the threat of a war to get the Conclave assembled in the first place, after all."

"Well . . ." SUNN's Chief Voice scratched his chin thoughtfully. "I suppose the fact that they want to talk at all has to be a good sign. At least it's not what you expect out of the kind of murderous barbarians we've all assumed we were facing. And the possibility that it was all a mistake—that they thought our people were soldiers who'd attacked one of their people—genuinely hadn't occurred to me."

Perthis was a bit surprised by how unwillingly he made that admission, and he wondered *why* he was so unwilling. Was it that he'd invested so much in hating the "Arcanans" for what they'd done that he simply didn't want to give up his hate? Or was it what he'd Seen from Shaylar's final Voice transmission? He remembered once again Seeing Ghartoun chan Hagrahyl stand up with his hands empty . . . and go down again, choking on his life's blood.

Perthis was a man who'd spent his entire adult career in the news business. He knew, beyond any shadow of a doubt, that what he'd Seen from Shaylar was the truth. It was, quite literally, impossible for a Voice to lie about something like that in such a deep linkage to another Voice. But the professional newsman in him also recognized how even the truth could be misread, misinterpreted. Was that what had happened here?

It was entirely possible that it was, he admitted. And if it was, the fact that relatively few people on Sharona—Davir Perthis, included—had *ever* seen a violent death with their own eyes had undoubtedly contributed to it. The sheer, horrifying emotional impact of seeing that sort of carnage with your physical eyes would have been bad enough for someone who'd never seen it before. Going the extra step and Seeing it with the total clarity (and emotional overtones) which could only come from a powerful Voice trapped in the middle of it only made it infinitely worse.

"What about what they say happened to Shaylar?"

Elivath's question broke in on the Chief Voice's thoughts, and Perthis looked back up at him with a sour expression.

"They haven't really said all that much, when you come right down to it," he pointed out. "Aside from the fact that she wasn't killed outright—which we already knew—all we have is their claims that they tried to get her to one of their Healers before she died. Or that they could have done anything for her if they'd managed to reach one in time. We didn't get that from a Voice, either, you know. And either way, she's still dead, and *they* still killed her."

"So you think they're lying?"

"I didn't say that." Perthis realized he sounded a little defensive, and waved one hand. "All right, I admit I *thought* it. I'm having a hard time getting past my original image of them, I guess. But the fact is, Darl, that we *don't* have any sort of confirmation of a single thing they've said, and I'm just . . . uncomfortable with the fact."

"But if they did try to save her, and if it turns out they can prove it, don't you think it would make a difference with public opinion?"

"*If* they genuinely tried to save her life after making an honest mistake, then probably yes," Perthis said. "But that's a lot of ifs, Darl. They've still got a lot of talking to do, as far as I'm concerned, to explain how what were supposed to be a bunch of trained soldiers mistook someone standing up and holding out empty hands as an act of aggression. Mind you, I'm not saying mistakes like that can't happen. Gods know they've happened in our own past. I'm just saying that after actually Seeing the events from our crew's side, it's going to be hard to convince a lot of our people, including me, that that's what happened here."

He started to say something else, then stopped himself. He didn't know exactly how much Elivath actually knew about the rumors regarding the Voice messages to Emperor Zindel and the Conclave. The original message from Regiment-Captain Velvelig, informing the emperor and the Conclave that the Arcanans had asked for negotiations, had been released directly to the Voice network and the general public. The *follow-on* messages had not been, and neither had any of the Conclave's—or Zindel's—responses to Velvelig.

Ostensibly, that was to avoid further exacerbating public opinion by generating unreasonable expectations, on the one hand, or generating additional fury when the bobbles and stumbles which were undoubtedly inevitable in opening negotiations with a totally alien civilization occurred, on the other hand. Perthis supposed that the official reasoning made sense, but he'd picked up on a few very quiet rumors that it was because those follow-on messages from whoever was actually talking to these people included reports that the Arcanans weren't being completely truthful. He had no idea what they were supposed to be lying about, but the thought that they were lying at all was hardly reassuring.

"Well, let's assume it turns out they really did their best to save her life," Elivath said. "And that they really do want to settle this as peacefully as they can, given everything that's already happened. If all that's true, what kind of effect *do* you think it's going to have on the Conclave and the unification?"

"I don't know that I expect it to have *any* effect," Perthis replied. Elivath raised one skeptical eyebrow, and the Chief Voice shrugged. "By now," he pointed out, "the debate's taken on a life of its own. Besides, even if we manage to put the brakes on this current confrontation, we still know the bastards are out there, don't we? All of our conventional political equations are going to have to take them into account from now on."

"Do you really think so?"

Elivath grimaced and set down his tea cup. He sat turning it on its saucer for a moment, lips slightly pursed, while he gazed out of the green room's window at the Great Palace's well-lit grounds under the great, midnight-blue dome of the starstruck heavens. Then he returned his gaze to Perthis.

"I was talking to one of the Authority's theoreticians," the Voice correspondent said. "From the way he was talking, this may be the only point of contact we'll see with these people. So if we get control of it, or just seal it off, wouldn't that be more or less the end of it?"

"Only point of contact?"

Perthis leaned back in his own chair. To be totally honest, he'd never thought of Elivath as the sharpest pencil in SUNN's box. He respected the strength of Elivath's Talent, and his integrity, but he'd also always thought of Elivath as one of his correspondents who required rather more careful direction than many.

He knew Elivath *knew* he regarded him that way—that was one of the problems when Voices with powerful Talents worked with one another—but he also knew that both he and Elivath had qualities the other respected, as well. Still, he'd never really considered Elivath an *investigative* reporter. The correspondent was extraordinarily good at explaining even complicated concepts to his audience, once he'd mastered those concepts himself, but he usually needed them explained to *him* in the first place by the investigators who'd gone out and turned them up initially. Part of Perthis' job was to see to it that the proper experts were found to explain things to him, and he was unaccustomed to having Elivath go out and do the finding for himself, especially in technical matters. But if the correspondent had, indeed, turned up some new technical information, Perthis wanted to know about it.

"Why should this be the only point of contact?" the Chief Voice continued after a moment. "Aside from the fact that we've never had one before, which might predispose us to expect it to be the only one, that is."

"I'm not the best technical man we've got," Elivath pointed out mildly—and, Perthis thought, with considerable understatement. "We both know that. But according to this fellow, the latest models for how the multiverse works suggest that our particular universe is part of what I guess you might call a 'cable' of universes. Sort of like those stranded cables they used to hang the bridge across the Ylani Strait, I guess."

He waved one hand, frowning, as if he weren't completely satisfied with his own analogy. Not too surprisingly, Perthis reflected. *No one*, as far as he was aware, had ever come up with an analogy for the multiverse's structure that he really liked.

"Anyway, this fellow I was talking to says that all of the empirical and theoretical work that's been done suggests that all of the universes in the multiverse had the same common starting point. What caused them to . . . separate from one another were events that had multiple possible outcomes. Each possible outcome happened *somewhere*, and that started the separate, divergent universes."

He paused, one eyebrow raised, and Perthis nodded to indicate that he was still following. *That* part of the theory had been explained to everyone, over and over again. There might be an Arpathian septman somewhere so far up in the hills that they still hadn't invented fire who hadn't heard it, but everyone else was fully aware of it.

"Well," Elivath continued, "this guy I was talking to says that up until recently we always figured that whenever a new universe was created, it went off in its own unique direction. That each new universe radiated at what I guess you could think of as right angles to the universe it split off from because of the particular event that created it. But he says that that theory's been challenged lately, and that the brains' best *current* guess is that the universes that are most similar lie . . . parallel to one another, for want of a better word, instead. They're all 'headed the same direction,' so to speak, not racing away from each other."

"I got the same briefing when this whole thing blew up in our faces," Perthis agreed, nodding again. "In fact, they said something about the Calirath Glimpses proving the existence of *parallel* universes."

"Yeah." Elivath made a face. "I remember. It made my head hurt, actually."

"Only if you tried to follow the theory instead of the consequences," Perthis pointed out with a wry grin. "Just remember that the boffins think that what a Glimpse is is really a sort of precognitive peek across into those parallel universes, whereas a straight Precog is stuck looking along the event line in his *own* universe. A Glimpse isn't *true* precognition, but more of a . . . statistical process. They do have some unique capability in their Talent which lets them follow possible human actions and outcomes, but the unpredictability of human nature means they can't be sure what any particular human in any particular universe is going to do. What they can do, apparently, is see the possible actions and outcomes of a whole bunch of people simultaneously. The *same* people, living in parallel universes. And what their Glimpses are is the most common outcomes of all those actions."

"Like I say, it made my head hurt. It still does."

"Mine, too, if I'm going to be honest." Perthis grinned. "But, the main point, is that that's the reason the Caliraths can See the consequences of human actions when no one else can. And if the universes in question weren't really, really close to one another—really 'parallel,' and really similar to one another, I mean—then a Glimpse based on what's going to happen in any other universe—or universes, for that matter—wouldn't help when it comes to figuring out what's going to happen in *this* one."

"That's probably what this fellow was getting at when he said that the parallel universes stay 'close together,'" Elivath said. "But he also pointed out that where the *portals* form is where one universe 'runs into' another one, and since similar universes stay close together and . . . head in the same 'direction,' then it's the most *dissimilar* universes which are most likely to collide and form portals. He says that's the best current theory for why we've never run into humans before. As different from us as these people obviously are, they still almost have to come from a universe that's in our basic 'cable,' since there are humans in it at all."

"I think I see where you're headed with this," Perthis said slowly. In fact, he was impressed by Elivath's analysis. Of course, he realized the Voice hadn't come up with it on his own, but it was obvious he'd been thinking hard about it for some time.

"So your basic point," the Chief Voice continued, "is that since we're all . . . traveling along in this same direction of yours, the odds are against any of the universes in our 'cable' colliding with another universe in *their* 'cable.'"

"Exactly." Elivath nodded vigorously, and it was Perthis' turn to gaze out the window into the night while he thought.

"I'm not sure it follows," he said finally. "Mind you, Darl, I'd like it to. Given how murderous these bastards seem to be, I'd like it a lot, actually. But if I'm following the logic properly, then didn't we start a fresh 'cable' at the moment our universes made contact? What I mean is, isn't there a new batch of universes spreading out from the point at which our universe and their universe found the same portal cluster? And if that's true, aren't the strands of that new 'cable' all laying out parallel to one another . . . and at right angles, for want of a better description, to our original 'cables'?"

"Now my head really hurts," Elivath said plaintively, and Perthis chuckled.

"It's not that bad. Or, at least, I don't *think* it is," he said. "At the same time, it sort of underscores our basic problem, doesn't it? You and I are hardly multi-universal theorists, but from what I'm hearing out of the people who are, they don't really have any idea at all what the ultimate consequences of this contact are likely to be. We may never find ourselves sharing another portal with these people, or we might find ourselves running into them every time we turn around! At any rate, I think we have to plan on the basis that we *could* be running into them again and again."

"And," Elivath said, cocking his head, "you see this as an opportunity to put Ternathia in charge of the planet, anyway."

Perthis managed not to blink, although the shrewdness of the correspondent's observation had taken him considerably aback. *I think I've been underestimating him,* the Chief Voice thought after a moment. *Either that, or I've been an awful lot more obvious about my little manipulations than I ever meant to be!* He gazed at Elivath for several seconds, then shrugged.

"I suppose you're right," he conceded. "Oh, I started out feeling that way simply because of the threat these people represented. I figured *somebody* had to be in charge if we were going to respond to them the way they obviously deserved, and Zindel was absolutely the best person I could think of for the job." The Chief Voice's lips twitched humorlessly. "For one thing, he's so damned levelheaded I figured he'd probably help restrain my own murderous impulses if they needed restraining.

"I still do think we need a world government that can not simply take advantage of whatever we manage to negotiate with these people this time around, but keep an eye on them for the future. But I'll admit that I've been more and more impressed with the possibilities of a world government—especially one with Ternathia's traditions behind it—for dealing with all the rest of our problems, too."

"Somebody to make the children behave right here on Sharona, you mean?" Elivath asked, but Perthis shook his head.

"That's probably part of it," he conceded, "but not all of it. Not by a long shot."

He paused briefly, trying to decide how best to say what he was thinking. It was odd. He was a professional newsman, yet putting his own thoughts into words in a conversation like this one often refused to come easily for him.

"We do have some problem children here on Sharona that need somebody to look after them until they finish growing up," he continued seriously at last. "But in realistic terms, and especially given the safety valve the portals have given us, the nations whose problems are a simple lack of maturity aren't any particular threat to the rest of us. Unfortunately, that's not true for *all* of our problem children."

"You're thinking about Uromathia, aren't you?" Elivath challenged.

"Mostly," Perthis admitted. "But even the current problems with Uromathia are almost all due to Chava, when you come right down to it. I mean, Uromathians in general sometimes seem to me to walk around with a king-sized chip on their collective shoulder, especially where Ternathia is concerned. But by and large, they're not really any more jingoistic or just naturally nasty than anyone else. The fact that their current emperor—and all three of his sons, as far as I can tell—are certifiable lunatics, now, though . . . *that's* a problem.

"On the one hand, that means getting rid of him (and of them) would solve our present difficulties with Uromathia. But, on the other hand, it means the *next* Chava—whether he's Uromathian or from somewhere else entirely—will simply present his own clutch of problems. Putting someone like Ternathia in charge of a world government with the mechanisms in place to deal with future Chavas as they arise will save us all an awful lot of grief down the road. Whatever happens at Hell's Gate."

"Assuming someone like Chava doesn't wind up in charge of it, instead," Elivath pointed out.

"That's not going to happen," Perthis said firmly.

Elivath looked rather more skeptical than the Chief Voice, but he didn't disagree. He couldn't, really, and Perthis knew it.

It had become painfully evident, even to Chava Busar, that his own candidacy for Emperor of Sharona had been a complete nonstarter. Only his closest neighbors had voted for him, and they'd obviously done it more because they were afraid of him (and how he might react if they *hadn't* voted for him) than because they'd thought he'd make a good planetary emperor. The fact that *anyone* outside his own empire had voted for him, coupled with the military and economic clout of that empire, gave him a degree of bargaining power when it came to the terms under which Uromathia might accept the Conclave's decision, but that was about it.

And it's enough, Perthis thought glumly.

"So you think this new compromise the Committee on Unification is supposed to be getting ready to report out is going to go through?" Elivath said.

"That's what Tarlin thinks," Perthis replied.

"He said so?"

Elivath sounded surprised, and Perthis laughed. Tarlin Bolsh and his international news division's analysts were notorious for covering their posteriors carefully when it came time to prognosticate on major international events. Without a Glimpse for guidance—and there weren't any Caliraths working for SUNN—precognition was pretty much useless when it came to political events, and it often seemed to Perthis that the analysts were more concerned with not being *wrong* than they were with being right.

"More or less . . . although he wasn't prepared to admit it for public consumption," the Chief Voice said dryly, and it was Elivath's turn to laugh.

"On the other hand," Perthis continued, his smile fading, "I think he's probably right."

"If I were Zindel, I wouldn't want Chava marrying into *my* family," Elivath said sourly.

"Neither would I," Perthis agreed. "But, as Tarlin pointed out, Chava's picked his demands pretty shrewdly. He's right, after all. Intermarriage *has* always been part of the traditional Ternathian approach to guaranteeing the inclusion of 'subject peoples'—although I *hate* the way Chava keeps throwing around that particular term—in the mainstream of their Empire." The Chief Voice shrugged. "If we're going to institute a planet-wide Ternathian Empire under the Calirath Dynasty, then demanding that the heir to the throne has to marry someone from the *Uromathian* royalty actually makes a lot of sense."

"In a perfect world," Elivath snorted. "In this world, it's going to make Chava Busar Janaki chan Calirath's father-in-law. Now, does that strike *you* as a marriage made in heaven?"

"Not by a long shot," Perthis said again. "But Janaki's a Calirath, and they've been making dynastic marriages for as long as anyone can remember. For that matter, for as far back as the oldest histories go! They haven't all worked out very well on a personal level, of course, but Janaki's going to understand the political necessities. And let's be fair, Darl. Whatever we may think of Chava, Uromathia is still the second most powerful nation on Sharona, and there are an awful lot of Uromathians. They *deserve* to be fairly represented in any world government. And if *they* aren't represented, what does that say to everyone else? You and I may be confident that Zindel chan Calirath isn't going to produce some sort of tyranny, but if we expect countries all over the planet to surrender their national sovereignty to him, then they need to *know* he's prepared to be reasonable about inclusiveness, honesty, fairness . . . and access to power."

"Maybe. No," Elivath grimaced, "not 'maybe.' You're right. But I don't think Zindel's especially happy about the prospect of sharing grandkids with Chava!"

"Given the fact that there probably aren't two men on the face of the entire planet who loathe each other more than he and Chava do, that's probably just a bit of an understatement." Perthis' tone was drier than a Shurkhali summer wind. "Of course, he knows Chava knows that, too. That's why he's dug in his heels so hard over 'resisting' the entire marriage proposal. Tarlin says his people figure it's Zindel's way of telling Chava that it's the *only* one of Uromathia's demands that Chava's going to get. And, frankly, I think Chava's entirely prepared to settle for it. He knows he can't possibly put a planetary crown on his own head; he's too hated and distrusted for that. So the best he can realistically hope for is to put it on a grandson's head. He'll settle for that, especially since somebody like him will figure that, if he's patient, sooner or later a possibility for him to ... improve his own position is going to present itself."

"Now *there's* a charming possibility," Elivath said sourly.

"I wouldn't be very happy if it worked out that way, myself," Perthis said more mildly. "On the other hand, you—and Chava, for that matter—might want to think about how long Ternathia's been playing this sort of game."

The Chief Voice showed his teeth in a smile that was really quite unpleasant, Elivath thought.

"Chava Busar thinks he's clever, and in a brutal sort of way, he is," Perthis said. "And he thinks Uromathia is an ancient empire, and that he's a ruthless sort of fellow. Both of those are true, too. But Ternathia's one hell of a lot more ancient, and the fact that the Caliraths have traditionally put their subjects' best interests first doesn't mean *they* aren't ruthless. In fact, Darl, if you go back and look at Ternathian history, I think you'll discover that nobody's *ever* been more ruthless than a Calirath when there was no other way to win. And do you really think Chava is even in the same league as Zindel chan Calirath when it comes to *intelligent* ruthlessness?"

Elivath opened his mouth. Then he stopped, looking thoughtful, and his frown turned slowly into a smile of its own.

"Actually, when you put it that way," he said finally, "no."

CHAPTER
FORTY-NINE

HADRIGN THALMAYR LAY rigidly on his side on the white-
sheeted bed in the airy, sunlit room. His eyes were screwed
tightly shut, beads of sweat stood out on his forehead, and his fists
were clenched so tightly that his nails had cut bleeding crescents
into his palms.

The breeze through the open window moved gently, almost caress-
ingly across him. He could hear the distant but unmistakable sounds
of a drill field: voices shouting orders in a foreign language, whistles
shrilling at irregular intervals, the occasional clatter of weapons as
troops went through their own version of the manual of arms, and
the deep-voiced sound of drill formations counting cadence. The
air was cool, the distant background noise—deeply familiar to any
professional soldier, despite the fact that he couldn't understand a
single word of the orders he overheard—only made the quiet around
him even more soothing, and he could almost literally physically
feel the relaxing, comforting peacefulness which had settled over
this place.

It was all reassuringly calm and normal . . . and its very normality
only made his terror and helpless rage still worse.

The man sitting in the chair beside his bed spoke again, in that
same utterly incomprehensible, comforting voice, but Thalmayr wasn't
fooled. He squeezed his eyelids even more tightly together and bit
his lip, welcoming the pain of the bite as it helped him summon
all of his resistance while that insidious, loathsome *touch* slid once
again across the surface of his mind.

It took all he could do not to moan or whimper in terror. He
called up all of his hatred, all of his fear and disgust, to bolster his
defiance, but it was hard. Hard.

He never knew exactly how long it lasted this time. Sometimes the man behind that lying, soothing voice stayed longer; sometimes he gave up sooner, and left. But he always came back, Thalmayr thought despairingly. And he always *would* come back, again and again. Until, finally, he managed to breach his victim's defenses at last, and the mere thought of what would happen then filled Hadrign Thalmayr with horror.

But eventually, finally, his tormentor gave up . . . this time. The commander of one hundred lay rigidly still, refusing to move or even open his eyes until he was *positive* the other man had truly left. That he wasn't just waiting, lurking above the bed like a vulture.

He lay there for a long time, then slowly and cautiously let his eyes slip back open. The chair beside the bed was empty, and he heaved a tremendous sigh of relief and finally allowed himself to relax, at least a bit.

He wanted to roll over onto his back, but the sandbags holding him on his side prevented it. Which, he admitted, was just as well, given the incision across his spine.

His teeth clenched again as he thought about that wound and all the pain their so-called "healers" had inflicted upon him. Butchers— barbarians! He'd been right about them all along, and he cursed Sir Jasak Olderhan in vicious mental silence as he remembered the other hundred's precious "*shardonai.*"

I should've fed the pair of them to the nearest godsdamned dragon! he thought savagely. *Them and all their fucking friends!*

He'd long since figured out that that sneaky little bitch with her bruised face and pitiful "poor me" eyes had somehow managed to get a message out to her butchering friends. He still didn't know how, but the way they'd flung her name at him again and again in their questioning proved she had . . . and the way they kept battering at his own mind suggested several ugly possibilities as to *how* she had.

The whole time that fucking idiot Olderhan was standing there "protecting her," she was busy telling her friends where we were and how to come find us and kill us! It's the only way they could've known she was still alive!

His molars ground together. It was all her fault. *She* was the one who'd brought the attack in on Thalmayr's command. It wasn't *his* fault. There was no way he could possibly have known what the little bitch was doing, that she'd managed to bring an entire godsdamned *regiment* down on him! If it hadn't been for *her*, his men would still be alive. *Magister Halathyn* would still be alive.

And Hadrign Thalmayr wouldn't be the half-paralyzed prisoner of the butchers who'd started all of this by massacring that brainless incompetent Olderhan's men in the first place. The butchers who'd somehow transported him over what had to be hundreds, if not thousands, of miles without his remembering a single thing about the journey. The butchers who cut open the flesh of helpless captives in some obscene pretense of trying to "help them," and then, when they were weakened by the pain, tried to rape away any useful information in their minds.

Well, they might break him in the end. *Any* man could be broken by enough torture, enough cruelty, and he had no way of knowing what other, even more horrendous powers of mental destruction they might yet be able to bring to bear upon him. But they wouldn't find it easy. He swore that to himself yet again, repeating it like a precious mantra of defiance, while despair poured over him with the gentle, soothing breeze.

*   *   *

"Frankly, Sir," Company-Captain Golvar Silkash said, "I'm at a loss." The Healers' Corps officer shook his head, his eyes unhappy. "I've done all *I* can, and Tobis is still trying, but I've *never* had a patient with this man's attitude. I just don't know what else we can do to get through to him."

Namir Velvelig grunted unhappily. It wasn't the first time Silkash had reported the same things to him, but the regiment-captain kept hoping that somehow, some way, *something* would change. But it didn't, of course, he thought moodily, playing with the mug of tea on his desk. Silkash had a matching mug in his left hand, but the Healer had been ignoring it ever since he sat down.

"Is Tobis right, do you think?" he asked.

"What? About the man having at least a trace of Talent of his own?"

"Yes. *Could* that be what's going on?"

"I suppose it could," Silkash said with a grimace. "Tobis knows a lot more about that sort of thing than I do, but I think even he's shooting blind on this one. We just plain don't have any experience with people who've never even *heard* of Talents!"

Velvelig grunted again, gazing out his window, where the steadily setting sun sank slowly behind the Sky Bloods, as if he imagined he could somehow find the answers he needed out there in the bronze and copper glow gilding the mountains. Company-Captain Silkash was the finest surgeon and medical doctor with whom Namir Velvelig had ever had the pleasure of serving. But, unlike the majority of the

Healers' Corps's commissioned officers—or Platoon-Captain Tobis Makree, his assistant surgeon, for that matter—he had no Talent at all. That put Silkash at a distinct disadvantage when it came to trying to analyze the Arcanan prisoner's reaction to Makree's Healing Talent. And, as Silkash had just pointed out, *no one* had ever had to deal with a patient who didn't even know what the Healing Talent *was*!

"How's chan Tergis coming with their language, Sir?" Silkash asked, as much for a frustrated change of subject as out of genuine curiosity, and Velvelig grunted yet a third time. It was remarkable, the surgeon reflected, just how expressive his CO's grunts could actually be, and he wondered if all Arpathians were like that. Velvelig's first grunt had expressed unhappiness; the second had expressed both agreement and frustration; and the third had expressed frustration and anger. Which, now that Silkash thought about it, was a logical enough progression *whenever* it came to dealing with these maddening "Arcanans," whether collectively or as individuals.

"Not well," the regiment-captain amplified after a moment. "We're keeping him so damned busy relaying messages up-chain from chan Baskay and chan Tesh that he really doesn't have a whole lot of time to devote to the project. And even when he does, he's running into the same sort of noncooperation Tobis seems to be encountering with this Thalmayr idiot."

The regiment-captain paused, then forced himself to be fair.

"I suppose, if I'd been captured—especially after the sort of massacre these people got put through—I wouldn't be in any hurry to cooperate with my jailers, either. After all, they're probably as imbued as our own people with the idea that it's their duty to refuse to give the enemy any useful information. And despite the total incompetence of their commander, it's obvious these are elite troops."

"If you say so, Sir," Silkash said dubiously. Velvelig raised an eyebrow at him, and the surgeon shrugged. "I know I've only seen them since they got here, but they don't exactly look like 'elite troops' to me."

"No?" Velvelig gazed at him speculatively, then snorted. "They seem a bit demoralized to you, do they? Sullen? Uncooperative? Silently resentful?"

"Yes, Sir. All of those." Silkash cocked his head to one side. "Why?"

"Because that's exactly the reaction I'd expect out of elite troops who'd suffered the sort of pounding these men survived. Think about it, Silky. From chan Tesh's reports, it's obvious they never even suspected we could fire on them *through* a portal. Their CO—such as he was, and what there was of him—went down in the first volley, which decapitated their entire command structure. The mortar rounds coming in on them must've been the most terrifying thing they'd ever experienced. Chan Tesh was *massacring* them—literally—and they couldn't even shoot back. So how did they react?"

Silkash's perplexity was obvious, and Velvelig waved his tea mug for impatient emphasis.

"They *charged*, Silky. They came out of their fortifications, got up out of their protective holes *under fire*—which is harder than hells for *anyone* to do, trust me—and they charged straight *into the fire that was killing them*." He shook his head. "Whatever we may think of what they did to the Chalgyn crew, and however stupidly they may have been commanded when chan Tesh hit them, these men were magnificent soldiers. In fact, I'll absolutely guarantee you that that idiot Thalmayr didn't have a thing to do with training them. Not these men. They were so much better than he was that there's no comparison. And that's exactly why so many of them got killed. Instead of turning around and running away, instead of breaking, they *charged* in an almost certainly spontaneous effort to get their own weapons into action on the far side of the portal. It's probably the bloody-minded septman in me, but I'm prepared to forgive men for a lot when they show that kind of guts."

"I guess I hadn't thought about it quite that way," Silkash admitted after a moment.

"No, I didn't think you had. But it also explains a lot about their present attitude, I imagine. These men weren't used to the idea that they could be beaten. They *expected* to win. And *if* they were going to lose, they never would have believed that anyone could have simply . . . wiped them out for the loss of barely half a dozen men on the other side. They're smart enough to have figured out that it was because they were up against weapons they had no experience fighting and had an idiot for a CO, but that's an intellectual understanding, not an emotional one. It doesn't get down inside a soldier's guts and heart where his belief in himself lives. Defeat is one thing for an elite unit at that level; abject, humiliating, *total* defeat is something else again. So they're bitter, ashamed, and convinced that they've failed their country, their honor, and themselves. But instead of simply collapsing, what have they done?

"They've dug in and refused to cooperate with us in any way, that's what they've done," Velvelig continued, once again answering his own question. "Maybe, in time—and especially if these negotiations actually go somewhere—that may change. I've been trying to help that change along; that's why I've been so insistent on our men treating them not just correctly, but with dignity. In the meantime, though, I'm not surprised by their attitude."

"Now that you've got me thinking in the same direction, neither am I," Silkash conceded. "But Tobis is probably right that their lack of familiarity with Talented people is also a factor. First, because they don't have a clue what chan Tergis is trying to accomplish, which sort of automatically precludes the possibility of cooperating, even if they wanted to. And, second, because if any of them *do* have a touch of Talent of their own, they might well react the same way Thalmayr is."

"Probably," Velvelig agreed. "Which, I'm afraid, brings us back to Thalmayr." The Arpathian's lips twisted briefly with all of the contempt he refused to feel for Thalmayr's unfortunate subordinates. "Just what is his prognosis?"

"Physically?" Silkash shrugged. "I can understand why Petty-Captain chan Rodair sent him on to us here at Fort Ghartoun, but I really wish he hadn't. For several reasons."

"Such as?"

"As much as I've grown to dislike the man, Sir, I'm a Healer. My Healer's Oath requires me to treat any patient with compassion and respect, and to offer him the very best treatment possible. That's why chan Rodair wanted him here at Ghartoun, because he thought the damage to Thalmayr's spine might be amenable to surgical intervention. Well, he was wrong. For that matter, *I* was wrong when I first examined the man. I think it may have been because I wanted so badly for chan Rodair to have been right, but that doesn't change the fact that we were *both* wrong. So we subjected him to a completely unnecessary—and useless—operation. That's bad enough, but even worse, whatever it is that's causing him to be so resistant to Tobis' efforts to get at his mental and emotional traumas is also hampering our efforts at pain management. So we've inflicted that additional suffering on him, as well."

"That's hardly your fault," Velvelig said. "You were doing the best you could for him, under very difficult circumstances."

"Oh, I know that, Sir. And so does Tobis. The problem is, I rather doubt *Thalmayr* does. And it doesn't change our responsibilities towards him, either."

"Well, we already knew the man was an idiot," Velvelig said in a comforting way. "No reason he shouldn't be an idiot about that, too, I suppose."

"I hadn't . . . quite looked at it that way, Sir." Silkash found that he was experiencing an unanticipated difficulty not smiling.

"Then you should. But I noticed that you prefaced your remarks by referring to his physical recovery. So, how do his mental and emotional prospects shape up?"

"It's really hard to be sure about that when our Talented Healer can't even reach the man. Still, as near as Tobis can tell, he's at least managed to divert Thalmayr's drive towards suicide."

"Which even Thalmayr should admit is a positive step!" Velvelig snorted.

"Assuming that he gives Tobis credit for it, yes, Sir. Of course, if he doesn't understand what Tobis is doing in the first place, he probably doesn't."

"No, I'm sure he doesn't," Velvelig said glumly. "You know, I really wish Prince Janaki hadn't brought us this particular guest."

"At least dropping him off with us helped get the prince out of the combat zone, Sir. That's got to be a plus, however you look at it."

"It certainly does." Velvelig sipped more tea, gazing ruminatively out the window once more. The sun was almost gone, he noticed, leaving the mountain summits etched dark and black, looming against the afterglow. He was going to have to light the lamps, he thought.

"If you don't mind my asking, Sir," Silkash said out of the gathering dimness after a moment, "you mentioned how busy chan Tergis is passing messages back up-chain. How well *are* the negotiations going?"

"I don't mind your asking, but if I had the answer to that, I wouldn't be a regiment-captain sitting out here at the ass-end of nowhere," Velvelig said dryly. "I'd be making my fortune as a Precog back home."

He drank a little more tea, set his mug back down on the desktop, got out a box of matches. He lit the lamps, replaced the glass chimneys and adjusted the wicks, then tipped his chair back and folded his hands behind his head.

"Chan Baskay and Rothag are still convinced these people are lying about entirely too many things for my peace of mind," he admitted. "What bothers me most about it isn't that diplomats . . . shade the truth. Gods know, they do that back home whenever they can, and if our diplomats didn't have Talents on the other side to keep them honest, they'd probably do a lot more of it. But if they're as urgently interested in negotiating some sort of permanent cease-fire as they claim to be, then I'd think they should have a lot more incentive to be at least forthcoming, if not completely honest. But they haven't really given us a lot more information. They seem almost obsessed with the little stuff, the fine details about *how* we're supposed to go about negotiating, rather than more substantive questions like what we're supposed to be negotiating *about*. And I don't much care for the attitude their military escort seems to be showing. There've been a couple of potentially ugly incidents already."

"What sort of incidents, Sir?"

"That's just it, they're the stupid kind. People who take umbrage or even insult from innocent remarks. Or people who insult *our* people, apparently by accident. Three times now, this Skirvon of theirs has suggested postponements in the talks themselves in order to 'let tempers cool.' I'm not there, of course, but I'm inclined to back chan Baskay's view. *I* think their troopers are actually under orders to *provoke* incidents as a deliberate delaying tactic and I've said as much in my own reports up-chain."

"But why would they be doing that, Sir?" Silkash's puzzlement showed.

"That's what neither chan Baskay nor I can understand," Velvelig admitted. "Logically, if all they want to do is waste our time, then why talk to us at all?"

"So you don't have any idea why they might be doing it?"

"Actually, chan Baskay's come up with one possible explanation that sort of makes sense. After all, one of the reasons *we* haven't pressed *them* harder is the delay in message turnaround between here and Sharona. We don't know exactly how these people communicate over long distances, but if they don't have Talents, they obviously don't have Voices. They *may* use this magic of theirs to do the same sort of things our Voices can do, but they may also have to physically transport messages, as well, and chan Baskay's suggested that their communications loop may well be even longer than ours. He thinks this Skirvon may be trying to kick grit into the works to slow things down until he can get definite orders—or maybe even until a more senior diplomat can arrive at Hell's Gate with official instructions from home about exactly what they are and aren't willing to settle for when it comes to possession of the cluster."

"And they're bothering to talk with us in the meantime because—?"

"I'm not sure, although I suppose it's possible they want to make sure we don't press on with our own exploration beyond the swamp portal. From Voice Kinlafia's Portal Sniffing, we know their entry portal for that universe isn't very close to the swamp portal, but that's really *all* we know. They might have some particularly important installation or colony much closer to it than that, and they might be trying to divert us from any exploration in its direction."

Velvelig shrugged, clearly unhappy with his own hypothesis.

"I don't say that's the only explanation. It's just the only one *I* can come up with. And, at least while we're negotiating, we're not shooting anymore. So, in some ways, it's as much to our advantage as to theirs to just keep right on talking. Besides," he grinned suddenly, "it gives *us* some time to get a 'real diplomat' in here to relieve poor chan Baskay!"

*   *   *

Commander of Two Thousand Mayrkos Harshu looked up from the paperwork in his PC as someone rapped gently and respectfully at the frame of his office doorway. His dark, intense eyes focused like a hunting gryphon on the officer standing in the open door. Then he laid his sarkolis crystal stylus on his blotter, much the way another man might have sheathed a sword.

"Enter," he said, and acting Commander of Five Hundred Alivar Neshok obeyed.

"I assume you're here for the afternoon briefing?" Harshu said, raising his eyebrows, and Neshok nodded.

"Yes, Sir, I am. May I go ahead and set up for it?"

"Of course you can, Five Hundred," Harshu said testily. "Unless my memory fails, that's why you're *here*, isn't it?"

The two thousand had a near-fetish for not "wasting time." Especially with what he considered pointless, unnecessary questions. Of course, he also had a reputation for cutting people off at the knees if they made mistakes because they were too stupid or too lazy to ask questions. Which could make things rather . . . difficult upon occasion.

"Yes, Sir," Neshok said, and moved quickly, uncasing his own crystal and bringing it swiftly on-line. He felt Two Thousand Harshu's impatient eyes on him while he made his preparations, but he found them far less intimidating than some of his fellow officers did. He had an even more powerful patron of his own, after all. Besides, he was far too well aware of the opportunities of his present assignment to worry about the two thousand's famed temper tantrums.

And that asshole Olderhan probably thought he'd spiked my career with his godsdamned shardonai, the acting five hundred thought with a mental sneer. *Gods! He's even stupider than Two Thousand mul Gurthak told me he was.*

Neshok hadn't enjoyed the reaming-out mul Gurthak had given him in front of Olderhan and the two diplomats. Nobody would have, and he'd labored under the additional suspicion that mul Gurthak intended to leave him swinging in the wind if Olderhan lodged any formal protests about Neshok's behavior when he got back to Garth Showma. But he'd wronged the two thousand. Mul Gurthak had simply been covering his own back, and Neshok's brevet promotion to his present rank and his assignment as Two Thousand Harshu's senior intelligence analyst was sufficient proof of mul Gurthak's continuing confidence in him.

And if it hadn't been for Olderhan's insistence on extending shar-don to that arrogant little bitch and her husband—and "Magister Kelbryan's" backing him up—the two thousand's plan would have worked, he reflected. *We didn't know she'd already managed to learn a civilized language, but that only would've made it easier to get her to talk. She'd damned well have told me anything I wanted her to by the time I got through with her.*

He let the fingertips of one hand brush the unsleeping eye insignia of the Intelligence Corps on his collar. He'd taken that off, at mul Gurthak's instructions, before he ever went to "greet" Olderhan and his prisoners. Aping the part of a line officer hadn't been all that difficult, however distasteful it might have been, and the two thousand had hoped a fellow line officer might have found it easier to separate Olderhan from his prisoners. And once they'd been separated and "administratively lost" somewhere at Fort Talon, it would all have turned out to have been a completely honest case of confused orders at a junior officer's level. Most unfortunate, of course, but just one of those things. Neshok had never doubted that Olderhan would have been furious, even if he'd gotten his prisoners back with only minor damage, but his own Intelligence superiors would have been quick to protect him, if only behind the scenes, if he'd managed to extract vital information first.

Well, that hadn't happened, but mul Gurthak clearly recognized the debt he owed Neshok for having made the attempt. That was why he'd been promoted and assigned to his present duty, which should allow him to acquire at least as many career points with his superiors.

And one of these days, I'll be in a position to give that smug, sanctimonious prick Olderhan exactly what he fucking well deserves, he thought viciously. Yet even as he thought it, he felt a tingle of remembered fear as he recalled the cold, fleering contempt in Sir Jasak Olderhan's dark eyes. And the fact that Olderhan's precious Second Andaran Scouts flunkies had actually been willing to take on his entire detachment if he'd so much as laid a finger on that little bitch.

He pushed the thought aside with a fresh promise of vengeance . . . and wished he could push aside the memory of a crackling corona of combat magic ready to strike and the steely-cold promise in Gadrial Kelbryan's lethal almond eyes, as well. Unfortunately . . .

Behind him, Two Thousand Harshu cleared his throat in his patented "get on with it" style, and Neshok shook himself free of his brooding thoughts.

"Beg pardon, Sir," he said. "I'm ready, now."

"Good." Harshu's tone added an unspoken "and it's about time," and Neshok ordered the office's spellware to dim the lights. Then he tapped his PC with the stylus, and a moving, living image glowed into being above Harshu's desk. The fidgeting two thousand stopped fidgeting instantly, as his fiercely intelligent eyes darted from place to place, carefully comparing the present image to the ones he'd seen before. As always, once the keen intellect behind those eyes had a fresh task to engage it, most of the affected impatience and hyperactivity disappeared quickly.

"As you can see, Sir, we're still getting very good imagery," he began.

"Yes, we are," Harshu agreed thoughtfully. "In fact, are we sure they don't know we are?" His eyes darted up from the small moving images of Sharonian soldiers to impale Neshok. "Could they possibly be setting all this up to show us what they *want* us to see?"

"No, Sir," Neshok said confidently, then snorted. "They're still pulling every boat up onto the island and turning it keel-up before they let anyone cross over into Hell's Gate." The Arcanans had adopted the Sharonian name for their contact universe. After all, as the Sharonian diplomat, Simrath, had pointed out at the time, it was grimly appropriate for both sides. "It's obvious Master Skirvon's observation is correct. The stupid, superstitious barbarians don't have a clue how magic works, so they aren't taking any chances . . . they think."

"It might not be a bad idea," Harshu said almost pleasantly, his eyes returning to the images before him, "to spend a little less time patting ourselves on our backs for cleverness and a little more time making certain we aren't underestimating the other side."

"Yes, Sir. Point taken," Neshok said just a bit more crisply. Harshu's notoriously short fuse with subordinates who he thought had screwed up might be as carefully cultivated as other parts of his reputation. Still, the stories about what had happened to people who'd *really* screwed up were ugly enough to dissuade even Neshok from relying upon his Intelligence patrons' protection.

"What I meant to say, Sir," he continued, "is that, as you know, we went to considerable lengths to convince them that the spell accumulators for the boats have to be attached to the keels. They haven't even looked inside the flotation tank under the after thwart, which—in the opinion of my staff and myself—strongly indicates that they don't have any idea we've hidden the real movement accumulator in there. And because they're still turning the boats upside down as a security measure, they're giving the recon crystals attached to their bottoms a three-hundred-sixty-degree field of view. It's not as good in terms of flexibility and total reach as we'd get if we could actually move them around, or as good as what a gryphon pass with an RC could give us, and their actual bivouac area is outside our zone from where they beach the boats. In other ways, though, it's actually better. The RC is close enough to get a good look at their fieldworks and their deployments, and it just sits there, which gives us an excellent opportunity to eavesdrop on anything they're saying within its scan area, as well."

Harshu glanced at him again, then nodded in grudgingly approving acceptance.

"Although the boat-mounted RCs never move," Neshok continued more confidently, "we have managed six RC walk-throughs." He smiled thinly. "Sending Master Skirvon's escort in dress uniform was a brilliant idea, Sir. I wish I'd thought of it myself." It never hurt to show a superior officer you knew how to give a subordinate credit for good ideas . . . especially when the superior officer in question already knew the idea in question had *come* from a subordinate. "They'd never seen our dress uniforms, so they didn't have any reason to suspect that the crystal mounted on that ridiculous horsehair crest on Fifty Narshu's helmet is actually a reconnaissance device, not just a particularly tasteless bit of decoration.

"At any rate, everything Narshu's RC has picked up only confirms what we're getting from the boat RCs."

"I see." Harshu frowned thoughtfully, leaning his folded forearms on his desk. "And is there confirmation about these two?" He twitched his head at the two Sharonians under the canvas sunshade at one end of the portal.

"Yes, Sir." Neshok nodded. "We're still not certain how they do what they're apparently doing, but thanks to the translation software Master Skirvon and Two Thousand mul Gurthak provided, we've definitely confirmed from their conversation and the chatter of their buddies that they're some sort of lookouts. And we've also confirmed that whatever it is they're doing, they can't do it *through* a portal any more than we could cast a spell through one. They rotate around the end of the portal on a quite rigid schedule, apparently to clear the blind spot the portal creates for them. We've watched them for days now, and they never deviate by more than a very few minutes from their set timing."

"I wish we had managed to determine exactly what it is they're doing," Harshu mused, and Neshok nodded.

"So do I, Sir, but there's just no way of guessing how these 'Talents' of theirs work. From what we've been able to overhear, it sounds as if the Talent this one is using—" he indicated the smaller of the two Sharonians "—works *sort of* like one of our scrying spells. It isn't the same, obviously. For one thing, they don't need a crystal to gather the image. And, for another, they appear to be able to sweep a general volume, rather than needing to know exactly where whatever they're trying to observe is within that volume. And, for a third thing—and we're not certain about this one, Sir; it's based on a couple of fairly cryptic remarks we've overheard and translated—he *appears* to be limited to the ability to detect living creatures."

"I suppose that could make sense," Harshu said thoughtfully. "If these Talents of theirs are all some kind of weird mental powers, then perhaps what they're picking up on is some sort of vibration or mental wave. Wouldn't get much of that off of a rock, I imagine."

"No, Sir."

"And you've managed to confirm their detection range, have you?" Harshu inquired.

"Ah, no, Sir," Neshok admitted. Harshu slanted his eyes sideways, looking back up at the acting five hundred, and Neshok grimaced. "So far, they haven't actually referred to their maximum range—not, at least, where any of our RCs have overheard them."

"That's not so good to hear, Five Hundred," Harshu observed. "It could have a rather significant effect on our military options, don't you agree?"

"Yes, Sir." Neshok refocused his own attention on the display rather than continuing to meet Harshu's gaze. Then he cleared his throat.

"Actually, Sir, we do have at least an approximation. Or perhaps I should say a bottom limit at which we *know* they can't 'see' us."

Harshu unfolded his arms and made a "go on" gesture with his right hand.

"As you know, Sir, we've been taking pains to conceal the existence of our dragons from them. And while I'm on the subject, Sir, the recorded take from the boat RCs confirms that they've never even dreamed about any sort of aerial capability for themselves and don't seem to have a clue that *we* have one." *Which,* he didn't add aloud, *just confirms what utter barbarians they are, doesn't it?* "Apparently they'd been wondering for some time how we got people in and out from the Second Andarans' base camp through all that muck and mire. Now that they've seen our boats, they think they know."

"Well, *that's* certainly good to hear."

"Yes, Sir. It is. And the fact that they don't know about dragons or gryphons clearly indicates that their lookouts haven't 'seen' our diplomats or their escort being flown in. We've been landing our people on an islet about forty miles from the portal and sending them the rest of the way in from there in the boats. Partly, that was because we needed an excuse to get the boats' RCs right up to the portal. But, just as importantly, we wanted to keep our dragons safely out of sight. We hadn't realized at the time that they had whatever kind of Talent this lookout of theirs is using—somehow Hundred Olderhan's *shardon* neglected to mention its existence to us, for some odd reason—but Master Skirvon and Five Hundred Klian agreed that it would be best to err on the side of caution. Fortunately, it would appear.

"At any rate, at forty miles, they haven't seen our people arriving. If they had, I'm positive someone would have remarked on it by now where our RCs could hear it. That both suggests that the dragons have remained safely unknown to them, and gives us a limit—forty miles—beyond which we ought to be safe from detection."

"Forty miles," Harshu murmured. "Call it thirty minutes for a dragon—twenty minutes, minimum."

"Yes, Sir. On the other hand, as I say, that's a *minimum* safe distance. His actual range for spotting us may be quite a bit shorter than that."

"And it may not be, too," Harshu replied tartly.

"No, Sir. As you say," Neshok agreed. "On the other hand, there is one other point." He paused until the two thousand looked at him again, then shrugged very slightly. "From a couple of things our RCs have overheard, while this fellow appears to be able to . . . sweep, for want of a better term, an entire volume, and while we don't really know how large a volume that is, it would seem that he does have to define the volume pretty carefully. We've watched him while he's doing whatever it is he's doing, and he sits very still, with his eyes closed, but his head turns slowly from side to side, as if he's looking at something behind his eyelids."

"And?" Harshu prompted.

"And he never tilts his head *back*, Sir."

Harshu frowned at him for a moment, and then the two thousand's eyes narrowed slightly.

"So you're suggesting that since they don't know about dragons, he's not looking *up*, just out?"

"That's what I think he's doing, Sir," Neshok said, and this time he chose not to mention that it was one of his noncommissioned analysts who'd actually first spotted the Sharonian lookout's head movements. "If they don't have any flight capability of their own, it would make a lot of sense for them to be concentrating on *surface* threats. After all, they wouldn't know there was any other kind, would they?"

"No, they wouldn't," Harshu agreed slowly.

His eyes were focused on something else, something only he could see, and they stayed that way for the better part of two minutes. Then they refocused on Neshok.

"Anything else? Anything new?" he asked.

"That's most of the new information, Sir. I've prepared a complete download for you, of course. Shall I transfer the file to your PC?"

"Yes, go ahead."

"Yes, Sir."

Neshok arranged the transfer with brisk efficiency. As he did, he noticed the headers for the documents Harshu had been working on when he arrived. Troop strengths and arrival schedules, the acting five hundred noted without very much surprise.

"There you are, Sir," he said as the little icon that indicated the file transfers were complete appeared in both crystals.

"Thank you." Harshu considered him for a moment or two, then nodded. "Aside from a certain tendency to denigrate the enemy, that was an excellent brief, Five Hundred," he said. "Keep up the good work . . . and try like hell not to let the fact that you dislike these people lead you into making the sorts of mistakes contempt produces. Am I clear?"

"Yes, Sir! You are, Sir!" Neshok said, bracing quickly to attention.

"Good. Carry on, Five Hundred."

"Yes, Sir."

Neshok turned with rather more than normal military precision and marched out of Harshu's office. The compliment on the quality of his work had felt good . . . which, of course, only made the sting of Harshu's admonition sharper.

Well, the two thousand was good at that sort of thing. It was one of his hallmarks. *Everybody* got a zinger from him every so often, Neshok reminded himself; far fewer got the compliment which had gone in front of this one.

He decided to concentrate on that as he stepped out onto the Fort Rycharn parade ground.

Rycharn wasn't much of a fort, he thought. About right for that broken down ass-kisser Klian to command. At the moment, though, it was crowded to the bursting point and beyond by the scores of dragons thronging its improvised dragonfield. There were more transports than Neshok had ever seen in one place in his entire life. The heavy transports' cargo pods were parked as neatly as possible around the field's perimeter, but there wasn't room to be *very* neat about it. The tactical transports and the battle dragons were based on the western side of the field, as far away from the fort's palisade and the troop encampments as they could get. Three of Two Thousand mul Gurthak's planned four reinforcement waves had arrived already, and the fourth was due within the next week.

And what happens then, I wonder? Neshok mused, listening to the sounds of the immensely overcrowded encampment. *Everybody's still being very careful to insist that no final decision's been made yet. I wonder just how true that actually is?*

He snorted wryly at the thought. From what mul Gurthak had said to him in his own private briefing before he was sent out here, especially about the importance of not allowing the enemy to tighten his grip on Hell's Gate even further, he was fairly certain what the Fort Talon commander had in mind. Of course, he could be wrong, and even if he wasn't, circumstances might have changed—depending on what Skirvon and Dastiri had been able to accomplish diplomatically—since Neshok had been sent forward himself. And there was also the problem that *Harshu* was the commander actually on the spot. Mul Gurthak couldn't push Harshu too hard without being rather more direct than Neshok was pretty sure the Mythalan two thousand wanted to be.

Which, of course, is the reason he sent me *out here, isn't it? A military commander's decisions are always based on the intelligence available to him. Which means that the fellow who provides him with that information has a better chance than most to . . . shape his probable command decisions.*

Commander of Five Hundred (Acting) Alivar Neshok smiled thinly as he gazed out across the ranks of dragons, the cargo pods, the white canvas tents of the waiting troopers, and the rows of field-dragons lined up so neatly in the artillery parks, and reflected upon the influence which had come to rest in his hands. It was a heavy responsibility, he told himself. One which had to be discharged carefully, thoughtfully.

And the fact that it put him in a position to help kick that sanctimonious, cowardly son-of-a-bitch Olderhan's gutless plans to just hand the biggest, most important portal cluster in history over to the enemy right in the balls was totally beside the point.

CHAPTER FIFTY

"YOU LOOK UNHAPPY, Five Hundred."

Sarr Klian looked up. Two Thousand Harshu sat across the table from him, holding his wine glass loosely cradled in his right hand. That table was covered with a white cloth and empty plates, for the two of them had just finished dining in what had been Klian's sitting room before Harshu arrived to take command of the steadily growing military power which had come to be based here at Fort Rycharn. Klian didn't resent giving up his quarters to the two thousand. Not precisely, at any rate. He did rather resent giving up his *office* space, but he knew that was silly. Harshu was the senior officer present. He needed the best facilities available, and it was inevitable that he should have them.

"Unhappy, Sir?" Klian repeated, and Harshu smiled.

"Sparring for time, are we, Five Hundred?"

His voice was almost gentle, at odds with his normal public persona, and he shifted his hand slightly, tilting his wine glass. The gleaming light elements of the wall-mounted lamps had been turned down, reducing their normal brilliance to a level more comfortable for dining, but they were bright enough to light a red glow in the heart of the glass.

"I suppose I am, Sir," Klian admitted levelly. He looked across the table into Harshu's eyes. "It's been my experience that when a superior officer makes that sort of statement, it's often the prelude to a . . . counseling session, shall we say?"

"Ah." Harshu's smile grew broader, and he cocked his head to one side. "I suppose that's a fair enough observation, Five Hundred. In this case, though, I'm genuinely curious about your thoughts. You've been sitting out here at the sharp end longer than anyone else. I don't say that automatically gives you any sort of special insight none of the rest of us can share, but I'm very well aware that I've come waltzing in and taken over your territory with less than three weeks' experience on the job, as it were."

"Curious about my thoughts about what, precisely, Sir?" Klian asked. "If you mean about being effectively superseded, I don't suppose any commanding officer worth his salt is ever happy to see that happen. But I'm certainly not sitting here nursing a sense of resentment over it. That would be pointless, at best, and stupid, at worst. I'm a five hundred, and what we're looking at out here right now is a five *thousand's* command—maybe even a ten thousand's. Exigencies of the service or not, there's no way I'd be fitted to command a force that size, even if I were the senior officer present."

"I think you actually mean that," Harshu observed. He sipped a little wine, then shrugged. "I'm relieved to hear it, too. After all, you're going to be in command of our logistics node here, no matter what happens. I can think of very few things better suited to trip someone up in a field command than having his logistics . . . creatively tangled, shall we say, by a resentful subordinate."

"I can assure you, Sir," Klian said just a bit stiffly, "that it never crossed my mind to—"

"I didn't mean to suggest it had," Harshu interrupted. "In fact, I meant to suggest rather the opposite. However," he set down his wine glass, plucked a roll out of the breadbasket between them, and began tearing it into small pieces and piling the fragments on the rim of his plate, "that wasn't the question I meant to get at earlier. It seems to me, Five Hundred, that you don't really approve of our contingency planning. I'd like to know why."

Klian sat very still for a moment, then drank from his own wine glass, mostly to buy a little more time to marshal his thoughts. Then he cleared his throat.

"Two Thousand," he said, "you're in command. Whether I 'approve' of your contingency planning or not is really beside the point, isn't it? Since you've asked, though, there are aspects of your plans—as I currently understand them, at any rate—that do cause me some concern."

"Specifically?" Harshu invited.

"Well," Klian sat back in his chair, folding his hands neatly on the tablecloth and wishing he didn't feel quite so much like an officer cadet who'd just been handed a trick question in his third-year tactics class, "I can't fault anything I've heard about your defensive planning, Sir. I think you're entirely right that without any equivalent of our dragons—and while I haven't seen Five Hundred Neshok's reports to you, I'm inclined to agree that the evidence clearly suggests they don't have any aerial capability—they'd be at a hopeless disadvantage trying to fight their way out of that swamp. They'd have to have a simply enormous advantage in manpower to slog through that kind of mud and muck—especially without any sort of spell-powered boats of their own—while fighting off continuous air attacks, no matter how good their weapons are.

"And no one could deny your legitimate responsibility to plan for possible *offensive* operations, either." The five hundred shrugged. "We're both soldiers, Sir. We both know that, ultimately, battles and wars are won by taking it to the enemy, not simply sitting still and letting him bring it to us. I guess what concerns me is the feel I'm picking up from the majority of your officers that they're actually *anticipating* offensive operations."

He paused, still looking levelly at Harshu, and the two thousand gazed back in silence for perhaps twenty seconds. Then it was Harshu's turn to shrug.

"I don't doubt that they are," he admitted calmly, and showed his teeth in a thin smile. "The bottom line, Five Hundred, is that the most important quality any soldier can have as he goes into battle is the offensive spirit. Even if we wind up standing totally on the defensive, having the troops thinking in terms of 'taking it to the enemy,' as you just said, won't hurt a thing. If we do go on the offense, on the other hand, there won't be time to turn everyone's thinking around if all we've been planning for is digging in and holding our ground."

"I can see that, Sir," Klian said in a neutral tone, and Harshu's smile grew wider.

"But you're still concerned," he observed. Klian started to say something else, but the two thousand waved it away. "No, that's all right, Five Hundred. I asked for your opinion, and I really want it. And I don't think your concerns are limited to the troops' attitude."

"Sir," Klian leaned forward slightly, "I guess I'm worried on two levels.

"First, however good our intelligence on their tactical dispositions right at the swamp portal, or even between there and Fallen Timbers, may be, we know literally nothing about these people's real military power. We don't have any clear indication of what their heavy weapons' capabilities may be, how close to the point of contact their major military bases may be, or how big they are. I know the current intelligence assessments are that they're not anticipating reinforcement within the next several weeks, but what does that actually tell us? We don't know anything about how big the reinforcement they *are* expecting might be, or what might be in the pipeline *behind* it. Even if we managed to punch right through everything they've got in the immediate vicinity, what happens when we run into their reserves? How does the fact that we'd presumably have better reconnaissance capabilities, thanks to our dragons and gryphons, play off against the superior *communications* these Voices of theirs give them? And how do these 'Talents' of theirs—including any we can't evaluate at all, because we've never seen them in action—play off against the capabilities our Gifts give us?

"Second, if Hundred Olderhan is right, and I believe he is, then all of this started out of a misunderstanding. A monumental fuck-up by Olderhan's second-in-command, followed by a bad judgment call on my own part, and what looks like terminal stupidity on the part of Hundred Thalmayr. If that's what it was, if neither side deliberately set out to create the situation, then surely the possibility of negotiating our way out of it really exists. I don't want to see that thrown away. And, if I may speak completely frankly, I'm concerned about how the other side would perceive any further offensive military action on our part. Especially after *we* initiated the diplomatic contact between us."

"It may surprise you to hear this, Five Hundred, but I think your concerns are well taken," Harshu said. Klian felt his eyebrows inch upwards, despite himself, and the two thousand chuckled harshly.

"I know I'm considered a loose dragon," he said. "And there's probably some truth to that, if I'm going to be honest. But I'm not blind to the risks and the potential costs you're talking about. The problem is that I have my instructions from Two Thousand mul Gurthak, and I can't allow myself to be paralyzed by all of the perfectly good arguments for doing nothing.

"The tactical concerns you've just put your finger on have given me the odd sleepless night since mul Gurthak handed this particular hot potato to me," he continued. "Trust me, I've thought about them a lot.

"At the moment, I'm inclined to think that the combination of our mobility and reconnaissance advantages would more than compensate for their Voices. We don't know how many of these Voices they've actually got, how far down through their formations they'd be available. Do they have them only at the battalion level? Or at the company level? I find it difficult to believe that they have them all the way down to the *platoon* level, and as I understand it, it takes a Voice at either end for the whole system to work. So in an actual combat situation, I suspect that our ability to see farther and more clearly, and the information that makes available to our commanders, would give us what amounted to a shorter command and control loop, even if we did have to send physical messages back and forth. Now, in a *strategic* sense, that certainly wouldn't be the case, and they'd probably have an edge in orchestrating troop movements at the operational level, as well. But how important would that be if we dominated in the *tactical* zone? How much use is a communication advantage, if you simply don't know what the other side is doing . . . and the other side *does* know that about you?"

He shrugged, as if to acknowledge the fact that neither one of them had the answer to that question.

"On the other hand, from the size of the forces they've got forward-deployed, and from the conversations our recon crystals have recorded, it seems pretty obvious that these people's transportation capabilities are even more inferior to ours than we'd originally thought. They're clearly dependent on unenhanced animal transport, and they're talking in terms of literally *months* before any substantial reinforcements can arrive. From the things they've said, however, they're also anticipating that those reinforcements will be substantial when they do arrive.

"Obviously, there are still some really big holes in our own ability to translate what they're saying. Even when we get the *words*, we don't always have the context to make sense out of them. Still, it's clear that they're bringing up a lot of combat power. Quite possibly more than we've been able to assemble. But they won't be able to get it into position for some time, whereas ours is almost completely into position now. And, of course, there's a corollary to that, because the striking power we'll have concentrated here by the end of next week represents everything currently available in this entire chain. We're going to be as strong as we're ever going to get—at least for the foreseeable future—very quickly now, whereas they apparently have substantial additional reinforcements ready to move in behind the ones they're currently expecting, as you yourself have just suggested. In other words, we're probably looking at the most favorable balance of forces we're likely to see, at least until the Commandery finds out what's going on and starts sending in additional forces, and that's going to take months yet.

"And, finally, there's the difficulty that what we're talking about here is the biggest, and almost certainly the most valuable, portal cluster in our history. From some of the things they've said, it seems apparent the same thing is true for them, and at the moment, they've got possession of it. If *we* had it, how quick would *we* be to give it up, or to share it? Especially with someone we regarded as murderous barbarians? Which," the two thousand's eyes suddenly bored into Klian's across the table, "is *precisely* how they think about us, judging from the RCs' take."

Klian looked back at his superior and wished he had an answer for those last two questions. Or that he quite dared to ask how important the possession of any portal cluster was compared to the possibility of a general war with another inter-universal civilization.

"I have to balance all of those questions and considerations against Two Thousand mul Gurthak's instructions and my own evaluation of the situation," Harshu continued after moment. "And, despite my loose-dragon reputation, I'll be honest and admit that it scares the tripes out of me. But that doesn't mean I don't have to do it anyway, now does it?"

"No, Sir. I guess not," Klian conceded. He wanted to ask just what Harshu's instructions from mul Gurthak were, but that information hadn't been volunteered, and he knew it wouldn't be.

"As far as the potential diplomatic consequences are concerned," Harshu said, "I'm like you, Five Hundred—a soldier. I was never trained as a diplomat, and I've never wanted to be one. Master Skirvon and Master Dastiri, on the other hand, *are* diplomats, and I assure you that I'm giving very serious consideration to their advice and conclusions. In his original briefing, Two Thousand mul Gurthak made the point to me that it would be foolish to neglect the resource they offer, and I have no intention of doing so."

Klian nodded, suppressing yet another of those nagging questions he wanted to ask but couldn't. He strongly suspected that Skirvon and Dastiri were making more than purely diplomatic assessments of the other side, and he wondered how much influence *those* "advice and conclusions" were going to have with Harshu.

Silence fell for several long moments, and then Harshu inhaled sharply and gave his head a little shake.

"Whatever we may end up doing, Five Hundred, I have no intention of doing *anything* until the rest of our assigned strength arrives three days from now. And Master Skirvon and Master Dastiri are due to report back to us here for 'consultations' the day after that. At this time, I can honestly tell you that I definitely have not decided in favor of launching any sort of offensive."

Klian's shoulders started to relax, but Harshu wasn't quite finished.

"I haven't firmly decided *against* it yet, either," he said. "I can't, not until I've heard what Skirvon and Dastiri have to say about these Sharonians' current attitude and fundamental posture. But," he looked into Klian's eyes very, very levelly, "I can't possibly justify delaying my decision much longer. Our logistics situation is going to be difficult enough, just trying to hold all of our dragons and troops here and keep them fed somehow. *You* know that better than anyone else. And even if that weren't true, *if* offensive operations seem unavoidable, then it would be criminally negligent of me to wait for the reinforcements they're expecting to actually get here."

*   *   *

"I wonder if Chava would accept a dinner invitation?" Zindel XXIV wondered aloud, as he gazed out across the Great Palace's immaculately landscaped grounds. The sun was high in a clear blue sky, and a not-so-small army of gardeners moved steadily across the grounds. The Great Palace and its gardens were so vast that not a hint of the normal city noises of Tajvana was audible here in the sitting room of his palatial suite, and he wished passionately that the realities behind that almost pastoral façade matched its appearances.

"I rather doubt he would, Your Majesty," Shamir Taje replied from behind him. "I may not think very much of the man's intelligence, and even less of his morals—assuming he has any—but he does seem to have quite well developed survival instincts."

"Are you suggesting he might think I was inviting him here with ulterior motives, Shamir?" the emperor demanded in injured tones, turning away from the window to look at his old friend.

"Oh, certainly not, Your Majesty," Taje said piously, and the emperor chuckled.

"Well, you're probably right. He wouldn't come. And, I suppose that if I'm going to be honest, I *would* have ulterior motives. Just think of all the room for unmarked graves the palace gardens offer. Just yesterday, I noticed a bed of flowers that looks like it could use some fertilizer."

Zindel's tone was light; the expression in his eyes wasn't.

"Your Majesty," the First Councilor said, "I wish, with all my heart, that we could simply ignore Chava. And I have to admit that some of our allies' suggestions that we should simply leave Uromathia out of any new world government are very tempting. Given time, the Uromathians would have to recognize how much their isolation was costing them, in both political and economic terms, and one of Chava's successors would undoubtedly find himself forced to reach some sort of rapprochement with us. Unfortunately, his most probable successor is one of those loathsome sons of his, which probably wouldn't be all that much of an improvement. And even that presupposes Chava would be willing to settle for that sort of ostracization long enough for a successor to enter the picture at all."

"And," Zindel said grimly, "it also overlooks the fact that we may just find ourselves needing Uromathia's military capabilities quite badly."

Taje started to say something, then visibly changed his mind. The emperor looked at him for a moment, then turned back to the window, clasping his hands behind them as he returned his gaze to the gardens.

"Go ahead, Shamir," he said.

"Your Majesty, they *are* talking to us at Fallen Timbers," Taje pointed out to his emperor's back.

"I'm aware of that. And I'm aware also that the analysts and pundits are having a field day with it. And, believe me, no one in the entire multiverse could more fervently hope that something comes of these negotiations."

The emperor's voice was calm, but his expression was grim as he watched birds fluttering through the grounds' groves of trees and imagined how his falcon, Charaeil, would have reacted to all those tasty treats.

It's a pity I can't invite her to dine on Chava, *instead*, he thought. And then, despite himself, he smiled. *Assuming, of course, that Finena would be willing to share.*

Then his smile faded, and he looked back over his shoulder at Taje. The First Councilor could see the same peaceful, tranquil scene outside the window, but there was something else entirely in his emperor's eyes. Something dark and terrible.

"I want us to settle this without anybody else getting killed, Shamir. But I'm Calirath. And in here," he tapped his temple, "what I've Glimpsed doesn't include a peaceful resolution."

"Your Majesty," Taje said gently, "not all Glimpses come to pass."

"But very few which haven't proven accurate have been this strong," Zindel countered. "And don't forget Andrin." He shook his head. "I haven't been saying her Talent is stronger than mine simply to bolster her stature in the Privy Council's eyes, you know. It *is* stronger, gods help her. It's not as developed as mine—she simply hasn't had the life experience to train it the way mine's been trained. But it's strong, Shamir. Strong."

His eyes were darker than ever, and his jaw tightened as he stared at something only he and his daughter could See. Then they refocused on the First Councilor.

"Peaceful coexistence isn't what she's Glimpsed, either," he said.

"But even if that's true, when do you and she See it happening?" Taje asked. The emperor quirked an eyebrow, and the First Councilor shrugged. "Even if these negotiations only buy us a few years—even just a few additional months—they'll be worth it, Your Majesty," he pointed out. "As you've been telling everyone for the last month and a half, we have a monumental task in front of us just to prepare for this sort of conflict. Every day we can buy could be invaluable."

"That's true enough," Zindel conceded. "Especially," he added grimly, "with Chava dragging his godsdamned feet this way."

"Well, at least he's finally stated what have to have been his real terms all along."

"I know." Zindel's expression changed subtly. Taje knew he would never have been able to describe the change to anyone else, yet it was instantly recognizable to someone who knew the emperor as well as he did. It was the expression of a weary, worried father, not a nation's ruler.

"I know," Zindel repeated quietly, "and I wish to all the gods that I could spare Janaki this."

"Your Majesty, you don't have to accept," Taje said. "We can send it back to the Committee on Unification with counter proposals of our own. Whatever he may think, Chava isn't really the sole arbiter of this process, you know. Or we could take Ronnel's advice and simply ignore Chava completely."

"Don't tempt me, Shamir," Zindel said grimly. He turned back to the window once again, letting his eyes feast on the peacefulness and calm. Yet even that small pleasure was flawed, because it was his job—his and his family's—to see to it that that peacefulness and calm were preserved. He wished he could be certain it was a job they could do. And he wished, almost as strongly, that there were some way he could spare his son the price of that preservation.

And how many godsdamned generations of our family have wished the same thing? he asked himself in a rare burst of self-pity. The question hovered in the back of his brain, but no sign of it colored his voice as he went on.

"As you've just said, we need all the time we can buy. I can't possibly justify wasting more of it in ultimately pointless maneuvers trying to avoid what has to be done. Chava's traded away a lot of bargaining points to get to this final demand—enough of them that his "reasonableness" has actually managed to sway a hefty minority of the delegates into actively espousing it on his behalf. Not only that, but this campaign of his of exhuming every single bone anyone's ever had to pick with Ternathia hasn't been totally useless from his perspective, either. He doesn't need a majority to spike the wheel of any modification of the Act he doesn't like, only a big enough *minority*."

"Of course he doesn't, Your Majesty," Taje agreed. "On the other hand, if you do decide to accept his terms on behalf of Ternathia, you've still got to get our allies in the Conclave to agree to it. I'm not at all sure that's going to be a simple proposition."

"You're thinking about Ronnel, I see," Zindel said dryly, and shook his head with a wry smile as he considered the Farnalian emperor. "I sometimes wish Ronnel weren't such a throwback to his ancestors. I can just see him charging the shield wall, foaming at the mouth, bellowing war cries, and whirling his ax around his head as he comes!"

"He's not quite *that* bad, Your Majesty," Taje protested, and Zindel snorted.

"He's *exactly* that bad," he corrected, "and he hates Chava with a pure and blinding passion. Of course, he's had more actual contact with Chava than we have, since he shares that section of border with Uromathia near the Scurlis. He hasn't told me exactly what Chava's done, but I've had enough reports from others to have a pretty shrewd idea. And Junni of Eniath's told me quite a bit—more, actually, than I suspect he realizes.

"So I understand why Ronnel's so passionately opposed to any sort of . . . accommodation with Uromathia. And if he thinks he could be any more opposed than I am to the notion of sharing grandchildren with Chava, he's sadly mistaken. But ultimately, he's going to have to swallow it, just like I am. We can't afford to split Sharona between Chava and his supporters and all the rest of us. And let's be honest here, Shamir—if we weren't the ones Chava was making that demand of, *we'd* probably think it wasn't unreasonable in light of the actual balance of power between Ternathia and Uromathia."

Taje had no choice but to nod.

"Very well." Zindel never turned away from the window. "Inform Representative Kinshe that Ternathia formally accepts Uromathia's proposed amendment of the draft Act of Unification. I suppose," his mouth twitched with just a trace of genuine humor, "that the crown of Sharona is worth a Uromathian daughter-in-law."

CHAPTER
FIFTY-ONE

Thaminar Kolmayr barely glanced at the banner headline on the morning issue of the *Gulf Point Daily News* their new press secretary had brought in. He didn't need to do any more than that, because he was intimately familiar with the story beneath that head- line. Indeed, he'd gotten depressingly good at political analysis over the past dreary, endless weeks.

Thaminar had never been a particularly political person before, but since the murder of their daughter, he and Shalassar had followed the news coming out of Tajvana with quiet, grieving intensity, for reasons very different from those motivating most other Sharonians. Everyone else was worried about who would rule them, and how their lives would change. Thaminar couldn't bear the thought of more change in their lives—not after the traumatic savagery of the "change" they'd already endured—but he knew it was inevitable. And however little interested he might have been in change for change's sake, he and Shalassar were profoundly interested in justice.

It had hurt desperately, seeing their daughter's photograph and name splashed across newspaper and magazine pages, or embedded in the telepathic Voicecasts. None of it carried anything approaching the sheer agony of Shaylar's final Voice message, but neither he nor Shalassar had the heart any longer to View those Voicecasts. Using their Voices at all, these last two months, kept bringing back the searing pain of their daughter's death. So they read the newspapers, instead, and told themselves they'd almost gotten used to seeing little Shaylar's picture everywhere they turned.

But the endless, aching grief had not yet passed, and he'd come to realize it never would truly heal. It had faded enough to let them pick up enough of the shattered pieces of their lives to move forward again, yet the pain remained, wrapped around the jagged, empty void her death had left in their hearts, and impossible to forget or assuage. To lose a child, no matter how, was agony. To literally *know* how she'd died, to have experienced with her the horror and terror of her final minutes of life and yet been forever unable to so much as touch her one last time . . .

Shalassar came in from the kitchen, carrying their breakfast on a tray. He wasn't especially hungry—he seldom was, these days—yet the steaming scent of the coffee was a comforting reminder of normal home life that he welcomed gratefully. They clung to such things, little rituals, familiar things done a thousand ordinary times, as a way of holding themselves together and getting them through each day.

Shalassar glanced at the headline. Just beneath it was yet another black-bordered photograph of Shaylar between the photographs of the only two men in the entire Conclave who truly mattered. The Conclave's delegates had already voted to create a united Empire of Sharona based on the Ternathian model and with Zindel chan Calirath as emperor. Uromathia's refusal to accept the outcome of that vote as binding upon it had created an enormous amount of anger, but no one had really been surprised. What had been at least a little surprising was the fact that Emperor Chava had managed to convince half a dozen smaller nations to stand with Uromathia by appealing to supposed ancient Ternathian wrongs.

Actually, Thaminar reflected, *it probably has less to do with "convincing" them to go along with him than it does with finding ways of threatening them into going along. He's supposed to be good at that, after all, and every one of them borders on Uromathia.*

However he'd gotten their support, it had given his protests an added degree of legitimacy. Thaminar didn't much care to admit that, but he couldn't deny it, either. Whether or not anyone liked it, Chava Busar and his adherents had positioned themselves well behind their single "reasonable demand." Now it remained to be seen whether the nations which had already accepted Zindel of Ternathia as their new world emperor were prepared to accept the amendment Chava had demanded.

"Do you think they'll accept?" Shalassar murmured, biting her lip gently as she set out the breakfast neither of them truly felt like eating.

"I don't know," Thaminar admitted. She paused, a plate of cut melon slices poised in her hand above the polished tabletop in the bright, sunlit dining nook, and looked up at him, and he shrugged.

"I would have thought that when Zindel accepted in Ternathia's name that that would have been the end of it. But apparently Chava is even less popular than I'd thought, difficult though that is to believe."

Shalassar surprised him with a slight smile, then shook her head.

"Do you really think there's significant opposition? Or is this another example of the papers needing to play up the drama to help circulation?"

"My dear, that's pretty cynical," Thaminar observed. "Not that it couldn't be true, too."

He smiled back at her, but the truth was that he didn't really know what was going through the minds of the men and women in Tajvana. On the one hand, it seemed remarkably cut and dried; on the other, some of the delegates—the reports suggested that Emperor Ronnel of Farnalia had probably had a little something to do with it—had dug in their heels in stubborn resistance. Apparently the thought of finding themselves one day living under the rule of Chava Busar's grandchild was more than they could stomach. They were a minority of the total Conclave, but they also included many of the strongest original supporters of the concept of a world empire. Besides, the Act of Unification had required a supermajority for its original ratification. The same supermajority would be required for any amendment of the original Act, and there were enough holdouts to put final approval very much up for grabs.

"In the end," he said, "I suppose it depends on whether or not Ronnel goes on holding out. According to everything I've read, he's one of Zindel's closest allies on almost everything else. I can't believe he won't eventually come around to Zindel's thinking on this issue. It's not as if it's *his* son who's going to have to marry one of Chava's daughters, anyway."

"Oh? And what about Fyysel? How reasonable was *he* when Chava's name was placed in nomination?" Shalassar challenged, and Thaminar grimaced.

She had a point, he conceded. Fyysel had strongly supported Halidar Kinshe's original proposal. But when Chava tried to put his own candidacy forward, Fyysel had spoken for his subjects' blazing outrage at the very suggestion. If, the King of Shurkhal had said bluntly, the world were stupid enough to ramrod Uromathia's ruler down Shurkhal's throat, it would discover that Shurkhali honor still burned hot and that Shurkhali men and women still knew how to fight a war.

Thaminar hadn't even tried to keep track of the number of times he'd read or heard the phrase "Death before Uromathia!" in his kingdom's newspapers and public debates. He'd been in total agreement with the sentiment, and he'd been well aware, through news reports, that Uromathia had done everything in its power to stir up old and vicious hatreds of Ternathia amongst those nations she'd once conquered in an effort to generate some sort of counterbalancing backlash against Zindel.

Despite the miserable failure of Chava's effort to put his own candidacy forward, he had succeeded in energizing a vociferous lunatic fringe almost everywhere outside the current-day boundaries of Ternathia. Fortunately, that fringe had found itself increasingly marginalized as the debate had raged. And as Zindel had emerged more and more strongly as a reasonable, moderate-minded, *honorable* man who steadfastly refused to allow his own allies to ram *his* candidacy down anyone's throat, the tide had shifted decisively in his favor.

Yet it remained to be seen whether or not Ternathia's ruler could talk his own "allies"—including King Fyysel—into accepting an arrangement which would guarantee Chava Busar's dynastic grasp on the crown of Sharona.

"I think, in the end, they'll have to accept," he said finally. "If *Zindel* is willing, how can they refuse? They intend to make him the emperor of all Sharona. Are they going to start right out by telling him he doesn't have the right to make this sort of decision for his own family?" Thaminar shook his head. "That's insane."

"And people don't regularly get insane where Chava is concerned?" Shalassar shot back.

"I don't have any easy answers for you, love," he said. "I wish I did. I wish I still *believed* in easy answers. But the only way we're going to find out is to wait until the votes are counted."

"I know, I know," Shalassar said, and managed to smile at him. He smiled back at her, then folded the paper and deliberately set it aside as she began spooning melon, grapes, and dates onto his plate. He wished that he could put his worries away as easily as he could discard the newspaper, but that wasn't going to happen. Today's vote was so critical that neither of them really *wanted* to think about it, but he knew they weren't going to be able to avoid it.

Which didn't mean they weren't both going to try to pretend they could.

"Do you have any delegations coming in today?" he asked, deliberately turning away from the vote in Tajvana and concentrating on their own lives, instead.

Shalassar gave him another smile, but he felt the terrible tension in her through their marriage bond. It was just as hard for her to let go of the Unification vote as it was for him.

"I'm not expecting any," she said, shaking her head. "That doesn't mean the bell won't ring anyway, of course."

Her smile turned a little less forced as she added the qualification. An ambassador to aquatic sentients couldn't do her job the way other diplomats did theirs, and Shalassar's life—and that of her family—had always reflected that inescapable reality.

Human-to-human ambassadors' jobs were almost boringly easy in comparison. They simply received written, verbal, or Voice messages about meeting dates, times, and places, then went and had them. They could actually calculate their calendars, at least for a day or so in advance.

The ambassadors assigned to serve the great apes—the mountain gorillas, chimpanzees, orangutans, baboons, some of the higher monkey species, and so on—lived far less organized lives. They couldn't expect comfortable quarters in the fashionable, diplomatic sections of Sharona's capital cities, because they had to live close to the populations they served. So they ended up parked out on the fringes of the wilderness areas set aside for the apes ... which allowed primate emissaries to simply walk up to their houses and knock on the door whenever they felt like it. Which they were notoriously prone to do. The apes were much less interested in the sort of formal, regimented protocols and scheduling humans preferred.

More often, of course, contact with the apes was actually initiated from the human side. The human ambassador would find himself compelled to trek out into the wilderness, seeking out the population of apes affected by a proposed development in their area—a construction site, road, or mine—in order to ask the apes' permission to build on their territory.

Sometimes no permission was forthcoming, but those cases tended to be the exception, not the rule. Usually, some sort of *quid pro quo* could be arrived at. Sometimes the agreements hammered out provided for moving the whole clan into an unoccupied region capable of sustaining them. Sometimes all it took was a gift of technology to help the clan improve its standard of living. More than one large cat had been unpleasantly surprised by sword-wielding chimps protecting their young and infirm, and most of the clans loved steel axheads and saws. Other clans had acquired access to medicines and Healers, paid for by the private developer or government negotiating the treaty.

Word of that sort of agreement generally spread to other clans in the region. Thaminar and Shalassar had smiled over one news story, in particular. The Nishani chimps had allowed mines to be developed in their clan's territory in exchange for medical care. Not to be outdone, the neighboring Minarti chimpanzee clan had plied *their* telepathic ambassador with questions about what humans might need or want from *them*. Once they'd discovered that several varieties of rare medicinal herbs which grew in profusion in their territory could be found virtually nowhere else, they'd offered to exchange them for the same medical care.

Horticulturists had been imported to coach the Minarti clan on propagation techniques designed to promote a cultivated supply of the herbs, rather than deplete the wild sources. The delighted chimpanzees had settled down to enjoy their improved health care, tending the plants upon which it depended, and everyone had been quite satisfied by the arrangement.

It was all very humanlike . . . which was one of the reasons it had amused Shalassar and Thaminar so much, since Shalassar's own experiences had been rather different.

For one thing, even chimpanzees had a far better developed sense of time—by human standards, at least—than the cetaceans did. There was, quite literally, no way to predict what hour of the day or night a whale or dolphin might suddenly come seeking the human ambassador. The denizens of the sea lived at an entirely different pace, and in a totally different environment, from humanity or its close cousins, and their perceptions and interests were shaped accordingly. If the cetaceans had even been aware of the Minarti clan's activities at all, they would have thought the entire business was unutterably boring.

Most of the land-dwelling sentients of Sharona (including the majority of humans) felt sorry for and smugly superior to the cetaceans, which had no hands and couldn't use human technology for much of anything. Most cetaceans, on the other hand, didn't think about the apes at all, except to feel sorry for and smugly superior to the hapless primates (including the majority of humans) who were stuck on dry land and unable to exploit a full three-quarters of their home planet's surface. They were totally disinterested in the goings-on of chimpanzees and mountain gorillas, although they'd been forced to modify that attitude where the humans who routinely crossed their home waters were involved.

Human beings might be unable to do much more than barely scratch the shallows of the cetaceans' endless oceans, but they did exploit at least some of the same territory. And since the emergence of Talents among them, it had been the humans who had initiated contact. No one—Shalassar included—quite understood how cetaceans maintained their historical record, but the fact that they did was beyond dispute. And because they did, they remembered the days in which even the greatest and most intelligent of them had been no more than one more food source for humanity . . . and how that had changed.

There were those, among the cetaceans, who remained wary of, even hostile towards, humanity because of things which had happened thousands upon thousands of years ago. More of them, though, remembered that humanity had altered its actions once it realized that it was dealing with other *intelligent* species. And even those who remained wary, recognized that at least some contact with human beings was inescapable.

That was where ambassadors like Shalassar stepped into the picture. She'd spent her life establishing contacts with the cetaceans, and even more than the ambassadors to the apes, she'd discovered that the nonhumans with whom she dealt had become the very center of her life and career. She wasn't simply their official conduit to land-dwelling humanity; she and her family had made friendships among the great whales, the dolphins and the porpoises, building intensely personal bridges across the inter-species gap.

Still, she *was* an ambassador, which meant she had more than a merely personal interest in the outcome of today's vote. She had a professional interest, as well, because if Zindel chan Calirath did, indeed, become the emperor of a united Sharona, he would also become Shalassar's ultimate superior. In essence, she'd find herself working for him, as *his* representative to the cetaceans, rather than for the Kingdom of Shurkhal. Which meant that somehow she'd have to find a way to explain to those aquatic intelligences just what sort of bizarre political convolutions those peculiar bipeds were up to now.

That thought brought her back to the vote once again, and she glanced at the clock on the mantle. It was nearly time for the SUNN Voicecast from Tajvana, and she suddenly felt Thaminar's arms wrap themselves around her from behind. She closed her eyes and leaned back against him, clinging to the love pouring through their marriage bond like another, even stronger set of arms, and he kissed the side of her neck.

"Let's go out to the beach," he said gruffly. "I don't want to stay inside."

Shalassar nodded, and they walked outside. They moved well down the beach from the house, past the official Embassy with its dock and bell, to a favorite spot well shaded by palms. Then they sat down on a blanket between the endless sweep of sea and sky. Shalassar sat in front of her husband, leaning back against the solidness of him, and treasured the cherishing strength of the arms about her.

Out here, there was enough sunlight and wind and sky to make the ache of loss feel smaller than it did enclosed by walls and a ceiling. They'd been spending a lot of time out here, in recent weeks, and Shalassar sighed as she leaned her head back against his chest. Memories slipped into their shared awareness. They saw Shaylar skipping down the beach, playing with her older brothers, building castles in the sand and hunting for shells. They saw her laughing in the surf, riding on the back of one of the dolphins who'd come as an emissary to the embassy.

They sat there for a long time, watching the birds wheeling overhead, listening to their inexpressibly lonely cries as they drifted against the vast infinity of sea and sky. Shalassar's people believed that the human soul rose like a seabird after death, singing its way into the sky in search of its final resting place in the heavens, out in the endless vastness of the ether where the gods dwelt. . . .

Shurkhali believed the soul was like a grain of the endless sands that swept across their arid homeland. When a Shurkhali died, his soul would be blown, like those grains of sand, back into the great drifts of souls that marched across the face of heaven, like the dunes of sand blowing across the face of Shurkhal. The soul of a person found worthy would be swept up and placed like a jewel in the diadem of heaven, to shine as a beacon to guide others on their way home.

Whether her journey had ended as a bird singing its way to heaven, or as a star shining in the diadem of the gods, Shaylar's parents had to believe their daughter had found the peace and happiness reserved for those who had lived life in joy and service to others. Surely her final action, safeguarding every living soul in Sharona by destroying the maps that might have led her killers here, had earned their child a place in the arms of the gods.

*   *   *

"Do you think Ronnel is *really* on our side?" Britham Dulan murmured quietly in Shamir Taje's ear.

Andrin knew she hadn't been supposed to overhear the Internal Affairs Councilor's question, but she'd always had remarkably acute hearing. And, she had to admit, she found Dulan's inquiry well taken. The Emperor of Farnalia was on his feet once more, his eyes crackling with fury, as he rebutted the comments of yet another of Chava Busar's allies.

He'd been doing a lot of that over the past several hours, as early morning turned into late afternoon, she reflected.

Taje's lips twitched in what could have been amusement or irritated agreement—or both, Andrin supposed—but the First Councilor didn't respond. Perhaps he was too well aware of all of the attention focused on the Ternathian delegation as the debate raged onward. Andrin wished he'd responded anyway, and, after a moment, she decided to take advantage of her own youthfulness. She didn't do it very often, but she *was* barely seventeen years old. There were times when being a teenager allowed her a degree of latitude the official adults around her were denied.

"Papa," she said quietly, looking up at her father in the chair beside hers, "why is Emperor Ronnel kicking up such a fuss?"

Zindel chan Calirath found himself restraining an abrupt temptation to burst into deep, rolling laughter. "Such a fuss" was precisely the right word for what his old friend was doing at the moment, although he rather doubted that anyone except his Andrin would have described it with such succinct accuracy. It took him a few seconds to be sure he had his voice under control, then he looked down at her and shook his head slightly.

"Ronnel is just a bit . . . stubborn," he said, with massive understatement. "To put it bluntly, he doesn't like Chava, he doesn't *trust* Chava, and he doesn't want Chava anywhere near the imperial succession. Not in any empire that *he* belongs to, at any rate."

"But if you don't object to it, then how can *he*?" she asked. "I mean, it doesn't seem very logical."

"Politics often *aren't* logical, 'Drin," he replied. "People think with their emotions at least as much as they do with their brains—probably more, I often think. Part of the art of ruling is to recognize that. To allow for it when it's likely to work against you, and to figure out how to *use* that same tendency when it can help to accomplish the things you have to accomplish.

"At the moment, though, Ronnel is convinced—in some cases for some pretty emotional reasons—that he has a lot of perfectly rational reasons to hate and distrust Chava. And he does, actually. To be honest, *most* people who know Chava have reasons to hate and distrust him."

He considered telling her about his intelligence reports on Chava's use of terror tactics against suspected opponents among his own people . . . and against his neighbors, as well. The "brigandage" which no one could ever quite stamp out in the mountains and valleys along his borders had been inexplicably on the upsurge over the last couple of decades—a period which just happened to coincide with his accession to the throne. And for some peculiar reason, it appeared to be directed primarily against people the Uromathian emperor didn't like very much. That was bad enough, but there were other, still darker reports which even Ternathian Imperial Intelligence hadn't been able to definitely confirm or rebut.

He thought about those reports as he looked down into his daughter's clear, sea-gray eyes, and decided not to share them. Someday he might have to, but that day had not arrived yet, and for all of her strength, she was still only a girl. *His* girl, and the father in him decided that just this once he would shelter her a little longer.

"No one is ever likely to confuse Chava with one of the paladins out of the old tales," he said instead. "Ronnel—and some of the other delegates—aren't about to forget that. And, to be perfectly honest, I suspect that the fact that Ronnel is one of my closer friends has something to do with his present attitude."

Andrin looked puzzled, and he squeezed her shoulder gently.

"I've told Ronnel this is how it has to be," he told her. "But he's not at all convinced that it's how I *want* it to be. Which is fair enough," he conceded, "since if I had any choice at all, I certainly wouldn't do something like this to Janaki! But the point is that Ronnel is convinced I made my decision for reasons of state, and he's furious at the thought of seeing me backed into this sort of corner by someone like Chava. And don't forget, he's Janaki's godfather, as well. Do think he really wants to see Janaki with Chava Busar as a father-in-law?"

Andrin shook her head with a grimace, and Zindel shrugged.

"To be perfectly honest, neither do I. But we don't seem to have a great deal of choice, and I know your brother, 'Drin. Once everything was explained to him, he'd make exactly the same decision I've made. Getting back to your question, though, it's the combination of Ronnel's own reasons to despise Chava, coupled with the fact that he's trying to 'defend' me from a decision he feels has been forced upon me, which accounts for his decision to oppose me on this particular issue. I did say," he reminded her, "that politics often aren't logical."

"But if this is *necessary*—?" she said, and he shrugged once again.

"Ronnel and I differ on just how necessary it is," he said. "I think we need Uromathia included from the outset. And I think we need to do it in a way which makes it perfectly clear to everyone that we've made an extra effort to accommodate Chava's reasonable demands. I think we can't afford to leave an excluded Uromathia sitting out there like some sort of canker, distracting us while we're trying to gear up for a major war against the Arcanans. And if we're going to include Uromathia, I want to do it in a way which cuts the legs out from under any future attempt on Chava's part to argue that we didn't meet him at least halfway.

"Ronnel's view is that the Conclave's already approved Unification and already approved my election as emperor. As far as he's concerned, the rest of Sharona can get along quite handily without Uromathia. In fact, I think he'd just as soon see Uromathia excluded in order to keep Chava as far away as possible from the levers of power. And the news that the Arcanans have initiated negotiations leaves Ronnel feeling less of a sense of urgency than he felt when unification was originally proposed. So where I'm willing—even determined, however little I like it—to include Uromathia, he's perfectly prepared to *exclude* it. And all he has to do to accomplish that is to prevent me from assembling a big enough supermajority to amend the original Act."

He smiled down at his daughter, but his eyes were dark.

"So you see, 'Drin, it's the very fact that he's my friend which is driving him to do everything in his power to defeat what I'm trying so hard to accomplish."

Andrin nodded slowly, but the youthful eyes looking up into his were just as dark, just as shadowed, and he knew. She'd Glimpsed what he had. Neither of them had Glimpsed it clearly—not yet—and, in many ways, that was even more terrifying than it would have been if they had. Over the millennia the Calirath Dynasty had discovered that the more deeply involved someone with the Calirath Talent was in the events he Glimpsed, and the more harshly those events impinged directly upon him, the harder it was to See that Glimpse's details sharply. That was what frightened Zindel chan Calirath now, because there was too much darkness, too much loss and pain, woven through the chaotic scenes he and Andrin had managed to Glimpse for him to force clarity upon them.

But because his daughter shared his Talent, she understood what Ronnel Karone—who did not—never could.

"I do see, Papa," she said quietly, laying her slender hand atop one of his. "Thank you for explaining to me."

CHAPTER
FIFTY-TWO

THE BRIGHT MORNING sunlight only made Sarr Klian's mood even darker by comparison.

The final draft of Two Thousand Harshu's reinforcements had arrived last night, and it was, Klian conceded, an impressive force. Mul Gurthak had managed to assemble even more fighting power than he'd projected in his original dispatches to Klian. He'd not only managed to dig up two complete Air Force talons, but he'd even come up with an additional four-dragon flight of the rare yellows. Klian hadn't expected that.

The Air Force's battle dragons were divided into flights and strikes on the basis of their breath weapons. The reds (the traditional colors of the original Mythalan war dragons bore very little resemblance to modern dragons' actual colors but still made a convenient shorthand for purposes of reference) were the fire-breathers, although it probably would have been more accurate to describe them as spitting fireballs. They'd been bred as a general attack type, although the "flight time" required for a fireball to reach its target made them less suitable for air-to-air combat.

The blacks were the lightning-breathers, who'd originally been developed expressly to fill that gap in dragon-versus-dragon combat. Their attacks delivered less total damage than a red's, but it was extremely focused. More importantly, it struck with literally "lightning-speed," which meant there wasn't any point in attempting to evade it the way someone might a fireball, if he was fast—and lucky—enough.

Both weapons sites were, of course, also effective against ground targets. No one in his right mind wanted to get in the way of dragon-spawned fireballs or lightning bolts, and it had been two hundred years since anyone had. But however little Klian might have liked the thought of being incinerated or flash-fried by lightning, the yellows were the ones that really gave him nightmares.

Almost every peace organization on Arcana—and a rather surprising number of officers within the Air Force itself—had tried repeatedly to have the yellows banned along with the weapons of mass destruction which had been outlawed when the Union was formed. Although the yellows' opponents hadn't succeeded in getting them completely banned, the Air Force had allowed their numbers to run down drastically. There simply weren't very many of them left, and Klian hadn't imagined that any of them were out here in the Lamia Chain. Nor could he imagine why they'd been sent in the first place, or what possible use anyone in the Commandery might have expected them to be.

Yellows were poison-breathers.

The shortest-ranged of all the dragons, they were also the most lethally effective against unprotected personnel. Their breath weapon had the largest area of effect, and without gas masks and a sound doctrine in their use, there was no defense against it.

They came in several varieties, the most deadly of which breathed what the Healers called a nerve-toxin that was uniformly lethal. Others breathed gases like chlorine, which were horrible enough but at least offered some possibility of survival if the wind was in your favor, or if you could get out of the gassed area quickly enough. But even a tiny concentration of the nerve-toxin was deadly once it was inhaled. There were rumors that the Mythalans had developed *contact* nerve-toxins during the Portal Wars. If that were true, at least they'd never been used, thankfully, but the existing varieties of yellows were more than enough to make Klian's skin crawl.

Especially now, as he stood on the Fort Rycharn parapet, gazing out across the crowded dragonfield at the rows upon rows of canvas tents. According to the latest returns, Harshu currently had two cavalry regiments and eight infantry battalions, plus artillery support, assembled under his command. That gave him over two thousand cavalry and almost nine thousand infantry, even before he counted the artillerists, the Air Force personnel, and the special combat engineer units. All told, Harshu had better than fourteen thousand men—as many men as many a full division could have boasted—and Klian felt a deep surge of inexpressible bitterness as he gazed out across that crowded encampment and thought how easily he might have contained this situation at the outset if he'd had it under *his* command.

Assuming you hadn't pissed it away the way you did Charlie Company, he told himself with bleak self-honesty.

He heard the flag above the fort cracking and popping in the crisp wind, and he was tempted to turn around and gaze back at the central office block. But he didn't. There wasn't any point. He'd already heard everything he needed to hear.

"Gentlemen," Two Thousand Harshu had told his assembled officers less than two hours ago, "Master Skirvon's latest dispatches make it quite clear the other side is not negotiating in good faith. That fact has become increasingly clear to him over the past several weeks, and he's communicated that conclusion to Two Thousand mul Gurthak. In addition, our reconnaissance has confirmed that the enemy actually on the portal are anticipating the arrival of substantial reinforcements within the next sixty to ninety days."

He'd paused, and Klian's heart had sunk into his boots. The five hundred had looked around at the silently watching faces, willing one of them to speak. When no one else had, he'd drawn a deep breath and lifted his own hand.

"Yes, Five Hundred Klian," Harshu had said.

"Excuse me, Sir. But if they aren't negotiating in good faith, what, exactly, does Master Skirvon think they *are* doing? Why talk to us in the first place?"

"They haven't requested a freeze on troop movements," Harshu had pointed out. "Obviously, that's because they believe—or hope, at any rate—that they can move their reinforcements to the front faster than we can. Unfortunately for them, they appear to be wrong. Master Skirvon's assessment is that they've basically been intent on buying time to bring those troops into play, without any intention of ever seriously attempting to resolve the differences between us peacefully. They continue to insist that the original confrontation was entirely *our* fault, and they've persistently refused to move beyond that to any discussion of the future possession of the portal cluster. Master Skirvon—who, I hardly need to remind anyone in this room, has by far the most personal experience in dealing with them—is of the opinion that they intend, at a bare minimum, to secure their own permanent and exclusive possession of Hell's Gate. Whether or not they intend to move *beyond* the cluster into our own territory is more than he's prepared to say at this point. That possibility cannot be overlooked, however."

Klian had hovered on the brink of pointing out that *Skirvon* hadn't requested any freezes on troop movements, either. But he hadn't said it. Harshu already knew that, and Klian had no doubt that Skirvon had waited to see what the other side proposed specifically as a test of the Sharonians' sincerity.

"Based on Master Skirvon's dispatches," Harshu had gone on, "Two Thousand mul Gurthak has authorized me to take preemptive action against the enemy, if, in my judgment, the situation requires it." Klian's plummeting heart had seemed to freeze as the two thousand paused briefly, then continued in measured tones. "He hasn't ordered us to attack, but he's eleven days away by dragon. As he says, he can't possibly be as good a judge of the immediate situation as we can here, at Fort Rycharn."

He'd surveyed the taut ranks of his officers. His eyes had challenged them to disagree with anything he'd said, but not a single voice had spoken. Not even Klian's.

"At the moment, we have a clear and overwhelming superiority. All of our reconnaissance confirms that they have less than one full regiment equivalent, and they remain in complete ignorance of our aerial capabilities. We have an equally overwhelming advantage in the speed with which we can move our troops. Given the fact that we know they have heavy reinforcements headed in our direction, I believe we have no option but to strike quickly and decisively."

Klian's jaw had tightened as he heard the words he'd dreaded from the beginning of the meeting, but Harshu hadn't been finished.

"Our immediate objective, obviously, is to secure Hell's Gate and control of its portal cluster," he'd said. "Two Thousand mul Gurthak has made it quite clear that the Union can't afford to leave it in Sharona's possession. Especially not given the fact that they may well have designs upon even more Arcanan territory. However, while the seizure of Hell's Gate itself ought to be a relatively straightforward proposition, given the balance of forces currently available, *holding* it may be quite another matter, given the hostile forces we know are already headed in this direction. To be blunt, we need additional defensive depth, especially given the size of the Sharonians' entry portal to that universe. We can't possibly adequately defend a portal that size with the forces currently available to us.

"Accordingly, I've decided that we'll continue through Hell's Gate. Thanks to Magister Halathyn's final discovery, we're equipped with portal detection devices of unparalleled range and sensitivity. If necessary, we can survey for, locate, and secure all of the portals in a given universe far more quickly than was ever possible before. Our objective, however, will be to get as far forward as we can. Ideally, I'd prefer to find another portal, no larger than our own swamp portal, to use as a chokepoint against the inevitable Sharonian counterattack.

Failing that, I want enough depth for us to use our air power to hammer them mercilessly as they advance, and rip apart their supply lines behind their spearheads. It's essential that we buy enough time for the Commandery to dispatch heavy reinforcements of our own, and we can't do that by standing passively on the defensive in Hell's Gate."

Still no one had spoken, and he'd shaken his head slowly.

"I realize that if we continue beyond Hell's Gate we'll be clearly and unambiguously moving into Sharonian territory. That, of course, would constitute an act of war by anyone's definition. But there's no point in deceiving ourselves, gentlemen. The moment we attack Hell's Gate, we *will* be at war with these people."

He'd said it unflinchingly, and continued in the same level tones.

"I don't say that lightly. Nonetheless, as Two Thousand mul Gurthak has pointed out, leaving Sharona in possession of Hell's Gate, *and* a foothold in our own territory, constitutes an unacceptable risk to the security and interests of the Union of Arcana. As soldiers in the Union Army, it's our duty to protect that security and those interests. I intend to do so. And once we've opened the ball by attacking at all, it would be criminally negligent of us to fail to act in accordance with the military realities and imperatives of our mission. The diplomats can sort out who's responsible for what and which of their universes we're prepared to hand back at the negotiating table, after the shooting is over. Our job is to make sure that when they sit down at that table, they sit down with the winning cards already in their hands. Is that clearly understood?"

Heads had nodded all around the room, and he'd nodded back.

"Good," he'd said, then showed his teeth in a feral smile.

"Now, as I'm sure we're all aware, the greatest single disadvantage we face are these 'Voices' of the Sharonians. Frankly, I'm not convinced they represent as much of a threat as some of us have suggested. It doesn't matter what kind of messages they pass along if they don't have the military wherewithal to stand up to us, after all. Nonetheless, I could be wrong about that, and even if I'm not, denying the enemy information about your own movements is one of the cardinal principles of warfare.

"I confess that I'd given this problem considerable thought without hitting on a solution to it. I wasn't the only one thinking about it, though, and Five Hundred Neshok has come up with an approach which may just work. It has its downsides," his expression had gone grimmer, "and it's more complicated than I'd prefer in an ideal world. In the world we've got, though, I think it may just work.

"Five Hundred?"

He'd gestured for Neshok to stand. The intelligence officer had obeyed, and as he'd explained the concept he'd come up with, Klian had understood exactly why Harshu's expression had been less than delighted.

Now, as he stood on the parapet in the clean morning air, he felt . . . dirty. And frightened. He had no doubt that Harshu was right about the immediate tactical situation. Nor did he doubt that the two thousand's initial operational plan would succeed.

But what happened after that? What happened when the Sharonians discovered that they'd been attacked yet again? And that this time no Arcanan could claim it had been a simple "misunderstanding"?

Neshok keeps calling these people "barbarians," the five hundred thought almost despairingly. *Harshu's always careful to avoid doing that himself, but it's there in the way he* thinks *about them. I don't know how much of that stems from the fact that it's what Neshok keeps feeding him in his intelligence analyses, and how much of it comes from inside his own head, but I've* met *Shaylar and her husband. Whatever these people may be, they aren't "barbarians," and after what they already did to Charlie Company, they're not going to be military pushovers, either, even if they don't have magic. Am I the only one who sees that?*

He had no answer to that question. Or not one that didn't terrify him, at any rate.

*   *   *

The sun wheeled slowly overhead. Neither of them even tried to tune into the real-time Voicecasts of the ferocious Conclave session they knew was raging in Tajvana. Near the noon hour, the staff King Fyysel had assigned to them brought a beautiful little luncheon out to them, and they made a show of trying to eat it, although neither of them could work up much enthusiasm.

"The debate has been furious," Dalisar Tharsayl, the head of their new staff said as he watched them nibble at the food. "The Emperor of Farnalia keeps shouting about Chava's 'extortion' and 'blackmail.' The King of Hinorea keeps responding with rants about Ternathian 'crimes against humanity' from two thousand years ago and demanding to know just why Emperor Ronnel seems so eager to put his good friend Zindel on the throne of Sharona, yet so bitterly opposed to accepting any Uromathian representation in the dynasty he intends to 'foist off upon the rest of us.'"

He shook his head, his expression a mixture of bemusement, anger, and concern, and Shalassar lifted her gaze to his.

"Did you expect anything else?" she asked, and he shook his head again, harder.

"No, Lady," he conceded. "I've given up expecting rationality out of human beings under any circumstances. Why should I expect that to change under *these*? Ancient prejudices and resentments, coupled with opportunism where the possibility of power is involved, are more than enough to reduce any semblance of reason to pure emotional chaos."

Shalassar surprised herself with a ghost of a laugh, and he smiled. Then he half-bowed in her direction.

"The debate continues," he said, "but I truly believe it's winding towards a conclusion. Our king has spoken several times, and surely everyone in the entire world must know how much King Fyysel—and all of our people—loathe and despise all Chava stands for. Yet the king speaks steadily and powerfully in favor of accepting the modification to the Act of Unification. To those who oppose the amendment, he points out that they intend to make Zindel of Ternathia Emperor of all Sharona, their ruler, and asks if they expect this man to be a mere figurehead. And if they don't, then why do they propose to begin his reign by questioning his competence to decide upon the political acceptability of the marriage of his own heir?"

Thaminar couldn't quite keep the surprise out of his eyes, and Tharsayl smiled crookedly.

"I wouldn't say His Majesty makes the argument cheerfully, Master Kolmayr," he said. "Indeed, the mere thought that his children must someday bow to Chava Busar's get, even knowing that any child of Prince Janaki will also be *Zindel's* grandchild, must be taking years off of his life. But," the chief of staff's smile vanished, "he's determined to accept it. Believe me," Tharsayl looked at both of them, "the Act of Unification will be amended and sustained. King Fyysel—and Emperor Zindel—will settle for no less than the creation of a world government capable of fighting any war, meeting any foe. It will happen, and justice *will* be done for your daughter."

Shalassar's eyes burned, and Thaminar reached out to grip her hand fiercely.

"Thank you," she got out, and King Fyysel's servant bowed deeply. Then he departed, directing the rest of the staff with silent gestures as they carried away the remnants of lunch.

*   *   *

"Ladies and Gentlemen of the Conclave, may I have your attention please."

Orem Limana's voice was tired but clear and strong, and the huge chamber of the Emperor Garim Chancellery stilled. It didn't happen instantly, but it did happen quickly, and Davir Perthis smiled tensely at Tarlin Bolsh in the Universal News Network booth high above the chancellery floor. A corner of his own Talent was tapped into the Voicecast going out from Darl Elivath, but most of his attention was on the Conclave before him.

It all came down to this, he thought. Everything he'd done, all of the corners he'd cut where the letter of his profession's official ethics were concerned. All of the delegates' debates, all of the horsetrading and the convincing . . . and the threats, and the browbeating. *All* of it came down to this moment, and this final vote.

He'd never thought for a moment that it would be this close, but no one was prepared to predict whether or not the vote to amend the Act of Unification would succeed.

Who would have thought that Ronnel Karone would fight so hard against Zindel's obvious wishes?

The Chief Voice shook his head, bemused by the way the bizarre convolutions of politics could surprise him even now. The spectacle of Ternathia's oldest and closest ally fighting to the last ditch against a *Ternathian* proposal would have been one for the history books even if the issue in question hadn't been so grave.

"What do you think?" he whispered to Bolsh.

"I don't," the International News Division chief replied out of the corner of his mouth, never taking his own eyes from Limana. "And I'm not sticking my neck out with a guess, either, so don't try to get one out of me. By my count, it's going to come right down to the finish line."

"*You're* a lot of help!"

"Sorry," Bolsh grunted. "You want accurate predictions about something like this, hire a Calirath."

"I—" Perthis began, then shut his mouth as the chancellery finally settled into the sort of silence that hurt a man's ears.

"Ladies and Gentlemen of the Conclave," Limana repeated into the stillness, "the vote has been tabulated. Chairman Kinshe?"

Halidar Kinshe, the chairman of the Committee on Unification, stood with a sheaf of papers in his hand.

"Ladies and Gentlemen," he said, "the motion before this Conclave was to amend Section Three of Article Two of the previously approved Act of Unification, by the addition of the following subsection."

He looked down at the papers in his hand and read in a slow, clear voice, giving each delegation's Voices the time to guarantee a clean translation to its delegates.

"Article Two, Section Three, Subsection Fourteen: It shall be agreed
that the Heir to the co-joined Thrones of the Empires of Ternathia
and Sharona shall, within three months of the ratification of this
Act of Unification by all Parties, wed a Royal Princess of Uromathia,
and that the Issue of this Marriage shall in perpetuity displace the
claim of any other Individual, Dynasty, or Nation upon the Crown
of the Empire of Sharona."

He paused and cleared his throat.

"The vote in favor of amending the Act by the addition of the
preceding subsection is four hundred and sixty-three in favor, two
hundred and thirty-seven opposed. The motion to amend," he drew
a deep breath, "is carried."

*　　　*　　　*

The sun had continued to wheel steadily overhead. Now, at last,
it was sliding down the sky and painting the western heavens in
glorious colors as it descended. The day had faded nearly into dusk,
and a chill breeze had begun to blow in across the water, when
Tharsayl reappeared. He walked down the beach in the loose white
robes which marked him instantly as a royal servant and gave them
a profound bow.

"It is done," he murmured.

Shalassar's heart shivered under Thaminar's arm, and they looked
up into Tharsayl's face, more than half-dreading, even now, what they
might see there. The chief of staff loomed up across the last of the
golden sunset as he straightened and looked back at them.

"The amendment was sustained by a single vote more than was
required, and Uromathia, as was agreed, has formally ratified the
Act," he said simply. "We have a new Emperor: Zindel chan Calirath.
Zindel XXIV of Ternathia . . . and Zindel the First of Sharona."

Thaminar's breath exploded out of him. Until it lifted, he hadn't
truly realized how heavy the weight of his fear had been. Despite
all he'd said to Shalassar, all the arguments logic and reason could
present, he'd been so afraid that at the last minute . . .

"Mother Marthea," he whispered, feeling Shalassar's matching relief
rippling through her, "thank you for this mercy."

A burst of light dazzled their eyes for just an instant; then the
sun slipped down past the edge of the world, and he realized that
their long vigil here by the sea had come to its close, after all.

"Let me take you in, love," he murmured to Shalassar. "You're
cold and tired."

She turned in his arms, peering up into his eyes, and then her eyes
lit with their first real smile since the dreadful news had arrived.

"So are you," she said. "And . . . I'm actually hungry."

She sounded almost surprised, and Thaminar crushed her close for just a moment, nearly weeping with relief. Then he stood and reached down, pulling her up from the sand, and walked slowly with her back to the home they'd made together over so many years.

They were just passing the dock, when the bell rang. The sound startled them, and they paused. Then Shalassar gave Thaminar's hand an apologetic squeeze and hurried out onto the dock. He and Tharsayl followed her more slowly, then stopped.

It was a dolphin. There was just enough light to see its sleek hide, glistening wetly where the elegant snout had lifted out of the water to reach the bell pull, and Shalassar knelt down beside it, resting one hand on the dolphin's head, just behind one large, liquid eye.

Those eyes had always seemed to Thaminar to watch her—and him—with deep and endless curiosity whenever one of these beautiful, mysterious creatures came calling at their dock. But there was something different about it, this time, and he stiffened as Shalassar's breath caught in obvious surprise.

The dolphin made a sharp staccato, chittering noise that sounded . . . happy, somehow. Thaminar wasn't actually able to Hear the dolphins his wife Spoke with. But he could sometimes feel echoes of her conversations through their marriage bond, and the dolphin's reaction felt light and buoyant in a way he couldn't explain. It lingered for several moments, then rolled slightly in the water, nodding its head deliberately toward Thaminar and Tharsayl. And then it uttered a strange burbling sound and slipped away from the dock.

It submerged, but only for an instant. Then its dorsal fin reappeared, cutting through the water with a dark V-shaped wake until the entire dolphin suddenly exploded out of the water once more. It leapt into the air, droplets of spray flying high enough to catch the fringe of the setting sun and glitter like a shower of topazes and rubies. The dolphin made a complete flip, three feet above the dark water, then splashed back into its mysterious world and was gone.

Shalassar straightened slowly, turning away from the waves, and Thaminar felt her sense of wonder through the marriage bond.

"They wanted to know if we'd decided yet," she said. "They wanted to know if we'd decided who would lead us."

"They *what?*"

Thaminar wasn't quite sure he'd heard her preposterous statement correctly. In all the years she'd served as an ambassador, the dolphins had never taken notice of human political affairs. Not like this.

She crossed the dock to his side and slipped one arm around him.

She stood beside him, leaning her head against his shoulder, gazing at the spot where the emissary had vanished from sight.

"They knew, somehow, that we were making this choice today," she said softly. "Marthea alone knows how—tonight, I could actually believe She told them! But however they learned about it, they knew. So one of them came to ask, when the light went. He was an emissary I'd never met before, but it felt as if he must be very important in the pod in which he travels, and he was very concerned when he asked."

"What did he say when you told him?" Tharsayl asked in an almost reverent voice, and a smile of wonder spread slowly across her face.

"He didn't say anything. Yet I felt a burst of joy, one unlike anything I've ever sensed in dolphin-kind before. I don't understand it. You may tell King Fyysel that, Dalisar. I don't understand it, but . . . the dolphins are pleased—very pleased—that Zindel chan Calirath has been chosen to lead us. It felt—"

She hesitated, biting her lip.

"Lady?" Tharsayl prompted gently, and she met his gaze in the steadily darkening evening.

"It felt as though their emissary had reached a decision. A desperately important decision. It's very difficult to put dolphin-speech into human words, but they've decided something. I'm sure of it. Decided something critical, but whether or not they ever tell us what it is . . ."

She shrugged and held out her palms in a gesture indicating helplessness.

"We may never know. But I find it very intriguing that the dolphins, at least, are paying attention to what happens to human politics. That's never happened before."

"Never?" Tharsayl asked almost sharply, and she shook her head.

"Never. The cetaceans are remarkably indifferent to most of us land-dwellers, on the whole. The great whales are more indifferent than the dolphins or orcas, who are naturally curious souls. But even the dolphins, who enjoy playing with us in the water and almost always help swimmers in trouble, have never shown any interest in how we govern ourselves. Their only 'political concerns' have always been strictly limited to how our actions, our plans, might affect them, and *vice versa*, not how we reached our decisions in the first place."

Tharsayl stood frowning at the dark water, barely visible now, and his eyes were troubled.

"Crown Prince Danith had a remarkable story to tell his father, the day he came home from here, Lady. The day you learned what had happened."

Thaminar frowned. So did Shalassar.

"When you were linked with the Portal Authority's Voice—" The chief of staff hesitated, clearly choosing his words with care. "There were dolphins here, in the floating ring, and one of the singing whales, and they . . . reacted to the news."

"Reacted?" Shalassar repeated with a frown. "Reacted how? To what?"

"There came a moment, a terrible moment, when you screamed, Lady," Tharsayl said. "And when you did, the sea came alive. They leapt from the water—all of them. His Highness said . . . He said the sound that broke from them was unearthly, horrifying. A sound of *rage*."

Shalassar's eyes went wide in shock. She stared at the chief of staff, and Tharsayl shook his head slowly.

"Representative Kinshe said your pain was so great, Lady, that it spilled across into their minds. They were *angry*, Lady. Both the representative and His Highness agreed on that."

"But *why?*" Shalassar half-whispered, her eyes meeting Thaminar's equally dumbfounded gaze. "I could understand grief. Most of the emissaries who come here knew Shaylar, watched her grow up. Many of them, of the dolphins and orcas, at least, have played with her in the water. But *anger?* I've never felt anger from a cetacean." She turned a baffled look on Tharsayl. "Why did they say it was anger?"

"I don't know, Lady, but they both felt the same thing. The sound was a sound of rage, and their anger was so deep, so powerful, that Lady Kinshe-Falis Felt it through her Healing Talent. The singing whale came completely out of the water, Lady. It stood on its tail and bellowed so loudly it shook the windows."

Shalassar gasped and her hand tightened on Thaminar's forearm.

"They don't *do* that!" she protested. "They just *don't.*"

Neither man spoke, and Shalassar shivered, abruptly and oddly frightened as the night closed in around them.

"I want to go inside now," she said in a small voice.

Thaminar nodded and slipped his arm around her once again, steadying her on the walk back to their home. She was more shaken, he realized, than she'd been by anything since the day the news from Hell's Gate had shattered their world.

He glanced back once at the dark water, where the vast sweep of black sea met the equally vast bowl of mostly-black sky. A faint glow remained visible on the western horizon, where the sun had set beyond the coast of Ricathia, but stars were already visible in the eastern sky and overhead.

Why were the cetaceans *angry* over Shaylar's death? Why were they so interested in the outcome of the day's vote? The world which had been so quiet and predictable for the vast majority of his life seemed very cold and frightening tonight. And under other skies, he knew, there were Sharonians even closer to the danger that loomed, out there in the darkness.

Keep them safe, Mother Marthea, he prayed with a sudden fervor he couldn't explain. *Keep us all safe. . . .*

Then they reached the house, with its warm gas lamps to dispel the cold and frightened feelings which had overwhelmed them all on the darkened dock. Merely closing the door felt like an act of preservation, somehow. An act that barred the way against the evil that lay waiting, out there in the multi-universal darkness.

He helped Shalassar into a chair, poured whiskey into three glasses, and handed them around. While they sipped their whiskey and felt safe behind the closed door, here inside these walls where the lights were warm and comforting, he wondered again what the cetaceans were planning . . . and why he'd felt that sudden, deep surge of fear.

Keep them safe, he found himself praying once more. *Please, keep them safe.*

*   *   *

"All right, One Thousand Toralk," Commander of Two Thousand Mayrkos Harshu said to his senior Air Force commander as the early afternoon sunlight burned down across Fort Rycharn. "Let's get these dragons in the air."

Watch for *Hell Hath No Fury*
by David Weber & Linda Evans
Coming in March 2007